PENGUIN CLASSICS

HUMPHRY CLINKER

TOBIAS SMOLLETT was born near Dumbarton in Scotland in 1721. He was educated at local schools and then at the University of Glasgow, which he left without a degree. He was apprenticed as a surgeon in the city, but in 1739, with a manuscript tragedy in his pocket, he went to London. In 1740 he sailed with the fleet to the West Indies as surgeon's mate on HMS *Chichester*. He was present at the disastrous attack on Cartagena and visited Jamaica. He settled in London in 1744 and practised – unsuccessfully – as a surgeon. *The Adventures of Roderick Random*, Smollett's first novel, appeared in 1748. Drawing on his own experiences, the book is a series of adventures depicting the travels of a Scottish hero; its exposé of London life foreshadows some of the themes in *Humphry Clinker*. In 1751 appeared *The Adventures of Peregrine Pickle*, and translations of *Gil Blas* in 1749 and *Don Quixote* in 1755. *The Adventures of Ferdinand Count Fathom* (1753) pioneered the Gothic horrors which became popular later in the century.

Smollett's last years were marred by sickness and disappointment. In 1760 he was fined £100 and sentenced to three months' imprisonment for a bitter attack on Admiral Knowles (who had commanded the West Indies expedition) in the *Critical Review*, which with two others he had founded in 1756 and edited until 1762. He then edited, with little success, *The Briton*, a weekly periodical supporting the unpopular Scottish Prime Minister, Lord Bute. Ill-health sent him abroad in 1763, and in 1766 he published his entertaining and acerbic *Travels through France and Italy*, which earned him, from Sterne, the nickname of 'Smelfungus'. He returned for a last visit to Scotland and Bath and then finally left England in 1768, dying aged fifty at Monte Nero, near Leghorn. *Humphry Clinker* was published in the year of his death, 1771.

JEREMY LEWIS worked in publishing for much of his life after leaving Trinity College, Dublin, in 1965, and was a director of Chatto & Windus for ten years. He was Deputy Editor of the *London Magazine* from 1991 to 1994 and is now Commissioning Editor of *The Oldie* and the Editor-at-Large of the *Literary Review*.

He has written two volumes of autobiography, *Playing for Time* (Collins, 1987) and *Kindred Spirits* (HarperCollins, 1995), and edited *The Vintage Book of Office Life* (1998). His biographies of Cyril Connolly and Tobias Smollett were published by Jonathan Cape and *Penguin Special: The Life and Times of Allen Lane* is available in Penguin. He is working on a book about the Greene family and the third volume of his memoirs, *Grub Street Irregular*, was published by HarperCollins in 2008. The Secretary of the R. S. Surtees Society and a Fellow of the Royal Society of Literature, he is married with two daughters and lives near Richmond Park.

SHAUN REGAN lectures on eighteenth-century and Romantic literature at Queen's University, Belfast. With Brean Hammond, he is the author of *Making the Novel: Fiction and Society in Britain, 1660–1789* (Palgrave Macmillan, 2006). He has published articles on Laurence Sterne, François Rabelais and Scriblerian satire and has essays forthcoming on Olaudah Equiano's *The Interesting Narrative*.

TOBIAS SMOLLETT

Humphry Clinker

Edited by SHAUN REGAN
With an Introduction by JEREMY LEWIS

PENGUIN BOOKS

PENGUIN CLASSICS

Published by the Penguin Group
Penguin Books Ltd, 80 Strand, London WC2R 0RL, England
Penguin Group (USA) Inc., 375 Hudson Street, New York, New York 10014, USA
Penguin Group (Canada), 90 Eglinton Avenue East, Suite 700, Toronto, Ontario, Canada M4P 2Y3
(a division of Pearson Penguin Canada Inc.)
Penguin Ireland, 25 St Stephen's Green, Dublin 2, Ireland (a division of Penguin Books Ltd)
Penguin Group (Australia), 250 Camberwell Road, Camberwell, Victoria 3124, Australia
(a division of Pearson Australia Group Pty Ltd)
Penguin Books India Pvt Ltd, 11 Community Centre, Panchsheel Park, New Delhi – 110 017, India
Penguin Group (NZ), 67 Apollo Drive, Rosedale, North Shore 0632, New Zealand
(a division of Pearson New Zealand Ltd)
Penguin Books (South Africa) (Pty) Ltd, 24 Sturdee Avenue, Rosebank, Johannesburg 2196, South Africa

Penguin Books Ltd, Registered Offices: 80 Strand, London WC2R 0RL, England

www.penguin.com

First published in 1771
This edition first published in Penguin Classics 2008
1

Introduction and Chronology copyright © Jeremy Lewis, 2008
Further Reading © Jeremy Lewis and Shaun Regan, 2008
Note on the Text © Angus Ross, 1967
End notes copyright © Shaun Regan, 2008
All rights reserved

The moral right of the editors has been asserted

Set in 10.25/12.25 pt PostScript Adobe Sabon
Typeset by Rowland Phototypesetting Ltd, Bury St Edmunds, Suffolk
Printed in England by Clays Ltd, St Ives plc

ISBN: 978-0-141-44142-9

www.greenpenguin.co.uk

Penguin Books is committed to a sustainable future
for our business, our readers and our planet.
The book in your hands is made from paper
certified by the Forest Stewardship Council

Mixed Sources
Product group from well-managed
forests and other controlled sources
www.fsc.org Cert no. SA-COC-1592
© 1996 Forest Stewardship Council

Contents

Introduction

Generally regarded as Tobias Smollett's greatest novel, *The Expedition of Humphry Clinker* was published in June 1771, just three months before Smollett's death at the age of fifty. He had left England for the last time three years earlier, and from his Italian exile he conjured up the figure of Matthew Bramble, a gout-ridden, crusty, seemingly misanthropic country squire, who travels round England and Scotland with his nephew Jery, his niece Lydia, his termagant sister Tabitha ('a maiden of forty-five, exceedingly starched, vain, and ridiculous', p. 12), a Welsh maidservant, and his manservant, Humphry Clinker; and as they jolt across country in their cramped and uncomfortable carriage, and move between one raucous and overcrowded set of rooms and another, Bramble rails against the degeneracy of the times and evokes in lurid detail a world which he finds increasingly uncongenial. Like Squire Bramble, Smollett suffered from poor health and was prone to hypochondria; but whereas Bramble pined for the 'clear, elastic, salutary air' (p. 133) and the peace and quiet of his home deep in the Monmouthshire countryside, Smollett spent most of his working life in the incestuous, feud-ridden world of Grub Street and literary London. He left England partly for reasons of health and partly because he could no longer stand the life he was leading. He was embattled in his lifetime and, in a curious way, he has been embattled ever since.

Although he is dutifully listed among the founders of the English novel – along with Samuel Richardson, Laurence Sterne, and his great rival, Henry Fielding – Smollett has been an unjustly neglected figure for far too long. He was highly regarded in his lifetime, and he was a major – and very obvious – influence on the young Charles Dickens[1]: but then he fell from grace, and has remained in limbo ever since. The late Victorians were shocked by his coarseness, his brutality and his lavatorial humour; academic critics, who prefer their novelists to be difficult and obscure (like Sterne) or sententious and long-winded (like Fielding), were disconcerted by his bluntness and pointed out that his characters were, in essence, humours or grotesques, incapable of ambiguity, introspection or change, and therefore unworthy of notice. George Orwell and V. S. Pritchett were keen admirers, but they remained lone voices; and since their essays appeared more than half a century ago, the silence has descended again, at least on this side of the Atlantic.[2] For those intrepid spirits who want to sample one of the funniest, most boisterous and most observant of British novelists, *Humphry Clinker* is the perfect place to start. Like Smollett's other great novel, *The Adventures of Roderick Random* (1748), it has the energy and pace of the picaresque, and a poignancy and a mellowness unexpected in so hard-boiled a novelist; and although Smollett is often dismissed as a literary bruiser, incapable of subtlety and the finer shades of meaning, *Humphry Clinker* is an extraordinarily sophisticated piece of work, an epistolary novel which interlaces and counterpoints five very different narrative voices and, as some critics have pointed out, anticipates James Joyce in its use of puns and double entendres. Like *Roderick Random* it has strong elements of autobiography and, since Smollett's life is as little known as his writing, a brief résumé might be in order, combining the high points of his career with the themes that run throughout his work.

Tobias Smollett was born near Dunbarton in the west of Scotland in March 1721. His family home was poised between Loch Lomond and the Clyde: in later years he would look back on the green hills of his childhood as a paradise lost, and nowhere more eloquently than in the Scottish scenes in *Humphry Clinker*, when Squire Bramble and his party visit Scotland for the first time. Smollett was descended from a long line of soldiers and lawyers, and his grandfather, Sir James, had been one of the commissioners appointed to negotiate the terms of the Act of Union of 1707, whereby the Scottish Parliament voted itself out of existence and the United Kingdom came into being. Union with England provided endless opportunities for ambitious young Scots, not least in the armed forces, the colonies and in medicine, but it was a mixed blessing. Many Scots, Smollett among them, found themselves torn between a prickly pride in their country of origin and a desire to prove themselves as Britons, taking full advantage of this wider stage. Draughty baronial halls were knocked down in favour of Palladian villas, beards gave way to periwigs, and Scots dialect came to be seen as parochial and a source of embarrassment. Although later in the century, the Edinburgh of the economist Adam Smith, the philosopher David Hume, the biographer James Boswell and the architect Robert Adam would be hailed as the Athens of the North, a sense of provincial insecurity endured, and Scots with social, political, intellectual or literary pretensions did their best to speak and sound like their equivalents in London. A Scot who spent most of his life in England, Smollett embodied this ambivalence. As an influential magazine editor, he abominated the use of 'Scotticisms' by his contributors, and his eyes grew moist when, gazing across the English Channel from Boulogne after a long absence abroad, he spotted the White Cliffs of Dover; yet he consorted almost exclusively with fellow-exiles in London and deeply resented the vicious Scottophobia that prevailed in eighteenth-century England. 'I am heartily sick of this land of indifference and phlegm where the finer sensations of the soul are not felt, and felicity is held to consist in stupefying port and overgrown buttocks of beef, where genius is lost, learning undervalued and taste altogether extinguished, and ignorance prevails to such a degree that one of our Chelsea club asked me if the weather was good when I crossed the sea from Scotland,' he once complained to his old friend the Church of Scotland minister Alexander Carlyle. The Scots were regarded by the English as clannish, ambitious outsiders who took the best jobs and looked after their own, and ridiculed as lice-ridden, boorish 'Sawnies',[3] devoted to kilts and porridge. On his rare return visits to Scotland Smollett must have shared Squire Bramble's outrage at the anti-Scottish slogans encountered on the road north, and he used the cantankerous, spindle-shanked figure of Lieutenant Obadiah Lismahago, Tabitha's lugubrious admirer, to give vent to Scottish feelings of resentment and frustration – while noting that, for all his patriotic spleen, the bad-tempered old soldier was happy to spend the evening of his days south of the border.

After attending the grammar school in Dunbarton, the fourteen-year-old Smollett enrolled at Glasgow University, where he was imbued with the traditional mixture of Greek, Latin, logic, science and metaphysics. Whereas Oxford and Cambridge were sinking into the torpor described by the English historian Edward Gibbon in his *Memoirs* (1796), the Scottish universities had far more to offer the enquiring student, and Smollett acquired a breadth of knowledge that would serve him well as a journalist and editor, enabling him to write seemingly learned pieces on Antarctica and the Hottentots of south-west Africa, and review books on bleaching and the history of South America. At the same time he trained as a surgeon-apothecary. Scotland has been famous for its doctors and its medical schools since the eighteenth century, and once again the training provided was far superior to that available south of the border, where the Greek physician Galen (*c.* 130 – *c.* 200) remained on the syllabus and medieval beliefs in hot and cold 'humours' were still in circulation. In England, at least, medicine remained a strictly hierarchical profession in which physicians were the aristocrats of the medical world, commanding large fees and looking down on surgeons and apothecaries as mere mechanics. Physicians assessed their patients' health by external symptoms only, by smell, colour, sound and taste (urine-sampling was a hazard of the profession); surgeons did the dirty work, lancing boils, letting blood, administering enemas, drawing teeth and setting limbs, while the still humbler apothecaries made up the medicines prescribed by the physicians. But Scottish medicine was far more open to developments on the Continent, and in particular the teachings of the great Hermann Boerhaave of Leyden.[4]

Medical students were taught anatomy and spent long hours working and watching in hospitals, and the old distinctions between the three branches of medicine became increasingly blurred and irrelevant. Much to the irritation of well-heeled and often ineffective English physicians, Scottish surgeon-physicians – the precursors of the modern general practitioner – began to offer their services, not least in the colonies and the armed services.

Smollett's medical career was brief and inglorious – he was thought to lack the emollient bedside manner expected of the society physician – but his training as a surgeon-apothecary strongly influenced his work as a novelist, in terms of both subject matter and approach. He was sceptical about his fellow-practitioners and their claims to knowledge – as Squire Bramble observes, 'the sum of all your medical discoveries amounts to this, that the more you study the less you know' (p. 29) – and his novels are populated by quacks, bogus apothecaries and predatory physicians circling like crows round the rakes and rich old ladies of Bath. Physical ailments loom large in *Humphry Clinker* – Bramble's letters are addressed to his doctor back in Wales, and in his opening tirade he complains that he is rigid with constipation – and, although shady doctors are less in evidence than in the earlier novels, a fine specimen is encountered in the pump room at Bristol Hot Wells, early on in Bramble's perambulations round the country. Like many of his contemporaries, Smollett relished lavatorial jokes and details, and the dubious Dr L—n (based on the German physician Diederich Wessel Linden) renders his listeners faint with horror as he reminds them how 'every person who pretended to nauseate the smell of another's excretions, snuffed up his own with particular complacency' (citing in evidence a Grand Duke of Tuscany), and tells them that he himself, 'when he happened to be low-spirited, or fatigued with business, found immediate relief and uncommon satisfaction from hanging over the stale contents of a close-stool, while his servant stirred it about under his nose.' (p. 23).

Doctors have few illusions, and Smollett is the most unillusioned of English novelists: his novels are peopled with conmen, pimps, highwaymen, vulgar nouveaux riches, loose women, drunkards and decadent grandees, and they have a ferocity and energy that make Fielding seem pallid by comparison. Smollett is also a very physical writer, flinching from the din and the filth and the stench of eighteenth-century England, yet recording it with a vigour reminiscent of the narrative paintings of his great contemporary William Hogarth, or the rumbustious scenes of Thomas Rowlandson,[5] that great master of the overflowing bosom and the pendulous paunch: like many writers of a satirical and conservative disposition, Smollett is wary of abstractions, impatient of elevated asides (he mocked Fielding as 'that sagacious moraliser') and lays great store on surface appearances. His characters reflect the training of a medical man brought up to judge by what he can see and smell and touch. His novels pulsate with bottlenoses and carbuncles and gammy legs and other unflattering physical attributes: like Dickens and R. S. Surtees,[6] the great Victorian hunting novelist and Smollett's only rival as the hard man of English letters, he takes careful note of his characters' looks and clothes, and if he seems to take less interest in what goes on inside their heads, he makes up for the omission by the energy and comicality of their movements about the fictional stage.

His medical training completed, Smollett – like so many of his fellow Scots in the years after the Act of Union – made the long journey south to seek his fortune. No sooner had he arrived in the capital, armed with introductions to fellow Scots in exile, than the War of Jenkins's Ear broke out in 1739: the British complained that Spanish coastguards in the Caribbean were making unprovoked assaults on ships going about their lawful business, while the Spaniards were only too well aware that the British wanted to get a share of the lucrative South American trade. Smollett enlisted in the Navy as a surgeon's mate, joined HMS *Chichester*, and found himself heading out to the West Indies to engage the dastardly Spaniards. He took part in the siege of Cartagena, the port on the coast of Colombia where the great Spanish treasure galleons took on their cargoes. Yellow fever took a far heavier toll of British soldiers and sailors than enemy action, and Smollett was so infuriated by the dithering and incompetence of Admiral Vernon[7] and Brigadier Wentworth that he raged about the subject for years to come, eventually earning himself a spell in the King's Bench Prison for libelling one of those involved. The naval scenes in *Roderick Random* include a mad and tyrannical captain, floggings, high seas and enemy action, and paved the way for the nineteenth-century naval novels of Captain Marryat,[8] Robert Louis Stevenson's *Treasure Island* (1883), Herman Melville's *Billy Budd* (1891) and C. S. Forester's Hornblower stories in the 1930s; but although voluble, kindly seadogs with wooden legs make welcome appearances in *Roderick Random* and *The Adventures of Peregrine Pickle* (1751), the naval motif is less in evidence in *Humphry Clinker*.

While in the West Indies, Smollett met and married Anne Lassells, a Jamaican heiress, and although Squire Bramble, aghast at the vulgarity and opulence of the nouveaux riches in Bath, rages against 'planters, negro-drivers, and hucksters, from our American plantations, enriched they know not how' (p. 44), the Smolletts had no compunction about selling off a slave or a parcel of land whenever funds ran low. Back in London, Smollett practised briefly as a doctor before opting instead for the literary life. Shortly before leaving Scotland, he had written a blank-verse play entitled *The Regicide*, and he set about trying to persuade a theatre manager to put it on. Smollett had no talent whatsoever as a playwright, and suffered agonies of humiliation and despair as his wretched play was taken up, kept in limbo for months on end, and eventually rejected. Despite his gruff exterior Smollett was easily wounded and bore grudges longer than most. In his first two novels, *Roderick Random* and *Peregrine Pickle*, he took elaborate comical revenge on the two great theatre managers of the day, David Garrick[9] and James Quin, both of whom had spurned *The Regicide*. Garrick eventually redeemed himself by staging Smollett's naval farce *The Reprisal: or the Tars of Old England* at Covent Garden in 1757, and although Smollett had earlier ridiculed Quin as an over-histrionic ham, much given to beating his brow and sonorous rumblings, the booming old thespian is more kindly treated in *Humphry Clinker*. Squire Bramble and his party come across him in Bath. 'I was once vastly entertained with your playing the Ghost of Gimlet at Drury-lane, when you rose up through the stage, with a white face and red eyes, and spoke of *quails upon the frightful porcofine* – Do, pray, spout a little the Ghost of Gimlet,' he is told by Tabitha Bramble, whose malapropisms are as evident in her speech as in her letters home. 'Madam (said Quin, with a glance of ineffable disdain) the Ghost of Gimlet is laid, never to rise again' (p. 62).

When, in 1737, the authorities learned that an anonymous play entitled *The Golden Rump* made reference to George II's flatulence and piles, Sir Robert Walpole rushed through legislation whereby all plays had to be approved by the Lord Chamberlain. Writers like Fielding abandoned the theatre for the novel, and in due course Smollett followed their example. *Roderick Random* was published anonymously, as was customary, and to Smollett's intense irritation many readers assumed it had been written by Fielding. The fact that Fielding's *The History of Tom Jones* (1749) sold many more copies than *Roderick Random* was a further source of jealousy and resentment, and a foretaste of what lay ahead. Although in temperament at least the two novelists were poles apart – Fielding has a sunny, optimistic view of human nature, whereas Smollett tends to assume the worst – they have invariably been compared ever since, almost always in Fielding's favour. But *Roderick Random* sold well enough to enable the Smolletts and their young daughter Elizabeth to move out of central London to Chelsea, then a self-contained village accessible by stagecoach.

Although, like many novelists since, Smollett denied that his first novel was lightly disguised autobiography, much of it is based on his own experiences. Roderick Random is a hot-tempered, proud young Scot, trained as a medic, who sets out to London to seek his fortune, joins the Navy as a ship's surgeon, and tries to make his name as a playwright. However, his rackety adventures in Covent Garden pubs and with ladies of ill repute may well have owed more to the imagination, since Smollett seems to have been a faithful if undemonstrative spouse, and there is no evidence of his having enjoyed a wild and riotous youth. As an admirer of Cervantes's *Don Quixote de la Mancha* (1605–15) and Alain-René Lesage's *Gil Blas* (1715–35) – both of which he translated[10] – Smollett is the

great master of the picaresque novel in English, and although
all his novels, including *Humphry Clinker*, are essentially picaresque, *Roderick Random* is the purest example of this fast-
moving, loose-limbed, anecdotal form, in which a young man
sets out to seek his fortune and undergoes endless tribulations
before reaching a happy ending; and its energy, vigour and
narrative pace are reminiscent of those other great Scots adventure stories, Stevenson's *Kidnapped* (1886) and John
Buchan's *The Thirty-Nine Steps* (1915). *Roderick Random* and
Humphry Clinker are the only novels by Smollett which are
still worth reading. *The Life and Adventures of Sir Launcelot
Greaves* (1762) is a dim reworking of *Don Quixote*, and tells
of how an eccentric and lovelorn gentleman, clad in a rusty suit
of armour, travels round England putting the world to rights;
The Adventures of Ferdinand Count Fathom (1753) is regarded
as a precursor of the Gothic novel, and its saturnine hero,
the quintessence of evil, briefly and implausibly resurfaces in
Humphry Clinker as the self-effacing Dr Grieve, mysteriously
redeemed and humbly devoted to the common good; *Peregrine
Pickle* has its redeeming moments, but is over-long and frequently tedious, and its bullying hero is almost too loathsome
to be borne. Like many of his contemporaries, Smollett seems
to have shared Peregrine Pickle's liking for sadistic practical
jokes, usually involving laxatives, emetics and what is delicately
referred to as 'double evacuation' (pp. 195, 338), and they
make their presence felt in *Humphry Clinker*, more often than
not at Lismahago's expense. Despite the boorish pranks, *Peregrine Pickle* was much admired by the young Charles Dickens,
who used the picaresque form to fine effect in early novels
like *Pickwick Papers* (1837) and *Nicholas Nickleby* (1838-9),
while excising the sexual and lavatorial scenes in deference to
Victorian sensibilities.

With his medical career behind him, Smollett became a full-
time writer and editor, rivalled only by Dr Johnson[11] in his
devotion to the literary life: in addition to his five novels, he
wrote a multi-volume *Complete History of England* (1757-8),
a masterly travel book, *Travels through France and Italy*
(1766), a scathing and scatological political satire, poems,

plays, innumerable book reviews and a disquisition on the waters of Bath. He also translated and co-edited the five-volume *Works of Voltaire* (1761–5), and edited and contributed to a forty-four-volume *Universal History* (1759–66), as well as writing *A Compendium of Authentic and Entertaining Voyages* (1756) and a gazetteer to the British Isles, and editing the standard two-volume work on obstetrics. He founded and edited the *Critical Review*, which survived until 1817 and was the *Times Literary Supplement* of its day, writing some 250 anonymous reviews himself and commissioning others from Dr Johnson, David Hume, William Hunter[12] and, possibly, Adam Smith and Samuel Richardson. Smollett founded two other magazines as well, the politically motivated *The Briton* and the *British Magazine*, in which *Sir Launcelot Greaves* was published in serial form, thereby setting an example that would be followed by Smollett's Victorian successors. He was a shrewd and hard-headed negotiator at a time when writers were coming to depend on the marketplace rather than rich patrons for their living, and the world of publishing was assuming a form still familiar to us today: the lapsing of the 1662 Licensing Act, which restricted the number of licensed booksellers and printers, had led to a proliferation of newspapers, magazines and books, all of which provided work for indigent hacks; the passing of the 1709 Copyright Act gave authors an unprecedented degree of protection and, although most writers were paid a flat fee for their work, it was possible to negotiate further payments in the event of a book being reprinted.

Because he was such a busy and influential figure in the literary world, Smollett was both courted and abused. Authors and reviewers sought his favours and his patronage, but savaged him behind his back, accusing him of running the *Critical Review* in the interest of his fellow Scots to the exclusion of the English. Despite occasional and long-awaited remittances from Jamaica, money was always in short supply, and Smollett, never the most robust of men, wore himself out and ruined his health through overwork. He is, with William Makepeace Thackeray, George Gissing, Cyril Connolly and Julian Maclaren-Ross, one of the great chroniclers of literary life, and his novels abound with exhausted hacks struggling to meet deadlines, knocking out reviews, exchanging waspish, incestuous gossip and grumbling over the parsimony of publishers.[13] Smollett was a keen supporter of his fellow scribes: like many hot-tempered reactionaries, he was, at heart, a kindly man, ready to support and encourage other writers, and generous with his time and his money. Though well aware of the treachery of his guests, many of whom were second-rate poseurs or would-be writers unable to convert eloquence in speech into words on the page, he used to invite assorted hacks to his house every Sunday for beer and beef; and as such he makes an extended appearance in *Humphry Clinker* as Mr S— (see p. 140), strolling under the filbert trees in his Chelsea garden.

Smollett could hold his own in the world of literary pugilism, but when he strayed into the political arena he was hopelessly out of his depth. Although he was never a Member of Parliament, Smollett's politics were identical to those of Matthew Bramble: he thought the world was going to the dogs, he loathed both the aristocratic Whig grandees and the nouveaux riches who had made their money in the City or the colonies and were busy buying up country estates and marrying their daughters into the aristocracy, and he attributed most of the ills of the world to luxury. For old-fashioned Tories and Country Whigs – the political groupings with whom Smollett had most in common – eighteenth-century society was blighted by faction and corruption: the Whig aristocracy was irremediably compromised and only the country gentleman, impervious to corruption, contemptuous of faction and with the independence that wealth bestows, was equipped to take a detached, disinterested view of the national interest. Since he seldom ventured out of London, Smollett's experience of English country gentlemen was more theoretical than practical, but he would have agreed with those who held up *The Spectator*'s Sir Roger de Coverley – a just and exemplary JP, and the 'best master in the world'[14] – as the embodiment of the wise and benevolent 'patriarch', and the polar opposite of those upstart 'patricians' who had made their fortunes as stock-jobbers or slave-owners, and bought their estates off the peg. For Smollett and those who thought like him, luxury was the most pernicious manifestation of all they detested in the new order. Luxury had been responsible for the downfall of Ancient Rome, whereby austere, public-spirited republican virtues gave way to the moral and political degeneration of the pleasure-loving Empire; luxury was irrational, urban and subversive, dissolving hierarchies and the bonds of mutual dependence, and was held responsible for rioting, insubordination, gin-drinking, bear-baiting, widespread vulgarity, tea-drinking among the lower orders, fashionable vicars and homosexuality. After the Treaty of Aix-la-Chapelle (1748) had concluded hostilities with France and brought to an end the War of the Austrian Succession, Smollett noted 'an irresistible tide of luxury and excess' as English tourists poured across the Channel and exposed themselves to the corrupting influence of the French;[15] and nowhere more so than among the vulgarians and arrivistes whom Squire Bramble so abominated during his reluctant visit to Bath, 'the very centre of racket and dissipation' (p. 41). 'Intoxicated by the flow of wealth, they affected to rival the luxury and magnificence of their superiors. They laid aside all decorum; became lewd, insolent, intemperate and riotous. All principles and even decency was gradually abolished,' Smollett noted in his history of England,[16] while Squire Bramble observed that 'all these absurdities arise from the general tide of luxury, which hath overspread the nation and swept away all, even the very dregs of the people' (p. 44).

By the 1750s such notions were running counter to the spirit of the age. Since the end of the seventeenth century those economists who emphasized the benefits of competition, enterprise and freedom from governmental restraints had begun to prevail over the mercantilists, with their belief in order, stability and government supervision. Adam Smith promoted the notion of specialization and the division of labour, of society as a machine in which partial or 'factional' interests had a part to play, while Bernard de Mandeville in *The Fable of the Bees* (1714) suggested that 'private vices' like greed, vanity and selfishness promoted 'public benefits', and that the creation of wealth by the few benefited the many by creating work and spreading money through society.[17] Neither Dr Johnson nor David Hume shared Smollett's loathing of luxury, but Smollett was un-moved. *Humphry Clinker* – or at least Squire Bramble's contri-butions to it – is permeated with his views, in the letters from Bath and London, and the cautionary tale of his old friend Mr Baynard, a hapless country gentleman who married a woman devoted to luxury, frittered away his fortune, and saw his com-fortable home converted into a sterile mausoleum of modish bad taste.

Smollett's contempt for the contemporary political scene is made obvious in *Humphry Clinker*, not least in those comical episodes in which Squire Bramble and his nephew Jery Melford encounter the blithering Duke of Newcastle (p. 111), the quin-tessence of the Whig Supremacy and the great survivor of eighteenth-century politics; Squire Bramble's indignation when he discovers that Humphry Clinker has Methodist leanings (p. 154) reflects Smollett's own adherence to the Thirty-Nine Articles as bulwarks of social order and stability.[18] The *Critical Review* was a conservative organ in that works which adhered to neo-classical rules were preferred to anything with a whiff of the Romantic, the disorderly or the subversive – its great rival and precursor, the *Monthly Review*, was more liberal-minded – but apart from libelling Admiral Charles Knowles[19] after the disastrous Rochefort expedition during the Seven Years War against France, for which he was duly fined and imprisoned, Smollett steered clear of politics until, to his dismay, he found himself doing battle with that self-proclaimed champion of Liberty, the Press and the common man, John Wilkes.

Charming, cross-eyed and hideously ugly – a keen ladies' man, he once boasted that he could talk away his face in half an hour – Wilkes had been one of Smollett's few English friends: his daughter Polly went to the same school in Chelsea as Elizabeth Smollett, and when Dr Johnson's black manservant Francis Barber was press-ganged into the Navy, Smollett wrote to Wilkes on behalf of the 'Great Cham' (as he famously nick-named Johnson) and secured his release. But their friendship could not survive the vicious outbreak of Scottophobia which followed the appointment of George III's old tutor, the Earl of Bute, as the First (i.e. Prime) Minister in 1762. Bute appointed

Smollett to edit a magazine, *The Briton*, which would defend his ministry and the peace negotiations following the Seven Years War. Ably assisted by another literary bruiser, the clergyman-poet Charles Churchill, Wilkes responded with the infamous magazine the *North Briton*, which was far livelier and more scurrilous than its anaemic rival, ridiculing its editor and portraying the Scots as a race of bare-buttocked thistle-eaters. Smollett was bruised and enraged by Wilkes's diatribes against the Scots, and he loathed his old friend's readiness to inflame and exploit the prejudices of the urban masses. 'The mob is a monster I never could abide,' says Squire Bramble. 'I detest the whole of it, as a mass of ignorance, presumption, malice, and brutality' (p. 45).

Adrift in the world of politics, exhausted by his literary labours, and in poor health, Smollett was close to breaking point. 'If I go on writing as I have proceeded for some years, my hand will be paralytic, and my brain dried to a snuff. I would not wish my greatest enemy a greater curse than the occupation of author, in which capacity I have toiled myself into an habitual asthma, and been baited like a bear by all the hounds of Grub Street,' he told a correspondent in Jamaica.[20] And then, in the spring of 1763, his beloved daughter died at the age of fifteen. Overwhelmed by 'unutterable sorrow',[21] the Smolletts decided to pack up their Chelsea house and take themselves abroad. After travelling round France, they spent ten months in Nice, where Smollett indulged his passion for bathing in the sea and noted, apropos the use of human excrement as manure, that 'the jakes [lavatories] of a Protestant family, who eat *gras* [fat] every day, bears a much higher price than the privy of a good Catholic, who lives maigre for one half of the year. The vaults belonging to the convent of Minims are not worth emptying.'[22] From Nice they were rowed in an open felucca to the Ligurian coast, travelling as far south as Rome before finally heading home after an absence of two years. The result of this journey was one of the great travel books in the language, the wonderfully bad-tempered and vigorous *Travels through France and Italy*, in which Smollett grumbles at length about the filthy state of French lavatories, bedbugs, surly Italian innkeepers, mincing Parisian *petits maîtres* and all the other horrors that awaited the intrepid British traveller on the far side of the Channel. Laurence Sterne, whom the Smolletts encountered in Montpellier, caricatured his fellow novelist in *A Sentimental Journey through France and Italy* (1768) as 'Smelfungus', the boorish embodiment of the xenophobic Briton, who does nothing but complain when abroad and is blind to the beauties of Italian art and architecture. Smollett's dislike of poseurs and self-professed aesthetes may well have provoked him into playing the part of the philistine, for the Italian letters in his *Travels* reveal a detailed if unorthodox knowledge of Classical and Renaissance art, while in the *Critical Review* he was a knowledgeable and enthusiastic supporter of English painters and engravers. As the preamble to *Humphry Clinker* suggests, travel books consisting of letters were much in vogue; although most of Smollett's 'letters' were written after the event, *Travels through France and Italy* was a fine example of its kind, and the epistolary form, the curmudgeonly narrator and the detailed observation of the manners and morals of those encountered en route almost certainly influenced the tone and structure of Smollett's last novel.

On their return to England in 1765 the Smolletts took a house in Golden Square, just round the corner from his Scottish friend William Hunter's lecture hall and anatomy collection. They spent the winter of 1765 in Bath and the following May Smollett paid his last visit to Scotland. Like Squire Bramble and his party, the Smolletts travelled north via Harrogate, spent time in Edinburgh and Glasgow (which Bramble calls 'one of the prettiest towns in Europe', p. 273), and visited Loch Lomond, Inverary, Jura, Islay and Mull. While in Scotland Smollett wrote the elegiac 'Ode to Leven-Water', which was later incorporated into *Humphry Clinker* (p. 277), but if Smollett's conversation was as lively as ever, his old friend the Scottish physician John Moore was 'much affected by the dismal alterations which had now taken place in his face and person', and noted how he seemed 'greatly affected by rheumatic pains, and was seized besides with an ulcer on his arm'.[23]

Back in London, literary life was as demanding as ever.

Smollett no longer edited the *Critical Review*, but he continued working on the multi-volume *Universal History*, added a fifth volume to his *Complete History of England*, ridiculed the politicians of the day in his scatological *The History and Adventures of an Atom* (1769), translated the French writer François Fenelon's *Les Aventures de Télémaque* (1699) as *The Adventures of Telemachus, son of Ulysses* (1776), and wrote much of an eight-volume compendium-cum-gazetteer, *The Present State of All Nations* (1768–9), the Scottish sections of which were incorporated, almost verbatim, in *Humphry Clinker*. But there was little now to hold him in England, and in the autumn of 1768 the Smolletts moved to Italy, where he died some three years later.

'It galls me to the soul to think how much that poor dear man suffered while he wrote that novel,' Anne Smollett declared after his death,[24] but for all its author's suffering and Squire Bramble's diatribes against the evils of the age, the lasting impression of *Humphry Clinker* is mellow, and even benign. It is also extremely funny: so much so that one often laughs out loud, even when Lismahago, a battered veteran of North American frontier wars, describes how he and a companion were scalped and tortured by a party of Miami Indians, and how Ensign Murphy was eventually burned at the stake, 'singing, as his death song, the *Drimmendoo*, in concert with Mr Lismahago, who was present at the solemnity' (p. 215). Hard-boiled as he seemed, Smollett – like Dickens – delighted in implausible coincidences and happy endings: Roderick Random, after being buffeted by fate like all true picaresque heroes, meets a melancholy, middle-aged Scot in an obscure part of South America who turns out to be his long lost father and bequeaths him a fortune, so enabling him to marry the decent but dreary girl of his dreams and settle down in his ancestral acres in Scotland, surrounded by grateful tenants and far removed from the corruption and temptations of London life; and – as the reader will eventually discover – *Humphry Clinker* has its fair share of similar improbabilities, including the parentage of its eponymous hero.

Those who find such scenes too saccharine can draw comfort

from the novel's documentary qualities: Smollett is the most
observant of novelists, describing with a horrified relish the
adulteration of Londoners' food and drink or the squalor
endured by those who flock to Bath to drink or wallow in its
waters ('what a delicate beveridge is every day quaffed by the
drinkers; medicated with the sweat and dirt, and dandriff; and
the abominable discharges of various kinds, from twenty different diseased bodies, parboiling in the kettle below', pp. 54–5).
Nor does he shy from including 'real life' characters in the
novel, among them James Quin, who is 'carried home with six
good bottles of claret under his belt' (p. 69), Samuel Derrick,
the Master of Ceremonies at Bath and a former colleague on
the *Critical Review*, the Duke of Newcastle and, of course,
Smollett himself. Meanwhile, readers with a taste for puns,
usually obscene, will find much to enjoy in the letters from
Tabitha Bramble and Win Jenkins, neither of whom have much
mastery of spelling: 'the holy bands of mattermoney' (p. 391)
is a particularly fine example, but others include 'cuntry' for
'country', 'turd' for 'third', 'beshits' for 'beseeches' and 'asterisks' for 'hysterics'.

Such wordplay has a distinctly modern quality, as does the
cunning way in which Smollett interlaces and contrasts his five
narrative voices. The same scene will often be described by
different narrators, and from very different points of view:
Bramble, like his creator, hates Bath and all it stands for, and
has to be dragged to London's famous pleasure gardens at
Ranelagh and Vauxhall, whereas his nephew Jery and his love-
sick niece Lydia are delighted by all they see. An epistolary
novel involving five letter writers is, in technical terms at least,
far more advanced than anything attempted by Samuel
Richardson or Frances (Fanny) Burney,[25] but Squire Bramble
dominates the proceedings, partly because the other members
of his party offer little opposition (Jery keeps the story going,
Lydia is suitably anodyne, Tabitha and Win Jenkins are there
for the jokes, and Humphry Clinker alone is denied a narrative
voice). Bramble gives voice to his creator's views and prejudices,
and he is the great exception to the notion that Smollett's
characters are little more than one-dimensional caricatures,

strong on colour but lacking any depth or substance. The kindly
misanthrope and the curmudgeon with the heart of gold were
familiar figures in the literature of the time, and Matthew
Bramble, Smollett's fictional alter ego, is a fine example of the
breed. Jery begins by finding him too cantankerous to be borne,
but soon realizes that 'his peevishness arises partly from bodily
pain, and partly from a natural excess of mental sensibility; for,
I suppose, the mind as well as the body, is in some cases endued
with a morbid excess of sensation' (p. 22), and that his uncle
'affects misanthropy, in order to conceal the sensibility of a
heart, which is tender, even to a degree of weakness' (p. 35).
Bramble, for his part, declares that his 'misanthropy increases
every day – The longer I live, I find the folly and the fraud of
mankind grow more and more intolerable' (p. 56), yet in every
letter home to Dr Lewis he worries about the welfare of his
tenants and arranges for them to be benefited in cash or in kind.
'When he is free from pain, he is the best-tempered man upon
earth; so gentle, so generous, so charitable, that every body
loves him,' (p. 48) we learn; and the same could be said of his
creator.

Although Smollett was only in his late forties when he wrote
Humphry Clinker, his last novel has a valedictory note, and
nowhere more so than in the pages devoted to the scenes of his
childhood. 'I have met with more kindness, hospitality, and
rational entertainment, in a few weeks, than ever I received
in any other country during the whole course of my life,'
(p. 257) Squire Bramble tells us. Uncorrupted by luxury, as
green and lush as he remembered, the Clyde Valley and Loch
Lomond seem like a vanished Arcadia, the lost idyll of a man
of whom V. S. Pritchett once wrote that 'generosity and goodness of heart go together with an impetuous temper and a touch
of hypochondria', and that 'his protest and his hypochondria
suggest that he felt the pleasure and the agony of a man who
has a skin too few.'[26] We should be reading Smollett again, for
his anger, his energy, his frankness, his comicality, his coarseness and, above all, his ability to tell a good story. He deserves
to be better remembered.

Jeremy Lewis

NOTES

1. The novels in which Smollett's influence is most apparent are
    The Pickwick Papers (1837), *Nicholas Nickleby* (1838–9) and
    The Old Curiosity Shop (1841). He made explicit his admiration
    for Smollett in *David Copperfield* (1849–50).

2. George Orwell's essay 'Tobias Smollett: Scotland's Best Novelist'
    was published in *Tribune* on 22 September 1944. It can be found
    in Volume 16 of *The Complete Works of George Orwell*, ed.
    Peter Davison (London: Secker & Warburg, 1998), pp. 408–10.
    V. S. Pritchett's essays 'The Shocking Surgeon' and 'The Unhappy
    Traveller' first appeared in the *New Statesman* and are available
    in his *Complete Essays* (London: Chatto & Windus, 1991),
    pp. 161–5 and 425–9.

3. A corruption of 'Sandy' – itself short for Alexander, a popular
    Scottish Christian name.

4. Hermann Boerhaave (1668–1738) was a professor of medicine,
    botany and chemistry at the University of Leyden in Holland.
    Under his guidance, it became the leading medical school in
    Europe and (unlike their English equivalents) many Scottish
    surgeons and physicians studied there.

5. Thomas Rowlandson (1756–1827) illustrated some of Smollett's
    novels, long after their author's death.

6. R. S. Surtees (1805–64) is best remembered as the creator of Mr
    Jorrocks, the hunting grocer. His best novels are *Mr Sponge's
    Sporting Tour* (1853) and *Mr Facey Romford's Hounds* (1865).

7. Admiral Edward Vernon (1684–1757) is best remembered for
    capturing Porto Bello from the Spaniards in the early months of
    the War of Jenkins's Ear (1739–41) and for attempting to reduce
    drunkenness in the Navy by replacing raw spirits with 'grog', a
    mixture of rum and water named after his grogram cloak.

8. Frederick Marryat (1792–1848) was a naval captain turned
    novelist. Eagerly devoured by Victorian and Edwardian children,
    his best-remembered stories are *Mr Midshipman Easy* (1836)
    and *The Children of the New Forest* (1847).

9. David Garrick (1717–79), the actor and manager of Drury Lane
    Theatre, visited Smollett in the King's Bench Prison in 1761 after
    he was found guilty of libel.

10. Smollett could read French more easily than he could speak it.
    His Spanish was almost certainly non-existent. His 'translation'

of *Don Quixote* was a paraphrase of a recent translation by the Irish painter Charles Jervas (*c.* 1675–1739) and repeated many of the elementary mistakes made by his predecessor.

11. Samuel Johnson (1709–84), the great lexicographer, poet, critic and essayist, founded and edited almost as many magazines as Smollett. Although the two men were never, in Smollett's words, 'cater-cousins' (close friends), Dr Johnson occasionally visited the Chelsea China Manufactory next to Smollett's house in Chelsea, and may well have called in on Smollett at the same time.

12. The Scottish anatomist and obstetrician William Hunter (1718–83) spent his working life in London, and was a close friend of Smollett.

13. William Makepeace Thackeray (1811–63) provided an entertaining account of literary life in his novel *Pendennis* (1848–50), while the grimmest account is that given in *New Grub Street* (1891) by George Gissing (1857–1903). Cyril Connolly (1903–74) warned about the 'pram in the hall' and other snares awaiting the unwary writer in his *Enemies of Promise* (1938). Julian Maclaren-Ross (1912–64) was the great chronicler of Soho literary life, most memorably in his posthumous *Memoirs of the Forties* (1965).

14. Richard Steele and Joseph Addison, *Selections from the Tatler and the Spectator*, ed. Angus Ross (London: Penguin, 1988), p. 216.

15. Tobias Smollett, *The History of England from the Revolution to the Death of George the Second* (London, 1804), Volume III, p. 275.

16. Ibid, Volume I, p. 175.

17. Bernard de Mandeville (1670–1733) was a Dutch-born physician and philosopher who settled in London. His *Fable of the Bees, or Private Vices, Public Benefits* (1714, 1723) suggested that even prostitutes and highwaymen could prove 'a blessing to the whole society' since they stimulated demand and encouraged the circulation of money. In France his book was burned by the public hangman.

18. Drawn up during the reign of Elizabeth I, the Thirty-Nine Articles provide the doctrinal foundations of the Church of England.

19. Charles Knowles (*c.* 1704–77), a pompous but effective sailor, spent much of his career in the Caribbean.

20. Letter 67 to John Harvie (December 1759) in *The Letters of*

Tobias Smollett, ed. Lewis M. Knapp (Oxford: Oxford University Press, 1970), p. 85.

21. Letter 90 to Richard Smith (May 1763). Ibid., p. 114.
22. Letter 22 in Tobias Smollett, *Travels through France and Italy*, ed. Frank Felsenstein (Oxford: Oxford University Press, 1981), p. 178.
23. John Moore, 'The Life of T. Smollett, M.D.' in *The Works of Tobias Smollett, M.D.*, ed. James P. Bowne, Volume I (London: Bickers & Sons, 1872), p. 134.
24. Letter from Ann Smollett to Archibald Hamilton (28 May 1773). Quoted in Lewis M. Knapp, 'Ann Smollett, Wife of Tobias Smollett', *Proceedings of the Modern Languages Association (PMLA)*, Volume 45, No. 4 (December 1930), pp. 1035–49.
25. Best remembered for *Evelina, or A Young Lady's Entrance into the World* (1778), Frances Burney (1752–1840) was, with Richardson, the great exponent of the epistolary novel in England. Like *Humphry Clinker, Evelina* contains vivid accounts of the pleasure gardens at Vauxhall and Ranelagh.
26. V. S. Pritchett, 'The Shocking Surgeon' in *The Living Novel* (London: Chatto & Windus, 1946), p. 20.

Chronology

1721 Tobias George Smollett is born in Dalquhurn, Cardross, near Dunbarton, Scotland, the second son of Archibald and Barbara Smollett.

1723 Death of Archibald Smollett.

*c.***1727** Smollett is sent to Dunbarton Grammar School.

*c.***1735** Smollett enrols at Glasgow University and studies there for three years.

He works for an apothecary in a dispensary in Glasgow.

1736 Smollett is apprenticed to John Gordon, a surgeon in Glasgow.

1739 Smollett leaves for London, with *The Regicide* in his pocket.

Outbreak of the War of Jenkins's Ear.

1740 Smollett joins HMS *Chichester* as a surgeon's mate.

1741 Takes part in the abortive siege of Cartagena, the Spanish treasure port in Colombia.

1741–4 Smollett remains in the West Indies; marries Anne Lassells of Kingston, Jamaica.

1744 Smollett returns to London; lives for a time in Downing Street, where he practices as a doctor.

Begins his futile attempts to place *The Regicide* with theatre managers. His first piece of writing is published – a poem entitled 'A New Song', set to music by James Oswald.

1746 Publication of Smollett's poem 'The Tears of Scotland', mourning the Battle of Culloden.

1747 Anne Smollett joins her husband from Jamaica.

1748 Birth of their daughter, Elizabeth.

Publication of *The Adventures of Roderick Random*.

1749 Publication of Smollett's translation of Lesage's *Gil Blas*.

The Regicide is published by subscription.

1750 The Smolletts move from Beaufort Street, off the Strand, to Monmouth House, Lawrence Street, Chelsea.

Smollett visits Paris with his friend John Moore.

1751 Publication of *The Adventures of Peregrine Pickle*.

1752 Publication of *An Essay on the External Use of Water*.

1753 Publication of *The Adventures of Ferdinand Count Fathom*.

Smollett spends five months in Scotland.

1754 Publication of Smollett's translation of the *Journal Œconomique* (itself the work of various hands), under the title *Select Essays on Commerce, Agriculture, Mines, Fisheries and Other Useful Subjects*.

1755 Publication of Smollett's 'translation' of *Don Quixote*.

1756 Publication of the seven-volume *A Compendium of Authentic and Entertaining Voyages*, which includes 'An Account of the Expedition against Cartagena'.

First publication of the monthly *Critical Review*, founded by Smollett and edited by him until 1763.

1757 Smollett's play *The Reprisal: or the Tars of Old England* is staged by David Garrick at Drury Lane.

1757–8 Publication of the multi-volume *Complete History of England*.

1760 First publication of the *British Magazine*, founded and edited by Smollett.

Smollett is found guilty of libelling Admiral Sir Charles Knowles.

1761 Publication of *The Adventures of Sir Launcelot Greaves*, initially in serial form in the *British Magazine*.

Smollett spends three months in the King's Bench Prison.

1761–5 Jointly edits and translates the *Works of Voltaire*.

1762 First publication of *The Briton*, founded and edited by Smollett.

1763 Death of Elizabeth Smollett. The Smolletts leave Chelsea and spend the next two years abroad, living for nine months in Nice and travelling through France and Italy.

1765 The Smolletts return to England; they take a house in Golden Square, and spend the winter in Gay Street, Bath.

Publication of *The Continuation of the Complete History of England*.

1766 Publication of *Travels through France and Italy*.

Smollett visits Scotland for the last time; visits Edinburgh, Glasgow, Loch Lomond, Inverary, Jura, Islay and Mull.

1768 Publication of *The Present State of All Nations*.

The Smolletts leave England for the last time and settle in Livorno (Leghorn) on the Italian coast.

1769 Publication of *The History and Adventures of an Atom*.

1771 Publication of *The Expedition of Humphry Clinker*.

Death of Tobias Smollett, aged fifty.

Further Reading

SMOLLETT

Basker, James G., *Tobias Smollett: Critic and Journalist* (London: Associated University Presses, 1988).

Beasley, Jerry C., *Tobias Smollett: Novelist* (London: University of Georgia Press, 1998).

Bold, Alan (ed.), *Smollett: Author of the First Distinction* (London: Vision, 1982).

Boucé, Paul-Gabriel, *The Novels of Tobias Smollett*, trans. Antonia White (London: Longman, 1976).

Douglas, Aileen, *Uneasy Sensations: Smollett and the Body* (Chicago: University of Chicago Press, 1995).

Gibson, William L., *Art and Money in the Writings of Tobias Smollett* (Lewisburg, PA: Bucknell University Press, 2007).

Kahrl, George M., *Tobias Smollett: Traveller–Novelist, etc.* (Chicago: University of Chicago Press, 1945).

Kelly, Lionel (ed.), *Smollett: The Critical Heritage* (London: Routledge & Kegan Paul, 1987).

Knapp, Lewis M., *Tobias Smollett: Doctor of Men and Manners* (Princeton NJ: Princeton University Press, 1949).

——(ed.), *The Letters of Tobias Smollett* (Oxford: Clarendon Press, 1970).

Lewis, Jeremy, *Tobias Smollett* (London: Jonathan Cape, 2003).

Martz, Louis L., *The Later Career of Tobias Smollett* (New York: Yale University Press, 1942).

Rousseau, G. S., *Tobias Smollett: Essays of Two Decades* (Edinburgh: T & T Clark, 1982).

Sekora, John, *Luxury: The Concept in Western Thought, Eden to Smollett* (London: Johns Hopkins University Press, 1977).

GENERAL BACKGROUND

Barrell, John, *English Literature in History, 1730–80: An Equal, Wide Survey* (London: Hutchinson, 1983).

Brewer, John, *The Pleasures of the Imagination* (London: HarperCollins, 1997).

Colley, Linda, *Britons: Forging the Nation, 1707–1837* (London: Yale University Press, 1992).

Crawford, Robert, *Devolving English Literature* (Oxford: Oxford University Press, 1992).

Herman, Arthur, *The Scottish Enlightenment: The Scots' Invention of the Modern World* (London: Fourth Estate, 2002).

Kernan, Alvin B., *Printing Technology, Letters and Samuel Johnson* (Princeton, NJ: Princeton University Press, 1987).

Simpson, Kenneth, *The Protean Scot: The Crisis of Identity in Eighteenth-Century Scottish Literature* (Aberdeen: Aberdeen University Press, 1988).

Speck, W. A., *Society and Literature in England, 1700–60* (Dublin: Gill and Macmillan, 1983).

HUMPHRY CLINKER: SOME RECENT DISCUSSIONS

Evans, James E., '"An Honest Scar Received in the Service of My Country": Lismahago's Colonial Perspective in *Humphry Clinker*', *Philological Quarterly*, 79:4 (Fall, 2000), 483–99.

Gottlieb, Evan '"Fools and Prejudice": Sympathy and National Identity in the Scottish Enlightenment and *Humphry Clinker*', *Eighteenth-century Fiction*, 18:1 (Fall, 2005), 81–106.

Hammond, Brean, and Shaun Regan, *Making the Novel: Fiction and Society in Britain, 1660–1789* (Basingstoke: Palgrave Macmillan, 2006), pp. 204–215.

Jacobsen, Susan L., ' "The Tinsel of the Times": Smollett's Argument Against Conspicuous Consumption in *Humphry Clinker*', *Eighteenth-century Fiction*, 9 (1996–97), 71–88.

McKeon, Michael, 'Aestheticising the Critique of Luxury: Smollett's *Humphry Clinker*', in *Luxury in the Eighteenth Century: Debates, Desires and Delectable Goods*, ed. Maxine Berg and Elizabeth Eger (Basingstoke: Palgrave Macmillan, 2003), pp. 57–67.

Richetti, John, *The English Novel in History, 1700–1780* (London: Routledge, 1999), pp. 181–92.

Rosenblaum, Michael, 'Smollett's *Humphry Clinker*'. in *The Cambridge Companion to the Eighteenth-Century Novel*, ed. John Richetti (Cambridge: Cambridge University Press, 1996), pp. 175–97.

Weed, David M., 'Sentimental Misogyny and Medicine in *Humphry Clinker*', *Studies in English Literature*, 37 (1997), pp. 535–52.

A Note on the Text

THERE are two distinct 'first' editions of *Humphry Clinker*, different type-settings but with identical imprints, and both with the misprint MDCLXXI on the title page of volume I. Another edition was printed in the same year, and a fourth in 1772. The relationship between these texts is complicated. F. B. Newman gives the most accessible information about the matter to date in 'A Consideration of the Bibliographical Problems connected with the First Edition of *Humphry Clinker*' in *Papers of the Bibliographical Society of America* 44 (1950), pp. 340–71; see also A. H. Smith, *The Printing and Publication of Early Editions of the Novels of . . . Smollett*, unpublished Ph.D. thesis, the University of London (1975). Smollett was not in England when the book was set up, and neither of the 'first' editions is without textual puzzles. The present text is based on a copy of the 1772 edition, for the use of which the editor thanks Mr F. W. Liebert of Yale University. Typographical variations, particularly in the punctuation, and in the use of dashes, have been normalized to the forms closest to modern use. Some gross misprints have been silently corrected, and on occasion readings from the earlier editions have been adopted. The end of each of Smollett's three volumes is marked *.

THE
EXPEDITION
OF
HUMPHRY CLINKER.

By the AUTHOR of
RODERICK RANDOM.

***

IN THREE VOLUMES.
VOL. I.

***

——Quorſum bæc tam putida tendunt,
Furcifer ? ad te, inquam——— Hor.

***

LONDON,
Printed for W. Johnston, in Ludgate-Street ;
and B. Collins, in Saliſbury.
MDCLXXI.

To Mr HENRY DAVIS, Bookseller, in London.

ABERGAVENNY, Aug. 4.

RESPECTED SIR,

I have received your esteemed favour of the 13th ultimo, whereby it appeareth, that you have perused those same Letters, the which were delivered unto you by my friend the reverend Mr Hugo Behn; and I am pleased to find you think they may be printed with a good prospect of success; in as much as the objections you mention, I humbly conceive, are such as may be redargued,[1] if not entirely removed — And, first, in the first place, as touching what prosecutions may arise from printing the private correspondence of persons still living, give me leave, with all due submission, to observe, that the Letters in question were not written and sent under the seal of secrecy; that they have no tendency to the *mala fama*,[2] or prejudice of any person whatsoever; but rather to the information and edification of mankind: so that it becometh a sort of duty to promulgate them *in usum publicum*,[3] Besides, I have consulted Mr Davy Higgins, an eminent attorney of this place, who, after due inspection and consideration, declareth, That he doth not think the said Letters contain any matter which will be held actionable in the eye of the law. Finally, if you and I should come to a right understanding, I do declare *in verbo sacerdotis*,[4] that, in case of any such prosecution, I will take the whole upon my own shoulders, even *quoad*[5] fine and imprisonment, though, I must confess, I should not care to undergo flagellation: *Tam ad turpitudinem, quam ad amaritudinem pœnœ spectans*[6] —

Secondly, concerning the personal resentment of Mr Justice Lismahago, I may say, *non flocci facio*[7] – I would not willingly vilipend[8] any Christian, if, peradventure, he deserveth that epithet: albeit, I am much surprised that more care is not taken to exclude from the commission all such vagrant foreigners as may be justly suspected of disaffection to our happy constitution, in church and state — God forbid that I should be so uncharitable, as to affirm positively, that the said Lismahago is no better than a Jesuit in disguise; but this I will assert and maintain, *totis viribus*,[9] that, from the day he qualified, he has never been once seen *intra templi parietes*,[10] that is to say, within the parish church.

Thirdly, with respect to what passed at Mr Kendal's table, when the said Lismahago was so brutal in his reprehensions, I must inform you, my good Sir, that I was obliged to retire, not by fear arising from his minatory[11] reproaches, which, as I said above, I value not of a rush; but from the sudden effect produced by a barbel's row, which I had eaten at dinner, not knowing, that the said row is at certain seasons violently cathartic, as Galen observeth in his chapter περι ιχθυς.[12]

Fourthly, and lastly, with reference to the manner in which I got possession of these Letters, it is a circumstance that concerns my own conscience only; sufficeth it to say, I have fully satisfied the parties in whose custody they were; and, by this time, I hope I have also satisfied you in such ways, that the last hand may be put to our agreement, and the work proceed with all convenient expedition; in which I hope I rest,

Respected Sir,

Your very humble servant,

JONATHAN DUSTWICH.

P.S. I propose, *Deo volente*,[13] to have the pleasure of seeing you in the great city, towards All-hallowtide,[14] when I shall be glad to treat with you concerning a parcel of MS. sermons, of a certain clergyman deceased; a cake of the right leaven, for the present taste of the public. *Verbum sapienti, &c.*[15]

J. D.

To the Revd. Mr JONATHAN DUSTWICH, at —.

SIR,

I received yours in course of post, and shall be glad to treat with you for the M.S. which I have delivered to your friend Mr Behn; but can by no means comply with the terms proposed. Those things are so uncertain – Writing is all a lottery – I have been a loser by the works of the greatest men of the age — I could mention particulars, and name names; but don't choose it – The taste of the town is so changeable. Then there have been so many letters upon travels lately published – What between Smollett's, Sharp's, Derrick's, Thicknesse's, Baltimore's, and Baretti's, together with Shandy's Sentimental Travels, the public seems to be cloyed with that kind of entertainment[1] – Nevertheless, I will, if you please, run the risque of printing and publishing, and you shall have half the profits of the impression — You need not take the trouble to bring up your sermons on my account – No body reads sermons but Methodists and Dissenters — Besides, for my own part, I am quite a stranger to that sort of reading; and the two persons, whose judgment I depended upon in those matters, are out of the way; one is gone abroad, carpenter of a man of war;[2] and the other has been silly enough to abscond, in order to avoid a prosecution for blasphemy – I'm a great loser by his going off – He has left a manual of devotion half finished on my hands, after having received money for the whole copy — He was the soundest divine, and had the most orthodox pen of all my people; and I never knew his judgment fail, but in flying from his bread and butter on this occasion.

By owning you was not put in bodily fear by Lismahago, you preclude yourself from the benefit of a good plea, over and above the advantage of binding him over. In the late war,[3] I inserted in my evening paper, a paragraph that came by the post, reflecting upon the behaviour of a certain regiment in battle. An officer of said regiment came to my shop, and, in the presence of my wife and journeyman, threatened to cut off my ears — As I exhibited marks of bodily fear more ways than one,

to the conviction of the bye-standers, I bound him over; my
action lay, and I recovered. As for flagellation, you have nothing
to fear, and nothing to hope, on that head – There has been but
one printer flogged at the cart's tail[4] these thirty years; that was
Charles Watson; and he assured me it was no more than a
flea-bite. C— S—[5] has been threatened several times by the
House of L—;[6] but it came to nothing. If an information[7]
should be moved for, and granted against you, as the editor of
those Letters, I hope you will have honesty and wit enough to
appear and take your trial — If you should be sentenced to the
pillory, your fortune is made – As times go, that's a sure step
to honour and preferment. I shall think myself happy if I can
lend you a lift;[8] and am, very sincerely,

Yours,

LONDON, Aug. 10th.   HENRY DAVIS.

Please my kind service to your neighbour, my cousin Madoc
— I have sent an Almanack and Court-kalendar,[9] directed for
him at Mr Sutton's, bookseller, in Gloucester, carriage paid,
which he will please to accept as a small token of my regard.
My wife, who is very fond of toasted cheese,[10] presents her
compliments to him, and begs to know if there's any of that
kind, which he was so good as to send us last Christmas, to be
sold in London.

H. D.

HUMPHRY CLINKER

To Dr Lewis.

Doctor,

The pills are good for nothing – I might as well swallow snow-balls to cool my reins[1] – I have told you over and over how hard I am to move; and at this time of day, I ought to know something of my own constitution. Why will you be so positive? Prithee send me another prescription – I am as lame and as much tortured in all my limbs as if I was broke upon the wheel:[2] indeed, I am equally distressed in mind and body – As if I had not plagues enough of my own, those children of my sister are left me for a perpetual source of vexation – what business have people to get children to plague their neighbours? A ridiculous incident that happened yesterday to my niece Liddy, has disordered me in such a manner, that I expect to be laid up with another fit of the gout – perhaps, I may explain myself in my next. I shall set out to-morrow morning for the Hot Well at Bristol,[3] where I am afraid I shall stay longer than I could wish. On the receipt of this send Williams thither with my saddle-horse and the *demi pique*.[4] Tell Barns to thresh out the two old ricks, and send the corn to market, and sell it off to the poor at a shilling a bushel under market price. – I have received a snivelling letter from Griffin, offering to make a public submission and pay costs. I want none of his submissions, neither will I pocket any of his money – The fellow is a bad neighbour, and I desire to have nothing to do with him: but as he is purse-proud, he shall pay for his insolence: let him give five pounds to the poor of the parish, and I will withdraw my action; and in the mean time you may tell Prig to stop proceedings. – Let Morgan's widow have the Alderney cow, and forty shillings to clothe her children: but don't say a syllable of the matter to any living soul – I'll make her pay when she is able. I desire you will lock up all my drawers, and keep the keys till meeting; and be sure you take the iron chest with my papers into your own custody – Forgive all this trouble from,

Dear Lewis,
Your affectionate
GLOUCESTER, April 2.   M. BRAMBLE

To Mrs GWYLLIM, house-keeper at Brambleton-hall.

MRS GWILLIM,
   When this cums to hand, be sure to pack up in the trunk male that stands in my closet, to be sent me in the Bristol waggon without loss of time, the following articles, viz. my rose collard neglejay,[1] with green robins, my yellow damask, and my black velvet suit, with the short hoop; my bloo quilted petticot, my green manteel, my laced apron, my French commode, Macklin head and lappets,[2] and the litel box with my jowls. Williams may bring over my bum-daffee,[3] and the viol with the easings of Dr Hill's dockwater,[4] and Chowder's lacksitif. The poor creature has been terribly constuprated ever since we left huom. Pray take particular care of the house while the family is absent. Let there be a fire constantly kept in my brother's chamber and mine. The maids, having nothing to do, may be sat a spinning. I desire you'll clap a pad-luck on the wind-seller, and let none of the men have excess to the strong bear[5] — don't forget to have the gate shit every evening before dark – The gardnir and the hind may lie below in the landry, to partake the house, with the blunderbuss and the great dog; and I hope you'll have a watchful eye over the maids. I know that hussy, Mary Jones, loves to be rumping with the men. Let me know if Alderney's calf be sould yet, and what he fought[6] — if the ould goose be sitting; and if the cobler has cut Dicky,

and how the pore anemil bore the operation. No more at present, but rests,

Yours,

GLOSTAR, April 2.   TABITHA[7] BRAMBLE

To Mrs MARY JONES, at Brambleton-hall.

DEAR MOLLY,

Heaving this importunity, I send my love to you and Saul, being in good health, and hoping to hear the same from you; and that you and Saul will take my poor kitten to bed with you this cold weather. We have been all in a sad taking here at Glostar – Miss Liddy had like to have[1] run away with a player-man,[2] and young master and he would adone themselves a mischief; but the squire applied to the mare, and they were bound over. — Mistress bid me not speak a word of the matter to any Christian soul – no more I shall; for, we servints should see all and say nothing — But what was worse than all this, Chowder has had the misfortune to be worried by a butcher's dog, and came home in a terrible pickle — Mistress was taken with the asterisks,[3] but they soon went off. The doctor was sent for to Chowder, and he subscribed a repository,[4] which did him great service — thank God he's now in a fair way to do well – pray take care of my box and the pillyber,[5] and put them under your own bed; for, I do suppose, madam Gwyllim will be a prying into my secrets, now my back is turned. John Thomas is in good health, but sulky. The squire gave away an ould coat to a poor man; and John says as how 'tis robbing him of his parquisites. — I told him, by his agreement he was to receive no vails; but he says as how there's a difference betwixt vails and perquisites;[6] and so there is for sartain. We are all going to the Hot Well, where I shall drink your health in a glass of water, being,

Dear Molly,

Your humble servant to command,

GLOSTAR, April 2nd.   W. JENKINS

To Sir WATKIN PHILLIPS, Bart. of Jesus college, Oxon.[1]

DEAR PHILLIPS,

As I have nothing more at heart than to convince you I am incapable of forgetting, or neglecting the friendship I made at college, I now begin that correspondence by letters, which you and I agreed, at parting, to cultivate. I begin it sooner than I intended, that you may have it in your power to refute any idle reports which may be circulated to my prejudice at Oxford, touching a foolish quarrel, in which I have been involved on account of my sister, who had been some time settled here in a boarding-school. When I came hither with my uncle and aunt (who are our guardians) to fetch her away, I found her a fine tall girl, of seventeen, with an agreeable person; but remarkably simple, and quite ignorant of the world. This disposition, and want of experience, had exposed her to the addresses of a person – I know not what to call him, who had seen her at a play; and, with a confidence and dexterity peculiar to himself, found means to be recommended to her acquaintance. It was by the greatest accident I intercepted one of his letters; as it was my duty to stifle this correspondence in its birth, I made it my business to find him out, and tell him very freely my sentiments of the matter. The spark did not like the stile I used, and behaved with abundance of mettle. Though his rank in life (which, by the bye, I am ashamed to declare) did not entitle him to much deference; yet as his behaviour was remarkably spirited, I admitted him to the privilege of a gentleman, and something might have happened, had not we been prevented. – In short, the business took air, I know not how, and made abundance of noise – recourse was had to justice — I was obliged to give my word and honour, &c. and to-morrow morning we set out for Bristol Wells, where I expect to hear from you by the return of the post. — I have got into a family of originals, whom I may one day attempt to describe for your amusement. My aunt, Mrs Tabitha Bramble, is a maiden of forty-five, exceedingly starched, vain, and ridiculous. – My uncle is an odd kind of humorist,[2] always on the fret, and so unpleasant in his manner, that rather than be obliged to keep him company, I'd resign all claim to the inheritance of his estate. – Indeed his being tortured by the gout may have soured his temper, and, perhaps, I may like him better on further acquaintance; certain it is, all his servants and neighbours in the country are fond of him, even to a degree of enthusiasm,[3] the reason of which I cannot as yet comprehend. Remember me to Griffy Price, Gwyn, Mansel, Basset, and all the rest of my old Cambrian companions. — Salute[4] the bed-maker in my name – give my service to the cook, and pray take care of poor Ponto, for the sake of his old master, who is, and ever will be,

Dear Phillips,
Your affectionate friend,
and humble servant,

GLOUCESTER, April 2.   JER. MELFORD

To Mrs JERMYN at her house in Gloucester.

DEAR MADAM,

Having no mother of my own, I hope you will give me leave to disburden my poor heart to you, who have always acted the part of a kind parent to me, ever since I was put under your care. – Indeed, and indeed, my worthy governess may believe me, when I assure her, that I never harboured a thought that was otherwise than virtuous; and, if God will give me grace, I shall never behave so as to cast a reflection on the care you have taken in my education. I confess I have given just cause of offence by my want of prudence and experience. I ought not to have listened to what the young man said; and it was my duty to have told you all that passed, but I was ashamed to mention it; and then he behaved so modest and respectful, and seemed to be so melancholy and timorous, that I could not find in my heart to do any thing that should make him miserable and desperate. As for familiarities, I do declare, I never once allowed him the favour of a salute; and as to the few letters that passed between us, they are all in my uncle's hands, and I hope they contain nothing contrary to innocence and honour. – I am still persuaded that he is not what he appears to be: but time will discover — mean while I will endeavour to forget a connexion, which is so displeasing to my family. I have cried without ceasing, and have not tasted any thing but tea, since I was hurried away from you; nor did I once close my eyes for three nights running. — My aunt continues to chide me severely when we are by ourselves; but I hope to soften her in time, by humility and submission. — My uncle, who was so dreadfully passionate in the beginning, has been moved by my tears and distress; and is now all tenderness and compassion; and my brother is reconciled to me on my promise to break off all correspondence with that unfortunate youth; but, notwithstanding all their indulgence, I shall have no peace of mind till I know my dear and ever honoured governess has forgiven her poor, disconsolate, forlorn,

Affectionate humble servant,

till death,

Clifton, April 6.   Lydia Melford

To Miss Lætitia Willis, at Gloucester.

My Dearest Letty,

I am in such a fright, lest this should not come safe to hand by the conveyance of Jarvis the carrier, that I beg you will write me, on the receipt of it, directing to me, under cover, to Mrs Winifred Jenkins, my aunt's maid, who is a good girl, and has been so kind to me in my affliction, that I have made her my confidant; as for Jarvis, he was very shy of taking charge of my letter and the little parcel, because his sister Sally had like to have lost her place on my account: indeed I cannot blame the man for his caution; but I have made it worth his while. – My dear companion and bed-fellow, it is a grievous addition to my other misfortunes, that I am deprived of your agreeable company and conversation, at a time when I need so much the comfort of your good humour and good sense; but, I hope, the friendship we contracted at boarding-school, will last for life – I doubt not but on my side it will daily increase and improve, as I gain experience, and learn to know the value of a true friend. – O, my dear Letty! what shall I say about poor Mr Wilson? I have promised to break off all correspondence, and, if possible, to forget him: but, alas! I begin to perceive that will not be in my power. As it is by no means proper that the picture should remain in my hands, lest it should be the occasion of more mischief, I have sent it to you by this opportunity, begging you will either keep it safe till better times, or return it to Mr Wilson himself, who, I suppose, will make it his business to see you at the usual place. If he should be low-spirited at my sending back his picture, you may tell him I have no occasion for a picture, while the original continues engraved on my — But no; I would not have you tell him that neither; because there must be an end of our correspondence – I wish he may forget me, for the sake of his own peace; and yet if he should, he must be a barbarous — But it is impossible — poor Wilson cannot be false and inconstant: I beseech him not to write to me, nor attempt to see me for some time; for, considering the resentment and passionate temper of my brother Jery, such an attempt might be attended with consequences which would make us all miserable for life – let us trust to time and the chapter of accidents; or rather to that Providence which will not fail, sooner or later, to reward those that walk in the paths of honour and virtue.[1] I would offer my love to the young ladies; but it is not fit that any of them should know you have received this letter. – If we go to Bath,[2] I shall send you my simple remarks upon that famous center of polite amusement, and every other place we may chance to visit; and I flatter myself that my dear Miss Willis will be punctual in answering the letters of her affectionate,

CLIFTON, April 6.   LYDIA MELFORD

To Dr Lewis.

Dear Lewis,

I have followed your directions with some success, and might have been upon my legs by this time, had the weather permitted me to use my saddle-horse. I rode out upon the Downs last Tuesday, in the forenoon, when the sky, as far as the visible horizon, was without a cloud; but before I had gone a full mile, I was overtaken instantaneously by a storm of rain that wet me to the skin in three minutes – whence it came the devil knows; but it has laid me up (I suppose) for one fortnight. It makes me sick to hear people talk of the fine air upon Clifton-downs: How can the air be either agreeable or salutary, where the demon of vapours descends in a perpetual drizzle? My confinement is the more intolerable, as I am surrounded with domestic vexations. – My niece has had a dangerous fit of illness, occasioned by that cursed incident at Gloucester, which I mentioned in my last. — She is a poor good-natured simpleton, as soft as butter, and as easily melted – not that she's a fool – the girl's parts are not despicable, and her education has not been neglected; that is to say, she can write and spell, and speak French, and play upon the harpsichord; then she dances finely, has a good figure, and is very well inclined; but, she's deficient in spirit, and so susceptible – and so tender forsooth! – truly, she has got a languishing eye, and reads romances.[1] — Then there's her brother, 'squire Jery, a pert jackanapes,[2] full of college-petulance and self-conceit; proud as a German count, and as hot and hasty as a Welch mountaineer. As for that fantastical animal, my sister Tabby, you are no stranger to her qualifications – I vow to God, she is sometimes so intolerable, that I almost think she's the devil incarnate come to torment me for my sins; and yet I am conscious of no sins that ought to entail such family-plagues upon me – why the devil should not I shake off these torments at once? I an't married to Tabby, thank Heaven! nor did I beget the other two: let them choose another guardian: for my part I an't in a condition to take care of myself; much less to superintend the conduct of giddy-headed

boys and girls. You earnestly desire to know the particulars of
our adventure at Gloucester, which are briefly these, and I hope
they will go no further: – Liddy had been so long cooped up in
a boarding-school, which, next to a nunnery, is the worst kind
of seminary that ever was contrived for young women, that she
became as inflammable as touch-wood; and going to a play in
holiday-time, – 'sdeath,[3] I'm ashamed to tell you! she fell in love
with one of the actors – a handsome young fellow that goes by
the name of Wilson. The rascal soon perceived the impression
he had made, and managed matters so as to see her at a house
where she went to drink tea with her governess. – This was the
beginning of a correspondence, which they kept up by means
of a jade of a milliner, who made and dressed caps for the girls
at the boarding-school. When we arrived at Gloucester, Liddy
came to stay at lodgings with her aunt, and Wilson bribed the
maid to deliver a letter into her own hands; but it seems Jery
had already acquired so much credit with the maid (by what
means he best knows) that she carried the letter to him, and so
the whole plot was discovered. The rash boy, without saying a
word of the matter to me, went immediately in search of Wilson;
and, I suppose, treated him with insolence enough. The theatrical hero was too far gone in romance to brook such usage: he
replied in blank verse, and a formal challenge ensued. They
agreed to meet early next morning and decide the dispute with
sword and pistol. I heard nothing at all of the affair, till Mr
Morley came to my bed-side in the morning, and told me he
was afraid my nephew was going to fight, as he had been
overheard talking very loud and vehement with Wilson at the
young man's lodgings the night before, and afterwards went
and bought powder and ball at a shop in the neighbourhood. I
got up immediately, and upon inquiry found he was just going
out. I begged Morley to knock up the mayor, that he might
interpose as a magistrate, and in the mean time I hobbled after
the squire, whom I saw at a distance walking at a great pace
towards the city gate – in spite of all my efforts, I could not
come up till our two combatants had taken their ground, and
were priming their pistols. An old house luckily screened me
from their view; so that I rushed upon them at once, before I

was perceived. They were both confounded, and attempted to make their escape different ways; but Morley coming up with constables, at that instant, took Wilson into custody, and Jery followed him quietly to the mayor's house. All this time I was ignorant of what had passed the preceding day; and neither of the parties would discover a tittle of the matter. The mayor observed that it was great presumption in Wilson, who was a stroller, to proceed to such extremities with a gentleman of family and fortune; and threatened to commit him on the vagrant act.[4] – The young fellow bustled up with great spirit, declaring he was a gentleman, and would be treated as such; but he refused to explain himself further. The master of the company being sent for, and examined, touching the said Wilson, said the young man had engaged with him at Birmingham about six months ago; but never would take his salary; that he had behaved so well in his private character, as to acquire the respect and good-will of all his acquaintance, and that the public owned his merit as an actor was altogether extraordinary. — After all, I fancy, he will turn out to be a run-away prentice from London. – The manager offered to bail him for any sum, provided he would give his word and honour that he would keep the peace; but the young gentleman was on his high ropes,[5] and would by no means lay himself under any restrictions: on the other hand, Hopeful was equally obstinate; till at length the mayor declared, that if they both refused to be bound over, he would immediately commit Wilson as a vagrant to hard labour. I own I was much pleased with Jery's behaviour on this occasion: he said, that rather than Mr Wilson should be treated in such an ignominious manner, he would give his word and honour to prosecute the affair no further while they remained at Gloucester – Wilson thanked him for his generous manner of proceeding, and was discharged. On our return to our lodgings, my nephew explained the whole mystery; and I own I was exceedingly incensed – Liddy being questioned on the subject, and very severely reproached by that wild-cat my sister Tabby, first swooned away, then dissolving in a flood of tears, confessed all the particulars of the correspondence, at the same time giving up three letters, which was all she had received from her admirer. The last, which Jery intercepted, I send you inclosed, and when you have read it, I dare say you won't wonder at the progress the writer had made in the heart of a simple girl, utterly unacquainted with the characters of mankind. Thinking it was high time to remove her from such a dangerous connexion, I carried her off the very next day to Bristol; but the poor creature was so frightened and fluttered, by our threats and expostulations, that she fell sick the fourth day after our arrival at Clifton, and continued so ill for a whole week, that her life was despaired of. It was not till yesterday that Dr Rigge[6] declared her out of danger. You cannot imagine what I have suffered, partly from the indiscretion of this poor child, but much more from the fear of losing her entirely. This air is intolerably cold, and the place quite solitary – I never go down to the Well without returning low-spirited; for there I meet with half a dozen poor emaciated creatures, with ghostly looks, in the last stage of a consumption,[7] who have made shift to linger through the winter like so many exotic plants languishing in a hot-house; but in all appearance, will drop into their graves before the sun has warmth enough to mitigate the rigour of this ungenial spring. – If you think the Bath-water will be of any service to me, I will go thither so soon as my niece can bear the motion of the coach. — Tell Barns I am obliged to him for his advice; but don't choose to follow it. If Davis voluntarily offers to give up the farm, the other shall have it; but I will not begin at this time of day to distress my tenants, because they are unfortunate, and cannot make regular payments: I wonder that Barns should think me capable of such oppression – As for Higgins, the fellow is a notorious poacher, to be sure; and an impudent rascal to set his snares in my own paddock; but, I suppose, he thought he had some right (especially in my absence) to partake of what nature seems to have intended for common use – you may threaten him in my name, as much as you please, and if he repeats the offence, let me know it before you have recourse to justice. — I know you are a great sportsman, and oblige many of your friends: I need not tell you to make use of my grounds; but it may be necessary to hint, that I am more afraid of my fowling-piece than of my game. When you can spare two or three brace of partridges, send them over by the stagecoach, and tell Gwyllim that she forgot to pack up my flannel and wide shoes in the trunk-mail – I shall trouble you as usual, from time to time, till at last I suppose you will be tired of corresponding with

Your assured friend,

CLIFTON, April 17.   M. BRAMBLE

To Miss LYDIA MELFORD.

Miss Willis has pronounced my doom — you are going away, dear Miss Melford! – you are going to be removed, I know not whither! what shall I do? which way shall I turn for consolation? I know not what I say – all night long have I been tossed in a sea of doubts and fears,[1] uncertainty and distraction, without being able to connect my thoughts, much less to form any consistent plan of conduct – I was even tempted to wish that I had never seen you; or that you had been less amiable, or less compassionate to your poor Wilson; and yet it would be detestable ingratitude in me to form such a wish, considering how much I am indebted to your goodness, and the ineffable pleasure I have derived from your indulgence and approbation – Good God! I never heard your name mentioned without emotion! the most distant prospect of being admitted to your company, filled my whole soul with a kind of pleasing alarm! as the time approached, my heart beat with redoubled force, and every nerve thrilled with a transport of expectation; but, when I found myself actually in your presence; — when I heard you speak; – when I saw you smile; when I beheld your charming eyes turned favourably upon me; my breast was filled with such tumults of delight, as wholly deprived me of the power of utterance, and wrapt me in a delirium of joy! — encouraged by your sweetness of temper and affability, I ventured to describe the feelings of my heart – even then you did not check my presumption – you pitied my sufferings and gave me leave to hope – you put a favourable – perhaps too favourable a construction, on my appearance – certain it is, I am no player in love – I speak the language of my own heart; and have no prompter but nature. — Yet there is something in this heart, which I have not yet disclosed. — I flattered myself – But, I will not — I must not proceed – Dear Miss Liddy! for Heaven's sake, contrive, if possible, some means of letting me speak to you before you leave Gloucester; otherwise, I know not what will – But I begin to rave again. – I will endeavour to bear this trial with fortitude – while I am capable of reflecting upon your tenderness and truth, I surely have no cause to despair – a cloud hangs over me, and there is a dreadful weight upon my spirits! While you stay in this place, I shall continually hover about your lodgings, as the parted soul is said to linger about the grave where its mortal comfort lies. — I know, if it is in your power, you will task your humanity – your compassion – shall I add, your affection? – in order to assuage the almost intolerable disquiet that torments the heart of your afflicted,

GLOUCESTER, March 31.   WILSON

To Sir WATKIN PHILLIPS, of Jesus college, Oxon.

HOT WELL, April 18.

DEAR PHILLIPS,

I give Mansel credit for his invention, in propagating the report that I had a quarrel with a mountebank's merry Andrew[1] at Gloucester: but I have too much respect for every appendage of wit, to quarrel even with the lowest buffoonery; and therefore I hope Mansel and I shall always be good friends. I cannot, however, approve of his drowning my poor dog Ponto, on purpose to convert Ovid's pleonasm[2] into a punning epitaph, – *deerant quoque Littora Ponto*:[3] for, that he threw him into the Isis,[4] when it was so high and impetuous, with no other view than to kill the fleas, is an excuse that will not hold water – But I leave poor Ponto to his fate, and hope Providence will take care to accommodate Mansel with a drier death.

As there is nothing that can be called company at the Well, I am here in a state of absolute rustication:[5] This, however, gives me leisure to observe the singularities in my uncle's character, which seems to have interested your curiosity. The truth is, his disposition and mine, which, like oil and vinegar, repelled one another at first, have now begun to mix by dint of being beat up together. I was once apt to believe him a complete Cynic;[6] and that nothing but the necessity of his occasions could compel him to get within the pale of society – I am now of another opinion. I think his peevishness arises partly from bodily pain, and partly from a natural excess of mental sensibility; for, I suppose, the mind as well as the body, is in some cases endued with a morbid excess of sensation.

I was t'other day much diverted with a conversation that passed in the Pump-room, betwixt him and the famous Dr L—n,[7] who is come to ply at the Well for patients. My uncle was complaining of the stink, occasioned by the vast quantity of mud and slime which the river leaves at low ebb under the windows of the Pump-room. He observed, that the exhalations arising from such a nuisance, could not but be prejudicial to the weak lungs of many consumptive patients, who came to drink the water. The Doctor overhearing this remark, made up to him, and assured him he was mistaken. He said, people in general were so misled by vulgar prejudices that philosophy was hardly sufficient to undeceive them. Then humming thrice, he assumed a most ridiculous solemnity of aspect, and entered into a learned investigation of the nature of stink. He observed, that stink, or stench, meant no more than a strong impression on the olfactory nerves; and might be applied to substances of the most opposite qualities; that in the Dutch language, *stinken* signifies the most agreeable perfume, as well as the most fetid odour, as appears in Van Vloudel's translation of Horace,[8] in that beautiful ode, *Quis multa gracilis*, &c. – The words *liquidis perfusus odoribus*, he translates *van civet & moschata gestinken*:[9] that individuals differed *toto cœlo*[10] in their opinion of smells, which, indeed, was altogether as arbitrary as the opinion of beauty; that the French were pleased with the putrid effluvia of animal food; and so were the Hottentots in Africa, and the

Savages in Greenland; and that the Negroes on the coast of
Senegal would not touch fish till it was rotten; strong presump-
tions in favour of what is generally called *stink*, as those nations
are in a state of nature, undebauched by luxury,[11] unseduced
by whim and caprice: that he had reason to believe the stercoraceous[12] flavour, condemned by prejudice as a stink, was, in
fact, most agreeable to the organs of smelling; for, that every
person who pretended to nauseate the smell of another's
excretions, snuffed up his own with particular complacency;
for the truth of which he appealed to all the ladies and gentlemen then present: he said, the inhabitants of Madrid and
Edinburgh found particular satisfaction in breathing their
own atmosphere, which was always impregnated with stercoraceous effluvia: that the learned Dr B—, in his treatise on the
Four Digestions,[13] explains in what manner the volatile effluvia
from the intestines stimulate and promote the operations of the
animal economy: he affirmed, the last Grand Duke of Tuscany,
of the *Medicis* family,[14] who refined upon sensuality with
the spirit of a philosopher, was so delighted with that odour,
that he caused the essence of ordure to be extracted, and used
it as the most delicious perfume: that he himself (the doctor)
when he happened to be low-spirited, or fatigued with business,
found immediate relief and uncommon satisfaction from hanging over the stale contents of a close-stool,[15] while his servant
stirred it about under his nose; nor was this effect to be
wondered at, when we consider that this substance abounds
with the self-same volatile salts that are so greedily smelled to
by the most delicate invalids, after they have been extracted
and sublimed by the chemists. — By this time the company
began to hold their noses; but the doctor, without taking
the least notice of this signal, proceeded to shew that many
fetid substances were not only agreeable but salutary; such as
assa fœtida,[16] and other medicinal gums, resins, roots, and
vegetables, over and above burnt feathers, tan-pits,[17] candle-
snuffs, &c. In short, he used many learned arguments to persuade his audience out of their senses; and from *stench* made a
transition to *filth*, which he affirmed was also a mistaken idea,
in as much as objects so called, were no other than certain

modifications of matter, consisting of the same principles that
enter into the composition of all created essences, whatever they
may be: that in the filthiest production of nature, a philosopher
considered nothing but the earth, water, salt and air, of which
it was compounded; that, for his own part, he had no more
objections to drinking the dirtiest ditch-water, than he had to
a glass of water from the Hot Well, provided he was assured
there was nothing poisonous in the concrete.[18] Then addressing
himself to my uncle, 'Sir (said he) you seem to be of a dropsical
habit, and probably will soon have a confirmed *ascites*:[19] if I
should be present when you are tapped, I will give you a con-
vincing proof of what I assert, by drinking without hesitation
the water that comes out of your abdomen.'—The ladies made
wry faces at this declaration, and my uncle, changing colour,
told him he did not desire any such proof of his philosophy:
'But I should be glad to know (said he) what makes you think
I am of a dropsical habit?' 'Sir, I beg pardon (replied the Doctor)
I perceive your ancles are swelled, and you seem to have the
facies leucophlegmatica.[20] Perhaps, indeed, your disorder may
be *oedematous*,[21] or gouty, or it may be the *lues venerea*:[22]
If you have any reason to flatter yourself it is this last, sir, I
will undertake to cure you with three small pills, even if the
disease should have attained its utmost inveteracy. Sir, it is an
arcanum which I have discovered, and prepared with infinite
labour. – Sir, I have lately cured a woman in Bristol – a common
prostitute, sir, who had got all the worst symptoms of the
disorder; such as *nodi*, *tophi*, and *gummata*, *verrucæ*, *cristæ
Galli*, and a *serpiginous* eruption,[23] or rather a pocky itch all
over her body. — By the time she had taken the second pill,
sir, by Heaven! she was as smooth as my hand, and the third
made her sound and as fresh as a new born infant.' 'Sir
(cried my uncle peevishly) I have no reason to flatter myself
that my disorder comes within the efficacy of your nostrum.
But this patient you talk of may not be so sound at bottom
as you imagine.' 'I can't possibly be mistaken (rejoined the
philosopher) for I have had communication[24] with her three
times – I always ascertain my cures in that manner.' At this
remark, all the ladies retired to another corner of the room,

and some of them began to spit. – As to my uncle, though he was ruffled at first by the doctor's saying he was dropsical, he could not help smiling at this ridiculous confession and, I suppose, with a view to punish this original, told him there was a wart upon his nose, that looked a little suspicious. 'I don't pretend to be a judge of those matters (said he) but I understand that warts are often produced by the distemper; and that one upon your nose seems to have taken possession of the very key-stone of the bridge, which I hope is in no danger of falling.'[25] L—n seemed a little confounded at this remark, and assured him it was nothing but a common excrescence of the cuticula, but that the bones were all sound below; for the truth of this assertion he appealed to the touch, desiring he would feel the part. My uncle said it was a matter of such delicacy to meddle with a gentleman's nose, that he declined the office – upon which, the Doctor turning to me, intreated me to do him that favour. I complied with his request, and handled it so roughly, that he sneezed, and the tears ran down his cheeks, to the no small entertainment of the company, and particularly of my uncle, who burst out a-laughing for the first time since I have been with him; and took notice, that the part seemed to be very tender. 'Sir (cried the Doctor) it is naturally a tender part; but to remove all possibility of doubt, I will take off the wart this very night.'

So saying, he bowed, with great solemnity all round, and retired to his own lodgings, where he applied a caustic to the wart; but it spread in such a manner as to produce a considerable inflammation, attended with an enormous swelling; so that when he next appeared, his whole face was overshadowed by this tremendous nozzle; and the rueful eagerness with which he explained this unlucky accident, was ludicrous beyond all description. — I was much pleased with meeting the original of a character, which you and I have often laughed at in description; and what surprises me very much, I find the features in the picture, which has been drawn for him, rather softened than over-charged.

As I have something else to say; and this letter has run to an unconscionable length, I shall now give you a little respite, and

trouble you again by the very first post. I wish you would take
it in your head to retaliate these double strokes upon

Yours always,
J. MELFORD

To Sir WATKIN PHILLIPS, of Jesus college, Oxon.

HOT WELL, April 20.

DEAR KNIGHT,

I now sit down to execute the threat in the tail of my last.
The truth is, I am big with the secret, and long to be delivered.
It relates to my guardian, who, you know, is at present our
principal object in view.

T'other day, I thought I had detected him in such a state of
frailty, as would but ill become his years and character. There
is a decent sort of woman, not disagreeable in her person, that
comes to the Well, with a poor emaciated child, far gone in a
consumption. I had caught my uncle's eyes several times
directed to this person, with a very suspicious expression in
them, and every time he saw himself observed, he hastily withdrew them, with evident marks of confusion – I resolved to
watch him more narrowly, and saw him speaking to her privately in a corner of the walk. At length, going down to the
Well one day, I met her half way up the hill to Clifton, and
could not help suspecting she was going to our lodgings by
appointment, as it was about one o'clock, the hour when my
sister and I are generally at the Pump-room. – This notion
exciting my curiosity, I returned by a back-way, and got unper-
ceived into my own chamber, which is contiguous to my uncle's
apartment. Sure enough, the woman was introduced but not
into his bed-chamber; he gave her audience in a parlour; so that
I was obliged to shift my station to another room, where,
however, there was a small chink in the partition, through
which I could perceive what passed. – My uncle, though a little
lame, rose up when she came in, and setting a chair for her,

desired she would sit down: then he asked if she would take a dish of chocolate,[1] which she declined, with much acknowledgment. After a short pause, he said, in a croaking tone of voice, which confounded me not a little, 'Madam, I am truly concerned for your misfortunes; and if this trifle can be of any service to you, I beg you will accept it without ceremony.' So saying, he put a bit of paper into her hand, which she opening with great trepidation, exclaimed in an extacy, 'Twenty pounds! Oh, sir!' and sinking down upon a settee, fainted away – Frightened at this fit, and, I suppose, afraid of calling for assistance, lest her situation should give rise to unfavourable conjectures, he ran about the room in distraction, making frightful grimaces; and, at length, had recollection enough to throw a little water in her face; by which application she was brought to herself: but, then her feeling took another turn. She shed a flood of tears, and cried aloud, 'I know not who you are: but, sure — worthy sir – generous sir! – the distress of me and my poor dying child – Oh! if the widow's prayers – if the orphan's tears of gratitude can ought avail – gracious Providence – Blessings! – shower down eternal blessings.' – Here she was interrupted by my uncle, who muttered in a voice still more and more discordant, 'For Heaven's sake be quiet, madam – consider – the people of the house – 'sdeath! can't you.' — All this time she was struggling to throw herself on her knees, while he seizing her by the wrists, endeavoured to seat her upon the settee, saying, 'Prithee – good now — hold your tongue' — At that instant, who should burst into the room but our aunt Tabby! of all antiquated maidens the most diabolically capricious — Ever prying into other people's affairs, she had seen the woman enter, and followed her to the door, where she stood listening, but probably could hear nothing distinctly, except my uncle's last exclamation; at which she bounded into the parlour in a violent rage, that dyed the tip of her nose of a purple hue, – 'Fy upon you, Matt! (cried she) what doings are these, to disgrace your own character, and disparage your family?' — Then, snatching the banknote out of the stranger's hand, she went on — 'How now, twenty pounds! – here is temptation with a witness! — Good-woman, go about your business — Brother, brother, I know not which most to admire; your concupissins,[2] or your extravagance!' — 'Good God (exclaimed the poor woman) shall a worthy gentleman's character suffer for an action that does honour to humanity?' By this time, uncle's indignation was effectually roused. His face grew pale, his teeth chattered, and his eyes flashed — 'Sister (cried he, in a voice like thunder) I vow to God, your impertinence is exceedingly provoking.' With these words, he took her by the hand, and, opening the door of communication, thrust her into the chamber where I stood, so affected by the scene, that the tears ran down my cheeks. Observing these marks of emotion, 'I don't wonder (said she) to see you concerned at the back-slidings of so near a relation; a man of his years and infirmities: These are fine doings, truly — This is a rare example, set by a guardian, for the benefit of his pupils[3] – Monstrous! incongruous! sophistical!' – I thought it was but an act of justice to set her to rights; and therefore explained the mystery – But she would not be undeceived, 'What (said she) would you go for to offer for to arguefy me out of my senses? Did'n't I hear him whispering to her to hold her tongue? Did'n't I see her in tears? Did'n't I see him struggling to throw her upon the couch? O filthy! hideous! abominable! Child, child, talk not to me of charity. — Who gives twenty pounds in charity? – But you are a stripling – You know nothing of the world — Besides, charity begins at home — Twenty pounds would buy me a complete suit of flowered silk, trimmings and all –' In short, I quitted the room, my contempt for her, and my respect for her brother, being increased in the same proportion. I have since been informed, that the person, whom my uncle so generously relieved, is the widow of an ensign, who has nothing to depend upon but the pension of fifteen pounds a year. The people of the Well-house give her an excellent character. She lodges in a garret, and works very hard at plain work,[4] to support her daughter, who is dying of a consumption. I must own, to my shame, I feel a strong inclination to follow my uncle's example, in relieving this poor widow; but, betwixt friends, I am afraid

of being detected in a weakness, that might entail the ridicule
of the company, upon,

Dear Phillips,
Yours always,
J. MELFORD

Direct your next to me at Bath; and remember me to all our
fellow-jesuits.

To Dr LEWIS.

HOT WELL, April 20.

I understand your hint. There are mysteries in physic, as
well as in religion; which we of the profane have no right to
investigate – A man must not presume to use his reason, unless
he has studied the categories, and can chop logic[1] by mode and
figure – Between friends, I think every man of tolerable parts
ought, at my time of day, to be both physician and lawyer, as
far as his own constitution and property are concerned. For my
own part, I have had an hospital these fourteen years within
myself, and studied my own case with the most painful attention; consequently may be supposed to know something of the
matter, although I have not taken regular courses of physiology
et cetera et cetera. — In short, I have for some time been of
opinion (no offence, dear Doctor) that the sum of all your
medical discoveries amounts to this, that the more you study
the less you know. – I have read all that has been written
on the Hot Wells, and what I can collect from the whole, is,
that the water contains nothing but a little salt, and calcarious[2]
earth, mixed in such inconsiderable proportion, as can have
very little, if any, effect on the animal economy. This being the
case, I think the man deserves to be fitted with a cap and
bells,[3] who for such a paultry advantage as this spring affords,
sacrifices his precious time, which might be employed in taking
more effectual remedies, and exposes himself to the dirt, the

stench, the chilling blasts, and perpetual rains, that render this place to me intolerable. If these waters, from a small degree of astringency, are of some service in the *diabetes*, *diarrhœa* and *night sweats*, when the secretions are too much increased, must not they do harm in the same proportion, where the humours are obstructed, as in the *asthma*, *scurvy*, *gout* and *dropsy*? – Now we talk of the *dropsy*, here is a strange fantastical oddity, one of your brethren, who harangues every day in the Pump-room, as if he was hired to give lectures on all subjects whatsoever – I know not what to make of him – Sometimes he makes shrewd remarks; at other times he talks like the greatest simpleton in nature – He has read a great deal; but without method or judgment, and digested nothing. He believes every thing he has read; especially if it has any thing of the marvellous in it; and his conversation is a surprizing hotch-potch of erudition and extravagance. — He told me t'other day, with great confidence, that my case was dropsical; or, as he called it, *leucophlegmatic*: A sure sign, that his want of experience is equal to his presumption; for, you know, there is nothing analogous to the dropsy in my disorder — I wish those impertinent fellows, with their ricketty understandings, would keep their advice for those that ask it — *Dropsy*, indeed! Sure I have not lived to the age of fifty-five, and had such experience of my own disorder, and consulted you and other eminent physicians, so often, and so long, to be undeceived by such a – But, without all doubt, the man is mad; and, therefore, what he says is of no consequence. I had, yesterday, a visit from Higgins, who came hither under the terror of your threats, and brought me in a present a brace of hares, which he owned he took in my ground; and I could not persuade the fellow that he did wrong, or that I would ever prosecute him for poaching – I must desire you will wink hard at the practices of this rascallion,[4] otherwise I shall be plagued with his presents, which cost me more than they are worth. — If I could wonder at any thing Fitzowen does, I should be surprized at his assurance in desiring you to solicit my vote for him at the next election for the county: for him, who opposed me, on the like occasion, with the most illiberal competition – You may tell him civilly, that I beg to be excused. Direct your next for me at Bath, whither I propose to remove to-morrow; not only on my own account, but for the sake of my niece, Liddy, who is like to relapse. The poor creature fell into a fit yesterday, while I was cheapening[5] a pair of spectacles, with a Jew-pedlar. — I am afraid there is something still lurking in that little heart of hers, which I hope a change of objects will remove. Let me know what you think of this half-witted Doctor's impertinent, ridiculous, and absurd notion of my disorder – So far from being dropsical, I am as lank in the belly as a grey-hound; and, by measuring my ancle with a pack-thread, I find the swelling subsides every day – From such doctors, good Lord deliver us![6] – I have not yet taken any lodgings in Bath; because there we can be accommodated at a minute's warning, and I shall choose for myself – I need not say your directions for drinking and bathing will be agreeable to,

Dear Lewis,
Yours ever,
MAT. BRAMBLE

P.S. I forgot to tell you, that my right ancle pits,[7] a symptom, as I take it, of its being *œdematous*, not *leucophlegmatic*.

To Miss LETTY WILLIS, at Gloucester.

HOT WELL, April 21.

MY DEAR LETTY,

I did not intend to trouble you again, till we should be settled at Bath; but having the occasion of Jarvis, I could not let it slip, especially as I have something extraordinary to communicate – O, my dear companion! What shall I tell you? for several days past there was a Jew-looking man, that plied at the Wells with a box of spectacles; and he always eyed me so earnestly, that I began to be very uneasy. At last, he came to our lodgings at Clifton, and lingered about the door, as if he wanted to speak to somebody — I was seized with an odd kind of fluttering, and begged Win to throw herself in his way: but the poor girl has weak nerves, and was afraid of his beard. My uncle, having occasion for new glasses, called him up stairs, and was trying a pair of spectacles, when the man, advancing to me, said in a whisper — O gracious! what d'ye think he said? – 'I am Wilson!' His features struck me that very moment — it was Wilson, sure enough! but so disguised, that it would have been impossible to know him, if my heart had not assisted in the discovery. I was so surprised, and so frightened that I fainted away, but soon recovered; and found myself supported by him on the chair, while my uncle was running about the room, with the spectacles on his nose, calling for help. I had no opportunity to speak to him; but looks were sufficiently expressive. He was payed for his glasses, and went away. Then I told Win who he was, and sent her after him to the Pump-room; where she spoke to him, and begged him in my name to withdraw from the place, that he might not incur the suspicion of my uncle or my brother, if he did not want to see me die of terror and vexation. The poor youth declared, with tears in his eyes, that he had something extraordinary to communicate; and asked, if she would deliver a letter to me: but this she absolutely refused, by my order. – Finding her obstinate in her refusal, he desired she would tell me that he was no longer a player, but a gentleman; in which character he would very soon avow his passion for me, without fear of censure or reproach — Nay, he even discovered his name and family, which, to my great grief, the simple girl forgot, in the confusion occasioned by her being seen talking to him by my brother, who stopt her on the road, and asked what business she had with that rascally Jew – She pretended she was cheapening a stay-hook, but was thrown into such a quandary, that she forgot the most material part of the information; and when she came home, went into an hysteric fit of laughing. This transaction happened three days ago, during which he has not appeared, so that I suppose he has gone. Dear Letty! you see how Fortune takes pleasure in persecuting your poor friend. If you should see him at Gloucester – or if you have seen him, and know his real name and family, pray keep me no longer in suspense — And yet, if he is under no obligation to keep himself longer concealed, and has a real affection for me, I should hope he will, in a little time, declare himself to my relations. Sure, if there is nothing unsuitable in the match, they won't be so cruel as to thwart my inclinations – O what happiness would then be my portion! I can't help indulging the thought, and pleasing my fancy with such agreeable ideas; which after all, perhaps, will never be realized – But, why should I despair? who knows what will happen? – We set out for Bath to-morrow, and I am almost sorry for it; as I begin to be in love with solitude, and this is a charming romantic place. The air is so pure; the Downs are so agreeable; the furz in full blossom; the ground enamelled with daisies, and primroses, and cowslips; all the trees bursting into leaves, and the hedges already clothed with their vernal livery; the mountains covered with flocks of sheep and tender bleating wanton lambkins playing, frisking, and skipping from side to side; the groves resound with the notes of blackbird, thrush, and linnet; and all night long sweet Philomel[1] pours forth her ravishingly delightful song. Then, for variety, we go down to the *nymph of Bristol spring*,[2] where the company is assembled before dinner; so good natured, so free, so easy; and there we drink the water so clear, so pure, so mild, so charmingly maukish.[3] There the fun is so chearful and reviving; the weather so soft; the walk so agreeable; the prospect so amusing; and the ships and boats going up and down the river, close under the windows of the Pump-room, afford such an enchanting variety of moving pictures, as require a much abler pen than mine to describe. To make this place a perfect paradise to me, nothing is wanting but an agreeable companion and sincere friend; such as my dear miss Willis hath been, and I hope still will be, to her ever faithful.

LYDIA MELFORD

Direct for me, still under cover, to Win; and Jarvis will take care to convey it safe. Adieu.

To Sir WATKIN PHILLIPS, of Jesus college, Oxon.

BATH, April 24.

DEAR PHILLIPS,

You have, indeed, reason to be surprised, that I should have concealed my correspondence with miss Blackerby from you, to whom I disclosed all my other connexions of that nature; but the truth is, I never dreamed of any such commerce, till your last informed me, that it had produced something which could not be much longer concealed. It is a lucky circumstance, however, that her reputation will not suffer any detriment, but rather derive advantage from the discovery; which will prove, at least, that it is not quite so rotten as most people imagined – For my own part, I declare to you, in all the sincerity of friendship, that, far from having any amorous intercourse with the object in question, I never had the least acquaintance with her person; but, if she is really in the condition you describe, I suspect Mansel to be at the bottom of the whole. His visits to that shrine were no secret; and this attachment, added to some good offices, which you know he has done me, since I left *Alma-mater*,[1] give me a right to believe him capable of saddling me with this scandal, when my back was turned — Nevertheless, if my name can be of any service to him, he is welcome to make use of it; and if the woman should be abandoned enough to swear his bantling to me, I must beg the favour of you to compound with the parish: I shall pay the penalty without repining; and you will be so good as to draw upon me immediately for the sum required — On this occasion, I act by the advice of my uncle; who says I shall have good-luck if I pass through life without being obliged to make many more compositions of the same kind. The old gentleman told me last night, with great good-humour, that betwixt the age of twenty and forty, he had been obliged to provide for nine bastards, sworn to him by women whom he never saw – Mr Bramble's character, which seems to interest you greatly, opens and improves upon me every day. – His singularities afford a rich mine of entertainment; his understanding, so far as I can judge, is well cultivated;

his observations on life are equally just, pertinent, and un-common. He affects misanthropy, in order to conceal the sensi-bility of a heart, which is tender, even to a degree of weakness. This delicacy of feeling, or soreness of the mind, makes him timorous and fearful; but then he is afraid of nothing so much as of dishonour; and although he is exceedingly cautious of giving offence, he will fire at the least hint of insolence or ill-breeding. – Respectable as he is, upon the whole, I can't help being sometimes diverted by his little distresses; which provoke him to let fly the shafts of his satire, keen and penetrating as the arrows of Teucer[2] – Our aunt, Tabitha, acts upon him as a perpetual grind-stone – She is, in all respects, a striking contrast to her brother — But I reserve her portrait for another occasion.

Three days ago we came hither from the Hot Well, and took possession of the first floor of a lodging-house, on the South Parade;[3] a situation which my uncle chose, for its being near the Bath, and remote from the noise of carriages. He was scarce warm in the lodgings when he called for his night-cap, his wide shoes, and flannel; and declared himself invested with the gout in his right foot; though, I believe it had as yet reached no farther than his imagination. It was not long before he had reason to repent his premature declaration; for our aunt Tabitha found means to make such a clamour and confusion, before the flannels could be produced from the trunk, that one would have imagined the house was on fire. All this time, uncle sat boiling with impatience, biting his fingers, throwing up his eyes, and muttering ejaculations; at length he burst into a kind of convulsive laugh, after which he hummed a song; and when the hurricane was over, exclaimed 'Blessed be God for all things!' This, however, was but the beginning of his troubles. Mrs Tabitha's favourite dog Chowder, having paid his compli-ments to a female turnspit[4] of his own species, in the kitchen, involved himself in a quarrel with no fewer than five rivals, who set upon him at once, and drove him up stairs to the dining-room door, with hideous noise: there our aunt and her woman, taking arms in his defence, joined the concert; which became truly diabolical. This fray being with difficulty suppressed, by the intervention of our own footman and the cook-maid of the

house, the squire had just opened his mouth, to expostulate
with Tabby, when the town-waits,[5] in the passage below, struck
up their music (if music it may be called) with such a sudden
burst of sound, as made him start and stare, with marks of
indignation and disquiet. He had recollection enough to send
his servant with some money to silence those noisy intruders;
and they were immediately dismissed, though not without some
opposition on the part of Tabitha, who thought it but reasonable that he should have more music for his money. Scarce had
he settled this knotty point, when a strange kind of thumping
and bouncing was heard right overhead, in the second story, so
loud and violent, as to shake the whole building. I own I was
exceedingly provoked at this new alarm; and before my uncle
had time to express himself on the subject, I ran up stairs, to
see what was the matter. Finding the room-door open, I entered
without ceremony, and perceived an object, which I cannot
now recollect without laughing to excess – It was a dancing
master,[6] with his scholar, in the act of teaching. The master was
blind of one eye, and lame of one foot, and led about the room
his pupil; who seemed to be about the age of threescore, stooped
mortally, was tall, raw-boned, hard-favoured, with a woollen
night-cap on his head; and he had stript off his coat, that he
might be more nimble in his motions – Finding himself intruded
upon, by a person he did not know, he forthwith girded himself
with a long iron sword, and advancing to me, with a peremptory air, pronounced, in a true Hibernian[7] accent, 'Mister What
d'ye callum, by my saoul and conscience, I am very glad to sea
you, if you are after coming in the way of friendship; and indeed,
and indeed now, I believe you are my friend sure enough, gra;[8]
though I never had the honour to sea your face before, my dear;
for becaase you come like a friend, without any ceremony at
all, at all' – I told him the nature of my visit would not admit
of ceremony; that I was come to desire he would make less
noise, as there was a sick gentleman below, whom he had no
right to disturb with such preposterous doings. 'Why, look-ye
now, young gentleman (replied this original) perhaps, upon
another occasion, I might shivilly request you to explain the
maining of that hard word, *prepasterous:* but there's a time for

all things, honey' – So saying, he passed me with great agility, and, running down stairs, found our foot-man at the dining-room door, of whom he demanded admittance, to pay his respects to the stranger. As the fellow did not think proper to refuse the request of such a formidable figure, he was immediately introduced, and addressed himself to my uncle in these words: 'Your humble servant, good sir, – I'm not so *prepasterous*, as your son calls it, but I know the rules of shivility – I'm a poor knight of Ireland, my name is sir Ulic Mackilligut, of the county of Galway; being your fellow-lodger, I'm come to pay my respects, and to welcome you to the South Parade, and to offer my best services to you, and your good lady, and your pretty daughter; and even to the young gentleman your son, though he thinks me a *prepasterous* fellow – You must know I am to have the honour to open a ball next door to-morrow with lady Mac Manus; and being rusted in my dancing, I was refreshing my memory with a little exercise; but if I had known there was a sick person below, by Christ! I would have sooner danced a hornpipe[9] upon my own head, than walk the softest minuet over yours.' – My uncle, who was not a little startled at his first appearance, received his compliment with great complacency, insisted upon his being seated, thanked him for the honour of his visit, and reprimanded me for my abrupt expostulation with a gentleman of his rank and character. Thus tutored, I asked pardon of the knight, who, forthwith starting up, embraced me so close, that I could hardly breathe; and assured me, he loved me as his own soul. At length, recollecting his night-cap, he pulled it off in some confusion; and, with his bald-pate uncovered, made a thousand apologies to the ladies, as he retired – At that instant, the Abbey bells[10] began to ring so loud, that we could not hear one another speak; and this peal, as we afterwards learned, was for the honour of Mr Bullock, an eminent cowkeeper of Tottenham,[11] who had just arrived at Bath, to drink the waters for indigestion. Mr Bramble had not time to make his remarks upon the agreeable nature of this serenade, before his ears were saluted with another concert that interested him more nearly. Two negroes, belonging to a Creole gentleman,[12] who lodged in the same house, taking their station at a window in the stair-case, about ten feet from our dining-room door, began to practise upon the French-horn;[13] and being in the very first rudiments of execution, produced such discordant sounds, as might have discomposed the organs of an ass — You may guess what effect they had upon the irritable nerves of uncle; who, with the most admirable expression of splenetic[14] suprize in his countenance, sent his man to silence these dreadful blasts, and desire the musicians to practise in some other place, as they had no right to stand there and disturb all the lodgers in the house. Those sable performers, far from taking the hint, and withdrawing, treated the messenger with great insolence; bidding him carry his compliments to their master, colonel Rigworm, who would give him a proper answer, and a good drubbing into the bargain; in the mean time they continued their noise, and even endeavoured to make it more disagreeable; laughing between whiles, at the thoughts of being able to torment their betters with impunity. Our 'squire, incensed at the additional insult, immediately dispatched the servant, with his compliments to colonel Rigworm, requesting that he would order his blacks to be quiet, as the noise they made was altogether intolerable – To this message, the Creole colonel replied, that his horns had a right to sound on a common staircase; that there they should play for his diversion; and that those who did not like the noise, might look for lodgings elsewhere. Mr Bramble no sooner received this reply, than his eyes began to glisten, his face grew pale, and his teeth chattered. After a moment's pause, he slipt on his shoes, without speaking a word, or seeming to feel any further disturbance from the gout in his toes. Then snatching his cane, he opened the door and proceeded to the place where the black trumpeters were posted. There, without further hesitation, he began to belabour them both; and exerted himself with such astonishing vigour and agility, that both their heads and horns were broken in a twinkling, and they ran howling down stairs to their master's parlour-door. The squire, following them half way, called aloud, that the colonel might hear him, 'Go, rascals, and tell your master what I have done; if he thinks himself injured, he knows where to come for satisfaction. As for you, this is but an earnest of what you shall receive, if ever you presume to blow a horn again here, while I stay in the house.' So saying, he retired to his apartment, in expectation of hearing from the West Indian; but the colonel prudently declined any farther prosecution of the dispute. My sister Liddy was frighted into a fit, from which she was no sooner recovered, than Mrs Tabitha began a lecture upon patience; which her brother interrupted with a most significant grin, 'True, sister, God increase my patience and your discretion. I wonder (added he) what sort of sonata we are to expect from this overture, in which the devil, that presides over horrid sounds, hath given us such variations of discord — The trampling of porters, the creaking and crashing of trunks, the snarling of curs, the scolding of women, the squeaking and squalling of fiddles and hautboys[15] out of tune, the bouncing of the Irish baronet over-head, and the bursting, belching, and brattling of the French-horns in the passage (not to mention the harmonious peal that still thunders from the Abbey steeple) succeeding one another without interruption, like the different parts of the same concert, have given me such an idea of what a poor invalid has to expect in this temple, dedicated to Silence and Repose, that I shall certainly shift my quarters to-morrow, and endeavour to effectuate my retreat before Sir Ulic opens the ball with my lady Mac Manus; a conjunction that bodes me no good.' This intimation was by no means agreeable to Mrs Tabitha, whose ears were not quite so delicate as those of her brother – She said it would be great folly to move from such agreeable lodgings, the moment they were comfortably settled. She wondered he should be such an enemy to music and mirth. She heard no noise but of his own making: it was impossible to manage a family in dumb-shew. He might harp as long as he pleased upon her scolding; but she never scolded, except for his advantage; but he would never be satisfied, even tho'f she should sweat blood and water in his service – I have a great notion that our aunt, who is now declining into the most desperate state of celibacy, had formed some design upon the heart of Sir Ulic Mackilligut, which she feared might be frustrated by our abrupt departure from these lodgings. Her brother, eyeing her askance, 'Pardon me, sister (said he) I should be a savage, indeed, were I insensible of my own felicity, in having such a mild, complaisant, good-humoured, and considerate companion and housekeeper; but as I have got a weak head, and my sense of hearing is painfully acute, before I have recourse to plugs of wool and cotton, I'll try whether I can't find another lodging, where I shall have more quiet and less music.' He accordingly dispatched his man upon this service; and next day he found a small house in Milsham-street,[16] which he hires by the week. Here, at least, we enjoy convenience and quiet within doors, as much as Tabby's temper will allow; but the squire still complains of flying pains in the stomach and head, for which he bathes and drinks the waters. He is not so bad, however, but that he goes in person to the pump, the rooms, and the coffee-houses; where he picks up continual food for ridicule and satire. If I can glean any thing for your amusement, either from his observation or my own, you shall have it freely, though I am afraid it will poorly compensate the trouble of reading these tedious insipid letters of,

Dear Phillips,

Yours always,

J. MELFORD

To Dr LEWIS.

BATH, April 23.

DEAR DOCTOR,

If I did not know that the exercise of your profession has habituated you to the hearing of complaints, I should make a conscience of troubling you with my correspondence, which may be truly called *the lamentations of Matthew Bramble*.[1] Yet I cannot help thinking I have some right to discharge the overflowings of my spleen upon you, whose province it is to remove those disorders that occasioned it; and let me tell you, it is no small alleviation of my grievances, that I have a sensible friend, to whom I can communicate my crusty humours, which, by retention, would grow intolerably acrimonious.

You must know, I find nothing but disappointment at Bath; which is so altered, that I can scarce believe it is the same place that I frequented about thirty years ago. Methinks I hear you say, 'Altered it is, without all doubt: but then it is altered for the better; a truth which, perhaps, you would own without hesitation, if you yourself was not altered for the worse.' The reflection may, for aught I know, be just. The inconveniences which I overlooked in the high-day of health, will naturally strike with exaggerated impression on the irritable nerves of an invalid, surprised by premature old age, and shattered with long-suffering – But, I believe, you will not deny, that this place, which Nature and Providence seem to have intended as a resource from distemper and disquiet, is become the very centre of racket and dissipation. Instead of that peace, tranquillity, and ease, so necessary to those who labour under bad health, weak nerves, and irregular spirits; here we have nothing but noise, tumult, and hurry; with the fatigue and slavery of maintaining a ceremonial, more stiff, formal, and oppressive, than the etiquette of a German elector. A national hospital it may be, but one would imagine that none but lunatics are admitted; and truly, I will give you leave to call me so, if I stay much longer at Bath. — But I shall take another opportunity to explain my sentiments at greater length on this subject – I was impatient to see the boasted improvements in architecture, for which the upper parts of the town have been so much celebrated and t'other day I made a circuit of all the new buildings. The Square,[2] though irregular, is, on the whole, pretty well laid out, spacious, open, and airy; and, in my opinion, by far the most wholesome and agreeable situation in Bath, especially the upper side of it; but the avenues to it are mean, dirty, dangerous, and indirect. Its communication with the Baths, is through the yard of an inn,[3] where the poor trembling valetudinarian is carried in a chair, betwixt the heels of a double row of horses, wincing under the curry-combs of grooms and postilions, over and above the hazard of being obstructed, or over-turned by the carriages which are continually making their exit or their entrance – I suppose after some chairmen shall have been maimed, and a few lives lost by those accidents, the corporation will think, in earnest, about providing a more safe and commodious passage. The Circus[4] is a pretty bauble, contrived for shew, and looks like Vespasian's amphitheatre[5] turned outside in. If we consider it in point of magnificence, the great number of small doors belonging to the separate houses, the inconsiderable height of the different orders, the affected ornaments of the architrave, which are both childish and misplaced, and the areas projecting into the street, surrounded with iron rails, destroy a good part of its effect upon the eye; and, perhaps, we shall find it still more defective, if we view it in the light of convenience. The figure of each separate dwelling-house, being the segment of a circle, must spoil the symmetry of the rooms, by contracting them towards the street windows, and leaving a larger sweep in the space behind. If, instead of the areas and iron rails, which seem to be of very little use, there had been a corridore with arcades all round, as in Covent-garden,[6] the appearance of the whole would have been more magnificent and striking; those arcades would have afforded an agreeable covered walk, and sheltered the poor chairmen and their carriages from the rain, which is here almost perpetual. At present, the chairs stand soaking in the open street, from morning to night, till they become so many boxes of wet leather, for the benefit of the gouty and rheumatic, who are transported in them from place to place. Indeed this is a shocking inconvenience that extends over the whole city; and, I am persuaded, it produces infinite mischief to the delicate and infirm; even the close chairs, contrived for the sick, by standing in the open air, have their frize[7] linings impregnated like so many spunges, with the moisture of the atmosphere, and those cases of cold vapour must give a charming check to the perspiration of a patient, piping hot from the Bath, with all his pores wide open.

But, to return to the Circus; it is inconvenient from its situation, at so great a distance from all the markets, baths, and places of public entertainment. The only entrance to it, through Gay-street,[8] is so difficult, steep, and slippery, that in wet weather, it must be exceedingly dangerous, both for those that ride in carriages, and those that walk a-foot; and when the

street is covered with snow, as it was for fifteen days successively
this very winter,[9] I don't see how any individual could go either
up or down, without the most imminent hazard of broken
bones. In blowing weather, I am told, most of the houses in
this hill are smothered with smoke, forced down the chimneys,
by the gusts of wind reverberated from the hill behind, which
(I apprehend likewise) must render the atmosphere here more
humid and unwholesome than it is in the square below; for the
clouds, formed by the constant evaporation from the baths and
rivers in the bottom, will, in their ascent this way, be first
attracted and detained by the hill that rises close behind the
Circus, and load the air with a perpetual succession of vapours:
this point, however, may be easily ascertained by means of an
hygrometer, or a paper of salt of tartar exposed to the action
of the atmosphere. The same artist who planned the Circus,
has likewise projected a Crescent;[10] when that is finished, we
shall probably have a Star; and those who are living thirty years
hence, may, perhaps, see all the signs of the Zodiac exhibited
in architecture at Bath. These, however fantastical, are still
designs that denote some ingenuity and knowledge in the architect; but the rage of building has laid hold on such a number of
adventurers, that one sees new houses starting up in every
out-let and every corner of Bath; contrived without judgment,
executed without solidity, and stuck together with so little
regard to plan and propriety, that the different lines of the new
rows and buildings interfere with, and intersect one another in
every different angle of conjunction. They look like the wreck
of streets and squares disjointed by an earthquake, which hath
broken the ground into a variety of holes and hillocks; or as if
some Gothic devil had stuffed them altogether in a bag, and
left them to stand higgledy piggledy, just as chance directed.
What sort of a monster Bath will become in a few years, with
those growing excrescences, may be easily conceived: but the
want of beauty and proportion is not the worst effect of these
new mansions; they are built so slight, with the soft crumbling
stone found in this neighbourhood, that I shall never sleep
quietly in one of them, when it blowed (as the sailors say) a
cap-full of wind; and, I am persuaded, that my hind,[11] Roger

Williams, or any man of equal strength, would be able to push his foot through the strongest part of their walls, without any great exertion of his muscles. All these absurdities arise from the general tide of luxury, which hath overspread the nation, and swept away all, even the very dregs of the people. Every upstart of fortune, harnessed in the trappings of the mode,[12] presents himself at Bath, as in the very focus of observation – Clerks and factors from the East Indies, loaded with the spoil of plundered provinces; planters, negro-drivers, and hucksters, from our American plantations, enriched they know not how; agents, commissaries, and contractors, who have fattened, in two successive wars,[13] on the blood of the nation; usurers, brokers, and jobbers of every kind; men of low birth, and no breeding, have found themselves suddenly translated into a state of affluence, unknown to former ages; and no wonder that their brains should be intoxicated with pride, vanity, and presumption. Knowing no other criterion of greatness, but the ostentation of wealth, they discharge their affluence without taste or conduct, through every channel of the most absurd extravagance; and all of them hurry to Bath, because here, without any further qualification, they can mingle with the princes and nobles of the land. Even the wives and daughters of low tradesmen, who, like shovel-nosed sharks, prey upon the blubber of those uncouth whales of fortune, are infected with the same rage of displaying their importance; and the slightest indisposition serves them for a pretext to insist upon being conveyed to Bath, where they may hobble country-dances[14] and cotillons[15] among lordlings, squires, counsellors, and clergy. These delicate creatures from Bedfordbury, Butcher-row, Crutched-friers, and Botolph-lane,[16] cannot breathe in the gross air of the Lower Town, or conform to the vulgar rules of a common lodging-house; the husband, therefore, must provide an entire house, or elegant apartments in the new buildings. Such is the composition of what is called the fashionable company at Bath; where a very inconsiderable proportion of genteel people are lost in a mob of impudent plebeians, who have neither understanding nor judgment, nor the least idea of propriety and decorum; and seem to enjoy nothing so much as an opportunity of insulting their betters.

Thus the number of people, and the number of houses continue to increase; and this will ever be the case, till the streams that swell this irresistible torrent of folly and extravagance, shall either be exhausted, or turned into other channels, by incidents and events which I do not pretend to foresee. This, I own, is a subject on which I cannot write with any degree of patience; for the mob[17] is a monster I never could abide, either in its head, tail, midriff, or members; I detest the whole of it, as a mass of ignorance, presumption, malice, and brutality; and, in this term of reprobation, I include, without respect of rank, station, or quality, all those of both sexes, who affect its manners, and court its society.

But I have written till my fingers are crampt, and my nausea begins to return – By your advice, I sent to London a few days ago for half a pound of Gengzeng;[18] though I doubt much, whether that which comes from America is equally efficacious with what is brought from the East Indies. Some years ago a friend of mine paid sixteen guineas for two ounces of it; and, in six months after, it was sold in the same shop for five shillings the pound. In short, we live in a vile world of fraud and sophistication;[19] so that I know nothing of equal value with the genuine friendship of a sensible man; a rare jewel! which I cannot help thinking myself in possession of, while I repeat the old declaration, that I am, as usual,

Dear Lewis,
Your affectionate
M. BRAMBLE

After having been agitated in a short hurricane, on my first arrival, I have taken a small house in Milsham-street, where I am tolerably well lodged, for five guineas a week. I was yesterday at the Pump-room,[20] and drank about a pint of water, which seems to agree with my stomach; and to-morrow morning I shall bathe, for the first time; so that in a few posts you may expect farther trouble; mean while, I am glad to find that the inoculation[21] has succeeded so well with poor Joyce, and that her face will be but little marked — If my friend Sir Thomas was a single man, I would not trust such a handsome wench in his family; but as I have recommended her, in a particular manner, to the protection of lady G—, who is one of the best women in the world, she may go thither without hesitation as soon as she is quite recovered and fit for service – Let her mother have money to provide her with necessaries, and she may ride behind her brother on Bucks; but you must lay strong injunctions on Jack, to take particular care of the trusty old veteran, who has faithfully earned his present ease by his past services.

To Miss WILLIS, at Gloucester.

BATH, April 26.

MY DEAREST COMPANION,

The pleasure I received from yours, which came to hand yesterday, is not to be expressed. Love and friendship are, without doubt, charming passions; which absence serves only to heighten and improve. Your kind present of the garnet bracelets, I shall keep as carefully as I preserve my own life; and I beg you will accept, in return, my heart-housewife,[1] with the tortoise-shell memorandum-book, as a trifling pledge of my unalterable affection.

Bath is to me a new world — All is gayety, good-humour, and diversion. The eye is continually entertained with the splendour of dress and equipage; and the ear with the sound of coaches, chairs, and other carriages. *The merry bells ring round,*[2] from morn till night. Then we are welcomed by the city-waits in our own lodgings; we have music in the Pump-room every morning, cotillons every forenoon in the rooms, balls twice a week, and concerts every other night, besides private assemblies and parties without number – As soon as we were settled in lodgings, we were visited by the Master of the Ceremonies;[3] a pretty little gentleman, so sweet, so fine, so civil, and polite, that in our country he might pass for the prince of

Wales; then he talks so charmingly, both in verse and prose, that you would be delighted to hear him discourse; for you must know he is a great writer, and has got five tragedies ready for the stage. He did us the favour to dine with us, by my uncle's invitation; and next day squired my aunt and me to every part of Bath; which, to be sure, is an earthly paradise. The Square, the Circus, and the Parades, put you in mind of the sumptuous palaces represented in prints and pictures; and the new, buildings, such as Princes-row, Harlequin's-row, Bladud's-row,[4] and twenty other rows, look like so many enchanted castles, raised on hanging terraces.

At eight in the morning, we go in dishabille[5] to the Pump-room; which is crowded like a Welsh fair; and there you see the highest quality, and the lowest trades folks, jostling each other, without ceremony, hail-fellow well-met. The noise of the music playing in the gallery, the heat and flavour of such a crowd, and the hum and buz of their conversation, gave me the head-ach and vertigo the first day; but, afterwards, all these things became familiar, and even agreeable. – Right under the Pump-room windows is the King's Bath;[6] a huge cistern, where you see the patients up to their necks in hot water. The ladies wear jackets and petticoats of brown linen, with chip hats,[7] in which they fix their handkerchiefs to wipe the sweat from their faces; but, truly, whether it is owing to the steam that surrounds them, or the heat of the water, or the nature of the dress, or to all these causes together, they look so flushed, and so frightful, that I always turn my eyes another way — My aunt, who says every person of fashion should make her appearance in the bath, as well as in the abbey church, contrived a cap with cherry-coloured ribbons to suit her complexion, and obliged Win to attend her yesterday morning in the water. But, really, her eyes were so red, that they made mine water as I viewed her from the Pump-room; and as for poor Win, who wore a hat trimmed with blue, what betwixt her wan complexion and her fear, she looked like the ghost of some pale maiden, who had drowned herself for love. When she came out of the bath, she took assafœtida drops, and was fluttered all day; so that we could hardly keep her from going into hysterics:[8] but her mistress says it will do her good; and poor Win curtsies, with the tears in her eyes. For my part, I content myself with drinking about half a pint of the water every morning.

The pumper, with his wife and servant, attend within a bar; and the glasses, of different sizes, stand ranged in order before them, so you have nothing to do but to point at that which you choose, and it is filled immediately, hot and sparkling from the pump. It is the only hot water I could ever drink, without being sick – Far from having that effect, it is rather agreeable to the taste, grateful to the stomach, and reviving to the spirits. You cannot imagine what wonderful cures it performs – My uncle began with it the other day; but he made wry faces in drinking, and I'm afraid he will leave it off — The first day we came to Bath, he fell into a violent passion; beat two black-a-moors, and I was afraid he would have fought with their master; but the stranger proved a peaceable man. To be sure, the gout had got into his head, as my aunt observed; but, I believe, his passion drove it away; for he has been remarkably well ever since. It is a thousand pities he should ever be troubled with that ugly distemper; for, when he is free from pain, he is the best-tempered man upon earth; so gentle, so generous, so charitable, that every body loves him; and so good to me, in particular, that I shall never be able to shew the deep sense I have of his tenderness and affection.

Hard by the Pump-room, is a coffee-house for the ladies; but my aunt says, young girls are not admitted, insomuch as the conversation turns upon politics, scandal, philosophy, and other subjects above our capacity; but we are allowed to accompany them to the booksellers shops, which are charming places of resort; where we read novels, plays, pamphlets, and newspapers, for so small a subscription as a crown a quarter; and in these offices of intelligence (as my brother calls them) all the reports of the day, and all the private transactions of the Bath, are first entered and discussed. From the bookseller's shop, we make a tour through the milliners and toymen;[9] and commonly stop at Mr Gill's, the pastry-cook,[10] to take a jelly, a tart, or a small bason of vermicelli. There is, moreover, another place of entertainment on the other side of the water, opposite to the

Grove,[11] to which the company cross over in a boat — It is called Spring-garden;[12] a sweet retreat, laid out in walks and ponds, and parterres of flowers; and there is a long-room for breakfasting and dancing. As the situation is low and damp, and the season has been remarkably wet, my uncle won't suffer me to go thither, lest I should catch cold: but my aunt says it is all a vulgar prejudice; and, to be sure, a great many gentlemen and ladies of Ireland frequent the place, without seeming to be the worse for it. They say, dancing at Spring-gardens, when the air is moist, is recommended to them as an excellent cure for the rheumatism. I have been twice at the play; where, notwith-standing the excellence of the performers, the gayety of the company, and the decorations of the theatre,[13] which are very fine, I could not help reflecting, with a sigh, upon our poor homely representations at Gloucester – But this, in confidence to my dear Willis – You know my heart, and will excuse its weakness. —

After all, the great scenes of entertainment at Bath, are the two public rooms;[14] where the company meet alternately every evening – They are spacious, lofty, and, when lighted up, appear very striking. They are generally crowded with well-dressed people, who drink tea in separate parties, play at cards, walk, or sit and chat together, just as they are disposed. Twice a-week there is a ball; the expence of which is defrayed by a voluntary subscription among the gentlemen; and every subscriber has three tickets. I was there Friday last with my aunt, under the care of my brother, who is a subscriber; and Sir Ulic Mackilligut recommended his nephew, captain O Donaghan, to me as a partner; but Jery excused himself, by saying I had got the head-ach; and, indeed, it was really so, though I can't imagine how he knew it. The place was so hot, and the smell so different from what we are used to in the country, that I was quite feverish when we came away. Aunt says it is the effect of a vulgar constitution, reared among woods and mountains; and, that as I become accustomed to genteel company, it will wear off. – Sir Ulic was very complaisant, made her a great many high-flown compliments; and, when we retired, handed her with great ceremony to her chair. The captain, I believe, would have done me the same favour; but my brother seeing him advance, took me under his arm, and wished him good night. The Captain is a pretty man, to be sure; tall and strait, and well made; with light-grey eyes, and a Roman nose; but there is a certain boldness in his look and manner, that puts one out of countenance – But I am afraid I have put you out of all patience with this long unconnected scrawl; which I shall therefore conclude, with assuring you, that neither Bath, nor London, nor all the diversions of life, shall ever be able to efface the idea of my dear Letty, from the heart of her ever affectionate

LYDIA MELFORD

To Mrs MARY JONES, at Brambleton-hall.

DEAR MOLLY JONES,

Heaving got a frank,[1] I now return your fever, which I received by Mr Higgins, at the Hot Well, together with the stockings, which his wife footed for me; but now they are of no survice. No body wears such things in this place – O Molly! you that live in the country have no deception of our doings at Bath. Here is such dressing, and fidling, and dancing, and gadding, and courting and plotting – O gracious! if God had not given me a good stock of discretion, what a power of things might not I reveal, consarning old mistress and young mistress; Jews with beards that were no Jews; but handsome Christians, without a hair upon their sin, strolling with spectacles, to get speech of Miss Liddy. But she's a dear sweet soul, as innocent as the child unborn.[2] She has tould me all her inward thoughts, and disclosed her passion for Mr Wilson; and that's not his name neither; and thof he acted among the player-men, he is meat for their masters;[3] and she has gi'en me her yellow trollopea;[4] which Mrs Drab, the mantymaker,[5] says will look very well when it is scowred and smoaked with silfur — You knows as how, yellow fitts my fizzogmony.[6] God he knows what havock I shall make among the mail sex, when I make my first appearance in this killing collar, with a full soot of gaze, as good as new, that I bought last Friday of madam Friponeau, the French mullaner — Dear girl, I have seen all the fine shews of Bath; the Prades, the Squires, and the Circlis, the Crashit, the Hottogon, and Bloody Buildings, and Harry King's row;[7] and I have been twice in the Bath with mistress, and na'r a smoak upon our backs, hussy — The first time I was mortally afraid, and flustered all day; and after-wards made believe that I had got the heddick; but mistress said, if I didn't go I should take a dose of bumtaffy; and so remembering how it worked Mrs Gwyllim a pennorth, I chose rather to go again with her into the Bath, and then I met with an axident. I dropt my petticoat, and could not get it up from the bottom. – But what did that signify; they mought laff, but they could see nothing; for I was up to the sin in water. To be sure, it threw me into such a gum-bustion, that I know not what I said, nor what I did, nor how they got me out, and rapt me in a blanket – Mrs Tabitha scoulded a little when we got home; but she knows as I know what's what — Ah Laud help you! – There is Sir Yury Micligut, of Balnaclinch, in the cunty of Kalloway – I took down the name from his gentleman, Mr O Frizzle, and he has got an estate of fifteen hundred a year – I am sure he is both rich and generous — But you nose, Molly, I was always famous for keeping secrets; and so he was very safe in trusting me with his flegm for mistress; which, to be sure is very honourable; for Mr O Frizzle assures me, he values not her portion a brass varthing[8] — And, indeed, what's poor ten thousand pounds to a Baron Knight of his fortune? and, truly, I told Mr O Frizzle that was all she had trust to — As for John Thomas, he's a morass fellor – I vow, I thought he would a[9] fit with Mr O Frizzle, because he axed me to dance with him at Spring Garden – But God he knows I have no thoughts eyther of wan or t'other.

As for house news, the worst is, Chowder has fallen off greatly from his stomick – He eats nothing but white meats, and not much of that; and wheezes, and seems to be much bloated. The doctors think he is threatened with a dropsy – Parson Marrofat, who has got the same disorder, finds great benefit from the waters; but Chowder seems to like them no better than the squire; and mistress says, if his case don't take a favourable turn, she will sartinly carry him to Aberga'ny,[10] to drink goat's whey – To be sure, the poor dear honymil is lost for want of axercise; for which reason, she intends to give him an airing once a-day upon the Downs, in a post-chaise[11] – I have already made very creditable connexions in this here place; where, to be sure, we have the very squintasense of satiety — Mrs Patcher, my lady Kilmacullock's woman, and I are sworn sisters. She has shewn me all her secrets, and learned me to wash gaze, and refrash rusty silks and bumbeseens,[12] by boiling them with winegar, chamberlye,[13] and stale beer. My short sack and apron luck as good as new from the shop, and my pumpydoor[14] as fresh as a rose, by the help of turtle-water[15] – But this is all Greek and Latten to you, Molly — If we should come to Aberga'ny, you'll be within a day's ride of us; and then we shall see wan another, please God — If not, remember me in your prayers, as I shall do by you in mine; and take care of my kitten, and give my kind sarvice to Sall; and this is all at present, from your beloved friend and sarvent,

BATH, April 26.   W. JENKINS

To Mrs GWYLLIM, house-keeper at Brambleton-hall.

I am astonished that Dr Lewis should take upon him to give away Alderney, without my privity and concurrants – What signifies my brother's order? My brother is little better than Non-compus.[1] He would give away the shirt off his back,[2] and the teeth out of his head; nay, as for that matter, he would have ruinated the family with his ridiculous charities, if it had not been for my four quarters – What between his willfullness and his waste, his trumps, and his frenzy, I lead the life of an indented slave. Alderney gave four gallons a-day, ever since the calf was sent to market. There is so much milk out of my dairy, and the press must stand still: but I won't loose a cheese pairing; and the milk shall be made good, if the sarvents should go without butter. If they must needs have butter, let them make it of sheep's milk; but then my wool will suffer for want of grace; so that I must be a loser on all sides — Well, patience is like a stout Welsh poney; it bears a great deal, and trots a great way; but it will tire at the long run. Before its long, perhaps I may shew Matt, that I was not born to be the household drudge to my dying day – Gwyn rites from Crickhowel, that the price of flannel is fallen three-farthings an ell; and that's another good penny out of my pocket – When I go to market to sell, my commodity stinks; but when I want to buy the commonest thing, the owner pricks it up under my nose; and it can't be had for love nor money – I think everything runs cross at Brambleton hall – You say the gander has broke the eggs; which is a phinumenon I don't understand: for when the fox carried off the old goose last year, he took her place, and hatched the eggs, and partected the goslings like a tender parent – Then you tell me the thunder has soured two barrels of beer in the seller. But how the thunder should get there, when the seller was double-locked, I can't comprehend. Howsomever, I won't have the beer thrown out, till I see it with my own eyes. Perhaps, it will recover – At least it will serve for vinegar to the sarvents. – You may leave off the fires in my brother's chamber and mine, as it is unsartain when we return. — I hope, Gwyllim, you'll take care there is no waste; and have an eye to the maids, and keep them to their spinning. I think they may go very well without beer in hot weather – it serves only to inflame the blood, and set them a-gog after the men. Water will make them fair and keep them cool and tamperit. Don't forget to put up in the portmantel, that cums with Williams, along with my riding-habit, hat, and feather, the viol of purl water,[3] and the tincktur for my stomach; being as how I am much troubled with flutterencies. This is all at present, from

Yours,

BATH, April 26.   TABITHA BRAMBLE

To Dr Lewis.

Dear Dick,

I have done with the waters; therefore your advice comes a
day too late – I grant that physic is no mystery of your making. I
know it is a mystery in its own nature; and, like other mysteries,
requires a strong gulp of faith to make it go down – Two days
ago, I went into the King's Bath, by the advice of our friend
Ch—,[1] in order to clear the strainer of the skin, for the benefit
of a free perspiration; and the first object that saluted my eye,
was a child full of scrophulous ulcers, carried in the arms of
one of the guides, under the very noses of the bathers. I was so
shocked at the sight, that I retired immediately with indignation
and disgust – Suppose the matter of those ulcers, floating on
the water, comes in contact with my skin, when the pores are
all open, I would ask you what must be the consequence? —
Good Heaven, the very thought makes my blood run cold! we
know not what sores may be running into the water while we
are bathing, and what sort of matter we may thus imbibe; the
king's-evil,[2] the scurvy, the cancer, and the pox; and, no doubt,
the heat will render the *virus* the more volatile and penetrating.
To purify myself from all such contamination, I went to the duke
of Kingston's private Bath,[3] and there I was almost suffocated for
want of free air; the place was so small, and the steam so stifling.

After all, if the intention is no more than to wash the skin, I
am convinced that simple element is more effectual than any
water impregnated with salt and iron; which, being astringent,
will certainly contract the pores, and leave a kind of crust upon
the surface of the body. But I am now as much afraid of
drinking, as of bathing; for, after a long conversation with the
Doctor, about the construction of the pump and the cistern, it
is very far from being clear with me, that the patients in the
Pump-room don't swallow the scourings of the bathers. I can't
help suspecting, that there is, or may be, some regurgitation
from the bath into the cistern of the pump. In that case, what
a delicate beveridge is every day quaffed by the drinkers; medicated with the sweat and dirt, and dandriff; and the abominable

discharges of various kinds, from twenty different diseased bodies, parboiling in the kettle below. In order to avoid this filthy composition, I had recourse to the spring that supplies the private baths on the Abbey-green; but I at once perceived something extraordinary in the taste and smell; and, upon inquiry, I find that the Roman baths in this quarter, were found covered by an old burying ground, belonging to the Abbey; through which, in all probability, the water drains in its passage; so that as we drink the decoction of living bodies at the Pump-room, we swallow the strainings of rotten bones and carcasses at the private bath – I vow to God, the very idea turns my stomach! – Determined, as I am, against any farther use of the Bath waters, this consideration would give me little disturbance, if I could find any thing more pure, or less pernicious, to quench my thirst; but, although the natural springs of excellent water are seen gushing spontaneous on every side, from the hills that surround us, the inhabitants, in general, make use of well-water, so impregnated with nitre, or alum, or some other villainous mineral, that it is equally ungrateful to the taste, and mischievous to the constitution. It must be owned, indeed, that here, in Milsham-street, we have a precarious and scanty supply from the hill; which is collected in an open bason in the Circus, liable to be defiled with dead dogs, cats, rats, and every species of nastiness, which the rascally populace may throw into it, from mere wantonness and brutality.—

Well, there is no nation that drinks so hoggishly as the English — What passes for wine among us, is not the juice of the grape. It is an adulterous mixture, brewed up of nauseous ingredients, by dunces, who are bunglers in the art of poison-making; and yet we, and our forefathers, are and have been poisoned by this cursed drench, without taste or flavour – The only genuine and whole-some beveridge in England, is London porter,[4] and Dorchester table-beer; but as for your ale and your gin, your cyder and your perry,[5] and all the trashy family of made wines, I detest them as infernal compositions, contrived for the destruction of the human species – But what have I to do with the human species? except a very few friends, I care not if the whole was —.

Heark ye, Lewis, my misanthropy increases every day – The longer I live, I find the folly and the fraud of mankind grow more and more intolerable – I wish I had not come from Brambleton-hall; after having lived in solitude so long, I cannot bear the hurry and impertinence of the multitude; besides, every thing is sophisticated in these crowded places. Snares are laid for our lives in every thing we eat or drink: the very air we breathe, is loaded with contagion. We cannot even sleep, without risque of infection. I say, infection – This place is the rendezvous of the diseased – You won't deny, that many diseases are infectious; even the consumption itself, is highly infectious. When a person dies of it in Italy, the bed and bedding are destroyed; the other furniture is exposed to the weather and the apartment white-washed, before it is occupied by any other living soul. You'll allow, that nothing receives infection sooner, or retains it longer, than blankets, feather-beds, and matrasses — 'Sdeath! how do I know what miserable objects have been stewing in the bed where I now lie! – I wonder, Dick, you did not put me in mind of sending for my own matrasses – But, if I had not been an ass, I should not have needed a rememberancer — There is always some plaguy reflection that rises up in judgment against me, and ruffles my spirits – Therefore, let us change the subject.

I have other reasons for abridging my stay at Bath – You know sister Tabby's complexion – If Mrs Tabitha Bramble had been of any other race, I should certainly have considered her as the most – But, the truth is, she has found means to interest my affection; or, rather, she is beholden to the force of prejudice, commonly called the ties of blood. Well, this amiable maiden has actually commenced a flirting correspondence with an Irish baronet of sixty-five. His name is Sir Ulic Mackilligut. He is said to be much out at elbows; and, I believe, has received false intelligence with respect to her fortune. Be that as it may, the connexion is exceedingly ridiculous, and begins already to excite whispers. For my part, I have no intention to dispute her free-agency; though I shall fall upon some expedient to undeceive her paramour, as to the point which he has principally in view. But I don't think her conduct is a proper example for Liddy, who has also attracted the notice of some coxcombs[6] in the Rooms; and Jery tells me, he suspects a strapping fellow, the knight's nephew, of some design upon the girl's heart. I shall, therefore, keep a strict eye over her aunt and her, and even shift the scene, if I find the matter grow more serious – You perceive what an agreeable task it must be, to a man of my kidney, to have the cure of such souls as these. – But, hold, you shall not have another peevish word (till the next occasion) from

Yours,

BATH, April 28.   MATT. BRAMBLE

To Sir WATKIN PHILLIPS, of Jesus college, Oxon.

DEAR KNIGHT,

I think those people are unreasonable, who complain that Bath is a contracted circle, in which the same dull scenes perpetually revolve, without variation – I am, on the contrary, amazed to find so small a place so crowded with entertainment and variety. London itself can hardly exhibit one species of diversion, to which we have not something analogous at Bath, over and above those singular advantages that are peculiar to the place. Here, for example, a man has daily opportunities of seeing the most remarkable characters of the community. He sees them in their natural attitudes and true colours; descended from their pedestals, and divested of their formal draperies, undisguised by art and affectation – Here we have ministers of state, judges, generals, bishops, projectors, philosophers, wits, poets, players, *chemists*, *fiddlers*, and *buffoons*.[1] If he makes any considerable stay in the place, he is sure of meeting with some particular friend, whom he did not expect to see; and to me there is nothing more agreeable than such casual rencounters – Another entertainment, peculiar to Bath, arises from the general mixture of all degrees assembled in our public rooms, without distinction of rank or fortune. This is what my uncle reprobates, as a monstrous jumble of heterogeneous principles;

a vile mob of noise and impertinence, without decency or subordination. But this chaos is to me a source of infinite amusement.

I was extremely diverted last ball-night to see the Master of the Ceremonies leading, with great solemnity, to the upper end of the room, an antiquated Abigail,[2] dressed in her lady's cast-clothes; whom he (I suppose) mistook for some countess just arrived at the Bath. The ball was opened by a Scotch lord, with a mulatto heiress from St Christopher's;[3] and the gay colonel Tinsel danced all the evening with the daughter of an eminent tinman from the borough of Southwark[4] – Yesterday morning, at the Pump-room, I saw a broken-winded Wapping landlady[5] squeeze through a circle of peers, to salute her brandy-merchant, who stood by the window, propped upon crutches; and a paralytic attorney of Shoe-lane,[6] in shuffling up to the bar, kicked the shins of the chancellor of England,[7] while his lordship, in a cut bob,[8] drank a glass of water at the pump. I cannot account for my being pleased with these incidents, any other way, than by saying they are truly ridiculous in their own nature, and serve to heighten the humour in the farce of life, which I am determined to enjoy as long as I can.

Those follies, that move my uncle's spleen, excite my laughter. He is as tender as a man without a skin; who cannot bear the slightest touch without flinching. What tickles another would give him torment; and yet he has what we may call lucid intervals, when he is remarkably facetious – Indeed, I never knew a hypochondriac so apt to be infected with good-humour. He is the most risible misanthrope I ever met with. A lucky joke, or any ludicrous incident, will set him a-laughing immoderately, even in one of his most gloomy paroxysms; and, when the laugh is over, he will curse his own imbecility. In conversing with strangers, he betrays no marks of disquiet – He is splenetic with his familiars only; and not even with them, while they keep his attention employed; but when his spirits are not exerted externally, they seem to recoil and prey upon himself — He has renounced the waters with execration; but he begins to find a more efficacious, and, certainly, a much more palatable remedy in the pleasures of society. He has discovered some old friends, among the invalids of Bath; and, in particular, renewed his acquaintance with the celebrated James Quin,[9] who certainly did not come here to drink water. You cannot doubt, but that I had the strongest curiosity to know this original; and it was gratified by Mr Bramble, who has had him twice at our house to dinner.

So far as I am able to judge, Quin's character is rather more respectable than it has been generally represented. His *bon mots* are in every witling's mouth; but many of them have a rank flavour, which one would be apt to think was derived from a natural grossness of idea. I suspect, however, that justice has not been done the author, by the collectors of those *Quiniana*; who have let the best of them slip through their fingers, and only retained such as were suited to the taste and organs of the multitude. How far he may relax in his hours of jollity, I cannot pretend to say; but his general conversation is conducted by the nicest rules of propriety; and Mr James Quin is, certainly, one of the best bred men in the kingdom. He is not only a most agreeable companion; but (as I am credibly informed) a very honest man; highly susceptible of friendship, warm, steady, and even generous in his attachments, disdaining flattery, and incapable of meanness and dissimulation. Were I to judge, however, from Quin's eye alone, I should take him to be proud, insolent, and cruel. There is something remarkably severe and forbidding in his aspect; and, I have been told, he was ever disposed to insult his inferiors and dependants. — Perhaps that report has influenced my opinion of his looks — You know we are the fools of prejudice. Howsoever that may be, I have as yet seen nothing but his favourable side, and my uncle, who frequently confers with him, in a corner, declares he is one of the most sensible men he ever knew – He seems to have a reciprocal regard for old Squaretoes,[10] whom he calls by the familiar name of Matthew, and often reminds of their old tavern-adventures: on the other hand, Matthew's eyes sparkle whenever Quin makes his appearance – Let him be never so jarring and discordant, Quin puts him in tune; and, like treble and bass in the same concert, they make excellent music together – T'other day, the conversation turning upon Shakespeare, I could not help saying, with some emotion, that I would give an hundred guineas to see Mr Quin act the part of Falstaff; upon which, turning to me with a smile, 'And I would give a thousand, young gentleman (said he) that I could gratify your longing.' My uncle and he are perfectly agreed in their estimate of life; which Quin says, would stink in his nostrils, if he did not steep it in claret.

I want to see this phenomenon in his cups; and have almost prevailed upon uncle to give him a small turtle at the Bear.[11] In the mean time, I must entertain you with an incident, that seems to confirm the judgment of those two cynic philosophers. I took the liberty to differ in opinion from Mr Bramble, when he observed, that the mixture of people in the entertainments of this place was destructive of all order and urbanity; that it rendered the plebeians insufferably arrogant and troublesome, and vulgarized the deportment and sentiments of those who moved in the upper spheres of life. He said such a preposterous coalition would bring us into contempt with all our neighbours; and was worse, in fact, than debasing the gold coin of the nation. I argued, on the contrary, that those plebeians who discovered such eagerness to imitate the dress and equipage of their superiors, would likewise, in time, adopt their maxims and their manners, be polished by their conversation, and refined by their example; but when I appealed to Mr Quin, and asked if he did not think that such an unreserved mixture would improve the whole mass? – 'Yes (said he) as a plate of marmalade would improve a pan of sirreverence.'[12]

I owned I was not much conversant in high-life, but I had seen what were called polite assemblies in London and else-where; that those of Bath seemed to be as decent as any; and that, upon the whole, the individuals that composed it, would not be found deficient in good manners and decorum. 'But let us have recourse to experience (said I) – Jack Holder, who was intended for a parson, has succeeded to an estate of two thousand a year, by the death of his elder brother. He is now at the Bath, driving about in a phaeton and four,[13] with French horns. He has treated with turtle and claret at all the taverns in Bath and Bristol, till his guests are gorged with good chear: he has bought a dozen suits of fine clothes, by the advice of the

Master of the Ceremonies, under whose tuition he has entered himself: he has lost hundreds at billiards to sharpers, and taken one of the nymphs of Avon-street[14] into keeping; but, finding all these channels insufficient to drain him of his current cash, his counsellor has engaged him to give a general tea-drinking to-morrow at Wiltshire's room. In order to give it the more eclat, every table is to be furnished with sweet-meats[15] and nosegays;[16] which, however, are not to be touched till notice is given by the ringing of a bell, and then the ladies may help themselves without restriction. This will be no bad way of trying the company's breeding.'

'I will abide by that experiment (cried my uncle) and if I could find a place to stand secure, without the vortex of the tumult, which I know will ensue, I would certainly go thither and enjoy the scene.' Quin proposed that we should take our station in the music-gallery, and we took his advice. Holder had got thither before us, with his horns perdue, but we were admitted. The tea-drinking passed as usual, and the company having risen from the tables, were sauntering in groupes, in expectation of the signal for attack, when the bell beginning to ring, they flew with eagerness to the dessert, and the whole place was instantly in commotion. There was nothing but justling, scrambling, pulling, snatching, struggling, scolding, and screaming. The nosegays were torn from one another's hands and bosoms; the glasses and china went to wreck; the tables and floors were strewed with comfits. Some cried; some swore; and the tropes and figures of Billingsgate[17] were used without reserve in all their native zest and flavour; nor were those flowers of rhetoric unattended with significant gesticulation. Some snapped their fingers; some forked them out; some clapped their hands, and some their back-sides; at length, they fairly proceeded to pulling caps, and every thing seemed to presage a general battle; when Holder ordered his horns to sound a charge, with a view to animate the combatants, and inflame the contest; but this manœuvre produced an effect quite contrary to what he expected. It was a note of reproach that roused them to an immediate sense of their disgraceful situation. They were ashamed of their absurd deportment, and suddenly desisted.

They gathered up their caps, ruffles, and handkerchiefs; and great part of them retired in silent mortification.

Quin laughed at this adventure; but my uncle's delicacy was hurt. He hung his head in manifest chagrin, and seemed to repine at the triumph of his judgment – Indeed, his victory was more complete than he imagined; for, as we afterwards learned, the two amazons who singularized themselves most in the action, did not come from the purlieus of Puddle-dock,[18] but from the courtly neighbourhood of St James's palace.[19] One was a baroness, and the other, a wealthy knight's dowager – My uncle spoke not a word, till we had made our retreat good to the coffee-house; where, taking off his hat and wiping his forehead, 'I bless God (said he) that Mrs Tabitha Bramble did not take the field to-day!' 'I would pit her for a cool hundred (cried Quin) against the best shake-bag[20] of the whole main.' The truth is, nothing could have kept her at home but the accident of her having taken physic before she knew the nature of the entertainment. She has been for some days furbishing up an old suit of black velvet, to make her appearance as Sir Ulic's partner at the next ball.

I have much to say of this amiable kinswoman; but she has not been properly introduced to your acquaintance. She is remarkably civil to Mr Quin; of whose sarcastic humour she seems to stand in awe; but her caution is no match for her impertinence. 'Mr Gwynn (said she the other day) I was once vastly entertained with your playing the Ghost of Gimlet at Drury-lane, when you rose up through the stage, with a white face and red eyes, and spoke of *quails upon the frightful porcofine*[21] – Do, pray, spout a little the Ghost of Gimlet.' 'Madam (said Quin, with a glance of ineffable disdain) the Ghost of Gimlet is laid, never to rise again' — Insensible of this check, she proceeded: 'Well, to be sure, you looked and talked so like a real ghost; and then the cock crowed so natural. I wonder how you could teach him to crow so exact, in the very nick of time; but, I suppose, he's game[22] – An't he game, Mr Gwynn?' 'Dunghill,[23] madam.' – 'Well, dunghill, or not dunghill, he has got such a clear counter-tenor, that I wish I had such another at Brambleton-hall, to wake the maids of a morning. Do you know where I could find one of his brood?' 'Probably in the work-house at St Giles's parish,[24] madam; but I protest I know not his particular mew!'[25] My uncle, frying with vexation, cried, 'Good God, sister, how you talk! I have told you twenty times, that this gentleman's name is not Gwynn.' — 'Hoity toity, brother mine (she replied) no offence, I hope – Gwynn is an honorable name, of true old British extraction — I thought the gentleman had been come of Mrs Helen Gwynn,[26] who was of his own profession; and if so be that were the case, he might be of king Charles's breed, and have royal blood in his veins.' — 'No, madam (answered Quin, with great solemnity) my mother was not a whore of such distinction — True it is, I am sometimes tempted to believe myself of royal descent; for my inclinations are often arbitrary – If I was an absolute prince, at this instant, I believe I should send for the head of your cook in a charger – She has committed felony, on the person of that John Dory,[27] which is mangled in a cruel manner, and even presented without sauce – O tempora! O mores!'[28]

This good-humoured sally turned the conversation into a less disagreeable channel – But, lest you should think my scribble as tedious as Mrs Tabby's clack, I shall not add another word, but that I am as usual

Yours,

BATH, April 30.   J. MELFORD

To Dr LEWIS.

DEAR LEWIS,

I received your bill upon Wiltshire, which was punctually honoured; but as I don't choose to keep so much cash by me, in a common lodging house, I have deposited 250l. in the bank of Bath, and shall take their bills for it in London, when I leave this place, where the season draws to an end – You must know, that now being a-foot, I am resolved to give Liddy a glimpse of London. She is one of the best hearted creatures I ever knew, and gains upon my affection every day – As for Tabby, I have dropt such hints to the Irish baronet, concerning her fortune, as, I make no doubt, will cool the ardour of his addresses. Then her pride will take the alarm; and the rancour of stale maidenhood being chafed, we shall hear nothing but slander and abuse of Sir Ulic Mackilligut – This rupture, I foresee, will facilitate our departure from Bath; where, at present, Tabby seems to enjoy herself with peculiar satisfaction. For my part, I detest it so much, that I should not have been able to stay so long in the place if I had not discovered some old friends; whose conversation alleviates my disgust – Going to the coffee-house one forenoon, I could not help contemplating the company, with equal surprize and compassion — We consisted of thirteen individuals; seven lamed by the gout, rheumatism, or palsy; three maimed by accident; and the rest either deaf or blind. One hobbled, another hopped, a third dragged his legs after him like a wounded snake, a fourth straddled betwixt a pair of long crutches, like the mummy of a felon hanging in chains; a fifth was bent into a horizontal position, like a mounted tele-scope, shoved in by a couple of chairmen; and a sixth was the bust of a man, set upright in a wheel machine,[1] which the waiter moved from place to place.

Being struck with some of their faces, I consulted the subscription-book; and, perceiving the names of several old friends, began to consider the groupe with more attention. At length I discovered rear-admiral Balderick, the companion of my youth, whom I had not seen since he was appointed lieuten-ant of the *Severn*. He was metamorphosed into an old man, with a wooden leg and a weatherbeaten face, which appeared the more ancient from his grey locks, that were truly venerable – Sitting down at the table, where he was reading a news-paper, I gazed at him for some minutes, with a mixture of pleasure and regret, which made my heart gush with tenderness; then, taking him by the hand, 'Ah, Sam (said I) forty years ago I little thought' – I was too much moved to proceed. 'An old friend, sure enough! (cried he, squeezing my hand, and surveying me eagerly through his glasses) I know the looming of the vessel, though she has been hard strained since we parted; but I can't heave up the name' — The moment I told him who I was, he exclaimed, 'Ha! Matt, my old fellow cruizer, still afloat!' And, starting up, hugged me in his arms. His transport, however, boded me no good; for, in saluting me, he thrust the spring of his spectacles into my eye, and, at the same time, set his wooden stump upon my gouty toe; an attack that made me shed tears in sad earnest — After the hurry of our recognition was over, he pointed out two of our common friends in the room: the bust was what remained of colonel Cockril, who had lost the use of his limbs in making an American campaign; and the telescope proved to be my college chum, sir Reginald Bently; who, with his new title, and unexpected inheritance, commenced fox-hunter, without having served his apprenticeship to the mystery; and, in consequence of following the hounds through a river, was seized with an inflammation of his bowels, which has contracted him into his present attitude.

Our former correspondence was forthwith renewed, with the most hearty expressions of mutual good-will, and as we had met so unexpectedly, we agreed to dine together that very day at the tavern. My friend Quin, being luckily unengaged, obliged us with his company; and, truly, this was the most happy day I have passed these twenty years. You and I, Lewis, having been always together, never tasted friendship in this high goût,[2] contracted from long absence. I cannot express the half of what I felt at this casual meeting of three or four companions, who had been so long separated, and so roughly treated by the storms of life. It was a renovation of youth; a kind of resuscitation of the dead, that realized those interesting dreams, in which we sometimes retrieve our ancient friends from the grave. Perhaps my enjoyment was not the less pleasing for being mixed with a strain of melancholy, produced by the remembrance of past scenes, that conjured up the ideas of some endearing connexions, which the hand of Death has actually dissolved.

The spirits and good humour of the company seemed to triumph over the wreck of their constitutions. They had even philosophy enough to joke upon their own calamities; such is the power of friendship, the sovereign cordial of life – I afterwards found, however, that they were not without their moments, and even hours of disquiet. Each of them apart, in succeeding conferences, expatiated upon his own particular grievances; and they were all malcontents at bottom – Over and above their personal disasters, they thought themselves unfortunate in the lottery of life. Balderick complained, that all the recompence he had received for his long and hard service, was the half-pay of a rear-admiral. The colonel was mortified to see himself over-topped by upstart generals, some of whom he had once commanded; and, being a man of a liberal turn, could ill put up with a moderate annuity, for which he had sold his commission. As for the baronet, having run himself considerably in debt, on a contested election, he has been obliged to relinquish his seat in parliament, and his seat in the country at the same time, and put his estate to nurse; but his chagrin, which is the effect of his own misconduct, does not affect me half so much as that of the other two, who have acted honourable and distinguished parts on the great theatre, and are now reduced to lead a weary life in this stew-pan of idleness and insignificance. They have long left off using the waters, after having experienced their inefficacy. The diversions of the place they are not in a condition to enjoy. How then do they make shift to pass their time? In the forenoon they crawl out to the Rooms or the coffeehouse, where they take a hand at whist, or descant upon the General Advertiser;[3] and their evenings they murder in private parties, among peevish invalids, and insipid old women – This is the case with a good number of individuals, whom nature seems to have intended for better purposes.

About a dozen years ago, many decent families, restricted to small fortunes, besides those that came hither on the score of health, were tempted to settle at Bath, where they could then live comfortably, and even make a genteel appearance, at a small expence: but the madness of the times has made the place too hot for them, and they are now obliged to think of other migrations – Some have already fled to the mountains of Wales, and others have retired to Exeter. Thither, no doubt, they will be followed by the flood of luxury and extravagance, which will drive them from place to place to the very Land's End; and there, I suppose, they will be obliged to ship themselves to some other country. Bath is become a mere sink of profligacy and extortion. Every article of house-keeping is raised to an enormous price; a circumstance no longer to be wondered at, when we know that every petty retainer of fortune piques himself upon keeping a table, and thinks it is for the honour of his character to wink at the knavery of his servants, who are in a confederacy with the market-people; and, of consequence, pay whatever they demand. Here is now a mushroom of opulence, who pays a cook seventy guineas a week for furnishing him with one meal a day. This portentous frenzy is become so contagious, that the very rabble and refuse of mankind are infected. I have known a negro-driver, from Jamaica, pay over-night, to the master of one of the rooms, sixty-five guineas for tea and coffee to the company, and leave Bath next morning, in such obscurity, that not one of his guests had the slightest idea of his person, or even made the least inquiry about his name. Incidents of this kind are frequent; and every day teems with fresh absurdities, which are too gross to make a thinking man merry. — But I feel the spleen creeping on me apace; and therefore will indulge you with a cessation, that you may have no unnecessary cause to curse your correspondence with,

Dear Dick,
Yours ever,

BATH, May 5.   MAT. BRAMBLE

To Miss LÆTITIA WILLIS, at Gloucester.

MY DEAR LETTY,

I wrote you at great length by the post, the twenty-sixth of last month, to which I refer you for an account of our proceedings at Bath; and I expect your answer with impatience. But, having this opportunity of a private hand, I send you two dozen of Bath rings; six of the best of which I desire you will keep for yourself, and distribute the rest among the young ladies, our common friends, as you shall think proper — I don't know how you will approve of the mottoes; some of them are not much to my own liking; but I was obliged to take such as I could find ready manufactured – I am vexed, that neither you nor I have received any further information of a certain person – Sure it cannot be wilful neglect! – O my dear Willis! I begin to be visited by strange fancies, and to have some melancholy doubts; which, however, it would be ungenerous to harbour without further inquiry – My uncle, who has made me a present of a very fine set of garnets, talks of treating us with a jaunt to London; which, you may imagine, will be highly agreeable; but I like Bath so well, that I hope he won't think of leaving it till the season is quite over; and yet, betwixt friends, something has happened to my aunt, which will probably shorten our stay in this place.

Yesterday, in the forenoon, she went by herself to a break-fasting in one of the rooms; and, in half an hour, returned in great agitation, having Chowder along with her in the chair. I believe some accident must have happened to that unlucky animal, which is the great source of all her troubles. Dear Letty! what a pity it is, that a woman of her years and discretion, should place her affection upon such an ugly, ill-conditioned cur, that snarls and snaps at every body. I asked John Thomas, the footman who attended her, what was the matter? and he did nothing but grin. A famous dog-doctor was sent for, and undertook to cure the patient, provided he might carry him home to his own house; but his mistress would not part with him out of her own sight — She ordered the cook to warm cloths, which she applied to his bowels, with her own hand. She gave up all thoughts of going to the ball in the evening; and when Sir Ulic came to drink tea, refused to be seen; so that he went away to look for another partner. My brother Jery whistles and dances. My uncle sometimes shrugs up his shoul-ders, and sometimes bursts out a-laughing. My aunt sobs and scolds by turns; and her woman, Win. Jenkins, stares and wonders with a foolish face of curiosity;[1] and, for my part, I am as curious as she, but ashamed to ask questions.

Perhaps time will discover the mystery; for if it was any thing that happened in the Rooms, it cannot be long concealed – All I know is, that last night at supper, miss Bramble spoke very disdainfully of Sir Ulic Mackilligut, and asked her brother if he intended to keep us sweltering all the summer at Bath? 'No, sister Tabitha (said he, with an arch smile) we shall retreat before the Dog-days[2] begin; though I make no doubt, that with a little temperance and discretion, our constitutions might be kept cool enough all the year, even at Bath.' As I don't know the meaning of this insinuation, I won't pretend to make any remarks upon it at present: hereafter, perhaps, I may be able to explain it more to your satisfaction — In the mean time, I beg you will be punctual in your correspondence, and continue to love your ever faithful

BATH, May 6.   LYDIA MELFORD

To Sir WATKIN PHILLIPS, of Jesus college, Oxon.

So then Mrs Blackerby's affair has proved a false alarm, and I have saved my money? I wish, however, her declaration had not been so premature; for though my being thought capable of making her a mother, might have given me some credit, the reputation of an intrigue with such a cracked pitcher does me no honour at all — In my last I told you I had hopes of seeing Quin, in his hours of elevation at the tavern which is the temple of mirth and good fellowship; where he, as priest of Comus,[1] utters the inspirations of wit and humour — I have had that satisfaction. I have dined with his club at the Three Tuns,[2] and had the honour to sit him out. At half an hour past eight in the evening, he was carried home with six good bottles of claret under his belt; and it being then Friday, he gave orders that he should not be disturbed till Sunday at noon — You must not imagine that this dose had any other effect upon his conversation, but that of making it more extravagantly entertaining – He had lost the use of his limbs, indeed, several hours before we parted, but he retained all his other faculties in perfection; and as he gave vent to every whimsical idea as it rose, I was really astonished at the brilliancy of his thoughts, and the force of his expression. Quin is a real voluptuary in the articles of eating and drinking; and so confirmed an epicure,[3] in the common acceptation of the term, that he cannot put up with ordinary fare. This is a point of such importance with him, that he always takes upon himself the charge of catering; and a man admitted to his mess, is always sure of eating delicate victuals, and drinking excellent wine – He owns himself addicted to the delights of the stomach, and often jokes upon his own sensuality; but there is nothing selfish in this appetite — He finds that good chear unites good company, exhilerates the spirits, opens the heart, banishes all restraint from conversation, and promotes the happiest purposes of social life. – But Mr James Quin is not a subject to be discussed in the compass of one letter; I shall therefore, at present, leave him to his repose, and call another of a very different complexion.

You desire to have further acquaintance with the person of our aunt, and promise yourself much entertainment from her connexion with Sir Ulic Mackilligut: but in this hope you are baulked already; that connexion is dissolved. The Irish baronet is an old hound, that, finding her carrion, has quitted the scent – I have already told you, that Mrs Tabitha Bramble is a maiden of forty-five. In her person, she is tall, raw-boned, aukward, flat-chested, and stooping; her complexion is sallow and freckled; her eyes are not grey, but greenish, like those of a cat, and generally inflamed; her hair is of a sandy, or rather dusty hue; her forehead low; her nose long, sharp, and, towards the extremity, always red in cool weather; her lips skinny, her mouth extensive, her teeth straggling and loose, of various colours and conformation; and her long neck shrivelled into a thousand wrinkles – In her temper, she is proud, stiff, vain, imperious, prying, malicious, greedy, and uncharitable. In all likelihood, her natural austerity had been soured by disappointment in love; for her long celibacy is by no means owing to her dislike of matrimony: on the contrary, she has left no stone unturned to avoid the reproachful epithet of old maid.[4]

Before I was born, she had gone such lengths in the way of flirting with a recruiting officer, that her reputation was a little singed. She afterwards made advances to the curate of the parish, who dropped some distant hints about the next presentation to the living, which was in her brother's gift; but finding that was already promised to another, he flew off at a tangent; and Mrs Tabby, in revenge, found means to deprive him of his cure. Her next lover was lieutenant of a man of war, a relation of the family, who did not understand the refinements of the passion, and expressed no aversion to grapple with cousin Tabby in the way of marriage; but before matters could be properly adjusted, he went out on a cruise, and was killed in an engagement with a French frigate. Our aunt, though baffled so often, did not yet despair – She layed all her snares for Dr Lewis, who is the *fidus Achates*⁵ of my uncle. She even fell sick upon the occasion, and prevailed with Matt to interpose in her behalf with his friend; but the Doctor, being a shy cock, would not be caught with chaff, and flatly rejected the proposal: so that Mrs Tabitha was content to exert her patience once more, after having endeavoured in vain to effect a rupture betwixt the two friends; and now she thinks proper to be very civil to Lewis, who is become necessary to her in the way of his profession.

These, however, are not the only efforts she has made towards a nearer conjunction with our sex. Her fortune was originally no more than a thousand pounds; but she gained an accession of five hundred by the death of a sister, and the lieutenant left her three hundred in his will. These sums she has more than doubled, by living free of all expence, in her brother's house; and dealing in cheese and Welsh flannel, the produce of his flocks and dairy. At present her capital is increased to about four thousand pounds; and her avarice seems to grow every day more and more repacious: but even this is not so intolerable as the perverseness of her nature, which keeps the whole family in disquiet and uproar. She is one of those geniuses who find some diabolical enjoyment in being dreaded and detested by their fellow-creatures.

I once told my uncle, I was surprised that a man of his disposition could bear such a domestic plague, when it could be so easily removed – The remark made him sore, because it seemed to tax him with want of resolution – Wrinkling up his nose, and drawing down his eye-brows, 'A young fellow (said he) when he first thrusts his snout into the world, is apt to be surprised at many things which a man of experience knows to be ordinary and unavoidable – This precious aunt of yours is become insensibly a part of my constitution – Damn her! She's a *noli me tangere*[6] in my flesh, which I cannot bear to be touched or tampered with.' I made no reply; but shifted the conversation. He really has an affection for this original; which maintains its ground in defiance of common sense, and in despite of that contempt which he must certainly feel for her character and understanding. Nay, I am convinced, that she has likewise a most virulent attachment to his person; though her love never shews itself but in the shape of discontent; and she persists in tormenting him out of pure tenderness – The only object within doors upon which she bestows any marks of affection, in the usual stile, is her dog Chowder; a filthy cur from Newfoundland,[7] which she had in a present from the wife of a skipper in Swansey[8] – One would imagine she had distinguished this beast with her favour on account of his ugliness and ill-nature, if it was not, indeed, an instinctive sympathy, between his disposition and her own. Certain it is, she caresses him without ceasing; and even harasses the family in the service of this cursed animal, which, indeed, has proved the proximate cause of her breach with Sir Ulic Mackilligut.

You must know, she yesterday wanted to steal a march of poor Liddy, and went to breakfast in the Room without any other companion than her dog, in expectation of meeting with the Baronet, who had agreed to dance with her in the evening – Chowder no sooner made his appearance in the Room, than the Master of the Ceremonies, incensed at his presumption, ran up to drive him away, and threatened him with his foot; but the other seemed to despise his authority, and displaying a formidable case of long, white, sharp teeth, kept the puny monarch[9] at bay – While he stood under some trepidation, fronting his antagonist, and bawling to the waiter, Sir Ulic Mackilligut came to his assistance; and seeming ignorant of the connexion between this intruder and his mistress, gave the former such a kick in the jaws, as sent him howling to the door — Mrs Tabitha, incensed at this outrage, ran after him, squalling in a tone equally disagreeable; while the Baronet followed her on one side, making apologies for his mistake; and Derrick on the other, making remonstrances upon the rules and regulations of the place.

Far from being satisfied with the Knight's excuses, she said she was sure he was no gentleman; and when the Master of the Ceremonies offered to hand her into the chair, she rapped him over the knuckles with her fan. My uncle's footman being still at the door, she and Chowder got into the same vehicle, and were carried off amidst the jokes of the chairmen and other populace — I had been riding out on Clerkendown, and happened to enter just as the *fracas* was over – The Baronet, coming up to me with an affected air of chagrin, recounted the adventure; at which I laughed heartily, and then his countenance cleared up. 'My dear soul (said he) when I saw a sort of a wild baist, snarling with open mouth at the Master of the Ceremonies, like the red cow going to devour Tom Thumb,[10] I could do no less than go to the assistance of the little man; but I never dreamt the baist was one of Mrs Bramble's attendants — O! if I had, he might have made his breakfast upon Derrick and welcome – But you know, my dear friend, how natural it is for us Irishmen to blunder, and to take the wrong sow by the ear – However, I will confess judgment, and cry her mercy; and it is to be hoped, a penitent sinner may be forgiven.'[11] I told him, that as the offence was not voluntary of his side, it was to be hoped he would not find her implacable.

But, in truth, all this concern was dissembled. In his approaches of gallantry to Mrs Tabitha, he had been misled by a mistake of at least six thousand pounds, in the calculation of her fortune; and in this particular he was just undeceived. He, therefore, seized the first opportunity of incurring her displeasure decently, in such a manner as would certainly annihilate the correspondence; and he could not have taken a more effectual method, than that of beating her dog. When he presented himself at our door, to pay his respects to the offended fair,[12] he was refused admittance, and given to understand that he should never find her at home for the future. She was not so inaccessible to Derrick, who came to demand satisfaction for the insult she had offered to him, even in the verge of his own court. She knew it was convenient to be well with the Master of the Ceremonies, while she continued to frequent the Rooms; and, having heard he was a poet, began to be afraid of making her appearance in a ballad or lampoon. – She therefore made excuses for what she had done, imputing it to the flutter of her spirits; and subscribed handsomely for his poems: so that he was perfectly appeased, and overwhelmed her with a profusion of compliment. He even solicited a reconciliation with Chowder; which, however, the latter declined; and he declared, that if he could find a precedent in the annals of the Bath, which he would carefully examine for that purpose, her favourite should be admitted to the next public breakfasting – But, I believe, she will not expose herself or him to the risque of a second disgrace – Who will supply the place of Mackilligut in her affections, I cannot foresee; but nothing in the shape of man can come amiss. Though she is a violent church-woman, of the most intolerant zeal, I believe in my conscience she would have no objection, at present, to treat on the score of matrimony with an Anabaptist, Quaker, or Jew; and even ratify the treaty at the expense of her own conversion. But, perhaps, I think too hardly of this kinswoman; who, I must own, is very little beholden to the good opinion of

Yours,

BATH, May 6.   J. MELFORD

To Dr Lewis.

You ask me, why I don't take the air a-horseback, during this fine weather? – In which of the avenues of this paradise would you have me take that exercise? Shall I commit myself to the high-roads of London or Bristol, to be stifled with dust, or pressed to death in the midst of post-chaises, flying-machines,[1] waggons, and coal-horses; besides the troops of fine gentlemen that take to the highway, to shew their horsemanship; and the coaches of fine ladies, who go thither to shew their equipages?

Shall I attempt the Downs, and fatigue myself to death in climbing up an eternal ascent, without any hopes of reaching the summit? Know then, I have made divers desperate leaps at those upper regions; but always fell backward into this vapour-pit, exhausted and dispirited by those ineffectual efforts; and here we poor valetudinarians pant and struggle, like so many Chinese gudgeons,[2] gasping in the bottom of a punch-bowl. By Heaven it is a kind of enchantment! If I do not speedily break the spell, and escape, I may chance to give up the ghost in this nauseous stew of corruption — It was but two nights ago, that I had like to have made my public exit, at a minute's warning. One of my greatest weaknesses is that of suffering myself to be over-ruled by the opinion of people, whose judgment I despise — I own, with shame and confusion of face, that importunity of any kind I cannot resist. This want of courage and constancy is an original flaw in my nature, which you must have often observed with compassion, if not with contempt. I am afraid some of our boasted virtues may be traced up to this defect. —

Without further preamble, I was persuaded to go to a ball, on purpose to see Liddy dance a minuet with a young petulant jackanapes, the only son of a wealthy undertaker[3] from London, whose mother lodges in our neighbourhood, and has contracted an acquaintance with Tabby. I sat a couple of long hours, half stifled, in the midst of a noisome crowd; and could not help wondering that so many hundreds of those that rank as rational creatures, could find entertainment in seeing a succession of insipid animals, describing the same dull figure for a whole evening, on an area, not much bigger than a taylor's shop-board. If there had been any beauty, grace, activity, magnificent dress, or variety of any kind howsoever absurd, to engage the attention, and amuse the fancy, I should not have been surprised; but there was no such object: it was a tiresome repetition of the same languid, frivolous scene, performed by actors that seemed to sleep in all their motions – The continual swimming of these phantoms before my eyes, gave me a swimming of the head; which was also affected by the fouled air, circulating through such a number of rotten human bellows — I therefore retreated towards the door, and stood in the passage to the next room, talking to my friend Quin; when an end being put to the minuets, the benches were removed to make way for the country-dances; and the multitude rising at once, the whole atmosphere was put in commotion. Then, all of a sudden, came rushing upon me an Egyptian gale,[4] so impregnated with pestilential vapours, that my nerves were overpowered, and I dropt senseless upon the floor.

You may easily conceive what a clamour and confusion this accident must have produced, in such an assembly – I soon recovered, however, and found myself in an easy chair, supported by my own people – Sister Tabby, in her great tenderness, had put me to the torture, squeezing my hand under her arm, and stuffing my nose with spirit of hartshorn,[5] till the whole inside was excoriated. I no sooner got home, than I sent for Doctor Ch—, who assured me I needed not be alarmed, for my swooning was entirely occasioned by an accidental impression of fetid effluvia upon nerves of uncommon sensibility. I know not how other people's nerves are constructed; but one would imagine they must be made of very coarse materials, to stand the shock of such a horrid assault. It was, indeed, *a compound of villainous smells*,[6] in which the most violent stinks, and the most powerful perfumes, contended for the mastery. Imagine to yourself a high exalted essence of mingled odours, arising from putrid gums, imposthumated lungs, sour flatulencies, rank armpits, sweating feet, running sores and issues, plasters, ointments, and embrocations, hungary-water,[7] spirit of lavender, assafœtida drops, musk, harts-horn, and sal volatile;[8] besides a thousand frowzy steams, which I could not analyse. Such, O Dick! is the fragrant æther we breathe in the polite assemblies of Bath – Such is the atmosphere I have exchanged for the pure, elastic, animating air of the Welsh mountains — *O Rus, quando te aspiciam!*[9] – I wonder what the devil possessed me –

But few words are best: I have taken my resolution – You may well suppose I don't intend to entertain the company with a second exhibition – I have promised, in an evil hour, to proceed to London, and that promise shall be performed, but my stay in the metropolis shall be brief. I have, for the benefit of my health, projected an expedition to the North, which, I hope, will afford some agreeable pastime. I have never travelled farther that way than Scarborough; and, I think, it is a reproach upon me, as a British freeholder, to have lived so long without making an excursion to the other side of the Tweed. Besides, I have some relations settled in Yorkshire, to whom it may not be improper to introduce my nephew and his sister – At present, I have nothing to add, but that Tabby is happily disentangled from the Irish Baronet; and that I will not fail to make you acquainted, from time to time, with the sequel of our adventures: a mark of consideration, which, perhaps, you would willingly dispense with in

Your humble servant,

BATH, May 8.   M. BRAMBLE

To Sir WATKIN PHILLIPS, of Jesus college, Oxon.

DEAR PHILLIPS,

A few days ago we were terribly alarmed by my uncle's fainting at the ball – He has been ever since cursing his own folly, for going thither at the request of an impertinent woman. He declares, he will sooner visit a house infected with the plague, than trust himself in such a nauseous spital[1] for the future, for he swears the accident was occasioned by the stench of the crowd; and that he would never desire a stronger proof of our being made of very gross materials, than our having withstood the annoyance, by which he was so much discomposed. For my part, I am very thankful for the coarseness of my organs, being in no danger of ever falling a sacrifice to the delicacy of my nose. Mr Bramble is extravagantly delicate in all his sensations, both of soul and body. I was informed by Dr Lewis, that he once fought a duel with an officer of the horseguards,[2] for turning aside to the Park-wall, on a necessary occasion, when he was passing with a lady under his protection. His blood rises at every instance of insolence and cruelty, even where he himself is no way concerned; and ingratitude makes his teeth chatter. On the other hand, the recital of a generous, humane, or grateful action, never fails to draw from him tears of approbation, which he is often greatly distressed to conceal.

Yesterday, one Paunceford[3] gave tea, on particular invitation – This man, after having been long buffetted by adversity, went abroad; and Fortune, resolved to make him amends for her former coyness, set him all at once up to the very ears in affluence. He has now emerged from obscurity, and blazes out in all the tinsel of the times. I don't find that he is charged with any practices that the law deems dishonest, or that his wealth has made him arrogant and inaccessible; on the contrary, he takes great pains to appear affable and gracious. But, they say, he is remarkable for shrinking from his former friendships, which were generally too plain and home-spun to appear amidst his present brilliant connexions; and that he seems uneasy at sight of some old benefactors, whom a man of honour would take pleasure to acknowledge – Be that as it may, he had so effectually engaged the company at Bath, that when I went with my uncle to the coffeehouse in the evening, there was not a soul in the room but one person, seemingly in years, who sat by the fire, reading one of the papers. Mr Bramble, taking his station close by him, 'There is such a crowd and confusion of chairs in the passage to Simpson's (said he) that we could hardly get along — I wish those minions of fortune would fall upon more laudable ways of spending their money. – I suppose, Sir, you like this kind of entertainment as little as I do?' 'I cannot say I have any great relish for such entertainments,' answered the other, without taking his eyes off the paper — 'Mr Serle (resumed my uncle) I beg pardon for interrupting you; but I can't resist the curiosity I have to know if you received a card on this occasion?'

The man seemed surprised at this address, and made some pause, as doubtful what answer he should make. 'I know my curiosity is impertinent (added my uncle) but I have a particular reason for asking the favour.' 'If that be the case (replied Mr Serle) I shall gratify you without hesitation, by owning that I have had no card. But, give me leave, Sir, to ask in my turn, what reason you think I have to expect such an invitation from the gentleman who gives tea?' 'I have my own reasons (cried Mr Bramble, with some emotion) and am convinced, more than ever, that this Paunceford is a contemptible fellow.' 'Sir (said the other, laying down the paper) I have not the honour to know you; but your discourse is a little mysterious, and seems to require some explanation. The person you are pleased to treat so cavalierly, is a gentleman of some consequence in the community; and, for aught you know, I may also have my particular reasons for defending his character' — 'If I was not convinced of the contrary (observed the other) I should not have gone so far' – 'Let me tell you, Sir (said the stranger, raising his voice) you have gone too far, in hazarding such reflections' —

Here he was interrupted by my uncle; who asked peevishly if he was Don Quixote[4] enough, at this time of day, to throw down his gauntlet as champion for a man who had treated him with such ungrateful neglect. 'For my part (added he) I shall never quarrel with you again upon this subject; and what I have said now, has been suggested as much by my regard for you, as by my contempt of him' — Mr Serle, then pulling off his spectacles, eyed uncle very earnestly, saying, in a mitigated tone, 'Surely I am much obliged — Ah, Mr Bramble! I now recollect your features, though I have not seen you these many years.' 'We might have been less strangers to one another (answered the squire) if our correspondence had not been interrupted, in consequence of a misunderstanding, occasioned by this very —, but no matter – Mr Serle, I esteem your character; and my friendship, such as it is, you may freely command.' 'The offer is too agreeable to be declined (said he); I embrace it very cordially; and, as the first fruits of it, request that you will change this subject, which, with me, is a matter of peculiar delicacy.'

My uncle owned he was in the right, and the discourse took a more general turn. Mr Serle passed the evening with us at our lodgings; and appeared to be intelligent, and even entertaining; but his disposition was rather of a melancholy hue. My uncle says he is a man of uncommon parts, and unquestioned probity: that his fortune, which was originally small, has been greatly hurt by a romantic spirit of generosity, which he has often displayed, even at the expence of his discretion, in favour of worthless individuals —— That he had rescued Paunceford from the lowest distress, when he was bankrupt, both in means and reputation – That he had espoused his interests with a degree of enthusiasm, broke with several friends, and even drawn his sword against my uncle, who had particular reasons for questioning the moral character of the said Paunceford: that, without Serle's countenance and assistance, the other never could have embraced the opportunity, which has raised him to this pinnacle of wealth: that Paunceford, in the first transports of his success, had written, from abroad, letters to different correspondents, owning his obligations to Mr Serle, in the warmest terms of acknowledgement, and declared he considered himself only as a factor for the occasions of his best friend: that, without doubt, he had made declarations of the same nature to his benefactor himself, though this last was always silent and reserved on the subject; but for some years, those tropes and figures of rhetoric had been disused; that, upon his return to England, he had been lavish in his caresses to Mr Serle, invited him to his house, and pressed him to make it his own: that he had overwhelmed him with general professions, and affected to express the warmest regard for him, in company of their common acquaintance; so that every body believed his gratitude was as liberal as his fortune; and some went so far as to congratulate Mr Serle on both.

All this time Paunceford carefully and artfully avoided particular discussions with his old patron, who had too much spirit to drop the most distant hint of balancing the account of obligation: that, nevertheless, a man of his feelings could not but resent this shocking return for all his kindness: and, therefore, he withdrew himself from the connexion, without coming to the least explanation or speaking a syllable on the subject to any living soul; so that now their correspondence is reduced to a slight salute with the hat, when they chance to meet in any public place; an accident that rarely happens, for their walks lie different ways. Mr Paunceford lives in a palace, feeds upon dainties, is arrayed in sumptuous apparel, appears in all the pomp of equipage, and passes his time among the nobles of the land. Serle lodges in Stall-street, up two pair of stairs backwards, walks a-foot in a Bath-rug, eats for twelve shillings a-week, and drinks water as preservative against the gout and gravel[5] — Mark the vicissitude. Paunceford once resided in a garret; where he subsisted upon sheep's-trotters and cow-heel, from which commons he was translated to the table of Serle, that ever abounded with good-chear; until want of economy and retention reduced him to a slender annuity in his decline of years, that scarce affords the bare necessaries of life – Paunceford, however, does him the honour to speak of him still, with uncommon regard; and to declare what pleasure it would give him to contribute in any shape to his convenience: 'But you know (he never fails to add) he's a shy kind of a man – And then such a perfect philosopher, that he looks upon all superfluities with the most sovereign contempt.'

Having given you this sketch of squire Paunceford, I need not make any comment on his character, but leave it at the mercy of your own reflection; from which I dare say, it will meet with as little quarter as it has found with

Yours always,

BATH, May 10.   J. MELFORD

To Mrs MARY JONES, at Brambleton-hall.

DEAR MOLLY,

We are all upon the ving – Hey for London, girl! – Fecks! we have been long enough here; for we're all turned tipsy turvy — Mistress has excarded Sir Ulic for kicking of Chowder; and I have sent O Frizzle away, with a flea in his ear[1] – I've shewn him how little I minded his tinsy and his long tail – A fellor, who would think for to go, for to offer, to take up with a dirty trollop under my nose — I ketched him in the very feet, coming out of the housemaids garret. – But I have gi'en the dirty slut a siserary.[2] O Molly! the sarvants at Bath are devils in garnet – They lite the candle at both ends – Here's nothing but ginketting, and wasting, and thieving and tricking, and trigging; and then they are never content – They won't suffer the 'squire and mistress to stay any longer; because they have been already above three weeks in the house; and they look for a couple of ginneys a-piece at our going away; and this is a parquisite they expect every month in the season; being as how no family has a right to stay longer than four weeks in the same lodgings; and so the cuck swears she will pin the dish-clout[3] to mistress's tail; and the house-maid vows, she'll put cowitch[4] in master's bed, if so be he don't discamp without furder ado – I don't blame them for making the most of their market, in the way of vails and parquisites; and I defy the devil to say I am a tail-carrier, or ever brought a poor servant into trouble —— But then they oft to have some conscience, in vronging those that be sarvants like themselves — For you must no, Molly, I missed three-quarters of blond lace, and a remnant of muslin, and my silver thimble; which was the gift of true love; they were all in my work-basket, that I left upon the table in the sarvants-hall, when mistresses bell rung; but if they had been under lock and kay, 'twould have been all the same; for there are double keys to all the locks in Bath; and they say as how the very teeth an't safe in your head, if you sleep with your mouth open – And so says I to myself, *them things could not go without hands; and so I'll watch their waters*: and so I did with a vitness; for then it was I found Bett consarned with O Frizzle. And as the cuck had thrown her slush at me, because I had taken part with Chowder, when he fit with the turnspit, I resolved to make a clear kitchen, and throw some of her fat into the fire. I ketched the chare-woman going out with her load in the morning, before she thought I was up, and brought her to mistress with her whole cargo – Marry, what do'st think she had got in the name of God? Her buckets were foaming full of our best bear, and her lap was stuffed with a cold tongue, part of a buttock of beef, half a turkey, and a swinging[5] lump of butter, and the matter of ten mould kandles, that had scarce ever been lit. The cuck brazened it out, and said it was her rite to rummage the pantry; and she was ready for to go before the mare: that he had been her potticary[6] many years, and would never think of hurting a poor sarvant, for giving away the scraps of the kitchen — I went another way to work with madam Betty, because she had been saucy, and called me skandelus names; and said O Frizzle couldn't abide me, and twenty other odorous falsehoods. I got a varrant from the mare, and her box being sarched by the constable, my things came out sure enuff; besides a full pound of vax candles, and a nite-cap of mistress, that I could sware to on my cruperal oaf[7] – O! then madam Mopstick came upon her merry bones;[8] and as the squire wouldn't hare of a pursecution, she scaped a skewering: but the longest day she has to live, she'll remember your

Humble sarvant,

BATH, May 15   W. JENKINS

If the hind should come again, before we be gone, pray send me the shift and apron, with the vite gallow manky[9] shoes; which you'll find in my pillowber – Sarvice to Saul –

To Sir WATKIN PHILLIPS, Bart. of Jesus college, Oxon.

You are in the right, dear Phillips; I don't expect regular answers to every letter – I know a college-life is too circumscribed to afford materials for such quick returns of communication. For my part, I am continually shifting the scene, and surrounded with new objects; some of which are striking enough. I shall therefore conclude my journal for your amusement; and, though, in all appearance, it will not treat of very important or interesting particulars, it may prove, perhaps, not altogether uninstructive and unentertaining.

The music and entertainments of Bath are over for this season; and all our gay birds of passage have taken their flight to Bristol-well, Tunbridge, Brighthelmstone, Scarborough, Harrowgate,[1] &c. Not a soul is seen in this place, but a few broken-winded parsons, waddling like so many crows along the North Parade. There is always a great shew of the clergy at Bath: none of your thin, puny, yellow, hectic[2] figures, exhausted

with abstinence, and hardy study, labouring under the *morbi eruditorum*,[3] but great overgrown dignitaries and rectors, with rubi-
cund noses and gouty ancles, or broad bloated faces, dragging
along great swag bellies; the emblems of sloth and indigestion.

Now we are upon the subject of parsons, I must tell you a
ludicrous adventure, which was achieved the other day by Tom
Eastgate, whom you may remember on the foundation of
Queen's.[4] He had been very assiduous to pin himself upon
George Prankley, who was a gentleman-commoner[5] of Christ-
church, knowing the said Prankley was heir to a considerable
estate, and would have the advowson of a good living,[6] the
incumbent of which was very old and infirm. He studied his
passions, and flattered them so effectually, as to become his
companion and counsellor; and, at last, obtained of him a
promise of the presentation, when the living should fall. Prankley, on his uncle's death, quitted Oxford, and made his first
appearance in the fashionable world at London; from whence
he came lately to Bath, where he has been exhibiting himself
among the bucks and gamesters of the place. Eastgate followed
him hither; but he should not have quitted him for a moment,
at his first emerging into life. He ought to have known he
was a fantastic, foolish, fickle fellow, who would forget his
college-attachments the moment they ceased appealing to his
senses. Tom met with a cold reception from his old friend; and
was, moreover, informed, that he had promised the living to
another man, who had a vote in the county, where he proposed
to offer himself a candidate at the next general election. He
now remembered nothing of Eastgate, but the freedoms he had
used to take with him, while Tom had quietly stood his butt,[7]
with an eye to the benefice; and those freedoms he began to
repeat in common-place sarcasms on his person and his cloth,
which he uttered in the public coffeehouse, for the entertainment of the company. But he was egregiously mistaken in giving
his own wit credit for that tameness of Eastgate, which had
been entirely owing to prudential considerations. These being
now removed, he retorted his repartee with interest, and found
no great difficulty in turning the laugh upon the aggressor; who,
losing his temper, called him names, and asked, *If he knew*

whom he talked to? After much altercation, Prankley, shaking his cane, bid him hold his tongue, otherwise he could dust his cassock[8] for him. 'I have no pretensions to such a valet (said Tom) but if you should do me that office, and overheat yourself, I have here a good oaken towel at your service.'

Prankley was equally incensed and confounded at this reply. After a moment's pause, he took him aside towards the window; and, pointing to the clump of firs, on Clerken-down, asked in a whisper, if he had spirit enough to meet him there, with a case of pistols, at six o'clock to-morrow morning. Eastgate answered in the affirmative; and, with a steady countenance, assured him, he would not fail to give him the rendezvous at the hour he mentioned. So saying, he retired; and the challenger stayed some time in manifest agitation. In the morning, East-gate, who knew his man, and had taken his resolution, went to Prankley's lodgings, and roused him by five o'clock.

The squire, in all probability, cursed his punctuality in his heart, but he affected to talk big; and having prepared his artillery overnight, they crossed the water at the end of the South Parade. In their progress up the hill, Prankley often eyed the parson, in hopes of perceiving some reluctance in his countenance; but as no such marks appeared, he attempted to intimidate him by word of mouth. 'If these flints do their office (said he) I'll do thy business in a few minutes.' 'I desire you will do your best (replied the other); for my part, I come not here to trifle. Our lives are in the hands of God; and one of us already totters on the brink of eternity' — This remark seemed to make some impression upon the squire, who changed coun-tenance, and with a faultering accent observed, 'That it ill became a clergyman to be concerned in quarrels and blood-shed' — 'Your insolence to me (said Eastgate) I should have bore with patience, had not you cast the most infamous reflec-tions upon my order, the honour of which I think myself in duty bound to maintain, even at the expence of my heart's blood; and surely it can be no crime to put out of the world a profligate wretch, without any sense of principle, morality, or religion' — 'Thou may'st take away my life (cried Prankley, in great perturbation) but don't go to murder my character. —

What! has't got no conscience?' 'My conscience is perfectly
quiet (replied the other); and now, Sir, we are upon the spot –
Take your ground as near as you please; prime your pistol; and
the Lord, of his infinite mercy, have compassion upon your
miserable soul!'

This ejaculation he pronounced in a loud solemn tone, with
his hat off, and his eyes lifted up; then drawing a large horse-
pistol, he presented, and put himself in a posture of action.
Prankley took his distance, and endeavoured to prime, but his
hand shook with such violence, that he found this operation
impracticable – His antagonist, seeing how it was with him,
offered his assistance, and advanced for that purpose; when the
poor squire, exceedingly alarmed at what he had heard and
seen, desired the action might be deferred till next day, as he
had not settled his affairs. 'I ha'n't made my will (said he); my
sisters are not provided for; and I just now recollect an old
promise, which my conscience tells me I ought to perform – I'll
first convince thee, that I'm not a wretch without principle, and
then thou shalt have an opportunity to take my life, which thou
seem'st to thirst after so eagerly.'

Eastgate understood the hint; and told him, that one day
should break no squares:[9] adding, 'God forbid that I should be
the means of hindering you from acting the part of an honest
man, and a dutiful brother' — By virtue of this cessation, they
returned peaceably together. Prankley forthwith made out the
presentation of the living, and delivered it to Eastgate, telling
him at the same time, he had now settled his affairs, and was
ready to attend him to the Fir-grove; but Tom declared he could
not think of lifting his hand against the life of so great a
benefactor – He did more: when they next met at the coffeehouse, he asked pardon of Mr Prankley, if in his passion he had
said any thing to give him offence; and the squire was so
gracious as to forgive him with a cordial shake of the hand,
declaring, that he did not like to be at variance with an old
college companion – Next day, however, he left Bath abruptly;
and then Eastgate told me all these particulars, not a little
pleased with the effects of his own sagacity, by which he has
secured a living worth 160l. *per annum.*

Of my uncle, I have nothing at present to say; but that we set out to-morrow for London *en famille*. He and the ladies, with the maid and Chowder in a coach; I and the man-servant a-horseback. The particulars of our journey you shall have in my next, provided no accident happens to prevent,

Yours ever,

BATH, May 17.   J. MELFORD

To Dr LEWIS.

DEAR DICK,

I shall to-morrow set out for London, where I have bespoke lodgings, at Mrs Norton's in Golden-square.[1] Although I am no admirer of Bath, I shall leave it with regret; because I must part with some old friends, whom, in all probability, I shall never see again. In the course of coffeehouse conversation, I had often heard very extraordinary encomiums passed on the performances of Mr T—,[2] a gentleman residing in this place, who paints landscapes for his amusement. As I have no great confidence in the taste and judgment of coffeehouse connoisseurs, and never received much pleasure from this branch of the art, those general praises made no impression at all on my curiosity; but, at the request of a particular friend, I went yesterday to see the pieces, which had been so warmly commended – I must own I am no judge of painting, though very fond of pictures. I don't imagine that my senses would play me so false, as to betray me into admiration of any thing that was very bad; but, true it is, I have often overlooked capital beauties, in pieces of extraordinary merit. – If I am not totally devoid of taste, however, this young gentleman of Bath is the best landscape-painter now living: I was struck with his performances in such a manner, as I had never been by painting before. His trees not only have a richness of foliage and warmth of colouring, which delights the view; but also a certain magnificence in the disposition and spirit in the expression, which I cannot describe. His management of the *chiaro oscuro*, or light

and shadow, especially gleams of sunshine, is altogether
wonderful, both in the contrivance and execution; and he is so
happy in his perspective, and marking his distances at sea, by a
progressive series of ships, vessels, capes, and promontories,
that I could not help thinking, I had a distant view of thirty
leagues upon the back-ground of the picture. If there is any
taste for ingenuity left in a degenerate age, fast sinking into
barbarism, this artist, I apprehend, will make a capital figure,
as soon as his works are known.

Two days ago, I was favoured with a visit by Mr Fitzowen;
who, with great formality, solicited my vote and interest at
the general election. I ought not to have been shocked at the
confidence of this man; though it was remarkable, considering
what had passed between him and me on a former occasion —
These visits are mere matter of form, which a candidate makes
to every elector; even to those who, he knows, are engaged in
the interest of his competitor, lest he should expose himself to
the imputation of pride, at a time when it is expected he should
appear humble. Indeed, I know nothing so abject as the
behaviour of a man canvassing for a seat in parliament —
This mean prostration (to borough-electors, especially) has, I
imagine, contributed in a great measure to raise that spirit of
insolence among the vulgar; which, like the devil, will be found
very difficult to lay. Be that as it may, I was in some confusion
at the effrontery of Fitzowen; but I soon recollected myself, and
told him, I had not yet determined for whom I should give my
vote, nor whether I should give it for any. – The truth is, I look
upon both candidates in the same light; and should think myself
a traitor to the constitution of my country, if I voted for either.
If every elector would bring the same consideration home to
his conscience, we should not have such reason to exclaim
against the venality of p—ts.[3] But we all are a pack of venal
and corrupted rascals; so lost to all sense of honesty, and all
tenderness of character, that, in a little time, I am fully persuaded, nothing will be infamous but virtue and public-spirit.

G. H—,[4] who is really an enthusiast in patriotism, and represented the capital in several successive parliaments, declared
to me t'other day, with the tears in his eyes, that he had lived

above thirty years in the city of London, and dealt in the way of commerce with all the citizens of note in their turns; but that, as he should answer to God, he had never, in the whole course of his life, found above three or four whom he could call thoroughly honest: a declaration which was rather mortifying than surprising to me; who have found so few men of worth in the course of my acquaintance, that they serve only as exceptions; which, in the grammarian's phrase, confirm and prove a general canon[5] — I know you will say, G. H— saw imperfectly through the mist of prejudice, and I am rankled by the spleen – Perhaps, you are partly in the right; for I have perceived that my opinion of mankind, like mercury in the thermometer, rises and falls according to the variations of the weather.

Pray settle accompts with Barnes; take what money of mine is in his hands, and give him acquittance. If you think Davis has stock or credit enough to do justice to the farm, give him a discharge for the rent that is due: this will animate his industry; for I know that nothing is so discouraging to a farmer as the thoughts of being in arrears with his landlord. He becomes dispirited, and neglects his labour; and so the farm goes to wreck. Tabby has been clamouring for some days about the lamb's skin, which Williams, the hind, begged of me, when he was last at Bath. Prithee take it back, paying the fellow the full value of it, that I may have some peace in my own house; and let him keep his own counsel, if he means to keep his place – O! I shall never presume to despise or censure any poor man, for suffering himself to be henpecked; conscious how I myself am obliged to truckle to a domestic demon; even though (blessed be God) she is not yoked with me for life, in the matrimonial waggon – She has quarrelled with the servants of the house about vails; and such intolerable scolding ensued on both sides, that I have been fain to appease the cook and chambermaid by stealth. Can't you find some poor gentleman of Wales, to take this precious commodity off the hands of

Yours,

BATH, May 19.   MATT. BRAMBLE

To Dr Lewis.

DOCTER LEWS,

Give me leaf to tell you, methinks you mought employ your talons better, than to encourage servants to pillage their masters – I find by Gwyllim, that Villiams has got my skin; for which he is an impotent rascal. He has not only got my skin, but, moreover, my butter-milk to fatten his pigs; and, I suppose, the next thing he gets, will be my pad[1] to carry his daughter to church and fair: Roger gets this, and Roger gets that; but I'd have you to know, I won't be rogered[2] at this rate by any ragmatical fellow in the kingdom – And I am surprised, docter Lews, you would offer to put my affairs in composition with the refuge and skim of the hearth. I have toiled and moyled to a good purpuss, for the advantage of Matt's family, if I can't safe as much owl as will make me an under petticoat. As for the butter-milk, ne'er a pig in the parish shall thrust his snout in it, with my good-will. There's a famous physician at the Hot Well, that prescribes it to his patience, when the case is consumptive; and the Scots and Irish have begun to drink it already, in such quantities, that there is not a drop left for the hogs in the whole neighbourhood of Bristol. I'll have our butter-milk barrelled up, and sent twice a-week to Aberginny, where it may be sold for a half-penny the quart; and so Roger may carry his pigs to another market – I hope, Docter, you will not go to put any more such phims in my brother's head, to the prejudice of my pockat; but rather give me some raisins (which hitherto you have not done) to subscribe myself

Your humble servant,

BATH, May 19.   TAB. BRAMBLE

To Sir WATKIN PHILLIPS, of Jesus college, Oxon.

DEAR PHILLIPS,

Without waiting for your answer to my last, I proceed to give
you an account of our journey to London, which has not been
wholly barren of adventure. Tuesday last the 'squire took his
place in a hired coach and four, accompanied by his sister and
mine, and Mrs Tabby's maid, Winifrid Jenkins, whose province
it was to support Chowder on a cushion in her lap. I could
scarce refrain from laughing when I looked into the vehicle,
and saw that animal sitting opposite to my uncle, like any other
passenger. The squire, ashamed of his situation, blushed to the
eyes: and, calling to the postilions to drive on, pulled the glass
up in my face. I, and his servant, John Thomas, attended them
on horseback.

Nothing worth mentioning occurred, till we arrived on the
edge of Marlborough Downs.[1] There one of the four horses
fell, in going down hill at a round trot; and the postilion behind,
endeavouring to stop the carriage, pulled it on one side into a
deep rut, where it was fairly[2] overturned. I had rode on about
two hundred yards before; but, hearing a loud scream, galloped
back and dismounted, to give what assistance was in my power.
When I looked into the coach, I could see nothing distinctly,
but the nether end of Jenkins, who was kicking her heels and
squalling with great vociferation. All of a sudden, my uncle
thrust up his bare pate, and bolted through the window, as
nimble as a grasshopper, having made use of poor Win's posteriors as a step to rise in his ascent – The man (who had
likewise quitted his horse) dragged this forlorn damsel, more
dead than alive, through the same opening. Then Mr Bramble,
pulling the door off its hinges with a jerk, laid hold on Liddy's
arm, and brought her to the light; very much frighted, but little
hurt. It fell to my share to deliver our aunt Tabitha, who had
lost her cap in the struggle, and being rather more than half
frantic, with rage and terror, was no bad representation of one
of the sister Furies[3] that guard the gates of hell — She expressed
no sort of concern for her brother, who ran about in the cold,

without his periwig, and worked with the most astonishing agility, in helping to disentangle the horses from the carriage: but she cried, in a tone of distraction, 'Chowder! Chowder! my dear Chowder! my poor Chowder is certainly killed!'

This was not the case – Chowder, after having tore my uncle's leg in the confusion of the fall, had retreated under the seat, and from thence the footman drew him by the neck; for which good office, he bit his fingers to the bone. The fellow, who is naturally surly, was so provoked at this assault, that he saluted his ribs with a hearty kick, exclaiming, 'Damn the nasty son of a bitch, and them he belongs to!' A benediction, which was by no means lost upon the implacable virago[4] his mistress – Her brother, however, prevailed upon her to retire into a peasant's house, near the scene of action, where his head and hers were covered, and poor Jenkins had a fit — Our next care was to apply some sticking plaister to the wound in his leg, which exhibited the impression of Chowder's teeth; but he never opened his lips against the delinquent — Mrs Tabby, alarmed at this scene, 'You say nothing, Matt (cried she); but I know your mind – I know the spite you have to that poor unfortunate animal! I know you intend to take his life away!' 'You are mistaken, upon my honour! (replied the squire, with a sarcastic smile) I should be incapable of harbouring any such cruel design against an object so amiable and inoffensive; even if he had not the happiness to be your favourite.'

John Thomas was not so delicate. The fellow, whether really alarmed for his life, or instigated by the desire of revenge, came in, and bluntly demanded, that the dog should be put to death; on the supposition, that if ever he should run mad hereafter, he, who had been bit by him, would be infected – My uncle calmly argued upon the absurdity of his opinion, observing, that he himself was in the same predicament, and would certainly take the precaution he proposed, if he was not sure he ran no risque of infection. Nevertheless, Thomas continued obstinate; and, at length declared, that if the dog was not shot immediately, he himself would be his executioner — This declaration opened the flood-gates of Tabby's eloquence, which would have shamed the first-rate oratress of Billingsgate. The footman retorted in the same stile; and the squire dismissed him from his service, after having prevented me from giving him a good horse-whipping for his insolence.

The coach being adjusted, another difficulty occurred – Mrs Tabitha absolutely refused to enter it again, unless another driver could be found to take the place of the postilion; who, she affirmed, had overturned the carriage from malice aforethought – After much dispute, the man resigned his place to a shabby country fellow, who undertook to go as far as Marlborough, where they could be better provided; and at that place we arrived about one o'clock, without farther impediment. Mrs Bramble, however, found new matter of offence; which, indeed, she has a particular genius for extracting at will from almost every incident in life. We had scarce entered the room at Marlborough, where we stayed to dine, when she exhibited a formal complaint against the poor fellow who had superseded the postilion. She said he was such a beggarly rascal that he had ne'er a shirt to his back, and had the impudence to shock her sight by shewing his bare posteriors, for which act of indelicacy he deserved to be set in the stocks. Mrs Winifred Jenkins confirmed the assertion, with respect to his nakedness, observing, at the same time, that he had a skin as fair as alabaster.

'This is a heinous offence, indeed (cried my uncle) let us hear what the fellow has to say in his own vindication.' He was accordingly summoned, and made his appearance, which was equally queer and pathetic. He seemed to be about twenty years of age, of a middling size, with bandy legs, stooping shoulders, high forehead, sandy locks, pinking[5] eyes, flat nose, and long chin – but his complexion was of a sickly yellow; his looks denoted famine, and the rags that he wore could hardly conceal what decency requires to be covered — My uncle, having surveyed him attentively, said, with an ironical expression in his countenance, 'An't you ashamed, fellow, to ride postilion without a shirt to cover your backside from the view of the ladies in the coach?' 'Yes, I am, an please your noble honour (answered the man) but necessity has no law, as the saying is — And more than that, it was an accident — My breeches cracked behind, after I had got into the saddle' — 'You're an impudent varlet (cried Mrs Tabby) for presuming to ride before persons of fashion without a shirt' — 'I am so, an please your worthy ladyship (said he) but I am a poor Wiltshire lad – I ha'n't a shirt in the world, that I can call my own, nor a rag of clothes, and please your ladyship, but what you see – I have no friend nor relation upon earth to help me out — I have had the fever and ague these six months, and spent all I had in the world upon doctors, and to keep soul and body together; and, saving your ladyship's good presence, I han't broke bread these four and twenty hours.'

Mrs Bramble, turning from him, said, she had never seen such a filthy tatterdemalion,[6] and bid him begone; observing, that he would fill the room full of vermin – Her brother darted a significant glance at her, as she retired with Liddy into another apartment, and then asked the man if he was known to any person in Marlborough? – When he answered, that the landlord of the inn had known him from his infancy; mine host was immediately called, and being interrogated on the subject, declared that the young fellow's name was Humphry Clinker.[7] That he had been a love begotten babe, brought up in the work-house, and put out apprentice by the parish to a country black-smith, who died before the boy's time was out: that he had for some time worked under his ostler, as a helper and extra postilion, till he was taken ill of the ague, which disabled him from getting his bread: that, having sold or pawned every thing he had in the world for his cure and subsistence, he became so miserable and shabby, that he disgraced the stable, and was dismissed; but that he never heard any thing to the prejudice of his character in other respects. 'So that the fellow being sick and destitute (said my uncle) you turned him out to die in the streets.' 'I pay the poor's rate[8] (replied the other) and I have no right to maintain idle vagrants, either in sickness or health; besides, such a miserable object would have brought a discredit upon my house.'

'You perceive (said the 'squire, turning to me) our landlord is a Christian of bowels – Who shall presume to censure the morals of the age, when the very publicans exhibit such examples of humanity? — Heark ye, Clinker, you are a most notorious offender — You stand convicted of sickness, hunger, wretchedness, and want – But, as it does not belong to me to punish criminals, I will only take upon me the task of giving you a word of advice – Get a shirt with all convenient dispatch, that your nakedness may not henceforward give offence to travelling gentlewomen, especially maidens in years.'

So saying, he put a guinea[9] into the hand of the poor fellow, who stood staring at him in silence, with his mouth wide open, till the landlord pushed him out of the room.

In the afternoon, as our aunt stept into the coach, she observed, with some marks of satisfaction, that the postilion, who rode next to her, was not a shabby wretch like the raga-muffin who had drove them into Marlborough. Indeed, the difference was very conspicuous: this was a smart fellow, with a narrow brimmed hat, with gold cording, a cut bob, a decent blue jacket, leather-breeches, and a clean linen shirt, puffed above the waist-band. When we arrived at the Castle on Spin-Hill,[10] where we lay, this new postilion was remarkably assidu-ous in bringing in the loose parcels; and, at length, displayed the individual countenance of Humphry Clinker, who had metamorphosed himself in this manner, by relieving from pawn part of his own clothes, with the money he had received from Mr Bramble.

Howsoever pleased the rest of the company were with such a favourable change in the appearance of this poor creature it soured on the stomach of Mrs Tabby, who had not yet digested the affront of his naked skin — She tossed her nose in disdain, saying, she supposed her brother had taken him into favour, because he had insulted her with his obscenity: that a fool and his money were soon parted; but that if Matt intended to take the fellow with him to London, she would not go a foot further that way — My uncle said nothing with his tongue, though his looks were sufficiently expressive; and next morning Clinker did not appear, so that we proceeded without further alterca-tion to Salt-hill,[11] where we proposed to dine – There, the first person that came to the side of the coach, and began to adjust the footboard, was no other than Humphry Clinker – When I handed out Mrs Bramble, she eyed him with a furious look, and passed into the house – My uncle was embarrassed, and asked him peevishly, what had brought him hither? The fellow said, his honour had been so good to him, that he had not the heart to part with him; that he would follow him to the world's end, and serve him all the days of his life,[12] without fee or reward.

Mr Bramble did not know whether to chide or laugh at this declaration — He foresaw much contradiction on the side of Tabby; and on the other hand, he could not but be pleased with the gratitude of Clinker, as well as with the simplicity of his character – 'Suppose I was inclined to take you into my service (said he) what are your qualifications? what are you good for?' 'An please your honour (answered this original) I can read and write, and do the business of the stable indifferent well — I can dress a horse, and shoe him, and bleed and rowel[13] him; and, as for the practice of sow-gelding, I won't turn my back on e'er a he in the county of Wilts — Then I can make hog's puddings and hob-nails, mend kettles and tin sauce-pans.' – Here uncle burst out a-laughing; and inquired what other accomplishments he was master of – 'I know something of single-stick, and psalmody (proceeded Clinker); I can play upon the Jew's-harp, sing Black-ey'd Susan, Arthur-o'Bradley, and divers other songs; I can dance a Welsh jig, and Nancy Dawson;[14] wrestle a fall with any lad of my inches, when I'm in heart; and, under correction, I can find a hare when your honour wants a bit of game.' 'Foregad! thou are a complete fellow (cried my uncle, still laughing) I have a good mind to take thee into my family — Prithee, go and try if thou can'st make peace with my sister – Thou ha'st given her much offence by shewing her thy naked tail.'

Clinker accordingly followed us into the room, cap in hand, where, addressing himself to Mrs Tabitha, 'May it please your ladyship's worship (cried he) to pardon and forgive my offences, and, with God's assistance, I shall take care that my tail shall never rise up in judgment against me, to offend your ladyship again — Do, pray, good, sweet, beautiful lady, take compassion on a poor sinner – God bless your noble countenance; I am sure you are too handsome and generous to bear malice – I will

serve you on my bended knees, by night and by day, by land
and by water; and all for the love and pleasure of serving such
an excellent lady.'

This compliment and humiliation had some effect upon
Tabby; but she made no reply; and Clinker, taking silence for
consent, gave his attendance at dinner. The fellow's natural
aukwardness and the flutter of his spirits were productive of
repeated blunders in the course of his attendance – At length,
he spilt part of a custard upon her right shoulder; and, starting
back, trod upon Chowder, who set up a dismal howl — Poor
Humphry was so disconcerted at this double mistake, that he
dropt the china dish, which broke into a thousand pieces; then,
falling down upon his knees, remained in that posture gaping,
with a most ludicrous aspect of distress — Mrs Bramble flew
to the dog, and, snatching him in her arms, presented him to
her brother saying, 'This is all a concerted scheme against this
unfortunate animal, whose only crime is its regard for me –
Here it is, kill it at once, and then you'll be satisfied.'

Clinker, hearing these words, and taking them in the literal
acceptation, got up in some hurry, and seizing a knife from the
side-board, cried, 'Not here, an please your ladyship – It will
daub the room – Give him to me, and I'll carry him to the ditch
by the roadside' — To this proposal he received no other
answer, than a hearty box on the ear, that made him stagger to
the other side of the room. 'What! (said she to her brother) am
I to be affronted by every mangy hound that you pick up on
the highway? I insist upon your sending this rascallion about
his business immediately' — 'For God's sake, sister, compose
yourself (said my uncle) and consider that the poor fellow is
innocent of any intention to give you offence' – 'Innocent as
the babe unborn' (cried Humphry). 'I see it plainly (exclaimed
this implacable maiden), he acts by your direction; and you are
resolved to support him in his impudence – This is a bad return
for all the services I have done you; for nursing you in your
sickness, managing your family, and keeping you from ruining
yourself by your own imprudence — But now you shall part
with that rascal or me, upon the spot, without farther loss of
time; and the world shall see whether you have more regard for

your own flesh and blood, or for a beggarly foundling taken
from the dunghill.'

Mr Bramble's eyes began to glisten, and his teeth to chatter.
'If stated fairly (said he, raising his voice) the question is,
whether I have spirit to shake off an intolerable yoke, by one
effort of resolution, or meanness enough to do an act of cruelty
and injustice, to gratify the rancour of a capricious woman –
Heark ye, Mrs Tabitha Bramble, I will now propose an alternative in my turn – Either discard your four-footed favourite, or
give me leave to bid you eternally adieu – For I am determined
that he and I shall live no longer under the same roof; and *to
dinner with what appetite you may*'[15] — Thunderstruck at this
declaration, she sat down in a corner; and, after a pause of
some minutes, 'Sure I don't understand you, Matt! (said she)'
'And yet I spoke in plain English' — answered the 'squire,
with a peremptory look. 'Sir (resumed this virago, effectually
humbled), it is your prerogative to command, and my duty to
obey. I can't dispose of the dog in this place; but if you'll allow
him to go in the coach to London, I give you my word, he shall
never trouble you again.'

Her brother, entirely disarmed by this mild reply, declared,
she could ask him nothing in reason that he would refuse;
adding, 'I hope, sister, you have never found me deficient in
natural affection.' Mrs Tabitha immediately rose, and, throwing her arms about his neck, kissed him on the cheek: he
returned her embrace with great emotion. Liddy sobbed, Win.
Jenkins cackled, Chowder capered, and Clinker skipped about,
rubbing his hands for joy of this reconciliation.

Concord being thus restored, we finished our meal with comfort; and in the evening arrived at London, without having met
with any other adventure. My aunt seems to be much mended
by the hint she received from her brother. She has been graciously pleased to remove her displeasure from Clinker, who is
now retained as a footman; and in a day or two will make his
appearance in a new suit of livery;[16] but as he is little acquainted
with London, we have taken an occasional valet, whom I intend
hereafter to hire as my own servant. We lodge in Golden-square,
at the house of one Mrs Norton, a decent sort of a woman,

who takes great pains to make us all easy. My uncle proposes to make a circuit of all the remarkable scenes of this metropolis, for the entertainment of his pupils; but as both you and I are already acquainted with most of those he will visit, and with some others he little dreams of, I shall only communicate what will be in some measure new to your observation. Remember me to our Jesuitical friends, and believe me ever,

Dear knight,

Yours affectionately,

LONDON, May 24.   J. MELFORD

To Dr Lewis.

DEAR DOCTOR,

   London is literally new to me; new in its streets, houses, and even in its situation; as the Irishman said, 'London is now gone out of town.'[1] What I left open fields, producing hay and corn, I now find covered with streets and squares, and palaces, and churches. I am credibly informed, that in the space of seven years, eleven thousand new houses have been built in one quarter of Westminster, exclusive of what is daily added to other parts of this unwieldy metropolis. Pimlico and Knightsbridge are now almost joined to Chelsea and Kensington; and if this infatuation continues for half a century, I suppose the whole county of Middlesex will be covered with brick.

   It must be allowed, indeed, for the credit of the present age, that London and Westminster are much better paved and lighted than they were formerly.[2] The new streets are spacious, regular, and airy; and the houses generally convenient. The bridge at Blackfriars[3] is a noble monument of taste and public-spirit. — I wonder how they stumbled upon a work of such magnificence and utility. But, notwithstanding these improvements, the capital is become an overgrown monster; which, like a dropsical head, will in time leave the body and extremities without nourishment and support.[4] The absurdity will appear in its full force, when we consider that one sixth part of the natives of this whole extensive kingdom is crowded within the bills of mortality.[5] What wonder that our villages are depopulated, and our farms in want of day-labourers? The abolition of small farms is but one cause of the decrease of population. Indeed, the incredible increase of horses and black cattle, to answer the purposes of luxury, requires a prodigious quantity of hay and grass, which are raised and managed without much labour; but a number of hands will always be wanted for the different branches of agriculture, whether the farms be large or small. The tide of luxury has swept all the inhabitants from the open country — The poorest squire, as well as the richest peer, must have his house in town, and make a figure with an extraordinary number of domestics. The plough-boys, cow-herds, and lower hinds are debauched and seduced by the appearance and discourse of those coxcombs in livery, when they make their summer excursions. They desert their dirt and drudgery, and swarm up to London, in hopes of getting into service, where they can live luxuriously and wear fine clothes, without being obliged to work; for idleness is natural to man — Great numbers of these, being disappointed in their expectation, become thieves and sharpers; and London being an immense wilderness, in which there is neither watch nor ward of any signification, nor any order or police, affords them lurking-places as well as prey.

There are many causes that contribute to the daily increase of this enormous mass; but they may be all resolved into the grand source of luxury and corruption – About five and twenty years ago, very few, even of the most opulent citizens of London, kept any equipage, or even any servants in livery. Their tables produced nothing but plain boiled and roasted, with a bottle of port and a tankard of beer. At present, every trader in any degree of credit, every broker and attorney, maintains a couple of footmen, a coachman, and postilion. He has his town-house, and his country-house, his coach, and his post-chaise. His wife and daughters appear in the richest stuffs, bespangled with diamonds. They frequent the court, the opera, the theatre, and the masquerade. They hold assemblies at their own houses: they make sumptuous entertainments, and treat with the richest wines of Bordeaux, Burgundy, and Champagne. The substantial tradesman, who wont to pass his evenings at the ale-house for fourpence half-penny, now spends three shillings at the tavern, while his wife keeps card-tables at home; she must likewise have fine clothes, her chaise, or pad, with country lodgings, and go three times a week to public diversions. Every clerk, apprentice, and even waiter of tavern or coffeehouse, maintains a gelding by himself, or in partnership, and assumes the air and apparel of a petit maitre[6] — The gayest places of public entertainment are filled with fashionable figures; which, upon inquiry, will be found to be journeymen taylors, serving-men, and abigails, disguised like their betters.

In short, there is no distinction or subordination left — The different departments of life are jumbled together – The hod-carrier, the low mechanic, the tapster, the publican, the shopkeeper, the pettifogger,[7] the citizen, and courtier, *all tread upon the kibes of one another*:[8] actuated by the demons of profligacy and licentiousness, they are seen every where rambling, riding, rolling, rushing, justling, mixing, bouncing, cracking, and crashing in one vile ferment of stupidity and corruption – All is tumult and hurry; one would imagine they were impelled by some disorder of the brain, that will not suffer them to be at rest. The foot-passengers run along as if they were pursued by bailiffs. The porters and chairmen trot with their burthens. People, who keep their own equipages, drive through the streets at full speed. Even citizens, physicians, and apothecaries, glide in their chariots like lightening. The hackney-coachmen make their horses smoke, and the pavement shakes under them; and I have actually seen a waggon pass through Piccadilly at the hand-gallop.[9] In a word, the whole nation seems to be running out of their wits.

The diversions of the times are not ill suited to the genius of this incongruous monster, called *the public*. Give it noise, confusion, glare, and glitter; it has no idea of elegance and propriety – What are the amusements of Ranelagh?[10] One half of the company are following at the other's tails, in an eternal circle; like so many blind asses in an olive-mill, where they can neither discourse, distinguish, nor be distinguished; while the other half are drinking hot water, under the denomination of tea, till nine or ten o'clock at night, to keep them awake for the rest of the evening. As for the orchestra, the vocal music especially, it is well for the performers that they cannot be heard distinctly. Vauxhall[11] is a composition of baubles, overcharged with paltry ornaments, ill conceived, and poorly executed; without any unity of design, or propriety of disposition. It is an unnatural assembly of objects, fantastically illuminated in broken masses; seemingly contrived to dazzle the eyes and divert the imagination of the vulgar – Here a wooden lion, there a stone statue; in one place, a range of things like coffeehouse boxes, covered a-top; in another, a parcel of ale-house benches; in a third, a puppet-show representation of a tin cascade; in a fourth, a gloomy cave of a circular form, like a sepulchral vault half lighted; in a fifth, a scanty flip of grass-plat, that would not afford pasture sufficient for an ass's colt. The walks, which nature seems to have intended for solitude, shade, and silence, are filled with crowds of noisy people, sucking up the nocturnal rheums of an aguish climate; and through these gay scenes, a few lamps glimmer like so many farthing candles.

When I see a number of well dressed people, of both sexes, sitting on the covered benches, exposed to the eyes of the mob; and, which is worse, to the cold, raw, night-air, devouring sliced beef, and swilling port, and punch, and cyder, I can't help compassionating their temerity; while I despise their want of taste and decorum; but, when they course along those damp and gloomy walks, or crowd together upon the wet gravel, without any other cover than the cope of Heaven, listening to a song, which one half of them cannot possibly hear, how can I help supposing they are actually possessed by a spirit, more absurd and pernicious than any thing we meet with in the precincts of Bedlam?[12] In all probability, the proprietors of this, and other public gardens of inferior note, in the skirts of the metropolis, are, in some shape, connected with the faculty of physic, and the company of undertakers; for, considering that eagerness in the pursuit of what is called pleasure, which now predominates through every rank and denomination of life, I am persuaded that more gouts, rheumatisms, catarrhs, and consumptions are caught in these nocturnal pastimes, *sub dio*,[13] than from all the risques and accidents to which a life of toil and danger is exposed.

These, and other observations, which I have made in this excursion, will shorten my stay at London, and send me back with a double relish to my solitude and mountains; but I shall return by a different route from that which brought me to town. I have seen some old friends, who constantly resided in this virtuous metropolis, but they are so changed in manners and disposition, that we hardly know or care for one another – In our journey from Bath, my sister Tabby provoked me into a transport of passion; during which, like a man who has drank himself pot-valiant,[14] I talked to her in such a stile of authority and resolution, as produced a most blessed effect. She and her dog have been remarkably quiet and orderly ever since this expostulation. How long this agreeable calm will last, Heaven above knows – I flatter myself, the exercise of travelling has been of service to my health; a circumstance which encourages me to proceed in my projected expedition to the North. But I must, in the mean time, for the benefit and amusement of my pupils, explore the depths of this chaos; this misshapen and monstrous capital, without head or tail, members or proportion.

Thomas was so insolent to my sister on the road, that I was obliged to turn him off abruptly, betwixt Chippenham and Marlborough, where our coach was overturned. The fellow was always sullen and selfish; but, if he should return to the country, you may give him a character for honesty and sobriety; and, provided he behaves with proper respect to the family, let him have a couple of guineas in the name of

Yours always,

MATT. BRAMBLE

LONDON, May 20.

To Miss LÆTITIA WILLIS, at Gloucester.

MY DEAR LETTY,

Inexpressible was the pleasure I received from yours of the 25th, which was last night put into my hands by Mrs Brentford, the milliner, from Gloucester — I rejoice to hear that my worthy governess is in good health, and, still more, that she no longer retains any displeasure towards her poor Liddy. I am sorry you have lost the society of the agreeable Miss Vaughn; but, I hope you won't have cause much longer to regret the departure of your school companions, as I make no doubt but your parents will, in a little time, bring you into the world, where you are so well qualified to make a distinguished figure. When that is the case, I flatter myself you and I shall meet again, and be happy together; and even improve the friendship which we contracted in our tender years — This at least I can promise – It shall not be for the want of my utmost endeavours, if our intimacy does not continue for life.

About five days ago we arrived in London, after an easy journey from Bath; during which, however, we were over-turned, and met with some other little incidents, which, had like to have occasioned a misunderstanding betwixt my uncle and aunt; but now, thank God, they are happily reconciled: we live in harmony together, and every day make parties to see the wonders of this vast metropolis, which, however, I cannot pretend to describe; for I have not as yet seen one hundredth part of its curiosities, and I am quite in a maze of admiration.

The cities of London and Westminster are spread out into an incredible extent. The streets, squares, rows, lanes, and alleys, are innumerable. Palaces, public buildings, and churches rise in every quarter; and, among these last, St Paul's appears with the most astonishing pre-eminence. They say it is not so large as St Peter's at Rome; but, for my own part, I can have no idea of any earthly temple more grand and magnificent.

But even these superb objects are not so striking as the crowds of people that swarm in the streets. I at first imagined that some great assembly was just dismissed, and wanted to stand aside till the multitude should pass; but this human tide continues to flow, without interruption or abatement, from morn till night. Then there is such an infinity of gay equipages, coaches, chariots, chaises, and other carriages, continually rolling and shifting before your eyes, that one's head grows giddy looking at them; and the imagination is quite confounded with splendour and variety. Nor is the prospect by water less grand and astonishing than that by land: you see three stupendous bridges,[1] joining the opposite banks of a broad, deep, and rapid river; so vast, so stately, so elegant, that they seem to be the work of the giants; betwixt them, the whole surface of the Thames is covered with small vessels, barges, boats, and wherries, passing to and fro; and below the three bridges, such a prodigious forest of masts, for miles together, that you would think all the ships in the universe were here assembled. All that you read of wealth and grandeur in the Arabian Nights' Entertainment, and the Persian Tales,[2] concerning Bagdad, Diarbekir, Damascus, Ispahan, and Samarkand, is here realized.

Ranelagh looks like the inchanted palace of a genie, adorned with the most exquisite performances of painting, carving, and gilding, enlightened with a thousand golden lamps, that emulate the noon-day sun; crowded with the great, the rich, the gay, the happy, and the fair; glittering with cloth of gold and silver, lace, embroidery, and precious stones. While these exulting sons and daughters of felicity tread this round of pleasure, or regale in different parties, and separate lodges, with fine imperial tea and other delicious refreshments, their ears are entertained with the most ravishing delights of music, both instrumental and vocal. There I heard the famous Tenducci,[3] a thing from Italy – It looks for all the world like a man, though they say it is not. The voice, to be sure, is neither man's nor woman's; but it is more melodious than either; and it warbled so divinely, that, while I listened, I really thought myself in paradise.

At nine o'clock, in a charming moonlight evening, we embarked at Ranelagh for Vauxhall, in a wherry so light and slender that we looked like so many fairies sailing in a nutshell. My uncle, being apprehensive of catching cold upon the water, went round in the coach, and my aunt would have accompanied him, but he would not suffer me to go by water if she went by land; and therefore she favoured us with her company, as she perceived I had a curiosity to make this agreeable voyage — After all, the vessel was sufficiently loaded; for, besides the waterman, there was my brother Jery, and a friend of his, one Mr Barton, a country gentleman, of a good fortune, who had dined at our house – The pleasure of this little excursion was, however, damped, by my being sadly frighted at our landing; where there was a terrible confusion of wherries, and a crowd of people bawling, and swearing, and quarrelling: nay, a parcel of ugly-looking fellows came running into the water, and laid hold of our boat with great violence, to pull it a-shore; nor would they quit their hold till my brother struck one of them over the head with his cane. But this flutter was fully recompensed by the pleasures of Vauxhall; which I no sooner entered, than I was dazzled and confounded with the variety of beauties that rushed all at once upon my eye. Image to yourself, my dear Letty, a spacious garden, part laid out in delightful walks, bounded with high hedges and trees, and paved with gravel; part exhibiting a wonderful assemblage of the most picturesque[4] and striking objects, pavilions, lodges, groves, grottoes, lawns, temples and cascades; porticoes, colonades, and rotundos; adorned with pillars, statues, and painting: the whole illuminated with an infinite number of lamps, disposed in different figures of suns, stars, and constellations; the place crowded with the gayest company, ranging through those blissful shades, or supping in different lodges on cold collations, enlivened with mirth, freedom, and good humour, and animated by an excellent band of music. Among the vocal performers I had the happiness to hear the celebrated Mrs —,[5] whose voice was loud and shrill, that it made my head ake through excess of pleasure.

In about half an hour after we arrived we were joined by my uncle, who did not seem to relish the place. People of experience and infirmity, my dear Letty, see with very different eyes from those that such as you and I make use of – Our evening's entertainment was interrupted by an unlucky accident. In one of the remotest walks we were surprised with a sudden shower, that set the whole company a-running, and drove us in heaps, one upon another, into the rotunda; where my uncle, finding himself wet, began to be very peevish and urgent to be gone. My brother went to look for the coach, and found it with much difficulty; but as it could not hold us all, Mr Barton stayed behind. It was some time before the carriage could be brought up to the gate, in the confusion, notwithstanding the utmost endeavours of our new footman, Humphry Clinker, who lost his scratch periwig,[6] and got a broken head[7] in the scuffle. The moment we were seated, my aunt pulled off my uncle's shoes, and carefully wrapped his poor feet in her capuchin;[8] then she gave him a mouth-ful of cordial, which she always keeps in her pocket, and his clothes were shifted as soon as we arrived at lodgings; so that, blessed be God, he escaped a severe cold, of which he was in great terror.

As for Mr Barton, I must tell you in confidence, he was a little particular; but, perhaps, I mistake his complaisance; and I wish I may, for his sake – You know the condition of my poor heart: which, in spite of hard usage – And yet I ought not to complain: nor will I, till farther information.

Besides Ranelagh and Vauxhall, I have been at Mrs Cornelys' assembly,[9] which, for the rooms, the company, the dresses, and decorations, surpasses all description; but as I have no great turn for card playing, I have not yet entered thoroughly into the spirit of the place: indeed I am still such a country hoyden,[10] that I could hardly find patience to be put in a condition to appear, yet, as I was not above six hours under the hands of the hair-dresser, who stuffed my head with as much black wool as would have made a quilted petticoat; and, after all, it was the smallest head in the assembly, except my aunt's – She, to be sure, was so particular with her rumpt gown[11] and petticoat, her scanty curls, her lappet-head,[12] deep triple ruffles, and high stays, that every body looked at her with surprise: some whispered, and some tittered; and lady Griskin, by whom we were introduced, flatly told her, she was twenty good years behind the fashion.

Lady Griskin is a person of fashion, to whom we have the

honour to be related. She keeps a small rout[13] at her own house, never exceeding ten or a dozen card-tables, but these are frequented by the best company in town – She has been so obliging as to introduce my aunt and me to some of her particular friends of quality, who treat us with the most familiar good-humour: we have once dined with her, and she takes the trouble to direct us in all our motions. I am so happy as to have gained her good-will to such a degree, that she sometimes adjusts my cap with her own hands; and she has given me a kind invitation to stay with her all the winter. This, however, has been cruelly declined by my uncle who seems to be (I know not how) prejudiced against the good lady; for, whenever my aunt happens to speak in her commendation, I observe that he makes wry faces, though he says nothing — Perhaps, indeed, these grimaces may be the effect of pain arising from the gout and rheumatism, with which he is sadly distressed — To me, however, he is always good-natured and generous, even beyond my wish. Since we came hither, he has made me a present of a suit of clothes, with trimmings and laces, which cost more money than I shall mention; and Jery, at his desire, has given me my mother's diamond crops, which are ordered to be set a-new; so that it won't be his fault if I do not glitter among the stars of the fourth or fifth magnitude. I wish my weak head may not grow giddy in the midst of all this gallantry and dissipation; though, as yet, I can safely declare, I could gladly give up all these tumultuous pleasures, for country solitude, and a happy retreat with those we love; among whom, my dear Willis will always possess the first place in the breast of her

Ever affectionate,

LONDON, May 31.   LYDIA MELFORD

To Sir WATKIN PHILLIPS, of Jesus college, Oxon.

DEAR PHILLIPS,

I send you this letter, franked by our old friend Barton; who is as much altered as it was possible for a man of his kidney to be – Instead of the careless, indolent sloven we knew at Oxford, I found him a busy talkative politician; a petit-maître in his dress, and a ceremonious courtier in his manners. He has not gall enough in his constitution to be enflamed with the rancour of party, so as to deal in scurrilous invectives; but, since he obtained a place, he is become a warm partizan of the ministry, and sees every thing through such an exaggerating medium, as to me, who am happily of no party, is altogether incomprehensible — Without all doubt, the fumes of faction not only disturb the faculty of reason, but also pervert the organs of sense; and I would lay a hundred guineas to ten, that if Barton on one side, and the most conscientious patriot in the opposition on the other, were to draw, upon honour, the picture of the k[ing] or m[inisters], you and I, who are still uninfected, and unbiased, would find both painters equally distant from the truth. One thing, however, must be allowed for the honour of Barton, he never breaks out into illiberal abuse, far less endeavours, by infamous calumnies, to blast the moral character of any individual on the other side.

Ever since we came hither, he has been remarkably assiduous in his attention to our family; an attention, which, in a man of his indolence and avocations, I should have thought altogether odd, and even unnatural, had not I perceived that my sister Liddy had made some impression upon his heart. I cannot say that I have any objection to his trying his fortune in this pursuit: if an opulent estate and a great flock of good-nature are sufficient qualifications in a husband, to render the marriage-state happy for life, she may be happy with Barton; but, I imagine, there is something else required to engage and secure the affection of a woman of sense and delicacy: something which nature has denied our friend – Liddy seems to be of the same opinion. When he addresses himself to her in discourse, she seems to listen with reluctance, and industriously avoids all particular communication; but in proportion to her coyness, our aunt is coming.[1] Mrs Tabitha goes more than half way to meet his advances; she mistakes, or affects to mistake, the meaning of his courtesy, which is rather formal and fulsome; she returns his compliments with hyperbolical interest, she persecutes him with her civilities at table, she appeals to him for ever in conversation, she sighs, and flirts, and ogles, and by her hideous affectation and impertinence, drives the poor courtier to the very extremity of his complaisance; in short, she seems to have undertaken the siege of Barton's heart, and carries on her approaches in such a desperate manner, that I don't know whether he will not be obliged to capitulate. In the mean time, his aversion to this inamorata struggling with his acquired affability, and his natural fear of giving offence, throws him into a kind of distress which is extremely ridiculous.

Two days ago, he persuaded my uncle and me to accompany him to St James's, where he undertook to make us acquainted with the persons of all the great men in the kingdom; and, indeed, there was a great assemblage of distinguished characters, for it was a high festival at court. Our conductor performed his promise with great punctuality. He pointed out almost every individual of both sexes, and generally introduced them to our notice, with a flourish of panegyrick[2] — Seeing the king approach, 'There comes (said he) the most amiable sovereign that ever swayed the sceptre of England: the *deliciæ humani generis*;[3] Augustus, in patronizing merit; Titus Vespasian in generosity; Trajan in beneficence; and Marcus Aurelius in philosophy.'[4] 'A very honest kind-hearted gentleman (added my uncle) he's too good for the times. A king of England should have a spice of the devil in his composition.' Barton, then turning to the duke of C[umberland],[5] proceeded, – 'You know the duke, that illustrious hero, who trode rebellion under his feet, and secured us in possession of every thing we ought to hold dear, as Englishmen and Christians. Mark what an eye, how penetrating, yet pacific! what dignity in his mien! what humanity in his aspect — Even malice must own, that he is one of the greatest officers in Christendom.' 'I think he is (said Mr Bramble) but who are these young gentlemen that stand beside him?' 'Those! (cried our friend) those are his royal nephews;[6] the princes of the blood. Sweet young princes! the sacred pledges of the Protestant line; so spirited, so sensible, so princely' — 'Yes; very sensible! very spirited! (said my uncle, interrupting him) but see the queen![7] ha, there's the queen! –

There's the queen! let me see — Let me see — Where are my glasses? ha! there's meaning in that eye — There's sentiment – There's expression – Well, Mr Barton, what figure do you call next?' The next person he pointed out, was the favourite *yearl*;[8] who stood solitary by one of the windows – 'Behold yon northern star (said he) *shorn of his beams*'[9] —— 'What! the Caledonian luminary, that lately blazed so bright in our hemisphere! methinks, at present, it glimmers through a fog; like Saturn without his ring, bleak, and dim, and distant – Ha, there's the other great phenomenon, the grand pensionary,[10] that weathercock of patriotism that veers about in every point of the political compass, and still feels the wind of popularity in his tail. He too, like a portentous comet, has risen again above the court-horizon; but how long he will continue to ascend, it is not easy to foretell, considering his great eccentricity – Who are those two satellites[11] that attend his motions?' When Barton told him their names, 'To their characters (said Mr Bramble) I am no stranger. One of them, without a drop of red blood in his veins, has a cold intoxicating vapour in his head; and rancour enough in his heart to inoculate and affect a whole nation. The other is (I hear) intended for a share in the ad[ministratio]n, and the pensionary vouches for his being duly qualified – The only instance I ever heard of his sagacity, was his deserting his former patron, when he found him declining in power, and in disgrace with the people. Without principle, talent, or intelligence, he is ungracious as a hog, greedy as a vulture, and thievish as a jackdaw; but, it must be owned, he is no hypocrite. He pretends to no virtue, and takes no pains to disguise his character – His ministry will be attended with one advantage, no man will be disappointed by his breach of promise, as no mortal ever trusted to his word. I wonder how lord — first discovered this happy genius, and for what purpose lord — has now adopted him: but one would think, that as amber has a power to attract dirt, and straws, and chaff, a minister is endued with the same kind of faculty, to *lick up every knave and blockhead in his way*'[12] — His eulogium was interrupted by the arrival of the old duke of N—;[13] who, squeezing into the circle with a busy face of importance, thrust his head into every countenance, as if he had been in search of somebody, to whom he wanted to impart something of great consequence – My uncle, who had been formerly known to him, bowed as he passed; and the duke seeing himself saluted so respectfully by a well-dressed person, was not slow in returning the courtesy — He even came up, and, taking him cordially by the hand, 'My dear friend, Mr A—[14] (said he) I am rejoiced to see you – How long have you been come from abroad? – How did you leave our good friends the Dutch? The king of Prussia[15] don't think of another war, ah? — He's a great king! a great conqueror! a very great conqueror! Your Alexanders and Hannibals were nothing at all to him, sir —— Corporals! drummers! dross! mere trash — Damned trash, heh?' — His grace being by this time out of breath, my uncle took the opportunity to tell him he had not been out of England, that his name was Bramble, and that he had the honour to sit in the last parliament but one of the late king, as representative for the borough of Dymkymraig.[16] 'Odso!'[17] (cried the duke) I remember you perfectly well, my dear Mr Bramble — You was always a good and loyal subject — a stanch friend to administration — I made your brother an Irish bishop' – 'Pardon me, my lord (said the squire) I once had a brother, but he was a captain in the army' — 'Ha! (said his grace) he was so – He was, indeed! But who was the Bishop then! Bishop Blackberry – Sure it was bishop Blackberry – Perhaps some relation of yours' —— 'Very likely, my lord (replied my uncle); the Blackberry is the fruit of the Bramble – But, I believe, the bishop is not a berry of our bush' – 'No more he is – No more he is, ha, ha, ha! (exclaimed the duke) there you gave me a scratch, good Mr Bramble, ha, ha, ha! – Well, I shall be glad to see you at Lincoln's-inn-fields – You know the way — Times are altered. Though I have lost the power, I retain the inclination – Your very humble servant, good Mr Blackberry' —— So saying, he shoved to another corner of the room. 'What a fine old gentleman! (cried Mr Barton) what spirits! what a memory! – He never forgets an old friend.' 'He does me too much honour (observed our squire) to rank me among the number – Whilst I sat in parliament, I never voted with the ministry but three times, when my conscience told me they were in the right: however, if he still keeps levee, I will carry my nephew thither, that he may see, and learn to avoid the scene; for, I think, an English gentleman never appears to such disadvantage, as at the levee of a minister – Of his grace I shall say nothing at present, but that for thirty years he was the constant and common butt of ridicule and execration. He was generally laughed at as an ape in politics, whose office and influence served only to render his folly the more notorious; and the opposition cursed him, as the indefatigable drudge of a first-mover,[18] who was justly stiled and stigmatized as the father of corruption: but this ridiculous ape, this venal drudge, no sooner lost the places he was so ill qualified to fill, and unfurled the banners of faction, than he was metamorphosed into a pattern of public virtue; the very people who reviled him before, now extolled him to the skies, as a wise, experienced statesman, chief pillar of the Protestant succession, and corner stone of English liberty. I should be glad to know how Mr Barton reconciles these contradictions, without obliging us to resign all title to the privilege of common sense.' 'My dear sir (answered Barton) I don't pretend to justify the extravagations of the multitude; who, I suppose, were as wild in their former censure, as in the present praise: but I shall be very glad to attend you on Thursday next to his grace's levee; where, I'm afraid, we shall not be crowded with company; for, you know, there's a wide difference between his present office of president of the council, and his former post of first lord commissioner of the treasury.'[19]

This communicative friend having announced all the remarkable characters of both sexes, that appeared at court, we resolved to adjourn, and retired. At the foot of the stair-case, there was a crowd of lacqueys and chairmen, and in the midst of them stood Humphry Clinker, exalted upon a stool, with his hat in one hand, and a paper in the other, in the act of holding forth to the people – Before we could inquire into the meaning of this exhibition, he perceived his master, thrust the paper into his pocket, descended from his elevation, bolted through the crowd, and brought up the carriage to the gate.

My uncle said nothing till we were seated, when, after having looked at me earnestly for some time, he burst out a-laughing, and asked if I knew upon what subject Clinker was holding forth to the mob — 'If (said he) the fellow is turned mounte-bank, I must turn him out of my service, otherwise he'll make Merry Andrews of us all' — I observed, that, in all probability, he had studied medicine under his master, who was a farrier.

At dinner, the squire asked him, if he had ever practised physic? 'Yes, and please your honour (said he) among brute beasts; but I never meddle with rational creatures.' 'I know not whether you rank in that class the audience you was haranguing in the court at St. James's, but I should be glad to know what kind of powders you was distributing; and whether you had a good sale' — 'Sale, sir! (cried Clinker) I hope I shall never be base enough to sell for gold and silver, what freely comes of God's grace. I distributed nothing, an like your honour, but a word of advice to my fellows in servitude and sin.' 'Advice! concerning what?' 'Concerning profane swearing, an please your honour; so horrid and shocking, that it made my hair stand on end.' 'Nay, if thou can'st cure them of that disease, I shall think thee a wonderful doctor indeed' — 'Why not cure them, my good master? the hearts of those poor people are not so stubborn as your honour seems to think — Make them first sensible that you have nothing in view but their good, then they will listen with patience, and easily be convinced of the sin and folly of a practice that affords neither profit nor pleasure'[20] – At this remark, our uncle changed colour, and looked round the company, conscious that his *own withers were not altogether unwrung*.[21] 'But, Clinker (said he) if you should have eloquence enough to persuade the vulgar to resign those tropes and figures of rhetoric, there will be little or nothing left to distinguish their conversation from that of their betters.' 'But then your honour knows, their conversation will be void of offence; and, at the day of judgment, there will be no distinction of persons.'[22]

Humphry going down stairs to fetch up a bottle of wine, my uncle congratulated his sister upon having such a reformer in the family; when Mrs Tabitha declared, he was a sober civilized fellow; very respectful, and very industrious; and, she believed, a good Christian into the bargain. One would think, Clinker must really have some very extraordinary talent, to ingratiate himself in this manner with a virago of her character, so fortified against him with prejudice and resentment; but the truth is, since the adventure of Salt-hill, Mrs Tabby seems to be entirely changed. She has left off scolding the servants, an exercise which was grown habitual, and even seemed necessary to her constitution; and is become so indifferent to Chowder, as to part with him in a present to lady Griskin, who proposes to bring the breed of him into fashion. Her ladyship is the widow of Sir Timothy Griskin, a distant relation of our family. She enjoys a jointure of five hundred pounds a-year, and makes shift to spend three times that sum. Her character before marriage was a little equivocal; but at present she lives in the *bon ton*,[23] keeps card-tables, gives private suppers to select friends, and is visited by persons of the first fashion – She has been remarkably civil to us all, and cultivates my uncle with the most particular regard; but the more she strokes him, the more his bristles seem to rise – To her compliments he makes very laconic and dry returns – T'other day she sent us a pottle of fine strawberries, which he did not receive without signs of disgust, muttering from the Æneid, *timeo Danaos et Dona ferentes*.[24] She has twice called for Liddy, of a forenoon, to take an aïrïng in the coach; but Mrs Tabby was always so alert (I suppose by his direction) that she never could have the niece without her aunt's company – I have endeavoured to sound Square-toes on this subject; but he carefully avoids all explanation.

I have now, dear Phillips, filled a whole sheet, and if you have read it to an end, I dare say, you are as tired as

Your humble servant,

LONDON, June 2.   J. MELFORD

To Dr LEWIS.

Yes, Doctor, I have seen the British Museum;[1] which is a noble collection, and even stupendous, if we consider it was made by a private man, a physician, who was obliged to make his own fortune at the same time: but great as the collection is, it would appear more striking if it was arranged in one spacious saloon, instead of being divided into different apartments, which it does not entirely fill – I could wish the series of medals was connected, and the whole of the animal, vegetable, and mineral kingdoms completed, by adding to each, at the public expence, those articles that are wanting. It would likewise be a great improvement, with respect to the library, if the deficiencies were made up, by purchasing all the books of character that are not to be found already in the collection – They might be classed in centuries, according to the dates of their publication, and catalogues printed of them and the manuscripts, for the information of those that want to consult, or compile from such authorities. I could also wish, for the honour of the nation, that there was a complete apparatus for a course of mathematics, mechanics, and experimental philosophy; and a good salary settled upon an able professor, who should give regular lectures on these subjects.

But this is all idle speculation, which will never be reduced to practice – Considering the temper of the times, it is a wonder to see any institution whatsoever established for the benefit of the public. The spirit of party is risen to a kind of phrenzy, unknown to former ages, or rather degenerated to a total extinction of honesty and candour – You know I have observed, for some time, that the public papers are become the infamous vehicles of the most cruel and perfidious defamation: every rancorous knave — every desperate incendiary, that can afford to spend half a crown or three shillings, may skulk behind the press of a newsmonger, and have a stab at the first character in the kingdom, without running the least hazard of detection or punishment.

I have made acquaintance with a Mr Barton, whom Jery knew at Oxford; a good sort of a man, though most ridiculously warped in his political principles; but his partiality is the less offensive, as it never appears in the stile of scurrility and abuse. He is a member of parliament, and a retainer to the court; and his whole conversation turns upon the virtues and perfections of the ministers, who are his patrons. T'other day, when he was

bedaubing one of those worthies, with the most fulsome praise,
I told him I had seen the same nobleman characterised very
differently, in one of the daily-papers; indeed, so stigmatized,
that if one half of what was said of him was true, he must
be not only unfit to rule, but even unfit to live: that those
impeachments had been repeated again and again, with the
addition of fresh matter; and that as he had taken no steps
towards his own vindication, I began to think there was some
foundation for the charge. 'And pray, Sir (said Mr Barton),
what steps would you have him take? – Suppose he should
prosecute the publisher, who screens the anonymous accuser,
and bring him to the pillory for a libel; this is so far from being
counted a punishment, *in terrorem*,[2] that it will probably make
his fortune. The multitude immediately take him into their
protection, as a martyr to the cause of defamation, which they
have always espoused — They pay his fine, they contribute to
the increase of his stock, his shop is crowded with customers,
and the sale of his paper rises in proportion to the scandal it
contains. All this time the prosecutor is inveighed against as a
tyrant and oppressor, for having chosen to proceed by the way
of information, which is deemed a grievance; but if he lays an
action for damages, he must prove the damage, and I leave you
to judge, whether a gentleman's character may not be brought
into contempt, and all his views in life blasted by calumny,
without his being able to specify the particulars of the damage
he has sustained.

'This spirit of defamation is a kind of heresy, that thrives
under persecution. *The liberty of the press* is a term of great
efficacy; and like that of the *Protestant religion*, has often served
the purposes of sedition – A minister, therefore, must arm
himself with patience, and bear those attacks without repining –
Whatever mischief they may do in other respects, they certainly
contribute, in one particular, to the advantages of government;
for those defamatory articles have multiplied papers in such a
manner, and augmented their sale to such a degree, that the duty
upon stamps and advertisements[3] has made a very considerable
addition to the revenue.' Certain it is, a gentleman's honour is
a very delicate subject to be handled by a jury, composed of

men, who cannot be supposed remarkable either for sentiment or impartiality – In such a case, indeed, the defendant is tried, not only by his peers, but also by his party; and I really think, that of all patriots, he is the most resolute who exposes himself to such detraction, for the sake of his country – If, from the ignorance or partiality of juries, a gentleman can have no redress from law, for being defamed in a pamphlet or news-paper, I know but one other method of proceeding against the publisher, which is attended with some risque, but has been practised successfully, more than once, in my remembrance – A regiment of horse was represented, in one of the newspapers, as having misbehaved at Dettingen;[4] a captain of that regiment broke the publisher's bones, telling him, at the same time, if he went to law, he should certainly have the like salutation from every officer of the corps. Governor — took the same satisfac-tion on the ribs of an author, who traduced him by name in a periodical paper – I know a low fellow of the same class, who, being turned out of Venice for his impudence and scurrility, retired to Lugano, a town of the Grisons[5] (a free people, God wot)[6] where he found a printing press, from whence he squirted his filth at some respectable characters in the republic, which he had been obliged to abandon. Some of these, finding him out of the reach of legal chastisement, employed certain useful instruments, such as may be found in all countries, to give him the bastinado;[7] which, being repeated more than once, effectually stopt the current of his abuse.

As for the liberty of the press, like every other privilege, it must be restrained within certain bounds; for if it is carried to a branch of law, religion, and charity, it becomes one of the greatest evils that ever annoyed the community. If the lowest ruffian may stab your good name with impunity in England, will you be so uncandid as to exclaim against Italy for the practice of common assassination? To what purpose is our property secured, if our moral character is left defenceless? People thus baited, grow desperate; and the despair of being able to preserve one's character, untainted by such vermin, produces a total neglect of fame; so that one of the chief incite-ments to the practice of virtue is effectually destroyed.

Mr Barton's last consideration, respecting the stamp-duty, is equally wise and laudable with another maxim which has been long adopted by our financiers, namely, to connive at drunkenness, riot, and dissipation, because they inhance the receipt of the excise;[8] not reflecting, that in providing this temporary convenience, they are destroying the morals, health, and industry of the people — Notwithstanding my contempt for those who flatter a minister,.I think there is something still more despicable in flattering a mob. When I see a man of birth, education, and fortune, put himself on a level with the dregs of the people, mingle with low mechanics, feed with them at the same board, and drink with them in the same cup, flatter their prejudices, harangue in praise of their virtues, expose themselves to the belchings of their beer, the fumes of their tobacco, the grossness of their familiarity, and the impertinence of their conversation, I cannot help despising him, as a man guilty of the vilest prostitution, in order to effect a purpose equally selfish and illiberal.

I should renounce politics the more willingly, if I could find other topics of conversation discussed with more modesty and candour; but the dæmon of party seems to have usurped every department of life. Even the world of literature and taste is divided into the most virulent factions, which revile, decry, and traduce the works of one another. Yesterday, I went to return an afternoon's visit to a gentleman of my acquaintance, at whose house I found one of the authors of the present age, who has written with some success – As I had read one or two of his performances, which gave me pleasure, I was glad of this opportunity to know his person; but his discourse and deportment destroyed all the impressions which his writings had made in his favour. He took upon him to decide dogmatically upon every subject, without deigning to shew the least cause for his differing from the general opinions of mankind, as if it had been our duty to acquiesce in the *ipse dixit*[9] of this new Pythagoras. He rejudged the characters of all the principal authors, who had died within a century of the present time; and, in this revision, paid no sort of regard to the reputation they had acquired — Milton was harsh and prosaic; Dryden, languid and verbose; Butler and Swift without humour; Congreve, without wit; and Pope destitute of any sort of poetical merit[10] – As for his contemporaries, he could not bear to hear one of them mentioned with any degree of applause – They were all dunces, pedants, plagiaries, quacks, and impostors; and you could not name a single performance, but what was tame, stupid, and insipid. It must be owned, that this writer had nothing to charge his conscience with, on the side of flattery; for I understand, he was never known to praise one line that was written, even by those with whom he lived on terms of good fellowship. This arrogance and presumption, in depreciating authors, for whose reputation the company may be interested, is such an insult upon the understanding, as I could not bear without wincing.

I desired to know his reasons for decrying some works, which had afforded me uncommon pleasure; and, as demonstration did not seem to be his talent, I dissented from his opinion with great freedom. Having been spoiled by the deference and humility of his hearers, he did not bear contradiction with much temper; and the dispute might have grown warm, had it not been interrupted by the entrance of a rival bard,[11] at whose appearance he always quits the place — They are of different cabals, and have been at open war these twenty years — If the other was dogmatical, this genius was declamatory: he did not discourse, but harangue; and his orations were equally tedious and turgid. He too pronounces *ex cathedra*[12] upon the characters of his contemporaries; and though he scruples not to deal out praise, even lavishly, to the lowest reptile in Grub-street[13] who will either flatter him in private, or mount the public rostrum as his panegyrist, he damns all the other writers of the age, with the utmost insolence and rancour – One is a blunderbuss, as being a native of Ireland; another, a half-starved louse of literature, from the banks of the Tweed; a third, an ass, because he enjoys a pension from the government; a fourth, the very angel of dulness, because he succeeded in a species of writing in which this Aristarchus[14] had failed; a fifth, who presumed to make strictures upon one of his performances, he holds as a bug in criticism, whose stench is more offensive than his sting – In short, except himself and his myrmidons,[15] there is not a man of genius or learning in the three kingdoms. As for the success of those, who have written without the pale of this confederacy, he imputes it entirely to want of taste in the public; not considering, that to the approbation of that very tasteless public, he himself owes all the consequence he has in life.

Those originals are not fit for conversation. If they would maintain the advantage they have gained by their writing, they should never appear but upon paper – For my part, I am shocked to find a man have sublime ideas in his head, and nothing but illiberal sentiments in his heart – The human soul will be generally found most defective in the article of candour – I am inclined to think, no mind was ever wholly exempt from envy; which, perhaps, may have been implanted, as an instinct essential to our nature. I am afraid we sometimes palliate this vice, under the spacious name of emulation. I have known a person remarkably generous, humane, moderate, and apparently self-denying, who could not hear even a friend commended, without betraying marks of uneasiness; as if that commendation had implied an odious comparison to his prejudice, and every wreath of praise added to the other's character, was a garland plucked from his own temples. This is a malignant species of jealousy, of which I stand acquitted in my own conscience — Whether it is a vice, or an infirmity, I leave you to inquire.

There is another point, which I would much rather see determined; whether the world was always as contemptible, as it appears to me at present? — If the morals of mankind have not contracted an extraordinary degree of depravity, within these thirty years, then must I be infected with the common vice of old men, *difficilis, querulus, laudator temporis acti*;[16] or, which is more probable, the impetuous pursuits and avocations of youth have formerly hindered me from observing those rotten parts of human nature, which now appear so offensively to my observation.

We have been at court, and 'change,[17] and every where; and every where we find food for spleen, and subject for ridicule – My new servant, Humphry Clinker, turns out a great original: and Tabby is a changed creature — She has parted with Chowder;

and does nothing but smile, like Malvolio in the play[18] — I'll be hanged if she is not acting a part which is not natural to her disposition, for some purpose which I have not yet discovered.

With respect to the characters of mankind, my curiosity is quite satisfied: I have done with the science of men, and must now endeavour to amuse myself with the novelty of things. I am, at present, by a violent effort of the mind, forced from my natural bias; but this power ceasing to act, I shall return to my solitude with redoubled velocity. Every thing I see, and hear, and feel, in this great reservoir of folly, knavery, and sophistication, contributes to inhance the value of a country life, in the sentiments of

Yours always,
LONDON, June 2.   MATT. BRAMBLE

To Mrs MARY JONES, at Brambleton-hall.

DEAR MARY JONES,
    Lady Griskin's botler, Mr Crumb, having got 'squire Barton to frank me a kiver, I would not neglect to let you know how it is with me, and the rest of the family.

I could not rite by John Thomas, for because he went away in a huff, at a minutes' warning. He and Chowder could not agree, and so they fitt upon the road, and Chowder bitt his thumb, and he swore he would do him a mischief, and he spoke saucy to mistress, whereby the squire turned him off in gudgeon; and by God's providence we picked up another footman, called Umphry Klinker; a good sole as ever broke bread; which shews that a scalded cat may prove a good mouser, and a hound be staunch, thof he has got narro hare on his buttocks; but the proudest nose may be bro't to the grinestone, by sickness and misfortunes.

O Molly! what shall I say of London? All the towns that ever I beheld in my born-days, are no more than Welsh barrows and crumlecks[1] to this wonderful sitty! Even Bath itself is but a fillitch,[2] in the naam of God — One would think there's no end of the streets, but the land's end. Then there's such a power of people, going hurry skurry! Such a racket of coxes! Such a noise, and haliballoo! So many strange sites to be seen! O gracious! my poor Welsh brain has been spinning like a top ever since I came hither! And I have seen the Park, and the paleass of Saint Gimses,[3] and the king's and the queen's magisterial pursing, and the sweet young princes, and the hillyfents, and pye bald ass,[4] and all the rest of the royal family.

Last week I went with mistress to the Tower, to see the crowns and wild beastis;[5] and there was a monstracious lion, with teeth half a quarter long; and a gentleman bid me not go near him, if I wasn't a maid; being as how he would roar, and tear, and play the dickens[6] – Now I had no mind to go near him; for I cannot abide such dangerous honeymils,[7] not I — but, mistress would go; and the beast kept such a roaring and bouncing, that I tho't he would have broke his cage and devoured us all; and the gentleman tittered forsooth; but I'll go to death upon it, I will, that my lady is as good a firchin,[8] as the child unborn; and, therefore, either the gentleman told a fib, or the lion oft to be set in the stocks for bearing false witness agin his neighbour; for the commandment sayeth, *Thou shalt not bear false witness against thy neighbour.*[9]

I was afterwards of a party at Sadler's-wells,[10] where I saw such tumbling and dancing upon ropes and wires, that I was frightened and ready to go into a fit – I tho't it was all inchantment; and, believing myself bewitched, began for to cry — You knows as how the witches in Wales fly upon broom-sticks: but here was flying without any broom-stick, or thing in the varsal world, and firing of pistols in the air, and blowing of trumpets, and swinging, and rolling of wheel-barrows upon a wire (God bless us!) no thicker than a sewing-thread; that, to be sure, they must deal with the devil! — A fine gentleman, with a pig's-tail, and a golden sord by his side, come to comfit me, and offered for to treat me with a pint of wind; but I would not stay; and so, in going through the dark passage, he began to shew his cloven futt, and went for to be rude: my fellow-sarvant, Umphry Klinker, bid him be sivil, and he gave the young man a dowse in the chops; but, I fackins, Mr Klinker wa'n't long in his debt

— with a good oaken sapling he dusted his doublet, for all his golden cheese toaster; and, fipping me under his arm, carried me huom, I nose not how, being I was in such a flustration – But, thank God! I'm now vaned from all such vanities; for what are all those rarities and vagaries to the glory that shall be revealed hereafter?[11] O Molly! let not your poor heart be puffed up with vanity.[12]

I had almost forgot to tell you, that I have had my hair cut and pippered, and singed, and bolstered, and buckled, in the newest fashion, by a French freezer[13] – *Parley vow Francey – Vee madmansell* – I now carries my head higher than arrow private gentlewoman of Vales. Last night, coming huom from the meeting, I was taken by lamp-light for an iminent poulterer's daughter, a great beauty – But as I was saying, this is all vanity and vexation of spirit[14] – The pleasures of London are no better than sower whey and stale cyder, when compared to the joys of the new Gerusalem.

Dear Mary Jones! An please God when I return, I'll bring you a new cap, with a turkey-shell coom, and a pyehouse sermon, that was preached in the Tabernacle;[15] and I pray of all love, you will mind your vriting and your spilling; for, craving your pardon, Molly, it made me suet to disseyffer your last scrabble, which was delivered by the hind at Bath – O, voman! voman! if thou had'st but the least consumption of what pleasure we scullers have, when we can cunster the crabbidst buck off hand, and spell the ethnitch vords without lucking at the primmer. As for Mr Klinker, he is qualified to be a clerk to a parish – But I'll say no more – Remember me to Saul – poor sole! it goes to my hart to think she don't yet know her letters – But all in God's good time – It shall go hard, but I will bring her the A B C in gingerbread; and that, you nose, will be learning to her taste.

Mistress says, we are going a long gurney to the North; but go where we will, I shall ever be,

Dear Mary Jones,

Yours with true infection

LONDON, June 3.   WIN. JENKINS

To Sir WATKIN PHILLIPS, of Jesus college, Oxon.

DEAR WAT,

I mentioned in my last, my uncle's design of going to the duke of N—'s levee; which design has been executed accordingly. His grace has been so long accustomed to this kind of homage, that though the place he now fills does not imply the tenth part of the influence, which he exerted in his former office, he has given his friends to understand, that they cannot oblige him in any thing more, than in contributing to support the shadow of that power, which he no longer retains in substance; and therefore he has still public days, on which they appear at his levee.

My uncle and I went thither with Mr Barton, who, being one of the duke's adherents, undertook to be our introducer – The room was pretty well filled with people, in a great variety of dress; but there was no more than one gown and cassock,[1] though I was told his grace had, while he was minister, preferred almost every individual that now filled the bench of bishops in the house of lords; but in all probability, the gratitude of the clergy is like their charity, which shuns the light – Mr Barton was immediately accosted by a person well stricken in years, tall, and raw-boned, with a hook-nose, and an arch leer, that indicated, at least, as much cunning as sagacity. Our conductor saluted him, by the name of captain C—, and afterwards informed us he was a man of shrewd parts, whom the government occasionally employed in secret services – But I have had the history of him more at large, from another quarter — He had been, many years ago, concerned in fraudulent practices, as a merchant, in France; and being convicted of some of them, was sent to the gallies, from whence he was delivered by the interest of the late duke of Ormond,[2] to whom he had recommended himself in letter, as his name-sake and relation – He was in the sequel, employed by our ministry as a spy; and in the war of 1740, traversed all Spain, as well as France, in the disguise of a capuchin, at the extreme hazard of his life, in as much as the court of Madrid had actually got scent of him, and given orders to apprehend him at St Sebastian's, from whence he had fortunately retired but a few hours before the order arrived. This and other hair-breadth 'scapes he pleaded so effectually as a merit with the English ministry, that they allowed him a comfortable pension, which he now enjoys in his old age – He has still access to all the ministers, and is said to be consulted by them on many subjects, as a man of uncommon understanding and great experience – He is, in fact, a fellow of some parts, and invincible assurance; and, in his discourse, he assumes such an air of self-sufficiency, as may very well impose upon some of the shallow politicians, who now labour at the helm of administration. But, if he is not belied, this is not the only imposture of which he is guilty — They say, he is at bottom not only a Roman-catholic, but really a priest; and while he pretends to disclose to our state-pilots all the springs that move the cabinet of Versailles, he is actually picking up intelligence for the service of the French minister — Be that as it may, captain C— entered into conversation with us in the most familiar manner, and treated the duke's character without any ceremony – 'This wise-acre³ (said he) is still a-bed; and, I think, the best thing he can do, is to sleep on till Christmas; for, when he gets up, he does nothing but expose his own folly. – Since Grenville was turned out,⁴ there has been no minister in this nation worth the meal that whitened his peri-wig – They are so ignorant, they scarce know a crab from a cauliflower; and then they are such dunces, that there's no making them comprehend the plainest proposition — In the beginning of the war, this poor half-witted creature told me, in a great fright, that thirty thousand French had marched from Acadie to Cape Breton — "Where did they find transports? (said I)" "Transports! (cried he) I tell you they marched by land" — "By land to the island of Cape Breton?" "What! is Cape Breton an island?" "Certainly." "Ha! are you sure of that?" When I pointed it out in the map, he examined it earnestly with his spectacles; then, taking me in his arms, "My dear C—! (cried he) you always bring us good news – Egad! I'll go directly, and tell the king that Cape Breton is an island."'

He seemed disposed to entertain us with more anecdotes of this nature, at the expense of his grace, when he was interrupted by the arrival of the Algerine ambassador; a venerable Turk, with a long white beard, attended by his dragoman, or interpreter, and another officer of his household, who had got no stockings to his legs — Captain C— immediately spoke with an air of authority to a servant in waiting, bidding him go and tell the duke to rise, as there was a great deal of company come, and, among others, the ambassador from Algiers — Then, turning to us, 'This poor Turk (said he) notwithstanding his grey beard, is a green-horn[5] — He has been several years resident in London, and still is ignorant of our political revolutions. This visit is intended for the prime minister of England; but you'll see how this wise duke will receive it as a mark of attachment to his own person' — Certain it is, the duke seemed eager to acknowledge the compliment — A door opened, he suddenly bolted out; with a shaving-cloth under his chin, his face frothed up to the eyes with soap lather; and running up to the ambassador, grinned hideous in his face – 'My dear Mahomet! (said he) God love your long beard, I hope the dey will make you a horsetail[6] at the next promotion, ha, ha, ha! — Have but a moment's patience, and I'll send to you in a twinkling,' — So saying, he retired into his den, leaving the Turk in some confusion. After a short pause, however, he said something to his interpreter, the meaning of which I had great curiosity to know, as he turned up his eyes while he spoke, expressing astonishment, mixed with devotion — We were gratified by means of the communicative captain C—, who conversed with the dragoman, as an old acquaintance. Ibrahim, the ambassador, who had mistaken his grace for the minister's fool, was no sooner undeceived by the interpreter, than he exclaimed to this effect — 'Holy prophet! I don't wonder that this nation prospers, seeing it is governed by the counsel of ideots; a series of men, whom all good mussulmen revere as the organs of immediate inspiration!' Ibrahim was favoured with a particular audience of short duration; after which the duke conducted him to the door, and then returned to diffuse his gracious looks among the crowd of his worshippers.

As Mr Barton advanced to present me to his grace, it was my fortune to attract his notice, before I was announced – He forth-with met me more than half way, and, seizing me by the hand, 'My dear Sir Francis! (cried he) this is so kind – I vow to Gad! I am so obliged – Such attention to a poor broken minister – Well – Pray when does your excellency set sail? – For God's sake have a care of your health, and eat stewed prunes[7] in the passage – Next to your own precious health, pray, my dear excellency, take care of the Five Nations – Our good friends the Five Nations – The Toryrories, the Maccolmacks, the Out-o'the-ways, the Crickets, and the Kickshaws[8] – Let 'em have plenty of blankets, and stinkubus, and wampum;[9] and your excellency won't fail to scour the kettle, and boil the chain, and bury the tree, and plant the hatchet – Ha, ha, ha!' When he had uttered this rhapsody, with his usual precipitation, Mr Barton gave him to understand, that I was neither Sir Francis, nor St Francis, but simply Mr Melford, nephew to Mr Bramble; who, stepping forward, made his bow at the same time. 'Odso! no more it is Sir Francis – (said this wise statesman) Mr Melford, I'm glad to see you – I sent you an engineer to fortify your dock – Mr Bramble – your servant, Mr Bramble – How d'ye, good Mr Bramble? Your nephew is a pretty young fellow – Faith and troth, a very pretty fellow! – His father is my old friend – How does he hold it? Still troubled with that damned disorder, ha?' 'No, my lord (replied my uncle), all his troubles are over – He has been dead these fifteen years.' 'Dead! how – Yes faith! now I remember: he is dead sure enough – Well, and how – does the young gentleman stand for Haverford West? or – a – what d'ye – My dear Mr Milfordhaven,[10] I'll do you all the service in my power – I hope I have some credit left' — My uncle then gave him to understand, that I was still a minor; and that we had no intention to trouble him at present, for any favour whatsoever – 'I came hither with my nephew (added he) to pay our respects to your grace; and I may venture to say, that his views and mine are at least as disinterested as those of any individual in this assembly.' 'My dear Mr Brambleberry! you do me infinite honour – I shall always rejoice to see you and your hopeful nephew, Mr Milfordhaven – My credit, such as it is, you may command – I wish we had more friends of your kidney.'

Then, turning to captain C—, 'Ha, C—! (said he) what news,

C—? How does the world wag? ha!' 'The world wags much after the old fashion, my lord (answered the captain): the politicians of London and Westminster have begun again to wag their tongues against your grace; and your short-lived popularity wags like a feather, which the next puff of antiministerial calumny will blow away' – 'A pack of rascals (cried the duke) – Tories, Jacobites, rebels; one half of them would wag their heels at Tyburn,[11] if they had their deserts' – So saying, he wheeled about; and going round the levee, spoke to every individual, with the most courteous familiarity; but he scarce ever opened his mouth without making some blunder, in relation to the person or business of the party with whom he conversed; so that he really looked like a comedian, hired to burlesque the character of a minister – At length, a person of a very prepossessing appearance coming in, his grace ran up, and, hugging him in his arms, with the appellation of 'My dear Ch—s!' led him forthwith into the inner apartment, or *Sanctum Sanctorum* of this political temple. 'That (said captain C—) is my friend C— T—,[12] almost the only man of parts who has any concern in the present administration – Indeed, he would have no concern at all in the matter, if the ministry did not find it absolutely necessary to make use of his talents upon some particular occasions – As for the common business of the nation, it is carried on in a constant routine by the clerks of the different offices, otherwise the wheels of government would be wholly stopt amidst the abrupt succession of ministers, every one more ignorant than his predecessor — I am thinking what a fine hovel we should be in, if all the clerks of the treasury, the secretaries, of the war-office, and the admiralty, should take it in their heads to throw up their places in imitation of the great pensioner – But, to return to C— T—; he certainly knows more than all the ministry and all the opposition, if their heads were laid together, and talks like an angel on a vast variety of subjects – He would really be a great man, if he had any consistency or stability of character – Then, it must be owned, he wants courage, otherwise he would never allow himself to be cowed by the great political bully,[13] for whose understanding he has justly a very great contempt. I have seen him as much afraid of that overbearing Hector,[14] as ever schoolboy was of his pedagogue; and yet this Hector, I shrewdly suspect, is no more than a craven at bottom – Besides this defect, C— has another, which he is at too little pains to hide – There's no faith to be given to his assertions, and no trust to be put in his promises – However, to give the devil his due, he's very good-natured; and even friendly, when close urged in the way of solicitation – As for principle, that's out of the question – In a word, he is a wit and an orator, extremely entertaining, and he shines very often at the expence even of those ministers to whom he is a retainer – This is a mark of great imprudence, by which he has made them all his enemies, whatever face they may put upon the matter; and sooner or later he'll have cause to wish he had been able to keep his own counsel – I have several times cautioned him on this subject; but 'tis all preaching to the desert[15] – His vanity runs away with his discretion' —— I could not help thinking the captain himself might have been the better for some hints of the same nature – His panegyric, excluding principle and veracity, puts me in mind of a contest I once overheard, in the way of altercation, betwixt two apple-women in Spring-garden[16] — One of those viragos having hinted something to the prejudice of the other's moral character, her antagonist, setting her hands in her sides, replied – 'Speak out, hussy – I scorn your malice – I own I'm both a whore and a thief; and what more have you to say? – Damn you, what more have you to say? baiting that, which all the world knows, I challenge you to say black is the white of my eye' – We did not wait for Mr T—'s coming forth; but after captain C— had characterised all the originals in waiting, we adjourned to a coffeehouse, where we had buttered muffins and tea to breakfast, the said captain still favouring us with his company — Nay, my uncle was so diverted with his anecdotes, that he asked him to dinner, and treated him with a fine turbot, to which he did ample justice — That same evening I spent at the tavern with some friends, one of whom let me into C—'s character, which Mr Bramble no sooner understood, than he expressed some concern for the connexion he had made, and resolved to disengage himself from it without ceremony.

We are become members of the Society for the Encouragement of the Arts,[17] and have assisted at some of their deliberations, which were conducted with equal spirit and sagacity –
My uncle is extremely fond of the institution, which will certainly be productive of great advantages to the public, if, from
its democratical form, it does not degenerate into cabal and
corruption – You are already acquainted with his aversion to
the influence of the multitude, which, he affirms, is incompatible
with excellence, and subversive of order – Indeed his detestation
of the mob has been heightened by fear, ever since he fainted
in the room at Bath; and this apprehension has prevented him
from going to the Little Theatre in the Hay-market,[18] and other
places of entertainment, to which, however, I have had the
honour to attend the ladies.

It grates old Square-toes to reflect, that it is not in his power
to enjoy even the most elegant diversions of the capital, without
the participation of the vulgar; for they now thrust themselves
into all assemblies, from a ridotto[19] at St James's, to a hop[20] at
Rotherhithe.[21]

I have lately seen our old acquaintance Dick Ivy, who we
imagined had died of dram-drinking; but he is lately emerged
from the Fleet, by means of a pamphlet which he wrote and
published against the government with some success. The sale
of this performance enabled him to appear in clean linen, and
he is now going about soliciting subscriptions for his Poems;
but his breeches are not yet in the most decent order.

Dick certainly deserves some countenance for his intrepidity
and perseverance – It is not in the power of disappointment,
nor even of damnation, to drive him to despair – After some
unsuccessful essays in the way of poetry, he commenced brandy-
merchant, and I believe his whole stock ran out through his
own bowels; then he consorted with a milk-woman, who kept
a cellar in Petty France:[22] but he could not make his quarters
good; he was dislodged and driven up stairs into the kennel by
a corporal in the second regiment of foot-guards – He was
afterwards the laureat of Blackfriars, from whence there was a
natural transition to the Fleet.[23] – As he had formerly miscarried
in panegyric, he now turned his thoughts to satire, and really

seems to have some talent for abuse. If he can hold out till the meeting of the parliament, and be prepared for another charge, in all probability Dick will mount the pillory, or obtain a pension, in either of which events his fortune will be made — Mean while he has acquired some degree of consideration with the respectable writers of the age; and as I have subscribed for his works, he did me the favour t'other night to introduce me to a society of those geniuses; but I found them exceedingly formal and reserved – They seemed afraid and jealous of one another, and sat in a state of mutual repulsion, like so many particles of vapour, each surrounded by its own electrified atmosphere. Dick, who has more vivacity than judgment, tried more than once to enliven the conversation; sometimes making an effort at wit, sometimes letting off a pun, and sometimes discharging a conundrum; nay, at length he started a dispute upon the hackneyed comparison betwixt blank verse and rhyme, and the professors opened with great clamour; but, instead of keeping to the subject, they launched out into tedious dissertations on the poetry of the ancients; and one of them, who had been a school-master, displayed his whole knowledge of prosody, gleaned from Disputer and Ruddiman.[24] At last, I ventured to say, I did not see how the subject in question could be at all elucidated by the practice of the ancients, who certainly had neither blank verse nor rhyme in their poems, which were measured by feet, whereas ours are reckoned by the number of syllables – This remark seemed to give umbrage to the pedant, who forthwith involved himself in a cloud of Greek and Latin quotations, which nobody attempted to dispel – A confused hum of insipid observations and comments ensued; and, upon the whole, I never passed a duller evening in my life – Yet, without all doubt, some of them were men of learning, wit, and ingenuity. As they are afraid of making free with one another, they should bring each his butt, or whet-stone, along with him, for the entertainment of the company – My uncle says, he never desires to meet with more than one wit at a time — One wit, like a knuckle of ham in soup, gives a zest and flavour to the dish; but more than one serves only to spoil the pottage – And now I'm afraid I have given you an unconscionable mess,

without any flavour at all; for which, I suppose, you will bestow
your benedictions upon

Your friend,
and servant

LONDON, June 5.   J. MELFORD

*

To Dr LEWIS.

DEAR LEWIS,

Your fable of the monkey and the pig,[1] is what the Italians
call *ben trovata*:[2] but I shall not repeat it to my apothecary,
who is a proud Scotchman, very thin skinned, and, for aught I
know, may have his degree in his pocket[3] – A right Scotchman
has always two strings to his bow, and is *in utrumque paratus*[4] –
Certain it is, I have not 'scaped a scouring; but, I believe, by means
of that scouring, I have 'scaped something worse, perhaps a tedious fit of the gout or rheumatism; for my appetite began to flag,
and I had certain croakings in the bowels, which boded me no
good — Nay, I am not yet quite free of these remembrances,
which warn me to be gone from this centre of infection —

What temptation can a man of my turn and temperament
have, to live in a place where every corner teems with fresh
objects of detestation and disgust? What kind of taste and
organs must those people have, who really prefer the adulterate
enjoyments of the town to the genuine pleasures of a country
retreat? Most people, I know, are originally seduced by vanity,
ambition, and childish curiosity; which cannot be gratified, but
in the *busy haunts of men*:[5] but, in the course of this gratification, their very organs of sense are perverted, and they become
habitually lost to every relish of what is genuine and excellent
in its own nature.

Shall I state the difference between my town grievances, and
my country comforts? At Brambleton-hall, I have elbow-room
within doors, and breathe a clear, elastic, salutary air — I enjoy
refreshing sleep, which is never disturbed by horrid noise, nor

interrupted, but in a-morning, by the sweet twitter of the mart-
let at my window – I drink the virgin lymph, pure and chrystal-
line as it gushes from the rock, or the sparkling beveridge,
home-brewed from malt of my own making; or I indulge with
cyder, which my own orchard affords; or with claret of the best
growth, imported for my own use, by a correspondent on whose
integrity I can depend; my bread is sweet and nourishing, made
from my own wheat, ground in my own mill, and baked in my
own oven; my table is, in a great measure, furnished from my
own ground; my five-year old mutton, fed on the fragrant
herbage of the mountains, that might vie with venison in juice
and flavour; my delicious veal, fattened with nothing but the
mother's milk, that fills the dish with gravy; my poultry from
the barn-door, that never knew confinement, but when they
were at roost; my rabbits panting from the warren; my game
fresh from the moors; my trout and salmon struggling from the
stream; oysters from their native banks; and herrings, with
other sea fish, I can eat in four hours after they are taken – My
sallads, roots, and pot-herbs, my own garden yields in plenty
and perfection; the produce of the natural soil, prepared by
moderate cultivation. The same soil affords all the different
fruits which England may call her own, so that my dessert is
every day fresh-gathered from the tree; my dairy flows with
nectarious tides of milk and cream, from whence we derive
abundance of excellent butter, curds, and cheese; and the refuse
fattens my pigs, that are destined for hams and bacon – I go to
bed betimes, and rise with the sun – I make shift to pass the
hours without weariness or regret, and am not destitute of
amusements within doors, when the weather will not permit
me to go abroad – I read, and chat, and play at billiards, cards
or back-gammon – Without doors, I superintend my farm, and
execute plans of improvements, the effects of which I enjoy
with unspeakable delight – Nor do I take less pleasure in seeing
my tenants thrive under my auspices, and the poor live comfortably by the employment which I provide – You know I have
one or two sensible friends, to whom I can open all my heart;
a blessing which, perhaps, I might have sought in vain among
the crowded scenes of life: there are a few others of more

humble parts, whom I esteem for their integrity; and their conversation I find inoffensive, though not very entertaining. Finally, I live in the midst of honest men, and trusty dependents, who, I flatter myself, have a disinterested attachment to my person — You, yourself, my dear Doctor, can vouch for the truth of these assertions.

Now, mark the contrast at London – I am pent up in frowzy lodgings, where there is not room enough to swing a cat; and I breathe the steams of endless putrefaction; and these would, undoubtedly, produce a pestilence, if they were not qualified by the gross acid of sea-coal, which is itself a pernicious nuisance to lungs of any delicacy of texture: but even this boasted corrector cannot prevent those languid, sallow looks, that distinguish the inhabitants of London from those ruddy swains that lead a country-life — I go to bed after midnight, jaded and restless from the dissipations of the day – I start every hour from my sleep, at the horrid noise of the watchmen[6] bawling the hour through every street, and thundering at every door; a set of useless fellows, who serve no other purpose but that of disturbing the repose of the inhabitants; and by five o'clock I start out of bed, in consequence of the still more dreadful alarm made by the country carts, and noisy rustics bellowing green pease under my window. If I would drink water, I must quaff the maukish contents of an open aqueduct,[7] exposed to all manner of defilement; or swallow that which comes from the river Thames, impregnated with all the filth of London and Westminster — Human excrement is the least offensive part of the concrete, which is composed of all the drugs, minerals, and poisons, used in mechanics and manufacture, enriched with the putrefying carcasses of beasts and men; and mixed with the scourings of all the wash-tubs, kennels, and common sewers, within the bills of mortality.

This is the agreeable potation, extolled by the Londoners, as the finest water in the universe – As to the intoxicating potion, sold for wine, it is a vile, unpalatable, and pernicious sophistication, balderdashed[8] with cyder, corn-spirit, and the juice of sloes. In an action at law, laid against a carman for having staved[9] a cask of port, it appeared from the evidence of the cooper, that there were not above five gallons of real wine in the whole pipe, which held above a hundred, and even that had been brewed and adulterated by the merchant at Oporto. The bread I eat in London, is a deleterious paste, mixed up with chalk, alum, and bone-ashes; insipid to the taste, and destructive to the constitution. The good people are not ignorant of this adulteration; but they prefer it to wholesome bread, because it is whiter than the meal of corn: thus they sacrifice their taste and their health, and the lives of their tender infants, to a most absurd gratification of a mis-judging eye; and the miller, or the baker, is obliged to poison them and their families, in order to live by his profession. The same monstrous depravity appears in their veal, which is bleached by repeated bleedings, and other villainous arts, till there is not a drop of juice left in the body, and the poor animal is paralytic before it dies; so void of all taste, nourishment, and savour, that a man might dine as comfortably on a white fricassee of kid-skin gloves; or chip hats from Leghorn.

As they have discharged the natural colour from their bread, their butchers-meat, and poultry, their cutlets, ragouts, fricassees and sauces of all kinds; so they insist upon having the complexion of their pot-herbs mended, even at the hazard of their lives. Perhaps, you will hardly believe they can be so mad as to boil their greens with brass halfpence, in order to improve their colour; and yet nothing is more true – Indeed, without this improvement in the colour, they have no personal merit. They are produced in an artificial soil, and taste of nothing but the dunghills, from whence they spring. My cabbage, cauliflower, and 'sparagus in the country, are as much superior in flavour to those that are sold in Covent-garden, as my heath-mutton is to that of St James's-market; which in fact, is neither lamb nor mutton, but something betwixt the two, gorged in the rank fens of Lincoln and Essex, pale, coarse, and frowzy – As for the pork, it is an abominable carnivorous animal, fed with horse-flesh and distillers' grains; and the poultry is all rotten, in consequence of a fever, occasioned by the infamous practice of sewing up the gut, that they may be the sooner fattened in coops, in consequence of this cruel retention.

Of the fish, I need say nothing in this hot weather, but that it comes sixty, seventy, fourscore, and a hundred miles by land-carriage; a circumstance sufficient without any comment, to turn a Dutchman's stomach, even if his nose was not saluted in every alley with the sweet flavour of *fresh* mackarel, selling by retail – This is not the season for oysters; nevertheless, it may not be amiss to mention, that the right Colchester[10] are kept in slime-pits, occasionally overflowed by the sea; and that the green colour, so much admired by the voluptuaries of this metropolis, is occasioned by the vitriolic scum, which rises on the surface of the stagnant and stinking water – Our rabbits are bred and fed in the poulterer's cellar, where they have neither air nor exercise, consequently they must be firm in flesh, and delicious in flavour; and there is no game to be had for love or money.

It must be owned, the Covent-garden affords some good fruit; which, however, is always engrossed by a few individuals of overgrown fortune, at an exorbitant price; so that little else than the refuse of the market falls to the share of the community; and that is distributed by such filthy hands, as I cannot look at without loathing. It was but yesterday that I saw a dirty barrow-bunter[11] in the street, cleaning her dusty fruit with her own spittle; and, who knows but some fine lady of St James's parish might admit into her delicate mouth those very cherries, which had been rolled and moistened between the filthy, and, perhaps, ulcerated chops of a St Giles's huckster – I need not dwell upon the pallid, contaminated mash, which they call strawberries; soiled and tossed by greasy paws through twenty baskets crusted with dirt; and then presented with the worst milk, thickened with the worst flour, into a bad likeness of cream: but the milk itself should not pass unanalysed, the produce of faded cabbage-leaves and sour draff,[12] lowered with hot water, frothed with bruised snails, carried through the streets in open pails, exposed to foul rinsings, discharged from doors and windows, spittle, snot, and tobacco-quids from foot passengers, overflowings from mud carts, spatterings from coach wheels, dirt and trash chucked into it by roguish boys for the joke's sake, the spewings of infants, who have slabbered in the tin-measure, which is thrown back in that condition among the milk, for the benefit of the next customer; and, finally, the vermin that drops from the rags of the nasty drab[13] that vends this precious mixture, under the respectable denomination of milk-maid.

I shall conclude this catalogue of London dainties, with that table-beer, guiltless of hops and malt, vapid and nauseous; much fitter to facilitate the operation of a vomit, than to quench thirst and promote digestion; the tallowy rancid mass, called butter, manufactured with candle grease and kitchen stuff; and their fresh eggs, imported from France and Scotland. — Now, all these enormities might be remedied with a very little attention to the article of police, or civil regulation; but the wise patriots of London have taken it into their heads, that all regulation is inconsistent with liberty; and that every man ought to live in his own way, without restraint — Nay, as there is not sense enough left among them, to be discomposed by the nuisance I have mentioned, they may, for aught I care, wallow in the mire of their own pollution.

A companionable man will, undoubtedly put up with many inconveniences for the sake of enjoying agreeable society. A facetious friend of mine used to say, the wine could not be bad, where the company was agreeable; a maxim which, however, ought to be taken *cum grano salis*:[14] but what is the society of London, that I should be tempted, for its sake, to mortify my senses, and compound with such uncleanness as my soul abhors? All the people I see, are too much engrossed by schemes of interest or ambition, to have any room left for sentiment or friendship — Even in some of my old acquaintance, those schemes and pursuits have obliterated all traces of our former connexion — Conversation is reduced to party disputes, and illiberal altercation – Social commerce, to formal visits and card-playing – If you pick up a diverting original by accident, it may be dangerous to amuse yourself with his oddities — He is generally a tartar[15] at bottom; a sharper, a spy, or a lunatic. Every person you deal with endeavours to over-reach you in the way of business; you are preyed upon by idle mendicants, who beg in the phrase of borrowing, and live upon the spoils of the stranger — Your tradesmen are without conscience, your friends without affection, and your dependents without fidelity. ——

My letter would swell into a treatise, were I to particularize every cause of offence that fills up the measure of my aversion to this, and every other crowded city – Thank Heaven! I am not so far sucked into the vortex, but that I can disengage myself without any great effort of philosophy – From this wild uproar of knavery, folly, and impertinence, I shall fly with double relish to the serenity of retirement, the cordial effusions of unreserved friendship, the hospitality and protection of the rural gods; in a word, the *jucunda oblivia vitæ*,[16] which Horace himself had not taste enough to enjoy. –

I have agreed for a good travelling-coach and four, at a guinea a day, for three months certain; and next week we intend to begin our journey to the North, hoping still to be with you by the latter end of October — I shall continue to write from every stage where we make any considerable halt, as often as anything occurs, which I think can afford you the least amusement. In the mean time, I must beg you will superintend the œconomy of Barns, with respect to my hay and corn harvests; assured that my ground produces nothing but what you may freely call your own — On any other terms I should be ashamed to subscribe myself

Your unvariable friend,

LONDON, June 8.   MATT. BRAMBLE

To Sir WATKIN PHILLIPS, Bart. of Jesus college, Oxon.

DEAR PHILLIPS,

In my last, I mentioned my having spent an evening with a society of authors, who seemed to be jealous and afraid of one another. My uncle was not at all surprised to hear me say I was disappointed in their conversation. 'A man may be very entertaining and instructive upon paper (said he), and exceedingly dull in common discourse. I have observed, that those

who shine most in private company, are but secondary stars in
the constellation of genius – A small stock of ideas is more
easily managed, and sooner displayed, than a great quantity
crowded together. There is very seldom any thing extraordinary
in the appearance and address of a good writer; whereas a
dull author generally distinguishes himself by some oddity or
extravagance. For this reason, I fancy, that an assembly of
Grubs must be very diverting.'

My curiosity being excited by this hint, I consulted my friend
Dick Ivy, who undertook to gratify it the very next day, which
was Sunday last. – He carried me to dine with S—,[1] whom you
and I have long known by his writings. – He lives in the skirts
of the town, and every Sunday his house is opened to all unfortunate brothers of the quill, whom he treats with beef, pudding,
and potatoes, port, punch, and Calvert's entire butt beer.[2] – He
has fixed upon the first day of the week for the exercise of his
hospitality, because some of his guests could not enjoy it on
any other, for reasons that I need not explain.[3] I was civilly
received in a plain, yet decent habitation, which opened backwards into a very pleasant garden, kept in excellent order; and,
indeed, I saw none of the outward signs of authorship, either
in the house or the landlord, who is one of those few writers of
the age that stand upon their own foundation, without patronage, and above dependence. If there was nothing characteristic
in the entertainer, the company made ample amends for his
want of singularity.

At two in the afternoon, I found myself one of ten messmates
seated at table; and, I question, if the whole kingdom could
produce such another assemblage of originals. Among their
peculiarities, I do not mention those of dress, which may be
purely accidental. What struck me were oddities originally produced by affectation, and afterwards confirmed by habit. One
of them wore spectacles at dinner, and another his hat flapped;[4]
though (as Ivy told me) the first was noted for having a seaman's
eye, when a bailiff was in the wind; and the other was never
known to labour under any weakness or defect of vision, except
about five years ago, when he was complimented with a couple
of black eyes by a player, with whom he had quarrelled in his

drink. A third wore a laced stocking, and made use of crutches, because, once in his life, he had been laid up with a broken leg, though no man could leap over a stick with more agility. A fourth had contracted such an antipathy to the country, that he insisted upon sitting with his back towards the window that looked into the garden, and when a dish of cauliflower was set upon the table, he snuffed up volatile salts to keep him from fainting; yet this delicate person was the son of a cottager, born under a hedge, and had many years run wild among asses on a common. A fifth affected distraction – When spoke to, he always answered from the purpose – sometimes he suddenly started up, and rapped out a dreadful oath – sometimes he burst out a-laughing – then he folded his arms, and sighed – and then, he hissed like fifty serpents.

At first I really thought he was mad, and, as he sat near me, began to be under some apprehensions for my own safety, when our landlord, perceiving me alarmed, assured me aloud that I had nothing to fear. 'The gentleman (said he) is trying to act a part for which he is by no means qualified – if he had all the inclination in the world, it is not in his power to be mad. His spirits are too flat to be kindled into frenzy.' ''Tis no bad p-p-puff, how-ow-ever (observed a person in a tarnished laced coat): aff-ffected m-madness w-will p-pass for w-wit w-with nine-ninet-teen out of t-twenty.' – 'And affected stuttering for humour: replied our landlord, tho', God knows, there is an affinity betwixt them.' It seems, this wag, after having made some abortive attempts in plain speaking, had recourse to this defect, by means of which he frequently extorted the laugh of the company, without the least expence of genius; and that imperfection, which he had at first counterfeited, was now become so habitual, that he could not lay it aside.

A certain winking genius, who wore yellow gloves at dinner, had, on his first introduction, taken such offence at S—, because he looked and talked, and ate and drank like any other man, that he spoke contemptuously of his understanding ever after, and never would repeat his visit, until he had exhibited the following proof of his caprice. Wat Wyvil, the poet,[5] having made some unsuccessful advances towards an intimacy with

S—, at last gave him to understand, by a third person, that he had written a poem in his praise, and a satire against his person; that if he would admit him to his house, the first should be immediately sent to press; but that if he persisted in declining his friendship, he would publish his satire without delay. S— replied, that he looked upon Wyvil's panegyrick, as in effect, a species of infamy, and would resent it accordingly with a good cudgel; but if he published the satire, he might deserve his compassion, and had nothing to fear from his revenge. Wyvil having considered the alternative, resolved to mortify S— by printing the panegyrick, for which he received a sound drubbing. Then he swore the peace against the aggressor, who, in order to avoid a prosecution at law, admitted him to his good graces. It was the singularity in S—'s conduct, on this occasion, that reconciled him to the yellow-gloved philosopher, who owned he had some genius, and from that period cultivated his acquaintance.

Curious to know upon what subjects the several talents of my fellow-guests were employed, I applied to my communicative friend Dick Ivy, who gave me to understand, that most of them were, or had been, understrappers, or journeymen, to more creditable authors, for whom they translated, collated, and compiled, in the business of bookmaking; and that all of them had, at different times, laboured in the service of our landlord, though they had now set up for themselves in various departments of literature. Not only their talents, but also their nations and dialects were so various, that our conversation resembled the confusion of tongues at Babel. We had the Irish brogue, the Scotch accent, and foreign idiom, twanged off by the most discordant vociferation; for as they all spoke together, no man had any chance to be heard, unless he could bawl louder than his fellows. It must be owned, however, there was nothing pedantic in their discourse; they carefully avoided all learned disquisitions, and endeavoured to be facetious; nor did their endeavours always miscarry —— some droll repartee passed, and much laughter was excited; and if any individual lost his temper so far as to transgress the bounds of decorum, he was effectually checked by the master of the feast, who exerted a sort of paternal authority over this irritable tribe.

The most learned philosopher of the whole collection, who had been expelled the university for atheism, has made great progress in a refutation of lord Bolingbroke's metaphysical works,[6] which is said to be equally ingenious and orthodox; but, in the mean time, he has been presented to the grand jury as a public nuisance, for having blasphemed in an ale-house on the Lord's day. The Scotchman gives lectures on the pronunciation of the English language, which he is now publishing by subscription.

The Irishman is a political writer, and goes by the name of my Lord Potatoe. He wrote a pamphlet in vindication of a minister, hoping his zeal would be rewarded with some place or pension; but, finding himself neglected in that quarter, he whispered about, that the pamphlet was written by the minister himself, and he published an answer to his own production. In this, he addressed the author under the title of *your lordship* with such solemnity, that the public swallowed the deceit, and bought up the whole impression. The wise politicians of the metropolis declared they were both masterly performances, and chuckled over the flimsy reveries of an ignorant garretteer, as the profound speculations of a veteran statesman, acquainted with all the secrets of the cabinet. The imposture was detected in the sequel, and our Hibernian pamphleteer retains no part of his assumed importance, but the bare title of *my lord*, and the upper part of the table at the potatoe-ordinary in Shoelane.

Opposite to me sat a Piedmontese, who had obliged the public with a humorous satire, intituled, *The Ballance of the English Poets*,[7] a performance which evinced the great modesty and taste of the author, and, in particular, his intimacy with the elegancies of the English language. The sage, who laboured under the αγροφοβια, or *horror of green fields*, had just finished a treatise on practical agriculture, though, in fact, he had never seen corn growing in his life, and was so ignorant of grain, that our entertainer, in the face of the whole company, made him own, that a plate of hominy was the best rice pudding he had ever eat.

The stutterer had almost finished his travels through Europe and part of Asia, without ever budging beyond the liberties of the King's Bench,[8] except in term-time, with a tipstaff[9] for his companion; and as for little Tim Cropdale, the most facetious member of the whole society, he had happily wound up the catastrophe of a virgin tragedy, from the exhibition of which he promised himself a large fund of profit and reputation. Tim had made shift to live many years by writing novels, at the rate of five pounds a volume; but that branch of business is now engrossed by female authors, who publish merely for the propagation of virtue, with so much ease and spirit, and delicacy, and knowledge of the human heart, and all in the serene tranquillity of high life, that the reader is not only inchanted by their genius, but reformed by their morality.

After dinner, we adjourned into the garden, where, I observed, Mr S— gave a short separate audience to every individual in a small remote filbert walk,[10] from whence most of them dropt off one after another, without further ceremony; but they were replaced by fresh recruits of the same clan, who came to make an afternoon's visit; and, among others, a spruce bookseller, called Birkin, who rode his own gelding, and made his appearance in a pair of new jemmy boots,[11] with massy spurs of plate. It was not without reason, that this midwife of the Muses used exercise a-horseback, for he was too fat to walk a-foot, and he underwent some sarcasms from Tim Cropdale, on his unwieldy size and inaptitude for motion. Birkin, who took umbrage at this poor author's petulance in presuming to joke upon a man so much richer than himself, told him, he was not so unwieldy but that he could move the Marshalsea court[12] for a writ, and even overtake him with it, if he did not very speedily come and settle accounts with him, respecting the expence of publishing his last ode to the king of Prussia, of which he had sold but three, and one of them was to Whitfield the methodist. Tim affected to receive this intimation with good humour, saying, he expected in a post or two, from Potsdam, a poem of thanks from his Prussian majesty, who knew very well how to pay poets in their own coin; but, in the mean time, he proposed, that Mr Birkin and he should run three times round the garden for a bowl of punch, to be drank at Ashley's[13] in the evening, and he would run boots against stockings. The

bookseller, who valued himself upon his mettle, was persuaded
to accept the challenge, and he forthwith resigned his boots
to Cropdale, who, when he had put them on, was no bad
representation of captain Pistol in the play.[14]

Every thing being adjusted, they started together with great
impetuosity, and, in the second round, Birkin had clearly the
advantage, *larding the lean earth as he puff'd along*.[15] Cropdale
had no mind to contest the victory further; but, in a twinkling,
disappeared through the back-door of the garden, which
opened into a private lane, that had communication with the
high road. – The spectators immediately began to hollow, 'Stole
away!' and Birkin set off in pursuit of him with great eagerness;
but he had not advanced twenty yards in the lane, when a thorn
running into his foot, sent him hopping back into the garden,
roaring with pain, and swearing with vexation. When he was
delivered from this annoyance by the Scotchman, who had been
bred to surgery, he looked about him wildly, exclaiming, 'Sure,
the fellow won't be such a rogue as to run clear away with my
boots!' Our landlord, having reconnoitered the shoes he had
left, which, indeed, hardly deserved that name, 'Pray (said he),
Mr Birkin, wa'n't your boots made of calf-skin?' 'Calf-skin or
cow-skin (replied the other) I'll find a slip of sheep-skin[16] that
will do this business – I lost twenty pounds by his farce which
you persuaded me to buy – I am out of pocket five pounds by
his damn'd ode; and now this pair of boots, bran new, cost me
thirty shillings, as per receipt – But this affair of the boots is
felony – transportation.[17] — I'll have the dog indicted at the
Old Bailey[18] – I will, Mr S—. I will be reveng'd, even though
I should lose my debt in consequence of his conviction.'

Mr S— said nothing at present, but accommodated him with
a pair of shoes; then ordered his servant to rub him down, and
comfort him with a glass of rum-punch, which seemed, in a
great measure, to cool the rage of his indignation. 'After all
(said our landlord) this is no more than a *humbug* in the way
of wit, though it deserves a more respectable epithet, when
considered as an effort of invention. Tim, being (I suppose)
out of credit with the cordwainer,[19] fell upon this ingenious
expedient to supply the want of shoes, knowing that Mr Birkin,

who loves humour, would himself relish the joke upon a little recollection. Cropdale literally lives by his wit, which he has exercised upon all his friends in their turns. He once borrowed my poney for five or six days to go to Salisbury, and sold him in Smithfield[20] at his return. This was a joke of such a serious nature, that, in the first transports of my passion, I had some thoughts of prosecuting him for horse-stealing; and even when my resentment had in some measure subsided, as he industriously avoided me, I vowed, I would take satisfaction on his ribs with the first opportunity. One day, seeing him at some distance in the street, coming towards me, I began to prepare my cane for action, and walked in the shadow of a porter, that he might not perceive me soon enough to make his escape; but, in the very instant I had lifted up the instrument of correction, I found Tim Cropdale metamorphosed into a miserable blind wretch, feeling his way with a long stick from post to post, and rolling about two bald unlighted orbs instead of eyes. I was exceedingly shocked at having so narrowly escaped the concern and disgrace that would have attended such a misapplication of vengeance: but, next day, Tim prevailed upon a friend of mine to come and solicit my forgiveness, and offer his note, payable in six weeks, for the price of the poney. – This gentleman gave me to understand, that the blind man was no other than Cropdale, who having seen me advancing, and guessing my intent, had immediately converted himself into the object aforesaid – I was so diverted at the ingenuity of the evasion, that I agreed to pardon his offence, refusing his note, however, that I might keep a prosecution for felony hanging over his head, as a security for his future good behaviour — But Timothy would by no means trust himself in my hands till the note was accepted – then he made his appearance at my door as a blind beggar, and imposed in such a manner upon my man, who had been his old acquaintance and pot-companion, that the fellow threw the door in his face, and even threatened to give him the bastinado. Hearing a noise in the hall, I went thither, and immediately recollecting the figure I had passed in the street, accosted him by his own name, to the unspeakable astonishment of the footman.'

Birkin declared he loved a joke as well as another; but asked if any of the company could tell where Mr Cropdale lodged, that he might send him a proposal about restitution, before the boots should be made away with. 'I would willingly give him a pair of new shoes (said he), and half a guinea into the bargain, for the boots, which fitted me like a glove; and I shan't be able to get the fellows of them till the good weather for riding is over.' The stuttering wit declared, that the only secret which Cropdale ever kept, was the place of his lodgings; but he believed, that, during the heats of summer, he commonly took his repose upon a bulk,[21] or indulged himself, in fresco, with one of the kennel-nymphs, under the portico of St Martin's church.[22] 'Pox on him! (cried the bookseller) he might as well have taken my whip and spurs – In that case, he might have been tempted to steal another horse, and then he would have rid to the devil of course.'

After coffee, I took my leave of Mr S—, with proper acknowledgments of his civility, and was extremely well pleased with the entertainment of the day, though not yet satisfied, with respect to the nature of this connexion, betwixt a man of character in the literary world, and a parcel of authorlings, who, in all probability, would never be able to acquire any degree of reputation by their labours. On this head I interrogated my conductor, Dick Ivy, who answered me to this effect – 'One would imagine S— had some view to his own interest, in giving countenance and assistance to those people, whom he knows to be bad men, as well as bad writers; but, if he has any such view, he will find himself disappointed; for if he is so vain as to imagine he can make them subservient to his schemes of profit or ambition, they are cunning enough to make him their property in the mean time. There is not one of the company you have seen to-day (myself excepted) who does not owe him particular obligations — One of them he bailed out of a spunging-house,[23] and afterwards paid the debt – another he translated into his family, and clothed, when he was turned out half naked from jail in consequence of an act for the relief of insolvent debtors[24] – a third, who was reduced to a woollen night cap, and lived upon sheeps trotters, up three pair of stairs backward in Butcher-row, he took into present pay and free

quarters, and enabled him to appear as a gentleman, without
having the fear of sheriff's officers before his eyes. Those who
are in distress he supplies with money when he has it, and with
his credit when he is out of cash. When they want business,
he either finds employment for them in his own service, or
recommends them to booksellers to execute some project he
has formed for their subsistence. They are always welcome to
his table (which though plain, is plentiful) and to his good
offices as far as they will go, and when they see occasion, they
make use of his name with the most petulant familiarity; nay,
they do not even scruple to arrogate to themselves the merit of
some of his performances, and have been known to sell their
own lucubrations as the produce of his brain. The Scotchman
you saw at dinner once personated him at an ale-house in
West-Smithfield and, in the character of S—, had his head
broke by a cow-keeper, for having spoke disrespectfully of the
Christian religion; but he took the law of him in his own person,
and the assailant was fain to give him ten pounds to withdraw
his action.'

I observed, that all this appearance of liberality on the side
of Mr S— was easily accounted for, on the supposition that
they flattered him in private, and engaged his adversaries in
public; and yet I was astonished, when I recollected that I often
had seen this writer virulently abused in papers, poems, and
pamphlets, and not a pen was drawn in his defence – 'But
you will be more astonished (said he) when I assure you,
those very guests whom you saw at his table to-day, were the
authors of great part of that abuse; and he himself is well
aware of their particular favours, for they are all eager to detect
and betray one another.' 'But this is doing the devil's work
for nothing (cried I). What should induce them to revile their
benefactor without provocation?' 'Envy (answered Dick) is
the general incitement; but they are galled by an additional
scourge of provocation. S— directs a literary journal,[25] in which
their productions are necessarily brought to trial; and though
many of them have been treated with such lenity and favour as
they little deserved, yet the slightest censure, such as, perhaps,
could not be avoided with any pretensions to candour and

impartiality, has rankled in the hearts of those authors to such a degree, that they have taken immediate vengeance on the critic in anonymous libels, letters, and lampoons. Indeed, all the writers of the age, good, bad, and indifferent, from the moment he assumed this office, became his enemies, either professed or in petto,[26] except those of his friends who knew they had nothing to fear from his strictures; and he must be a wiser man than me who can tell what advantage or satisfaction he derives from having brought such a nest of hornets about his ears.'

I owned, that was a point which might deserve consideration; but still I expressed a desire to know his real motives for continuing his friendship to a set of rascals equally ungrateful and insignificant. – He said, he did not pretend to assign any reasonable motive; that, if the truth must be told, the man was, in point of conduct, a most incorrigible fool; that, though he pretended to have a knack at hitting off characters, he blundered strangely in the distribution of his favours, which were generally bestowed on the most undeserving of those who had recourse to his assistance; that, indeed, this preference was not so much owing to want of discernment as to want of resolution, for he had not fortitude enough to resist the importunity even of the most worthless; and, as he did not know the value of money, there was very little merit in parting with it so easily; that his pride was gratified in seeing himself courted by such a number of literary dependents; that, probably, he delighted in hearing them expose and traduce one another; and, finally, from their information, he became acquainted with all the transactions of Grub-street, which he had some thoughts of compiling for the entertainment of the public.

I could not help suspecting, from Dick's discourse, that he had some particular grudge against S—, upon whose conduct he had put the worst construction it would bear; and, by dint of cross-examination, I found he was not at all satisfied with the character which had been given in the Review of his last performance, though it had been treated civilly in consequence of the author's application to the critic. By all accounts, S— is not without weakness and caprice; but he is certainly good-humoured and civilized; nor do I find that there is any thing overbearing, cruel, or implacable in his disposition.

I have dwelt so long upon authors, that you will perhaps suspect I intend to enroll myself among the fraternity; but, if I were actually qualified for the profession, it is at best but a desperate resource against starving, as it affords no provision for old age and infirmity. Salmon,[27] at the age of fourscore, is now in a garret, compiling matter, at a guinea a sheet, for a modern historian, who, in point of age, might be his grand-child; and Psalmonazar,[28] after having drudged half a century in the literary mill, in all the simplicity and abstinence of an Asiatic, subsists upon the charity of a few booksellers, just sufficient to keep him from the parish, – I think Guy,[29] who was himself a bookseller, ought to have appropriated one wing or ward of his hospital to the use of decayed authors; though indeed, there is neither hospital, college, nor work-house, within the bills of mortality, large enough to contain the poor of this society, composed, as it is, from the refuse of every other profession.

I know not whether you will find any amusement in this account of an odd race of mortals, whose constitution had, I own, greatly interested the curiosity of

Yours,

LONDON, June 10.   J. MELFORD

To Miss LÆTITIA WILLIS, at Gloucester.

MY DEAR LETTY,

There is something on my spirits, which I should not venture to communicate by the post, but having the opportunity of Mrs Brentwood's return, I seize it eagerly, to disburthen my poor heart, which is oppressed with fear and vexation. – O Letty! what a miserable situation it is, to be without a friend to whom one can apply for counsel and consolation in distress! I hinted in my last, that one Mr Barton had been very particular in his civilities: I can no longer mistake his meaning – he has formally professed himself my admirer; and, after a thousand assiduities, perceiving I made but a cold return to his addresses, he had recourse to the mediation of lady Griskin, who has acted the part of a very warm advocate in his behalf: — but, my dear Willis, her ladyship over acts her part – she not only expatiates on the ample fortune, the great connexions, and the unblemished character of Mr Barton, but she takes the trouble to catechise me; and, two days ago, peremptorily told me, that a girl of my age could not possibly resist so many considerations, if her heart was not pre-engaged.

This insinuation threw me into such a flutter, that she could not but observe my disorder; and, presuming upon the discovery, insisted upon my making her the confidante of my passion. But, although I had not such command of myself as to conceal the emotion of my heart, I am not such a child as to disclose its secret to a person who would certainly use them to its prejudice. I told her, it was no wonder if I was out of countenance at her introducing a subject of conversation so unsuitable to my years and inexperience; that I believed Mr Barton was a very worthy gentleman, and I was much obliged to him for his good opinion; but the affections were involuntary, and mine, in particular, had as yet made no concessions in his favour. She shook her head with an air of distrust that made me tremble; and observed, that if my affections were free, they would submit to the decision of prudence, especially when enforced by the authority of those who had a right to direct my conduct. This remark implied a design to interest my uncle or my aunt, perhaps my brother, in behalf of Mr Barton's passion; and I am sadly afraid that my aunt is already gained over. Yesterday in the forenoon, he had been walking with us in the Park, and stopping in our return at a toy-shop, he presented her with a very fine snuff-box, and me with a gold etuis,[1] which I resolutely refused, till she commanded me to accept it on pain of her displeasure: nevertheless, being still unsatisfied with respect to the propriety of receiving this toy, I signified my doubts to my brother, who said he would consult my uncle on the subject, and seemed to think Mr Barton had been rather premature in his presents.

What will be the result of this consultation, Heaven knows; but I am afraid it will produce an explanation with Mr Barton, who will, no doubt, avow his passion, and solicit their consent to a connexion which my soul abhors; for, my dearest Letty, it is not in my power to love Mr Barton, even if my heart was untouched by any other tenderness. Not that there is any thing disagreeable about his person, but there is a total want of that nameless charm which captivates and controuls the inchanted spirit – at least, he appears to me to have this defect; but if he had all the engaging qualifications which a man can possess, they would be excited in vain against that constancy, which, I flatter myself, is the characteristic of my nature. No, my dear Willis, I may be involved in fresh troubles, and I believe I shall, from the importunities of this gentleman and the violence of my relations; but my heart is incapable of change.

You know I put no faith in dreams; and yet I have been much disturbed by one that visited me last night. – I thought I was in a church, where a certain person, whom you know, was on the point of being married to my aunt; that the clergyman was Mr Barton, and that poor forlorn I, stood weeping in a corner, half naked, and without shoes or stockings. – Now, I know there is nothing so childish as to be moved by those vain illusions; but, nevertheless, in spite of all my reason, this hath made a strong impression upon my mind, which begins to be very gloomy. Indeed, I have another more substantial cause of affliction – I have some religious scruples, my dear friend, which lie heavy on my conscience. – I was persuaded to go to the Tabernacle, where I heard a discourse that affected me deeply. – I have prayed fervently to be enlightened, but as yet I am not sensible of these inward motions, those operations of grace, which are the signs of a regenerated spirit; and therefore I begin to be in terrible apprehensions about the state of my poor soul. Some of our family have had very uncommon accessions, particularly my aunt and Mrs Jenkins, who sometimes speak as if they were really inspired; so that I am not like to want for either exhortation or example, to purify my thoughts, and recall them from the vanities of this world, which, indeed, I would willingly resign, if it was in my power; but to make this sacrifice, I must be enabled by such assistance from above as hath not yet been indulged to

Your unfortunate friend,

June 10.   LYDIA MELFORD

To Sir WATKIN PHILLIPS, of Jesus college, Oxon.

DEAR PHILLIPS,

The moment I received your letter, I began to execute your commission – With the assistance of mine host at the Bull and Gate,[1] I discovered the place to which your fugitive valet had retreated, and taxed him with his dishonesty – The fellow was in manifest confusion at sight of me, but he denied the charge with great confidence, till I told him, that if he would give up the watch, which was a family piece, he might keep the money and the clothes, and go to the devil his own way, at his leisure; but if he rejected this proposal, I would deliver him forthwith to the constable, whom I had provided for that purpose, and he would carry him before the justice without further delay. After some hesitation, he desired to speak with me in the next room, where he produced the watch, with all its appendages, and I have delivered it to our landlord, to be sent you by the first safe conveyance – So much for business.

I shall grow vain, upon your saying you find entertainment in my letters; barren, as they certainly are, of incident and importance, because your amusement must arise, not from the matter, but from the manner, which you know is all my own – Animated, therefore, by the approbation of a person, whose nice taste and consummate judgment I can no longer doubt, I will chearfully proceed with our memoirs – As it is determined we shall set out next week for Yorkshire, I went to-day in the forenoon with my uncle to see a carriage, belonging to a coach-maker in our neighbourhood – Turning down a narrow lane, behind Longacre,[2] we perceived a crowd of people standing at a door; which, it seems, opened into a kind of a methodist meeting, and were informed, that a footman was then holding

forth to the congregation within. Curious to see this phœno-
menon, we squeezed into the place with much difficulty; and
who should this preacher be, but the identical Humphry
Clinker. He had finished his sermon, and given out a psalm,
the first stave of which he sung with peculiar graces — But if we
were astonished to see Clinker in the pulpit, we were altogether
confounded at finding all the females of our family among the
audience – There was lady Griskin, Mrs Tabitha Bramble, Mrs
Winifred Jenkins, my sister Liddy, and Mr Barton, and all of
them joined in the psalmody, with strong marks of devotion.

   I could hardly keep my gravity on this ludicrous occasion;
but old Square-toes was differently affected – The first thing
that struck him, was the presumption of his lacquey, whom he
commanded to come down, with such an air of authority as
Humphry did not think proper to disregard. He descended
immediately, and all the people were in commotion. Barton
looked exceedingly sheepish, lady Griskin flirted her fan, Mrs
Tabby groaned in spirit, Liddy changed countenance, and Mrs
Jenkins sobbed as if her heart was breaking – My uncle, with a
sneer, asked pardon of the ladies, for having interrupted their
devotion, saying, he had particular business with the preacher,
whom he ordered to call a hackney-coach. This being immediately brought up to the end of the lane, he handed Liddy into
it, and my aunt and I following him, we drove home, without
taking any further notice of the rest of the company, who still
remained in silent astonishment.

   Mr Bramble, perceiving Liddy in great trepidation, assumed
a milder aspect, bidding her be under no concern, for he was
not at all displeased at any thing she had done – 'I have no
objection (said he) to your being religiously inclined; but I don't
think my servant is a proper ghostly director for a devotee of
your sex and character – if, in fact (as I rather believe) your
aunt is not the sole conductress of this machine' — Mrs Tabitha
made no answer, but threw up the whites of her eyes, as if in
the act of ejaculation – Poor Liddy, said, she had no right to
the title of a devotee; that she thought there was no harm in
hearing a pious discourse, even if it came from a footman,
especially as her aunt was present; but that if she had erred

from ignorance, she hoped he would excuse it, as she could not bear the thoughts of living under his displeasure. The old gentleman, pressing her hand with a tender smile, said she was a good girl, and that he did not believe her capable of doing any thing that could give him the least umbrage or disgust.

When we arrived at our lodgings, he commanded Mr Clinker to attend him up stairs, and spoke to him in these words — 'Since you are called upon by the spirit to preach and to teach, it is high time to lay aside the livery of an earthly master; and for my part, I am unworthy to have an apostle in my service' – 'I hope (said Humphry) I have not failed in my duty to your honour – I should be a vile wretch if I did, considering the misery from which your charity and compassion relieved me – but having an inward admonition of the spirit —' 'An admonition of the devil – (cried the squire, in a passion) What admonition, you blockhead? – What right has such a fellow as you to set up for a reformer?' 'Begging your honour's pardon (replied Clinker) may not the new light of God's grace shine upon the poor and the ignorant in their humility, as well as upon the wealthy, and the philosopher in all his pride of human learning?' 'What you imagine to be the new light of grace (said his master) I take to be a deceitful vapour, glimmering through a crack in your upper story – In a word, Mr Clinker, I will have no light in my family but what pays the king's taxes,[3] unless it be the light of reason, which you don't pretend to follow.'

'Ah, sir! (cried Humphry) the light of reason, is no more in comparison to the light I mean, than a farthing candle to the sun at noon'[4] – 'Very true (said uncle), the one will serve to shew you your way, and the other to dazzle and confound your weak brain – Heark ye, Clinker, you are either an hypocritical knave, or a wrong-headed enthusiast; and in either case, unfit for my service – If you are a quack in sanctity and devotion, you will find it an easy matter to impose upon silly women, and others of crazed understanding, who will contribute lavishly for your support – If you are really seduced by the reveries of a disturbed imagination, the sooner you lose your senses entirely, the better for yourself and the community. In that case, some charitable person might provide you with a dark room and clean straw in Bedlam, where it would not be in your power to infect others with your fanaticism; whereas, if you have just reflection enough left to maintain the character of a chosen vessel[5] in the meetings of the godly, you and your hearers will be misled by a Will-i'the-wisp,[6] from one error into another, till you are plunged into religious frenzy; and then, perhaps, you will hang yourself in despair' — 'Which the Lord of his infinite mercy forbid! (exclaimed the affrighted Clinker) It is very possible I may be under the temptation of the devil, who wants to wreck me on the rocks of spiritual pride – Your honour says, I am either a knave or a madman; now, as I'll assure your honour, I am no knave, it follows that I must be mad; therefore, I beseech your honour, upon my knees, to take my case into consideration, that means may be used for my recovery' —

The 'squire could not help smiling at the poor fellow's simplicity, and promised to take care of him, provided he would mind the business of his place, without running after the new light of methodism: but Mrs Tabitha took offence at his humility, which she interpreted into poorness of spirit and worldly mindedness – She upbraided him with the want of courage to suffer for conscience sake[7] — She observed, that if he should lose his place for bearing testimony to the truth, Providence would not fail to find him another, perhaps more advantageous; and, declaring that it could not be very agreeable to live in a family where an inquisition was established, retired to another room in great agitation.

My uncle followed her with a significant look, then, turning to the preacher, 'You hear what my sister says – If you cannot live with me upon such terms as I have prescribed, the vineyard of methodism lies before you, and she seems very well disposed to reward your labour' – 'I would not willingly give offence to any soul upon earth (answered Humphry); her ladyship has been very good to me, ever since we came to London; and surely she has a heart turned for religious exercises; and both she and lady Griskin sing psalms and hymns like two cherubims — But, at the same time, I'm bound to love and obey your honour – It becometh not such a poor ignorant fellow as me, to hold dispute with gentlemen of rank and learning – As for

the matter of knowledge, I am no more than a beast in comparison of your honour; therefore I submit; and, with God's grace,
I will follow you to the world's end, if you don't think me too
far gone to be out of confinement' –

His master promised to keep him for some time longer on
trial; then desired to know in what manner lady Griskin and
Mr Barton came to join their religious society, he told him, that
her ladyship was the person who first carried my aunt and
sister to the Tabernacle, whither he attended them, and had
his devotion kindled by Mr W—'s preaching:[8] that he was
confirmed in this new way, by the preacher's sermons, which
he had bought and studied with great attention: that his discourse and prayers had brought over Mrs Jenkins and the
house-maid to the same way of thinking; but as for Mr Barton,
he had never seen him at service before this day, when he came
in company with lady Griskin — Humphry, moreover, owned
that he had been encouraged to mount the rostrum, by the
example and success of a weaver, who was much followed as a
powerful minister: that on his first trial he found himself under
such strong impulsions, as made him believe he was certainly
moved by the spirit; and that he had assisted in lady Griskin's,
and several private houses, at exercises of devotion.

Mr Bramble was no sooner informed, that her ladyship had
acted as the primum mobile[9] of this confederacy, than he concluded she had only made use of Clinker as a tool, subservient
to the execution of some design, to the true secret of which he
was an utter stranger – He observed, that her ladyship's brain
was a perfect mill for projects; and that she and Tabby had
certainly engaged in some secret treaty, the nature of which he
could not comprehend. I told him I thought it was no difficult
matter to perceive the drift of Mrs Tabitha, which was to
ensnare the heart of Barton, and that in all likelihood my lady
Griskin acted as her auxiliary: that this supposition would
account for their endeavours to convert him to methodism; an
event which would occasion a connexion of souls that might
be easily improved into a matrimonial union.

My uncle seemed to be much diverted by the thoughts of this
scheme's succeeding; but I gave him to understand, that Barton

was pre-engaged: that he had the day before made a present of an etuis to Liddy, which her aunt had obliged her to receive, with a view, no doubt, to countenance her own accepting of a snuff-box at the same time; that my sister having made me acquainted with this incident, I had desired an explanation of Mr Barton, who declared his intentions were honourable, and expressed his hope that I would have no objections to his alliance; that I had thanked him for the honour he intended our family; but told him, it would be necessary to consult her uncle and aunt, who were her guardians; and their approbation being obtained, I could have no objection to his proposal; though I was persuaded that no violence would be offered to my sister's inclinations, in a transaction that so nearly interested the happiness of her future life: that he had assured me, he should never think of availing himself of a guardian's authority, unless he could render his addresses agreeable to the young lady herself; and that he would immediately demand permission of Mr and Mrs Bramble, to make Liddy a tender of his hand and fortune.

The squire was not insensible to the advantages of such a match, and declared he would promote it with all his influence; but when I took notice that there seemed to be an aversion on the side of Liddy, he said he would sound her on the subject; and if her reluctance was such as would not be easily overcome, he would civilly decline the proposal of Mr Barton; for he thought that, in the choice of a husband a young woman ought not to sacrifice the feelings of her heart for any consideration upon earth – 'Liddy is not so desperate (said he) as to worship fortune at such an expence.' I take it for granted, this whole affair will end in smoke; though there seems to be a storm brewing in the quarter of Mrs Tabby, who sat with all the sullen dignity of silence at dinner, seemingly pregnant with complaint and expostulation. As she had certainly marked Barton for her own prey, she cannot possibly favour his suit to Liddy; and therefore I expect something extraordinary will attend his declaring himself my sister's admirer. This declaration will certainly be made in form, as soon as the lover can pick up resolution enough to stand the brunt of Mrs Tabby's disappointment; for he is, without doubt, aware of her designs upon his person — The particulars of the *denouement* you shall know in due season: mean while I am

Always yours,

LONDON, June 10. J. MELFORD

To Dr Lewis.

DEAR LEWIS,

The deceitful calm was of short duration. I am plunged again in a sea of vexation, and the complaints in my stomach and bowels are returned; so that I suppose I shall be disabled from prosecuting the excursion I had planned – What the devil had I to do, to come a plague hunting with a leash of females in my train? Yesterday my precious sister (who, by the bye, has been for some time a professed methodist) came into my apartment, attended by Mr Barton, and desired an audience with a very stately air – 'Brother (said she), this gentleman has something to propose, which I flatter myself will be the more acceptable, as it will rid you of a troublesome companion.' Then Mr Barton proceeded to this effect – 'I am, indeed, extremely ambitious of being allied to your family, Mr Bramble, and I hope you will see no cause to interpose your authority.' 'As for authority (said Tabby, interrupting him with some warmth), I know of none that he has a right to use on this occasion — If I pay him the compliment of making him acquainted with the step I intend to take, it is all he can expect in reason – This is as much as I believe he would do by me, if he intended to change his own situation in life – In a word, brother, I am so sensible of Mr Barton's extraordinary merit, that I have been prevailed upon to alter my resolution of living a single life, and to put my happiness in his hands, by vesting him with a legal title to my person and fortune, such as they are. The business at present, is to have the writings drawn; and I shall be obliged to you, if you will recommend a lawyer to me for that purpose' –

You may guess what an effect this overture had upon me; who, from the information of my nephew, expected that Barton was to make a formal declaration of his passion for Liddy; I could not help gazing in silent astonishment, alternately at Tabby, and her supposed admirer, who last hung his head in the most aukward confusion for a few minutes, and then retired on pretence of being suddenly seized with a vertigo — Mrs Tabitha affected much concern, and would have had him make use of a bed in the house; but he insisted upon going home, that he might have recourse of some drops, which he kept for such emergencies, and his innamorata[1] acquiesced – In the mean time I was exceedingly puzzled at this adventure (though I suspected the truth) and did not know in what manner to demean myself towards Mrs Tabitha, when Jery came in and told me, he had just seen Mr Barton alight from his chariot at lady Griskin's door – This incident seemed to threaten a visit from her ladyship, with which we were honoured accordingly, in less than half an hour – 'I find (said she) there has been a match of cross purposes among you good folks; and I'm come to set you to rights' – So saying, she presented me with the following billet[2] —

DEAR SIR,

I no sooner recollected myself from the extreme confusion I was thrown into, by that unlucky mistake of your sister, than I thought it my duty to assure you, that my devoirs to Mrs Bramble never exceeded the bounds of ordinary civility; and that my heart is unalterably fixed upon Miss Liddy Melford, as I had the honour to declare to her brother, when he questioned me upon that subject – Lady Griskin has been so good as to charge herself, not only with the delivery of this note, but also with the task of undeceiving Mrs Bramble, for whom I have the most profound respect and veneration, though my affection being otherwise engaged is no longer in the power of

Sir,

Your very humble servant,

RALPH BARTON.

Having cast my eyes over this billet, I told her ladyship, that I would no longer retard the friendly office she had undertaken:

and I and Jerry forthwith retired into another room. There we soon perceived the conversation grow very warm betwixt the two ladies; and, at length, could distinctly hear certain terms of altercation, which we could no longer delay interrupting, with any regard to decorum. When we entered the scene of contention, we found Liddy had joined the disputants, and stood trembling betwixt them, as if she had been afraid they would have proceeded to something more practical than words — Lady Griskin's face was like the full moon in a storm of wind, glaring, fiery, and portentous; while Tabby looked grim and ghastly, with an aspect breathing discord and dismay. – Our appearance put a stop to their mutual revilings; but her ladyship turning to me, 'Cousin (said she) I can't help saying I have met with a very ungrateful return from this lady, for the pains I have taken to serve her family' – 'My family is much obliged to your ladyship (cried Tabby, with a kind of hysterical giggle); but we have no right to the good offices of such an honourable go-between.' 'But, for all that, good Mrs Tabitha Bramble (resumed the other), I shall be content with the reflection, That virtue is its own reward; and it shall not be my fault, if you continue to make yourself ridiculous – Mr Bramble, who has no little interest of his own to serve, will, no doubt, contribute all in his power to promote a match betwixt Mr Barton and his niece, which will be equally honourable and advantageous; and, I dare say, Miss Liddy herself will have no objection to a measure so well calculated to make her happy in life' — 'I beg your ladyship's pardon (exclaimed Liddy, with great vivacity) I have nothing but misery to expect from such a measure; and I hope my guardians will have too much compassion, to barter my peace of mind for any consideration of interest or fortune' – 'Upon my word, Miss Liddy! (said she) you have profited by the example of your good aunt — I comprehend your meaning, and will explain it when I have a proper opportunity — In the mean time, I shall take my leave – Madam, your most obedient, and devoted humble servant,' said she, advancing close up to my sister, and curtsying so low, that I thought she intended to squat herself down on the floor — This salutation Tabby returned with equal solemnity; and the expression of the two faces, while they continued in this attitude, would be no bad subject for a pencil like that of the incomparable Hogarth,[3] if any such should ever appear again, in these times of dullness and degeneracy.

Jery accompanied her ladyship to her house, that he might have an opportunity to restore the etuis to Barton, and advise him to give up his suit, which was so disagreeable to his sister, against whom, however, he returned much irritated – Lady Griskin had assured him that Liddy's heart was pre-occupied; and immediately the idea of Wilson recurring to his imagination, his family-pride took the alarm – He denounced vengeance against the adventurer, and was disposed to be very peremptory with his sister; but I desired he would suppress his resentment, until I should have talked with her in private.

The poor girl, when I earnestly pressed her on this head, owned with a flood of tears, that Wilson had actually come to the Hot Well at Bristol, and even introduced himself into our lodgings as a Jew pedlar; but that nothing had passed betwixt them, further than her begging him to withdraw immediately, if he had any regard for her peace of mind: that he had disappeared accordingly, after having attempted to prevail upon my sister's maid, to deliver a letter; which, however, she refused to receive, though she had consented to carry a message, importing that he was a gentleman of a good family; and that, in a very little time, he would avow his passion in that character – She confessed, that although he had not kept his word in this particular, he was not yet altogether indifferent to her affection; but solemnly promised, she would never carry on any correspondence with him, or any other admirer, for the future, without the privity and approbation of her brother and me.

By this declaration, she made her own peace with Jery; but the hot-headed boy is more than ever incensed against Wilson, whom he now considers as an impostor, that harbours some infamous design upon the honour of his family — As for Barton, he was not a little mortified to find his present returned, and his addresses so unfavourably received; but he is not a man to be deeply affected by such disappointments; and I know not whether he is not as well pleased with being discarded by Liddy,

as he would have been with a permission to prosecute his
pretensions, at the risque of being every day exposed to the
revenge or machinations of Tabby, who is not to be slighted
with impunity. – I had not much time to moralize on these
occurrences; for the house was visited by a constable and his
gang, with a warrant from justice Buzzard,[4] to search the box
of Humphry Clinker, my footman, who was just apprehended
as a highwayman – This incident threw the whole family into
confusion. My sister scolded the constable for presuming to
enter the lodgings of a gentleman on such an errand, without
having first asked, and obtained permission; her maid was
frightened into fits, and Liddy shed tears of compassion for the
unfortunate Clinker, in whose box, however, nothing was
found to confirm the suspicion of robbery.

For my own part, I made no doubt of the fellow's being
mistaken for some other person, and I went directly to the
justice, in order to procure his discharge; but there I found the
matter much more serious than I expected – Poor Clinker stood
trembling at the bar, surrounded by thief-takers; and at a little
distance, a thick, squat fellow, a postilion, his accuser, who had
seized him on the street, and swore positively to his person,
that the said Clinker had, on the 15th day of March last, on
Blackheath, robbed a gentleman in a post-chaise, which he (the
postilion) drove – This deposition was sufficient to justify his
commitment; and he was sent accordingly to Clerkenwell
prison,[5] whither Jery accompanied him in the coach, in order
to recommend him properly to the keeper, that he may want
for no convenience which the place affords.

The spectators, who assembled to see this highwayman, were
sagacious enough to discern something very villainous in his
aspect; which (begging their pardon) is the very picture of
simplicity; and the justice himself put a very unfavourable construction upon some of his answers, which, he said, savoured
of the ambiguity and equivocation of an old offender; but, in
my opinion, it would have been more just and humane to
impute them to the confusion into which we may suppose a
poor country lad to be thrown on such an occasion. I am still
persuaded he is innocent; and, in this persuasion, I can do no

less than use my utmost endeavours that he may not be oppressed – I shall, to-morrow, send my nephew to wait on the gentleman who was robbed, and beg he will have the humanity to go and see the prisoner; that, in case he should find him quite different from the person of the highwayman, he may bear testimony in his behalf – Howsoever it may fare with Clinker, this cursed affair will be to me productive of intolerable chagrin – I have already caught a dreadful cold, by rushing into the open air from the justice's parlour, where I had been stewing in the crowd; and though I should not be laid up with the gout, as I believe I shall, I must stay at London for some weeks, till this poor devil comes to his trial at Rochester; so that, in all probability, my northern expedition is blown up.

If you can find any thing in your philosophical budget, to console me in the midst of these distresses and apprehensions, pray let it be communicated to

Your unfortunate friend,

LONDON, June 12.   MATT. BRAMBLE

To Sir WATKIN PHILLIPS, of Jesus college, Oxon.

DEAR WAT,

The farce is finished, and another piece of a graver cast brought upon the stage. — Our aunt made a desperate attack upon Barton, who had no other way of saving himself, but by leaving her in possession of the field, and avowing his pretensions to Liddy, by whom he has been rejected in his turn. – Lady Griskin acted as his advocate and agent on this occasion, with such zeal as embroiled her with Mrs Tabitha, and a high scene of altercation passed betwixt these two religionists, which might have come to action, had not my uncle interposed. They are however reconciled, in consequence of an event which hath involved us all in trouble and disquiet. You must know, the poor preacher, Humphry Clinker, is now exercising his ministry among the felons in Clerkenwell prison – A postilion having sworn a robbery against him, no bail could be taken, and he was committed to jail, notwithstanding all the remonstrances and interest my uncle could make in his behalf.

All things considered, the poor fellow cannot possibly be guilty, and yet, I believe, he runs some risque of being hanged. – Upon his examination, he answered with such hesitation and reserve as persuaded most of the people, who crowded the place, that he was really a knave, and the justice's remarks confirmed their opinion. Exclusive of my uncle and myself, there was only one person who seemed inclined to favour the culprit. – He was a young man, well dressed, and, from the manner in which he cross-examined the evidence, we took it for granted, that he was a student in one of the inns of court.[1] – He freely checked the justice for some uncharitable inferences he made to the prejudice of the prisoner, and even ventured to dispute with his worship on certain points of law.

My uncle, provoked at the unconnected and dubious answers of Clinker, who seemed in danger of falling a sacrifice to his own simplicity, exclaimed, 'In the name of God, if you are innocent, say so.' 'No (cried he) God forbid that I should call myself innocent, while my conscience is burthened with sin.' 'What then, you did commit this robbery?' resumed his master. 'No, sure (said he) blessed be the Lord, I'm free of that guilt.'

Here the justice interposed, observing, that the man seemed inclined to make a discovery by turning king's evidence,[2] and desired the clerk to take his confession; upon which Humphry declared, that he looked upon confession to be a popish fraud, invented by the whore of Babylon.[3] The Templar affirmed, that the poor fellow was *non compos*; and exhorted the justice to discharge him as a lunatic. — 'You know very well (added he) that the robbery in question was not committed by the prisoner.'

The thief-takers grinned at one another; and Mr Justice Buzzard replied with great emotion, 'Mr Martin, I desire you will mind your own business; I shall convince you one of these days that I understand mine.' In short, there was no remedy; the mittimus[4] was made out, and poor Clinker sent to prison in a hackney-coach, guarded by the constable, and accompanied by your humble servant. By the way, I was not a little surprised to hear this retainer to justice bid the prisoner to keep up his spirits, for that he did not at all doubt but that he would get off for a few weeks confinement – He said, his worship knew very well that Clinker was innocent of the fact, and that the real highwayman who robbed the chaise, was no other than that very individual Mr Martin, who had pleaded so strenuously for honest Humphry.

Confounded at this information, I asked, 'Why then is he suffered to go about at his liberty, and this poor innocent fellow treated as a malefactor?' 'We have exact intelligence of all Mr Martin's transactions (said he); but as yet there is not evidence sufficient for his conviction; and as for this young man, the justice could do no less than commit him, as the postilion swore point-blank to his identity.' 'So if this rascally postilion should persist in the falsity to which he is sworn (said I), this innocent lad may be brought to the gallows.'

The constable observed, that he would have time enough to prepare for his trial, and might prove an *alibi*; or, perhaps, Martin might be apprehended and convicted for another fact; in which case, he might be prevailed upon to take this affair upon himself; or, finally, if these chances should fail, and the evidence stand good against Clinker, the jury might recommend him to mercy, in consideration of his youth, especially if this should appear to be the first fact of which he had been guilty.

Humphry owned he could not pretend to recollect where he had been on the day when the robbery was committed, much less prove a circumstances of that kind so far back as six months, though he knew he had been sick of the fever and ague, which, however, did not prevent him from going about – then, turning up his eyes, he ejaculated, 'The Lord's will be done! if it be my fate to suffer, I hope I shall not disgrace the faith of which, though unworthy, I make profession.'

When I expressed my surprize that the accuser should persist in charging Clinker, without taking the least notice of the real robber who stood before him, and to whom, indeed, Humphry bore not the smallest resemblance; the constable (who was himself a thief-taker) gave me to understand, that Mr Martin was the best qualified for business of all the gentlemen on the road he had ever known; that he had always acted on his own bottom, without partner or correspondent, and never went to work but when he was cool and sober; that his courage and presence of mind never failed him; that his address was genteel, and his behaviour void of all cruelty and insolence; that he never encumbered himself with watches or trinkets, nor even with bank-notes, but always dealt for ready money, and that in the current coin of the kingdom; and that he could disguise himself and his horse in such a manner, that, after the action, it was impossible to recognize either the one or the other – 'This great man (said he) has reigned paramount in all the roads within fifty miles of London above fifteen months, and has done more business in that time, than all the rest of the profession put together; for those who pass through his hands are so delicately dealt with, that they have no desire to give him the least disturbance; but for all that, his race is almost run – he is now fluttering about justice, like a moth about a candle – there are so many lime-twigs[5] laid in his way, that I'll bet a cool hundred, he swings before Christmas.'

Shall I own to you, that this portrait, drawn by a ruffian, heightened by what I myself had observed in his deportment, has interested me warmly in the fate of poor Martin, whom nature seems to have intended for a useful and honourable member of that community upon which he now preys for subsistence? It seems, he lived some time as a clerk to a timber-merchant, whose daughter Martin having privately married, was discarded, and his wife turned out of doors. She did not long survive her marriage; and Martin, turning fortune-hunter, could not supply his occasions any other way, than by taking to the road, in which he has travelled hitherto with uncommon success. – He pays his respects regularly to Mr Justice Buzzard, the thief-catcher-general of this metropolis, and sometimes they smoke a pipe together very lovingly, when the conversation generally turns upon the nature of evidence. – The justice has given him fair warning to take care of himself, and he has received his caution in good part. – Hitherto he has baffled all the vigilance, art, and activity of Buzzard and his emissaries, with such conduct as would have done honour to the genius of a Cæsar or a Turenne;[6] but he has one weakness, which has proved fatal to all the heroes of his tribe, namely, an indiscreet devotion to the fair sex, and in all probability, he will be attacked on this defenceless quarter.

Be that as it may, I saw the body of poor Clinker consigned to the gaoler of Clerkenwell, to whose indulgence I recommended him so effectually, that he received him in the most hospitable manner, though there was a necessity for equipping him with a suit of irons, in which he made a very rueful appearance. The poor creature seemed as much affected by my uncle's kindness, as by his own misfortune. When I assured him, that nothing should be left undone for procuring his enlargement, and making his confinement easy in the mean time, he fell down on his knees, and kissing my hand, which he bathed with his tears, 'O 'squire! (cried he, sobbing) what shall I say? – I can't – no, I can't speak – my poor heart is bursting with gratitude to you and my dear – dear – generous – noble benefactor.'

I protest, the scene became so pathetic,[7] that I was fain to force myself away, and returned to my uncle, who sent me in the afternoon with a compliment to one Mr Mead, the person who had been robbed on Black-heath. As I did not find him at home, I left a message, in consequence of which he called at our lodgings this morning, and very humanely agreed to visit the prisoner. By this time, lady Griskin had come to make her formal compliments of condolance to Mrs Tabitha, on this domestic calamity; and that prudent maiden, whose passion was now cooled, thought proper to receive her ladyship so civilly, that a reconciliation immediately ensued. These two ladies resolved to comfort the poor prisoner in their own persons, and Mr Mead and I 'squired them to Clerkenwell, my uncle being detained at home by some slight complaints in his stomach and bowels.

The turnkey, who received us at Clerkenwell, looked remarkably sullen; and when we enquired for Clinker, 'I don't care, if the devil had him (said he); here has been nothing but canting and praying since the fellow entered the place. – Rabbit him![8] the tap will be ruined – we han't sold a cask of beer, nor a dozen of wine, since he paid his garnish[9] – the gentlemen get drunk with nothing but your damned religion. — For my part, I believe as how your man deals with the devil. – Two or three as bold hearts as ever took the air upon Hounslow,[10] have been blubbering all night; and if the fellow an't speedily removed by Habeas Corpus,[11] or otherwise, I'll be damn'd if there's a grain of true spirit left within these walls – we shan't have a soul to do credit to the place, or make his exit like a true born English-man – damn my eyes! there will be nothing but snivelling in the cart – we shall all die like so many psalm-singing weavers.'

In short, we found that Humphry was, at that very instant, haranguing the felons in the chapel; and that the gaoler's wife and daughter, together with my aunt's woman, Win Jenkins, and our house-maid, were among the audience, which we immediately joined. I never saw any thing so strongly pictur-esque as this congregation of felons clanking their chains, in the midst of whom stood orator Clinker, expatiating in a trans-port of fervor, on the torments of hell, denounced in scripture against evil-doers, comprehending murderers, robbers, thieves, and whore mongers. The variety of attention exhibited in the faces of those ragamuffins, formed a groupe that would not have disgraced the pencil of a Raphael.[12] In one, it denoted admiration; in another, doubt; in a third, disdain; in a fourth, contempt; in a fifth, terror; in a sixth, derision; and in a seventh, indignation. – As for Mrs Winifred Jenkins, she was in tears, overwhelmed with sorrow; but whether for her own sins, or the misfortune of Clinker, I cannot pretend to say. The other females seemed to listen with a mixture of wonder and devotion. The gaoler's wife declared he was a saint in trouble, saying, she wished from her heart there was such another good soul, like him, in every gaol in England.

Mr Mead, having earnestly surveyed the preacher, declared his appearance was so different from that of the person who robbed him on Black-heath, that he could freely make oath he was not the man: but Humphry himself was by this time pretty well rid of all apprehensions of being hanged; for he had been the night before solemnly tried and acquitted by his fellow prisoners, some of whom he had already converted to methodism. He now made proper acknowledgments for the

honour of our visit, and was permitted to kiss the hands of the
ladies, who assured him, he might depend upon their friendship
and protection. Lady Griskin, in her great zeal, exhorted his
fellow-prisoners to profit by the precious opportunity of having
such a saint in bonds among them, and turn over a new leaf for
the benefit of their poor souls; and, that her admonition might
have the greater effect, she reinforced it with her bounty.

While she and Mrs Tabby returned in the coach with the two
maid-servants, I waited on Mr Mead to the house of justice
Buzzard, who, having heard his declaration, said his oath could
be of no use at present, but that he would be a material evidence
for the prisoner at his trial; so that there seems to be no remedy
but patience for poor Clinker; and, indeed, the same virtue, or
medicine, will be necessary for us all, the squire in particular,
who had set his heart upon his excursion to the northward.

While we were visiting honest Humphry in Clerkenwell
prison, my uncle received a much more extraordinary visit at
his own lodgings. Mr Martin, of whom I have made such
honourable mention, desired permission to pay him his
respects, and was admitted accordingly. He told him, that having observed him, at Mr Buzzard's, a good deal disturbed by
what had happened to his servant, he had come to assure him
he had nothing to apprehend for Clinker's life; for, if it was
possible that any jury could find him guilty upon such evidence,
he, Martin himself, would produce in court a person, whose
deposition would bring him off clear as the sun at noon. – Sure,
the fellow would not be so romantic[13] as to take the robbery
upon himself! – He said, the postilion was an infamous fellow,
who had been a dabbler in the same profession, and saved his
life at the Old Bailey by impeaching his companions; that being
now reduced to great poverty, he had made this desperate push,
to swear away the life of an innocent man, in hopes of having
the reward upon his conviction; but that he would find himself
miserably disappointed, for the justice and his myrmidons[14]
were determined to admit of no interloper in this branch of
business; and that he did not at all doubt but that they would
find matter enough to shop the evidence[15] himself before the
next gaol-delivery. He affirmed, that all these circumstances

were well known to the justice; and that his severity to Clinker was no other than a hint to his master to make him a present in private, as an acknowledgment of his candour and humanity.

This hint, however, was so unpalatable to Mr Bramble, that he declared, with great warmth, he would rather confine himself for life to London, which he detested, than be at liberty to leave it tomorrow, in consequence of encouraging corruption in a magistrate. Hearing, however, how favourable Mr Mead's report had been for the prisoner, he is resolved to take the advice of counsel in what manner to proceed for his immediate enlargement. I make no doubt, but that in a day or two this troublesome business may be discussed; and in this hope we are preparing for our journey. If our endeavours do not miscarry, we shall have taken the field before you hear again from

Yours,

LONDON, June 11.   J. MELFORD

To Dr LEWIS.

Thank Heaven! dear Lewis, the clouds are dispersed, and I have now the clearest prospect of my summer campaign, which, I hope, I shall be able to begin to-morrow. I took the advice of counsel with respect to the case of Clinker, in whose favour a lucky incident has intervened. The fellow who accused him, has had his own battery turned upon himself. – Two days ago he was apprehended for a robbery on the highway, and committed, on the evidence of an accomplice. Clinker, having moved for a writ of *habeas corpus*, was brought before the lord chief justice,[1] who, in consequence of an affidavit of the gentleman who had been robbed, importing that the said Clinker was not the person who stopped him on the highway, as well as in consideration of the postilion's character and present circumstances, was pleased to order, that my servant should be admitted to bail, and he has been discharged accordingly, to the unspeakable satisfaction of our whole family, to which he has recommended himself in an extraordinary manner, not only by his obliging

deportment, but by his talents of preaching, praying, and singing psalms, which he has exercised with such effect, that even
Tabby respects him as a chosen vessel. If there was any thing
like affectation or hypocrisy in this excess of religion, I would
not keep him in my service; but, so far as I can observe, the
fellow's character is downright simplicity, warmed with a kind
of enthusiasm, which renders him very susceptible of gratitude
and attachment to his benefactors.

As he is an excellent horseman, and understands farriery, I
have bought a stout gelding for his use, that he may attend us
on the road, and have an eye to our cattle, in case the coachman
should not mind his business. My nephew, who is to ride his
own saddle-horse, has taken, upon trial, a servant just come
from abroad with his former master, Sir William Strollop, who
vouches for his honesty. The fellow, whose name is Dutton,
seems to be a petit maitre. – He has got a smattering of French,
bows, and grins, and shrugs, and takes snuff *a la mode de
France*, but values himself chiefly upon his skill and dexterity
in hair-dressing. – If I am not much deceived by appearance, he
is, in all respects, the very contrast of Humphry Clinker.

My sister has made up matters with lady Griskin; though, I
must own, I should not have been sorry to see that connexion
entirely destroyed: but Tabby is not of a disposition to forgive
Barton, who, I understand, is gone to his seat in Berkshire for
the summer season. I cannot help suspecting, that in the treaty
of peace, which has been lately ratified betwixt those two
females, it is stipulated, that her ladyship shall use her best
endeavours to provide an agreeable help-mate for our sister
Tabitha, who seems to be quite desperate in her matrimonial
designs. Perhaps, the match-maker is to have a valuable consideration in the way of brokerage, which she will most certainly deserve, if she can find any man in his senses, who will
yoke with Mrs Bramble from motives of affection or interest.

I find my spirits and my health affect each other reciprocally
– that is to say, every thing that discomposes my mind, produces
a correspondent disorder in my body; and my bodily complaints
are remarkably mitigated by those considerations that dissipate
the clouds of mental chagrin. – The imprisonment of Clinker

brought on those symptoms which I mentioned in my last, and now they are vanished at his discharge. – It must be owned, indeed, I took some of the tincture of ginseng, prepared according to your prescription, and found it exceedingly grateful to the stomach; but the pain and sickness continued to return, after short intervals, till the anxiety of my mind was entirely removed, and then I found myself perfectly at ease. We have had fair weather these ten days, to the astonishment of the Londoners, who think it portentous. If you enjoy the same indulgence in Wales, I hope Barns has got my hay made, and safe cocked by this time. As we shall be in motion for some weeks, I cannot expect to hear from you as usual; but I shall continue to write from every place at which we make any halt, that you may know our track, in case it should be necessary to communicate any thing to

Your assured friend,

LONDON, June 14.   MATT. BRAMBLE

To Mrs MARY JONES, at Brambleton-hall, &c.

DEAR MARY,

Having the occasion of my cousin Jenkins of Aberga'ny, I send you, as a token, a turkey-shell comb, a kiple of yards of green ribbon, and a sarment upon the nothingness of good works, which was preached in the Tabernacle; and you will also receive a horn-buck[1] for Saul, whereby she may learn her letters; for I'm much consarned about the state of her poor sole – and what are all the pursuits of this life to the consarns of that immortal part? – What is life but a veil of affliction? O Mary! the whole family have been in such a constipation! – Mr Clinker has been in trouble, but the gates of hell have not been able to prevail again him.[2] — His virtue is like poor gould, seven times tried in the fire. He was tuck up for a rubbery, and had before gustass Busshard, who made his mittamouse; and the pore youth was sent to prison upon the false oaf of a willian, that wanted to sware his life away for the looker of cain.[3]

The 'squire did all in his power, but could not prevent his being put in chains, and confined among common manufactors, where he stood like an innocent sheep in the midst of wolves and tygers.[4] Lord knows what mought have happened to this pyehouse young man, if master had not applied to Apias Korkus, who lives with the ould bailiff, and is, they say, five hundred years old (God bless us!), and a congeror: but, if he be, sure I am he don't deal with the devil, otherwise he couldn't have fought out Mr Clinker, as he did, in spite of stone walls, iron bolts, and double locks, that flew open at his command;[5] for ould Scratch[6] has not a greater enemy upon hearth than Mr Clinker, who is, indeed, a very powerful labourer in the Lord's vineyard. I do no more than yuse the words of my good lady, who has got the infectual calling; and, I trust, that even myself, though unworthy, shall find grease to be excepted. — Miss Liddy has been touch'd to the quick, but is a little timorsome: howsomever, I make no doubt, but she, and all of us, will be brought, by the endeavours of Mr Clinker, to produce blessed fruit of generation and repentance.[7] — As for master and the young 'squire, they have as yet had narro glimpse of the new light. — I doubt as how their harts are hardened by worldly wisdom, which, as the pyebill saith, is foolishness in the sight of God.[8]

O Mary Jones, pray without seizing[9] for grease to prepare you for the operations of this wonderful instrument, which, I hope, will be exorcised this winter upon you and others at Brambleton-hall. — To-morrow, we are to set out in a cox and four for Yorkshire; and, I believe, we shall travel that way far, and far, and farther than I can tell; but I shan't go so far as to forget my friends; and Mary Jones will always be remembered as one of them by her

Humble sarvant,
LONDON, June 14.   WIN. JENKINS

To Mrs GWYLLIM, house-keeper at Brambleton-hall.

MRS GWYLLIM,

I can't help thinking it very strange, that I never had an answer to the letter I wrote you some weeks ago from Bath, concerning the sour bear, the gander, and the maids eating butter, which I won't allow to be wasted. — We are now going upon a long journey to the north, whereby I desire you will redouble your care and circumflexion, that the family may be well managed in our absence; for, you know, you must render account, not only to your earthly master, but also to him that is above; and if you are found a good and faithful sarvant,[1] great will be your reward in haven.[2] I hope there will be twenty stun of cheese ready for market by the time I get huom, and as much owl spun, as will make half a dozen pair of blankets; and that the savings of the butter-milk will fetch me a good penny before Martinmass,[3] as the two pigs are to be fed for baking with bitchmast[4] and acrons.

I wrote to doctor Lews for the same porpuss, but he never had the good manners to take the least notice of my letter; for which reason, I shall never favour him with another, though he beshits me on his bended knees. You will do well to keep a watchful eye over the hind Villiams, who is one of his amissories, and, I believe, no better than he should be at bottom. God forbid that I should lack christian charity; but charity begins at huom, and sure nothing can be a more charitable work than to rid the family of such vermine. I do suppose, that the bindled cow has been had to the parson's bull, that old Moll has had another litter of pigs, and that Dick is become a mighty mouser. Pray order every thing for the best, and be frugal, and keep the maids to their labour – If I had a private opportunity, I would send them some hymns to sing instead of profane ballads; but, as I can't, they and you must be contented with the prayers of

Your assured friend,

T. BRAMBLE

To Sir WATKIN PHILLIPS, Bart. of Jesus college, Oxon.

DEAR PHILLIPS,

The very day after I wrote my last, Clinker was set at liberty – As Martin had foretold, the accuser was himself committed for a robbery, upon unquestionable evidence. He had been for some time in the snares of the thief-taking society; who, resenting his presumption in attempting to incroach upon their monopoly of impeachment, had him taken up and committed to Newgate, on the deposition of an accomplice, who has been admitted as evidence for the king. The postilion being upon record as an old offender, the chief justice made no scruple of admitting Clinker to bail, when he perused the affidavit of Mr Mead, importing that the said Clinker was not the person that robbed him on Black-heath; and honest Humphry was discharged – When he came home, he expressed great eagerness to pay his respects to his master, and here his elocution failed him, but his silence was pathetic;[1] he fell down at his feet and embraced his knees, shedding a flood of tears, which my uncle did not see without emotion – He took snuff in some confusion; and, putting his hand in his pocket, gave him his blessing in something more substantial than words – 'Clinker (said he), I am so well convinced, both of your honesty and courage, that I am resolved to make you my life-guardman on the highway.'

He was accordingly provided with a case of pistols, and a carbine[2] to be flung a-cross his shoulders; and every other preparation being made, we set out last Thursday, at seven in the morning; my uncle, with the three women in the coach; Humphry, well mounted on a black gelding bought for his use; myself a-horseback, attended by my new valet, Mr Dutton, an exceeding coxcomb, fresh from his travels, whom I have taken upon trial – The fellow wears a solitaire,[3] uses paint,[4] and takes rappee[5] with all the grimace of a French marquis. At present, however, he is in riding-dress, jack-boots[6] leather breeches, a scarlet waistcoat, with gold binding, a laced hat, a hanger, a French posting-whip in his hand, and his hair *en queue*.[7]

Before we had gone nine miles, my horse lost one of his

shoes; so that I was obliged to stop at Barnet to have another, while the coach proceeded at an easy pace over the common. About a mile short of Hatfield, the postilions, stopping the carriage, gave notice to Clinker that there were two suspicious fellows a-horseback, at the end of a lane, who seemed waiting to attack the coach. Humphry forthwith apprised my uncle, declaring he would stand by him to the last drop of his blood; and unflinging his carbine, prepared for action. The 'squire had pistols in the pockets of the coach, and resolved to make use of them directly; but he was effectually prevented by his female companions, who flung themselves about his neck, and screamed in concert – At that instant, who should come up at a hand-gallop, but Martin, the highway-man, who, advancing to the coach, begged the ladies would compose themselves for a moment; then, desiring Clinker to follow him to the charge, he pulled a pistol out of his bosom, and they rode up together to give battle to the rogues, who, having fired at a great distance, fled a-cross the common. They were in pursuit of the fugitives when I came up, not a little alarmed at the shrieks in the coach, where I found my uncle in a violent rage, without his periwig, struggling to disentangle himself from Tabby and the other two, and swearing with great vociferation. Before I had time to interpose, Martin and Clinker returned from the pursuit, and the former payed his compliments with great politeness, giving us to understand, that the fellows had scampered off, and that he believed they were a couple of raw 'prentices from London. He commended Clinker for his courage, and said, if we would give him leave, he would have the honour to accompany us as far as Stevenage, where he had some business.

The 'squire, having recollected and adjusted himself, was the first to laugh at his own situation: but it was not without difficulty, that Tabby's arms could be untwisted from his neck; Liddy's teeth chattered, and Jenkins was threatened with a fit as usual. I had communicated to my uncle the character of Martin, as it was described by the constable, and he was much struck with its singularity – He could not suppose the fellow had any design on our company, which was so numerous and well armed; he therefore thanked him, for the service he had just done them, said he would be glad of his company, and asked him to dine with us at Hatfield. This invitation might not have been agreeable to the ladies, had they known the real profession of our guest, but this was a secret to all, except my uncle and myself – Mrs Tabitha, however, would by no means consent to proceed with a case of loaded pistols in the coach, and they were forthwith discharged in complaisance to her and the rest of the women.

Being gratified in this particular, she became remarkably good-humoured, and at dinner behaved in the most affable manner to Mr Martin, with whose polite address and agreeable conversation she seemed to be much taken. After dinner, the landlord accosting me in the yard, asked with a significant look, if the gentleman that rode the sorrel belonged to our company? – I understand his meaning, but answered *no*; that he had come up with us on the common, and helped us to drive away two fellows, that looked like highwaymen – He nodded three times distinctly, as much as to say, he knows his cue. Then he inquired, if one of those men was mounted on a bay mare, and the other on a chestnut gelding with a white streak down his forehead? and being answered in the affirmative, he assured me they had robbed three post-chaises this very morning – I inquired, in my turn, if Mr Martin was of his acquaintance; and, nodding thrice again, he answered, that *he had seen the gentleman*.

Before we left Hatfield, my uncle, fixing his eyes on Martin with such expression as is more easily conceived than described, asked, if he often travelled that road? and he replied with a look which denoted his understanding the question, that he very seldom did business in that part of the country. In a word, this adventurer favoured us with his company to the neighbourhood of Stevenage, where he took his leave of the coach and me, in very polite terms, and turned off upon a cross-road, that led to a village on the left – At supper, Mrs Tabby was very full in the praise of Mr Martin's good-sense and good-breeding, and seemed to regret that she had not a further opportunity to make some experiment upon his affection. In the morning, my uncle was not a little surprised to receive, from the waiter a billet couched in these words –

Sir,

I could easily perceive from your looks, when I had the honour to converse with you at Hatfield, that my character is not unknown to you; and, I dare say you won't think it strange, that I should be glad to change my present way of life, for any other honest occupation, let it be ever so humble, that will afford me bread in moderation, and sleep in safety – Perhaps you may think I flatter, when I say, that from the moment I was witness to your generous concern in the cause of your servant, I conceived a particular esteem and veneration for your person; and yet what I say is true. I should think myself happy, if I could be admitted into your protection and service, as house-steward, clerk, butler, or bailiff, for either of which places I think myself tolerably well qualified; and, sure I am, I should not be found deficient in gratitude and fidelity – At the same time, I am very sensible how much you must deviate from the common maxims of discretion, even in putting my professions to the trial; but I don't look upon you as a person that thinks in the ordinary stile; and the delicacy of my situation, will, I know, justify this address to a heart warmed with beneficence and compassion – Understanding you are going pretty far north, I shall take an opportunity to throw myself in your way again, before you reach the borders of Scotland; and, I hope, by that time, you will have taken into consideration, the truly distressful case of,

honoured sir,

your very humble,

and devoted servant,

Edward Martin

The 'squire, having perused this letter, put it into my hand, without saying a syllable; and when I had read it we looked at each other in silence. From a certain sparkling in his eyes, I discovered there was more in his heart, than he cared to express with his tongue, in favour of poor Martin; and this was precisely my own feeling, which he did not fail to discern, by the same means of communication – 'What shall we do (said he) to save this poor sinner from the gallows, and make him a useful member of the commonwealth; and yet the proverb says, Save a thief from the gallows, and he'll cut your throat.' I told him I really believed Martin was capable of giving the proverb the lie; and that I should heartily concur in any step he might take in favour of his solicitation. We mutually resolved to deliberate upon the subject, and, in the mean time, proceeded on our journey. The roads, having been broken up by the heavy rains in the spring, were so rough, that although we travelled very slowly, the jolting occasioned such pain to my uncle, that he was become exceedingly peevish when we arrived at this place, which lies about eight miles from the postroad, between Wetherby and Boroughbridge.

Harrigate-water,[8] so celebrated for its efficacy in the scurvy and other distempers, is supplied from a copious spring, in the hollow of a wild common, round which, a good many houses have been built for the convenience of the drinkers, though few of them are inhabited. Most of the company lodge at some distance, in five separate inns,[9] situated in different parts of the commons, from whence they go every morning to the well, in their own carriages. The lodgers of each inn form a distinct society, that eat together; and there is a commodious public room, where they breakfast in disabille, at separate tables, from eight o'clock till eleven, as they chance or chuse to come in – Here also they drink tea in the afternoon, and play at cards or dance in the evening. One custom, however, prevails, which I looked upon as a solecism[10] in politeness – The ladies treat with tea in their turns; and even girls of sixteen are not exempted from this shameful imposition — There is a public ball by subscription every night at one of the houses, to which all the company from the others are admitted by tickets; and, indeed, Harrigate treads upon the heels of Bath, in the articles of gaiety and dissipation – with this difference, however, that here we are more sociable and familiar. One of the inns is already full up to the very garrets, having no less than fifty lodgers, and as many servants. Our family does not exceed thirty-six; and I should be sorry to see the number augmented, as our accommodations won't admit of much increase.

At present, the company is more agreeable than one could expect from an accidental assemblage of persons, who are utter

strangers to one another – There seems to be a general disposition among us to maintain good-fellowship, and promote the
purposes of humanity, in favour of those who come hither on
the score of health. I see several faces which we left at Bath,
although the majority are of the Northern counties, and many
come from Scotland for the benefit of these waters – In such a
variety, there must be some originals, among whom Mrs
Tabitha Bramble is not the most inconsiderable – No place
where there is such an intercourse between the sexes, can be
disagreeable to a lady of her views and temperament – She has
had some warm disputes at table, with a lame parson from
Northumberland, on the new birth, and the insignificance of
moral virtue; and her arguments have been reinforced by an
old Scotch lawyer, in a tye periwig, who, though he has lost his
teeth, and the use of his limbs, can still wag his tongue with
great volubility. He has paid her such fulsome compliments,
upon her piety and learning, as seem to have won her heart;
and she, in her turn, treats him with such attention as indicates
a design upon his person; but, by all accounts, he is too much
of a fox to be inveigled into any snare that she can lay for his
affection.

We do not propose to stay long at Harrigate, though, at
present, it is our headquarters, from whence we shall make
some excursions, to visit two or three of our rich relations, who
are settled in this country. – Pray, remember me to all our
friends of Jesus, and allow me to be still.

Yours affectionately

HARRIGATE, June 23.   J. MELFORD

To Dr LEWIS.

DEAR DOCTOR,

Considering the tax we pay for turnpikes, the roads of this
county constitute a most intolerable grievance. Between
Newark and Weatherby, I have suffered more from jolting and
swinging than ever I felt in the whole course of my life, although

the carriage is remarkably commodious and well hung, and the postilions were very careful in driving. I am now safely housed at the New Inn,[1] at Harrigate, whither I came to satisfy my curiosity, rather than with any view of advantage to my health; and, truly, after having considered all the parts and particulars of the place, I cannot account for the concourse of people one finds here, upon any other principle but that of caprice, which seems to be the character of our nation.

Harrigate is a wild common, bare and bleak, without tree or shrub, or the least signs of cultivation; and the people who come to drink the water, are crowded together in paltry inns, where the few tolerable rooms are monopolized by the friends and favourites of the house, and all the rest of the lodgers are obliged to put up with dirty holes, where there is neither space, air, nor convenience. My apartment is about ten feet square; and when the folding bed is down, there is just room sufficient to pass between it and the fire. One might expect, indeed, that there would be no occasion for a fire at Midsummer; but here the climate is so backward, that an ash tree, which our landlord has planted before my window, is just beginning to put forth its leaves; and I am fain to have my bed warmed every night.

As for the water, which is said to have effected so many surprising cures, I have drank it once, and the first draught has cured me of all desire to repeat the medicine. – Some people say it smells of rotten eggs, and others compare it to the scourings of a foul gun. – It is generally supposed to be strongly impregnated with sulphur; and Dr Shaw, in his book upon mineral water,[2] says, he has seen flakes of sulphur floating in the well – *Pace tanti viri;*[3] I, for my part, have never observed any thing like sulphur, either in or about the well, neither do I find that any brimstone has ever been extracted from the water. As for the smell, if I may be allowed to judge from my own organs, it is exactly that of bilge-water; and the saline taste of it seems to declare that it is nothing else than salt water putrified in the bowels of the earth. I was obliged to hold my nose with one hand, while I advanced the glass to my mouth with the other; and after I had made shift to swallow it, my stomach could hardly retain what it had received. – The only effects it produced were sickness, griping, and insurmountable disgust. – I can hardly mention it without puking. – The world is strangely misled by the affectation of singularity. I cannot help suspecting, that this water owes its reputation in a great measure to its being so strikingly offensive. – On the same kind of analogy, a German doctor[4] has introduced hemlock and other poisons, as specifics, into the *materia medica*. – I am persuaded, that all the cures ascribed to the Harrigate water, would have been as efficaciously, and infinitely more agreeably performed, by the internal and external use of sea-water.[5] Sure I am, this last is much less nauseous to the taste and smell, and much more gentle in its operation as a purge, as well as more extensive in its medical qualities.

Two days ago we went across the country to visit 'squire Burdock,[6] who married a first cousin of my father, an heiress, who brought him an estate of a thousand a-year. This gentleman is a declared opponent of the ministry in parliament; and having an opulent fortune, piques himself upon living in the country, and maintaining *old English hospitality* – By the bye, this is a phrase very much used by the English themselves both in words and writing; but I never heard of it out of the island, except by way of irony and sarcasm. What the hospitality of our forefathers has been I should be glad to see recorded, rather in the memoirs of strangers who have visited our country, and were the proper objects and judges of such hospitality, than in the discourse and lucubrations of the modern English, who seem to describe it from theory and conjecture. Certain it is, we are generally looked upon by foreigners, as a people totally destitute of this virtue; and I never was in any country abroad, where I did not meet with persons of distinction, who complained of having been inhospitably used in Great Britain. A gentleman of France, Italy, or Germany, who has entertained and lodged an Englishman at his house, when he afterwards meets with his guest at London, is asked to dinner at the Saracen's-head, the Turk's-head, the Boar's-head, or the Bear, eats raw beef and butter, drinks execrable port, and is allowed to pay his share of the reckoning.

But to return from this digression, which my feeling for the honour of my country obliged me to make — our Yorkshire cousin has been a mighty fox-hunter *before the Lord*;[7] but now he is too fat and unwieldy to leap ditches and five-bar gates; nevertheless, he still keeps a pack of hounds, which are well exercised; and his huntsman every night entertains him with the adventures of the day's chace, which he recites in a tone and terms that are extremely curious and significant. In the mean time, his broad brawn is scratched by one of his grooms. — This fellow, it seems, having no inclination to curry any beast out of the stable, was at great pains to scollop his nails in such a manner that the blood followed at every stroke. – He was in hopes that he would be dismissed from this disagreeable office, but the event turned out contrary to his expectation. – His master declared he was the best scratcher in the family; and now he will not suffer any other servant to draw a nail upon his carcase.

The 'squire's lady is very proud, without being stiff or in-accessible. — She receives even her inferiors in point of fortune with a kind of arrogant civility; but then she thinks she has a right to treat them with the most ungracious freedoms of speech, and never fails to let them know she is sensible of her own superior affluence – In a word, she speaks well of no living soul, and has not one single friend in the world. Her husband hates her mortally; but, although the brute is sometimes so very powerful in him that he will have his own way, he generally truckles to her dominion, and dreads, like a school-boy, the lash of her tongue. On the other hand, she is afraid of provoking him too far, lest he should make some desperate effort to shake off her yoke. – She, therefore, acquiesces in the proofs he daily gives of his attachment to the liberty of an English freeholder, by saying and doing, at his own table, whatever gratifies the brutality of his disposition, or contributes to the ease of his person. The house, though large, is neither elegant nor comfort-able. – It looks like a great inn, crowded with travellers, who dine at the landlord's ordinary, where there is a great profusion of victuals and drink, but mine host seems to be misplaced; and I would rather dine upon filberts with a hermit, than feed upon venison with a hog. The footmen might be aptly compared to the waiters of a tavern, if they were more serviceable and less rapacious; but they are generally insolent and inattentive, and so greedy, that, I think, I can dine better, and for less expence, at the Star and Garter in Pall mall, than at our cousin's castle in Yorkshire. The 'squire is not only accommodated with a wife, but he is also blessed with an only son, about two and twenty, just returned from Italy, a complete fidler and *dillettante*;[8] and he slips no opportunity of manifesting the most perfect contempt for his own father.

When we arrived, there was a family of foreigners at the house, on a visit to this virtuoso, with whom they had been acquainted at the Spa; it was the count de Melville, with his lady,[9] on their way to Scotland. Mr Burdock had met with an accident, in consequence of which both the count and I would have retired but the young gentleman and his mother insisted upon our staying dinner; and their serenity seemed to be so little ruffled by what had happened, that we complied with their invitation. The 'squire had been brought home over night in his post-chaise, so terribly belaboured about the pate, that he seemed to be in a state of stupefaction, and had ever since remained speechless. A country apothecary, called Grieve, who lived in a neighbouring village, having been called to his assistance, had let him blood, and applied a poultice to his head, declaring, that he had no fever, nor any other bad symptom but the loss of speech, if he really had lost that faculty. But the young 'squire said this practitioner was an *ignorantaccio*, that there was a fracture in the *cranium*, and that there was a necessity for having him trepanned without loss of time. His mother, espousing this opinion, had sent an express to York for a surgeon to perform the operation, and he was already come with his 'prentice and instruments. Having examined the patient's head, he began to prepare his dressings; though Grieve still retained his first opinion that there was no fracture, and was the more confirmed in it as the 'squire had passed the night in profound sleep, uninterrupted by any catching or convulsion. The York surgeon said he could not tell whether there was a fracture, until he should take off the scalp; but, at any rate, the operation might be of service in giving vent to any blood that

might be extravasated, either above or below the *dura mater*.
The lady and her son were clear for trying the experiment; and
Grieve was dismissed with some marks of contempt, which,
perhaps, he owed to the plainness of his appearance. He seemed
to be about the middle age, wore his own black hair without
any sort of dressing; by his garb, one would have taken him for
a quaker, but he had none of the stiffness of that sect, on the
contrary he was very submissive, respectful, and remarkably
taciturn.

Leaving the ladies in an apartment by themselves, we
adjourned to the patient's chamber, where the dressings and
instruments were displayed in order upon a pewter dish. The
operator, laying aside his coat and periwig, equipped himself
with a night-cap, apron, and sleeves, while his 'prentice and
footman, seizing the 'squire's head, began to place it in a proper
posture. — But mark what followed. – The patient, bolting
upright in the bed, collared each of these assistants with the
grasp of Hercules, exclaiming, in a bellowing tone, 'I ha'n't
lived so long in Yorkshire to be trepanned by such vermin as
you;' and leaping on the floor, put on his breeches quietly, to
the astonishment of us all. The Surgeon still insisted upon the
operation, alleging it was now plain that the brain was injured,
and desiring the servants put him into bed again; but nobody
would venture to execute his orders, or even to interpose: when
the 'squire turned him and his assistants out of doors, and
threw his apparatus out at the window. Having thus asserted
his prerogative, and put on his cloaths with the help of a valet,
the count, with my nephew and me, were introduced by his
son, and received with his usual stile of rustic civility; then
turning to signor Macaroni,[10] with a sarcastic grin, 'I tell thee
what, Dick (said he), a man's scull is not to be bored every time
his head is broken; and I'll convince thee and thy mother, that
I know as many tricks as e'er an old fox in the West Riding.'

We afterwards understood he had quarrelled at a public
house with an exciseman, whom he challenged to a bout at
single stick, in which he had been worsted; and that the shame
of this defeat had tied up his tongue. As for madam, she had
shewn no concern for his disaster, and now heard of his recov-

ery without emotion – She had taken some little notice of my sister and niece, though rather with a view to indulge her own petulance, than out of any sentiment of regard to our family. – She said Liddy was a fright, and ordered her woman to adjust her head before dinner; but she would not meddle with Tabby, whose spirit, she soon perceived, was not to be irritated with impunity. At table, she acknowledged me so far as to say she had heard of my father; though she hinted, that he had dis-obliged her family by making a poor match in Wales. She was disagreeably familiar in her enquiries about our circumstances; and asked, if I intended to bring up my nephew to the law. I told her, that, as he had an independent fortune, he should follow no profession but that of a country gentleman; and that I was not without hopes of procuring for him a seat in parlia-ment — 'Pray cousin (said she), what may his fortune be?' When I answered, that, with what I should be able to give him, he would have better than two thousand a year, she replied, with a disdainful toss of her head, that it would be impossible for him to preserve his independence on such a paultry provision.

Not a little nettled at this arrogant remark, I told her, I had the honour to sit in parliament with her father, when he had little more than half that income; and I believed there was not a more independent and incorruptible member in the house. 'Ay; but times are changed (cried the 'squire) – Country gentle-men now-a-days live after another fashion. – My table alone stands me in a cool thousand a quarter, though I raise my own stock, import my own liquors, and have every thing at the first hand. – True it is, I keep open house, and receive all comers, for the honour of Old England.' 'If that be the case (said I), 'tis a wonder you can maintain it at so small an expence; but every private gentleman is not expected to keep a *caravanserai*[11] for the accommodation of travellers: indeed, if every individual lived in the same stile, you would not have such a number of guests at your table, of consequence your hospitality would not shine so bright for the glory of the West Riding.' The young 'squire, tickled by this ironical observation, exclaimed, 'O *che burla!*'[12] – his mother eyed me in silence with a supercilious air; and the father of the feast, taking a bumper of October,[13] 'My

service to you, cousin Bramble (said he), I have always heard
there was something keen and biting in the air of the Welch
mountains.'

I was much pleased with the count de Melville, who is sensible, easy, and polite; and the countess is the most amiable
woman I ever beheld. In the afternoon they took leave of their
entertainers, and the young gentleman, mounting his horse,
undertook to conduct their coach through the park, while one
of their servants rode round to give notice to the rest, whom
they had left at a public house on the road. The moment their
backs were turned, the censorious dæmon took possession of
our Yorkshire landlady and our sister Tabitha — The former
observed, that the countess was a good sort of a body, but
totally ignorant of good breeding, consequently aukward in her
address. The squire said, he did not pretend to the breeding of
any thing but colts; but that the jade would be very handsome,
if she was a little more in flesh. 'Handsome! (cried Tabby) she
has indeed a pair of black eyes without any meaning; but then
there is not a good feature in her face.' 'I know not what you
call good features in Wales (replied our landlord); but they'll
pass in Yorkshire.' Then turning to Liddy, he added, 'What say
you, my pretty Redstreak?[14] – what is your opinion of the
countess?' 'I think (cried Liddy, with great emotion), she's an
angel.' Tabby chid her for talking with such freedom in company; and the lady of the house said, in a contemptuous tone,
she supposed miss had been brought up at some country
boarding-school.

Our conversation was suddenly interrupted by the young
gentleman, who galloped into the yard all aghast, exclaiming,
that the coach was attacked by a great number of highwaymen.
My nephew and I rushed out, found his own and his servant's
horse ready saddled in the stable, with pistols in the caps —
We mounted instantly, ordering Clinker and Dutton to follow
with all possible expedition; but notwithstanding all the speed
we could make, the action was over before we arrived, and the
count with his lady, safe lodged at the house of Grieve, who
had signalized himself in a very remarkable manner on this
occasion. At the turning of a lane, that led to the village where

the count's servants remained, a couple of robbers a-horseback suddenly appeared, with their pistols advanced: one kept the coachman in awe, and the other demanded the count's money, while the young 'squire went off at full speed, without ever casting a look behind. The count desiring the thief to withdraw his pistol, as the lady was in great terror, delivered his purse without making the least resistance; but not satisfied with this booty, which was pretty considerable, the rascal insisted upon rifling her of her ear-rings and necklace, and the countess screamed with affright. Her husband, exasperated at the violence with which she was threatened, wrested the pistol out of the fellow's hand, and turning it upon him, snapped it in his face; but the robber knowing there was no charge in it, drew another from his bosom, and in all probability would have killed him on the spot, had not his life been saved by a wonderful interposition. Grieve, the apothecary, chancing to pass that very instant, ran up to the coach, and with a crab-stick, which was all the weapon he had, brought the fellow to the ground with the first blow; then seizing his pistol, presented it at his colleague, who fired his piece at random, and fled without further opposition. The other was secured by the assistance of the count and the coachman; and his legs being tied under the belly of his own horse, Grieve conducted him to the village, whither also the carriage proceeded. It was with great difficulty the countess could be kept from swooning; but at last she was happily conveyed to the house of the apothecary, who went into the shop to prepare some drops for her, while his wife and daughter administered to her in another apartment.

I found the count standing in the kitchen with the parson of the parish, and expressing much impatience to see his protector, whom as yet he had scarce found time to thank for the essential service he had done him and the countess. – The daughter passing at the same time with a glass of water, monsieur de Melville could not help taking notice of her figure, which was strikingly engaging. – 'Ay (said the parson), she is the prettiest girl, and the best girl in all my parish: and if I could give my son an estate of ten thousand a year, he should have my consent to lay it at her feet. If Mr Grieve had been as solicitous about getting money, as he has been in performing all the duties of a primitive Christian, Fy would not have hung so long upon his hands.' 'What is her name?' said I. 'Sixteen years ago (answered the vicar) I christened her by the names of Seraphina Melvilia.' 'Ha! what! how! (cried the count eagerly) sure, you said Seraphina Melvilia.' 'I did (said he); Mr Grieve told me those were the names of two noble persons abroad, to whom he had been obliged for more than life.'

The count, without speaking another syllable, rushed into the parlour, crying, 'This is your god-daughter, my dear.' Mrs Grieve, then seizing the countess by the hand, exclaimed with great agitation, 'O madam! – O sir! — I am – I am your poor Elinor. — This is my Seraphina Melvilia — O child! these are the count and countess of Melville, the generous – the glorious benefactors of thy once unhappy parents.'

The countess rising from her seat threw her arms about the neck of the amiable Seraphina, and clasped her to her breast with great tenderness, while she herself was embraced by the weeping mother. This moving scene was completed by the entrance of Grieve himself, who falling on his knees before the count, 'Behold (said he) a penitent, who at length can look upon his patron without shrinking.' 'Ah, Ferdinand! (cried he, raising and folding him in his arms) the playfellow of my infancy – the companion of my youth! — Is it to you then I am indebted for my life?' 'Heaven has heard my prayer (said the other), and given me an opportunity to prove myself not altogether unworthy of your clemency and protection.' He then kissed the hand of the countess, while monsieur de Melville saluted his wife and lovely daughter, and all of us were greatly affected by this pathetic recognition.

In a word, Grieve was no other than Ferdinand count Fathom, whose adventures were printed many years ago. Being a sincere convert to virtue, he had changed his name, that he might elude the enquiries of the count, whose generous allowance he determined to forego, that he might have no dependence but upon his own industry and moderation. He had accordingly settled in this village as a practitioner in surgery and physic, and for some years wrestled with all the miseries of indigence, which, however, he and his wife had borne with the most exemplary resignation. At length, by dint of unwearied attention to the duties of his profession, which he exercised with equal humanity and success, he had acquired a tolerable share of business among the farmers and common people, which enabled him to live in a decent manner. He had been scarce ever seen to smile; was unaffectedly pious; and all the time he could spare from the avocations of his employment, he spent in educating his daughter, and in studying for his own improvement. – In short, the adventurer Fathom was, under the name of Grieve, universally respected among the commonalty of this district, as a prodigy of learning and virtue. These particulars I learned from the vicar, when we quitted the room, that they might be under no restraint in their mutual effusions. I make no doubt that Grieve will be pressed to leave off business, and re-unite himself to the count's family; and as the countess seemed extremely fond of his daughter, she will, in all probability, insist upon Seraphina's accompanying her to Scotland.

Having paid our compliments to these noble persons, we returned to the 'squire's, where we expected an invitation to pass the night, which was wet and raw; but it seems, 'squire Burdock's hospitality reached not so far for the honour of Yorkshire; we therefore departed in the evening, and lay at an inn, where I caught cold.

In hope of riding it down before it could take fast hold on my constitution, I resolved to visit another relation, one Mr Pimpernel, who lived about a dozen miles from the place where we lodged. Pimpernel being the youngest of four sons, was bred an attorney at Furnival's inn;[15] but all his elder brothers dying, he got himself called to the bar for the honour of his family, and soon after this preferment, succeeded to his father's estate which was very considerable. He carried home with him all the knavish chicanery of the lowest pettifogger,[16] together with a wife whom he had purchased of a drayman for twenty pounds; and he soon found means to obtain a *dedimus*[17] as an acting justice of peace. He is not only a sordid miser in his disposition, but his avarice is mingled with a spirit of despotism, which is truly diabolical. – He is a brutal husband, an unnatural parent, a harsh master, an oppressive landlord, a litigious neighbour, and a partial magistrate — Friends he has none; and in point of hospitality and good breeding, our cousin Burdock is a prince in comparison of this ungracious miscreant, whose house is the lively representation of a gaol. Our reception was suitable to the character I have sketched. Had it depended upon the wife, we should have been kindly treated. – She is really a good sort of a woman, in spite of her low original, and well respected in the country; but she has not interest enough in her own house to command a draught of table beer, far less to bestow any kind of education on her children, who run about, like ragged colts, in a state of nature. – Pox on him! he is such a dirty fellow, that I have not patience to prosecute the subject.

By that time we reached Harrigate, I began to be visited by certain rheumatic symptoms. The Scotch lawyer, Mr Micklewhimmen, recommended a hot bath of these waters so earnestly, that I was over-persuaded to try the experiment. – He had used it often with success and always stayed an hour in the bath, which was a tub filled with Harrigate water, heated for the purpose. If I could hardly bear the smell of a single tumbler when cold, you may guess how my nose was regaled by the streams arising from a hot bath of the same fluid. At night, I was conducted into a dark hole on the ground floor, where the tub smoaked and stunk like the pot of Acheron,[18] in one corner, and in another stood a dirty bed provided with thick blankets, in which I was to sweat after coming out of the bath. My heart seemed to die within me when I entered this dismal bagnio, and found my brain assaulted by such insufferable effluvia. I cursed Micklewhimmen for not considering that my organs were formed on this side of the Tweed; but being ashamed to recoil upon the threshold, I submitted to the process.

After having endured all but real suffocation for above a quarter of an hour in the tub, I was moved to the bed and wrapped in blankets. – There I lay a full hour panting with intolerable heat; but not the least moisture appearing on my skin, I was carried to my own chamber, and passed the night without closing an eye, in such a flutter of spirits as rendered me the most miserable wretch in being. I should certainly have run distracted, if the rarefaction of my blood, occasioned by that Stygian bath,[19] had not burst the vessels, and produced a violent hæmorrhage, which, though dreadful and alarming, removed the horrible disquiet – I lost two pounds of blood, and more, on this occasion; and find myself still weak and languid; but, I believe, a little exercise will forward my recovery, and therefore I am resolved to set out to-morrow for York, in my way to Scarborough, where I propose to brace up my fibres by sea-bathing, which, I know, is one of your favourite specificks. There is, however, one disease, for which you have found as yet no specific, and that is old age, of which this tedious unconnected epistle is an infallible symptom; *what*, therefore, *cannot be cured, must be endured*, by you, as well as by

Yours,

HARRIGATE, June 26.   MATT. BRAMBLE

To Sir WATKIN PHILLIPS, Bart. of Jesus college, Oxon.

DEAR KNIGHT,

The manner of living at Harrigate was so agreeable to my disposition, that I left the place with some regret – Our aunt Tabby would have probably made some objection to our departing so soon, had not an accident embroiled her with Mr Micklewhimmen, the Scotch advocate, on whose heart she had been practising, from the second day after our arrival – That original, though seemingly precluded from the use of his limbs, had turned his genius to good account – In short, by dint of groaning, and whining, he had excited the compassion of the company so effectually, that an old lady, who occupied the very best apartment in the house, gave it up for his ease and convenience. When his man led him into the Long Room,[1] all the females were immediately in commotion – One set an elbow-chair; another shook up the cushion; a third brought a stool; and a fourth a pillow, for the accommodation of his feet – Two ladies (of whom Tabby was always one) supported him into the dining-room, and placed him properly at the table; and his taste was indulged with a succession of delicacies, culled by their fair hands. All this attention he repaid with a profusion of compliments and benedictions, which were not the less agreeable for being delivered in the Scottish dialect. As for Mrs Tabitha, his respects were particularly addressed to her, and he did not fail to mingle them with religious reflections, touching free grace, knowing her bias to methodism, which he also professed upon a calvinistical[2] model.

For my part, I could not help thinking this lawyer was not such an invalid as he pretended to be. I observed he ate very heartily three times a day; and though his bottle was marked *stomachic tincture*, he had recourse to it so often, and seemed to swallow it with such peculiar relish, that I suspected it was not compounded in the apothecary's shop, or the chemist's laboratory. One day, while he was earnest in discourse with Mrs Tabitha, and his servant had gone out on some occasion or other, I dexterously exchanged the labels, and situation of his bottle and mine; and having tasted his tincture, found it was excellent claret. I forthwith handed it about me to some of my neighbours, and it was quite emptied before Mr Micklewhimmen had occasion to repeat his draught. At length, turning about, he took hold of my bottle, instead of his own, and, filling a large glass, drank to the health of Mrs Tabitha – It had scarce touched his lips, when he perceived the change which had been put upon him, and was at first a little out of countenance – He seemed to retire within himself, in order to deliberate, and in half a minute his resolution was taken; addressing himself to our quarter, 'I give the gentleman credit for his wit (said he); it was a gude practical joke; but sometimes *hi joci in seria ducunt mala*[3] – I hope for his own sake he has na drank all the liccor; for it was a vara poorful infusion of jallap[4] in Bourdeaux wine; at its possable he may ha ta'en sic a dose as will produce a terrible catastrophe in his ain booels –'

By far the greater part of the contents had fallen to the share of a young clothier from Leeds, who had come to make a figure at Harrigate, and was, in effect a great coxcomb in his way. It was with a view to laugh at his fellow-guests, as well as to mortify the lawyer, that he had emptied the bottle, when it came to his turn, and he had laughed accordingly: but now his mirth gave way to his apprehension – He began to spit, to make wry faces, and writhe himself into various contorsions – 'Damn the stuff! (cried he) I thought it had a villainous twang – pah! He that would cozen a Scot, mun get oope betimes, and take Old Scratch for his counsellor –' 'In troth mester what d'ye ca'um (replied the lawyer), your wit has run you into a filthy puddle – I'm truly consarned for your waeful case – The best advice I can give you, in sic a delemma, is to send an express to Rippon[5] for doctor Waugh,[6] without delay, and, in the mean time, swallow all the oil and butter you can find in the hoose, to defend your poor stomach and intastines from the villication[7] of the particles of the jallap, which is vara violent, even when taken in moderation.'

The poor clothier's torments had already begun: he retired, roaring with pain, to his own chamber; the oil was swallowed, and the doctor sent for; but before he arrived, the miserable patient had made such discharges upwards and downwards, that nothing remained to give him further offence; and this double evacuation, was produced by imagination alone; for what he had drank was genuine wine of Bourdeaux, which the lawyer had brought from Scotland for his own private use. The clothier, finding the joke turn out so expensive and disagreeable, quitted the house next morning, leaving the triumph to Mickle-whimmen, who enjoyed it internally without any outward signs of exultation – on the contrary, he affected to pity the young man for what he had suffered; and acquired fresh credit from this shew of moderation.

It was about the middle of the night, which succeeded this adventure, that the vent of the kitchen chimney being foul, the soot took fire, and the alarm was given in a dreadful manner – Every body leaped naked[8] out of bed, and in a minute the whole house was filled with cries and confusion – There was two stairs in the house, and to these we naturally ran; but they were both so blocked up, by the people pressing one upon another, that it seemed impossible to pass, without throwing down and trampling upon the women. In the midst of this anarchy, Mr Mickle-whimmen, with a leathern portmanteau on his back, came running as nimble as a buck along the passage; and Tabby in her underpetticoat, endeavouring to hook him under the arm, that she might escape through his protection, he very fairly pushed her down, crying, 'Na, na, gude faith, charity begins at hame!' Without paying the least respect to the shrieks and intreaties of his female friends, he charged through the midst of the crowd, overturning every thing that opposed him; and actually fought his way to the bottom of the stair-case – By this time Clinker had found a ladder by which he entered the window of my uncle's chamber, where our family was assembled, and proposed that we should make our exit successively by that conveyance. The 'squire exhorted his sister to begin the descent; but, before she could resolve, her woman, Mrs Winifred Jenkins, in a transport of terror, threw herself out at the window upon the ladder, while Humphry dropped upon the ground, that he might receive her in her descent — This maiden was just as she had started out of bed, the moon shone very bright, and a fresh breeze of wind blowing, none of Mrs Winifred's beauties could possibly escape the view of the fortunate Clinker, whose heart was not able to withstand the united force of so many charms; at least I am much mistaken, if he has not been her humble slave from that moment – He received her in his arms, and, giving her his coat to protect her from the weather, ascended again with admirable dexterity.

At that instant, the landlord of the house called out with an audible voice, that the fire was extinguished, and the ladies had nothing further to fear: this was a welcome note to the audience, and produced an immediate effect; the shrieking ceased, and a confused sound of expostulation ensued. I conducted Mrs Tabitha and my sister to their own chamber, where Liddy fainted away; but was soon brought to herself. Then I went to offer my services to the other ladies, who might want assistance – They were all scudding through the passage to their several apartments; and as the thoroughfair was lighted by two lamps, I had a pretty good observation of them in their transit; but as most of them were naked to the smock, and all their heads shrouded in huge nightcaps, I could not distinguish one face from another, though I recognized some of their voices – These were generally plaintive; some wept, some scolded, and some prayed – I lifted up one poor old gentlewoman, who had been overturned and sore bruised by a multitude of feet; and this was also the case with the lame person from Northumberland, whom Micklewhimmen had in his passage overthrown, though not with impunity, for the cripple, in falling, gave him such a good pelt on the head with his crutch, that the blood followed.

As for this lawyer, he waited below till the hurly burly was over, and then stole softly to his own chamber, from whence he did not venture to make a second sally till eleven in the forenoon, when he was led into the Public Room, by his own servant and another assistant, groaning most woefully, with a bloody napkin round his head. But things were greatly altered – The selfish brutality of his behaviour on the stairs had steeled their hearts against all his arts and address — Not a soul offered to accommodate him with a chair, cushion, or footstool; so that he was obliged to sit down on a hard bench – In that position, he looked around with a rueful aspect, and, bowing very low, said in a whining tone, 'Your most humble servant, ladies – Fire is a dreadful calamity' – 'Fire purifies gold, and it ties friendship,' cried Mrs Tabitha, bridling. 'Yea, madam (replied Micklewhimmen); and it trieth discretion also' – 'If discretion consists in forsaking a friend in adversity, you are eminently possessed of that virtue' (resumed our aunt). — 'Na, madam (rejoined the advocate), well I wot, I cannot claim any merit from the mode of my retreat – Ye'll please to observe, ladies, there are twa independent principles that actuate our nature – One is instinct, which we have in common with the brute creation, and the other is reason – Noo, in certain great emergencies, when the faculty of reason is suspended, instinct taks the lead, and when this predominates, having no affinity with reason, it pays no sort of regard to its connections; it only operates for the preservation of the individual, and that by the most expeditious and effectual means; therefore, begging your pardon, ladies, I'm no accountable in *foro conscientiæ*[9] for what I did, while under the influence of this irresistible pooer.'

Here my uncle interposing, 'I should be glad to know (said he), whether it was instinct that prompted you to retreat with bag and baggage; for, I think, you had a portmanteau on your shoulder' – The lawyer answered, without hesitation, 'Gif I might tell my mind freely, withoot incuring the suspicion of presumption, I should think it was something superior to either reason or instinct which suggested that measure, and this on a twafold accoont: in the first place, the portmanteau contained the writings of a worthy nobleman's estate; and their being burnt would have occasioned a loss that could not be repaired; secondly, my good angel seems to have laid the portmanteau on my shoulders, by way of defence, to sustain the violence of a most inhuman blow, from the crutch of a reverend clergyman, which, even in spite of that medium, hath wounded me sorely, even unto the pericranium.' 'By your own doctrine (cried the parson, who chanced to be present), I am not accountable for the blow, which was the effect of instinct.' 'I crave your pardon, reverend sir (said the other), instinct never acts but for the preservation of the individual; but your preservation was out of the case — you had already received the damage, and therefore the blow must be imputed to revenge, which is a sinful passion, that ill becomes any Christian, especially a protestant divine; and let me tell you, most reverend doctor, gin I had a mind to plea, the law would hauld my libel relevant.' 'Why, the damage is pretty equal on both sides (cried the parson); your head is broke, and my crutch is snapt in the middle – Now, if you will repair the one, I will be at the expence of curing the other.'

This sally raised the laugh against Micklewhimmen, who began to look grave; when my uncle, in order to change the discourse, observed, that instinct had been very kind to him in another respect; for it had restored to him the use of his limbs, which, in his exit, he had moved with surprising agility. — He replied, that it was the nature of fear to brace up the nerves; and mentioned some surprising feats of strength and activity performed by persons under the impulse of terror; but he complained that in his own particular, the effects had ceased when the cause was taken away – The 'squire said, he would lay a tea-drinking on his head, that he should dance a Scotch measure, without making a false step; and the advocate grin-

ning, called for the piper – A fidler being at hand, this original
started up, with his bloody napkin over his black tye-periwig,
and acquitted himself in such a manner as excited the mirth of
the whole company; but he could not regain the good graces of
Mrs Tabby, who did not understand the principle of instinct;
and the lawyer did not think it worth his while to proceed to
further demonstration.

From Harrigate, we came hither, by the way of York, and
here we shall tarry some days, as my uncle and Tabitha are
both resolved to make use of the waters. Scarborough, though
a paltry town, is romantic from its situation along a cliff that
over-hangs the sea. The harbour is formed by a small elbow of
land that runs out as a natural mole, directly opposite to the
town; and on that side is the castle, which stands very high, of
considerable extent, and, before the invention of gun-powder,
was counted impregnable. At the other end of Scarborough are
two public rooms[10] for the use of the company, who resort to
this place in the summer, to drink the waters and bathe in the
sea; and the diversions are pretty much on the same footing
here as at Bath. The Spa is a little way beyond the town, on this
side, under a cliff, within a few paces of the sea, and thither the
drinkers go every morning in dishabille; but the descent is by a
great number of steps, which invalids find very inconvenient.
Betwixt the well and the harbour, the bathing machines are
ranged along the beach, with all their proper utensils and
attendants — You have never seen one of these machines –
Image to yourself a small, snug, wooden chamber, fixed upon
a wheel-carriage, having a door at each end, and on each side
a little window above, a bench below – The bather, ascending
into this apartment by wooden steps, shuts himself in, and
begins to undress, while the attendant yokes a horse to the end
next the sea, and draws the carriage forwards, till the surface
of the water is on a level with the floor of the dressing-room,
then he moves and fixes the horse to the other end – The person
within being stripped, opens the door to the sea-ward, where
he finds the guide ready, and plunges headlong into the water
— After having bathed, he re-ascends into the apartment, by
the steps which had been shifted for that purpose, and puts on

his clothes at his leisure, while the carriage is drawn back again upon the dry land; so that he has nothing further to do, but to open the door, and come down as he went up – Should he be so weak or ill as to require a servant to put off and on his clothes, there is room enough in the apartment for half a dozen people. The guides who attend the ladies in the water, are of their own sex, and they and the female bathers have a dress of flannel for the sea; nay, they are provided with other conveniences for the support of decorum. A certain number of the machines are fitted with tilts, that project from the sea-ward ends of them, so as to screen the bathers from the view of all persons whatsoever – The beach is admirably adapted for this practice, the descent being gently gradual, and the sand soft as velvet; but then the machines can be used only at a certain time of the tide, which varies every day; so that sometimes the bathers are obliged to rise very early in the morning — For my part, I love swimming as an exercise, and can enjoy it at all times of the tide, without the formality of an apparatus – You and I have often plunged together into the Isis; but the sea is a much more noble bath, for health as well as pleasure. You cannot conceive what a flow of spirits it gives, and how it braces every sinew of the human frame. Were I to enumerate half the diseases which are every day cured by sea-bathing, you might justly say you had received a treatise, instead of a letter, from

Your affectionate friend
and servant,

SCARBOROUGH, July 1.   J. MELFORD

To Dr LEWIS.

I have not found all the benefit I expected at Scarborough, where I have been these eight days – From Harrigate we came hither by the way of York, where we stayed only one day to visit the Castle, the Minster and the Assembly-room.[1] The first, which was heretofore a fortress, is now converted to a prison, and is the best, in all respects, I ever saw, at home or abroad –

It stands in a high situation, extremely well ventilated; and has a spacious area within the walls, for the health and convenience of all the prisoners except those whom it is necessary to secure in close confinement — Even these last have all the comforts that the nature of their situation can admit. Here the assizes[2] are held, in a range of buildings erected for that purpose.

As for the Minster, I know not how to distinguish it, except by its great size and the height of its spire, from those other ancient churches in different parts of the kingdom, which used to be called monuments of Gothic architecture; but it is now agreed, that this stile is Saracen rather than Gothic;[3] and, I suppose, it was first imported into England from Spain, great part of which was under the dominion of the Moors. Those British architects who adopted this stile, don't seem to have considered the propriety of their adoption. The climate of the country, possessed by the Moors or Saracens, both in Africa and Spain, was so exceedingly hot and dry, that those who built places of worship for the multitude, employed their talents in contriving edifices that should be cool; and, for this purpose, nothing could be better adapted than those buildings; vast, narrow, dark, and lofty, impervious to the sun-beams, and having little communication with the scorched external atmosphere; but ever affording a refreshing coolness, like subterranean cellars in the heats of summer, or natural caverns in the bowels of huge mountains. But nothing could be more preposterous, than to imitate such a mode of architecture in a country like England, where the climate is cold, and the air eternally loaded with vapours; and where, of consequence, the builder's intention should be to keep the people dry and warm – For my part, I never entered the Abbey church at Bath but once, and the moment I stept over the threshold, I found myself chilled to the very marrow of my bones – When we consider, that in our churches, in general, we breathe a gross stagnated air, surcharged with damps from vaults, tombs, and charnel-houses,[4] may we not term them so many magazines of rheums, created for the benefit of the medical faculty? and safely aver, that more bodies are lost, than souls saved, by going to church, in the winter especially, which may be said to engross eight months in the year. I should be glad to know, what offence it would give to tender consciences, if the house of God was made more comfortable, or less dangerous to the health of valetudinarians; and whether it would not be an encouragement to piety, as well as the salvation of many lives, if the place of worship was well floored, wainscotted, warmed, and ventilated, and its area kept sacred from the pollution of the dead. The practice of burying in churches was the effect of ignorant superstition, influenced by knavish priests, who pretended that the devil could have no power over the defunct if he was interred in holy ground; and this indeed, is the only reason that can be given for consecrating all cemeteries, even at this day.

The external appearance of an old cathedral cannot be but displeasing to the eye of every man, who has any idea of propriety or proportion, even though he may be ignorant of architecture as a science; and the long slender spire puts one in mind of a criminal impaled with a sharp stake rising up through his shoulder – These towers, or steeples, were likewise borrowed from the Mahometans; who, having no bells, used such minarets for the purpose of calling the people to prayers – They may be of further use, however, for making observations and signals; but I would vote for their being distinct from the body of the church, because they serve only to make the pile more barbarous, or Saracenical.

There is nothing of this Arabic architecture in the Assembly Room, which seems to me to have been built upon a design of Palladio,[5] and might be converted into an elegant place of worship; but it is indifferently contrived for that sort of idolatry which is performed in it at present: the grandeur of the fane[6] gives a diminutive effect to the little painted divinities that are adorned in it, and the company, on a ball-night, must look like an assembly of fantastic fairies, revelling by moon-light among the columns of a Grecian temple.

Scarborough seems to be falling off, in point of reputation — All these places (Bath excepted) have their vogue, and then the fashion changes – I am persuaded, there are fifty spaws in England as efficacious and salutary as that of Scarborough, though they have not yet risen to fame; and, perhaps, never will, unless some medical encomiast should find an interest in displaying their virtues to the public view — Be that as it may, recourse will always be had to this place for the convenience of sea bathing, while this practice prevails; but it were to be wished, they would make the beach more accessible to invalids.

I have here met with my old acquaintance, H[ewet]t,[7] whom you have often heard me mention as one of the most original characters upon earth — I first knew him at Venice, and afterwards saw him in different parts of Italy, where he was well known by the nick-name of Cavallo Bianco, from his appearing always mounted on a pale horse, like Death in the Revelations.[8] You must remember the account I once gave you of a curious dispute he had at Constantinople, with a couple of Turks, in defence of the Christian religion; a dispute from which he acquired the epithet of Demonstrator – The truth is, H— owns no religion but that of nature;[9] but, on this occasion, he was stimulated to shew his parts, for the honour of his country – Some years ago, being in the Campidoglio at Rome, he made up to the bust of Jupiter, and, bowing very low, exclaimed in the Italian language, 'I hope, sir, if ever you get your head above water again, you will remember that I paid my respects to you in your adversity.' This sally was reported to the cardinal Camerlengo,[10] and by him laid before pope Benedict XIV,[11] who could not help laughing at the extravagance of the address, and said to the cardinal, 'Those English heretics think they have a right to go to the devil in their own way.'

Indeed H— was the only Englishman I ever knew, who had resolution enough to live in his own way, in the midst of foreigners; for, neither in dress, diet, customs, or conversation, did he deviate one tittle from the manner in which he had been brought up. About twelve years ago, he began a Giro or circuit, which he thus performed – At Naples, where he fixed his head-quarters, he embarked for Marseilles, from whence he travelled with a Voiturin[12] to Antibes – There he took his passage to Genoa and Lerici; from which last place he proceeded, by the way of Cambratina, to Pisa and Florence – After having halted some time in this metropolis, he set out with a Vetturino[13] for Rome, where he reposed himself a few weeks, and then continued his route for Naples, in order to wait for the next opportunity of embarkation – After having twelve times described this circle, he lately flew off at a tangent to visit some trees at his country-house in England, which he had planted above twenty years ago, after the plan of the double colonnade in the piazza of St Peter's at Rome — He came hither to Scarborough, to pay his respects to his noble friend and former pupil, the M— of G—,[14] and, forgetting that he is now turned of seventy, sacrificed so liberally to Bacchus, that next day he was seized with a fit of the apoplexy,[15] which has a little impaired his memory; but he retains all the oddity of his character in perfection, and is going back to Italy by the way of Geneva, that he may have a conference with his friend Voltaire,[16] about giving the last blow to the Christian superstition – He intends to take shipping here for Holland or Hamburgh; for it is a matter of great indifference to him at what part of the continent he first lands.

When he was going abroad the last time, he took his passage in a ship bound for Leghorn, and his baggage was actually embarked. In going down the river by water, he was by mistake put on board of another vessel under sail; and, upon inquiry understood she was bound to Petersburgh — 'Petersburgh, – Petersburgh – (said he) I don't care if I go along with you.' He forthwith struck a bargain with the captain; bought a couple of shirts of the mate, and was safe conveyed to the court of Muscovy, from whence he travelled by land to receive his baggage at Leghorn — He is now more likely than ever to execute a whim of the same nature; and I will hold any wager, that as he cannot be supposed to live much longer, according to the course of nature, his exit will be as odd as his life has been extravagant.*

* This gentleman crossed the sea to France, visited and conferred with Mr de Voltaire at Fernay, resumed his old circuit at Genoa, and died in 1767, at the house of Vanini[17] in Florence. Being taken with a suppression of urine, he resolved, in imitation of Pomponius Atticus,[18] to take himself off by abstinence; and this resolution he executed like an ancient Roman. He saw company to the last, cracked his jokes, conversed freely, and entertained his guests with music. On the third day of his fast, he found himself entirely freed of his complaint; but refused taking sustenance. He said the most disagreeable part

But, to return from one humourist to another, you must know I have received benefit, both from the chalybeate and the sea, and would have used them longer, had not a most ridiculous adventure, by making me the town-talk, obliged me to leave the place; for I can't bear the thoughts of affording a spectacle to the multitude — Yesterday morning, at six o'clock, I went down to the bathing-place, attended by my servant Clinker, who waited on the beach as usual – The wind blowing from the north, and the weather being hazy, the water proved so chill, that when I rose from my first plunge, I could not help sobbing and bawling out, from the effects of the cold. Clinker, who heard me cry, and saw me indistinctly a good way without the guide, buffetting the waves, took it for granted I was drowning, and rushing into the sea, clothes and all, overturned the guide in his hurry to save his master. I had swam out a few strokes, when hearing a noise, I turned about and saw Clinker, already up to his neck, advancing towards me, with all the wildness of terror in his aspect – Afraid he would get out of his depth, I made haste to meet him, when, all of a sudden, he seized me by one ear, dragged me bellowing with pain upon the dry beach, to the astonishment of all the people, men, and women, and children there assembled.

I was so exasperated by the pain of my ear, and the disgrace of being exposed in such an attitude, that, in the first transport I struck him down; then, running back into the sea, took shelter in the machine where my clothes had been deposited. I soon recollected myself so far as to do justice to the poor fellow, who, in great simplicity of heart, had acted from motives of fidelity and affection – Opening the door of the machine, which was immediately drawn on shore, I saw him standing by the wheel, dropping like a water-work, and trembling from head to foot; partly from cold, and partly from the dread of having offended his master – I made my acknowledgments for the blow he had received, assured him I was not angry, and insisted upon

---

of the voyage was past, and he should be a cursed fool indeed, to put about ship, when he was just entering the harbour. In these sentiments he persisted, without any marks of affectation, and thus finished his course with such ease and serenity, as would have done honour to the firmest Stoic of antiquity.

his going home immediately, to shift his clothes; a command which he could hardly find in his heart to execute, so well disposed was he to furnish the mob with further entertainment at my expence. Clinker's intention was laudable without all doubt, but, nevertheless, I am a sufferer by his simplicity – I have had a burning heat, and a strange buzzing noise in that ear, ever since it was so roughly treated; and I cannot walk the street without being pointed at; as the monster that was hauled naked a-shore upon the beach – Well, I affirm that folly is often more provoking than knavery, aye and more mischievous too; and whether a man had not better choose a sensible rogue, than an honest simpleton for his servant, is no matter of doubt with

Yours,

SCARBOROUGH, July 4.   MATT. BRAMBLE

To Sir WATKIN PHILLIPS, Bart of Jesus college, Oxon.

DEAR WAT,

We made a precipitate retreat from Scarborough, owing to the excessive delicacy of our 'Squire, who cannot bear the thoughts of being *prætereuntium digito monstratus*.[1]

One morning, while he was bathing in the sea, his man Clinker took it in his head that his master was in danger of drowning; and, in this conceit, plunging into the water, he lugged him out naked on the beach, and almost pulled off his ear in the operation. You may guess how this atchievement was relished by Mr Bramble, who is impatient, irascible, and has the most extravagant ideas of decency and decorum in the œconomy of his own person – In the first ebullition of his choler,[2] he knocked Clinker down with his fist; but he afterwards made him amends for his outrage, and, in order to avoid further notice of the people, among whom this incident had made him remarkable, he resolved to leave Scarborough next day.

We set out accordingly over the moors, by the way of Whitby, and began our journey betimes, in hopes of reaching Stockton that night; but in this hope we were disappointed – In the afternoon, crossing a deep gutter, made by a torrent, the coach was so hard strained, that one of the irons, which connect the frame, snapt, and the leather sling on the same side, cracked in the middle – The shock was so great, that my sister Liddy struck her head against Mrs Tabitha's nose with such violence that the blood flowed; and Win Jenkins was darted through a small window in that part of the carriage next the horses, where she stuck like a bawd in the pillory, till she was released by the hand of Mr Bramble. We were eight miles distant from any place where we could be supplied with chaises, and it was impossible to proceed with the coach, until the damage should be repaired – in this dilemma, we discovered a black-smith's forge on the edge of a small common, about half a mile from the scene of our disaster, and thither the postilions made shift to draw the carriage, slowly, while the company walked a-foot; but we found the black-smith had been dead some days; and his wife, who had been lately delivered, was deprived of her senses, under the care of a nurse, hired by the parish. We were exceedingly mortified at this disappointment, which, however, was surmounted by the help of Humphry Clinker, who is a surprising compound of genius and simplicity. Finding the tools of the defunct, together with some coals in the smithy, he unscrewed the damaged iron in a twinkling, and, kindling a fire, united the broken pieces with equal dexterity and dispatch – While he was at work upon this operation, the poor woman in the straw,[3] struck with the well-known sound of the hammer and anvil, started up, and, notwithstanding all the nurse's efforts, came running into the smithy, where, throwing her arms about Clinker's neck, 'Ah, Jacob (cried she) how could you leave me in such a condition?'

This incident was too pathetic to occasion mirth — it brought tears into the eyes of all present. The poor widow was put to bed again; and we did not leave the village without doing something for her benefit – Even Tabitha's charity was awakened on this occasion. As for the tender-hearted Humphry Clinker, he hammered the iron and wept at the same time – But his ingenuity was not confined to his own province of farrier and black-smith — It was necessary to join the leather sling, which had been broke; and this service he likewise performed, by means of a broken awl, which he new-pointed and ground, a little hemp, which he spun into lingels,[4] and a few tacks which he made for the purpose – Upon the whole, we were in a condition to proceed in little more than an hour; but even this delay obliged us to pass the night at Gisborough – Next day we crossed the Tees at Stockton, which is a neat agreeable town; and there we resolved to dine, with purpose to lie at Durham.

Whom should we meet in the yard, when we alighted, but Martin the adventurer? Having handed out the ladies, and conducted them into an apartment, where he payed his compliments to Mrs Tabby, with his usual address, he begged leave to speak to my uncle in another room; and there, in some confusion, he made an apology for having taken the liberty to trouble him with a letter at Stevenage. He expressed his hope, that Mr Bramble had bestowed some consideration on his unhappy case, and repeated his desire of being taken into his service.

My uncle, calling me into the room, told him, that we were both very well inclined to rescue him from a way of life that was equally dangerous and dishonourable; and that he should have no scruples in trusting to his gratitude and fidelity, if he had any employment for him, which he thought would suit his qualifications and his circumstances; but that all the departments he had mentioned in his letter, were filled up by persons of whose conduct he had no reason to complain; of consequence he could not, without injustice, deprive any one of them of his bread – Nevertheless, he declared himself ready to assist him in any feasible project, either with his purse or credit.

Martin seemed deeply touched at this declaration – The tear started in his eye, while he said, in a faultering accent – 'Worthy sir – your generosity oppresses me – I never dreamed of troubling you for any pecuniary assistance – indeed I have no occasion – I have been so lucky at billiards and betting in different places, at Buxton, Harrigate, Scarborough, and Newcastle races, that my stock in ready-money amounts to three hundred pounds, which I would willingly employ, in prosecuting some honest scheme of life; but my friend, justice Buzzard, has set so many springs for my life, that I am under the necessity of either retiring immediately to a remote part of the country, where I can enjoy the protection of some generous patron, or of quitting the kingdom altogether – It is upon this alternative that I now beg leave to ask your advice – I have had information of all your route, since I had the honour to see you at Stevenage; and, supposing you would come this way from Scarborough, I came hither last night from Darlington, to pay you my respects.'

'It would be no difficult matter to provide you with an asylum in the country (replied my uncle); but a life of indolence and obscurity would not suit with your active and enterprizing disposition – I would therefore advise you to try your fortune in the East Indies – I will give you a letter to a friend in London, who will recommend you to the direction, for a commission in the company's service;⁵ and if that cannot be obtained, you will at least be received as a volunteer – in which case, you may pay for your passage, and I shall undertake to procure you such credentials, that you will not be long without a commission.'

Martin embraced the proposal with great eagerness; it was therefore resolved, that he should sell his horse, and take a passage by sea for London, to execute the project without delay – In the mean time he accompanied us to Durham, where we took up our quarters for the night – Here, being furnished with letters from my uncle, he took his leave of us, with strong symptoms of gratitude and attachment, and set out for Sunderland, in order to embark in the first collier, bound for the river Thames. He had not been gone half an hour, when we were joined by another character, which promised something extraordinary – A tall, meagre figure, answering, with his horse, the description of Don Quixote mounted on Rozinante, appeared in the twilight at the inn door, while my aunt and Liddy stood at a window in the dining-room – He wore a coat, the cloth of which had once been scarlet, trimmed with Brandenburgs,⁶ now totally deprived of their metal, and he had holster-caps and housing of the same stuff and same antiquity. Perceiving ladies at the window above, he endeavoured to dismount with the most graceful air he could assume; but the ostler neglecting to hold the stirrup when he wheeled off his right foot, and stood with his whole weight on the other, the girth unfortunately gave way, the saddle turned, down came the cavalier to the ground, and his hat and perriwig falling off, displayed a head-piece of various colours, patched and plaistered in a woeful condition – The ladies, at the window above, shrieked with affright, on the supposition that the stranger had received some notable damages in his fall; but the greatest injury he had sustained arose from the dishonour of his descent, aggravated by the disgrace of exposing the condition of his cranium; for certain plebeians that were about the door, laughed aloud, in the belief that the captain had got either a scald head,[7] or a broken head, both equally opprobrious.

He forthwith leaped up in a fury, and snatching one of his pistols, threatened to put the ostler to death, when another squall from the women checked his resentment. He then bowed to the window, while he kissed the butt-end of his pistol, which he replaced; adjusted his wig in great confusion, and led his horse into the stable – By this time I had come to the door, and could not help gazing at the strange figure that presented itself to my view – He would have measured above six feet in height had he stood upright; but he stooped very much; was very narrow in the shoulders, and very thick in the calves of his legs, which were cased in black spatterdashes[8] – As for his thighs, they were long and slender, like those of a grasshopper; his face was, at least, half a yard in length, brown and shrivelled, with projecting cheek-bones, little grey eyes on the greenish hue, a large hook-nose, a pointed chin, a mouth from ear to ear, very ill furnished with teeth, and a high, narrow fore-head, well furrowed with wrinkles. His horse was exactly in the stile of its rider; a resurrection of dry bones,[9] which (as we afterwards learned) he valued exceedingly, as the only present he had ever received in his life.

Having seen this favourite steed properly accommodated in the stable, he sent up his compliments to the ladies, begging permission to thank them in person for the marks of concern they had shewn at his disaster in the court yard – As the 'squire said they could not decently decline his visit, he was shewn up stairs and paid his respects in the Scotch dialect, with much formality – 'Leddies (said he), perhaps ye may be scandaleezed at the appearance of my heed made, when it was uncovered by accident; but I can assure you, the condition you saw it in, is neither the effects of diseases, nor of drunkenness: but an honest scar received in the service of my country.' He then gave us to understand, that having been wounded at Ticonderoga,[10] in America, a party of Indians rifled him, scalped him, broke his scull with the blow of a tomahawk, and left him for dead on the field of battle; but that being afterwards found with signs of life, he had been cured in the French hospital, though the loss of substance could not be repaired; so that the scull was left naked in several places, and these he covered with patches.

There is no hold by which an Englishman is sooner taken than that of compassion – We were immediately interested in behalf of this veteran – Even Tabby's heart was melted; but our pity was warmed with indignation, when we learned, that in the course of two sanguinary wars, he had been wounded, maimed, mutilated, taken, and enslaved, without ever having attained a higher rank than that of lieutenant – My uncle's eyes gleamed, and his nether lip quivered, while he exclaimed, 'I vow to God, sir, your case is a reproach to the service – The injustice you have met with is so flagrant' — 'I must crave your pardon, sir (cried the other, interrupting him), I complain of no injustice – I purchased an ensigncy thirty years ago; and, in the course of service rose to a lieutenant, according to my seniority' – 'But in such a length of time (resumed the 'squire), you must have seen a great many young officers put over your head' – 'Nevertheless (said he), I have no cause to murmur – They bought their preferment with their money – I had no money to carry to market – that was my misfortune; but no body was to blame' – 'What! no friend to advance a sum of money?' (said Mr Bramble) 'Perhaps, I might have borrowed money for the purchase of a company (answered the other); but that loan must have been refunded; and I did not chuse to incumber myself with a debt of a thousand pounds, to be payed from an income of ten shillings a-day.' 'So you have spent the best part of your life (cried Mr Bramble), your youth, your blood, and your constitution, amidst the dangers, the difficulties, the horrors and hardships of a war, for the consideration of three or four shillings a-day – a consideration –' 'Sir (replied the Scot, with great warmth), you are the man that does me injustice, if you say or think I have been actuated by any such paltry consideration — I am a gentleman; and entered the service as other gentlemen do, with such hopes and sentiments as honourable ambition inspires – If I have not been lucky in the lottery of life, so neither do I think myself unfortunate – I owe to no man a farthing; I can always command a clean shirt, a mutton-chop, and a truss of straw; and when I die, I shall leave effects sufficient to defray the expence of my burial.'

My uncle assured him, he had no intention to give him the least offence, by the observations he had made; but, on the contrary, spoke from a sentiment of friendly regard to his interest – The lieutenant thanked him with a stiffness of civility, which nettled our old gentleman, who perceived that his moderation was all affected; for, whatsoever his tongue might declare, his whole appearance denoted dissatisfaction — In short, without pretending to judge of his military merit, I think I may affirm, that this Caledonian is a self-conceited pedant, aukward, rude, and disputacious – He has had the benefit of a school-education, seems to have read a good number of books, his memory is tenacious, and he pretends to speak several different languages; but he is so addicted to wrangling, that he will cavil at the clearest truths, and, in the pride of argumentation, attempt to reconcile contradictions — Whether his address and qualifications are really of that stamp which is agreeable to the taste of our aunt, Mrs Tabitha, or that indefatigable maiden is determined to shoot at every sort of game, certain it is she has begun to practice upon the heart of the lieutenant, who favoured us with his company to supper.

I have many other things to say of this man of war, which I shall communicate in a post or two; mean while, it is but reasonable that you should be indulged with some respite from those weary lucubrations of

Yours,

NEWCASTLE UPON TYNE, July 10.   J. MELFORD

To Sir WATKIN PHILLIPS, Bart. of Jesus college, Oxon.

DEAR PHILLIPS,

In my last I treated you with a high flavoured dish, in the character of the Scotch lieutenant, and I must present him once more for your entertainment. It was our fortune to feed upon him the best part of three days; and I do not doubt that he will start again in our way before we shall have finished our northern excursion. The day after our meeting with him at Durham proved so tempestuous that we did not choose to proceed on our journey; and my uncle persuaded him to stay till the weather should clear up, giving him, at the same time, a general invitation to our mess. The man has certainly gathered a whole budget of shrewd observations, but he brings them forth in such an ungracious manner as would be extremely disgusting, if it was not marked by that characteristic oddity which never fails to attract the attention – He and Mr Bramble discoursed, and even disputed, on different subjects in war, policy, the belles lettres, law, and metaphysics; and sometimes they were warmed into such altercation as seemed to threaten an abrupt dissolution of their society; but Mr Bramble set a guard over his own irascibility, the more vigilantly as the officer was his guest; and when, in spite of all his efforts, he began to wax warm, the other prudently cooled in the same proportion.

Mrs Tabitha chancing to accost her brother by the familiar diminutive of Matt, 'Pray, sir (said the lieutenant), 'is your name Matthias?' You must know it is one of our uncle's foibles to be ashamed of his name Matthew, because it is puritanical; and this question chagrined him so much, that he answered, 'No, by G—d!' in a very abrupt tone of displeasure. – The Scot took umbrage at the manner of his reply, and bristling up, 'If I had known (said he) that you did not care to tell your name, I should not have asked the question – The leddy called you Matt, and I naturally thought it was Matthias: – perhaps, it may be Methuselah, or Metrodorus, or Metellus, or Mathurinus, or Malthinnus, or Matamorus, or —' 'No (cried my uncle laughing), it is neither of those, captain: – my name is Matthew

Bramble, at your service. – The truth is, I have a foolish pique at the name of Matthew, because it favours of those canting hypocrites, who, in Cromwell's time, christened all their children by names taken from the scripture.' – 'A foolish pique indeed (cried Mrs Tabby), and even sinful, to fall out with your name because it is taken from holy writ. – I would have you to know, you was called after great-uncle Matthew ap Madoc ap Meredith, esquire, of Llanwysthin, in Montgomeryshire, justice of the *quorum*,[1] and *crusty ruttleorum*,[2] a gentleman of great worth and property, descended in a strait line, by the female side, from Llewellyn, prince of Wales.'[3]

This genealogical anecdote seemed to make some impression upon the North-Briton, who bowed very low to the descendant of Llewellyn, and observed that he himself had the honour of a scriptural nomination. The lady expressing a desire of knowing his address, he said, he designed himself Lieutenant Obadiah Lismahago; and in order to assist her memory, he presented her with a slip of paper inscribed with these three words, which she repeated with great emphasis, declaring, it was one of the most noble and sonorous names she had ever heard. He observed that Obadiah was an adventitious appellation, derived from his great-grandfather, who had been one of the original covenanters;[4] but Lismahago was the family surname, taken from a place in Scotland so called.[5] He likewise dropped some hints about the antiquity of his pedigree, adding, with a smile of self-denial, *Sed genus et proavos, et quæ non fecimus ipsi, vix ea nostra voco*,[6] which quotation he explained in deference to the ladies; and Mrs Tabitha did not fail to compliment him on his modesty in waving the merit of his ancestry, adding, that it was the less necessary to him, as he had such a considerable fund of his own. She now began to glew herself to his favour with the grossest adulation. – She expatiated upon the antiquity and virtues of the Scottish nation, upon their valour, probity, learning, and politeness. — She even descended to encomiums on his own personal address, his gallantry, good sense, and erudition. – She appealed to her brother, whether the captain was not the very image of our cousin governor Griffith. – She discovered a surprising eagerness to know the particulars of his

life, and asked a thousand questions concerning his atchiev-
ements in war; all which Mr Lismahago answered with a sort
of jesuitical[7] reserve, affecting a reluctance to satisfy her curiosity on a subject that concerned his own exploits.

By dint of her interrogations, however, we learned, that he
and ensign Murphy had made their escape from the French
hospital at Montreal, and taken to the woods, in hope of reaching some English settlement; but mistaking their route, they fell
in with a party of Miamis,[8] who carried them away in captivity.
The intention of these Indians was to give one of them as an
adopted son to a venerable sachem,[9] who had lost his own in
the course of the war, and to sacrifice the other according to
the custom of the country. Murphy, as being the younger and
handsomer of the two, was designed to fill the place of the
deceased, not only as the son of the sachem, but as the spouse
of a beautiful squaw, to whom his predecessor had been
betrothed; but in passing through the different whigwhams or
villages of the Miamis, poor Murphy was so mangled by the
women and children, who have the privilege of torturing all
prisoners in their passage, that, by the time they arrived at the
place of the sachem's residence, he was rendered altogether
unfit for the purposes of marriage: it was determined therefore,
in the assembly of the warriors, that ensign Murphy should be
brought to the stake, and that the lady should be given to
lieutenant Lismahago, who had likewise received his share of
torments, though they had not produced emasculation. – A
joint of one finger had been cut, or rather sawed off with a
rusty knife; one of his great toes was crushed into a mash
betwixt two stones; some of his teeth were drawn, or dug out
with a crooked nail; splintered reeds had been thrust up his
nostrils and other tender parts; and the calves of his legs had
been blown up with mines of gunpowder dug in the flesh with
the sharp point of the tomahawk.

The Indians themselves allowed that Murphy died with great
heroism, singing, as his death song, the *Drimmendoo*,[10] in concert with Mr Lismahago, who was present at the solemnity.
After the warriors and the matrons had made a hearty meal
upon the muscular flesh which they pared from the victim, and

had applied a great variety of tortures, which he bore without flinching, an old lady, with a sharp knife, scooped out one of his eyes, and put a burning coal in the socket. The pain of this operation was so exquisite that he could not help bellowing, upon which the audience raised a shout of exultation, and one of the warriors stealing behind him, gave him the *coup de grâce* with a hatchet.

Lismahago's bride, the squaw Squinkinacoosta, distinguished herself on this occasion. — She shewed a great superiority of genius in the tortures which she contrived and executed with her own hands. – She vied with the stoutest warrior in eating the flesh of the sacrifice; and after all the other females were fuddled with dram-drinking, she was not so intoxicated but that she was able to play the game of the platter with the conjuring sachem, and afterwards go through the ceremony of her own wedding, which was consummated that same evening. The captain had lived very happily with this accomplished squaw for two years, during which she bore him a son, who is now the representative of his mother's tribe; but, at length, to his unspeakable grief, she had died of a fever, occasioned by eating too much raw bear, which they had killed in a hunting excursion.

By this time, Mr Lismahago was elected sachem, acknowledged first warrior of the Badger tribe, and dignified with the name or epithet of Occacanastaogarora, which signifies *nimble as a weasel*; but all these advantages and honours he was obliged to resign, in consequence of being exchanged for the orator of the community, who had been taken prisoner by the Indians that were in alliance with the English. At the peace, he had sold out upon half pay, and was returned to Britain, with a view to pass the rest of his life in his own country, where he hoped to find some retreat where his slender finances would afford him a decent subsistence. Such are the outlines of Mr Lismahago's history, to which Tabitha *did seriously incline her ear*; – indeed, she seemed to be taken with the same charms that captivated the heart of Desdemona, who loved the Moor *for the dangers he had past*.[11]

The description of poor Murphy's sufferings, which threw

my sister Liddy into a swoon, extracted some sighs from the breast of Mrs Tabby: when she understood he had been rendered unfit for marriage, she began to spit, and ejaculated, 'Jesus, what cruel barbarians!' and she made wry faces at the lady's nuptial repast; but she was eagerly curious to know the particulars of her marriage-dress; whether she wore high-breasted stays or bodice, a robe of silk or velvet, and laces of Mechlin or minionette[12] — she supposed, as they were connected with the French, she used *rouge*, and had her hair dressed in the Parisian fashion. The captain would have declined giving a catagorical explanation of all these particulars, observing, in general, that the Indians were too tenacious of their own customs to adopt the modes of any nation whatsoever; he said, moreover, that neither the simplicity of their manners nor the commerce of their country, would admit of those articles of luxury which are deemed magnificence in Europe; and that they were too virtuous and sensible to encourage the introduction of any fashion which might help to render them corrupt and effeminate.

These observations served only to inflame her desire of knowing the particulars about which she had enquired; and, with all his evasion, he could not help discovering the following circumstances – that his princess had neither shoes, stockings, shift, nor any kind of linen – that her bridal dress consisted of a petticoat of red bays, and a fringed blanket, fastened about her shoulders with a copper skewer; but of ornaments she had great plenty. – Her hair was curiously plaited, and interwoven with bobbins of human bone – one eye-lid was painted green, and the other yellow; the cheeks were blue, the lips white, the teeth red, and there was a black list drawn down the middle of the forehead as far as the tip of the nose – a couple of gaudy parrot's feathers were stuck through the division of the nostrils – there was a blue stone set in the chin – her ear-rings consisted of two pieces of hickery, of the size and shape of drum-sticks – her arms and legs were adorned with bracelets of wampum – her breast glittered with numerous strings of glass beads – she wore a curious pouch, or pocket of woven grass, elegantly painted with various colours — about her neck was hung the fresh scalp of a Mohawk warrior, whom her deceased lover had lately slain in battle — and, finally, she was anointed from head to foot with bear's grease, which sent forth a most agreeable odour.

One would imagine that these paraphernalia would not have been much admired by a modern fine lady; but Mrs Tabitha was resolved to approve of all the captains connexions. — She wished, indeed, the squaw had been better provided with linen; but she owned there was much taste and fancy in her ornaments; she made no doubt, therefore, that madam Squinkinacoosta was a young lady of good sense and rare accomplishments, and a good christian at bottom. Then she asked whether his consort had been high-church or low-church, presbyterian or ana-baptist, or had been favoured with any glimmering of the new light of the gospel? When he confessed that she and her whole nation were utter strangers to the christian faith, she gazed at him with signs of astonishment, and Humphry Clinker, who chanced to be in the room, uttered a hollow groan.

After some pause, 'In the name of God, captain Lismahago (cried she), what religion do they profess?' 'As to religion, madam (answered the lieutenant), it is among those Indians a matter of great simplicity – they never heard of any *Alliance between Church and State*.[13] – They, in general, worship two contending principles; one the Fountain of all Good, the other the source of all evil. – The common people there, as in other countries, run into the absurdities of superstition; but sensible men pay adoration to a Supreme Being, who created and sustains the universe.' 'O! what pity (exclaimed the pious Tabby), that some holy man has not been inspired to go and convert these poor heathens!'[14]

The lieutenant told her, that while he resided among them, two French missionaries arrived, in order to convert them to the catholic religion; but when they talked of mysteries and revelations, which they could neither explain nor authenticate, and called in the evidence of miracles which they believed upon hearsay; when they taught that the Supreme Creator of Heaven and Earth had allowed his only Son, his own equal in power and glory, to enter the bowels of a woman, to be born as a human creature, to be insulted, flagellated, and even executed as a malefactor; when they pretended to create God himself, to swallow, digest, revive, and multiply him *ad infinitum*, by the help of a little flour and water, the Indians were shocked at the impiety of their presumption. – They were examined by the assembly of the sachems who desired them to prove the divinity of their mission by some miracle. – They answered, that it was not in their power. — 'If you were really sent by Heaven for our conversion (said one of the sachems), you would certainly have some supernatural endowments, at least you would have the gift of tongues, in order to explain your doctrine to the different nations among which you are employed; but you are so ignorant of our language, that you cannot express yourselves even on the most trifling subjects.'

In a word, the assembly were convinced of their being cheats, and even suspected them of being spies: they ordered them a bag of Indian corn a-piece, and appointed a guide to conduct them to the frontiers; but the missionaries having more zeal than discretion, refused to quit the vineyard. — They persisted in saying mass, in preaching, baptizing, and squabbling with the conjurers, or priests of the country, till they had thrown the whole community into confusion. – Then the assembly proceeded to try them as impious impostors, who represented the Almighty as a trifling, weak, capricious being, and pretended to make, unmake, and reproduce him at pleasure; they were, therefore, convicted of blasphemy and sedition, and condemned to the stake, where they died singing *Salve regina*,[15] in a rapture of joy, for the crown of martyrdom which they had thus obtained.

In the course of this conversation, lieutenant Lismahago dropt some hints by which it appeared he himself was a freethinker. Our aunt seemed to be startled at certain sarcasms he threw out against the creed of saint Athanasius[16] – He dwelt much upon the words, *reason*, *philosophy*, and *contradiction in terms* – he bid defiance to the eternity of hell-fire; and even threw such squibs at the immortality of the soul, as singed a little the whiskers of Mrs Tabitha's faith; for, by this time she began to look upon Lismahago as a prodigy of learning and sagacity. — In short, he could be no longer insensible to the advances she made towards his affection; and although there was something repulsive in his nature, he overcame it so far as to make some return to her civilities. – Perhaps, he thought it would be no bad scheme, in a superannuated lieutenant on half-pay, to effect a conjunction with an old maid, who, in all probability, had fortune enough to keep him easy and comfortable in the fag-end of his days – An ogling correspondence forthwith commenced between this amiable pair of originals – He began to sweeten the natural acidity of his discourse with the treacle of compliment and commendation — He from time to time offered her snuff, of which he himself took great quantities, and even made her a present of a purse of silk grass, woven by the hands of the amiable Squinkinacoosta, who had used it as a shot-pouch in her hunting expeditions.

From Doncaster northwards, all the windows of all the inns are scrawled with doggeral rhimes, in abuse of the Scotch nation; and what surprised me very much, I did not perceive one line written in the way of recrimination – Curious to hear what Lismahago would say on this subject, I pointed out to him a very scurrilous epigram against his countrymen, which was engraved on one of the windows of the parlour where we sat. — He read it with the most starched composure; and when I asked his opinion of the poetry, 'It is vara terse and vara poignant (said he); but with the help of a wat dish-clout, it might be rendered more clear and parspicuous. – I marvel much that some modern wit has not published a collection of these essays under the title of the *Glazier's Triumph over Sawney the Scot* — I'm persuaded it would be a vara agreeable offering to the patriots of London and Westminster.' When I expressed some surprize that the natives of Scotland, who travel this way, had not broke all the windows upon the road, 'With submission (replied the lieutenant), that were but shallow policy – it would only serve to make the satire more cutting and severe; and I think it is much better to let it stand in the window, than have it presented in the reckoning.'

My uncle's jaws began to quiver with indignation. —— He said, the scribblers of such infamous stuff deserved to be scourged at the cart's tail for disgracing their country with such monuments of malice and stupidity. – 'These vermin (said he) do not consider, that they are affording their fellow subjects, whom they abuse, continual matter of self-gratulation, as well as the means of executing the most manly vengeance that can be taken for such low, illiberal attacks. For my part, I admire the philosophic forbearance of the Scots, as much as I despise the insolence of those wretched libellers, which is akin to the arrogance of the village cock, who never crows but upon his own dunghill.' The captain, with an affectation of candour, observed, that men of illiberal minds were produced in every soil; that in supposing those were the sentiments of the English in general, he should pay too great a compliment to his own country, which was not of consequence enough to attract the envy of such a flourishing and powerful people.

Mrs Tabby broke forth again in praise of his moderation, and declared that Scotland was the soil which produced every virtue under heaven. – When Lismahago took his leave for the night, she asked her brother if the captain was not the prettiest gentleman he had ever seen; and whether there was not something wonderfully engaging in his aspect? – Mr Bramble having eyed her sometime in silence, 'Sister (said he), the lieutenant is, for aught I know, an honest man and a good officer – he has a considerable share of understanding, and a title to more encouragement than he seems to have met with in life; but I cannot, with a safe conscience, affirm, that he is the prettiest gentleman I ever saw; neither can I descern any engaging charm in his countenance, which, I vow to Gad, is, on the contrary, very hard-favoured and forbidding.'

I have endeavoured to ingratiate myself with this North-Briton, who is really a curiosity; but he has been very shy of my conversation ever since I laughed at his asserting that the English tongue was spoke with more propriety at Edinburgh than at London. Looking at me with a double squeeze of souring in his aspect, 'If the old definition be true (said he), that risibility is the distinguishing characteristic of a rational creature, the English are the most distinguished for rationality of any people I ever knew.' I owned, that the English were easily struck with any thing that appeared ludicrous, and apt to laugh accordingly; but it did not follow, that, because they were more given to laughter, they had more rationality than their neighbours: I said, such an inference would be an injury to the Scots, who were by no means defective in rationality, though generally supposed little subject to the impressions of humour.

The captain answered, that this supposition must have been deduced either from their conversation or their compositions, of which the English could not possibly judge with precision, as they did not understand the dialect used by the Scots in common discourse, as well as in their works of humour. When I desired to know what those works of humour were, he mentioned a considerable number of pieces, which he insisted were equal in point of humour to any thing extant in any language dead or living — He, in particular, recommended a collection of detached poems, in two small volumes, intituled, *The Ever-Green*, and the works of Allan Ramsay,[17] which I intend to provide myself with at Edinburgh. – He observed, that a North-Briton is seen to a disadvantage in an English company, because he speaks in a dialect that they can't relish, and in a phraseology which they don't understand. – He therefore finds himself under a restraint, which is a great enemy to wit and humour. – These are faculties which never appear in full lustre, but when the mind is perfectly at ease, and, as an excellent writer says, enjoys *her elbow-room*.[18]

He proceeded to explain his assertion that the English language was spoken with greater propriety at Edinburgh than in London. – He said, what we generally called the Scottish dialect was, in fact, true, genuine old English, with a mixture of some French terms and idioms, adopted in a long intercourse betwixt the French and Scotch nations; that the modern English, from affectation and false refinement, had weakened, and even corrupted their language, by throwing out the guttural sounds, altering the pronunciation and the quantity, and disusing many words and terms of great significance. In consequence of these innovations, the works of our best poets, such as Chaucer, Spenser, and even Shakespeare, were become, in many parts, unintelligible to the natives of South Britain, whereas the Scots, who retain the antient language, understand them without the help of a glossary. 'For instance (said he), how have your commentators been puzzled by the following expression in the *Tempest* – *He's gentle and not fearful*:[19] as if it was a para-logism[20] to say, that being *gentle*, he must of course be *cour-ageous*: but the truth is, one of the original meanings, if not the sole meaning, of that word was, *noble, high-minded*; and to this day, a Scotch woman, in the situation of the young lady in the *Tempest*, would express herself nearly in the same terms – Don't provoke him; for being gentle, that is, *high-spirited*, he won't tamely bear an insult. Spenser, in the very first stanza of his *Fairy Queen*, says,

A *gentle* knight was pricking on the plain;

which knight, far from being *tame* and fearful, was so stout that

Nothing did he dread, but ever was ydrad.[21]

To prove that we had impaired the energy of our language by false refinement, he mentioned the following words, which, though widely different in signification, are pronounced exactly in the same manner – *wright, write, right, rite*; but among the Scots, these words are as different in pronunciation, as they are in meaning and orthography; and this is the case with many others which he mentioned by way of illustration. – He, more-over, took notice, that we had (for what reason he could never learn) altered the sound of our vowels from that which is retained by all the nations in Europe; an alteration which rendered the language extremely difficult to foreigners, and made it almost impracticable to lay down general rules for orthography and pronunciation. Besides, the vowels were no longer simple sounds in the mouth of an Englishman, who pronounced both *i* and *u* as diphthongs.[22] Finally, he affirmed, that we mumbled our speech with our lips and teeth, and ran the words together without pause or distinction, in such a manner, that a foreigner, though he understood English tolerably well, was often obliged to have recourse to a Scotchman to explain what a native of England had said in his own language.

The truth of this remark was confirmed by Mr Bramble from his own experience; but he accounted for it on another principle. – He said, the same observation would hold in all languages; that a Swiss talking French was more easily understood than a Parisian, by a foreigner who had not made himself master of the language; because every language had its peculiar recitative,[23] and it would always require more pains, attention, and practice, to acquire both the words and the music, than to learn the words only; and yet no body would deny, that the one was imperfect without the other: he therefore apprehended, that the Scotchman and the Swiss were better understood by learners, because they spoke the words only, without the music, which they could not rehearse. One would imagine this check might have damped the North Briton; but it served only to agitate his humour for disputation. — He said, if every nation had its own recitative or music, the Scots had theirs, and the Scotchman who had not yet acquired the cadence of the English, would naturally use his own in speaking their language; therefore, if he was better understood than the native, his recitative must be more intelligible than that of the English; of consequence, the dialect of the Scots had an advantage over that of their fellow-subjects, and this was another strong presumption that the modern English had corrupted their language in the article of pronunciation.

The lieutenant was, by this time, become so polemical, that every time he opened his mouth out flew a paradox, which he maintained with all the enthusiasm of altercation; but all his paradoxes favoured strong of a partiality for his own country. He undertook to prove that poverty was a blessing to a nation; that *oatmeal* was preferable to *wheat-flour*; and that the worship of Cloacina,[24] in temples which admitted both sexes, and every rank of votaries promiscuously, was a filthy species of idolatry that outraged every idea of delicacy and decorum. I did not so much wonder at his broaching these doctrines, as at the arguments, equally whimsical and ingenious, which he adduced in support of them.

In fine, lieutenant Lismahago is a curiosity which I have not yet sufficiently perused; and therefore I shall be sorry when we lose his company, though, God knows, there is nothing very amiable in his manner or disposition. – As he goes directly to the south-west division of Scotland, and we proceed in the road to Berwick, we shall part to-morrow at a place called Feltonbridge; and, I dare say, this separation will be very grievous to our aunt Mrs Tabitha, unless she has received some flattering assurance of his meeting her again. If I fail in my purpose of entertaining you with these unimportant occurrences, they will at least serve as exercises of patience, for which you are indebted to

Yours always,

MORPETH, July 13.   J. MELFORD

To Dr LEWIS.

DEAR DOCTOR,

I have now reached the northern extremity of England, and see, close to my chamber-window, the Tweed gliding through the arches of that bridge[1] which connects this suburb to the town of Berwick. – Yorkshire you have seen, and therefore I shall say nothing of that opulent province. The city of Durham appears like a confused heap of stones and brick, accumulated so as to cover a mountain, round which a river winds its brawling course. The streets are generally narrow, dark, and unpleasant, and many of them almost impassible in consequence of their declivity. The cathedral is a huge gloomy pile; but the clergy are well lodged. — The bishop lives in a princely manner – the golden prebends keep plentiful tables – and, I am told, there is some good sociable company in the place; but the country, when viewed from the top of Gateshead-Fell, which extends to Newcastle, exhibits the highest scene of cultivation that ever I beheld. As for Newcastle, it lies mostly in a bottom, on the banks of the Tyne, and makes an appearance still more disagreeable than that of Durham; but it is rendered populous and rich by industry and commerce; and the country lying on both sides the river, above the town, yields a delightful prospect of agriculture and plantation. Morpeth and Alnwick are neat, pretty towns, and this last is famous for the castle which has belonged so many ages to the noble house of Piercy, earls of Northumberland.[2] – It is, doubtless, a large edifice, containing a great number of apartments, and stands in a commanding situation; but the strength of it seems to have consisted not so much in its site, or the manner in which it is fortified, as in the valour of its defendants.

Our adventures since we left Scarborough, are scarce worth reciting; and yet I must make you acquainted with my sister Tabby's progress in husband-hunting, after her disappointments at Bath and London. She had actually begun to practise upon a certain adventurer, who was in fact a highwayman by profession; but he had been used to snares much more danger-ous than any she could lay, and escaped accordingly. – Then she opened her batteries upon an old weather-beaten Scotch lieutenant, called Lismahago, who joined us at Durham, and is, I think, one of the most singular personages I ever encountered – His manner is as harsh as his countenance; but his peculiar turn of thinking, and his pack of knowledge made up of the remnants of rarities, rendered his conversation desirable, in spite of his pedantry and ungracious address. – I have often met with a crab-apple in a hedge, which I have been tempted to eat for its flavour, even while I was disgusted by its austerity. The spirit of contradiction is naturally so strong in Lismahago, that I believe in my conscience he has rummaged, and read, and studied with indefatigable attention, in order to qualify himself to refute established maxims, and thus raise trophies for the gratification of polemical pride. – Such is the asperity of his self-conceit, that he will not even acquiesce in a transient com-pliment made to his own individual in particular, or to his country in general.

When I observed, that he must have read a vast number of books to be able to discourse on such a variety of subjects, he declared he had read little or nothing, and asked how he should find books among the woods of America, where he had spent the greatest part of his life. My nephew remarking that the Scots in general were famous for their learning, he denied the imputation, and defied him to prove it from their works – 'The Scots (said he) have a slight tincture of letters, with which they make a parade among people who are more illiterate than themselves; but they may be said to float on the surface of science, and they have made very small advances in the useful arts.' 'At least (cried Tabby), all the world allows that the Scots behaved gloriously in fighting and conquering the savages of America.' 'I can assure you, madam, you have been misinformed (replied the lieutenant); in that continent the Scots did nothing more than their duty, nor was there one corps in his majesty's service that distinguished itself more than another. – Those who affected to extol the Scots for superior merit, were no friends to that nation.'

Though he himself made free with his countrymen, he would not suffer any other person to glance a sarcasm at them with impunity. One of the company chancing to mention lord B—'s inglorious peace,[3] the lieutenant immediately took up the cudgels in his lordship's favour, and argued very strenuously to prove that it was the most honourable and advantageous peace that England had ever made since the foundation of the monarchy. – Nay, between friends, he offered such reasons on this subject, that I was really confounded, if not convinced. – He would not allow that the Scots abounded above their proportion in the army and navy of Great-Britain, or that the English had any reason to say his countrymen had met with extraordinary encouragement in the service. – 'When a South and North-Briton (said he) are competitors for a place or commission, which is in the disposal of an English minister or an English general, it would be absurd to suppose that the preference will not be given to the native of England, who has so many advantages over his rival. – First and foremost, he has in his favour that laudable partiality, which, Mr Addison says, never fails to cleave to the heart of an Englishman;[4] secondly, he has more powerful connexions, and a greater share of parliamentary interest, by which those contests are generally decided; and lastly, he has a greater command of money to smooth the way to his success. For my own part (said he), I know no Scotch officer, who has risen in the army above the rank of a subaltern, without purchasing every degree of preferment either with money or recruits; but I know many gentlemen of that country, who, for want of money and interest, have grown grey in the rank of lieutenants; whereas very few instances of this ill-fortune are to be found among the natives of South-Britain. – Not that I would insinuate that my countrymen have the least reason to complain. – Preferment in the service, like success in any other branch of traffic, will naturally favour those who have the greatest stock of cash and credit, merit and capacity being supposed equal on all sides.'

But the most hardy of all this original's positions were these: – That commerce would, sooner or later, prove the ruin of every nation, where it flourishes to any extent – that the parliament was the rotten part of the British constitution – that the liberty of the press was a national evil – and that the boasted institution of juries, as managed in England, was productive of shameful perjury and flagrant injustice. He observed, that traffick was an enemy to all the liberal passions of the soul, founded on the thirst of lucre, a sordid disposition to take advantage of the necessities of our fellow creatures. — He affirmed, the nature of commerce was such, that it could not be fixed or perpetuated, but, having flowed to a certain height, would immediately begin to ebb, and so continue till the channels should be left almost dry; but there was no instance of the tide's rising a second time to any considerable influx in the same nation. Mean while the sudden affluence occasioned by trade, forced open all the sluices of luxury and overflowed the land with every species of profligacy and corruption; a total pravity of manners would ensue, and this must be attended with bankruptcy and ruin. He observed of the parliament, that the practice of buying boroughs, and canvassing for votes, was an avowed system of venality, already established on the ruins of principle, integrity, faith, and good order, in consequence of which the elected and the elector, and, in short, the whole body of the people, were equally and universally contaminated and corrupted. He affirmed, that of a parliament thus constituted, the crown would always have influence enough to secure a great majority in its dependence, from the great number of posts, places, and pensions it had to bestow; that such a parliament would (as it had already done) lengthen the term of its sitting and authority, whenever the prince should think it for his interest to continue the representatives, for, without doubt, they had the same right to protect their authority *ad infinitum*, as they had to extend it from three to seven years.[5] — With a parliament, therefore, dependent upon the crown, devoted to the prince, and supported by a standing army, garbled and modelled for the purpose, any king of England may, and probably some ambitious sovereign will, totally overthrow all the bulwarks of the constitution; for it is not to be supposed that a prince of high spirit will tamely submit to be thwarted in all his measures, abused and insulted by a populace of unbridled ferocity, when he has it in his power to crush all opposition under his feet with the concurrence of the legislature. He said, he should always consider the liberty of the press as a national evil, while it enabled the vilest reptile to soil the lustre of the most shining merit, and furnished the most infamous incendiary with the means of disturbing the peace and destroying the good order of the community. He owned, however, that under due restrictions, it would be a valuable privilege; but affirmed, that at present there was no law in England sufficient to restrain it within proper bounds.

With respect to juries, he expressed himself to this effect: — Juries are generally composed of illiterate plebeians, apt to be mistaken, easily misled, and open to sinister influence; for if either of the parties to be tried, can gain over one of the twelve jurors, he has secured the verdict in his favour; the juryman thus brought over will, in despight of all evidence and conviction, generally hold out till his fellows are fatigued, and harassed, and starved into concurrence; in which case the verdict is unjust, and the jurors are all perjured: but cases will often occur, when the jurors are really divided in opinion, and each side is convinced in opposition to the other; but no verdict will be received, unless they are unanimous, and they are all bound, not only in conscience, but by oath, to judge and declare according to their conviction. — What then will be the consequence? — They must either starve in company, or one side must sacrifice their conscience to their convenience, and join in a verdict which they believe to be false. This absurdity is avoided in Sweden, where a bare majority is sufficient; and in Scotland, where two thirds of the jury are required to concur in the verdict.

You must not imagine that all these deductions were made on his part, without contradictions on mine. – No – the truth is, I found myself piqued in point of honour, at his pretending to be so much wiser than his neighbours. – I questioned all his assertions, started innumerable objections, argued and wrangled with uncommon perseverance, and grew very warm, and even violent, in the debate. – Sometimes he was puzzled, and once or twice, I think, fairly refuted; but from those falls he rose again, like Antæus,[6] with redoubled vigour, till at length I was tired, exhausted, and really did not know how to proceed, when luckily he dropped a hint, by which he discovered he had been bred to the law; a confession which enabled me to retire from the dispute with a good grace, as it could not be supposed that a man like me, who had been bred to nothing, should be able to cope with a veteran in his own profession. I believe, however, that I shall for some time continue to chew the cud of reflection upon many observations which this original discharged.

Whether our sister Tabby was really struck with his conversation, or is resolved to throw at every thing she meets in the shape of a man, till she can fasten the matrimonial noose, certain it is, she has taken desperate strides towards the affection of Lismahago, who cannot be said to have met her half way, though he does not seem altogether insensible to her civilities. — She insinuated more than once how happy we should be to have his company through that part of Scotland which we proposed to visit, till at length he plainly told us, that his road was totally different from that which we intended to take; that, for his part, his company would be of very little service to us in our progress, as he was utterly unacquainted with the country, which he had left in his early youth, consequently, he could neither direct us in our enquiries, nor introduce us to any family of distinction. He said, he was stimulated by an irresistible impulse to revisit the *paternus lar*, or *patria domus*,[7] though he expected little satisfaction, inasmuch as he understood that his nephew, the present possessor, was but ill qualified to support the honour of the family. – He assured us, however, as we design to return by the west road, that he will watch our motions, and endeavour to pay his respects to us at Dumfries. – Accordingly he took his leave of us at a place half way betwixt Morpeth and Alnwick, and pranced away in great state, mounted on a tall, meagre, raw-boned, shambling grey gelding, without e'er a tooth in his head, the very counter-part of the rider; and, indeed, the appearance of the two was so picturesque, that I would give twenty guineas to have them tolerably presented on canvas.

Northumberland is a fine county, extending to the Tweed, which is a pleasant pastoral stream; but you will be surprised when I tell you that the English side of that river is neither so well cultivated nor so populous as the other. – The farms are thinly scattered, the lands uninclosed, and scarce a gentleman's seat is to be seen in some miles from the Tweed; whereas the Scots are advanced in crowds to the very brink of the river, so that you may reckon above thirty good houses, in the compass of a few miles, belonging to proprietors whose ancestors had fortified castles in the same situations, a circumstance that shews what dangerous neighbours the Scots must have formerly been to the northern counties of England.

Our domestic œconomy continues on the old footing. — My sister Tabby still adheres to methodism, and had the benefit of a sermon at Wesley's meeting in Newcastle;[8] but I believe the passion of love has in some measure abated the fervour of devotion both in her and her woman, Mrs Jenkins, about whose good graces there has been a violent contest betwixt my nephew's valet, Mr Dutton, and my man, Humphry Clinker. – Jery has been obliged to interpose his authority to keep the peace; and to him I have left the discussion of that important affair, which had like to have kindled the flames of discord in the family of

Yours always,

TWEEDMOUTH, July 15.   MATT. BRAMBLE

To Sir WATKIN PHILLIPS, Bart. at Oxon.

DEAR WAT,

In my two last you had so much of Lismahago, that I suppose you are glad he is gone off the stage for the present. – I must now descend to domestic occurrences. – Love, it seems, is resolved to assert his dominion over all the females of our family. — After having practised upon poor Liddy's heart, and played strange vagaries with our aunt Mrs Tabitha, he began to run riot in the affections of her woman, Mrs Winifred Jenkins, whom I have had occasion to mention more than once in the course of our memoirs. Nature intended Jenkins for something very different from the character of her mistress; yet custom and habit have effected a wonderful resemblance betwixt them in many particulars. Win, to be sure, is much younger and more agreeable in her person; she is likewise tender-hearted and benevolent, qualities for which her mistress is by no means remarkable, no more than she is for being of a timorous disposition, and much subject to fits of the mother,[1] which are the infirmities of Win's constitution: but then she seems to have adopted Mrs Tabby's manner with her cast cloaths. — She dresses and endeavours to look like her mistress, although her own looks are much more engaging. — She enters into her scheme of œconomy, learns her phrases, repeats her remarks, imitates her stile in scolding the inferior servants, and, finally, subscribes implicitly to her system of devotion. — This, indeed, she found the more agreeable, as it was in a great measure introduced and confirmed by the ministry of Clinker, with whose personal merit she seems to have been struck ever since he exhibited the pattern of his naked skin at Marlborough.

Nevertheless, though Humphry had this double hank upon her inclinations, and exerted all his power to maintain the conquest he had made, he found it impossible to guard it on the side of vanity, where poor Win was as frail as any female in the kingdom. In short, my rascal Dutton professed himself her admirer, and, by dint of his outlandish qualifications, threw his rival Clinker out of the saddle of her heart. Humphry may be compared to an English pudding, composed of good wholesome flour and suet, and Dutton to a syllabub or iced froth, which, though agreeable to the taste, has nothing solid or substantial. The traitor not only dazzled her with his second-hand finery, but he fawned, and flattered, and cringed – he taught her to take rappee, and presented her with a snuff-box of *papier mâché* – he supplied her with a powder for her teeth – he mended her complexion, and he dressed her hair in the Paris fashion – he undertook to be her French master and her dancing-master, as well as friseur, and thus imperceptibly wound himself into her good graces. Clinker perceived the progress he had made, and repined in secret. – He attempted to open her eyes in the way of exhortation, and finding it produced no effect had recourse to prayer. At Newcastle, while he attended Mrs Tabby to the methodist meeting his rival accompanied Mrs Jenkins to the play. He was dressed in a silk coat, made at Paris for his former master, with a tawdry waistcoat of tarnished brocade;[2] he wore his hair in a great bag with a huge solitaire, and a long sword dangled from his thigh. The lady was all of a flutter with faded lutestring, washed gauze, and ribbons three times refreshed; but she was most remarkable for the frisure of her head, which rose, like a pyramid, seven inches above the scalp, and her face was primed and patched from the chin up to the eyes; nay, the gallant himself had spared neither red nor white in improving the nature of his own complexion. In this attire, they walked together through the high street to the theatre, and as they passed for players ready dressed for acting, they reached it unmolested; but as it was still light when they returned, and by that time the people had got information of their real character and condition, they hissed and hooted all the way, and Mrs Jenkins was all bespattered with dirt, as well as insulted with the opprobrious name of *painted Jezabel*,[3] so that her fright and mortification threw her into an hysteric fit the moment she came home.

Clinker was so incensed at Dutton, whom he considered as the cause of her disgrace, that he upbraided him severely for having turned the poor woman's brain. The other affected to treat him with contempt, and mistaking his forbearance for want of courage, threatened to horse-whip him into good manners. Humphry then came to me, humbly begging I would give him leave to chastise my servant for his insolence – 'He has challenged me to fight him at sword's point (said he); but I might as well challenge him to make a horse-shoe, or a plough iron; for I know no more of the one than he does of the other. – Besides, it doth not become servants to use those weapons, or to claim the privilege of gentlemen to kill one another when they fall out; moreover, I would not have his blood upon my conscience for ten thousand times the profit or satisfaction I should get by his death; but if your honour won't be angry, I'll engage to gee 'en a good drubbing, that, may hap, will do 'en service, and I'll take care it shall do 'en no harm.' I said, I had no objection to what he proposed, provided he could manage matters so as not to be found the aggressor, in case Dutton should prosecute him for an assault and battery.

Thus licensed, he retired; and that same evening easily pro-voked his rival to strike the first blow, which Clinker returned with such interest that he was obliged to call for quarter, declar-ing, at the same time, that he would exact severe and bloody satisfaction the moment we should pass the border, when he could run him through the body without fear of the conse-quence. — This scene passed in presence of lieutenant Lisma-hago, who encouraged Clinker to hazard a thrust of cold iron with his antagonist. 'Cold iron (cried Humphry) I shall never use against the life of any human creature; but I am so far from being afraid of his cold iron, that I shall use nothing in my defence but a good cudgel, which shall always be at his service.' In the mean time, the fair cause of this contest, Mrs Winifred Jenkins, seemed overwhelmed with affliction, and Mr Clinker acted much on the reserve, though he did not presume to find fault with her conduct.

The dispute between the two rivals was soon brought to a very unexpected issue. Among our fellow-lodgers at Berwick, was a couple from London, bound to Edinburgh, on the voyage of matrimony. The female was the daughter and heiress of a pawnbroker deceased, who had given her guardians the slip, and put herself under the tuition of a tall Hibernian, who had conducted her thus far in quest of a clergyman to unite them in marriage, without the formalities required by the law of England. I know not how the lover had behaved on the road, so as to decline in the favour of his inamorata; but, in all probability, Dutton perceived a coldness on her side, which encouraged him to whisper, it was a pity she should have cast affections upon a taylor, which he affirmed the Irishman to be. This discovery completed her disgust, of which my man taking the advantage, began to recommend himself to her good graces, and the smooth-tongued rascal found no difficulty to insinuate himself into the place of her heart, from which the other had been discarded – Their resolution was immediately taken. In the morning, before day, while poor Teague[4] lay snoring a-bed, his indefatigable rival ordered a post-chaise, and set out with the lady for Coldstream, a few miles up the Tweed, where there was a parson who dealt in this branch of commerce, and there they were noosed, before the Irishman ever dreamt of the matter. But when he got up at six o'clock, and found the bird was flown, he made such a noise as alarmed the whole house. One of the first persons he encountered, was the postilion returned from Coldstream, where he had been witness to the marriage, and over and above an handsome gratuity, had received a bride's favour, which he now wore in his cap – When the forsaken lover understood they were actually married, and set out for London; and that Dutton had discovered to the lady, that he (the Hibernian) was a taylor, he had like to have run distracted. He tore the ribbon from the fellow's cap, and beat it about his ears. He swore he would pursue him to the gates of hell, and ordered a post-chaise and four to be got ready as soon as possible; but, recollecting that his finances would not admit of this way of travelling, he was obliged to countermand this order.

For my part, I knew nothing at all of what had happened, till the postilion brought me the keys of my trunk and portmanteau, which he had received from Dutton, who sent me his respects, hoping I would excuse him for his abrupt departure, as it was a step upon which his fortune depended – Before I had time to make my uncle acquainted with this event, the Irishman burst into my chamber, without any introduction, exclaiming, – 'By my soul, your sarvant has robbed me of five thousand pounds, and I'll have satisfaction, if I should be hanged tomorrow.' – When I asked him who he was, 'My name (said he) is Master Macloughlin – but it should be Leighlin Oneale, for I am come from Tier-Owen the Great;[5] and so I am as good a gentleman as any in Ireland; and that rogue, your sarvant, said I was a taylor, which was as big a lie as if he had called me the pope – I'm a man of fortune, and have spent all I had; and so being in distress, Mr Coshgrave, the fashioner in Shuffolk-street,[6] tuck me out, and made me his own private shecretary: by the same token, I was the last he bailed; for his friends obliged him to tie himself up, that he would bail no more above ten pounds; for why, becaase as how, he could not refuse any body that asked, and therefore in time would have robbed himself of his whole fortune, and, if he had lived long at that rate, must have died bankrupt very soon – and so I made my addresses to Miss Skinner, a young lady of five thousand pounds fortune, who agreed to take me for better nor worse; and, to be sure, this day would have put me in possession, if it had not been for that rogue, your sarvant, who came like a tief,[7] and stole away my property, and made her believe I was a taylor; and that she was going to marry the ninth part of a man:[8] but the devil burn my soul, if ever I catch him on the mountains of Tulloghobegly,[9] if I don't shew him that I'm nine times as good a man as he, or e'er a bug[10] of his country.'

When he had rung out his first alarm, I told him I was sorry he had allowed himself to be so jockied;[11] but it was no business of mine; and that the fellow who robbed him of his bride, had likewise robbed me of my servant – 'Didn't I tell you then (cried he) that Rogue was his true Christian name. – Oh if I had but one fair trust with him upon the sod, I'd give him lave to brag all the rest of his life.'

My uncle hearing the noise, came in, and being informed of this adventure, began to comfort Mr Oneale for the lady's elopement; observing that he seemed to have had a lucky escape, that it was better she should elope before, than after marriage – The Hibernian was of a very different opinion. He said, 'If he had been once married, she might have eloped as soon as she pleased; he would have taken care that she should not have carried her fortune along with her – Ah (said he) she's a Judas Iscariot, and has betrayed me with a kiss; and, like Judas, she carried the bag,[12] and has not left me money enough to bear my expences back to London; and so I'm come to this pass, and the rogue that was the occasion of it has left you without a sarvant, you may put me in his place; and by Jasus, it is the best thing you can do.' – I begged to be excused, declaring I could put up with any inconvenience, rather than treat as a footman the descendant of Tier-Owen the Great. I advised him to return to his friend, Mr Cosgrave, and take his passage from Newcastle by sea, towards which I made him a small present, and he retired, seemingly resigned to his evil fortune. I have taken upon trial a Scotchman, called Archy M'Alpin, an old soldier, whose last master, a colonel, lately died at Berwick. The fellow is old and withered; but he has been recommended to me for his fidelity, by Mrs Humphreys,[13] a very good sort of a woman, who keeps the inn at Tweedmouth, and is much respected by all the travellers on this road.

Clinker, without doubt, thinks himself happy in the removal of a dangerous rival, and he is too good a Christian, to repine at Dutton's success. Even Mrs Jenkins will have reason to congratulate herself upon this event, when she cooly reflects upon the matter; for, howsoever she was forced from her poise for a season, by snares laid for her vanity, Humphry is certainly the north-star to which the needle of her affection would have pointed at the long run. At present, the same vanity is exceedingly mortified, upon finding herself abandoned by her new admirer, in favour of another inamorata. She received the news with a violent burst of laughter, which soon brought on a fit of crying; and this gave the finishing blow to the patience of her mistress, which had held out beyond all expectation. She now opened all those floodgates of reprehension, which had been shut so long. She not only reproached her with her levity and indiscretion, but attacked her on the score of religion, declaring roundly that she was in a state of apostacy[14] and reprobation; and finally, threatened to send her a packing at this extremity of the kingdom. All the family interceded for poor Winifred, not even excepting her slighted swain, Mr Clinker, who, on his knees, implored and obtained her pardon.

There was, however, another consideration that gave Mrs Tabitha some disturbance. At Newcastle, the servants had been informed by some wag, that there was nothing to eat in Scotland, but *oat-meal* and *sheep's-heads*; and lieutenant Lismahago being consulted, what he said served rather to confirm than to refute the report. Our aunt being apprised of this circumstance, very gravely advised her brother to provide a sumpter horse with store of hams, tongues, bread, biscuit, and other articles for our subsistence, in the course of our peregrination, and Mr Bramble as gravely replied, that he would take the hint into consideration: but, finding no such provision was made, she now revived the proposal, observing that there was a tolerable market at Berwick, where we might be supplied; and that my man's horse would serve as a beast of burthen – The 'squire, shrugging his shoulders, eyed her askance with a look of ineffable contempt: and, after some pause, 'Sister (said he), I can hardly persuade myself you are serious.' She was so little acquainted with the geography of the island, that she imagined we could not go to Scotland but by sea;[15] and, after we had passed through the town of Berwick, when he told her we were upon Scottish ground, she could hardly believe the assertion – If the truth must be told, the South Britons in general are woefully ignorant in this particular. What, between want of curiosity, and traditional sarcasms, the effect of ancient animosity, the people at the other end of the island know as little of Scotland as of Japan.

If I had never been in Wales, I should have been more struck with the manifest difference in appearance betwixt the peasants and commonalty on different sides of the Tweed. The boors of Northumberland are lusty fellows, fresh complexioned, cleanly, and well cloathed; but the labourers in Scotland are generally lank, lean, hard-featured, sallow, soiled, and shabby, and their little pinched blue caps have a beggarly effect. The cattle are much in the same stile with their drivers, meagre, stunted, and ill equipt. When I talked to my uncle on this subject, he said,

'Though all the Scottish hinds would not bear to be compared with those of the rich counties of South Britain, they would stand very well in competition with the peasants of France, Italy, and Savoy – not to mention the mountaineers of Wales, and the red-shanks of Ireland.'[16]

We entered Scotland by a frightful moor of sixteen miles, which promises very little for the interior parts of the kingdom; but the prospect mended as we advanced. Passing through Dunbar, which is a neat little town, situated on the sea-side, we lay at a country inn,[17] where our entertainment far exceeded our expectation; but for this we cannot give the Scots credit, as the landlord is a native of England. Yesterday we dined at Haddington, which has been a place of some consideration, but is now gone to decay; and in the evening arrived at this metropolis, of which I can say very little. It is very romantic, from its situation on the declivity of a hill, having a fortified castle at the top, and a royal palace at the bottom.[18] The first thing that strikes the nose of a stranger, shall be nameless; but what first strikes the eye, is the unconscionable height of the houses, which generally rise to five, six, seven, and eight stories, and, in some places (as I am assured), to twelve. This manner of building, attended with numberless inconveniences, must have been originally owing to want of room. Certain it is, the town seems to be full of people: but their looks, their language, and their customs, are so different from ours, that I can hardly believe myself in Great-Britain.

The inn at which we put up[19] (if it may be so called) was so filthy and disagreeable in all respects, that my uncle began to fret, and his gouty symptoms to recur – Recollecting, however, that he had a letter of recommendation to one Mr Mitchelson,[20] a lawyer, he sent it by his servant, with a compliment, importing that we would wait upon him next day in person; but that gentleman visited us immediately, and insisted upon our going to his own house, until he could provide lodgings for our accommodation. We gladly accepted of his invitation, and repaired to his house, where we were treated with equal elegance and hospitality, to the utter confusion of our aunt, whose prejudices, though beginning to give way, were not yet entirely removed. To-day, by the assistance of our friend, we are settled in convenient lodgings, up four pair of stairs, in the High-street, the fourth story being, in this city, reckoned more genteel than the first. The air is, in all probability, the better; but it requires good lungs to breathe it at this distance above the surface of the earth. – While I do remain above it, whether higher or lower, provided I breathe at all,

I shall ever be,

Dear Phillips, yours,

July 18.   J. MELFORD

To Dr LEWIS.

DEAR LEWIS,

That part of Scotland contiguous to Berwick, nature seems to have intended as a barrier between two hostile nations. It is a brown desert of considerable extent, that produces nothing but heath and fern; and what rendered it the more dreary when we passed, there was a thick fog that hindered us from seeing above twenty yards from the carriage – My sister began to make wry faces, and use her smelling-bottle; Liddy looked blank, and Mrs Jenkins dejected; but in a few hours these clouds were dissipated; the sea appeared upon our right, and on the left the mountains retired a little, leaving an agreeable plain betwixt them and the beach; but, what surprised us all, this plain, to the extent of several miles, was covered with as fine wheat as ever I saw in the most fertile parts of South Britain — This plentiful crop is raised in the open field, without any inclosure, or other manure than the *alga marina*, or sea-weed, which abounds on this coast; a circumstance which shews that the soil and climate are favourable; but that agriculture in this country is not yet brought to that perfection which it has attained in England. Inclosures would not only keep the grounds warm, and the several fields distinct, but would also protect the crop from the high winds, which are so frequent in this part of the island.

Dunbar is well situated for trade, and has a curious bason, where ships of small burthen may be perfectly secure; but there is little appearance of business in the place – From thence, all the way to Edinburgh, there is a continual succession of fine seats, belonging to noblemen and gentlemen; and as each is surrounded by its own parks and plantation, they produce a very pleasing effect in a country which lies otherwise open and exposed. At Dunbar there is a noble park, with a lodge, belonging to the Duke of Roxburgh,[1] where Oliver Cromwell had his head-quarters, when Lesley, at the head of a Scotch army,[2] took possession of the mountains in the neighbour-hood, and hampered him in such a manner, that he would have been obliged to embark and get away by sea, had not the fanaticism of the enemy forfeited the advantage which they had obtained by their general's conduct – Their ministers, by exhortation, prayer, assurance, and prophecy, instigated them to go down and slay the Philistines in Gilgal,[3] and they quitted their ground accordingly, notwithstanding all that Lesley could do to restrain the madness of their enthusiasm — When Oliver saw them in motion, he exclaimed, 'Praised be the Lord, he hath delivered them into the hands of his servant!' and ordered his troops to sing a psalm of thanksgiving, while they advanced in order to the plain, where the Scots were routed with great slaughter.

In the neighbourhood of Haddington, there is a gentleman's house,[4] in the building of which, and the improvements about it, he is said to have expended forty thousand pounds: but I cannot say I was much pleased with either the architecture or the situation; though it has in front a pastoral stream, the banks of which are laid out in a very agreeable manner. I intended to pay my respects to Lord Elibank,[5] whom I had the honour to know at London many years ago. He lives in this part of Lothian; but was gone to the North, on a visit – You have often heard me mention this nobleman, whom I have long revered for his humanity and universal intelligence, over and above the entertainment arising from the originality of his character – At Musselburgh, however, I had the good-fortune to drink tea with my old friend Mr Cardonel;[6] and at his house I met with Dr C—,[7] the parson of the parish, whose humour and conversation inflamed me with a desire of being better acquainted with his person – I am not at all surprised that these Scots make their way in every quarter of the globe.

This place is but four miles from Edinburgh, towards which we proceeded along the sea-shore, upon a firm bottom of smooth sand, which the tide had left uncovered in its retreat —— Edinburgh, from this avenue, is not seen to much advantage – We had only an imperfect view of the Castle and upper parts of the town, which varied incessantly according to the inflexions of the road, and exhibited the appearance of detached spires and turrets, belonging to some magnificent edifice in ruins. The palace of Holyrood house stands on the left, as you enter the Canon-gate[8] – This is a street continued from hence to the gate called Nether Bow, which is now taken away;[9] so that there is no interruption for a long mile, from the bottom to the top of the hill on which the castle stands in a most imperial situation — Considering its fine pavement, its width, and the lofty houses on each side, this would be undoubtedly one of the noblest streets in Europe, if an ugly mass of mean buildings, called the Lucken-Booths,[10] had not thrust itself, by what accident I know not, into the middle of the way, like Middle-Row in Holborn.[11] The city stands upon two hills, and the bottom between them; and, with all its defects, may very well pass for the capital of a moderate kingdom. – It is full of people, and continually resounds with the noise of coaches and other carriages, for luxury as well as commerce. As far as I can perceive, here is no want of provisions – The beef and mutton are as delicate here as in Wales; the sea affords plenty of good fish; the bread is remarkably fine; and the water is excellent, though I'm afraid not in sufficient quantity to answer all the purposes of cleanliness and convenience; articles in which, it must be allowed, our fellow-subjects are a little defective – The water is brought in leaden pipes from a mountain in the neighbourhood, to a cistern on the Castle-hill, from whence it is distributed to public conduits in different parts of the city – From these it is carried in barrels, on the backs of male and female porters, up two, three, four, five, six, seven, and eight pairs of stairs, for the use of particular families — Every story is a complete house, occupied by a separate family; and the stair being common to them all, is generally left in a very filthy condition; a man must tread with great circumspection to get safe housed with unpolluted shoes – Nothing can form a stronger contrast, than the difference betwixt the outside and inside of the door; for the good-women of this metropolis are remarkably nice in the ornaments and propriety of their apartments, as if they were resolved to transfer the imputation from the individual to the public. You are no stranger to their method of discharging all their impurities from their windows, at a certain hour of the night, as the custom is in Spain, Portugal, and some parts of France and Italy – A practice to which I can by no means be reconciled; for notwithstanding all the care that is taken by their scavengers to remove this nuisance every morning by break of day, enough still remains to offend the eyes, as well as other organs of those whom use has not hardened against all delicacy of sensation.

The inhabitants seem insensible to these impressions, and are apt to imagine the disgust that we avow is little better than affectation; but they ought to have some compassion for strangers, who have not been used to this kind of sufferance; and consider, whether it may not be worth while to take some pains to vindicate themselves from the reproach that, on this account, they bear among their neighbours. As to the surprising height of their houses, it is absurd in many respects; but in one particular light I cannot view it without horror; that is, the dreadful situation of all the families above, in case the common staircase should be rendered impassable by a fire in the lower stories – In order to prevent the shocking consequences that must attend such an accident, it would be a right measure to open doors of communication from one house to another, on every story, by which the people might fly from such a terrible visitation. In all parts of the world, we see the force of habit prevailing over all the dictates of convenience and sagacity — All the people of business at Edinburgh, and even the genteel company, may be seen standing in crowds every day, from one to two in the afternoon, in the open street, at a place where formerly stood a market-cross,[12] which (by the bye) was a curious piece of Gothic architecture, still to be seen in lord Sommerville's garden[13] in this neighbourhood – I say, the people stand in the open street from the force of custom, rather than move a few yards to an Exchange that stands empty on one side, or to the Parliament-close on the other, which is a noble square adorned with a fine equestrian statue of king Charles II.[14] – The company thus assembled, are entertained with a variety of tunes, played upon a set of bells, fixed in a steeple hard by[15] – As these bells are well-toned, and the musician, who has a salary from the city, for playing upon them with keys, is no bad performer, the entertainment is really agreeable, and very striking to the ears of a stranger.

The public inns of Edinburgh are still worse than those of London; but by means of a worthy gentleman, to whom I was recommended, we have got decent lodgings in the house of a widow gentlewoman of the name of Lockhart;[16] and here I shall stay until I have seen every thing that is remarkable in and about this capital. I now begin to feel the good effects of exercise — I eat like a farmer, sleep from mid-night till eight in the morning without interruption, and enjoy a constant tide of spirits, equally distant from inanition and excess; but whatever ebbs or flows my constitution may undergo, my heart will still declare that I am,

> Dear Lewis,
> Your affectionate friend and servant,

EDR. July 18.   MATT. BRAMBLE

To Mrs MARY JONES, at Brambleton-hall.

DEAR MARY,

The 'squire has been so kind as to rap my bit of nonsense under the kiver of his own sheet – O, Mary Jones! Mary Jones! I have had trials and trembulation. God help me! I have been a vixen and a griffin[1] these many days – Sattin has had power to temp me in the shape of van Ditton, the young 'squire's wally de shamble;[2] but by God's grease he did not purvail – I thoft as how, there was no arm in going to a play at Newcastle, with my hair dressed in the Parish fashion; and as for the trifle of paint, he said as how my complexion wanted rouch, and so I let him put it on with a little Spanish owl;[3] but a mischievous mob of colliers, and such promiscous ribble rabble, that could bare no smut but their own, attacked us in the street, and called me *hoar* and *painted Issabel*, and splashed my close, and spoiled me a complete set of blond lace triple ruffles, not a pin the worse for the ware – They cost me seven good sillings, to lady Griskin's woman at London.

When I axed Mr Clinker what they meant by calling me Issabel, he put the byebill into my hand, and I read of van Issabel a painted harlot, that vas thrown out of a vindore, and the dogs came and licked her blood – But I am no harlot; and, with God's blessing, no dog shall have my poor blood to lick: marry, Heaven forbid, amen! As for Ditton, after all his court-ing, and his compliment, he stole away an Irishman's bride, and took a French leave[4] of me and his master; but I vally not his going a farting; but I have had hanger on his account – Mistriss scoulded like mad; thof I have the comfit that all the family took my part, and even Mr Clinker pleaded for me on his bended knee; thof, God he knows, he had raisins enuff to complain; but he's a good sole, abounding with Christian meek-ness, and one day will meet with his reward.

And now, dear Mary, we have got to Haddingborrough, among the Scots, who are civil enuff for our money, thof I don't speak their lingo – But they should not go for to impose upon foreigners; for the bills in their houses say, they have different *easements*[5] to let; and behold there is nurro geaks[6] in the whole kingdom, nor any thing for poor sarvants, but a barrel with a pair of tongs thrown a-cross; and all the chairs in the family are emptied into this here barrel once a-day; and at ten o'clock at night the whole cargo is flung out of a back windore that looks into some street or lane, and the maids calls *gardy loo*[7] to the passengers which signifies *Lord have mercy upon you!* and this is done every night in every house in Haddingborrough; so you may guess, Mary Jones, what a sweet savour comes from such a number of profuming pans; but they say it is wholesome, and, truly, I believe it is; for being in the vapours, and thinking of Issabel and Mr Clinker, I was going into a fit of astericks, when this fiff, saving your presence, took me by the nose so powerfully that I sneezed three times, and found myself wonderfully refreshed; and this to be sure is the raisin why there are no fits in Haddingborrough.

I was likewise made believe, that there was nothing to be had but *oat-meal* and *seeps-heads*; but if I hadn't been a fool, I mought have known there could be no *heads* without kerkasses — This very blessed day I dined upon a delicate leg of Velsh mutton and cully-flower; and as for the oat-meal, I leave that to the sarvants of the country, which are pore drudges, many of them without shoes or stockings – Mr Clinker tells me here is a great call of the gospel; but I wish, I wish some of our family be not fallen off from the rite way – O, if I was given to tail-baring, I have my own secrets to discover — There has been a deal of huggling and flurtation betwixt mistress and an ould Scotch officer, called Kismycago. He looks for all the orld like the scare-crow that our gardener has set up to frite away the sparrows; and what will come of it, the Lord knows; but come what will, it shall never be said that I menchioned a syllabub of the matter – Remember me kindly to Saul and the kitten — I hope they got the horn-buck, and will put it to a good yuse, which is the constant prayer of,

Dear Molly,

Your loving friend,

ADDINGBOROUGH, July 18.   WIN. JENKINS

To Sir WATKIN PHILLIPS, Bart. of Jesus college, Oxon.

DEAR PHILLIPS,

If I stay much longer at Edinburgh, I shall be changed into a downright Caledonian – My uncle observes, that I have already acquired something of the country accent. The people here are so social and attentive in their civilities to strangers, that I am insensibly sucked into the channel of their manners and customs, although they are in fact much more different from ours than you can imagine – That difference, however, which struck me very much at my first arrival, I now hardly perceive, and my ear is perfectly reconciled to the Scotch accent, which I find even agreeable in the mouth of a pretty woman – It is a sort of Doric dialect,[1] which gives an idea of amiable simplicity — You cannot imagine how we have been caressed and feasted in the *good town of Edinburgh* of which we are become free denizens and guild brothers, by the special favour of the magistracy.

I had a whimsical commission from Bath, to a citizen of this metropolis – Quin, understanding our intention to visit Edinburgh, pulled out a guinea, and desired the favour I would drink it at a tavern, with a particular friend and bottle-companion of his, Mr R— C—,[2] a lawyer of this city – I charged myself with the commission, and, taking the guinea, 'You see (said I) I have pocketed your bounty.' 'Yes (replied Quin, laughing); and a head-ake into the bargain, if you drink fair.' I made use of this introduction to Mr C—, who received me with open arms, and gave me the rendezvous, according to the cartel.[3] He had provided a company of jolly fellows, among whom I found myself extremely happy; and did Mr C— and Quin all the justice in my power; but, alas, I was no more than a tiro among a troop of veterans, who had compassion upon my youth and conveyed me home in the morning by what means I know not – Quin was mistaken, however, as to the head-ake; the claret was too good to treat me so roughly.

While Mr Bramble holds conferences with the graver literati of the place, and our females are entertained at visits by the Scotch ladies, who are the best and kindest creatures upon earth, I pass my time among the bucks of Edinburgh; who, with a great share of spirit and vivacity, have a certain shrewdness and self-command that is not often found among their neighbours, in the high-day of youth and exultation — Not a hint escapes a Scotchman that can be interpreted into offence by any individual in the company; and national reflections are never heard – In this particular, I must own, we are both unjust and ungrateful to the Scots; for, as far as I am able to judge, they have a real esteem for the natives of South-Britain; and never mention our country, but with expressions of regard – Nevertheless, they are far from being servile imitators of our modes and fashionable vices. All their customs and regulations of public and private œconomy, of business and diversion, are in their own stile. This remarkably predominates in their looks, their dress and manner, their music, and even their cookery. Our 'squire declares, that he knows not another people upon earth, so strongly marked with a national character – Now we are upon the article of cookery, I must own, some of their dishes are savoury, and even delicate; but I am not yet Scotch-man enough to relish their singed sheep's-head and haggice, which were provided at our request, one day at Mr Mitchel-son's, where we dined – The first put me in mind of the history of Congo, in which I had read of negroes' heads sold publickly in the markets;[4] the last, being a mess of minced lights, livers, suet, oat-meal, onions, and pepper, inclosed in a sheep's stomach, had a very sudden effect upon mine, and the delicate Mrs Tabby changed colour; when the cause of our disgust was instantaneously removed at the nod of our entertainer. The Scots, in general, are attached to this composition, with a sort of national fondness, as well as to their oat-meal bread; which is presented at every table, in thin triangular cakes, baked upon a plate of iron, called a girdle; and these, many of the natives, even in the higher ranks of life, prefer to wheaten-bread, which they have here in perfection – You know we used to vex poor Murray of Baliol-college,[5] by asking, if there was really no fruit but turnips in Scotland? — Sure enough, I have seen turnips make their appearance, not as a desert, but by way of *hors d'œuvres*, or whets, as radishes are served betwixt more sub-stantial dishes in France and Italy; but it must be observed, that the turnips of this country are as much superior in sweetness, delicacy, and flavour, to those in England, as a musk-melon is to the stock of a common cabbage. They are small and conical, of a yellowish colour, with a very thin skin; and, over and above their agreeable taste, are valuable for their antiscorbutic[6] quality – As to the fruit now in season, such as cherries, gooseberries, and currants, there is no want of them at Edinburgh; and in the gardens of some gentlemen, who live in the neighbourhood, there is now a very favourable appearance of apricots, peaches, nectarines, and even grapes: nay, I have seen a very fine shew of pineapples within a few miles of this metropolis. Indeed, we have no reason to be surprised at these particulars, when we consider how little difference there is, in fact, betwixt this climate and that of London.

All the remarkable places in the city and its avenues, for ten miles around, we have visited, much to our satisfaction. In the Castle are some royal apartments, where the sovereign occasionally resided; and here are carefully preserved the regalia of the kingdom, consisting of a crown, said to be of great value, a sceptre, and a sword of state, adorned with jewels – Of these symbols of sovereignty, the people are exceedingly jealous – A report being spread during the sitting of the union-parliament, that they were removed to London, such a tumult arose, that the lord commissioner would have been torn to pieces, if he had not produced them for the satisfaction of the populace.

The palace of Holyrood-house is an elegant piece of architecture, but sunk in an obscure, and, as I take it, unwholesome bottom, where one would imagine it had been placed on purpose to be concealed. The apartments are lofty, but unfurnished; and as for the pictures of the Scottish kings, from Fergus I. to king William, they are paultry daubings, mostly by the same hand,[7] painted either from the imagination, or porters hired to sit for the purpose. All the diversions of London we enjoy at Edinburgh, in a small compass. Here is a well conducted concert,[8] in which several gentlemen perform on different instruments – The Scots are all musicians – Every man you meet plays on the flute, the violin, or violoncello; and there is one nobleman, whose compositions are universally admired[9] – Our company of actors is very tolerable; and a subscription is now on foot for building a new theatre;[10] but their assemblies please me above all other public exhibitions.

We have been at the hunters' ball,[11] where I was really astonished to see such a number of fine women – The English, who have never crossed the Tweed, imagine erroneously, that the Scotch ladies are not remarkable for personal attractions; but, I can declare with a safe conscience, I never saw so many handsome females together, as were assembled on this occasion. At the Leith races,[12] the best company comes hither from the remoter provinces; so that, I suppose, we had all the beauty of the kingdom concentrated as it were into one focus; which was, indeed, so vehement, that my heart could hardly resist its power – Between friends, it has sustained some damage from the bright eyes of the charming miss R[ento]n,[13] whom I had the honour to dance with at the ball – The countess of Melville attracted all eyes, and the admiration of all present – She was accompanied by the agreeable miss Grieve, who made many conquests; nor did my sister Liddy pass unnoticed in the assembly – She is become a toast[14] at Edinburgh, by the name of the Fair Cambrian, and has already been the occasion of much wine-shed; but the poor girl met with an accident at the ball, which has given us great disturbance.

A young gentleman, the express image of that rascal Wilson, went up to ask her to dance a minuet; and his sudden appearance shocked her so much, that she fainted away – I call Wilson a rascal, because, if he had been really a gentleman, with honourable intentions, he would have, ere now, appeared in his own character – I must own, my blood boils with indignation when I think of that fellow's presumption; and Heaven confound me if I don't – But I won't be so womanish as to rail – Time will, perhaps, furnish occasion – Thank God, the cause of Liddy's disorder remains a secret. The lady directress of the ball,[15] thinking she was overcome by the heat of the place, had her conveyed to another room, where she soon recovered so well, as to return and join in the country dances, in which the Scotch lasses acquit themselves with such spirit and agility, as put their partners to the height of their mettle – I believe our aunt, Mrs Tabitha, had entertained hopes of being able to do some execution among the cavaliers at this assembly — She had been several days in consultation with milliners and mantua-makers, preparing for the occasion, at which she made her appearance in a full suit of damask, so thick and heavy,

that the sight of it alone, at this season of the year, was sufficient
to draw drops of sweat from any man of ordinary imagination
– She danced one minuet with our friend Mr Mitchelson, who
favoured her so far, in the spirit of hospitality and politeness;
and she was called out a second time by the young laird of
Ballymawhawple,[16] who, coming in by accident, could not
readily find any other partner; but as the first was a married
man, and the second payed no particular homage to her charms,
which were also over-looked by the rest of the company, she
became dissatisfied and censorious – At supper, she observed
that the Scotch gentlemen made a very good figure, when they
were a little improved by travelling; and therefore it was pity
they did not all take the benefit of going abroad – She said the
women were awkward, masculine creatures; that, in dancing,
they lifted their legs like so many colts; that they had no idea
of graceful motion, and put on their clothes in a frightful
manner; but if the truth must be told, Tabby herself was the
most ridiculous figure, and the worst dressed of the whole
assembly – The neglect of the male sex rendered her malcontent
and peevish; she now found fault with every thing at Edinburgh,
and teized her brother to leave the place, when she was suddenly
reconciled to it on a religious consideration — There is a sect of
fanaticks, who have separated themselves from the established
kirk, under the name of Seceders[17] – They acknowledge no
earthly head of the church, reject lay-patronage, and maintain
the methodist doctrines of the new birth, the new light, the
efficacy of grace, the insufficiency of works, and the operations
of the spirit. Mrs Tabitha, attended by Humphry Clinker, was
introduced to one of their conventicles, where they both
received much edification; and she has had the good fortune to
come acquainted with a pious Christian, called Mr Moffat,
who is very powerful in prayer, and often assists her in private
exercises of devotion.

I never saw such a concourse of genteel company at any races
in England, as appeared on the course of Leith – Hard by, in
the fields called the Links, the citizens of Edinburgh divert
themselves at a game called golf, in which they use a curious
kind of bats, tipt with horn, and small elastic balls of leather,

stuffed with feathers, rather less than tennis balls, but of a much harder consistence – This they strike with such force and dexterity from one hole to another, that they will fly to an incredible distance. Of this diversion the Scots are so fond, that when the weather will permit, you may see a multitude of all ranks, from the senator of justice to the lowest tradesman, mingled together in their shirts, and following the balls with the utmost eagerness – Among others, I was shewn one particular set of golfers, the youngest of whom was turned of fourscore — They were all gentlemen of independent fortunes, who had amused themselves with this pastime for the best part of a century, without having ever felt the least alarm from sickness or disgust; and they never went to bed, without having each the best part of a gallon of claret in his belly. Such uninterrupted exercise, co-operating with the keen air from the sea, must, without all doubt, keep the appetite always on edge, and steel the constitution against all the common attacks of distemper.

The Leith races gave occasion to another entertainment of a very singular nature – There is at Edinburgh a society or corporation of errand-boys, called cawdies, who ply in the streets at night with paper lanthorns, and are very serviceable in carrying messages – These fellows, though shabby in their appearance, and rudely familiar in their address, are wonderfully acute, and so noted for fidelity, that there is no instance of [a] cawdy's having betrayed his trust – Such is their intelligence, that they know, not only every individual of the place, but also every stranger, by that time he has been four and twenty hours in Edinburgh; and no transaction, even the most private, can escape their notice – They are particularly famous for their dexterity in executing one of the functions of Mercury; though, for my own part, I never employed them in this department of business – Had I occasion for any service of this nature, my own man, Archy M'Alpine, is as well qualified as e'er a cawdie in Edinburgh; and I am much mistaken, if he has not been heretofore of their fraternity. Be that as it may, they resolved to give a dinner and a ball at Leith, to which they formally invited all the young noblemen and gentlemen that were at the races; and this invitation was reinforced by an assurance that all the celebrated ladies of pleasure would grace the entertainment with their company. – I received a card on this occasion, and went thither with half a dozen of my acquaintance. – In a large hall the cloth was laid on a long range of tables joined together, and here the company seated themselves, to the number of about fourscore, lords, and lairds, and other gentlemen, courtezans and cawdies mingled together, as the slaves and their masters were in the time of the Saturnalia in ancient Rome. – The toast master, who sat at the upper end, was one Cawdie Fraser, a veteran pimp, distinguished for his humour and sagacity, well known and much respected in his profession by all the guests, male and female, that were here assembled. – He had bespoke the dinner and the wine: he had taken care that all his brethren should appear in decent apparel and clean linen; and he himself wore a periwig with three tails in honour of the festival. — I assure you the banquet was both elegant and plentiful, and seasoned with a thousand sallies, that promoted a general spirit of mirth and good humour. – After the desert, Mr Fraser proposed the following toasts, which I don't pretend to explain. – 'The best in Christendom.'[18] – 'Gibbs' contract.'[19] – 'The beggar's benison.'[20] – 'King and kirk.' – 'Great Britain and Ireland.' – Then, filling a bumper, and turning to me, 'Mester Malford (said he), may a' unkindness cease betwixt John Bull and his sister Moggy.'[21] – The next person he singled out, was a nobleman who had been long abroad. — 'Ma lord (cried Fraser), here is a bumper to a' those noblemen who have virtue enough to spend their rents in their ain country.' – He afterwards addressed himself to a member of parliament in these words: – 'Meester – I'm sure ye'll ha' nae objection to my drinking, disgrace and dule[22] to ilka Scot, that sells his conscience and his vote.' – He discharged a third sarcasm at a person very gaily dressed, who had risen from small beginnings, and made a considerable fortune at play. – Filling his glass, and calling him by name, 'Lang life (said he), to the wylie loon that gangs a-field with a toom poke at his lunzie,[23] and comes hame with a sackful of siller.' — All these toasts being received with loud bursts of applause, Mr Fraser called for pint glasses, and filled his own to the brim: then standing up, and all his brethren following his example, 'Ma lords and gentlemen (cried he), here is a cup of thanks for the great and undeserved honour you have done your poor errand-boys this day.' – So saying, he and they drank off their glasses in a trice, and quitting their seats, took their station each behind one of the other guests; – exclaiming, 'Noo we're your honours cawdies again.'

The nobleman who had bore the first brunt of Mr Fraser's satire, objected to his abdication. He said, as the company was assembled by invitation from the cawdies, he expected they were to be entertained at their expense. 'By no means, my lord (cried Fraser), I wad na be guilty of sic presumption for the wide warld – I never affronted a gentleman since I was born; and sure at this age, I wonnot offer an indignity to sic an honourable convention.' 'Well (said his Lordship) as you have expended some wit, you have a right to save your money. You have given me good counsel, and I take it in good part. As you have voluntarily quitted your seat, I will take your place with the leave of the good company, and think myself happy to be hailed, *Father of the Feast*.' He was forthwith elected into the chair, and complimented in a bumper in his new character.

The claret continued to circulate without interruption, till the glasses seemed to dance upon the table, and this, perhaps, was a hint to the ladies to call for music – At eight in the evening the ball began in another apartment: at midnight we went to supper; but it was broad day before I found the way to my lodgings; and, no doubt, his Lordship had a swinging bill to discharge.

In short, I have lived so riotously for some weeks, that my uncle begins to be alarmed on the score of my constitution, and very seriously observes, that all his own infirmities are owing to such excesses indulged in his youth – Mrs Tabitha says it would be more to the advantage of my soul as well as body, if, instead of frequenting these scenes of debauchery, I would accompany Mr Moffat and her to hear a sermon of the reverend Mr M'Corkindale. — Clinker often exhorts me, with a groan, to take care of my precious health; and even Archy M'Alpine, when he happens to be overtaken[24] (which is oftener the case than I could wish), reads me a long lecture upon temperance and sobriety; and is so very wise and sententious, that, if I could provide him with a professor's chair, I would willingly give up the benefit of his admonitions and service together; for I was tutor-sick at alma mater.

I am not, however, so much engrossed by the gaieties of Edinburgh, but that I find time to make parties in the family way. – We have not only seen all the villas and villages within ten miles of the capital, but we have also crossed the Firth, which is an arm of the sea seven miles broad, that divides Lothian from the shire, or, as the Scots call it, the *kingdom of Fife*. There is a number of large open sea-boats that ply on this passage from Leith to Kinghorn, which is a borough on the other side. In one of these our whole family embarked three days ago, excepting my sister, who, being exceedingly fearful of the water, was left to the care of Mrs Mitchelson. We had an easy and quick passage into Fife, where we visited a number of poor towns on the sea-side, including St Andrew's, which is the skeleton of a venerable city; but we were much better pleased with some noble and elegant seats and castles, of which there is a great number in that part of Scotland. Yesterday we took boat again on our return to Leith, with fair wind and agreeable weather; but we had not advanced half-way when the sky was suddenly overcast, and the wind changing, blew directly in our teeth; so that we were obliged to turn, or tack the rest of the way. In a word, the gale increased to a storm of wind and rain, attended with such a fog, that we could not see the town of Leith, to which we were bound, nor even the castle of Edinburgh, notwithstanding its high situation. It is not to be doubted but that we were all alarmed on this occasion. And at the same time, most of the passengers were seized with a nausea that produced violent retchings. My aunt desired her brother to order the boatmen to put back to Kinghorn, and this expedient he actually proposed; but they assured him there was no danger. Mrs Tabitha finding them obstinate, began to scold, and insisted upon my uncle's exerting his authority as a justice of the peace. Sick and peevish as he was, he could not help laughing at this wise proposal, telling her, that his commission did not extend so far, and, if it did, he should let the people take their own way; for he thought it would be great presumption in him to direct them in the exercise of their own profession. Mrs Winifred Jenkins made a general clearance with the assistance of Mr Humphry Clinker, who joined her both in prayer and ejaculation. – As he took it for granted that we should not be long in this world, he offered some spiritual consolation to Mrs Tabitha, who rejected it with great disgust, bidding him keep his sermons for those who had leisure to hear such nonsense. – My uncle sat, collected in himself, without speaking; my man Archy had recourse to a brandy-bottle, with which he made so free, that I imagined he had sworn to die of drinking any thing rather than sea-water: but the brandy had no more effect upon him in the way of intoxication, than if it had been sea-water in good earnest. – As for myself, I was too much engrossed by the sickness at my stomach, to think of any thing else. – Meanwhile the sea swelled mountains high, the boat pitched with such violence, as if it had been going to pieces; the cordage rattled, the wind roared; the lightning flashed, the thunder bellowed, and the rain descended in a deluge – Every time the vessel was put about, we ship'd a sea that drenched us all to the skin. – When, by dint of turning, we thought to have cleared the pier head, we were driven to leeward, and then the boatmen themselves began to fear that the tide would fail before we should fetch up our lee-way: the next trip, however, brought us into smooth water, and we were safely landed on the quay, about one o'clock in the afternoon. – 'To be sure (cried Tabby, when she found herself on *terra firma*),[25] we must all have perished, if we had not been the particular care of Providence.' – 'Yes (replied my uncle), but I am much of the honest high-lander's mind – after he had made such a passage as this: his friend told him he was much indebted to Providence; – "Certainly (said Donald), but, by my saul, mon, I'se ne'er trouble Providence again, so long as the brig of Stirling stands."' — You must know the brig, or bridge of Stirling, stands above twenty miles up the river Forth, of which this is the outlet – I don't find that our 'squire has suffered in his health from this adventure; but poor Liddy is in a peaking way – I'm afraid this unfortunate girl is uneasy in her mind; and this apprehension distracts me, for she is really an amiable creature.

We shall set out to-morrow or next day for Stirling and Glasgow; and we propose to penetrate a little way into the Highlands, before we turn our course to the southward – In the mean time, commend me to all our friends round Carfax,[26] and believe me to be, ever yours,

EDINBURGH, Aug. 8.   J. MELFORD

*

To Dr LEWIS.

I should be very ungrateful, dear Lewis, if I did not find myself disposed to think and speak favourably of this people, among whom I have met with more kindness, hospitality, and rational entertainment, in a few weeks, than ever I received in any other country during the whole course of my life. – Perhaps, the gratitude excited by these benefits may interfere with the impartiality of my remarks; for a man is as apt to be prepossessed by particular favours as to be prejudiced by private motives of disgust. If I am partial, there is, at least, some merit in my conversion from illiberal prejudices which had grown up with my constitution.

The first impressions which an Englishman receives in this country, will not contribute to the removal of his prejudices; because he refers every thing he sees to a comparison with the same articles in his own country; and this comparison is unfavourable to Scotland in all its exteriors, such as the face of the country in respect to cultivation, the appearance of the bulk of the people, and the language of conversation in general. – I am not so far convinced by Mr Lismahago's arguments, but that I think the Scots would do well, for their own sakes, to adopt the English idioms and pronunciation; those of

them especially, who are resolved to push their fortunes in
South-Britain — I know, by experience, how easily an Englishman is influenced by the ear, and how apt he is to laugh,
when he hears his own language spoken with a foreign or
provincial accent – I have known a member of the house of
commons speak with great energy and precision, without
being able to engage attention, because his observations were
made in the Scotch dialect, which (no offence to lieutenant
Lismahago) certainly gives a clownish air even to sentiments
of the greatest dignity and decorum. – I have declared my
opinion on this head to some of the most sensible men of this
country, observing, at the same time, that if they would employ
a few natives of England to teach the pronunciation of our
vernacular tongue, in twenty years there would be no difference,
in point of dialect, between the youth of Edinburgh and of
London.

The civil regulations of this kingdom and metropolis are
taken from very different models from those of England, except
in a few particular establishments, the necessary consequences
of the union.[1] – Their college of justice is a bench of great
dignity, filled with judges of character and ability. – I have
heard some causes tried before this venerable tribunal; and
was very much pleased with the pleadings of their advocates,
who are by no means deficient either in argument or elocution.
The Scottish legislation is founded, in a great measure, on the
civil law;[2] consequently, their proceedings vary from those of
the English tribunals; but, I think, they have the advantage of
us in their method of examining witnesses apart, and in the
constitution of their jury,[3] by which they certainly avoid the evil
which I mentioned in my last from Lismahago's observation.

The university of Edinburgh[4] is supplied with excellent professors in all the sciences; and the medical school, in particular,
is famous all over Europe. – The students of this art have the
best opportunity of learning it to perfection, in all its branches,
as there are different courses for the *theory of medicine* and the
practice of medicine; for *anatomy, chemistry, botany*, and the
materia medica, over and above those of *mathematics* and
experimental philosophy; and all these are given by men of

distinguished talents. What renders this part of education still more complete, is the advantage of attending the infirmary,[5] which is the best instituted charitable foundation that I ever knew. Now we are talking of charities, here are several hospitals,[6] exceedingly well endowed, and maintained under admirable regulations; and these are not only useful, but ornamental to the city. Among these, I shall only mention the general work-house, in which all the poor, not otherwise provided for, are employed, according to their different abilities, with such judgment and effect, that they nearly maintain themselves by their labour, and there is not a beggar to be seen within the precincts of this metropolis. It was Glasgow that set the example of this establishment, about thirty years ago. – Even the kirk of Scotland, so long reproached with fanaticism and canting, abounds at present with ministers celebrated for their learning, and respectable for their moderation. – I have heard their sermons with equal astonishment and pleasure. – The good people of Edinburgh no longer think dirt and cobwebs essential to the house of God. – Some of their churches have admitted such ornaments as would have excited sedition, even in England, a little more than a century ago; and psalmody is here practised and taught by a professor from the cathedral of Durham: – I should not be surprised, in a few years, to hear it accompanied with an organ.

Edinburgh is a hot-bed of genius. — I have had the good fortune to be made acquainted with many authors of the first distinction; such as the two Humes, Robertson, Smith, Wallace, Blair, Ferguson, Wilkie,[7] &c. and I have found them all as agreeable in conversation as they are instructive and entertaining in their writings. These acquaintances I owe to the friendship of Dr Carlyle, who wants nothing but inclination to figure with the rest upon paper. The magistracy of Edinburgh is changed every year by election, and seems to be very well adapted both for state and authority. – The *lord provost* is equal in dignity to the *lord mayor of London*; and the *four bailies* are equivalent to the rank of aldermen. – There is a *dean of guild*, who takes cognizance of mercantile affairs; a treasurer; a town-clerk; and the council is composed of deacons, one of whom is returned every year, in rotation, as representative of every company of artificers or handicraftsmen. Though this city, from the nature of its situation, can never be made either very convenient or very cleanly, it has, nevertheless, an air of magnificence that commands respect. – The castle is an instance of the sublime[8] in scite and architecture. – Its fortifications are kept in good order, and there is always in it a garrison of regular soldiers, which is relieved every year; but it is incapable of sustaining a siege carried on according to the modern operations of war. — The castle hill, which extends from the outward gate to the upper end of the high street, is used as a public walk for the citizens, and commands a prospect, equally extensive and delightful, over the county of Fife, on the other side of the Frith, and all along the sea-coast, which is covered with a succession of towns that would seem to indicate a considerable share of commerce; but, if the truth must be told, these towns have been falling to decay ever since the union, by which the Scots were in a great measure deprived of their trade with France. – The palace of Holyrood-house is a jewel in architecture, thrust into a hollow where it cannot be seen; a situation which was certainly not chosen by the ingenious architect, who must have been confined to the site of the old palace, which was a convent. Edinburgh is considerably extended on the south side, where there are divers little elegant squares built in the English manner; and the citizens have planned some improvements on the north, which, when put in execution, will add greatly to the beauty and convenience of this capital.

The sea-port is Leith, a flourishing town, about a mile from the city, in the harbour of which I have seen above one hundred ships lying all together. You must know, I had the curiosity to cross the Frith in a passage boat, and stayed two days in Fife, which is remarkably fruitful in corn, and exhibits a surprising number of fine seats, elegantly built, and magnificently furnished. There is an incredible number of noble houses in every part of Scotland that I have seen. – Dalkeith, Pinkie, Yester, and lord Hopton's [Hopetoun's],[9] all of them within four or five miles of Edinburgh, are princely palaces, in every one of which a sovereign might reside at his ease. – I suppose the Scots affect these monuments of grandeur. – If I may be allowed to mingle censure with my remarks upon a people I revere, I must observe, that their weak side seems to be vanity. – I am afraid that even their hospitality is not quite free of ostentation. – I think I have discovered among them uncommon pains taken to display their fine linen, of which, indeed, they have great plenty, their furniture, plate, housekeeping, and variety of wines, in which article, it must be owned, they are profuse, if not prodigal – A burgher of Edinburgh, not content to vie with a citizen of London, who has ten times his fortune, must excel him in the expence as well as elegance of his entertainments.

Though the villas of the Scotch nobility and gentry have generally an air of grandeur and state, I think their gardens and parks are not comparable to those of England; a circumstance the more remarkable, as I was told by the ingenious Mr Phillip Miller of Chelsea,[10] that almost all the gardeners of South-Britain were natives of Scotland. The verdure of this country is not equal to that of England. – The pleasure-grounds are, in my opinion, not so well laid out according to the *genius loci*;[11] nor are the lawns, and walks, and hedges kept in such delicate order. – The trees are planted in prudish[12] rows, which have not such an agreeable natural effect, as when they are thrown into irregular groupes, with intervening glades; and firs, which they generally raise around their houses, look dull and funereal in the summer season. — I must confess, indeed, that they yield serviceable timber, and good shelter against the northern blasts; that they grow and thrive in the most barren soil, and continually perspire a fine balsam of turpentine, which must render the air very salutary and sanative to lungs of a tender texture.

Tabby and I have been both frightened in our return by sea from the coast of Fife — She was afraid of drowning, and I of catching cold, in consequence of being drenched with sea-water; but my fears as well as hers, have been happily disappointed. — She is now in perfect health; I wish I could say the same of Liddy — Something uncommon is the matter with that poor girl; her colour fades, her appetite fails, and her spirits flag –

She is become moping and melancholy, and is often found in tears — Her brother suspects internal uneasiness on account of Wilson, and denounces vengeance against that adventurer. — She was, it seems, strongly affected at the ball by the sudden appearance of one Mr Gordon, who strongly resembles the said Wilson; but I am rather suspicious that she caught cold by being overheated with dancing. – I have consulted Dr Gregory,[13] an eminent physician of an amiable character, who advises the highland air, and the use of goat-milk whey, which, surely, cannot have a bad effect upon a patient who was born and bred among the mountains of Wales – The doctor's opinion is the more agreeable, as we shall find those remedies in the very place which I proposed as the utmost extent of our expedition – I mean the borders of Argyle.

Mr Smollett,[14] one of the judges of the commissary court, which is now sitting, has very kindly insisted upon our lodging at his country-house, on the banks of Lough-Lomond, about fourteen miles beyond Glasgow. For this last city we shall set out in two days, and take Stirling in our way, well provided with recommendations from our friends at Edinburgh, whom, I protest, I shall leave with much regret. I am so far from thinking it any hardship to live in this country, that, if I was obliged to lead a town life, Edinburgh would certainly be the headquarters of

Yours always,

EDIN., August 8.   MATT. BRAMBLE

To Sir WATKIN PHILLIPS, Bart. of Jesus college, Oxon.

DEAR KNIGHT,

I am now little short of the *Ultima Thule*,[1] if this appellation properly belongs to the Orkneys or Hebrides. These last are now lying before me, to the amount of some hundreds, scattered up and down the Deucalidonian sea,[2] affording the most picturesque and romantic prospect I ever beheld — I write this letter in a gentleman's house, near the town of Inverary which may be deemed the capital of the West Highlands, famous for nothing so much as for the stately castle³ begun, and actually covered in by the late duke of Argyle, at a prodigious expence – Whether it will ever be completely finished is a question. —

But, to take things in order — We left Edinburgh ten days ago; and the further North we proceed, we find Mrs Tabitha the less manageable; so that her inclinations are not of the nature of the loadstone; they point not towards the pole. What made her leave Edinburgh with reluctance at last, if we may believe her own assertions, was a dispute which she left unfinished with Mr Moffat, touching the eternity of hell torments. That gentleman, as he advanced in years, began to be sceptical on this head, till, at length, he declared open war against the common acceptation of the word *eternal*. He is now persuaded, that *eternal* signifies no more than an indefinite number of years; and that the most enormous sinner may be quit for *nine millions, nine hundred thousand, nine hundred and ninety-nine years of hell-fire*; which term or period, as he very well observes, forms but an inconsiderable drop, as it were, in the ocean of eternity – For this mitigation he contends, as a system agreeable to the ideas of goodness and mercy, which we annex to the supreme Being – Our aunt seemed willing to adopt this doctrine in favour of the wicked; but he hinted that no person whatever was so righteous as to be exempted entirely from punishment in a future state; and that the most pious Christian upon earth might think himself very happy to get off for a fast of seven or eight thousand years in the midst of fire and brimstone. Mrs Tabitha revolted at this dogma, which filled her at once with horror and indignation – She had recourse to the opinion of Humphry Clinker, who roundly declared it was the popish doctrine of purgatory, and quoted scripture in defence of the *fire everlasting, prepared for the devil and his angels*⁴ – The reverend master Mackcorkendal, and all the theologists and saints of that persuasion were consulted, and some of them had doubts about the matter; which doubts and scruples had begun to infect our aunt, when we took our departure from Edinburgh.

We passed through Linlithgow, where there was an elegant

royal palace,[5] which is now gone to decay, as well as the town itself – This too is pretty much the case with Stirling, though it still boasts of a fine old castle in which the kings of Scotland were wont to reside in their minority – But Glasgow is the pride of Scotland, and, indeed, it might very well pass for an elegant and flourishing city in any part of Christendom. There we had the good fortune to be received into the house of Mr Moore,[6] an eminent surgeon, to whom we were recommended by one of our friends at Edinburgh; and, truly, he could not have done us more essential service – Mr Moore is a merry facetious companion, sensible and shrewd, with a considerable fund of humour; and his wife an agreeable woman, well bred, kind, and obliging – Kindness, which I take to be the essence of good-nature and humanity, is the distinguishing character- istic of the Scotch ladies in their own country – Our landlord shewed us every thing, and introduced us to all the world at Glasgow; where, through his recommendation, we were com- plimented with the freedom of the town. Considering the trade and opulence of this place, it cannot but abound with gaiety and diversions — Here is a great number of young fellows that rival the youth of the capital in spirit and expence; and I was soon convinced, that all the female beauties of Scot- land were not assembled at the hunters ball in Edinburgh — The town of Glasgow flourishes in learning as well as in com- merce – Here is an university,[7] with professors in all the different branches of science, liberally endowed, and judiciously chosen – It was vacation time when I passed, so that I could not entirely satisfy my curiosity; but their mode of education is certainly preferable to ours in some respects – The students are not left to the private instruction of tutors; but taught in public schools or classes, each science by its particular professor or regent.[8]

My uncle is in raptures with Glasgow – He not only visited all the manufactures of the place, but made excursions all round to Hamilton, Paisley, Renfrew, and every other place within a dozen miles, where there was any thing remarkable to be seen in art or nature. I believe the exercise, occasioned by those jaunts, was of service to my sister Liddy, whose appetite and spirits begin to revive – Mrs Tabitha displayed her attractions as usual, and actually believed she had entangled one Mr Maclellan, a rich inkle-manufacturer,[9] in her snares; but when matters came to an explanation, it appeared that his attachment was altogether spiritual, founded upon an intercourse of devotion, at the meeting of Mr John Wesley;[10] who, in the course of his evangelical mission, had come hither in person – At length, we set out for the banks of Lough-Lomond, passing through the little borough of Dumbarton, or (as my uncle will have it) Dunbritton, where there is a castle, more curious than any thing of the kind I had ever seen – It is honoured with a particular description by the elegant Buchanan,[11] as an *arx inexpugnabilis*,[12] and, indeed, it must have been impregnable by the antient manner of besieging. It is a rock of considerable extent, rising with a double top, in an angle formed by the confluence of two rivers, the Clyde and the Leven; perpendicular and inaccessible on all sides, except in one place where the entrance is fortified; and there is no rising ground in the neighbourhood from whence it could be damaged by any kind of battery.

From Dumbarton, the West Highlands appear in the form of huge, dusky mountains, piled one over another; but this prospect is not at all surprising to a native of Glamorgan – We have fixed our headquarters at Cameron, a very neat country-house belonging to commissary Smollet, where we found every sort of accommodation we could desire — It is situated like a Druid's temple, in a grove of oak, close by the side of Lough-Lomond, which is a surprising body of pure transparent water, unfathomably deep in many places, six or seven miles broad, four and twenty miles in length, displaying above twenty green islands, covered with wood; some of them cultivated for corn, and many of them stocked with red deer – They belong to different gentlemen, whose seats are scattered along the banks of the lake, which are agreeably romantic beyond all conception. My uncle and I have left the women at Cameron, as Mrs Tabitha would by no means trust herself again upon the water, and to come hither it was necessary to cross a small inlet of the sea, in an open ferry-boat – This country appears more and more wild and savage the further we advance; and the people are as different from the Lowland Scots, in their looks, garb, and language, as the mountaineers of Brecknock are from the inhabitants of Herefordshire.

When the Lowlanders want to drink a chearupping-cup, they go to the public house, called the Change-house,[13] and call for a chopine of two-penny,[14] which is a thin, yeasty beverage, made of malt; not quite so strong as the table-beer of England – This is brought in a pewter stoop, shaped like a skittle, from whence it is emptied into a quaff; that is, a curious cup made of different pieces of wood, such as box and ebony, cut into little staves, joined alternately, and secured with delicate hoops, having two ears or handles – It holds about a gill,[15] is sometimes tipt round the mouth with silver, and has a plate of the same metal at bottom, with the landlord's cypher engraved. – The Highlanders, on the contrary, despise this liquor, and regale themselves with whisky;[16] a malt spirit, as strong as geneva,[17] which they swallow in great quantities, without any signs of inebriation. They are used to it from the cradle, and find it an excellent preservative against the winter cold, which must be extreme on these mountains – I am told that it is given with great success to infants, as a cordial in the confluent small-pox,[18] when the eruption seems to flag, and the symptoms grow unfavourable – The Highlanders are used to eat much more animal food than falls to the share of their neighbours in the Low-country – They delight in hunting; have plenty of deer and other game, with a great number of sheep, goats, and black-cattle running wild, which they scruple not to kill as venison, without being much at pains to ascertain the property.

Inverary is but a poor town, though it stands immediately under the protection of the duke of Argyle,[19] who is a mighty prince in this part of Scotland. The peasants live in wretched cabins, and seem very poor; but the gentlemen are tolerably well lodged, and so loving to strangers, that a man runs some risque of his life from their hospitality – It must be observed that the poor Highlanders are now seen to disadvantage – They have been not only disarmed by act of parliament, but also deprived of their ancient garb,[20] which was both graceful and convenient; and what is a greater hardship still, they are compelled to wear breeches; a restraint which they cannot bear with any degree of patience: indeed, the majority wear them, not in the proper place, but on poles or long staves over their shoulders — They are even debarred the use of their striped stuff called Tartane, which was their own manufacture, prized by them above all the velvets, brocades, and tissues of Europe and Asia. They now lounge along in loose great coats, of coarse russet,[21] equally mean and cumbersome, and betray manifest marks of dejection – Certain it is, the government could not have taken a more effectual method to break their national spirit.

We have had princely sport in hunting the stag on these mountains – These are the lonely hills of Morven, where Fingal and his heroes enjoyed the same pastime; I feel an enthusiastic pleasure when I survey the brown heath that Ossian wont to tread; and hear the wind whistle through the bending grass — When I enter our landlord's hall, I look for the suspended harp of that divine bard, and listen in hopes of hearing the aerial sound of his respected spirit – The poems of Ossian[22] are in every mouth – A famous antiquarian of this country, the laird of Macfarlane,[23] at whose house we dined a few days ago, can repeat them all in the original Gallick, which has a great affinity to the Welch, not only in the general sound, but also in a great number of radical words; and I make no doubt that they are both sprung from the same origin. I was not a little surprised, when asking a Highlander one day, if he knew where we should find any game? he replied, '*hu niel Sassenagh*', which signifies *no English*: the very same answer I should have received from a Welchman, and almost in the same words. The Highlanders have no other name for the people of the Low-country, but Sassenagh,[24] or Saxons; a strong presumption, that the Lowland Scots and the English are derived from the same stock — The peasants of these hills strongly resemble those of Wales in their looks, their manners, and habitations; every thing I see, and hear, and feel, seems Welch – The mountains, vales, and streams; the air and climate; the beef, mutton, and game, are all Welch – It must be owned, however, that this people are better provided than we in some articles – They have plenty of red deer and roebuck, which are fat and delicious at this season of the year – Their sea teems with amazing quantities of the finest fish in the world; and they find means to procure very good claret at a very small expence.

Our landlord is a man of consequence in this part of the country; a cadet from the family of Argyle and hereditary captain of one of his castles – His name, in plain English, is Dougal Campbell; but as there is a great number of the same appellation, they are distinguished (like the Welch) by patronimics;[25] and as I have known an antient Briton called Madoc ap-Morgan ap-Jenkin, ap-Jones, our Highland chief designs himself Dou'l Mac-amish mac-'oul ichian, signifying Dougal, the son of James, the son of Dougal, the son of John – He has travelled in the course of his education, and is disposed to make certain alterations in his domestic œconomy; but he finds it impossible to abolish the ancient customs of the family; some of which are ludicrous enough – His piper for example, who is an hereditary officer of the household, will not part with the least particle of his privileges. — He has a right to wear the kilt, or ancient Highland dress, with the purse, pistol, and durk – a broad yellow ribbon, fixed to the chanter-pipe, is thrown over his shoulder, and trails along the ground, while he performs the function of his minstrelsy; and this, I suppose, is analogous to the pennon or flag which was formerly carried before every knight in battle. — He plays before the laird every Sunday in his way to the kirk, which he circles three times, performing the family march which implies defiance to all the enemies of the clan; and every morning he plays a full hour by the clock, in the great hall, marching backwards and forwards all the time, with a solemn pace, attended by the laird's kinsmen, who seem much delighted with the music – In this exercise, he indulges them with a variety of pibrochs or airs, suited to the different passions, which he would either excite or assuage.

Mr Campbell himself, who performs very well on the violin, has an invincible antipathy to the sound of the Highland bagpipe, which sings in the nose with a most alarming twang, and, indeed, is quite intolerable to ears of common sensibility, when aggravated by the echo of a vaulted hall – He therefore begged the piper would have some mercy upon him, and dispense with this part of the morning service — A consultation of the clan being held on this occasion, it was unanimously agreed, that the laird's request could not be granted without a dangerous encroachment upon the customs of the family – The piper declared, he could not give up for a moment the privilege he derived from his ancestors; nor would the laird's relations forego an entertainment which they valued above all others – There was no remedy; Mr Campbell, being obliged to acquiesce, is fain to stop his ears with cotton; to fortify his head with three or four night-caps and every morning retire into the penetralia[26] of his habitation, in order to avoid this diurnal annoyance. When the music ceases, he produces himself at an open window that looks into the courtyard, which is by this time filled with a crowd of his vassals and dependents, who worship his first appearance, by uncovering their heads, and bowing to the earth with the most humble prostration. As all these people have something to communicate in the way of proposal, complaint, or petition, they wait patiently till the laird comes forth, and, following him in his walks, are favoured each with a short audience in his turn. Two days ago, he dispatched above an hundred different sollicitors, in walking with us to the house of a neighbouring gentleman, where we dined by invitation. Our landlord's house-keeping is equally rough and hospitable, and savours much of the simplicity of ancient times: the great hall, paved with flat stones, is about forty-five feet by twenty-two, and serves not only for a dining-room, but also for a bed-chamber, to gentlemen-dependents and hangers-on of the family. At night, half a dozen occasional beds are ranged on each side along the wall. These are made of fresh heath, pulled up by the roots, and disposed in such a manner as to make a very agreeable couch, where they lie, without any other covering than the plaid – My uncle and I were indulged with separate chambers and down beds which we begged to exchange for a layer of heath; and indeed I never slept so much to my satisfaction. It was not only soft and elastic, but the plant, being in flower, diffused an agreeable fragrance, which is wonderfully refreshing and restorative.

Yesterday we were invited to the funeral of an old lady, the grand-mother of a gentleman in this neighbourhood, and found ourselves in the midst of fifty people, who were regaled with a sumptuous feast, accompanied by the music of a dozen pipers. In short, this meeting had all the air of a grand festival; and the guests did such honour to the entertainment, that many of them could not stand when we were reminded of the business on which we had met. The company forthwith taking horse, rode in a very irregular cavalcade to the place of interment, a church, at the distance of two long miles from the castle. On our arrival, however, we found we had committed a small oversight, in leaving the corpse behind; so we were obliged to wheel about, and met the old gentle-woman half way, being carried upon poles by the nearest relations of her family, and attended by the *coronach*,[27] composed of a multitude of old hags, who tore their hair, beat their breasts, and howled most hideously. At the grave, the orator, or *senachie*, pronounced the panegyric of the defunct, every period being confirmed by a yell of the *coronach*. The body was committed to the earth, the pipers playing a pibroch all the time; and all the company standing uncovered. The ceremony was closed with the discharge of pistols; then we returned to the castle, resumed the bottle, and by midnight there was not a sober person in the family, the females excepted. The 'squire and I were, with some difficulty, permitted to retire with our landlord in the evening; but our entertainer was a little chagrined at our retreat; and afterwards seemed to think it a disparagement to his family, that not above a hundred gallons of whisky had been drunk upon such a solemn occasion. This morning we got up by four, to hunt the roebuck, and, in half an hour, found breakfast ready served in the hall. The hunters consisted of Sir George Colquhoun and me, as strangers (my uncle not chusing to be of the party), of the *laird in person, the laird's brother, the laird's brother's son, the laird's sister's son, the laird's father's brother's son*, and all their *foster brothers*, who are counted parcel of the family: but we were attended by an infinite number of *Gaelly's*,[28] or ragged Highlanders without shoes or stockings.

The following articles formed our morning's repast: one kit

of boiled eggs; a second, full of butter; a third full of cream; an entire cheese, made of goat's milk; a large earthen pot full of honey; the best part of a ham; a cold venison pasty; a bushel of oat meal, made in thin cakes and bannocks, with a small wheaten loaf in the middle for the strangers; a large stone bottle full of whisky, another of brandy, and a kilderkin[29] of ale. There was a ladle chained to the cream kit, with curious wooden bickers[30] to be filled from this reservoir. The spirits were drank out of a silver quaff, and the ale out of horns: great justice was done to the collation by the guests in general; one of them in particular ate above two dozen of hard eggs, with a proportionable quantity of bread, butter, and honey; nor was one drop of liquor left upon the board. Finally, a large roll of tobacco was presented by way of desert, and every individual took a comfortable quid, to prevent the bad effects of the morning air. We had a fine chace over the mountains, after a roebuck, which we killed, and I got home time enough to drink tea with Mrs Campbell and our 'squire. To-morrow we shall set out on our return for Cameron. We propose to cross the Frith of Clyde, and take the towns of Greenock and Port-Glasgow in our way. This circuit being finished, we shall turn our faces to the south, and follow the sun with augmented velocity, in order to enjoy the rest of the autumn in England, where Boreas[31] is not quite so biting as he begins already to be on the tops of these northern hills. But our progress from place to place shall continue to be specified in these detached journals of

Yours always,

ARGYLSHIRE, Sept. 3.   J. MELFORD

To Dr Lewis.

DEAR DICK,

About a fortnight is now elapsed, since we left the capital of Scotland, directing our course towards Stirling, where we lay – The castle of this place is such another as that of Edinburgh, and affords a surprising prospect of the windings of the river

Forth, which are so extraordinary, that the distance from hence to Alloa by land, is but forty miles, and by water it is twenty-four. Alloa is a neat thriving town, that depends in a great measure on the commerce of Glasgow, the merchants of which send hither tobacco and other articles, to be deposited in warehouses for exportation from the Frith of Forth. In our way hither we visited a flourishing iron-work,[1] where, instead of burning wood, they use coal, which they have the art of clearing in such a manner as frees it from the sulphur, that would otherwise render the metal too brittle for working. Excellent coal is found in almost every part of Scotland.

The soil of this district produces scarce any other grain but oats and barley; perhaps because it is poorly cultivated, and almost altogether uninclosed. The few inclosures they have consist of paultry walls of loose stones gathered from the fields, which indeed they cover, as if they had been scattered on purpose. When I expressed my surprize that the peasants did not disencumber their grounds of these stones; a gentleman, well acquainted with the theory as well as practice of farming, assured me that the stones, far from being prejudicial, were serviceable to the crop. This philosopher had ordered a field of his own to be cleared, manured and sown with barley, and the produce was more scanty than before. He caused the stones to be replaced, and next year the crop was as good as ever. The stones were removed a second time, and the harvest failed; they were again brought back, and the ground retrieved its fertility. The same experiment has been tried in different parts of Scotland with the same success – Astonished at this information, I desired to know in what manner he accounted for this strange phenomenon; and he said there were three ways in which the stones might be serviceable. They might possibly restrain an excess in the perspiration of the earth, analogous to colliquative sweats,[2] by which the human body is sometimes wasted and consumed. They might act as so many fences to protect the tender blade from the piercing winds of the spring; or, by multiplying the reflexion of the sun, they might increase the warmth, so as to mitigate the natural chilness of the soil and climate – But, surely this excessive perspiration might be more effectually checked by different kinds of manure, such as ashes, lime, chalk, or marl, of which last it seems there are many pits in this kingdom: as for the warmth, it would be much more equally obtained by inclosures; the cultivation would require less labour; and the ploughs, harrows, and horses, would not suffer half the damage which they now sustain.

These north-western parts are by no means fertile in corn. The ground is naturally barren and moorish. The peasants are poorly lodged, meagre in their looks, mean in their apparel, and remarkably dirty. This last reproach they might easily wash off, by means of those lakes, rivers, and rivulets of pure water, with which they are so liberally supplied by nature. Agriculture cannot be expected to flourish where the farms are small, the leases short, and the husbandman begins upon a rack rent,[3] without a sufficient stock to answer the purposes of improvement. The granaries of Scotland are the banks of the Tweed, the counties of East and Mid-Lothian, the Carse of Gowrie, in Perthshire, equal in fertility to any part of England, and some tracts in Aberdeenshire and Murray, where I am told the harvest is more early than in Northumberland, although they lie above two degrees farther north. I have a strong curiosity to visit many places beyond the Forth and the Tay, such as Perth, Dundee, Montrose, and Aberdeen, which are towns equally elegant and thriving; but the season is too far advanced to admit of this addition to my original plan.

I am so far happy as to have seen Glasgow, which, to the best of my recollection and judgment, is one of the prettiest towns in Europe; and, without all doubt, it is one of the most flourishing in Great Britain. In short, it is a perfect bee-hive in point of industry. It stands partly on a gentle declivity; but the greatest part of it is in a plain, watered by the river Clyde. The streets are straight, open, airy, and well paved; and the houses lofty and well built of hewn stone. At the upper end of the town, there is a venerable cathedral,[4] that may be compared with York-minster or West-minster; and, about the middle of the descent from this to the Cross, is the college, a respectable pile of building, with all manner of accommodation for the professors and students, including an elegant library, and an observatory well provided with astronomical instruments. The number of inhabitants is said to amount to thirty thousand; and marks of opulence and independency appear in every quarter of this commercial city, which, however, is not without its inconveniences and defects. The water of their public pumps is generally hard and brackish, an imperfection the less excusable, as the river Clyde runs by their doors, in the lower part of the town; and there are rivulets and springs above the cathedral, sufficient to fill a large reservoir with excellent water, which might be thence distributed to all the different parts of the city. It is of more consequence to consult the health of the inhabitants in this article, than to employ so much attention in beautifying their town with new streets, squares, and churches. Another defect, not so easily remedied, is the shallowness of the river, which will not float vessels of any burthen within ten or twelve miles of the city; so that the merchants are obliged to load and unload their ships at Greenock and Port-Glasgow, situated about fourteen miles nearer the mouth of the Frith, where it is about two miles broad.

The people of Glasgow have a noble spirit of enterprise – Mr Moore, a surgeon, to whom I was recommended from Edinburgh, introduced me to all the principal merchants of the place. Here I became acquainted with Mr Cochran,[5] who may be stiled one of the sages of this kingdom. He was first magistrate at the time of the last rebellion. I sat as member when he was examined in the house of commons, upon which occasion Mr P—[6] observed he had never heard such a sensible evidence given at that bar. I was also introduced to Dr John Gordon,[7] a patriot of a truly Roman spirit, who is the father of the linen manufacture in this place, and was the great promoter of the city workhouse, infirmary, and other works of public utility. Had he lived in ancient Rome, he would have been honoured with a statue at the public expence. I moreover conversed with one Mr G—ssf—d,[8] whom I take to be one of the greatest merchants in Europe. In the last war, he is said to have had at one time five and twenty ships with their cargoes, his own property, and to have traded for above half a million sterling a-year. The last war was a fortunate period for the commerce of Glasgow – The merchants, considering that their ships bound for America, launching out at once into the Atlantic by the north of Ireland, pursued a track very little frequented by privateers, resolved to insure one another, and saved a very considerable sum by this resolution, as few or none of their ships were taken — You must know I have a sort of national attachment to this part of Scotland – The great church dedicated to St Mongah, the river Clyde, and other particulars that smack of our Welch language and customs, contribute to flatter me with the notion, that these people are the descendants of the Britons, who once possessed this country. Without all question, this was a Cumbrian kingdom: its capital was Dumbarton (a corruption of Dunbritton) which still exists as a royal borough, at the influx of the Clyde and Leven, ten miles below Glasgow. The same neighbourhood gave birth to St Patrick, the apostle of Ireland, at a place where there is still a church and village, which retain his name. Hard by are some vestiges of the famous Roman wall, built in the reign of Antonine,[9] from the Clyde to the Forth, and fortified with castles, to restrain the incursions of the Scots or Caledonians, who inhabited the West-Highlands. In a line parallel to this wall, the merchants of Glasgow have determined to make a navigable canal[10] betwixt the two Firths which will be of incredible advantage to their commerce, in transporting merchandize from one side of the island to the other.

From Glasgow we travelled along the Clyde, which is a delightful stream, adorned on both sides with villas, towns, and villages. Here is no want of groves, and meadows, and corn-fields interspersed; but on this side of Glasgow, there is little other grain than oats and barley; the first are much better, the last much worse, than those of the same species in England. I wonder, there is so little rye, which is a grain that will thrive in almost any soil; and it is still more surprising, that the cultivation of potatoes should be so much neglected in the Highlands, where the poor people have not meal enough to supply them with bread through the winter. On the other side of the river are the towns of Paisley and Renfrew. The first, from an inconsiderable village, is become one of the most flourishing places of the kingdom, enriched by the linen, cambrick,[11]

flowered lawn,[12] and silk manufactures. It was formerly noted
for a rich monastery of the monks of Clugny, who wrote the
famous *Scoti-Chronicon*, called *The Black Book of Paisley*.[13]
The old abbey still remains, converted into a dwelling-house,
belonging to the earl of Dundonald.[14] Renfrew is a pretty town,
on the banks of Clyde, capital of the shire, which was heretofore
the patrimony of the Stuart family, and gave the title of baron
to the king's eldest son, which is still assumed by the prince of
Wales.

The Clyde we left a little on our left-hand at Dunbritton,
where it widens into an æstuary or frith, being augmented by
the influx of the Leven. On this spot stands the castle formerly
called Alcluyd, washed by these two rivers on all sides, except
a narrow isthmus,[15] which at every spring-tide is overflowed.
The whole is a great curiosity, from the quality and form of the
rock, as well as from the nature of its situation — We now
crossed the water of Leven, which, though nothing near so
considerable as the Clyde, is much more transparent, pastoral,
and delightful. This charming stream is the outlet of Lough-
Lomond, and through a tract of four miles pursues its winding
course, murmuring over a bed of pebbles, till it joins the Frith
at Dunbritton. A very little above its source, on the lake, stands
the house of Cameron, belonging to Mr Smollett, so
embosomed in an oak wood, that we did not see it till we were
within fifty yards of the door. I have seen the Lago di Garda,
Albano, De Vico, Bolsena, and Geneva, and, upon my honour,
I prefer Lough-Lomond to them all, a preference which is certainly owing to the verdant islands that seem to float upon its
surface, affording the most inchanting objects of repose to the
excursive view. Nor are the banks destitute of beauties, which
even partake of the sublime. On this side they display a sweet
variety of woodland, cornfield, and pasture, with several agreeable villas emerging as it were out of the lake, till, at some
distance, the prospect terminates in huge mountains covered
with heath, which being in the bloom, affords a very rich
covering of purple. Every thing here is romantic beyond imagination. This country is justly stiled the Arcadia of Scotland; and
I don't doubt but it may vie with Arcadia in every thing but

climate. — I am sure it excels it in verdure, wood, and water. – What say you to a natural bason of pure water, near thirty miles long, and in some places seven miles broad, and in many above a hundred fathom deep, having four and twenty habitable islands, some of them stocked with deer, and all of them covered with wood; containing immense quantities of delicious fish, salmon, pike, trout, perch, flounders, eels, and powans, the last a delicate kind of fresh-water herring peculiar to this lake; and finally communicating with the sea, by sending off the Leven, through which all those species (except the powan) make their exit and entrance occasionally?

Inclosed I send you the copy of a little ode to this river, by Dr Smollett, who was born on the banks of it, within two miles of the place where I am now writing. – It is at least picturesque and accurately descriptive, if it has no other merit. – There is an idea of truth in an agreeable landscape taken from nature, which pleases me more than the gayest fiction which the most luxuriant fancy can display.

I have other remarks to make; but as my paper is full, I must reserve them till the next occasion. I shall only observe at present, that I am determined to penetrate at least forty miles into the Highlands, which now appear like a vast fantastic vision in the clouds, inviting the approach of

Yours always,

CAMERON, Aug. 28.   MATT. BRAMBLE

ODE TO LEVEN-WATER[16]

On Leven's banks, while free to rove,
And tune the rural pipe to love;
I envied not the happiest swain
That ever trod th' Arcadian plain.

Pure stream! in whose transparent wave
My youthful limbs I wont to lave;
No torrents stain thy limpid source;
No rocks impede thy dimpling course,

That sweetly warbles o'er its bed,
With white, round, polish'd pebbles spread;
While, lightly pois'd, the scaly brood
In myriads cleave thy crystal flood;
The springing trout in speckled pride;
The salmon, monarch of the tide;
The ruthless pike, intent on war;
The silver eel, and motled par.*

Devolving from thy parent lake,
A charming maze thy waters make,
By bow'rs of birch, and groves of pine,
And hedges flow'r'd with eglantine.

Still on thy banks so gayly green,
May num'rous herds and flocks be seen,
And lasses chanting o'er the pail,
And shepherds piping in the dale,
And ancient faith that knows no guile,
And industry imbrown'd with toil,
And hearts resolv'd, and hands prepar'd,
The blessings they enjoy to guard.

To Dr Lewis.

DEAR DOCTOR,

If I was disposed to be critical, I should say this house of
Cameron is too near the lake, which approaches, on one side,
to within six or seven yards of the window. It might have been
placed in a higher site, which would have afforded a more
extensive prospect and a drier atmosphere; but this imperfection is not chargeable on the present proprietor, who purchased
it ready built, rather than be at the trouble of repairing his own

---

* The par is a small fish, not unlike the smelt, which it rivals in delicacy and
flavour.

family-house of Bonhill, which stands two miles from hence on the Leven, so surrounded with plantation, that it used to be known by the name of the Mavis (or thrush) Nest. Above that house is a romantic glen or clift of a mountain, covered with hanging woods having at bottom a stream of fine water that forms a number of cascades in its descent to join the Leven; so that the scene is quite enchanting. A captain of a man of war, who had made the circuit of the globe with Mr Anson,[1] being conducted to this glen, exclaimed, 'Juan Fernandez, by God!'

Indeed, this country would be a perfect paradise, if it was not, like Wales, cursed with a weeping climate, owing to the same cause in both, the neighbourhood of high mountains, and a westerly situation, exposed to the vapours of the Atlantic ocean. This air, however, notwithstanding its humidity, is so healthy, that the natives are scarce ever visited by any other disease than the small-pox, and certain cutaneous evils, which are the effects of dirty living, the great and general reproach of the commonalty of this kingdom. Here are a great many living monuments of longævity; and among the rest a person, whom I treat with singular respect, as a venerable druid, who has lived near ninety years, without pain or sickness, among oaks of his own planting.[2] – He was once proprietor of these lands; but being of a projecting spirit, some of his schemes miscarried, and he was obliged to part with his possession, which hath shifted hands two or three times since that period; but every succeeding proprietor hath done every thing in his power, to make his old age easy and comfortable. He has a sufficiency to procure the necessaries of life; and he and his old woman reside in a small convenient farm-house, having a little garden which he cultivates with his own hands. This ancient couple live in great health, peace, and harmony, and, knowing no wants, enjoy the perfection of content. Mr Smollet calls him the admiral, because he insists upon steering his pleasure-boat upon the lake; and he spends most of his time in ranging through the woods, which he declares he enjoys as much as if they were still his own property – I asked him the other day, if he was never sick, and he answered, Yes; he had a slight fever the year before the union. If he was not deaf, I should take much pleasure in his conversation; for he is very intelligent, and his memory is surprisingly retentive – These are the happy effects of temperance, exercise, and good nature — Notwithstanding all his innocence, however, he was the cause of great perturbation to my man Clinker, whose natural superstition has been much injured, by the histories of witches, fairies, ghosts, and goblins, which he has heard in this country – On the evening after our arrival, Humphry strolled into the wood, in the course of his meditation, and all at once the admiral stood before him, under the shadow of a spreading oak. Though the fellow is far from being timorous in cases that are not supposed preternatural, he could not stand the sight of this apparition, but ran into the kitchen, with his hair standing on end, staring wildly, and deprived of utterance. Mrs Jenkins, seeing him in this condition, screamed aloud, 'Lord have mercy upon us, he has seen something!' Mrs Tabitha was alarmed, and the whole house in confusion. When he was recruited with a dram, I desired him to explain the meaning of all this agitation; and, with some reluctance, he owned he had seen a spirit, in the shape of an old man with a white beard, a black cap, and a plaid nightgown. He was undeceived by the admiral in person, who, coming in at this juncture, appeared to be a creature of real flesh and blood.

Do you know how we fare in this Scottish paradise? We make free with our landlord's mutton, which is excellent, his poultry-yard, his garden, his dairy, and his cellar, which are all well stored. We have delicious salmon, pike, trout, perch, par, &c. at the door, for the taking. The Frith of Clyde, on the other side of the hill, supplies us with mullet, red and grey, cod, mackarel, whiting, and a variety of sea-fish, including the finest fresh herrings I ever tasted. We have sweet, juicy beef, and tolerable veal, with delicate bread from the little town of Dunbritton; and plenty of partridge, growse, heath cock, and other game in presents.

We have been visited by all the gentlemen in the neighbourhood, and they have entertained us at their houses, not barely with hospitality, but with such marks of cordial affection, as one would wish to find among near relations, after an absence of many years.

I told you, in my last, I had projected an excursion to the Highlands, which project I have now happily executed, under the auspices of Sir George Colquhoun, a colonel in the Dutch service, who offered himself as our conductor on this occasion. Leaving our women at Cameron, to the care and inspection of Lady H[elen] C[olquhoun], we set out on horseback for Inverary, the county town of Argyle, and dined on the road with the Laird of Macfarlane, the greatest genealogist I ever knew in any country, and perfectly acquainted with all the antiquities of Scotland.

The Duke of Argyle has an old castle in Inverary, where he resides when he is in Scotland; and hard by is the shell of a noble Gothic palace, built by the last duke, which, when finished, will be a great ornament to this part of the Highlands. As for Inverary, it is a place of very little importance.

This country is amazingly wild, especially towards the mountains, which are heaped upon the backs of one another, making a most stupendous appearance of savage nature, with hardly any signs of cultivation, or even of population. All is sublimity, silence, and solitude. The people live together in glens or bottoms, where they are sheltered from the cold and storms of winter: but there is a margin of plain ground spread along the sea side, which is well inhabited and improved by the arts of husbandry; and this I take to be one of the most agreeable tracts of the whole island; the sea not only keeps it warm, and supplies it with fish, but affords one of the most ravishing prospects in the whole world; I mean the appearance of the Hebrides, or Western Islands to the number of three hundred, scattered as far as the eye can reach, in the most agreeable confusion. As the soil and climate of the Highlands are but ill adapted to the cultivation of corn, the people apply themselves chiefly to the breeding and feeding of black cattle, which turn to good account. Those animals run wild all the winter, without any shelter or subsistence, but what they can find among the heath. When the snow lies so deep and hard, that they cannot penetrate to the roots of the grass, they make a diurnal progress, guided by a sure instinct, to the sea-side at low water, where they feed on the *alga marina*,[3] and other plants that grow upon the beach.

Perhaps this branch of husbandry, which required very little attendance and labour, is one of the principal causes of that idleness and want of industry, which distinguishes these mountaineers in their own country – When they come forth into the world, they become as diligent and alert as any people upon earth. They are undoubtedly a very distinct species from their fellow subjects of the Lowlands, against whom they indulge an ancient spirit of animosity; and this difference is very discernible even among persons of family and education. The Lowlanders are generally cool and circumspect, the Highlanders fiery and ferocious: but this violence of their passions serves only to inflame the zeal of their devotion to strangers, which is truly enthusiastic.

We proceeded about twenty miles beyond Inverary, to the house of a gentleman, a friend of our conductor, where we stayed a few days, and were feasted in such a manner, that I began to dread the consequence to my constitution.

Notwithstanding the solitude that prevails among these mountains, there is no want of people in the Highlands. I am credibly informed that the duke of Argyle can assemble five thousand men in arms, of his own clan and surname, which is Campbell; and there is besides a tribe of the same appellation, whose chief is the Earl of Breadalbine.[4] The Macdonalds are as numerous, and remarkably warlike: the Camerons, M'Leods, Frasers, Grants, M'Kenzies, M'Kays, M'Phersons, M'Intoshes, are powerful clans; so that if all the Highlanders, including the inhabitants of the Isles, were united, they could bring into the field an army of forty thousand fighting men, capable of undertaking the most dangerous enterprize. We have lived to see four thousand of them, without discipline, throw the whole kingdom of Great Britain into confusion. They attacked and defeated two armies of regular troops accustomed to service.[5] They penetrated into the centre of England; and afterwards marched back with deliberation, in the face of two other armies, through an enemy's country, where every precaution was taken to cut off their retreat. I know not any other people in Europe, who, without the use or knowledge of arms, will attack regular forces sword in hand, if their chief will head them in battle. When disciplined, they cannot fail of being excellent soldiers. They do not walk like the generality of mankind, but trot and bounce like deer, as if they moved upon springs. They greatly excel the Lowlanders in all the exercises that require agility; they are incredibly abstemious, and patient of hunger and fatigue; so steeled against the weather, that in travelling, even when the ground is covered with snow, they never look for a house, or any other shelter but their plaid, in which they wrap themselves up, and go to sleep under the cope of heaven. Such people, in quality of soldiers, must be invincible, when the business is to perform quick marches in a difficult country, to strike sudden strokes, beat up the enemy's quarters, harrass their cavalry, and perform expeditions without the formality of magazines, baggage, forage, and artillery. The chieftainship of the High-landers is a very dangerous influence operating at the extremity of the island, where the eyes and hands of government cannot be supposed to see [and] act with precision and vigour. In order to break the force of clanship, administration has always practised the political maxim, *Divide et impera*.[6] The legislature hath not only disarmed these mountaineers, but also deprived them of their antient garb, which contributed in a great measure to keep up their military spirit; and their slavish tenures are all dissolved by act of parliament; so that they are at present as free and independent of their chiefs, as the law can make them: but the original attachment still remains, and is founded on something prior to the *feudal system*, about which the writers of this age have made such a pother, as if it was a new discovery, like the *Copernican system*. Every peculiarity of policy, custom, and even temperament, is affectedly traced to this origin, as if the feudal constitution had not been common to almost all the natives of Europe. For my part, I expect to see the use of trunk-hose and buttered ale ascribed to the influence of the *feudal system*. The connection between the clans and their chiefs is, without all doubt, *patriarchal*.[7] It is founded on heredi-tary regard and affection, cherished through a long succession of ages. The clan consider the chief as their father, they bear his name, they believe themselves descended from his family, and they obey him as their lord, with all the ardour of filial love and veneration; while he, on his part, exerts a paternal authority, commanding, chastising, rewarding, protecting, and maintaining them as his own children. If the legislature would entirely destroy this connection, it must compel the Highlanders to change their habitation and their names. Even this experiment has been formerly tried without success — In the reign of James VI a battle was fought within a few short miles of this place, between two clans, the M'Gregors and the Colquhouns, in which the latter were defeated: the Laird of M'Gregor made such a barbarous use of his victory, that he was forfeited and outlawed by act of parliament: his lands were given to the family of Montrose, and his clan were obliged to change their name. They obeyed so far, as to call themselves severally Campbell, Graham, or Drummond, the surnames of the families of Argyle, Montrose, and Perth, that they might enjoy the protection of those houses; but they still added M'Gregor to their new appellation; and as their chief was deprived of his estate, they robbed and plundered for his subsistence. – Mr Cameron of Lochiel,[8] the chief of that clan, whose father was attainted for having been concerned in the last rebellion, returning from France in obedience to a proclamation and act of parliament, passed at the beginning of the late war, payed a visit to his own country, and hired a farm in the neighbourhood of his father's house, which had been burnt to the ground. The clan, though ruined and scattered, no sooner heard of his arrival than they flocked to him from all quarters, to welcome his return, and in a few days stocked his farm with seven hundred black cattle, which they had saved in the general wreck of their affairs: but their beloved chief, who was a promising youth, did not live to enjoy the fruits of their fidelity and attachment.

The most effectual method I know to weaken, and at length destroy this influence, is to employ the commonalty in such a manner as to give them a taste of property and independence – In vain the government grants them advantageous leases on the forfeited estates, if they have no property to prosecute the means of improvement – The sea is an inexhaustible fund of riches; but the fishery cannot be carried on without vessels, casks, salt, lines, nets, and other tackle. I conversed with a sensible man of this country, who, from a real spirit of patriotism had set up a fishery on the coast, and a manufacture of coarse linen, for the employment of the poor Highlanders. Cod is here in such plenty, that he told me he had seen several hundred taken on one line, at one hawl — It must be observed, however, that the line was of immense length, and had two thousand hooks, baited with muscles; but the fish was so superior to the cod caught on the banks of Newfoundland, that his correspondent at Lisbon sold them immediately at his own price, although Lent was just over when they arrived, and the people might be supposed quite cloyed with this kind of diet — His linen manufacture was likewise in a prosperous way, when the late war intervening, all his best hands were pressed into the service.

It cannot be expected, that the gentlemen of this country should execute commercial schemes to render their vassals independent; nor, indeed, are such schemes suited to their way of life and inclination; but a company of merchants might, with proper management, turn to good account a fishery established in this part of Scotland — Our people have a strange itch to colonize America, when the uncultivated parts of our own island might be settled to greater advantage.

After having rambled through the mountains and glens of Argyle, we visited the adjacent islands of Ila, Jura, Mull, and Icolmkill. In the first, we saw the remains of a castle, built in a lake, where Macdonald, lord or king of the isles, formerly resided.[9] Jura is famous for having given birth to one Mackcrain,[10] who lived one hundred and eighty years in one house, and died in the reign of Charles the Second. Mull affords several bays, where there is safe anchorage: in one of which, the Florida, a ship of the Spanish armada, was blown up by one of Mr Smollett's ancestors – About forty years ago, John duke of Argyle[11] is said to have consulted the Spanish registers, by which it appeared, that this ship had the military chest on board – He employed experienced divers to examine the wreck; and they found the hull of the vessel still entire, but so covered with sand, that they could not make their way between decks; however, they picked up several pieces of plate, that were scattered about in the bay, and a couple of fine brass cannon.

Icolmkill, or Iona, is a small island which St Columba chose for his habitation[12] – It was respected for its sanctity, and college or seminary of ecclesiastics – Part of its church is still standing, with the tombs of several Scottish, Irish, and Danish sovereigns, who were here interred – These islanders are very bold and dexterous watermen, consequently the better adapted to the fishery: in their manners they are less savage and impetuous than their countrymen on the continent; and they speak the Erse or Gaelick in its greatest purity.

Having sent round our horses by land, we embarked in the distinct of Cowal, for Greenock, which is a neat little town, on the other side of the Frith, with a curious harbour formed by three stone jetties, carried out a good way into the sea — Newport-Glasgow is such another place, about two miles higher up – Both have a face of business and plenty, and are supported entirely by the shipping of Glasgow, of which I counted sixty large vessels in these harbours — Taking boat again at Newport, we were in less than an hour landed on the other side, within two short miles of our head-quarters, where we found our women in good health and spirits – They had been two days before joined by Mr Smollett and his lady, to whom we have such obligations as I cannot mention, even to you, without blushing.

To-morrow we shall bid adieu to the Scotch Arcadia, and begin our progress to the southward, taking our way by Lanerk and Nithsdale, to the west borders of England. I have received so much advantage and satisfaction from this tour, that if my health suffers no revolution in the winter, I believe I shall be tempted to undertake another expedition to the Northern extremity of Caithness, unencumbered by those impediments which now clog the heels of,

Yours,

CAMERON, Sept. 6.   MATT. BRAMBLE

To Miss LÆTITIA WILLIS, at Gloucester.

MY DEAREST LETTY,

Never did poor prisoner long for deliverance, more than I have longed for an opportunity to disburthen my cares into your friendly bosom; and the occasion which now presents itself, is little less than miraculous – Honest Saunders Macawly, the travelling Scotchman, who goes every year to Wales, is now at Glasgow, buying goods, and coming to pay his respects to our family, has undertaken to deliver this letter into your own hand — We have been six weeks in Scotland, and seen the principal towns of the kingdom, where we have been treated with great civility — The people are very courteous; and the country being exceedingly romantic, suits my turn and inclinations — I contracted some friendships at Edinburgh, which is a large and lofty city, full of gay company; and, in particular, commenced an intimate correspondence with one miss R—t—n, an amiable young lady of my own age, whose charms seemed to soften, and even to subdue the stubborn heart of my brother Jery; but he no sooner left the place than he relapsed into his former insensibility — I feel, however, that this indifference is not the family constitution — I never admitted but one idea of love, and that has taken such root in my heart, as to be equally proof against all the pulls of discretion, and the frosts of neglect.

Dear Letty! I had an alarming adventure at the hunters ball in Edinburgh – While I sat discoursing with a friend in a corner, all at once the very image of Wilson stood before me, dressed exactly as he was in the character of Aimwell![1] It was one Mr Gordon, whom I had not seen before — Shocked at the sudden apparition, I fainted away, and threw the whole assembly in confusion — However, the cause of my disorder remained a secret to every body but my brother, who was likewise struck with the resemblance, and scolded after we came home – I am very sensible of Jery's affection, and know he spoke as well with a view to my own interest and happiness, as in regard to the honour of the family; but I cannot bear to have my wounds probed severely – I was not so much affected by the censure he passed upon my own indiscretion, as with the reflection he made on the conduct of Wilson – He observed, that if he was really the gentleman he pretended to be, and harboured nothing but honourable designs, he would have vindicated his pretensions in the face of day – This remark made a deep impression upon my mind — I endeavoured to conceal my thoughts; and this endeavour had a bad effect upon my health and spirits; so it was thought necessary that I should go to the Highlands, and drink the goat-milk-whey.

We went accordingly to Lough Lomond, one of the most enchanting spots in the whole world; and what with this remedy, which I had every morning fresh from the mountains, and the pure air, and chearful company, I have recovered my flesh and appetite; though there is something still at bottom, which it is not in the power of air, exercise, company, or medicine to remove — These incidents would not touch me so nearly, if I had a sensible confidant to sympathize with my affliction, and comfort me with wholesome advice – I have nothing of this kind, except Win Jenkins, who is really a good body in the main, but very ill qualified for such an office – The poor creature is weak in her nerves, as well as in her understanding; otherwise I might have known the true name and character of that unfortunate youth – But why do I call him *unfortunate?* perhaps the epithet is more applicable to me for having listened to the false professions of — But, hold! I have as yet no right, and sure I have no inclination to believe any thing to the prejudice of his honour – In that reflection I shall still exert my patience – As for Mrs Jenkins, she herself is really an object of compassion – Between vanity, methodism, and love, her head is almost turned. I should have more regard for her, however, if she had been more constant in the object of her affection; but, truly, she aimed at conquest, and flirted at the same time with my uncle's footman, Humphrey Clinker, who is really a deserving young man, and one Dutton, my brother's valet de chambre, a debauched fellow; who, leaving Win in the lurch, ran away with another man's bride at Berwick.

My dear Willis, I am truly ashamed of my own sex — We complain of advantages which the men take of our youth, inexperience, insensibility, and all that; but I have seen enough to believe, that our sex in general make it their business to ensnare the other; and for this purpose, employ arts which are by no means to be justified — In point of constancy, they certainly have nothing to reproach the male part of the creation – My poor aunt, without any regard to her years and imperfections, has gone to market with her charms in every place where she thought she had the least chance to dispose of her person, which, however, hangs still heavy on her hands – I am afraid she has used even religion as a decoy, though it has not answered her expectation – She has been praying, preaching, and catechising among the methodists, with whom this country abounds; and pretends to have such manifestations and revelations, as even Clinker himself can hardly believe, though the poor fellow is half crazy with enthusiasm. As for Jenkins, she affects to take all her mistress's reveries for gospel – She has also her heart-heavings and motions of the spirit; and God forgive me if I think uncharitably, but all this seems to me to be downright hypocrisy and deceit – Perhaps, indeed, the poor girl imposes on herself – She is generally in a flutter, and is much subject to vapours – Since we came to Scotland, she has seen apparitions, and pretends to prophesy — If I could put faith in all these supernatural visitations, I should think myself abandoned of grace; for I have neither seen, heard, nor felt anything of this nature, although I endeavour to discharge the duties of religion with all the sincerity, zeal, and devotion, that is in the power of,

> Dear Letty,
> your ever affectionate,

GLASGOW, Sept. 7.   LYDIA MELFORD

We are so far on our return to Brambleton-hall; and I would fain hope we shall take Gloucester in our way, in which case I shall have the inexpressible pleasure of embracing my dear Willis – Pray remember me to my worthy governess.

To Mrs MARY JONES, at Brambleton-hall.

DEAR MARY,

Sunders Macully, the Scotchman, who pushes directly for Vails, has promised to give it you into your own hand, and therefore I would not miss the opportunity to let you know as I am still in the land of the living:[1] and yet I have been on the brink of the other world since I sent you my last letter. – We went by sea to another kingdom called Fife, and coming back, had like to have gone to pot in a storm. – What between the frite and sickness, I thought I should have brought my heart up; even Mr Clinker was not his own man for eight and forty hours after we got ashore. – It was well for some folks that we scaped drownding; for mistress was very frexious, and seemed but indifferently prepared for a change; but, thank God, she was soon put in a better frame by the private exaltations of the reverend Mr Macrocodile. – We afterwards churned to Starling and Grascow, which are a kiple of handsome towns; and then we went to a gentleman's house at Loff-Loming, which is a wonderful sea of fresh water, with a power of hylands in the midst on't. – They say as how it has n'er a bottom, and was made by a musician[2] and, truly, I believe it; for it is not in the coarse of nature. – It has got *waves without wind, fish without fins, and a floating hyland;*[3] and one of them is a crutch-yard, where the dead are buried; and always before the person dies, a bell rings of itself to give warning.

O Mary! this is the land of congyration – The bell knolled when we were there – I saw lights, and heard lamentations. – The gentleman, our landlord, has got another house, which he was fain to quit, on account of a mischievous ghost, that would not suffer people to lie in their beds. – The fairies dwell in a hole of Kairmann,[4] a mounting hard by; and they steal away the good women that are in the straw, if so be as how there a'n't a horshoe nailed to the door: and I was shewn an ould vitch, called Elspath Ringavey, with a red petticoat, bleared eyes, and a mould of grey bristles on her sin. – That she mought do me no harm, I crossed her hand with a taster,[5] and bid her tell my fortune; and she told me such things – descriving Mr Clinker to a hair – but it shall ne'er be said, that I minchioned a word of the matter. – As I was troubled with fits, she advised me to bathe in the loff, which was holy water; and so I went in the morning to a private place along with the house-maid, and we bathed in our birth-day soot,[6] after the fashion of the country; and behold whilst we dabbled in the loff, sir George Coon started up with a gun; but we clapt our hands to our faces, and passed by him to the place where we had left our smocks – A civil gentleman would have turned his head another way. – My comfit is, he new not which was which; and, as the saying is, *all cats in the dark are grey.* — Whilst we stayed at Loff-Loming, he and our two 'squires went three or four days churning among the wild men of the mountings; a parcel of selvidges[7] that lie in caves among the rocks, devour young children, speak Velch, but the vords are different. Our ladies would not part with Mr Clinker, because he is so stout and so pyehouse, that he fears neither man nor devils, if so be as they don't take him by surprise. – Indeed, he was once so flurried by an operition, that he had like to have sounded.[8] – He made believe as if it had been the ould edmiral; but the old edmiral could not have made his air to stand on end, and his teeth to shatter; but he said so in prudence, that the ladies mought not be afear'd. Miss Liddy has been puny, and like to go into a decline – I doubt her pore art is too tinder – but the got's-fey has set her on her legs again. – You nows got's-fey is mother's milk to a Velch woman. As for mistress, blessed be God, she ails nothing. – Her stomick is good, and she improves in grease and godliness; but, for all that, she may have infections like other people, and I believe, she wouldn't be sorry to be called *your ladyship*, whenever sir George thinks proper to ax the question – But, for my part, whatever I may see or hear, not a praticle shall ever pass the lips of,

Dear Molly,

Your loving friend,

GRASCO, Sept. 7.   WIN. JENKINS

Remember me, as usual, to Sall. – We are now coming home, though not the nearest road. — I do suppose, I shall find the kitten a fine boar at my return.

To Sir WATKIN PHILLIPS, Bart. at Oxon.

DEAR KNIGHT,

Once more I tread upon English ground, which I like not the worse for the six weeks' ramble I have made among the woods and mountains of Caledonia; no offence to the *land of cakes, where bannocks grow upon straw.*[1] I never saw my uncle in such health and spirits as he now enjoys. Liddy is perfectly recovered; and Mrs Tabitha has no reason to complain. Nevertheless, I believe, she was, till yesterday, inclined to give the whole Scotch nation to the devil, as a pack of insensible brutes, upon whom her accomplishments had been displayed in vain. – At every place where we halted, did she mount the stage, and flourished her rusty arms, without being able to make one conquest. One of her last essays was against the heart of Sir George Colquhoun, with whom she fought all the weapons more than twice over. – She was grave and gay by turns – she moralized and methodized – she laughed, and romped, and danced, and sung, and sighed, and ogled, and lisped, and fluttered, and flattered – but all was preaching to the desart – The baronet, being a well-bred man, carried his civilities as far as she could in conscience expect, and, if evil tongues are to be believed, some degrees farther; but he was too much a veteran in gallantry, as well as in war, to fall into any ambuscade that she could lay for his affection – While we were absent in the Highlands, she practised also upon the laird of Ladrishmore, and even gave him the rendezvous in the wood of Drumscailloch; but the laird had such a reverend care of his own reputation, that he came attended with the parson of the parish, and nothing passed but spiritual communication. — After all these miscarriages, our aunt suddenly recollected lieutenant Lismahago, whom, ever since our first arrival at Edinburgh, she seemed to have utterly forgot; but now she expressed her hopes of seeing him at Dumfries, according to his promise.

We set out from Glasgow by the way of Lanerk, the county-town of Clydesdale, in the neighbourhood of which, the whole river Clyde, rushing down a steep rock, forms a very noble and stupendous cascade. Next day we were obliged to halt in a small borough, until the carriage, which had received some damage, should be repaired; and here we met with an incident which warmly interested the benevolent spirit of Mr Bramble – As we stood at the window of an inn that fronted the public prison, a person arrived on horseback, genteelly, tho' plainly, dressed in a blue frock, with his own hair cut short, and a gold-laced hat upon his head. – Alighting, and giving his horse to the landlord, he advanced to an old man who was at work in paving the street, and accosted him in these words: 'This is hard work for such an old man as you.' – So saying, he took the instrument out of his hand, and began to thump the pavement. – After a few strokes, 'Have you never a son (said he) to ease you of this labour?' 'Yes, an please your honour (replied the senior), I have three hopeful lads, but, at present, they are out of the way.' 'Honour not me (cried the stranger); but more becomes me to honour your grey hairs. – Where are those sons you talk of?' The ancient paviour said, his eldest son was a captain in the East Indies; and the youngest had lately inlisted as a soldier, in hopes of prospering like his brother. The gentleman desiring to know what was become of the second, he wiped his eyes, and owned, he had taken upon him his old father's debts, for which he was now in the prison hard by.

The traveller made three quick steps towards the jail, then turning short, 'Tell me (said he), has that unnatural captain sent you nothing to relieve your distress?' 'Call him not unnatural (replied the other); God's blessing be upon him! he sent me a great deal of money; but I made a bad use of it; I lost it by being security for a gentleman that was my landlord, and was stript of all I had in the world besides.' At that instant a young man, thrusting out his head and neck between two iron bars in the prison-window, exclaimed, 'Father! father! if my brother William is in life, that's he!' 'I am! – I am! – (cried the stranger, clasping the old man in his arms, and shedding a flood of tears) – I am your son Willy, sure enough!' Before the father, who was quite confounded, could make any return to this tenderness, a decent old woman bolting out from the door of a poor habitation, cried, 'Where is my bairn? where is my dear Willy?' – The captain no sooner beheld her, than he quitted his father, and ran into her embrace.

I can assure you, my uncle, who saw and heard every thing that passed, was as much moved as any one of the parties concerned in this pathetic recognition – He sobbed, and wept, and clapped his hands, and hollowed, and finally ran down into the street. By this time, the captain had retired with his parents, and all the inhabitants of the place were assembled at the door. – Mr Bramble, nevertheless, pressed thro' the crowd, and entering the house, 'Captain (said he), I beg the favour of your acquaintance — I would have travelled a hundred miles to see this affecting scene; and I shall think myself happy if you and your parents will dine with me at the public house.' The captain thanked him for his kind invitation, which, he said, he would accept with pleasure; but in the mean time, he could not think of eating or drinking, while his poor brother was in trouble. He forthwith deposited a sum equal to the debt in the hands of the magistrate, who ventured to set his brother at liberty without farther process; and then the whole family repaired to the inn with my uncle, attended by the crowd, the individuals of which shook their townsman by the hand, while he returned their caresses without the least sign of pride or affectation.

This honest favourite of fortune, whose name was Brown, told my uncle, that he had been bred a weaver, and, about eighteen years ago, had, from a spirit of idleness and dissipation, enlisted as a soldier in the service of the East-India company; that, in the course of duty, he had the good fortune to attract the notice and approbation of Lord Clive,[2] who preferred him from one step to another, till he attained the rank of captain and pay-master to the regiment, in which capacities he had honestly amassed above twelve thousand pounds, and, at the peace, resigned his commission. – He had sent several remittances to his father, who received the first only, consisting of one hundred pounds; the second had fallen into the hands of a bankrupt; and the third had been consigned to a gentleman of Scotland, who died before it arrived; so that it still remained to be accounted for by his executors. He now presented the old man with fifty pounds for his present occasions, over and above bank notes for one hundred, which he had deposited for his brother's release. — He brought along with him a deed ready executed, by which he settled a perpetuity of four-score pounds upon his parents, to be inherited by their other two sons after their decease. — He promised to purchase a commission for his youngest brother; to take the other as his own partner in a manufacture which he intended to set up, to give employment and bread to the industrious; and to give five hundred pounds, by way of dower, to his sister, who had married a farmer in low circumstances. – Finally, he gave fifty pounds to the poor of the town where he was born, and feasted all the inhabitants without exception.

My uncle was so charmed with the character of captain Brown, that he drank his health three times successively at dinner – He said, he was proud of his acquaintance; that he was an honour to his country, and had in some measure redeemed human nature from the reproach of pride, selfishness, and ingratitude. — For my part, I was as much pleased with the modesty as with the filial virtue of this honest soldier, who assumed no merit from his success, and said very little of his own transactions, though the answers he made to our inquiries were equally sensible and laconic. Mrs Tabitha behaved very graciously to him until she understood that he was going to make a tender of his hand to a person of low estate, who had been his sweet-heart while he worked as a journeyman weaver. – Our aunt was no sooner made acquainted with this design, than she starched up her behaviour with a double proportion of reserve; and when the company broke up, she observed with a toss of her nose, that Brown was a civil fellow enough, considering the lowness of his original; but that Fortune, though she had mended his circumstances, was incapable to raise his ideas, which were still humble and plebeian.

On the day that succeeded this adventure, we went some miles out of our road to see Drumlanrig, a seat belonging to the duke of Queensberry,[3] which appears like a magnificent palace erected by magic, in the midst of a wilderness. – It is indeed a princely mansion, with suitable parks and plantations, rendered still more striking by the nakedness of the surrounding country, which is one of the wildest tracts in all Scotland. – This wildness, however, is different from that of the Highlands; for here the mountains, instead of heath, are covered with a fine green swarth, affording pasture to innumerable flocks of sheep. But the fleeces of this country, called Nithsdale, are not comparable to the wool of Galloway, which is said to equal that of Salisbury plain. Having passed the night at the castle of Drumlanrig, by invitation from the duke himself, who is one of the best men that ever breathed, we prosecuted our journey to Dumfries, a very elegant trading town near the borders of England, where we found plenty of good provision and excellent wine, at very reasonable prices, and the accommodation as good in all respects as in any part of South-Britain. – If I was confined to Scotland for life, I would chuse Dumfries as the place of my residence. Here we made enquiries about captain Lismahago, of whom hearing no tidings, we proceeded by the Solway Frith, to Carlisle. You must know, that the Solway sands, upon which travellers pass at low water, are exceedingly dangerous, because, as the tide makes, they become quick in different places, and the flood rushes in so impetuously, that the passengers are often overtaken by the sea and perish.

In crossing these treacherous Syrtes[4] with a guide, we perceived a drowned horse, which Humphry Clinker, after due inspection, declared to be the very identical beast which Mr Lismahago rode when he parted with us at Feltonbridge in Northumberland. This information, which seemed to intimate that our friend the lieutenant had shared the fate of his horse, affected us all, and above all our aunt Tabitha, who shed salt tears, and obliged Clinker to pull a few hairs out of the dead horse's tail, to be worn in a ring as a remembrance of his master: but her grief and ours was not of long duration; for one of the first persons we saw in Carlisle, was the lieutenant *in propria persona*,[5] bargaining with a horse-dealer for another steed, in the yard of the inn where we alighted. – Mrs Bramble was the first that perceived him, and screamed as if she had seen a ghost; and, truly, at a proper time and place, he might very well have passed for an inhabitant of another world; for he was more meagre and grim than before. – We received him the more cordially for having supposed he had been drowned; and he was not deficient in expressions of satisfaction at this meeting. – He told us, he had enquired for us at Dumfries, and been informed by a travelling merchant from Glasgow, that we had resolved to return by the way of Coldstream. – He said, that in passing the sands without a guide, his horse had knocked up, and he himself must have perished, if he had not been providentially relieved by a return post-chaise. – He moreover gave us to understand, that his scheme of settling in his own country having miscarried, he was so far on his way to London, with a view to embark for North-America, where he intended to pass the rest of his days among his old friends the Miamis, and amuse himself in finishing the education of the son he had by his beloved Squinkinacoosta.

This project was by no means agreeable to our good aunt, who expatiated upon the fatigues and dangers that would attend such a long voyage by sea, and afterwards such a tedious journey by land – She enlarged particularly on the risque he would run, with respect to the concerns of his precious soul, among savages who had not yet received the glad tidings of salvation; and she hinted that his abandoning Great-Britain might, perhaps, prove fatal to the inclinations of some deserving person, whom he was qualified to make happy for life. My uncle, who is really a Don Quixote in generosity, understanding that Lismahago's real reason for leaving Scotland was the impossibility of subsisting in it with any decency upon the wretched provision of a subaltern's half-pay,[6] began to be warmly interested on the side of compassion. – He thought it very hard, that a gentleman who had served his country with honour, should be driven by necessity to spend his old age, among the refuse of mankind, in such a remote part of the world. – He discoursed with me upon the subject; observing, that he would willingly offer the lieutenant an asylum at Brambleton-hall, if he did not foresee that his singularities and humour of contradiction would render him an intolerable house-mate, though his conversation at some times might be both instructive and entertaining: but, as there seemed to be something particular in his attention to Mrs Tabitha, he and I agreed in opinion, that this intercourse should be encouraged and improved, if possible, into a matrimonial union; in which case there would be a comfortable provision for both; and they might be settled in a house of their own, so that Mr Bramble should have no more of their company than he desired.

In pursuance of this design, Lismahago has been invited to pass the winter at Brambleton-hall, as it will be time enough to execute his American project in the spring. – He has taken time to consider of this proposal; mean while, he will keep us company as far as we travel in the road to Bristol, where he has hopes of getting a passage for America. I make no doubt but that he will postpone his voyage, and prosecute his addresses to a happy consummation; and sure, if it produces any fruit, it must be of a very peculiar flavour. As the weather continues favourable, I believe, we shall take the Peak of Derbyshire and Buxton Wells in our way. — At any rate, from the first place where we make any stay, you shall hear again from

Yours always,

CARLISLE, Sep. 12.   J. MELFORD

To Dr Lewis.

DEAR DOCTOR,

The peasantry of Scotland are certainly on a poor footing all over the kingdom; and yet they look better, and are better cloathed than those of the same rank in Burgundy, and many other places of France and Italy; nay, I will venture to say they are better fed, notwithstanding the boasted wine of these foreign countries. The country people of North-Britain live chiefly on oat-meal, and milk, cheese, butter, and some garden-stuff, with now and then a pickled-herring, by way of delicacy; but flesh-meat they seldom or never taste; nor any kind of strong liquor, except two-penny, at times of uncommon festivity – Their breakfast is a kind of hasty pudding, of oat-meal or pease-meal, eaten with milk. They have commonly pottage for dinner, composed of cale or cole,[1] leeks, barley or big,[2] and butter; and this is reinforced with bread and cheese, made of skimmed-milk – At night they sup on sowens or flummery of oat-meal[3] – In a scarcity of oats, they use the meal of barley and pease, which is both nourishing and palatable. Some of them have potatoes; and you find parsnips in every peasant's garden – They are cloathed with a coarse kind of russet of their own making, which is both decent and warm – They dwell in poor huts, built of loose stones and turf, without any mortar, having a fire-place or hearth in the middle, generally made of an old mill-stone, and a hole at top to let out the smoke.

These people, however, are content, and wonderfully sagacious – All of them read the Bible, and are even qualified to dispute upon the articles of their faith; which in those parts I have seen, is entirely Presbyterian. I am told, that the inhabitants of Aberdeenshire are still more acute. I once knew a Scotch gentleman at London, who had declared war against this part of his countrymen; and swore that the impudence and knavery of the Scots, in that quarter, had brought a reproach upon the whole nation.

The river Clyde, above Glasgow, is quite pastoral; and the banks of it are every where adorned with fine villas. From the sea to its source, we may reckon the seats of many families of the first rank, such as the duke of Argyle at Roseneath, the earl of Bute in the isle of that name, the earl of Glencairn at Finlayston, lord Blantyre at Areskine, the dutchess of Douglas at Bothwell, duke Hamilton at Hamilton, the duke of Douglas at Douglas, and the earl of Hyndford at Carmichael. Hamilton is a noble palace, magnificently furnished; and hard by is the village of that name, one of the neatest little towns I have seen in any country. The old castle of Douglas being burned to the ground by accident, the late duke resolved, as head of the first family of Scotland, to have the largest house in the kingdom,

and ordered a plan for this purpose; but there was only one
wing of it finished when he died. It is to be hoped that his
nephew, who is now in possession of his great fortune,[4] will
complete the design of his predecessor – Clydesdale is in general
populous and rich, containing a great number of gentlemen,
who are independent in their fortune; but it produces more
cattle than corn – This is also the case with Tweedale, through
part of which we passed, and Nithsdale, which is generally
rough, wild, and mountainous – These hills are covered with
sheep; and this is the small delicious mutton, so much preferable
to that of the London-market. As their feeding costs so little,
the sheep are not killed till five years old, when their flesh,
juices, and flavour are in perfection; but their fleeces are much
damaged by the tar, with which they are smeared to preserve
them from the rot in winter, during which they run wild night
and day, and thousands are lost under huge wreaths of snow
— 'Tis pity the farmers cannot contrive some means to shelter
this useful animal from the inclemencies of a rigorous climate,
especially from the perpetual rains, which are more prejudicial
than the greatest extremity of cold weather.

On the little river Nid, is situated the castle of Drumlanrig,
one of the noblest seats in Great-Britain, belonging to the duke
of Queensberry; one of those few noblemen whose goodness of
heart does honour to human-nature – I shall not pretend to
enter into a description of this palace, which is really an instance
of the sublime in magnificence, as well as in situation, and puts
one in mind of the beautiful city of Palmyra, rising like a vision
in the midst of the wilderness. His grace keeps open house, and
lives with great splendour – He did us the honour to receive us
with great courtesy, and detain'd us all night, together with
above twenty other guests, with all their servants and horses to a
very considerable number – The dutchess[5] was equally gracious,
and took our ladies under her immediate protection. The longer
I live, I see more reason to believe that prejudices of education
are never wholly eradicated, even when they are discovered to
be erroneous and absurd. Such habits of thinking as interest
the grand passions, cleave to the human heart in such a manner,
that though an effort of reason may force them from their hold

for a moment, this violence no sooner ceases, than they resume their grasp with an increased elasticity and adhesion.

I am led into this reflection, by what passed at the duke's table after supper. The conversation turned upon the vulgar notions of spirits and omens, that prevail among the commonalty of North-Britain, and all the company agreed, that nothing could be more ridiculous. One gentleman, however, told a remarkable story of himself, by way of speculation – 'Being on a party of hunting in the North (said he), I resolved to visit an old friend, whom I had not seen for twenty years – So long he had been retired and sequestered from all his acquaintance, and lived in a moping melancholy way, much afflicted with lowness of spirits, occasioned by the death of his wife, whom he had loved with uncommon affection. As he resided in a remote part of the country, and we were five gentlemen with as many servants, we carried some provision with us from the next market town, lest we should find him unprepared for our reception. The roads being bad, we did not arrive at the house till two o'clock in the afternoon; and were agreeably surprised to find a very good dinner ready in the kitchen, and the cloth laid with six covers. My friend himself appeared in his best apparel at the gate, and received us with open arms telling me he had been expecting us these two hours – Astonished at this declaration, I asked who had given him intelligence of our coming? and he smiled without making any other reply – However, presuming upon our former intimacy, I afterwards insisted upon knowing; and he told me, very gravely, he had seen me in a vision of the second sight – Nay, he called in the evidence of his steward, who solemnly declared, that his master had the day before apprised him of my coming, with four other strangers, and ordered him to provide accordingly; in consequence of which intimation, he had prepared the dinner which we were now eating; and laid the covers according to the number foretold.' The incident we all owned to be remarkable, and I endeavoured to account for it by natural means. I observed, that as the gentleman was of a visionary turn, the casual idea, or remembrance of his old friend, might suggest those circumstances, which accident had for once realized; but that in all probability he had seen many visions of the same kind, which were never verified. None of the company directly dissented from my opinion; but from the objections that were hinted, I could plainly perceive that the majority were persuaded there was something more extraordinary in the case.

Another gentleman of the company, addressing himself to me, 'Without all doubt (said he), a diseased imagination is very apt to produce visions; but we must find some other method to account for something of this kind, that happened within these eight days in my neighbourhood — A gentleman of a good family, who cannot be deemed a visionary in any sense of the word, was near his own gate, in the twilight, visited by his grandfather, who has been dead these fifteen years – The spectre was mounted seemingly on the very horse he used to ride, with an angry and terrible countenance, and said something, which his grandson, in the confusion of fear, could not understand. But this was not all – He lifted up a huge horse whip, and applied it with great violence to his back and shoulders, on which I saw the impression with my own eyes. The apparition was afterwards seen by the sexton of the parish, hovering about the tomb where his body lies interred; as the man declared to several persons in the village, before he knew what had happened to the gentleman – Nay, he actually came to me as a justice of the peace, in order to make oath of these particulars, which, however, I declined administering. As for the grandson of the defunct, he is a sober, sensible, worldly minded fellow, too intent upon schemes of interest to give in to reveries. He would have willingly concealed the affair; but he bawled out in the first transport of his fear, and, running into the house, exposed his back and his sconce to the whole family; so that there was no denying it in the sequel. It is now the common discourse of the country, that this appearance and behaviour of the old man's spirit, portends some great calamity to the family, and the good-woman has actually taken to her bed in this apprehension.'

Though I did not pretend to explain this mystery, I said, I did not at all doubt, but it would one day appear to be a deception; and, in all probability, a scheme executed by some

enemy of the person who had sustained the assault; but still the
gentleman insisted upon the clearness of the evidence, and the
concurrence of testimony, by which two creditable witnesses,
without any communication one with another, affirmed the
appearance of the same man, with whose person they were
both well acquainted – From Drumlanrig we pursued the course
of the Nid to Dumfries, which stands seven miles above the
place where the river falls into the sea; and is, after Glasgow,
the handsomest town I have seen in Scotland – The inhabitants,
indeed, seem to have proposed that city as their model; not
only in beautifying their town and regulating its police, but also
in prosecuting their schemes of commerce and manufacture, by
which they are grown rich and opulent.

We re-entered England, by the way of Carlisle, where we
accidentally met with our friend Lismahago, whom we had in
vain inquired after at Dumfries and other places – It would
seem that the captain, like the prophets of old, is but little
honoured in his own country,[6] which he has now renounced
for ever – He gave me the following particulars of his visit to
his native soil – In his way to the place of his nativity, he learned
that his nephew had married the daughter of a burgeois, who
directed a weaving manufacture, and had gone into partnership
with his father-in-law: chagrined with this information, he had
arrived at the gate in the twilight, where he heard the sound of
treddles in the great hall, which had exasperated him to such
a degree, that he had like to have lost his senses: while he
was thus transported with indignation, his nephew chanced to
come forth, when, being no longer master of his passion, he
cried, 'Degenerate rascal! you have made my father's house a
den of thieves;'[7] and at the same time chastised him with his
horse-whip; then, riding round the adjoining village, he had
visited the burying-ground of his ancestors by moon-light; and,
having paid his respects to their *manes*,[8] travelled all night to
another part of the country — Finding the head of the family
in such a disgraceful situation, all his own friends dead or
removed from the places of their former residence, and the
expence of living increased to double of what it had been, when
he first left his native country, he had bid it an eternal adieu,

and was determined to seek for repose among the forests of America.

I was no longer at a loss to account for the apparition, which had been described at Drumlanrig; and when I repeated the story to the lieutenant, he was much pleased to think his resentment had been so much more effectual than he intended; and he owned, he might at such an hour, and in such an equipage, very well pass for the ghost of his father, whom he was said greatly to resemble —— Between friends, I fancy Lismahago will find a retreat without going so far as the wigwams of the Miamis. My sister Tabby is making continual advances to him, in the way of affection; and, if I may trust to appearances, the captain is disposed to take opportunity by the forelock. For my part, I intend to encourage this correspondence, and shall be glad to see them united – In that case, we shall find a way to settle them comfortably in our own neighbourhood. I, and my servants, will get rid of a very troublesome and tyrannic gouvernante; and I shall have the benefit of Lismahago's conversation, without being obliged to take more of his company than I desire; for though an olla⁹ is a high-flavoured dish, I could not bear to dine upon it every day of my life.

I am much pleased with Manchester, which is one of the most agreeable and flourishing towns in Great-Britain; and I perceive that this is the place which hath animated the spirit, and suggested the chief manufactures of Glasgow. We propose to visit Chatsworth, the Peak, and Buxton, from which last place we shall proceed directly homewards, though by easy journies. If the season has been as favourable in Wales as in the North, your harvest is happily finished; and we have nothing left to think of but our October, of which let Barns be properly reminded. You will find me much better in flesh than I was at our parting; and this short separation has given a new edge to those sentiments of friendship with which I always have been, and ever shall be,

Yours,

MANCHESTER, Sept. 15.   MATT. BRAMBLE

To Mrs GWYLLIM, house-keeper at Brambleton-hall.

MRS GWYLLIM,

It has pleased Providence to bring us safe back to England, and partake us in many pearls by land and water, in particular the *Devil's Harse a pike*, and *Hoyden's Hole*,[1] which hath got no bottom; and, as we are drawing huomwards, it may be proper to uprise you, that Brambleton-hall may be in condition to receive us, after this long gurney to the islands of Scotland. By the first of next month you may begin to make constant fires in my brother's chamber and mine; and burn a fagget every day in the yellow damask room: have the tester and curtains dusted, and the feather-bed and matrosses well haired, because, per-haps, with the blissing of haven, they may be yoosed on some occasion. Let the ould hogsheads be well skewred and seasoned for bear, as Mat is resolved to have his seller choak fool.

If the house was mine, I would turn over a new leaf —— I don't see why the sarvants of Wales shouldn't drink fair water, and eat hot cakes and barley cale, as they do in Scotland, without troubling the botcher above once a quarter – I hope you keep accunt of Roger's purseeding in reverence to the buttermilk. I expect my dew when I come huom, without baiting an ass,[2] I'll assure you. – As you must have layed a great many more eggs than would be eaten, I do suppose there is a power of turks, chick-ings, and guzzling about the house; and a brave kergo of cheese ready for market; and that the owl has been sent to Crick-howel, saving what the maids spun in the family.

Pray let the whole house and furniture have a thorough cleaning from top to bottom, for the honour of Wales; and let Roger search into, and make a general clearance of the slit holes, which the maids have in secret; for I know they are much given to sloth and uncleanness. I hope you have worked a reformation among them, as I exhorted you in my last, and set their hearts upon better things than they can find in junkitting and caterwauling with the fellows of the country.

As for Win Jenkins, she has undergone a perfect metamur-physis, and is become a new creeter from the ammunition of

Humphry Clinker, our new footman, a pious young man, who has laboured exceedingly, that she may bring forth fruits of repentance.[3] I make no doubt but he will take the same pains with that pert hussey Mary Jones, and all of you; and that he may have power given to penetrate and instill his goodness, even into your most inward parts, is the fervent prayer of

Your friend in the spirit,

Septr. 18.   TAB. BRAMBLE

To Dr Lewis.

DEAR LEWIS,

Lismahago is more paradoxical than ever. – The late gulp he had of his native air, seems to have blown fresh spirit into all his polemical faculties. I congratulated him the other day on the present flourishing state of his country, observing that the Scots were now in a fair way to wipe off the national reproach of poverty, and expressing my satisfaction at the happy effects of the union, so conspicuous in the improvement of their agriculture, commerce, manufactures, and manners – The lieutenant, screwing up his features into a look of dissent and disgust, commented on my remarks to this effect – 'Those who reproach a nation for its poverty, when it is not owing to the profligacy or vice of the people, deserve no answer. The Lacedæmonians were poorer than the Scots, when they took the lead among all the free states of Greece, and were esteemed above them all for their valour and their virtue. The most respectable heroes of ancient Rome, such as Fabricius, Cincinnatus, and Regulus,[1] were poorer than the poorest freeholder in Scotland; and there are at this day individuals in North-Britain, one of whom can produce more gold and silver than the whole republic of Rome could raise at those times when her public virtue shone with unrivalled lustre; and poverty was so far from being a reproach, that it added fresh laurels to her fame, because it indicated a noble contempt of wealth, which was proof against all the arts of corruption – If poverty be a subject for reproach, it follows that wealth is the object of esteem and veneration — In that case, there are Jews and others in Amsterdam and London, enriched by usury, peculation, and different species of fraud and extortion, who are more estimable than the most virtuous and illustrious members of the community. An absurdity which no man in his senses will offer to maintain. — Riches are certainly no proof of merit: nay they are often (if not most commonly) acquired by persons of sordid minds and mean talents: nor do they give any intrinsic worth to the possessor; but, on the contrary, tend to pervert his understanding, and render his morals more depraved. But, granting that poverty were really matter of reproach, it cannot be justly imputed to Scotland. No country is poor that can supply its inhabitants with the necessaries of life, and even afford articles for exportation. Scotland is rich in natural advantages: it produces every species of provision in abundance, vast herds of cattle and flocks of sheep, with a great number of horses; prodigious quantities of wool and flax, with plenty of copse wood, and in some parts large forests of timber. The earth is still more rich below than above the surface. It yields inexhaustible stores of coal, freestone, marble, lead, iron, copper, and silver, with some gold. The sea abounds with excellent fish, and salt to cure them for exportation; and there are creeks and harbours round the whole kingdom, for the convenience and security of navigation. The face of the country displays a surprising number of cities, towns, villas, and villages, swarming with people; and there seems to be no want of art, industry, government, and police: such a kingdom can never be called poor, in any sense of the word, though there may be many others more powerful and opulent. But the proper use of those advantages, and the present prosperity of the Scots, you seem to derive from the union of the two kingdoms!'

I said, I supposed he would not deny that the appearance of the country was much mended; that the people lived better, had more trade, and a greater quantity of money circulating since the union, than before. 'I may safely admit these premises (answered the lieutenant), without subscribing to your inference. The difference you mention, I should take to be the natural progress of improvement —— Since that period, other nations, such as the Swedes, the Danes, and in particular the French, have greatly increased in commerce, without any such cause assigned. Before the union, there was a remarkable spirit of trade among the Scots, as appeared in the case of their Darien company,[2] in which they had embarked no less than four hundred thousand pounds sterling; and in the flourishing state of the maritime towns in Fife, and on the eastern coast, enriched by their trade with France, which failed in consequence of the union. The only solid commercial advantage reaped from that measure, was the privilege of trading to the English plantations; yet, excepting Glasgow and Dumfries, I don't know any other Scotch towns concerned in that traffick. In other respects, I conceive the Scots were losers by the union. – They lost the independency of their state, the greatest prop of national spirit; they lost their parliament, and their courts of justice were subjected to the revision and supremacy of an English tribunal.'

'Softly, captain (cried I), you cannot be said to have lost your own parliament, while you are represented in that of Great-Britain.' 'True (said he, with a sarcastic grin), in debates of national competition, the sixteen peers and forty-five commoners of Scotland, must make a formidable figure in the scale, against the whole English legislature.' 'Be that as it may (I observed) while I had the honour to sit in the lower house, the Scotch members had always the majority on their side.' 'I understand you, Sir (said he), they generally side with the majority; so much the worse for their constituents. But even this evil is not the worst they have sustained by the union. Their trade has been saddled with grievous impositions, and every article of living severely taxed, to pay the interest of enormous debts, contracted by the English, in support of measures and connections in which the Scots had no interest nor concern.' I begged he would at least allow, that by the union the Scots were admitted to all the privileges and immunities of English subjects; by which means multitudes of them were provided for in the army and navy, and got fortunes in different parts of England, and its dominions. 'All these (said he) become English subjects to all intents and purposes, and are in a great measure lost to their mother-country. The spirit of rambling and adventure has been always peculiar to the natives of Scotland. If they had not met with encouragement in England, they would have served and settled, as formerly, in other countries, such as Muscovy, Sweden, Denmark, Poland, Germany, France, Piedmont, and Italy, in all which nations their descendants continue to flourish even at this day.'

By this time my patience began to fail and I exclaimed, 'For God's sake, what has England got by this union which, you say, has been so productive of misfortune to the Scots.' 'Great and manifold are the advantages which England derives from the union (said Lismahago, in a solemn tone). First and foremost, the settlement of the protestant succession, a point which the English ministry drove with such eagerness, that no stone was left unturned, to cajole and bribe a few leading men, to cram the union down the throats of the Scottish nation, who were surprisingly averse to the expedient. They gained by it a considerable addition of territory, extending their dominion to the sea on all sides of the island, thereby shutting up all back-doors against the enterprizes of their enemies. They got an accession of above a million of useful subjects, constituting a never-failing nursery of seamen, soldiers, labourers, and mechanics; a most valuable acquisition to a trading country, exposed to foreign wars, and obliged to maintain a number of settlements in all the four quarters of the globe. In the course of seven years, during the last war, Scotland furnished the English army and navy with seventy thousand men, over and above those who migrated to their colonies, or mingled with them at home in the civil departments of life. This was a very considerable and seasonable supply to a nation, whose people had been for many years decreasing in number, and whose lands and manufactures were actually suffering for want of hands. I need not remind you of the hackneyed maxim, that, to a nation in such circumstances, a supply of industrious people is a supply of wealth; nor repeat an observation, which is now received as an eternal truth, even among the English themselves, that the Scots who settle in South-Britain are remarkably sober, orderly, and industrious.'

I allowed the truth of this remark, adding, that by their industry, œconomy, and circumspection, many of them in England, as well as in her colonies, amassed large fortunes, with which they returned to their own country, and this was so much lost to South-Britain. — 'Give me leave, sir (said he), to assure you, that in your fact you are mistaken, and in your deduction erroneous. — Not one in two hundred that leave Scotland ever returns to settle in his own country; and the few that do return, carry thither nothing that can possibly diminish the stock of South-Britain; for none of their treasure stagnates in Scotland – There is a continual circulation, like that of the blood in the human body, and England is the heart, to which all the streams which it distributes are refunded and returned: nay, in consequence of that luxury which our connexion with England hath greatly encouraged, if not introduced, all the produce of our lands, and all the profits of our trade, are engrossed by the natives of South-Britain; for you will find that the exchange between the two kingdoms is always against Scotland; and that she retains neither gold nor silver sufficient for her own circulation. – The Scots, not content with their own manufactures and produce, which would very well answer all necessary occasions, seem to vie with each other in purchasing superfluities from England; such as broad-cloth, velvets, stuffs, silks, lace, furs, jewels, furniture of all sorts, sugar, rum, tea, chocolate and coffee; in a word, not only every mode of the most extravagant luxury, but even many articles of convenience, which they might find as good, and much cheaper in their own country. For all these particulars, I conceive, England may touch about one million sterling a-year. – I don't pretend to make an exact calculation; perhaps, it may be something less, and perhaps, a great deal more. The annual revenue arising from all the private estates of Scotland cannot fall short of a million sterling; and, I should imagine, their trade will amount to as much more. – I know the linen manufacture alone returns near half a million, exclusive of the home-consumption of that article. – If, therefore, North-Britain pays a ballance of a million annually to England, I insist upon it, that country is more valuable to her in the way of commerce, than any colony in her possession, over and above the other advantages which I have specified: therefore, they are no friends, either to England or to truth, who affect to depreciate the northern part of the united kingdom.'

I must own, I was at first a little nettled to find myself schooled in so many particulars. — Though I did not receive all his assertions as gospel, I was not prepared to refute them; and I cannot help now acquiescing in his remarks so far as to think, that the contempt for Scotland, which prevails too much on this side the Tweed, is founded on prejudice and error. — After some recollection, 'Well, captain (said I), you have argued stoutly for the importance of your own country: for my part, I have such a regard for our fellow-subjects of North-Britain, that I shall be glad to see the day, when your peasants can afford to give all their oats to their cattle, hogs, and poultry, and indulge themselves with good wheaten loaves, instead of such poor, unpalatable, and inflammatory diet.' Here again I brought my self into a premunire³ with the disputative Caledonian. He said he hoped he should never see the common people lifted out of that sphere for which they were intended by nature and the course of things; that they might have some reason to complain of their bread, if it were mixed, like that of Norway, with saw dust and fish-bones; but that oatmeal was, he apprehended, as nourishing and salutary as wheat-flour, and the Scots in general thought it at least as savoury. – He affirmed, that a mouse, which, in the article of self-preservation, might be supposed to act from infallible instinct, would always prefer oats to wheat, as appeared from experience; for, in a place where there was a parcel of each, that animal has never begun to feed upon the latter till all the oats were consumed: for their nutritive quality, he appealed to the hale, robust constitutions of the people who lived chiefly upon oatmeal; and, instead of being inflammatory, he asserted, that it was a cooling sub-acid, balsamic and mucilaginous;⁴ insomuch, that in all inflammatory distempers, recourse was had to water-gruel, and flummery made of oatmeal.

'At least (said I), give me leave to wish them such a degree of commerce as may enable them to follow their own inclinations.'

—— 'Heaven forbid! (cried this philosopher). Woe be to that nation, where the multitude is at liberty to follow their own inclinations! Commerce is undoubtedly a blessing, while restrained within its proper channels; but a glut of wealth brings along with it a glut of evils: it brings false taste, false appetite, false wants, profusion, venality, contempt of order, engendering a spirit of licentiousness, insolence, and faction, that keeps the community in continual ferment, and in time destroys all the distinctions of civil society; so that universal anarchy and uproar must ensue. Will any sensible man affirm, that the national advantages of opulence are to be sought on these terms?' 'No, sure; but I am one of those who think, that, by proper regulations, commerce may produce every national benefit, without the allay of such concomitant evils.'

So much for the dogmata of my friend Lismahago, whom I describe the more circumstantially, as I firmly believe he will set up his rest in Monmouthshire. Yesterday, while I was alone with him, he asked, in some confusion, if I should have any objection to the success of a gentleman and a soldier, provided he should be so fortunate as to engage my sister's affection. I answered without hesitation, that my sister was old enough to judge for herself; and that I should be very far from disapproving any resolution she might take in his favour. – His eyes sparkled at this declaration. He declared, he should think himself the happiest man on earth to be connected with my family; and that he should never be weary of giving me proofs of his gratitude and attachment. I suppose Tabby and he are already agreed; in which case, we shall have a wedding at Brambleton-hall, and you shall give away the bride. – It is the least thing you can do, by way of atonement for your former cruelty to that poor love-sick maiden, who has been so long a thorn in the side of

Yours,

Sept. 20.   MATT. BRAMBLE

We have been at Buxton; but, as I did not much relish either the company or the accommodations, and had no occasion for the water, we stayed but two nights in the place.

To Sir WATKIN PHILLIPS, Bart. of Jesus college, Oxon.

DEAR WAT,

Adventures begin to thicken as we advance to the southward. – Lismahago has now professed himself the admirer of our aunt, and carries on his addresses under the sanction of her brother's approbation; so that we shall certainly have a wedding by Christmas. I should be glad you was present at the nuptials, to help me throw the stocking,[1] and perform other ceremonies peculiar to that occasion. — I am sure it will be productive of some diversion; and, truly, it would be worth your while to come across the country on purpose to see two such original figures in bed together, with their laced night caps; he, the emblem of good cheer, and she, the picture of good nature. All this agreeable prospect was clouded, and had well nigh vanished entirely, in consequence of a late misunderstanding between the future brothers-in-law, which, however, is now happily removed.

A few days ago, my uncle and I, going to visit a relation, met with lord Oxmington at his house, who asked us to dine with him next day, and we accepted the invitation. — Accordingly, leaving our women under the care of captain Lismahago, at the inn where we had lodged the preceding night, in a little town, about a mile from his lordship's dwelling, we went at the hour appointed, and had a fashionable meal served up with much ostentation to a company of about a dozen persons, none of whom he had ever seen before. – His lordship is much more remarkable for his pride and caprice, than for his hospitality and understanding; and, indeed, it appeared, that he considered his guests merely as objects to shine upon, so as to reflect the lustre of his own magnificence – There was much state, but no courtesy; and a great deal of compliment without any conversation. – Before the desert was removed, our noble entertainer proposed three general toasts; then calling for a glass of wine, and bowing all round, wished us a good afternoon. This was the signal for the company to break up, and they obeyed it immediately, all except our 'squire who was greatly shocked at the manner of this dismission – He changed countenance, bit his lip in silence, but still kept his seat, so that his lordship found himself obliged to give us another hint, by saying, he should be glad to see us another time. 'There is no time like the present (cried Mr Bramble); your lordship has not yet drank a bumper to *the best in Christendom*.' 'I'll drink no more bumpers to-day (answered our landlord); and I am sorry to see you have drank too many. – Order the gentleman's carriage to the gate.' – So saying, he rose and retired abruptly; our 'squire starting up at the same time, laying his hand upon his sword, and eyeing him with a most ferocious aspect. The master having vanished in this manner, our uncle bad one of the servants to see what was to pay; and the fellow answering, 'This is no inn,' 'I cry you mercy (cried the other), I perceive it is not; if it were, the landlord would be more civil. – There's a guinea, however; take it, and tell your lord, that I shall not leave the country till I have had the opportunity to thank him in person for his politeness and hospitality.'

We then walked down stairs through a double range of lacqueys, and getting into the chaise, proceeded homewards. Perceiving the 'squire much ruffled, I ventured to disapprove of his resentment, observing, that as lord Oxmington was well known to have his brain very ill timbered, a sensible man should rather laugh, than be angry at his ridiculous want of breeding. – Mr Bramble took umbrage at my presuming to be wiser than he upon this occasion; and told me, that as he had always thought for himself in every occurrence in life, he would still use the same privilege, with my good leave.

When we returned to our inn, he closeted Lismahago; and having explained his grievance, desired that gentleman to go and demand satisfaction of lord Oxmington in his name. – The lieutenant charged himself with this commission, and immediately set out a-horseback for his lordship's house, attended, at his own request, by my man Archy Macalpine, who had been used to military service; and truly, if Macalpine had been mounted upon an ass, this couple might have passed for the knight of La Mancha and his 'squire Panza.[2] It was not till after some demur that Lismahago obtained a private audience, at which he formally defied his lordship to single combat, in the name of Mr Bramble, and desired him to appoint the time and place. Lord Oxmington was so confounded at this unexpected message, that he could not, for some time, make any articulate reply; but stood staring at the lieutenant with manifest marks of perturbation. At length, ringing a bell with great vehemence, he exclaimed, 'What! a commoner send a challenge to a peer of the realm! – Privilege! privilege! – Here's a person brings me a challenge from the Welshman that dined at my table – An impudent fellow. – My wine is not yet out of his head.'

The whole house was immediately in commotion. – Macalpine made a soldierly retreat with two horses; but the captain was suddenly surrounded and disarmed by the footmen, whom a French valet de chambre headed in this exploit; his sword was passed through a close-stool, and his person through the horse-pond. – In this plight he returned to the inn, half mad with his disgrace. – So violent was the rage of his indignation, that he mistook its object. – He wanted to quarrel with Mr Bramble; he said, he had been dishonoured on his account, and he looked for reparation at his hands. – My uncle's back was up in a moment; and he desired him to explain his pretensions. – 'Either compel lord Oxmington to give me satisfaction (cried he), or give it me in your own person.' 'The latter part of the alternative is the most easy and expeditious (replied the 'squire, starting up): if you are disposed for a walk, I'll attend you this moment.'

Here they were interrupted by Mrs Tabby, who had overheard all that passed. — She now burst into the room, and running betwixt them, in great agitation, 'Is this your regard for me (said she to the lieutenant), to seek the life of my brother?' Lismahago, who seemed to grow cool as my uncle grew hot, assured her he had a very great respect for Mr Bramble, but he had still more for his own honour, which had suffered pollution; but if that could be once purified, he should have no further cause of dissatisfaction. — The 'squire said, he should have thought it incumbent upon him to vindicate the lieutenant's honour; but, as he had now carved for himself, he might swallow and digest it as well as he could —— In a word, what betwixt the mediation of Mrs Tabitha, the recollection of the captain, who perceived he had gone too far, and the remonstrances of your humble servant, who joined them at this juncture, those two originals were perfectly reconciled; and then we proceeded to deliberate upon the means of taking vengeance for the insults they had received from the petulant peer; for, until that aim should be accomplished, Mr Bramble swore, with great emphasis, that he would not leave the inn where we now lodged, even if he should pass his Christmas on the spot.

In consequence of our deliberations, we next day, in the forenoon, proceeded in a body to his lordship's house, all of us, with our servants, including the coachman, mounted a-horseback, with our pistols loaded and ready primed. – Thus prepared for action, we paraded solemnly and slowly before his lordship's gate, which we passed three times in such a manner, that he could not but see us, and suspect the cause of our appearance. – After dinner we returned, and performed the same cavalcade, which was again repeated the morning following; but we had no occasion to persist in these manœuvres — About noon, we were visited by the gentleman, at whose house we had first seen lord Oxmington. – He now came to make apologies in the name of his lordship, who declared he had no intention to give offence to my uncle, in practising what had been always the custom of his house; and that as for the indignities which had been put upon the officer, they were offered without his Lordship's knowledge, at the instigation of his valet de chambre. – 'If that be the case (said my uncle, in a peremptory tone), I shall be contented with lord Oxmington's personal excuses; and I hope my friend will be satisfied with his lordship's turning that insolent rascal out of his service.' – 'Sir (cried Lismahago), I must insist upon taking personal vengeance for the personal injuries I have sustained.'

After some debate, the affair was adjusted in this manner. — His lordship, meeting us at our friend's house, declared he was sorry for what had happened; and that he had no intention to give umbrage. – The valet de chambre asked pardon of the lieutenant upon his knees, when Lismahago, to the astonishment of all present, gave him a violent kick on the face, which laid him on his back, exclaiming in a furious tone, '*Oui je te pardonne, gens foutre.*'[3]

Such was the fortunate issue of this perilous adventure, which threatened abundance of vexation to our family; for the 'squire is one of those who will sacrifice both life and fortune, rather than leave what they conceive to be the least speck or blemish upon their honour and reputation. His lordship had no sooner pronounced his apology, with a very bad grace, than he went away in some disorder, and, I dare say, he will never invite another Welchman to his table.

We forthwith quitted the field of this atchievement, in order to prosecute our journey; but we follow no determinate course. — We make small deviations, to see the remarkable towns, villas, and curiosities on each side of our route; so that we advance by slow steps towards the borders of Monmouthshire: but in the midst of these irregular motions, there is no abberration nor eccentricity in that affection with which I am, dear Wat,

Yours always,

Sept. 28.   J. MELFORD

To Dr Lewis.

DEAR DICK,

At what time of life may a man think himself exempted from the necessity of sacrificing his repose to the punctilios[1] of a contemptible world? I have been engaged in a ridiculous adventure, which I shall recount at meeting; and this, I hope, will not be much longer delayed, as we have now performed almost all our visits, and seen every thing that I think has any right to retard us in our journey homewards — A few days ago, understanding by accident, that my old friend Baynard was in the country, I would not pass so near his habitation without paying him a visit, though our correspondence had been interrupted for a long course of years.

I felt my self very sensibly affected by the idea of our past intimacy, as we approached the place where we had spent so many happy days together; but when we arrived at the house, I could not recognize any one of those objects, which had been so deeply impressed upon my remembrance – The tall oaks that shaded the avenue, had been cut down, and the iron gates at the end of it removed, together with the high wall that surrounded the court yard. The house itself, which was formerly a convent of Cistercian monks, had a venerable appearance: and along the front that looked into the garden, was a stone gallery, which afforded me many an agreeable walk, when I was disposed to be contemplative – Now the old front is covered with a screen of modern architecture; so that all without is Grecian, and all within Gothic – As for the garden, which was well stocked with the best fruit which England could produce, there is not now the least vestage remaining of trees, walls, or hedges — Nothing appears but a naked circus of loose sand, with a dry bason and a leaden triton in the middle.

You must know, that Baynard, at his father's death, had a clear estate of fifteen hundred pounds a-year, and was in other respects extremely well qualified to make a respectable figure in the commonwealth; but, what with some excesses of youth, and the expence of a contested election, he in a few years found himself encumbered with a debt of ten thousand pounds, which he resolved to discharge by means of a prudent marriage – He accordingly married a miss Thomson, whose fortune amounted to double the sum that he owed – She was the daughter of a citizen, who had failed in trade; but her fortune came by an uncle, who died in the East-Indies – Her own parents being dead, she lived with a maiden aunt, who had superintended her education; and, in all appearance, was well enough qualified for the usual purposes of the married state — Her virtues, however, stood rather upon a negative, than a positive foundation – She was neither proud, insolent, nor capricious, nor given to scandal, nor addicted to gaming, nor inclined to gallantry – She could read, and write, and dance, and sing, and play upon the harpsichord, and smatter French, and take a hand at whist and ombre; but even these accomplishments she possessed by halves – She excelled in nothing. Her conversation was flat, her stile mean, and her expression embarrassed – In a word, her character was totally insipid. Her person was not disagreeable; but there was nothing graceful in her address, nor engaging in her manners; and she was so ill qualified to do the honours of the house, that when she sat at the head of the table, one was always looking for the mistress of the family in some other place.

Baynard had flattered himself, that it would be no difficult matter to mould such a subject after his own fashion, and that she would chearfully enter into his views, which were wholly turned to domestic happiness. He proposed to reside always in the country, of which he was fond to a degree of enthusiasm; to cultivate his estate, which was very improvable; to enjoy the exercise of rural diversions; to maintain an intimacy of correspondence with some friends that were settled in his neighbourhood; to keep a comfortable house, without suffering his expence to exceed the limits of his income; and to find pleasure and employment for his wife in the management and avocations of her own family — This, however, was a visionary scheme, which he never was able to realize. His wife was as ignorant as a new-born babe of everything that related to the conduct of a family; and she had no idea of a country-life. Her understanding did not reach so far as to comprehend the first principles of discretion; and, indeed, if her capacity had been better than it was, her natural indolence would not have permitted her to abandon a certain routine, to which she had been habituated. She had not taste enough to relish any rational enjoyment; but her ruling passion[2] was vanity, not that species which arises from self-conceit of superior accomplishments, but that which is of a bastard and idiot nature, excited by shew and ostentation, which implies not even the least consciousness of any personal merit.

The nuptial peal of noise and nonsense being rung out in all the usual changes, Mr Baynard thought it high time to make her acquainted with the particulars of the plan which he had projected — He told her that his fortune, though sufficient to afford all the comforts of life, was not ample enough to command all the superfluities of pomp and pageantry, which, indeed, were equally absurd and intolerable – He therefore hoped she would have no objection to their leaving London in the spring, when he would take the opportunity to dismiss some unnecessary domestics, whom he had hired for the occasion of their marriage – She heard him in silence, and after some pause, 'So (said she) I am to be buried in the country!' He was so confounded at this reply, that he could not speak for some minutes: at length he told her, he was much mortified to find he had proposed anything that was disagreeable to her ideas – 'I am sure (added he) I meant nothing more than to lay down a comfortable plan of living within the bounds of our fortune, which is but moderate.' 'Sir (said she), you are the best judge of your own affairs — My fortune, I know, does not exceed twenty thousand pounds — Yet, even with that pittance, I might have had a husband who would not have begrudged me a house in London' – 'Good God! my dear (cried poor Baynard, in the utmost agitation), you don't think me so sordid – I only hinted what I thought – But, I don't pretend to impose –' 'Yes, sir (resumed the lady), it is your prerogative to command, and my duty to obey' –

So saying, she burst into tears and retired to her chamber, where she was joined by her aunt – He endeavoured to recollect himself, and act with vigour of mind on this occasion; but was betrayed by the tenderness of his nature, which was the greatest defect of his constitution. He found the aunt in tears, and the niece in a fit, which held her the best part of eight hours, at the expiration of which, she began to talk incoherently about *death* and her *dear husband*, who had sat by her all this time, and now pressed her hand to his lips, in a transport of grief and penitence for the offence he had given —— From thence forward, he carefully avoided mentioning the country; and they continued to be sucked deeper and deeper into the vortex of extravagance and dissipation, leading what is called a fashionable life in town – About the latter end of July, however, Mrs Baynard, in order to exhibit a proof of conjugal obedience, desired of her own accord, that they might pay a visit to his country house, as there was no company left in London. He would have excused himself from this excursion which was no part of the œconomical plan he had proposed; but she insisted upon making this sacrifice to his taste and prejudices, and away they went with such an equipage as astonished the whole country — All that remained of the season was engrossed by receiving and returning visits in the neighbourhood; and, in this intercourse it was discovered that sir John Chickwell had a house-steward and one footman in livery more than the complement of Mr Baynard's household. This remark was made by the aunt at table, and assented to by the husband, who observed that sir John Chickwell might very well afford to keep more servants than were found in the family of a man who had not half his fortune. Mrs Baynard ate no supper that evening; but was seized with a violent fit, which completed her triumph over the spirit of her consort. The two supernumerary servants were added – The family plate was sold for old silver, and a new service procured; fashionable furniture was provided, and the whole house turned topsy turvy.

At their return to London in the beginning of winter, he, with a heavy heart, communicated these particulars to me in confidence. Before his marriage, he had introduced me to the lady as his particular friend; and I now offered in that character, to lay before her the necessity of reforming her œconomy, if she had any regard to the interest of her own family, or complaisance for the inclinations of her husband – But Baynard declined my offer, on the supposition that his wife's nerves were too delicate to bear expostulation; and that it would only serve to overwhelm her with such distress as would make himself miserable.

Baynard is a man of spirit, and had she proved a termagant, he would have known how to deal with her; but, either by accident or instinct, she fastened upon the weak side of his soul, and held it so fast, that he has been in subjection ever since – I afterwards advised him to carry her abroad to France or Italy, where he might gratify her vanity for half the expence it cost him in England: and this advice he followed accordingly – She was agreeably flattered with the idea of seeing and knowing foreign parts, and foreign fashions; of being presented to sovereigns, and living familiarly with princes. She forthwith seized the hint which I had thrown out on purpose, and even pressed Mr Baynard to hasten his departure; so that in a few weeks they crossed the sea to France, with a moderate train, still including the aunt; who was her bosom counsellor, and abetted her in all her oppositions to her husband's will — Since that period, I have had little or no opportunity to renew our former correspondence – All that I knew of his transactions, amounted to no more than that after an absence of two years, they returned so little improved in œconomy, that they launched out into new oceans of extravagance, which at length obliged him to mortgage his estate – By this time she had bore him three children, of which the last only survives, a puny boy of twelve or thirteen, who will be ruined in his education by the indulgence of his mother.

As for Baynard, neither his own good sense, nor the dread of indigence, nor the consideration of his children, has been of force sufficient to stimulate him into the resolution of breaking at once the shameful spell by which he seems enchanted — With a taste capable of the most refined enjoyment, a heart glowing with all the warmth of friendship and humanity, and a disposition strongly turned to the more rational pleasures of a retired and country life, he is hurried about in a perpetual tumult, amidst a mob of beings pleased with rattles, baubles, and gew-gaws, so void of sense and distinction, that even the most acute philosopher would find it a very hard task to discover for what wise purpose of providence they were created — Friendship is not to be found; nor can the amusements for which he sighs be enjoyed within the rotation of absurdity, to which he is doomed for life. He has long resigned all views of improving his fortune by management and attention to the exercise of husbandry, in which he delighted; and as to domestic happiness, not the least glimpse of hope remains to amuse his imagination. Thus blasted in all his prospects, he could not fail to be overwhelmed with melancholy and chagrin, which have preyed upon his health and spirits in such a manner, that he is now threatened with a consumption.

I have given you a sketch of the man, whom the other day I went to visit – At the gate we found a great number of powdered

lacquies, but no civility – After we had sat a considerable time
in the coach, we were told, that Mr Baynard had rode out, and
that his lady was dressing; but we were introduced to a parlour,
so very fine and delicate, that in all appearance it was designed
to be seen only, not inhabited. The chairs and couches were
carved, gilt, and covered with rich damask, so smooth and
slick, that they looked as if they had never been sat upon. There
was no carpet upon the floor, but the boards were rubbed and
waxed in such a manner, that we could not walk, but were
obliged to slide along them; and as for the stove, it was too
bright and polished to be polluted with sea-coal, or stained by
the smoke of any gross material fire – When we had remained
above half an hour sacrificing to the inhospitable powers in
the *temple of cold reception*, my friend Baynard arrived, and
understanding we were in the house, made his appearance, so
meagre, yellow, and dejected, that I really should not have
known him, had I met with him in any other place — Running
up to me, with great eagerness, he strained me in his embrace,
and his heart was so full, that for some minutes he could
not speak – Having saluted us all round, he perceived our
uncomfortable situation, and conducting us into another apartment, which had fire in the chimney, called for chocolate —
Then, withdrawing, he returned with a compliment from his
wife, and, in the mean time, presented his son Harry, a shambling, blear-eyed boy, in the habit of a hussar;[3] very rude,
forward, and impertinent – His father would have sent him to
a boarding-school, but his mamma and aunt would not hear of
his lying out of the house; so that there was a clergyman engaged
as his tutor in the family.

   As it was but just turned of twelve, and the whole house was
in commotion to prepare a formal entertainment, I foresaw it
would be late before we dined, and proposed a walk to Mr
Baynard, that we might converse together freely. In the course
of this perambulation, when I expressed some surprize that he
had returned so soon from Italy, he gave me to understand,
that his going abroad had not at all answered the purpose, for
which he left England; that although the expence of living was
not so great in Italy as at home, respect being had to the same

rank of life in both countries, it had been found necessary for him to lift himself above his usual stile, that he might be on some footing with the counts, marquises, and cavaliers, with whom he kept company — He was obliged to hire a great number of servants, to take off a great variety of rich cloths, and to keep a sumptuous table for the fashionable scorocconi[4] of the country; who, without a consideration of this kind, would not have payed any attention to an untitled foreigner, let his family or fortune be ever so respectable – Besides, Mrs Baynard was continually surrounded by a train of expensive loungers, under the denominations of language-masters, musicians, painters, and ciceroni;[5] and had actually fallen into the disease of buying pictures and antiques upon her own judgment, which was far from being infallible – At length she met with an affront, which gave her disgust to Italy, and drove her back to England with some precipitation. By means of frequenting the dutchess of B[edford]'s conversazione,[6] while her grace was at Rome, Mrs Baynard became acquainted with all the fashionable people of that city, and was admitted to their assemblies without scruple – Thus favoured, she conceived too great an idea of her own importance, and when the dutchess left Rome, resolved to have a conversazione that should leave the Romans no room to regret her grace's departure. She provided hands for a musical entertainment, and sent biglietti of invitation[7] to every person of distinction; but not one Roman of the female sex appeared at her assembly – She was that night seized with a violent fit, and kept her bed three days, at the expiration of which she declared that the air of Italy would be the ruin of her constitution. In order to prevent this catastrophe, she was speedily removed to Geneva, from whence they returned to England by the way of Lyons and Paris. By the time they arrived at Calais, she had purchased such a quantity of silks, stuffs, and laces, that it was necessary to hire a vessel to smuggle them over, and this vessel was taken by a custom-house cutter; so that they lost the whole cargo, which had cost them above eight hundred pounds.

It now appears, that her travels had produced no effect upon her, but that of making her more expensive and fantastic than

ever:– She affected to lead the fashion, not only in point of
female dress, but in every article of taste and connoisseurship.
She made a drawing of the new facade to the house in the
country; she pulled up the trees, and pulled down the walls of
the garden, so as to let in the easterly wind, which Mr Baynard's
ancestors had been at great pains to exclude. To shew her taste
in laying out ground, she seized into her own hand a farm of
two hundred acres, about a mile from the house, which she
parcelled out into walks and shrubberies, having a great bason
in the middle, into which she poured a whole stream that turned
two mills, and afforded the best trout in the country. The
bottom of the bason, however, was so ill secured, that it would
not hold the water which strained through the earth, and made
a bog of the whole plantation: in a word, the ground which
formerly payed him one hundred and fifty pounds a year, now
cost him two hundred pounds a year to keep it in tolerable
order, over and above the first expence of trees, shrubs, flowers,
turf, and gravel. There was not an inch of garden ground left
about the house, nor a tree that produced fruit of any kind; nor
did he raise a truss of hay, or a bushel of oats for his horses,
nor had he a single cow to afford milk for his tea; far less did
he ever dream of feeding his own mutton, pigs, and poultry:
every article of housekeeping, even the most inconsiderable,
was brought from the next market town, at the distance of five
miles, and thither they sent a courier every morning to fetch
hot rolls for breakfast. In short, Baynard fairly owned that he
spent double his income, and that in a few years he should be
obliged to sell his estate for the payment of his creditors. He
said that his wife had such delicate nerves, and such imbecility
of spirit, that she could neither bear remonstrance, be it ever so
gentle, nor practise any scheme of retrenchment, even if she
perceived the necessity of such a measure. He had therefore
ceased struggling against the stream, and endeavoured to reconcile himself to ruin, by reflecting that his child at least would
inherit his mother's fortune, which was secured to him by the
contract of marriage.

The detail which he gave me of his affairs, filled me at
once with grief and indignation. I inveighed bitterly against the

indiscretion of his wife, and reproached him with his unmanly acquiescence under the absurd tyranny which she exerted. I exhorted him to recollect his resolution, and make one effectual effort to disengage himself from a thraldom, equally shameful and pernicious. I offered him all the assistance in my power. I undertook to regulate his affairs, and even to bring about a reformation in his family, if he would only authorise me to execute the plan I should form for his advantage. I was so affected by the subject, that I could not help mingling tears with my remonstrances, and Baynard was so penetrated with these marks of my affection, that he lost all power of utterance. He pressed me to his breast with great emotion, and wept in silence. At length he exclaimed, 'Friendship is undoubtedly the most precious balm of life! Your words, dear Bramble, have in a great measure recalled me from an abyss of despondence, in which I have been long overwhelmed – I will, upon honour, make you acquainted with a distinct state of my affairs, and, as far as I am able to go, will follow the course you prescribe. But there are certain lengths which my nature — The truth is, there are tender connexions, of which a batchelor has no idea – Shall I own my weakness? I cannot bear the thoughts of making that woman uneasy' – 'And yet (cried I), she has seen you unhappy for a series of years – unhappy from her misconduct, without ever shewing the least inclination to alleviate your distress' – 'Nevertheless (said he) I am persuaded she loves me with the most warm affection; but these are incongruities in the composition of the human mind which I hold to be inexplicable.'

I was shocked at his infatuation, and changed the subject, after we had agreed to maintain a close correspondence for the future – He then gave me to understand, that he had two neighbours, who, like himself, were driven by their wives at full speed, in the high road to bankruptcy and ruin. All the three husbands were of dispositions very different from each other, and, according to this variation, their consorts were admirably suited to the purpose of keeping them all three in subjection. The views of the ladies were exactly the same. They vied in grandeur, that is, in ostentation, with the wife of Sir Charles

Chickwell, who had four times their fortune; and she again piqued herself upon making an equal figure with a neighbouring peeress, whose revenue trebled her own. Here then was the fable of the frog and the ox,[8] realized in four different instances within the same county: one large fortune, and three moderate estates, in a fair way of being burst by the inflation of female vanity; and in three of these instances, three different forms of female tyranny were exercised. Mr Baynard was subjugated by practising upon the tenderness of his nature. Mr Milksan, being of a timorous disposition, truckled to the insolence of a termagant. Mr Sowerby, who was of a temper neither to be moved by fits, nor driven by menaces, had the fortune to be fitted with a helpmate, who assailed him with the weapons of irony and satire; sometimes sneering in the way of compliment; sometimes throwing out sarcastic comparisons, implying reproaches upon his want of taste, spirit, and generosity: by which means she stimulated his passions from one act of extravagance to another, just as the circumstances of her vanity required.

All these three ladies have at this time the same number of horses, carriages, and servants in and out of livery; the same variety of dress; the same quantity of plate and china; the like ornaments in furniture: and in their entertainments they endeavour to exceed one another in the variety, delicacy, and expence of their dishes. I believe it will be found upon enquiry, that nineteen out of twenty, who are ruined by extravagance, fall a sacrifice to the ridiculous pride and vanity of silly women, whose parts are held in contempt by the very men whom they pillage and enslave. Thank heaven, Dick, that among all the follies and weaknesses of human nature, I have not yet fallen into that of matrimony.

After Baynard and I had discussed all these matters at leisure, we returned towards the house, and met Jery with our two women, who had come forth to take the air, as the lady of the mansion had not yet made her appearance. In short, Mrs Baynard did not produce herself, till about a quarter of an hour before dinner was upon the table. Then her husband brought her into the parlour, accompanied by her aunt and son, and she received us with a coldness of reserve sufficient to freeze the very soul of hospitality. Though she knew I had been the intimate friend of her husband, and had often seen me with him in London, she shewed no marks of recognition or regard, when I addressed myself to her in the most friendly terms of salutation. She did not even express the common compliment of, *I am glad to see you*; or, *I hope you have enjoyed your health since we had the pleasure of seeing you*; or some such words of course: nor did she once open her mouth in the way of welcome to my sister and my niece: but sat in silence like a statue, with an aspect of insensibility. Her aunt, the model upon which she had been formed, was indeed the very essence of insipid formality but the boy was very pert and impudent, and prated without ceasing.

At dinner, the lady maintained the same ungracious indifference, never speaking but in whispers to her aunt; and as to the repast, it was made up of a parcel of kickshaws,[9] contrived by a French cook, without one substantial article adapted to the satisfaction of an English appetite. The pottage was little better than bread soaked in dishwashings, lukewarm. The ragouts looked as if they had been once eaten and half digested: the fricassees were involved in a nasty yellow poultice: and the rotis[10] were scorched and stinking, for the honour of the fumet.[11] The desert consisted of faded fruit and iced froth, a good emblem of our landlady's character; the table-beer was sour, the water foul, and the wine vapid; but there was a parade of plate and china, and a powdered lacquey stood behind every chair, except those of the master and mistress of the house, who were served by two valets dressed like gentlemen. We dined in a large old Gothic parlour, which was formerly the hall. It was now paved with marble, and, notwithstanding the fire which had been kindled about an hour, struck me with such a chill sensation, that when I entered it the teeth chattered in my jaws – In short, every thing was cold, comfortless, and disgusting, except the looks of my friend Baynard, which declared the warmth of his affection and humanity.

After dinner we withdrew into another apartment, where the boy began to be impertinently troublesome to my niece Liddy. He wanted a play-fellow, forsooth; and would have romped with her, had she encouraged his advances – He was even so impudent as to snatch a kiss, at which she changed countenance, and seemed uneasy; and though his father checked him for the rudeness of his behaviour, he became so outrageous as to thrust his hand in her bosom: an insult to which she did not tamely submit, though one of the mildest creatures upon earth. Her eyes sparkling with resentment, she started up, and lent him such a box in the ear, as sent him staggering to the other side of the room.

'Miss Melford (cried his father), you have treated him with the utmost propriety – I am only sorry that the impertinence of any child of mine should have occasioned this exertion of your spirit, which I cannot but applaud and admire.' His wife was so far from assenting to the candour of his apology, that she rose from the table, and, taking her son by the hand, 'Come, child (said she), your father cannot abide you.' So saying, she retired with this hopeful youth, and was followed by her gouvernante: but neither the one nor the other deigned to take the least notice of the company.

Baynard was exceedingly disconcerted; but I perceived his uneasiness was tinctured with resentment, and derived a good omen from this discovery. I ordered the horses to be put to the carriage, and, though he made some efforts to detain us all night, I insisted upon leaving the house immediately; but, before I went away, I took an opportunity of speaking to him again in private. I said every thing I could recollect, to animate his endeavours in shaking off those shameful trammels. I made no scruple to declare, that his wife was unworthy of that tender complaisance which he had shewn for her foibles: that she was dead to all the genuine sentiments of conjugal affection; insensible of her own honour and interest, and seemingly destitute of common sense and reflection. I conjured him to remember what he owed to his father's house, to his own reputation, and to his family, including even this unreasonable woman herself, who was driving on blindly to her own destruction. I advised him to form a plan for retrenching superfluous expence, and try to convince the aunt of the necessity for such a reformation, that she might gradually prepare her niece for its execution; and I exhorted him to turn that disagreeable piece of formality out of the house, if he should find her averse to his proposal.

Here he interrupted me with a sigh, observing that such a step would undoubtedly be fatal to Mrs Baynard – 'I shall lose all patience (cried I), to hear you talk so weakly – Mrs Baynard's fits will never hurt her constitution. I believe in my conscience they are all affected: I am sure she has no feeling for your distresses; and, when you are ruined, she will appear to have no feeling for her own.' Finally, I took his word and honour that he would make an effort, such as I had advised; that he would form a plan of œconomy, and, if he found it impracticable without my assistance, he would come to Bath in the winter, where I promised to give him the meeting, and contribute all in my power to the retrieval of his affairs – With this mutual engagement we parted; and I shall think myself supremely happy, if, by my means, a worthy man, whom I love and esteem, can be saved from misery, disgrace, and despair.

I have only one friend more to visit in this part of the country, but he is of a complexion very different from that of Baynard. You have heard me mention Sir Thomas Bullford, whom I knew in Italy. He is now become a country gentleman; but, being disabled by the gout from enjoying any amusement abroad, he entertains himself within doors, by keeping open house for all comers, and playing upon the oddities and humours of his company: but he himself is generally the greatest original at his table. He is very good-humoured, talks much, and laughs without ceasing. I am told that all the use he makes of his understanding at present, is to excite mirth, by exhibiting his guests in ludicrous attitudes. I know not how far we may furnish him with entertainment of this kind, but I am resolved to beat up his quarters, partly with a view to laugh with the knight himself, and partly to pay my respects to his lady, a good-natured sensible woman, with whom he lives upon very easy terms, although she has not had the good fortune to bring him an heir to his estate.

And now, dear Dick, I must tell you for your comfort, that you are the only man upon earth to whom I would presume to

send such a long-winded epistle, which I could not find in my
heart to curtail, because the subject interested the warmest
passions of my heart; neither will I make any other apology
to a correspondent who has been so long accustomed to the
impertinence of

Sept. 30.   MATT. BRAMBLE

To Sir WATKIN PHILLIPS, Bart. at Oxon.

DEAR KNIGHT,

I believe there is something mischievous in my disposition,
for nothing diverts me so much as to see certain characters
tormented with false terrors. — We last night lodged at the
house of Sir Thomas Bullford, an old friend of my uncle, a jolly
fellow, of moderate intellects, who, in spite of the gout, which
hath lamed him, is resolved to be merry to the last; and mirth
he has a particular knack in extracting from his guests, let
their humour be ever so caustic or refractory. — Besides our
company, there was in the house a fat-headed justice of the
peace, called Frogmore, and a country practitioner in surgery,
who seemed to be our landlord's chief companion and confidant. – We found the knight sitting on a couch, with his crutches
by his side, and his feet supported on cushions; but he received
us with a hearty welcome, and seemed greatly rejoiced at our
arrival. – After tea, we were entertained with a sonata on
the harpsichord by lady Bullford, who sung and played to
admiration; but Sir Thomas seemed to be a little asinine in the
article of ears, though he affected to be in raptures, and begged
his wife to favour us with an *arietta*[1] of her own composing. –
This *arietta*, however, she no sooner began to perform, than he
and the justice fell asleep; but the moment she ceased playing,
the knight waked snorting, and exclaimed, 'O *cara!*[2] what d'ye
think, gentlemen? Will you talk any more of your Pargolesi and
your Corelli?'[3] – At the same time, he thrust his tongue in one
cheek, and leered with one eye at the doctor and me, who sat
on his left hand. — He concluded the pantomime with a loud

laugh, which he could command at all times extempore. —
Notwithstanding his disorder, he did not do penance at supper,
nor did he ever refuse his glass when the toast went round, but
rather encouraged a quick circulation, both by precept and
example.

I soon perceived the doctor had made himself very necessary
to the baronet. — He was the whetstone of his wit, the butt of
his satire, and his operator in certain experiments of humour,
which were occasionally tried upon strangers. – Justice Frogmore was an excellent subject for this species of philosophy;
sleek and corpulent, solemn, and shallow, he had studied Burn[4]
with uncommon application, but he studied nothing so much
as the art of living (that is, eating) well — This fat buck had
often afforded good sport to our landlord; and he was frequently started with tolerable success, in the course of this
evening; but the baronet's appetite for ridicule seemed to be
chiefly excited by the appearance, address, and conversation
of Lismahago, whom he attempted in all different modes of
exposition; but he put me in mind of a contest that I once saw
betwixt a young hound and an old hedge-hog – The dog turned
him over and over, and bounced and barked, and mumbled;
but as often as he attempted to bite, he felt a prickle in his jaws,
and recoiled in manifest confusion; — The captain, when left
to himself, will not fail to turn his ludicrous side to the company, but if any man attempts to force him into that attitude, he
becomes stubborn as a mule, and unmanageable as an elephant
unbroke.

Divers tolerable jokes were cracked upon the justice, who eat
a most unconscionable supper, and, among other things, a large
plate of broiled mushrooms, which he had no sooner swallowed
than the doctor observed, with great gravity, that they were of
the kind called *champignons*, which in some constitutions has
a poisonous effect. – Mr Frogmore startled at this remark,
asked, in some confusion, why he had not been so kind as to
give him that notice sooner. – He answered, that he took it for
granted, by his eating them so heartily, that he was used to the
dish; but as he seemed to be under some apprehension, he
prescribed a bumper of plague water,[5] which the justice drank

off immediately, and retired to rest, not without marks of terror and disquiet.

At midnight we were shewn to our different chambers, and in half an hour, I was fast asleep in bed; but about three o'clock in the morning I was waked with a dismal cry of *Fire!* and starting up, ran to the window in my shirt. – The night was dark and stormy; and a number of people half-dressed ran backwards and forwards thro' the court-yard, with links and lanthorns, seemingly in the utmost hurry and trepidation. – Slipping on my cloaths in a twinkling, I ran down stairs, and, upon enquiry, found the fire was confined to a back-stair, which led to a detached apartment where Lismahago lay. — By this time, the lieutenant was alarmed by bawling at his window, which was in the second story, but he could not find his cloaths in the dark, and his room-door was locked on the outside. — The servants called to him, that the house had been robbed; that, without all doubt, the villains had taken away his cloaths, fastened the door, and set the house on fire, for the stair-case was in flames. — In this dilemma the poor lieutenant ran about the room naked like a squirrel in a cage, popping out his head at the window between whiles, and imploring assistance. – At length, the knight in person was brought out in his chair, attended by my uncle and all the family, including our aunt Tabitha, who screamed, and cried, and tore her hair, as if she had been distracted – Sir Thomas had already ordered his people to bring a long ladder which was applied to the captain's window, and now he exhorted him earnestly to descend. – There was no need of much rhetoric to persuade Lismahago, who forthwith made his exit by the window, roaring all the time to the people below to hold fast the ladder.

Notwithstanding the gravity of the occasion, it was impossible to behold this scene without being seized with an inclination to laugh. The rueful aspect of the lieutenant in his shirt, with a quilted night-cap fastened under his chin, and his long lank limbs and posteriors exposed to the wind, made a very picturesque appearance, when illumined by the links and torches which the servants held up to light him in his descent. – All the company stood round the ladder, except the knight, who sat in his chair, exclaiming from time to time, 'Lord, have mercy upon us! – save the gentleman's life! – mind your footing, dear captain! – softly! – stand fast! – clasp the ladder with both hands! – there! — well done, my dear boy! – O bravo! – an old soldier for ever! – bring a blanket — bring a warm blanket to comfort his poor carcase — warm the bed in the green room —— give me your hand, dear captain – I'm rejoiced to see thee safe and sound with all my heart.' Lismahago was received at the foot of the ladder by his inamorata, who snatching a blanket from one of the maids, wrapped it about his body; two men-servants took him under the arms, and a female conducted him to the green room, still accompanied by Mrs Tabitha, who saw him fairly put to bed. – During this whole transaction, he spoke not a syllable, but looked exceeding grim, sometimes at one, sometimes at another of the spectators, who now adjourned in a body to the parlour where we had supped, every one surveying another with marks of astonishment and curiosity.

The knight being seated in an easy chair, seized my uncle by the hand, and bursting into a long and loud laugh, 'Matt (cried he), crown me with oak, or ivy, or laurel, or parsely, or what you will, and acknowledge this to be a *coup de maitre*[6] in the way of waggery – ha, ha, ha! – Such *a camisciata, scagliata, beffata!*[7] O, *che roba!*[8] – O, what a subject! — O, what *carica-tura!*[9] — O, for a Rosa, a Rembrandt, a Schalken![10] – Zooks,[11] I'll give a hundred guineas to have it painted! – what a fine descent from the cross, or ascent to the gallows! what lights and shadows! – what a groupe below! – what expression above! — what an aspect! – did you mind the aspect? – ha, ha, ha! — and the limbs, and the muscles — every toe denoted terror! – ha, ha, ha! — then the blanket! – O, what *costume*! St Andrew! St Lazarus! St Barrabas! – ha, ha, ha!' 'After all then (cried Mr Bramble very gravely), this was no more than a false alarm. – We have been frightened out of our beds, and almost out of our senses, for the joke's sake.' 'Ay, and such a joke! (cried our landlord) such a farce! such a *denouement*! such a *catas-trophe*!'[12]

'Have a little patience (replied our 'squire); we are not yet come to the *catastrophe*; and pray God it may not turn out a tragedy instead of a farce. — The captain is one of those saturnine[13] subjects, who have no idea of humour. – He never laughs in his own person; nor can he bear that other people should laugh at his expence – Besides, if the subject had been properly chosen, the joke was too severe in all conscience.' ' 'Sdeath! (cried the knight) I could not have bated him an ace had he been my own father; and as for the subject, such another does not present itself once in half a century.' Here Mrs Tabitha interposing, and bridling up, declared, she did not see that Mr Lismahago was a fitter subject for ridicule than the knight himself; and that she was very much afraid, he would very soon find he had mistaken his man. — The baronet was a good deal disconcerted by this intimation, saying, that he must be a Goth and a barbarian, if he did not enter into the spirit of such a happy and humourous contrivance. – He begged, however, that Mr Bramble and this sister would bring him to reason; and this request was reinforced by lady Bullford, who did not fail to read the baronet a lecture upon his indiscretion, which lecture he received with submission on one side of his face, and a leer upon the other.

We now went to bed for the second time; and before I got up, my uncle had visited Lismahago in the green room, and used such arguments with him, that when we met in the parlour he seemed to be quite appeased. – He received the knight's apology with good grace, and even professed himself pleased at finding he had contributed to the diversion of the company. — Sir Thomas shook him by the hand, laughing heartily; and then desired a pinch of snuff, in token of perfect reconciliation – The lieutenant, putting his hand in his waistcoat pocket, pulled out, instead of his own Scotch mull,[14] a very fine gold snuff-box, which he no sooner perceived than he said, 'Here is a small mistake.' 'No mistake at all (cried the baronet): a fair exchange is no robbery. – Oblige me so far, captain, as to let me keep your mull as a memorial.' 'Sir (said the lieutenant), the mull is much at your service; but this machine I can by no means retain. – It looks like compounding a sort of felony in the code of honour. – Besides, I don't know but there may be another joke in this conveyance; and I don't find myself disposed to be brought upon the stage again. — I won't presume to make free with your pockets, but I beg you will put it up again with your own hand.' — So saying, with a certain austerity of aspect, he presented the snuff-box to the knight, who received it in some confusion, and restored the mull, which he would by no means keep except on the terms of exchange.

This transaction was like to give a grave cast to the conversation, when my uncle took notice that Mr Justice Frogmore had not made his appearance either at the night-alarm, or now at the general rendezvous. The baronet hearing Frogmore mentioned, 'Odso! (cried he) I had forgot the justice. – Pr'ythee, doctor, go and bring him out of his kennel.' – Then laughing till his sides were well shaken, he said he would shew the captain, that he was not the only person of the drama exhibited for the entertainment of the company. As to the night-scene, it could not affect the justice, who had been purposely lodged in the farther end of the house, remote from the noise, and lulled with a dose of opium into the bargain. In a few minutes, Mr Justice was led into the parlour in his nightcap and loose morning-gown, rolling his head from side to side, and groaning piteously all the way. – 'Jesu! neighbour Frogmore (exclaimed the baronet), what is the matter? – you look as if you was not a man for this world. — Set him down softly on the couch — poor gentleman! – Lord have mercy upon us! – What makes him so pale, and yellow, and bloated?' 'Oh, Sir Thomas! (cried the justice) I doubt 'tis all over with me — Those mushrooms I eat at your table have done my business[15] — ah! oh! hey!' 'Now the Lord forbid! (said the other) – what! man, have a good heart – How does thy stomach feel? – hah?'

To this interrogation he made no reply; but throwing aside his night-gown, discovered that his waist-coat would not meet upon his belly by five good inches at least. 'Heaven protect us all! (cried Sir Thomas) – what a melancholy spectacle! – never did I see a man so suddenly swelled, but when he was either just dead, or just dying. — Doctor, can'st thou do nothing for this poor object?' 'I don't think the case is quite desperate (said the surgeon), but I would advise Mr Frogmore to settle his affairs with all expedition; the parson may come and pray by

him, while I prepare a glyster[16] and an emetic draught.' The
justice, rolling his languid eyes, ejaculated with great fervency,
'Lord, have mercy upon us! Christ, have mercy upon us!'[17] —
Then he begged the surgeon, in the name of God, to dispatch –
'As for my worldly affairs (said he), they are all settled but one
mortgage, which must be left to my heirs – but my poor soul!
my poor soul! what will become of my poor soul? – miserable
sinner that I am!' 'Nay, pr'ythee, my dear boy, compose thyself
(resumed the knight); consider the mercy of heaven is infinite;
thou can'st not have any sins of a very deep dye on thy conscience, or the devil's in't.' 'Name not the devil (exclaimed the
terrified Frogmore), I have more sins to answer for than the
world dreams of. – Ah! friend, I have been sly – sly – damn'd
sly! — Send for the parson without loss of time, and put me to
bed, for I am posting to eternity.' – He was accordingly raised
from the couch, and supported by two servants, who led him
back to his room; but before he quitted the parlour, he intreated
the good company to assist him with their prayers. – He added,
'Take warning by me, who am suddenly cut off in my prime,
like a flower of the field;[18] and God forgive you, Sir Thomas,
for suffering such poisonous trash to be eaten at your table.'

He was no sooner removed out of hearing, than the baronet
abandoned himself to a violent fit of laughing, in which he was
joined by the greatest part of the company; but we could hardly
prevent the good lady from going to undeceive the patient, by
discovering, that while he slept his waistcoat had been strait-
ened by the contrivance of the surgeon; and that the disorder
in his stomach and bowels was occasioned by some antimonial
wine,[19] which he had taken over night, under the denomination
of plague-water. — She seemed to think that his apprehension
might put an end to his life: the knight swore he was no such
chicken, but a tough old rogue, that would live long enough to
plague all his neighbours. – Upon enquiry, we found his character did not intitle him to much compassion or respect, and
therefore we let our landlord's humour take its course. – A
glyster was actually administered by an old woman of the
family, who had been Sir Thomas's nurse, and the patient
took a draught made with oxymel of squills[20] to forward the

operation of the antimonial wine, which had been retarded by
the opiate of the preceding night. He was visited by the vicar,
who read prayers, and began to take an account of the state of
his soul, when those medicines produced their effect; so that
the parson was obliged to hold his nose while he poured forth
spiritual consolation from his mouth. The same expedient was
used by the knight and me, who, with the doctor, entered the
chamber at this juncture, and found Frogmore enthroned on
an easing-chair, under the pressure of a double evacuation. The
short intervals betwixt every heave he employed in crying for
mercy, confessing his sins, or asking the vicar's opinion of his
case; and the vicar answered, in a solemn snuffling tone, that
heightened the ridicule of the scene. The emetic having done its
office, the doctor interfered, and ordered the patient to be put
in bed again. When he examined the *egesta*,[21] and felt his pulse,
he declared that much of the *virus* was discharged, and, giving
him a composing draught, assured him he had good hopes of
his recovery. — This welcome hint he received with the tears
of joy in his eyes, protesting, that if he should recover, he would
always think himself indebted for his life to the great skill and
tenderness of his doctor, whose hand he squeezed with great
fervour; and thus he was left to his repose.

We were pressed to stay dinner, that we might be witnesses
of his resuscitation; but my uncle insisted upon our departing
before noon, that we might reach this town before it should be
dark. — In the mean-time, lady Bullford conducted us into
the garden to see a fishpond just finished, which Mr Bramble
censured as being too near the parlour, where the knight now
sat by himself, dozing in an elbow-chair after the fatigues of his
morning atchievement. — In this situation he reclined, with his
feet wrapped in flannel, and supported in a line with his body,
when the door flying open with a violent shock, lieutenant
Lismahago rushed into the room with horror in his looks,
exclaiming, 'A mad dog! a mad dog!' and throwing up the
window sash, leaped into the garden – Sir Thomas, waked by
this tremendous exclamation, started up, and forgetting his
gout, followed the lieutenant's example by a kind of instinctive
impulse. — He not only bolted thro' the window like an arrow

from a bow, but ran up to his middle in the pond before he gave the least sign of recollection. Then the captain began to bawl, 'Lord have mercy upon us! – pray, take care of the gentleman! — for God's sake, mind your footing, my dear boy! – get warm blankets – comfort his poor carcase – warm the bed in the green room.'

Lady Bullford was thunder-struck at this phænomenon, and the rest of the company gazed in silent astonishment, while the servants hastened to assist their master, who suffered himself to be carried back into the parlour without speaking a word. — Being instantly accommodated with dry clothes and flannels, comforted with a cordial, and replaced *in statu quo*, one of the maids was ordered to chafe his lower extremities, an operation in consequence of which his senses seemed to return and his good humour to revive. – As we had followed him into the room, he looked at every individual in his turn, with a certain ludicrous expression in his countenance, but fixed his eyes in particular upon Lismahago, who presented him with a pinch of snuff, and when he took it in silence, 'Sir Thomas Bullford (said he), I am much obliged to you for all your favours, and some of them I have endeavoured to repay in your own coin.' 'Give me thy hand (cried the baronet); thou hast indeed payed me *Scot and lot*;[22] and even left a balance in my hands, for which, in presence of this company, I promise to be account-able.' – So saying, he laughed very heartily, and even seemed to enjoy the retaliation which had been exacted at his own expence; but lady Bullford looked very grave; and in all prob-ability thought the lieutenant had carried his resentment too far, considering that her husband was valetudinary – but, according to the proverb, *he that will play at bowls must expect to meet with rubbers.*

I have seen a tame bear, very diverting when properly man-aged, become a very dangerous wild beast when teized·for the entertainment of the spectators. – As for Lismahago, he seemed to think the fright and the cold bath would have a good effect upon his patient's constitution: but the doctor hinted some apprehension that the gouty matter might, by such a sudden shock, be repelled from the extremities and thrown upon some

of the more vital parts of the machine. – I should be very sorry
to see this prognostic verified upon our facetious landlord, who
told Mrs Tabitha at parting, that he hoped she would remember
him in the distribution of the bride's favours, as he had taken
so much pains to put the captain's parts and mettle to the proof.
— After all, I am afraid our 'squire will appear to be the greatest
sufferer by the baronet's wit; for his constitution is by no means
calculated for night-alarms. – He has yawned and shivered all
day, and gone to bed without supper; so that, as we have got
into good quarters, I imagine we shall make a halt to-morrow;
in which case, you will have at least one day's respite from the
persecution of
Oct. 3.   J. MELFORD

To Mrs MARY JONES, at Brambleton-hall.

DEAR MARY JONES,

   Miss Liddy is so good as to unclose me in a kiver as fur as
Gloster, and the carrier will bring it to hand – God send us all
safe to Monmouthshire, for I'm quite jaded with rambling – 'Tis
a true saying, *live and learn* – O woman, what chuckling and
changing have I seen! – Well, there's nothing sartain in this
world — Who would have thought that mistriss, after all the
pains taken for the good of her prusias sole, would go for to
throw away her poor body? that she would cast the heys of
infection upon such a carrying-crow as Lashmihago! as old as
Mathewsullin,[1] as dry as a red herring, and as poor as a starved
veezel – O, Molly, hadst thou seen him come down the ladder,
in a shurt so scanty, that it could not kiver his nakedness! –
The young 'squire called him Dunquickset;[2] but he looked for
all the world like Cradoc-ap-Morgan, the ould tinker, that
suffered at Abergany for steeling of kettle[3] – Then he's a profane
scuffle, and, as Mr Clinker says, no better than an impfiddle,[4]
continually playing upon the pyebill and the new-burth – I
doubt he has as little manners as money; for he can't say a civil
word, much more make me a present of a pair of gloves for

goodwill; but he looks as if he wanted to be very forewood and familiar – O! that ever a gentlewoman of years and discretion should tare her air, and cry and disporridge herself for such a nubjack![5] as the song goes –

> I vow she would fain have a burd
> That bids such a price for an owl.[6]

but, for sartain, he must have dealt with some Scotch musician to bring her to this pass — As for me, I put my trust in the Lord; and I have got a slice of witch elm sowed in the gathers of my under petticoat; and Mr Clinker assures me, that by the new light of grease, I may deify the devil and all his works[7] — But I nose what I nose — If mistress should take up with Lashmyhago, this is no sarvice for me – Thank God, there's no want of places; and if it wan't for wan thing, I would – but, no matter – Madam Baynar's woman has twenty good pounds a-year and parquisites; and dresses like a parson of distinkson — I dined with her and the valley de shambles, with bags and golden jackets; but there was nothing kimfittable to eat, being as how they lived upon board, and having nothing but a piss of could cuddling[8] tart and some blamangey, I was tuck with the cullick, and a murcey it was that mistress had her viol of assings[9] in the cox.

But, as I was saying, I think for sartain this match will go forewood; for things are come to a creesus; and I have seen with my own hays, such smuggling — But I scorn for to exclose the secrets of the family; and if it wance comes to marrying, who nose but the frolick may go round – I believes as how, Miss Liddy would have no reversion if her swan would appear; and you would be surprised, Molly, to receive a bride's fever from your humble sarvant — but this is all suppository, dear girl; and I have sullenly promised to Mr Clinker, that neither man, woman, nor child shall no that arrow said a civil thing to me in the way of infection – I hope to drink your health at Brambleton-hall, in a horn of October, before the month be out – Pray let my bed be turned once a-day, and the windore opened, while the weather is dry; and burn a few billets with some brush in the footman's garret, and see their mattrash be dry as a bone: for both our gentlemen have got a sad could by lying in damp shits at sir Tummas Ballfart's. No more at present, but my sarvice to Saul and the rest of our fellow-sarvents, being,

Dear Mary Jones,

Always yours,

Oct. 4.   WIN. JENKINS

To Miss LÆTITIA WILLIS, at Gloucester.

MY DEAR LETTY,

This method of writing to you from time to time, without any hopes of an answer, affords me, I own, some ease and satisfaction in the midst of my disquiet, as it in some degree lightens the burthen of affliction: but it is at best a very imperfect enjoyment of friendship, because it admits of no return of confidence and good counsel — I would give the whole world to have your company for a single day – I am heartily tired of this itinerant way of life – I am quite dizzy with a perpetual succession of objects – Besides it is impossible to travel such a length of way, without being exposed to inconveniencies, dangers, and disagreeable accidents, which prove very grievous to a poor creature of weak nerves like me, and make me pay very dear for the gratification of my curiosity.

Nature never intended me for the busy world — I long for repose and solitude, where I can enjoy that disinterested friendship which is not to be found among crouds, and indulge those pleasing reveries that shun the hurry and tumult of fashionable society — Unexperienced as I am in the commerce of life, I have seen enough to give me a disgust to the generality of those who carry it on – There is such malice, treachery, and dissimulation, even among professed friends and intimate companions, as cannot fail to strike a virtuous mind with horror; and when Vice quits the stage for a moment, her place is immediately occupied by Folly, which is often too serious to excite any thing but compassion – Perhaps I ought to be silent on the foibles of my poor aunt; but with you, my dear Willis, I have no secrets; and, truly, her weaknesses are such as cannot be concealed. Since the first moment we arrived at Bath, she has been employed constantly in spreading nets for the other sex; and, at length, she has caught a superannuated lieutenant, who is in a fair way to make her change her name – My uncle and my brother seem to have no objection to this extraordinary match, which, I make no doubt, will afford abundance of matter for conversation and mirth; for my part, I am too sensible of my own weaknesses, to be diverted with those of other people — At present, I have something at heart that employs my whole attention, and keeps my mind in the utmost terror and suspence.

Yesterday in the forenoon, as I stood with my brother at the parlour window of an inn, where we had lodged, a person passed a-horseback, whom (gracious Heaven!) I instantly discovered to be Wilson! He wore a white riding-coat, with the cape buttoned up to his chin; looking remarkably pale, and passed at a round trot, without seeming to observe us — Indeed, he could not see us; for there was a blind that concealed us from the view. You may guess how I was affected at this apparition – The light forsook my eyes; and I was seized with such a palpitation and trembling, that I could not stand. I sat down upon a couch, and strove to compose myself, that my brother might not perceive my agitation; but it was impossible to escape his prying eyes – He had observed the object that alarmed me; and, doubtless, knew him at the first glance – He now looked at me with a stern countenance; then he ran out into the street, to see what road the unfortunate horseman had taken – He afterwards dispatched his man for further intelligence, and seemed to meditate some violent design. My uncle, being out of order, we remained another night at the inn; and all day long Jery acted the part of an indefatigable spy upon my conduct – He watched my very looks with such eagerness of attention, as if he would have penetrated into the utmost recesses of my heart – This may be owing to his regard for my honour, if it is not the effect of his own pride; but he is so hot, and violent, and unrelenting, that the sight of him alone throws me into a flutter; and really it will not be in my power to afford him any share of my affection, if he persists in persecuting me at this rate. I am afraid he has formed some scheme of vengeance, which will make me completely wretched! I am afraid he suspects some collusion from this appearance of Wilson. — Good God! did he really appear? or was it only a phantom, a pale spectre to apprise me of his death?

O Letty, what shall I do? – where shall I turn for advice and consolation? – shall I implore the protection of my uncle, who has been always kind and compassionate. – This must be my last resource. — I dread the thoughts of making him uneasy; and would rather suffer a thousand deaths than live the cause of dissension in the family. – I cannot conceive the meaning of Wilson's coming hither: — perhaps, it was in quest of us, in order to disclose his real name and situation: – but wherefore pass without staying to make the least enquiry? – My dear Willis, I am lost in conjecture. – I have not closed an eye since I saw him. – All night long have I been tossed about from one imagination to another. – The reflection finds no resting place. — I have prayed, and sighed, and wept plentifully. — If this terrible suspence continues much longer, I shall have another fit of illness, and then the whole family will be in confusion – If it was consistent with the wise purposes of Providence, would I were in my grave – But it is my duty to be resigned. — My dearest Letty, excuse my weakness – excuse these blots — my tears fall so fast that I cannot keep the paper dry – yet I ought to consider that I have as yet no cause to despair — but I am such a faint-hearted timorous creature!

Thank God, my uncle is much better than he was yesterday. — He is resolved to pursue our journey strait to Wales. — I hope we shall take Gloucester in our way – that hope chears my poor heart – I shall once more embrace my best beloved Willis, and pour all my griefs into her friendly bosom. — O heaven! is it possible that such happiness is reserved for

The dejected and forlorn

Oct. 4.   LYDIA MELFORD

To Sir WATKIN PHILLIPS, Bart. of Jesus college, Oxon.

DEAR WATKIN,

I yesterday met with an incident which I believe you will own to be very surprising – As I stood with Liddy at the window of the inn where we had lodged, who should pass by but Wilson a-horseback! – I could not be mistaken in the person, for I had a full view of him as he advanced; I plainly perceived by my sister's confusion that she recognized him at the same time. I was equally astonished and incensed at his appearance, which I could not but interpret into an insult, or something worse. I ran out at the gate, and, seeing him turn the corner of the street, I dispatched my servant to observe his motions, but the fellow was too late to bring me that satisfaction. He told me, however, that there was an inn, called the Red Lion, at that end of the town, where he supposed the horseman had alighted, but that he would not enquire without further orders. I sent him back immediately to know what strangers were in the house, and he returned with a report that there was one Mr Wilson lately arrived. In consequence of this information I charged him with a note directed to that gentleman, desiring him to meet me in half an hour in a certain field at the town's end, with a case of pistols, in order to decide the difference which could not be determined at our last rencounter: but I did not think proper to subscribe the billet. My man assured me he had delivered it into his own hand; and, that having read it, he declared he would wait upon the gentleman at the place and time appointed.

M'Alpine being an old soldier, and luckily sober at the time, I entrusted him with my secret. I ordered him to be within call, and, having given him a letter to be delivered to my uncle in case of accident, I repaired to the rendezvous, which was an inclosed field at a little distance from the highway. I found my antagonist had already taken his ground, wrapped in a dark horseman's coat, with a laced hat flapped over his eyes; but what was my astonishment, when, throwing off this wrapper, he appeared to be a person whom I had never seen before! He had one pistol stuck in a leather belt, and another in his hand

ready for action, and, advancing a few steps, called to know if
I was ready – I answered, 'No,' and desired a parley; upon
which he turned the muzzle of his piece towards the earth; then
replaced it in his belt, and met me half way – When I assured
him he was not the man I expected to meet, he said *it might be
so*: that he had received a slip of paper directed to Mr Wilson,
requesting him to come hither; and that as there was no other
in the place of that name, he naturally concluded the note was
intended for him, and him only — I then gave him to understand, that I had been injured by a person who assumed that
name, which person I had actually seen within the hour, passing
through the street on horseback; that hearing there was a Mr
Wilson at the Red Lion, I took it for granted he was the man,
and in that belief had writ the billet; and I expressed my surprize, that he, who was a stranger to me and my concerns,
should give me such a rendezvous, without taking the trouble
to demand a previous explanation — He replied, that there was
no other of his name in the whole country; that no such horseman had alighted at the Red Lion since nine o'clock, when he
arrived – that having had the honour to serve his majesty, he
thought he could not decently decline any invitation of this
kind, from what quarter soever it might come; and that if any
explanation was necessary, it did not belong to him to demand
it, but to the gentleman who summoned him into the field –
Vexed as I was at this adventure, I could not help admiring the
coolness of this officer, whose open countenance prepossessed
me in his favour. – He seemed to be turned of forty; wore his
own short black hair, which curled naturally about his ears,
and was very plain in his apparel – When I begged pardon for
the trouble I had given him, he received my apology with great
good humour. – He told me that he lived about ten miles off, at a
small farm-house, which would afford me tolerable lodging, if I
would come and take diversion of hunting with him for a few
weeks; in which case we might, perhaps, find out the man who
had given me offence – I thanked him very sincerely for his courteous offer, which, I told him, I was not at liberty to accept at
present, on account of my being engaged in a family party; and
so we parted, with mutual professions of good will and esteem.

Now tell me, dear knight, what am I to make of this singular adventure? – Am I to suppose that the horseman I saw was really a thing of flesh and blood, or a bubble that vanished into air? – or must I imagine Liddy knows more of the matter than she chuses to disclose? – If I thought her capable of carrying on any clandestine correspondence with such a fellow, I should at once discard all tenderness, and forget that she was connected with me by the ties of blood – But how is it possible that a girl of her simplicity and inexperience, should maintain such an intercourse, surrounded, as she is, with so many eyes, destitute of all opportunity, and shifting quarters every day of her life! – Besides, she has solemnly promised – No – I can't think the girl so base – so insensible to the honour of her family. — What disturbs me chiefly, is the impression which these occurrences seem to make upon her spirits – These are the symptoms from which I conclude that the rascal has still a hold on her affection – surely I have a right to call him a rascal, and to conclude that his designs are infamous. But it shall be my fault if he does not one day repent his presumption — I confess I cannot think, much less write on this subject, with any degree of temper or patience; I shall therefore conclude with telling you, that we hope to be in Wales by the latter end of the month: but before that period you will probably hear again from

your affectionate

Oct. 4.   J. MELFORD

To Sir WATKIN PHILLIPS, Bart. of Jesus college, Oxon.

DEAR PHILLIPS,

When I wrote you by last post, I did not imagine I should be tempted to trouble you again so soon: but I now sit down with a heart so full that it cannot contain itself; though I am under such agitation of spirits, that you are to expect neither method nor connexion in this address – We have been this day within a hair's breadth of losing honest Matthew Bramble, in consequence of a cursed accident, which I will endeavour to explain.

– In crossing the country to get into the post road, it was necessary to ford a river, and we that were a-horseback passed without any danger or difficulty; but a great quantity of rain having fallen last night and this morning, there was such an accumulation of water, that a mill-head gave way, just as the coach was passing under it, and the flood rushed down with such impetuosity, as first floated, and then fairly overturned the carriage in the middle of the stream – Lismahago and I, and the two servants, alighting instantaneously, ran into the river to give all the assistance in our power. – Our aunt, Mrs Tabitha, who had the good fortune to be uppermost, was already half way out of the coach window, when her lover approaching, disengaged her entirely; but, whether his foot slipt, or the bur-then was too great, they fell over head and ears in each others' arms. He endeavoured more than once to get up, and even to disentangle himself from her embrace, but she hung about his neck like a mill-stone (no bad emblem of matrimony), and if my man had not proved a stanch auxiliary, those two lovers would in all probability have gone hand in hand to the shades below – For my part, I was too much engaged to take any cognizance of their distress. – I snatched out my sister by the hair of the head, and, dragging her to the bank, recollected that my uncle had not yet appeared – Rushing again into the stream, I met Clinker hauling ashore Mrs Jenkins, who looked like a mermaid with her hair dishevelled about her ears; but, when I asked if his master was safe, he forthwith shook her from him, and she must have gone to pot, if a miller had not seasonably come to her relief. – As for Humphry, he flew like lightning, to the coach, that was by this time filled with water, and, diving into it, brought up the poor 'squire, to all appearance, deprived of life – It is not in my power to describe what I felt at this melancholy spectacle – it was such an agony as baffles all description! The faithful Clinker, taking him up in his arms, as if he had been an infant of six months, carried him ashore, howling most piteously all the way, and I followed him in a transport of grief and consternation – When he was laid upon the grass, and turned from side to side, a great quantity of water ran out at his mouth, then he opened his eyes, and fetched a deep sigh – Clinker perceiving these signs of life, immediately tied up his arm with a garter, and, pulling out a horse-fleam,[1] let him blood in the farrier stile. – At first a few drops only issued from the orifice; but the limb being chafed, in a little time the blood began to flow in a continued stream, and he uttered some incoherent words, which were the most welcome sounds that ever saluted my ear. There was a country inn hard by, the landlord of which had by this time come with his people to give their assistance. – Thither my uncle being carried, was undressed and put to bed, wrapped in warm blankets; but having been moved too soon, he fainted away, and once more lay without sense or motion, notwithstanding all the efforts of Clinker and the landlord, who bathed his temples with Hungary water, and held a smelling-bottle to his nose. As I had heard of the efficacy of salt in such cases, I ordered all that was in the house to be laid under his head and body; and whether this application had the desired effect, or nature of herself prevailed, he, in less than a quarter of an hour, began to breathe regularly, and soon retrieved his recollection, to the unspeakable joy of all the by-standers. As for Clinker, his brain seemed to be affected. – He laughed, and wept, and danced about in such a distracted manner, that the landlord very judiciously conveyed him out of the room. My uncle, seeing me dropping wet, comprehended the whole of what had happened, and asked if all the company was safe? – Being answered in the affirmative, he insisted upon my putting on dry clothes; and, having swallowed a little warm wine, desired he might be left to his repose. Before I went to shift myself, I inquired about the rest of the family – I found Mrs Tabitha still delirious from her fright, discharging very copiously the water she had swallowed. She was supported by the captain, distilling drops from his uncurled periwig, so lank and so dank, that he looked like Father Thames without his sedges, embracing Isis, while she cascaded in his urn.[2] Mrs Jenkins was present also, in a loose bed gown, without either cap or handkerchief; but she seemed to be as little *compos mentis* as her mistress, and acted so many cross purposes in the course of her attendance, that, between the two, Lismahago had occasion for all his philosophy. As for Liddy, I thought the poor girl would have actually lost her senses. The good woman of the house had shifted her linen, and put her into bed; but she was seized with the idea that her uncle had perished, and in this persuasion made a dismal out-cry; nor did she pay the least regard to what I said, when I solemnly assured her he was safe. Mr Bramble hearing the noise, and being informed of her apprehension, desired she might be brought into his chamber; and she no sooner received this intimation, than she ran thither half naked, with the wildest expression of eagerness in her countenance – Seeing the 'squire sitting up in the bed, she sprung forwards and throwing her arms about his neck, exclaimed in a most pathetic tone, 'Are you – Are you indeed my uncle – My dear uncle! – My best friend! My father! – Are you really living? or is it an illusion of my poor brain!' Honest Matthew was so much affected, that he could not help shedding tears, while he kissed her forehead, saying, 'My dear Liddy, I hope I shall live long enough to shew how sensible I am of your affection – But your spirits are fluttered, child – You want rest – Go to bed and compose yourself' – 'Well, I will (she replied) – but still methinks this cannot be real – The coach was full of water – My uncle was under us all – Gracious God! – You was under water – How did you get out; – tell me that? or I shall think this is all a deception' – 'In what manner I was brought out, I know as little as you do, my dear (said the 'squire); and, truly, that is a circumstance of which I want to be informed.' I would have given him a detail of the whole adventure, but he would not hear me until I should change my clothes; so that I had only time to tell him, that he owed his life to the courage and fidelity of Clinker: and having given him this hint, I conducted my sister to her own chamber.

This accident happened about three o'clock in the afternoon, and in little more than an hour the hurricane was all over; but as the carriage was found to be so much damaged, that it could not proceed without considerable repairs, a blacksmith and wheelwright were immediately sent for to the next market-town, and we congratulated ourselves upon being housed at an inn, which, though remote from the post-road, afforded exceeding good lodging. The women being pretty well composed, and the men all a-foot, my uncle sent for his servant, and, in the presence of Lismahago and me, accosted him in these words – 'So, Clinker, I find you are resolved I shan't die by water – As you have fished me up from the bottom at your own risque, you are at least entitled to all the money that was in my pocket, and there it is' – So saying, he presented him with a purse containing thirty guineas, and a ring nearly of the same value – 'God forbid! (cried Clinker), your honour shall excuse me – I am a poor fellow, but I have a heart – O! if your honour did but know how I rejoice to see – Blessed be his holy name,[3] that made me the humble instrument – But as for the lucre of gain, I renounce it – I have done no more than my duty – No more than I would have done for the most worthless of my fellow-creatures – No more than I would have done for captain Lismahago, or Archy Macalpine, or any sinner upon earth – But for your worship, I would go through fire as well as water'[4] — 'I do believe it, Humphry (said the 'squire); but as you think it was your duty to save my life at the hazard of your own, I think it is mine to express the sense I have of your extraordinary fidelity and attachment – I insist upon your receiving this small token of my gratitude; but don't imagine that I look upon this as an adequate recompence for the service you have done me – I have determined to settle thirty pounds a-year upon you for life; and I desire these gentlemen will bear witness to this my intention, of which I have a memorandum in my pocketbook.' 'Lord make me thankful for all these mercies! (cried Clinker, sobbing), I have been a poor bankrupt from the beginning – your honour's goodness found me, when I was – naked – when I was – sick and forlorn — I understand your honour's looks – I would not give offence – but my heart is very full – and if your worship won't give me leave to speak, – I must vent it in prayers to heaven for my benefactor.' When he quitted the room, Lismahago said, he should have a much better opinion of his honesty, if he did not whine and cant so abominably; but that he had always observed those weeping and praying fellows were hypocrites at bottom. Mr Bramble made no reply to this sarcastic remark, proceeding from the lieutenant's resentment of Clinker having, in pure simplicity of heart, ranked him with

M'Alpine and the sinners of the earth — The landlord being called to receive some orders about the beds, told the 'squire that his house was very much at his service, but he was sure he should not have the honour to lodge him and his company. He gave us to understand that his master who lived hard by, would not suffer us to be at a public house, when there was accommodation for us at his own; and that, if he had not dined abroad in the neighbourhood he would have undoubtedly come to offer his services at our first arrival. He then launched out in praise of that gentleman, whom he had served as butler, representing him as a perfect miracle of goodness and generosity. He said he was a person of great learning, and allowed to be the best farmer in the country: – that he had a lady who was as much beloved as himself, and an only son, a very hopeful young gentleman, just recovered from a dangerous fever, which had like to have proved fatal to the whole family; for, if the son had died, he was sure the parents would not have survived their loss — He had not yet finished the encomium of Mr Dennison, when this gentleman arrived in a post-chaise, and his appearance seemed to justify all that had been said in his favour. He is pretty well advanced in years, but hale, robust, and florid, with an ingenuous countenance, expressive of good sense and humanity. Having condoled with us on the accident which had happened, he said he was come to conduct us to his habitation, where we should be less incommoded than at such a paultry inn, and expressed his hope that the ladies would not be the worse for going thither in his carriage, as the distance was not above a quarter of a mile. My uncle having made a proper return to this courteous exhibition, eyed him attentively, and then asked if he had not been at Oxford, a commoner of Queen's college? When Mr Dennison answered, 'Yes,' with some marks of surprise – 'Look at me then (said our 'squire) and let us see if you can recollect the features of an old friend, whom you have not seen these forty years.' — The gentleman, taking him by the hand, and gazing at him earnestly, – 'I protest (cried he), I do think I recall the idea of Matthew Loyd of Glamorganshire, who was student of Jesus.' 'Well remembered, my dear friend, Charles Dennison (exclaimed my uncle, pressing him to his breast), I am that very identical Matthew Loyd of Glamorgan.' Clinker, who had just entered the room with some coals for the fire, no sooner heard these words, than throwing down the scuttle on the toes of Lismahago, he began to caper as if he was mad, crying – 'Matthew Loyd of Glamorgan! – O Providence! – Matthew Loyd of Glamorgan!' — Then, clasping my uncle's knees, he went on in this manner —— 'Your worship must forgive me – Matthew Loyd of Glamorgan! – O Lord, Sir! – I can't contain myself! – I shall lose my senses' – 'Nay, thou hast lost them already, I believe (said the 'squire, peevishly), prithee, Clinker, be quiet — What is the matter?' —— Humphry, fumbling in his bosom, pulled out an old wooden snuff-box, which he presented in great trepidation to his master, who, opening it immediately, perceived a small cornelian[5] seal, and two scraps of paper – At sight of these articles he started, and changed colour, and casting his eye upon the inscriptions – 'Ha! – how! – what! – where (cried he) is the person here named?' Clinker, knocking his own breast, could hardly pronounce these words – 'Here – here — here is Matthew Loyd, as the certificate sheweth – Humphry Clinker was the name of the farrier that took me 'prentice' – 'And who gave you these tokens?' said my uncle hastily – 'My poor mother on her death-bed' — replied the other – 'And who was your mother?' 'Dorothy Twyford, an please your honour, heretofore bar-keeper at the Angel at Chippenham.' – 'And why were not these tokens produced before?' 'My mother told me she had wrote to Glamorganshire, at the time of my birth, but had no answer; and that afterwards, when she made enquiry, there was no such person in that county.' 'And so in consequence of my changing my name and going abroad at that very time, thy poor mother and thou have been left to want and misery – I am really shocked at the consequence of my own folly.' – Then, laying his hand on Clinker's head, he added, 'Stand forth, Matthew Loyd – You see, gentlemen, how the sins of my youth rise up in judgment against me – Here is my direction written with my own hand, and a seal which I left at the woman's request; and this is a certificate of the child's baptism, signed by the curate of the parish.' The company were not a little surprised at this discovery, upon which Mr Dennison facetiously congratulated both the father and the son: for my part, I shook my new-found cousin heartily by the hand, and Lismahago complimented him with the tears in his eyes, for he had been hopping about the room, swearing in broad Scotch, and bellowing with the pain occasioned by the fall of the coalscuttle upon his foot. He had even vowed to drive the *saul* out of the body of that mad rascal: but, perceiving the unexpected turn which things had taken, he wished him joy of his good fortune, observing that it went very near his heart, as he was like to be a great toe out of pocket by the discovery – Mr Dennison now desired to know for what reason my uncle had changed the name by which he knew him at Oxford, and our 'squire satisfied him, by answering to this effect – 'I took my mother's name, which was Loyd, as heir to her lands in Glamorganshire; but when I came of age, I sold that property, in order to clear my paternal estate, and resumed my real name; so that I am now Matthew Bramble of Brambleton-hall in Monmouthshire, at your service; and this is my nephew, Jeremy Melford of Belfield, in the county of Glamorgan.' At that instant the ladies entering the room, he presented Mrs Tabitha as his sister, and Liddy as his niece. The old gentleman saluted them very cordially, and seemed struck with the appearance of my sister, whom he could not help surveying with a mixture of complacency and surprize — 'Sister (said my uncle), there is a poor relation that recommends himself to your good graces – The quondam Humphry Clinker is metamorphosed into Matthew Loyd; and claims the honour of being your carnal kinsman — in short, the rogue proves to be a crab of my own planting in the days of hot blood and unrestrained libertinism.' Clinker had by this time dropt upon one knee, by the side of Mrs Tabitha, who, eyeing him askance, and flirting her fan with marks of agitation, thought proper, after some conflict, to hold out her hand for him to kiss, saying, with a demure aspect, 'Brother, you have been very wicked: but I hope you'll live to see the folly of your ways – I am very sorry to say the young man, whom you have this day acknowledged, has more grace and religion, by the gift of God, than you with all your profane learning, and repeated opportunity – I do think he has got the trick of the eye, and the tip of the nose of my uncle Loyd of Flluydwellyn; and as for the long chin, it is the very moral of[6] the governor's – Brother, as you have changed his name pray change his dress also; that livery doth not become any person that hath got our blood in his veins.' — Liddy seemed much pleased with this acquisition to the family. – She took him by the hand, declaring she should always be proud to own her connexion with a virtuous young man, who had given so many proofs of his gratitude and affection to her uncle. – Mrs Winifred Jenkins, extremely fluttered between her surprize at this discovery, and the apprehension of losing her sweetheart, exclaimed in a giggling tone, – 'I wish you joy Mr Clinker – Floyd – I would say – hi, hi, hi! – you'll be so proud you won't look at your poor fellow servants, oh, oh, oh!' Honest Clinker owned he was overjoyed at his good fortune, which was greater than he deserved – 'But wherefore should I be proud? (said he) a poor object conceived in sin, and brought forth in iniquity,[7] nursed in a parish workhouse, and bred in a smithy — Whenever I seem proud, Mrs Jenkins, I beg of you to put me in mind of the condition I was in, when I first saw you between Chippenham and Marlborough.'

When this momentous affair was discussed to the satisfaction of all parties concerned, the weather being dry, the ladies declined the carriage; so that we walked all together to Mr Dennison's house, where we found the tea ready prepared by his lady, an amiable matron, who received us with all the benevolence of hospitality. – The house is old fashioned and irregular, but lodgeable and commodious. To the south it has the river in front, at the distance of a hundred paces; and on the north, there is a rising ground covered with an agreeable plantation; the greens and walks are kept in the nicest order, and all is rural and romantic. I have not yet seen the young gentleman, who is on a visit to a friend in the neighbourhood, from whose house he is not expected 'till to-morrow.

In the mean time, as there is a man going to the next market-town with letters for the post, I take this opportunity to send you the history of this day, which has been remarkably full of adventures; and you will own I give you them like a beef-steak at Dolly's,[8] *hot* and *hot*,[9] without ceremony and parade, just as they come from the recollection of

Yours,

J. MELFORD

To Dr LEWIS.

DEAR DICK,

Since the last trouble I gave you, I have met with a variety of incidents, some of them of a singular nature, which I reserve as a fund for conversation; but there are others so interesting, that they will not keep in *petto* till meeting.

Know then, it was a thousand pounds to a sixpence, that you should now be executing my will, instead of perusing my letter! Two days ago, our coach was overturned in the midst of a rapid river, where my life was saved with the utmost difficulty, by the courage, activity, and presence of mind of my servant Humphry Clinker — But this is not the most surprising circumstance of the adventure – The said Humphry Clinker proves to be Matthew Loyd, natural son of one Matthew Loyd of Glamorgan, if you know any such person – You see, Doctor, that notwithstanding all your philosophy, it is not without some reason that the Welchmen ascribe such energy to the force of blood – But we shall discuss this point on some future occasion.

This is not the only discovery which I made in consequence of our disaster – We happened to be wrecked upon a friendly shore — The lord of the manor is no other than Charles Dennison, our fellow-rake at Oxford – We are now happily housed with that gentleman, who has really attained to that pitch of rural felicity, at which I have been aspiring these twenty years in vain. He is blessed with a consort, whose disposition is suited to his own in all respects; tender, generous, and benevolent – She, moreover, possesses an uncommon share of understanding, fortitude, and discretion, and is admirably qualified to be his companion, confidant, counsellor, and coadjutrix.[1] These excellent persons have an only son, about nineteen years of age, just such a youth as they could have wished that Heaven would bestow to fill up the measure of their enjoyment – In a word, they know no other allay to their happiness, but their apprehension and anxiety about the life and concerns of this beloved object.

Our old friend, who had the misfortune to be a second brother,[2] was bred to the law, and even called to the bar; but he did not find himself qualified to shine in that province, and had very little inclination for his profession – He disobliged his father, by marrying for love, without any consideration of fortune; so that he had little or nothing to depend upon for some years but his practice, which afforded him a bare subsistence; and the prospect of an increasing family, began to give him disturbance and disquiet. In the mean time, his father dying, was succeeded by his elder brother, a fox-hunter and a sot, who neglected his affairs, insulted and oppressed his servants, and in a few years had well nigh ruined the estate, when he was happily carried off by a fever, the immediate consequence of a debauch. Charles, with the approbation of his wife, immediately determined to quit business, and retire into the country, although this resolution was strenuously and zealously opposed by every individual, whom he consulted on the subject. Those who had tried the experiment, assured him that he could not pretend to breathe in the country for less than the double of what his estate produced; that, in order to be upon the footing of a gentleman, he would be obliged to keep horses, hounds, carriages, with a suitable number of servants, and maintain an elegant table for the entertainment of his neighbours; that farming was a mystery, known only to those who had been bred up to it from the cradle, the success of it depending not only upon skill and industry, but also upon such attention and œconomy as no gentleman could be supposed to give or practise; accordingly, every attempt made by gentlemen miscarried, and not a few had been ruined by their prosecution of agriculture – Nay, they affirmed that he would find it cheaper to buy hay and oats for his cattle, and to go to market for poultry, eggs, kitchen herbs, and roots, and even the most inconsiderable article of house-keeping, than to have those articles produced on his own ground.

These objections did not deter Mr Dennison, because they were chiefly founded on the supposition, that he would be obliged to lead a life of extravagance and dissipation, which he and his consort equally detested, despised, and determined to avoid – The objects he had in view, were health of body, peace of mind,[3] and the private satisfaction of domestic quiet, unallayed by actual want, and uninterrupted by the fears of indigence – He was very moderate in his estimate of the necessaries, and even of the comforts of life – He required nothing but wholesome air, pure water, agreeable exercise, plain diet, convenient lodging, and decent apparel. He reflected, that if a peasant without education, or any great share of natural sagacity, could maintain a large family, and even become opulent upon a farm, for which he payed an annual rent of two or three hundred pounds to the landlord, surely he himself might hope for some success from his industry, having no rent to pay, but, on the contrary, three or four hundred pounds a year to receive – He considered, that the earth was an indulgent mother, that yielded her fruits to all her children without distinction. He had studied the theory of agriculture with a degree of eagerness and delight; and he could not conceive there was any mystery in the practice, but what he should be able to disclose by dint of care and application. With respect to household expence, he entered into a minute detail and investigation, by which he perceived the assertions of his friends were altogether erroneous – He found he should save sixty pounds a year in the single article of house-rent, and as much more in pocket-money and contingencies; that even butcher's-meat was twenty per cent. cheaper in the country than in London; but that poultry, and almost every other circumstance of house-keeping, might be had for less than one-half of what they cost in town; besides, a considerable saving on the side of dress, in being delivered from the oppressive imposition of ridiculous modes, invented by ignorance, and adopted by folly.

As to the danger of vying with the rich in pomp and equipage, it never gave him the least disturbance. He was now turned of forty, and, having lived half that time in the busy scenes of life, was well skilled in the science of mankind. There cannot be in nature a more contemptible figure than that of a man, who, with five hundred a year, presumes to rival in expence a neighbour who possesses five times that income – His ostentation, far from concealing, serves only to discover his indigence, and render his vanity the more shocking; for it attracts the eyes of censure, and excites the spirit of inquiry. There is not a family in the country, nor a servant in his own house, nor a farmer in the parish, but what knows the utmost farthing that his lands produce, and all these behold him with scorn or compassion. I am surprised that these reflections do not occur to persons in this unhappy dilemma, and produce a salutary effect; but the truth is, of all the passions incident to human nature, vanity is that which most effectually perverts the faculties of the understanding; nay, it sometimes becomes so incredibly depraved, as to aspire at infamy, and find pleasure in bearing the stigmas of reproach.

I have now given you a sketch of the character and situation of Mr Dennison, when he came down to take possession of this estate; but as the messenger, who carries the letters to the next town, is just setting off, I shall reserve what further I have to say on this subject, till the next post, when you shall certainly hear from

Yours always,

Oct. 8.   MATT. BRAMBLE

To Dr LEWIS.

Once more, dear doctor, I resume the pen for your amusement. – It was on the morning after our arrival that, walking out with my friend, Mr Dennison, I could not help breaking forth into the warmest expressions of applause at the beauty of the scene, which is really inchanting; and I signified, in particular, how much I was pleased with the disposition of some detached groves, that afforded at once shelter and ornament to his habitation.

'When I took possession of these lands, about two and twenty years ago (said he), there was not a tree standing within a mile of the house, except those of an old neglected orchard, which produced nothing but leaves and moss. – It was in the gloomy month of November, when I arrived, and found the house in such a condition, that it might have been justly stiled the *tower of desolation*.[1] – The court-yard was covered with nettles and docks, and the garden exhibited such a rank plantation of weeds as I had never seen before; – the window-shutters were falling in pieces, – the sashes broken; – and owls and jack-daws had taken possession of the chimnies. – The prospect within was still more dreary – All was dark, and damp, and dirty beyond description; – the rain penetrated in several parts of the roof; – in some apartments the very floors had given way; – the hangings were parted from the walls, and shaking in mouldy remnants; the glasses were dropping out of their frames; – the family-pictures were covered with dust; – and all the chairs and tables worm-eaten and crazy. — There was not a bed in the house that could be used, except one old-fashioned machine, with a high gilt tester and fringed curtains of yellow mohair, which had been, for aught I know, two centuries in the family. — In short, there was no furniture but the utensils of the kitchen; and the cellar afforded nothing but a few empty butts and barrels, that stunk so abominably, that I would not suffer any body to enter it until I had flashed a considerable quantity of gunpowder to qualify the foul air within.

'An old cottager and his wife, who were hired to lie in the house, had left it with precipitation, alledging, among other causes of retreat, that they could not sleep for frightful noises, and that my poor brother certainly walked after his death. – In a word, the house appeared uninhabitable; the barn, stable, and outhouses were in ruins; all the fences broken down, and the fields lying waste.

'The farmer who kept the key never dreamed I had any intention to live upon the spot – He rented a farm of sixty pounds, and his lease was just expiring. – He had formed a scheme of being appointed bailiff to the estate, and of con-verting the house and the adjacent grounds to his own use. – A hint of his intention I received from the curate at my first arrival; I therefore did not pay much regard to what he said by way of discouraging me from coming to settle in the country; but I was a little startled when he gave me warning that he should quit the farm at the expiration of his lease, unless I could abate considerably in the rent.

'At this period I accidentally became acquainted with a person, whose friendship laid the foundation of all my prosperity. In the next market-town I chanced to dine at an inn with a Mr Wilson, who was lately come to settle in the neighbourhood. – He had been lieutenant of a man of war, but quitted the sea in some disgust, and married the only daughter of farmer Bland, who lives in this parish, and has acquired a good fortune in the way of husbandry. – Wilson is one of the best natured men I ever knew; brave, frank, obliging, and ingenuous — He liked my conversation, I was charmed with his liberal manner; and acquaintance immediately commenced, and this was soon improved into a friendship without reserve. – There are characters which, like similar particles of matter, strongly attract each other. – He forthwith introduced me to his father-in-law, farmer Bland, who was well acquainted with every acre of my estate, of consequence well qualified to advise me on this occasion. — Finding I was inclined to embrace a country life, and even to amuse myself with the occupation of farming, he approved of my design – He gave me to understand that all my farms were underlett; that the estate was capable of great improvement; that there was plenty of chalk in the neighbourhood; and that my own ground produced excellent marle for manure. — With respect to the farm, which was like to fall into my hands, he said he would willingly take it at the present rent; but at the same time owned, that if I would expend two hundred pounds in enclosure, it would be worth more than double the sum.

'Thus encouraged, I began the execution of my scheme without further delay, and plunged into a sea of expence, though I had no fund in reserve, and the whole produce of the estate did not exceed three hundred pounds a year – In one week, my house was made weather-tight, and thoroughly cleansed from top to bottom; then it was well ventilated by throwing all the doors and windows open, and making blazing fires of wood in every chimney from the kitchen to the garrets. – The floors were repaired, the sashes new glazed, and out of the old furniture of the whole house, I made shift to fit up a parlour and three chambers in a plain yet decent manner. – The court-yard was cleared of weeds and rubbish, and my friend Wilson charged himself with the dressing of the garden; bricklayers were set at work upon the barn and stable; and labourers engaged to restore the fences, and begin the work of hedging and ditching, under the direction of farmer Bland, at whose recommendation I hired a careful hind to lie in the house, and keep constant fires in the apartments.

'Having taken these measures, I returned to London, where I forthwith sold off my household-furniture, and, in three weeks from my first visit, brought my wife hither to keep her Christmas. — Considering the gloomy season of the year, the dreariness of the place, and the decayed aspect of our habitation, I was afraid that her resolution would sink under the sudden transition from a town life to such a melancholy state of rustication; but I was agreeably disappointed. — She found the reality less uncomfortable than the picture I had drawn. — By this time indeed, things were mended in appearance – The out-houses had risen out of their ruins; the pigeon-house was rebuilt, and replenished by Wilson, who also put my garden in decent order, and provided a good stock of poultry, which made an agreeable figure in my yard; and the house, on the whole, looked like the habitation of human creatures. – Farmer Bland spared me a milch cow for my family, and an ordinary saddle-horse for my servant to go to market at the next town. – I hired a country lad for a footman, the hind's daughter was my house-maid, and my wife had brought a cook-maid from London.

'Such was my family when I began house-keeping in this place, with three hundred pounds in my pocket, raised from the sale of my superfluous furniture. – I knew we should find occupation enough through the day to employ our time; but I dreaded the long winter evenings; yet, for those too we found a remedy: — The curate, who was a single man, soon became so naturalized to the family, that he generally lay in the house; and his company was equally agreeable and useful. – He was a modest man, a good scholar, and perfectly well qualified to instruct me in such country matters as I wanted to know. – Mr Wilson brought his wife to see us, and she became so fond of Mrs Dennison, that she said she was never so happy as when she enjoyed the benefit of her conversation. – She was then a fine buxom country lass, exceedingly docile, and as good-natured as her husband Jack Wilson; so that a friendship ensued among the women, which hath continued to this day.

'As for Jack, he hath been my constant companion, counsellor, and commissary. — I would not for a hundred pounds you should leave my house without seeing him. — Jack is an universal genius – his talents are really astonishing: – He is an excellent carpenter, joiner, and turner, and a cunning artist in iron and brass. – He not only superintended my œconomy, but also presided over my pastimes – He taught me to brew beer, to make cyder, perry, mead, usquebaugh,[2] and plague-water; to cook several outlandish delicacies, such as *ollas*, *pepper-pots*, *pillaws*, *corys*, *chabobs*, and *stufatas*.[3] – He understands all manner of games from chess down to chuck-farthing,[4] sings a good song, plays upon the violin, and dances a hornpipe with surprising agility. – He and I walked, and rode, and hunted, and fished together, without minding the vicissitudes of the weather; and I am persuaded, that in a raw, moist climate, like this of England, continual exercise is as necessary as food to the preservation of the individual. – In the course of two and twenty years, there has not been one hour's interruption or abatement in the friendship subsisting between Wilson's family and mine; and, what is a rare instance of good fortune, that friendship is continued to our children. – His son and mine are nearly of the same age and the same disposition; they have been bred up together at the same school and college, and love each other with the warmest affection.

'By Wilson's means, I likewise formed an acquaintance with a sensible physician, who lives in the next market-town; and his sister, an agreeable old maiden, passed the Christmas holidays at our house. – Mean while I began my farming with great eagerness, and that very winter planted these groves that please you so much. – As for the neighbouring gentry, I had no trouble from that quarter during my first campaign; they were all gone to town before I settled in the country; and by the summer I had taken measures to defend myself from their attacks. – When a gay equipage came to my gates, I was never at home; those who visited me in a modest way, I received; and according to the remarks I made on their characters and conversation, either rejected their advances, or returned their civility – I was in general despised among the fashionable company, as a low fellow, both in breeding and circumstances; nevertheless, I found a few individuals of moderate fortune, who gladly adopted my stile of living; and many others would have acceded to our society, had they not been prevented by the pride, envy, and ambition of their wives and daughters. – Those, in times of luxury and dissipation, are the rocks upon which all the small estates in the country are wrecked.

'I reserved in my own hands, some acres of ground adjacent to the house, for making experiments in agriculture, according to the directions of Lyle, Tull, Hart, Duhamel,[5] and others who have written on this subject; and qualified their theory with the practical observations of farmer Bland, who was my great master in the art of husbandry. — In short, I became enamoured of a country life; and my success greatly exceeded my expectation — I drained bogs, burned heath, grubbed up furze[6] and fern; I planted copse and willows where nothing else would grow; I gradually inclosed all my farms, and made such improvements that my estate now yields me clear twelve hundred pounds a year – All this time my wife and I have enjoyed uninterrupted health, and a regular flow of spirits, except on a very few occasions, when our cheerfulness was invaded by such accidents as are inseparable from the condition of life. – I lost two children in their infancy, by the small-pox, so that I have one son only, in whom all our hopes are centered. – He went yesterday to visit a friend, with whom he has stayed all night, but he will be here to dinner. — I shall this day have the pleasure of presenting him to you and your family; and I flatter myself you will find him not altogether unworthy of our affection.

'The truth is, either I am blinded by the partiality of a parent, or he is a boy of very amiable character; and yet his conduct has given us unspeakable disquiet. – You must know, we had projected a match between him and a gentleman's daughter in the next county, who will in all probability be heiress of a considerable fortune; but, it seems, he had a personal disgust to the alliance. – He was then at Cambridge, and tried to gain time on various pretences; but being pressed in letters by his mother and me to give a definitive answer, he fairly gave his tutor the slip, and disappeared about eight months ago. – Before he took this rash step, he wrote me a letter, explaining his objections to the match, and declaring, that he would keep himself concealed until he should understand that his parents would dispense with his contracting an engagement that must make him miserable for life, and he prescribed the form of advertising in a certain newspaper, by which he might be apprized of our sentiments on this subject.

'You may easily conceive how much we were alarmed and afflicted by this elopement, which he had made without dropping the least hint to his companion Charles Wilson, who belonged to the same college. – We resolved to punish him with the appearance of neglect, in hopes that he would return of his own accord; but he maintained his purpose till the young lady chose a partner for herself; then he produced himself, and made his peace by the mediation of Wilson. – Suppose we should unite our families by joining him with your niece, who is one of the most lovely creatures I ever beheld. – My wife is already as fond of her as if she were her own child, and I have a presentiment that my son will be captivated by her at first sight.' 'Nothing could be more agreeable to all our family (said I) than such an alliance; but, my dear friend, candour obliges me to tell you, that I am afraid Liddy's heart is not wholly disengaged — there is a cursed obstacle' — 'You mean the young stroller at Gloucester (said he) – You are surprised that I should know this circumstance; but you will be more surprised when I tell you that stroller is no other than my son George Dennison – That was the character he assumed in his eclipse.' 'I am, indeed, astonished and overjoyed (cried I), and shall be happy beyond expression to see your proposal take effect.'

He then gave me to understand that the young gentleman, at

his emerging from concealment, had disclosed his passion for Miss Melford, the niece of Mr Bramble, of Monmouthshire. Though Mr Dennison little dreamed that this was his old friend Matthew Loyd, he nevertheless furnished his son with proper credentials, and he had been at Bath, London, and many other places in quest of us, to make himself and his pretensions known. – The bad success of his enquiry had such an effect upon his spirits, that immediately at his return he was seized with a dangerous fever, which overwhelmed his parents with terror and affliction; but he was now happily recovered, though still weak and disconsolate. My nephew joining us in our walk, I informed him of these circumstances, with which he was wonderfully pleased. He declared he would promote the match to the utmost of his power, and that he longed to embrace young Mr Dennison as his friend and brother. – Mean while, the father went to desire his wife to communicate this discovery gradually to Liddy, that her delicate nerves might not suffer too sudden a shock; and I imparted the particulars to my sister Tabby, who expressed some surprize, not altogether unmixed, I believe, with an emotion of envy; for, though she could have no objection to an alliance at once so honourable and advantageous, she hesitated in giving her consent on pretence of the youth and inexperience of the parties: at length, however, she acquiesced, in consequence of having consulted with captain Lismahago.

Mr Dennison took care to be in the way when his son arrived at the gate, and, without giving him time or opportunity to make any enquiry about the strangers, brought him up stairs to be presented to Mr Loyd and his family – The first person he saw when he entered the room, was Liddy, who, notwithstanding all her preparation, stood trembling in the utmost confusion – At sight of this object he was fixed motionless to the floor, and, gazing at her with the utmost eagerness of astonishment, exclaimed, 'Sacred heaven! what is this! – ha! wherefore –' Here his speech failing, he stood straining his eyes, in the most emphatic silence – 'George (said his father), this is my friend Mr Loyd.' Roused at this intimation, he turned and received my salute, when I said, 'Young gentleman, if you had trusted me with your secret at our last meeting, we should have parted upon better terms.' Before he could make any answer, Jery came round and stood before him with open arms. – At first, he started and changed colour; but after a short pause, he rushed into his embrace, and they hugged one another as if they had been intimate friends from their infancy: then he payed his respects to Mrs Tabitha, and advancing to Liddy, 'Is it possible (cried he), that my senses do not play me false! – that I see Miss Melford under my father's roof – that I am permitted to speak to her without giving offence – and that her relations have honoured me with their countenance and protection.' Liddy blushed, and trembled, and faltered – 'To be sure, sir (said she), it is a very surprising circumstance — a great – a providential — I really know not what I say – but I beg you will think I have said what's agreeable.'

Mrs Dennison interposing said, 'Compose yourselves, my dear children. – Your mutual happiness shall be our peculiar care.' The son going up to his mother, kissed one hand; my niece bathed the other with her tears; and the good old lady pressed them both in their turns to her breast. – The lovers were too much affected to get rid of their embarrassment for one day; but the scene was much enlivened by the arrival of Jack Wilson, who brought, as usual, some game of his own killing — His honest countenance was a good letter of recommendation. – I received him like a dear friend after a long separation; and I could not help wondering to see him shake Jery by the hand as an old acquaintance — They had, indeed, been acquainted some days, in consequence of a diverting incident, which I shall explain at meeting. – That same night a consultation was held upon the concerns of the lovers, when the match was formally agreed to, and all the marriage articles were settled without the least dispute. – My nephew and I promised to make Liddy's fortune five thousand pounds. Mr Dennison declared, he would make over one half of his estate immediately to his son, and that his daughter-in-law should be secured in a jointure of four hundred – Tabby proposed, that, considering their youth, they should undergo one year at least, of probation before the indissoluble knot should be tied; but the young gentleman being very impatient and importunate, and the scheme implying that the young couple should live in the house, under the wings of his parents, we resolved to make them happy without further delay.

As the law requires that the parties should be some weeks resident in the parish,[7] we shall stay here till the ceremony is performed. — Mr Lismahago requests that he may take the benefit of the same occasion; so that next Sunday the banns will be published for all four together. – I doubt I shall not be able to pass my Christmas with you at Brambleton-hall. – Indeed, I am so agreeably situated in this place, that I have no desire to shift my quarters; and I foresee, that when the day of separation comes, there will be abundance of sorrow on all sides. – In the mean time, we must make the most of those blessings which Heaven bestows. – Considering how you are tethered by your profession, I cannot hope to see you so far from home; yet the distance does not exceed a summer-day's journey, and Charles Dennison, who desires to be remembered to you, would be rejoiced to see his old compotator; but as I am now stationary, I expect regular answers to the epistles of

Yours invariably,

Oct. 11.   MATT. BRAMBLE

To Sir WATKIN PHILLIPS, Bart. at Oxon.

DEAR WAT,

Every day is now big with incident and discovery — Young Mr Dennison proves to be no other than that identical person whom I have execrated so long, under the name of Wilson – He had eloped from college at Cambridge, to avoid a match that he detested, and acted in different parts of the country as a stroller, until the lady in question made choice of a husband for herself; then he returned to his father, and disclosed his passion for Liddy, which met with the approbation of his parents, though the father little imagined that Mr Bramble was his old companion Matthew Loyd. The young gentleman, being impowered to make honourable proposals to my uncle and me, had been in search of us all over England, without effect; and he it was whom I had seen pass on horseback by the window of the inn, where I stood with my sister, but he little dreamed that we were in the house – As for the real Mr Wilson, whom I called forth to combat, by mistake, he is the neighbour and intimate friend of old Mr Dennison, and this connexion had suggested to the son the idea of taking that name while he remained in obscurity.

You may easily conceive what pleasure I must have felt on discovering that the honour of our family was in no danger from the conduct of a sister whom I love with uncommon affection; that, instead of debasing her sentiments and views to a wretched stroller, she had really captivated the heart of a gentleman, her equal in rank and superior in fortune; and that, as his parents approved of his attachment, I was on the eve of acquiring a brother-in-law so worthy of my friendship and esteem. George Dennison is, without all question, one of the most accomplished young fellows in England. His person is at once elegant and manly, and his understanding highly culti-vated. Tho' his spirit is lofty, his heart is kind; and his manner so engaging, as to command veneration and love, even from malice and indifference. When I weigh my own character with his, I am ashamed to find myself so light in the balance; but the comparison excites no envy – I propose him as a model for imitation – I have endeavoured to recommend myself to his friendship, and hope I have already found a place in his affec-tion. I am, however, mortified to reflect what flagrant injustice we every day commit, and what absurd judgment we form, in viewing objects through the falsifying mediums of prejudice and passion. Had you asked me a few days ago, the picture of Wilson the player, I should have drawn a portrait very unlike the real person and character of George Dennison – Without all doubt, the greatest advantage acquired in travelling and perusing mankind in the original, is that of dispelling those shameful clouds that darken the faculties of the mind, pre-venting it from judging with candour and precision.

The real Wilson is a great original, and the best tempered,

companionable man I ever knew – I question if ever he was angry or low-spirited in his life. He makes no pretensions to letters; but he is an adept in every thing else that can be either useful or entertaining. Among other qualifications, he is a complete sportsman, and counted the best shot in the county. He and Dennison, and Lismahago and I, attended by Clinker, went a-shooting yesterday, and made a great havock among the partridges – To-morrow we shall take the field against the woodcocks and snipes. In the evening we dance and sing, or play at commerce, loo, and quadrille.[1]

Mr Dennison is an elegant poet, and has written some detached pieces on the subject of his passion for Liddy, which must be very flattering to the vanity of a young woman – Perhaps he is one of the greatest theatrical geniuses that ever appeared. He sometimes entertains us with reciting favourite speeches from our best plays. We are resolved to convert the great hall into a theatre, and get up the *Beaux Stratagem* without delay – I think I shall make no contemptible figure in the character of *Scrub*; and Lismahago will be very great in *Captain Gibbet*[2] – Wilson undertakes to entertain the country people with *Harlequin Skeleton*,[3] for which he has got a jacket ready painted with his own hand.

Our society is really enchanting. Even the severity of Lismahago relaxes, and the vinegar of Mrs Tabby is remarkably dulcified,[4] ever since it was agreed that she should take precedency of her niece in being first noosed: for, you must know, the day is fixed for Liddy's marriage; and the banns for both couples have been already once published in the parish church. The Captain earnestly begged that one trouble might serve for all, and Tabitha assented with a vile affectation of reluctance. Her inamorato, who came hither very slenderly equipt, has sent for his baggage to London, which, in all probability, will not arrive in time for the wedding; but it is of no great consequence, as every thing is to be transacted with the utmost privacy – Meanwhile, directions are given for making out the contracts of marriage, which are very favourable for both females; Liddy will be secured in a good jointure;[5] and her aunt will remain mistress of her own fortune, except one half of the interest, which her husband shall have a right to enjoy for his natural life: I think this is as little in conscience as can be done for a man who yokes with such a partner for life.

These expectants seem to be so happy, that if Mr Dennison had an agreeable daughter, I believe I should be for making the third couple in this country dance. The humour seems to be infectious; for Clinker, alias Loyd, has a month's mind[6] to play the fool, in the same fashion, with Mrs Winifred Jenkins. He has even sounded me on the subject; but I have given him no encouragement to prosecute this scheme – I told him I thought he might do better, as there was no engagement nor promise subsisting; that I did not know what designs my uncle might have formed for his advantage; but I was of opinion, that he should not, at present, run the risque of disobliging him by any premature application of this nature – Honest Humphry protested he would suffer death sooner than do or say any thing that should give offence to the 'squire: but he owned he had a kindness for the young woman, and had reason to think she looked upon him with a favourable eye; that he considered this mutual manifestation of good will, as an engagement understood, which ought to be binding to the conscience of an honest man; and he hoped the 'squire and I would be of the same opinion, when we should be at leisure to bestow any thought about the matter – I believe he is in the right; and we shall find time to take his case into consideration – You see we are fixed for some weeks at least, and as you have had a long respite, I hope you will begin immediately to discharge the arrears due to

Your affectionate,

Oct. 14.   J. MELFORD

To Miss LÆTITIA WILLIS, at Gloucester.

MY DEAR, DEAR LETTY,

Never did I sit down to write in such agitation as I now feel – In the course of a few days, we have met with a number of incidents so wonderful and interesting, that all my ideas are

thrown into confusion and perplexity – You must not expect
either method or coherence in what I am going to relate – my
dearest Willis. Since my last, the aspect of affairs is totally
changed! – and so changed! – but I would fain give you a
regular detail — In passing a river about eight days ago, our
coach was overturned, and some of us narrowly escaped with
life – My uncle had well nigh perished — O Heaven, I cannot
reflect upon that circumstance without horror – I should have
lost my best friend, my father and protector, but for the resolution and activity of his servant Humphry Clinker, whom
Providence really seems to have placed near him for the necessity of this occasion. – I would not be thought superstitious; but
surely he acted from a stronger impulse than common fidelity
– Was it not the voice of nature that loudly called upon him to
save the life of his own father? for, O Letty, it was discovered
that Humphry Clinker was my uncle's natural son.

Almost at the same instant, a gentleman, who came to offer
us his assistance, and invite us to his house, turned out to be a
very old friend of Mr Bramble. — His name is Mr Dennison,
one of the worthiest men living; and his lady is a perfect saint
upon earth. They have an only son – who do you think is this
only son? – O Letty! – O gracious heaven! how my heart
palpitates, when I tell you that this only son of Mr Dennison's,
is that very identical youth who, under the name of Wilson, has
made such ravage in my heart! – Yes, my dear friend! Wilson
and I are now lodged in the same house, and converse together
freely – His father approves of his sentiments in my favour; his
mother loves me with all the tenderness of a parent; my uncle,
my aunt and my brother, no longer oppose my inclinations –
On the contrary, they have agreed to make us happy without
delay; and in three weeks or a month, if no unforeseen accident
intervenes, your friend Lydia Melford, will have changed her
name and condition – I say, if *no accident intervenes*, because
such a torrent of success makes me tremble! — I wish there
may not be something treacherous in this sudden reconciliation
of fortune – I have no merit – I have no title to such felicity.
Far from enjoying the prospect that lies before me, my mind is
harrassed with a continued tumult, made up of hopes and

wishes, doubts and apprehensions – I can neither eat nor sleep, and my spirits are in perpetual flutter. – I more than ever feel that vacancy in my heart, which your presence alone can fill. – The mind, in every disquiet, seeks to repose itself on the bosom of a friend; and this is such a trial as I really know not how to support without your company and counsel — I must, therefore, dear Letty, put your friendship to the test – I must beg you will come and do the last offices of maidenhood to your companion Lydia Melford.

This letter goes inclosed in one to our worthy governess, from Mrs Dennison, entreating her to interpose with your mamma, that you may be allowed to favour us with your company on this occasion; and I flatter myself that no material objection can be made to our request – The distance from hence to Gloucester, does not exceed one hundred miles, and the roads are good. – Mr Clinker, alias Loyd, shall be sent over to attend your motions – If you step into the post-chaise, with your maid Betty Barker, at seven in the morning, you will arrive by four in the afternoon at the half-way house, where there is good accommodation. There you shall be met by my brother and myself, who will next day conduct you to this place, where, I am sure, you will find yourself perfectly at your ease in the midst of an agreeable society. – Dear Letty, I will take no refusal – if you have any friendship — any humanity — you will come. — I desire that immediate application may be made to your mamma; and that the moment her permission is obtained, you will apprise

Your ever faithful,

Oct. 14.   LYDIA MELFORD

To Mrs JERMYN, at her house in Gloucester.

DEAR MADAM,

Though I was not so fortunate as to be favoured with an answer to the letter with which I troubled you in the spring, I still flatter myself that you retain some regard for me and my concerns. I am sure the care and tenderness with which I was treated, under your roof and tuition, demand the warmest returns of gratitude and affection on my part, and these sentiments, I hope, I shall cherish to my dying day – At present, I think it my duty to make you acquainted with the happy issue of that indiscretion by which I incurred your displeasure. — Ah! madam, the slighted Wilson is metamorphosed into George Dennison, only son and heir of a gentleman, whose character is second to none in England, as you may understand upon inquiry. My guardian, my brother and I, are now in his house; and an immediate union of the two families is to take place in the persons of the young gentleman and your poor Lydia Melford. – You will easily conceive how embarrassing this situation must be to a young inexperienced creature like me, of weak nerves and strong apprehensions; and how much the presence of a friend and confidant would encourage and support me on this occasion. You know, that of all the young ladies, Miss Willis was she that possessed the greatest share of my confidence and affection; and, therefore, I fervently wish to have the happiness of her company at this interesting crisis.

Mrs Dennison, who is the object of universal love and esteem, has, at my request, written to you on this subject, and I now beg leave to reinforce her sollicitations. – My dear Mrs Jermyn! my ever honoured governess! let me conjure you by that fondness which once distinguished your favourite Lydia! by that benevolence of heart, which disposes you to promote the happiness of your fellow-creatures in general! lend a favourable ear to my petition, and use your influence with Letty's mamma, that my most earnest desire may be gratified. Should I be indulged in this particular, I will engage to return her safe, and even to accompany her to Gloucester, where, if you will give me leave, I will present to you, under another name,

Dear Madam,

Your most affectionate

Humble servant,

And penitent,

LYDIA MELFORD

Oct. 14.

To Mrs MARY JONES, at Brambleton-hall.

O MARY JONES! MARY JONES!

I have met with so many axidents, suprisals, and ter-
rifications, that I am in a pafeck fantigo, and I believe I shall
never be my own self again. Last week I was dragged out of a
river like a drowned rat, and lost a bran-new night-cap, with a
sulfer stayhook, that cost me a good half-a-crown, and an odd
shoe of green gallow monkey; besides wetting my cloaths and
taring my smuck, and an ugly gash made in the back part of
my thy, by the stump of a tree – To be sure Mr Clinker tuck
me out of the cox; but he left me on my back in the water, to
go to the 'squire; and I mought have had a watry grave, if a
millar had not brought me to the dry land — But, O! what
choppings and changes girl – The player man that came after
Miss Liddy, and frightened me with a beard at Bristol Well, is
now matthew-murphy'd[1] into a fine young gentleman, son and
hare of 'squire Dollison – We are all together in the same house,
and all parties have agreed to the match, and in a fortnite the
surrymony will be performed.

But this is not the only wedding we are to have – Mistriss is
resolved to have the same frolick, in the naam of God! Last
Sunday in the parish crutch, if my own ars may be trusted, the
clerk called the banes of marridge betwixt Opaniah Lash-
meheygo, and Tapitha Brample, spinster; he mought as well
have called her inkle-weaver, for she never spun and hank of
yarn in her life – Young 'squire Dollison and Miss Liddy make
the second kipple; and there might have been a turd, but times
are changed with Mr Clinker – O Molly! what do'st think? Mr
Clinker is found to be a pye-blow of our own 'squire, and his
rite naam is Mr Matthew Loyd (thof God he nose how that can
be); and he is now out of livery, and wares ruffles – but I new
him when he was out at elbows,[2] and had not a rag to kiver his
pistereroes; so he need not hold his head so high – He is for
sartin very umble and compleasant, and purtests as how he has
the same regard as before; but that he is no longer his own
master, and cannot portend to marry without the 'squire's

consent – He says he must wait with patience, and trust to Providence, and such nonsense – But if so be as how his regard be the same, why stand shilly shally?[3] Why not strike while the iron is hot, and speak to the 'squire without loss of time? What subjection can the 'squire make to our coming together – Thof my father wan't a gentleman, my mother was an honest woman – I didn't come on the wrong side of the blanket,[4] girl – My parents were marred according to the right of holy mother crutch, in the face of men and angles – Mark that, Mary Jones.

Mr Clinker (Loyd I would say) had best look to his tackle[5] – There be other chaps[6] in the market, as the saying is — What would he say if I should except the soot and sarvice of the young 'squire's valley? Mr Machappy is a gentleman born, and has been abroad in the wars – He has a world of buck larning, and speaks French, and Ditch, and Scotch, and all manner of outlandish lingos; to be sure he's a little the worse for the ware, and is much given to drink; but then he's good-tempered in his liquor, and a prudent woman mought wind him about her finger – But I have no thoughts of him, I'll assure you — I scorn for to do, or to say, or to think any thing that mought give unbreech to Mr Loyd, without furder occasion – But then I have such vapours, Molly – I sit and cry by myself, and take ass of etida, and smill to burnt fathers, and kindal-snuffs; and I pray constantly for grease, that I may have a glimpse of the new-light, to shew me the way through this wretched veil of tares – And yet, I want for nothing in this family of love, where every sole is so kind and so courteous, that wan would think they are so many saints in haven. Dear Molly, I recommend myself to your prayers, being, with my sarvice to Saul,

your ever loving,

and discounselled friend,

Oct. 14.   WIN. JENKINS

To Dr Lewis.

DEAR DICK,

You cannot imagine what pleasure I have in seeing your handwriting, after such a long cessation on your side of our correspondence – Yet, Heaven knows, I have often seen your hand-writing with disgust – I mean, when it appeared in abbreviations of apothecary's Latin – I like your hint of making interest for the reversion of the collector's place, for Mr Lismahago, who is much pleased with the scheme, and presents you with his compliments and best thanks for thinking so kindly of his concerns – The man seems to mend, upon further acquaintance. That harsh reserve, which formed a disagreeable husk about his character, begins to peel off in the course of our communication — I have great hopes that he and Tabby will be as happily paired as any two draught animals[1] in the kingdom; and I make no doubt but that he will prove a valuable acquisition to our little society, in the article of conversation, by the fire-side in winter.

Your objection to my passing this season of the year at such a distance from home, would have more weight if I did not find myself perfectly at my ease where I am; and my health so much improved, that I am disposed to bid defiance to gout and rheumatism – I begin to think I have put myself on the superannuated list too soon, and absurdly sought for health in the retreats of laziness – I am persuaded that all valetudinarians are too sedentary, too regular, and too cautious — We should sometimes increase the motion of the machine, to *unclog the wheels of life*;[2] and now and then take a plunge amidst the waves of excess, in order to case-harden the constitution. I have even found a change of company as necessary as a change of air, to promote a vigorous circulation of the spirits, which is the very essence and criterion of good health.

Since my last, I have been performing the duties of friendship, that required a great deal of exercise, from which I hope to derive some benefit – Understanding, by the greatest accident in the world, that Mr Baynard's wife was dangerously ill of a pleuritic fever, I borrowed Dennison's post-chaise, and went across the country to his habitation, attended only by Loyd (quondam[3] Clinker) on horseback. – As the distance is not above thirty miles, I arrived about four in the afternoon, and meeting the physician at the door, was informed that his patient had just expired. – I was instantly seized with a violent emotion, but it was not grief. – The family being in confusion, I ran up stairs into the chamber, where, indeed, they were all assembled. – The aunt stood wringing her hands in a kind of stupefaction of sorrow, but my friend acted all the extravagancies of affliction — He held the body in his arms, and poured forth such a lamentation, that one would have thought he had lost the most amiable consort and valuable companion upon earth.

Affection may certainly exist independent of esteem; nay, the same object may be lovely in one respect, and detestable in another – The mind has a surprising faculty of accommodating, and even attaching itself, in such a manner, by dint of use, to things that are in their own nature disagreeable, and even pernicious, that it cannot bear to be delivered from them without reluctance and regret. Baynard was so absorbed in his delirium, that he did not perceive me when I entered, and desired one of the women to conduct the aunt into her own chamber. – At the same time I begged the tutor to withdraw the boy, who stood gaping in a corner, very little affected with the distress of the scene. – These steps being taken, I waited till the first violence of my friend's transport was abated, then disengaged him gently from the melancholy object, and led him by the hand into another apartment; though he struggled so hard, that I was obliged to have recourse to the assistance of his valet de chambre — In a few minutes, however, he recollected himself, and folding me in his arms, 'This (cried he), is a friendly office, indeed! — I know not how you came hither; but, I think, Heaven sent you to prevent my going distracted – O Matthew! I have lost my dear Harriet! – my poor, gentle, tender creature, that loved me with such warmth and purity of affection – my constant companion of twenty years! – She's gone – she's gone for ever! – Heaven and earth! where is she? — Death shall not part us!'

So saying, he started up, and could hardly be with-held from returning to the scene we had quitted – You will perceive it would have been very absurd for me to argue with a man that talked so madly. – On all such occasions, the first torrent of passion must be allowed to subside gradually. – I endeavoured to beguile his attention by starting little hints and insinuating other objects of discourse imperceptibly; and being exceedingly pleased in my own mind at this event, I exerted myself with such an extraordinary flow of spirits as was attended with success. — In a few hours, he was calm enough to hear reason, and even to own that Heaven could not have interposed more effectually to rescue him from disgrace and ruin. – That he might not, however, relapse into weaknesses for want of company, I passed the night in his chamber, in a little tent bed brought thither on purpose; and well it was I took this precaution, for he started up in bed several times, and would have played the fool, if I had not been present.

Next day he was in a condition to talk of business, and vested me with full authority over his household, which I began to exercise without loss of time, tho' not before he knew and approved of the scheme I had projected for his advantage. – He would have quitted the house immediately; but this retreat I opposed. — Far from encouraging a temporary disgust, which might degenerate into an habitual aversion, I resolved, if possible, to attach him more than ever to his Houshold Gods. – I gave directions for the funeral to be as private as was consistant with decency; I wrote to London, that an inventory and estimate might be made of the furniture and effects in his town-house, and gave notice to the landlord, that Mr Baynard should quit the premises at Lady-day;[4] I set a person at work to take account of every thing in the country-house, including horses, carriages, and harness; I settled the young gentleman at a boarding-school, kept by a clergyman in the neighbourhood, and thither he went without reluctance, as soon as he knew that he was to be troubled no more with his tutor, whom we dismissed. – The aunt continued very sullen, and never appeared at table, though Mr Baynard payed his respects to her every day in her own chamber; there also she held conferences with the waiting-women and other servants of the family: but, the moment her niece was interred, she went away in a post-chaise prepared for that purpose: she did not leave the house, however, without giving Mr Baynard to understand, that the wardrobe of her niece was the perquisite of her woman; accordingly that worthless drab received all the clothes, laces, and linen of her deceased mistress, to the value of five hundred pounds, at a moderate computation.

The next step I took was to disband that legion of supernumerary domestics, who had preyed so long upon the vitals of my friend: a parcel of idle drones, so intolerably insolent, that they even treated their own master with the most contemptuous neglect. They had been generally hired by his wife, according to the recommendation of her woman, and these were the only patrons to whom they payed the least deference. I had therefore uncommon satisfaction in clearing the house of these vermin. The woman of the deceased, and a chambermaid, a valet de chambre, a butler, a French cook, a master gardener, two footmen and a coachman, I payed off, and turned out of the house immediately, paying to each a month's wages in lieu of warning. Those whom I retained, consisted of the female cook, who had been assistant to the Frenchman, a house maid, an old lacquey, a postilion, and under-gardener. Thus I removed at once a huge mountain of expence and care from the shoulders of my friend, who could hardly believe the evidence of his own senses, when he found himself so suddenly and so effectually relieved. His heart, however, was still subject to vibrations of tenderness, which returned at certain intervals, extorting sighs, and tears, and exclamations of grief and impatience: but these fits grew every day less violent and less frequent, 'till at length his reason obtained a complete victory over the infirmities of his nature.

Upon an accurate enquiry into the state of his affairs, I find his debts amount to twenty thousand pounds, for eighteen thousand pounds of which sum his estate is mortgaged; and as he pays five per cent, interest, and some of his farms are unoccupied, he does not receive above two hundred pounds a year clear from his lands, over and above the interest of his wife's fortune, which produced eight hundred pounds annually.

For lightening this heavy burthen, I devised the following expedient – His wife's jewels, together with his superfluous plate and furniture in both houses, his horses and carriages, which are already advertised to be sold by auction, will, according to the estimate, produce two thousand five hundred pounds in ready money, with which the debt will be immediately reduced to eighteen thousand pounds – I have undertaken to find him ten thousand pounds at four per cent. by which means he will save one hundred a-year in the article of interest, and perhaps we shall be able to borrow the other eight thousand on the same terms. According to his own scheme of a country life, he says he can live comfortably for three hundred pounds a-year; but, as he has a son to educate, we will allow him five hundred; then there will be an accumulating fund of seven hundred a-year, principal and interest, to pay off the incumbrance; and, I think, we may modestly add three hundred, on the presumption of new-leasing and improving the vacant farms: so that, in a couple of years, I suppose there will be above a thousand a-year appropriated to liquidate a debt of sixteen thousand.

We forthwith began to class and set apart the articles designed for sale, under the direction of an upholder[5] from London; and, that nobody in the house might be idle, commenced our reformation without doors, as well as within. With Baynard's good leave, I ordered the gardener to turn the rivulet into its old channel, to refresh the fainting Naiads,[6] who had so long languished among mouldring roots, withered leaves, and dry pebbles – The shrubbery is condemned to extirpation; and the pleasure ground will be restored to its original use of corn-field and pasture – Orders are given for rebuilding the walls of the garden at the back of the house, and for planting clumps of firs, intermingled with beech and chestnut, at the east end, which is now quite exposed to the surly blasts that come from that quarter. All these works being actually begun, and the house and auction left to the care and management of a reputable attorney, I brought Baynard along with me in the chaise, and made him acquainted with Dennison, whose goodness of heart would not fail to engage his esteem and affection.

— He is indeed charmed with our society in general, and declares that he never saw the theory of true pleasure reduced to practice before. – I really believe it would not be an easy task to find such a number of individuals assembled under one roof, more happy than we are at present.

I must tell you, however, in confidence, I suspect Tabby of tergiversation.[7] – I have been so long accustomed to that original, that I know all the caprices of her heart, and can often perceive her designs while they are yet in embrio – She attached herself to Lismahago for no other reason but that she despaired of making a more agreeable conquest – At present, if I am not much mistaken in my observation, she would gladly convert the widowhood of Baynard to her own advantage. – Since he arrived, she has behaved very coldly to the captain, and strove to fasten on the other's heart, with the hooks of overstrained civility – These must be the instinctive efforts of her constitution, rather than the effects of any deliberate design; for matters are carried to such a length with the lieutenant, that she could not retract with any regard to conscience or reputation. Besides, she will meet with nothing but indifference or aversion on the side of Baynard, who has too much sense to think of such a partner at any time, and too much delicacy to admit a thought of any such connexion at the present juncture – Meanwhile, I have prevailed upon her to let him have four thousand pounds at four per cent towards paying off his mortage. Young Dennison has agreed that Liddy's fortune shall be appropriated to the same purpose, on the same terms. – His father will sell out three thousand pounds stock for his accommodation. – Farmer Bland has, at the desire of Wilson, undertaken for two thousand; and I must make an effort to advance what further will be required to take my friend out of the hands of the Philistines.[8] He is so pleased with the improvements made on his estate, which is all cultivated like a garden, that he has entered himself as a pupil in farming to Mr Dennison, and resolved to attach himself wholly to the practice of husbandry.

Every thing is now prepared for our double wedding. The marriage-articles for both couples are drawn and executed; and the ceremony only waits until the parties shall have been resident in the parish the term prescribed by law. Young Dennison betrays some symptoms of impatience; but, Lismahago bears this necessary delay with the temper of a philosopher. – You must know, the captain does not stand altogether on the foundation of personal merit. Besides his half-pay, amounting to two and forty pounds a year, this indefatigable œconomist has amassed eight hundred pounds, which he has secured in the funds. This sum arises partly from his pay's running up while he remained among the Indians; partly from what he received as a consideration for the difference between his full appointment and the half-pay, to which he is now restricted; and partly from the profits of a little traffick he drove in peltry,[9] during his sachemship among the Miamis.

Liddy's fears and perplexities have been much assuaged by the company of one Miss Willis, who had been her intimate companion at the boarding-school. Her parents had been earnestly sollicited to allow her making this friendly visit on such an extraordinary occasion; and two days ago she arrived with her mother, who did not chuse that she should come without a proper gouvernante. The young lady is very sprightly, handsome, and agreeable, and the mother a mighty good sort of a woman; so that their coming adds considerably to our enjoyment. But we shall have a third couple yoked in the matrimonial chain. Mr Clinker Loyd has made humble remonstrance through the canal of my nephew, setting forth the sincere love and affection mutually subsisting between him and Mrs Winifred Jenkins, and praying my consent to their coming together for life. I would have wished that Mr Clinker had kept out of this scrape; but as the nymph's happiness is at stake, and she has already some fits in the way of despondence, I, in order to prevent any tragical catastrophe, have given him leave to play the fool, in imitation of his betters; and I suppose we shall in time have a whole litter of his progeny at Brambleton-hall. The fellow is stout and lusty, very sober and conscientious; and the wench seems to be as great an enthusiast in love as in religion.

I wish you would think of employing him some other way, that the parish may not be overstocked — you know he has been bred a farrier, consequently belongs to the faculty; and as he is very docile, I make no doubt but, with your good instruction, he may be, in a little time, qualified to act as a Welch apothecary. Tabby, who never did a favour with a good grace, has consented, with great reluctance, to this match. Perhaps it hurts her pride, as she now considers Clinker in the light of a relation; but, I believe, her objections are of a more selfish nature. She declares she cannot think of retaining the wife of Matthew Loyd in the character of a servant; and she foresees, that on such an occasion the woman will expect some gratification for her past services. As for Clinker, exclusive of other considerations, he is so trusty, brave, affectionate, and alert, and I owe him such personal obligations, that he merits more than all the indulgence that can possibly be shewn him, by

Yours,

Oct. 26.   MATT. BRAMBLE

To Sir WATKIN PHILLIPS, Bart. at Oxon.

DEAR KNIGHT,

The fatal knots are now tied. The comedy is near a close; and the curtain is ready to drop: but, the latter scenes of this act I shall recapitulate in order – About a fortnight ago, my uncle made an excursion across the country, and brought hither a particular friend, one Mr Baynard, who has just lost his wife, and was for some time disconsolate, though by all accounts he had much more cause for joy than for sorrow at this event. — His countenance, however, clears up apace; and he appears to be a person of rare accomplishments. – But, we have received another still more agreeable reinforcement to our company, by the arrival of Miss Willis from Gloucester. She was Liddy's bosom friend at the boarding-school, and being earnestly sollicited to assist at the nuptials, her mother was so obliging as to grant my sister's request, and even to come with her in person. Liddy, accompanied by George Dennison and me, gave them the meeting half-way, and next day conducted them hither in safety. Miss Willis is a charming girl, and, in point of disposition, an agreeable contrast to my sister, who is rather too grave and sentimental[1] for my turn of mind. – The other is gay, frank, a little giddy, and always good-humoured. She has, moreover, a genteel fortune, is well born, and remarkably handsome. – Ah Phillips! if these qualities were permanent – if her humour would never change, nor her beauties decay, what efforts would I not make – But these are idle reflections – my destiny must one day be fulfilled.

At present we pass the time as agreeably as we can. – We have got up several farces, which afforded unspeakable entertainment by the effects they produced among the country people, who are admitted to all our exhibitions. – Two nights ago, Jack Wilson acquired great applause in Harlequin Skeleton, and Lismahago surprised us all in the character of Pierot. – His long lank sides, and strong marked features, were all peculiarly adapted to his part. — He appeared with a ludicrous stare, from which he had discharged all meaning: he adopted the impressions of fear and amazement so naturally, that many of the audience were infected by his looks; but when the skeleton held him in chace his horror became most divertingly picturesque, and seemed to endow him with such præternatural agility as confounded all the spectators. It was a lively representation of Death in pursuit of Consumption,[2] and had such an effect upon the commonalty, that some of them shrieked aloud, and others ran out of the hall in the utmost consternation.

This is not the only instance in which the lieutenant has lately excited our wonder. His temper, which had been soured and shrivelled by disappointment and chagrin, is now swelled out, and smoothed like a raisin in plumb-porridge. From being reserved and punctilious, he is become easy and obliging. He cracks jokes, laughs and banters, with the most facetious familiarity; and, in a word, enters into all our schemes of merriment and pastime – The other day his baggage arrived in the waggon from London, contained in two large trunks and a long deal box not unlike a coffin. The trunks were filled with his wardrobe, which he displayed for the entertainment of the company, and he freely owned, that it consisted chiefly of the *opima spolia*[3] taken in battle. What he selected for his wedding suit, was a tarnished white cloth faced with blue velvet, embroidered with silver; but, he valued himself most upon a tye-periwig,[4] in which he had made his first appearance as a lawyer above thirty years ago. This machine had been in buckle[5] ever since, and now all the servants in the family were employed to frizz it out for the occasion, which was yesterday celebrated at the parish church. George Dennison and his bride were distinguished by nothing extraordinary in their apparel. His eyes lightened with eagerness and joy, and she trembled with coyness and confusion. My uncle gave her away, and her friend Willis supported her during the ceremony.

But my aunt and her paramour took the pas,[6] and formed, indeed, such a pair of originals, as, I believe all England could not parallel. She was dressed in the stile of 1739; and the day being cold, put on a manteel of green velvet laced with gold: but this was taken off by the bridegroom, who threw over her shoulders a fur cloak of American sables, valued at fourscore guineas, a present equally agreeable and unexpected. Thus accoutred, she was led up to the altar by Mr Dennison, who did the office of her father: Lismahago advanced in the military step with his French coat reaching no farther than the middle of his thigh,[7] his campaign wig that surpasses all description, and a languishing leer upon his countenance, in which there seemed to be something arch and ironical. The ring, which he put upon her finger, he had concealed till the moment it was used. He now produced it with an air of self-complacency. It was a curious antique, set with rose diamonds: he told us afterwards, it had been in the family two hundred years and was a present from his grand-mother. These circumstances agreeably flattered the pride of our aunt Tabitha, which had already found uncommon gratification in the captain's generosity; for he had, in the morning, presented my uncle with a fine bear's skin, and a Spanish fowling-piece, and me with a case of pistols curiously mounted with silver. At the same time he gave Mrs Jenkins an Indian purse, made of silk grass, containing twenty crown pieces. You must know, this young lady, with the assistance of Mr Loyd, formed the third couple who yesterday sacrificed to Hymen.[8] I wrote to you in my last, that he had recourse to my mediation, which I employed successfully with my uncle; but Mrs Tabitha held out 'till the love-sick Jenkins had two fits of the mother; then she relented, and those two cooing turtles were caged for life – Our aunt made an effort of generosity in furnishing the bride with her superfluities of clothes and linen, and her example was followed by my sister; nor did Mr Bramble and I neglect her on this occasion. It was, indeed, a day of peace-offering. – Mr Dennison insisted upon Liddy's accepting two bank notes of one hundred pounds each, as pocket-money; and his lady gave her a diamond necklace of double that value. There was, besides, a mutual exchange of tokens among the individuals of the two families thus happily united.

As George Dennison and his partner were judged improper objects of mirth, Jack Wilson had resolved to execute some jokes on Lismahago, and after supper began to ply him with bumpers, when the ladies had retired; but the captain perceiving his drift, begged for quarter, alledging that the adventure, in which he had engaged, was a very serious matter; and that it would be more the part of a good Christian to pray that he might be strengthened, than to impede his endeavours to finish the adventure. – He was spared accordingly, and permitted to ascend the nuptial couch with all his senses about him. – There he and his consort sat in state, like Saturn and Cybele,[9] while the benediction posset[10] was drank; and a cake being broken over the head of Mrs Tabitha Lismahago, the fragments were distributed among the bystanders, according to the custom of the antient Britons, on the supposition that every person who eat of this hallowed cake, should that night have a vision of the man or woman whom Heaven designed should be his or her wedded mate.

The weight of Wilson's waggery fell upon honest Humphry and his spouse, who were bedded in an upper room, with the usual ceremony of throwing the stocking. — This being performed, and the company withdrawn, a sort of catter-wauling ensued, when Jack found means to introduce a real cat shod with walnut-shells, which galloping along the boards, made such a dreadful noise as effectually discomposed our lovers. — Winifred screamed aloud, and shrunk under the bed-cloaths – Mr Loyd, believing that Satan was come to buffet him *in propria persona*, laid aside all carnal thoughts, and began to pray aloud with great fervency. – At length, the poor animal, being more afraid than either, leaped into the bed, and meauled with the most piteous exclamation. – Loyd, thus informed of the nature of the annoyance, rose and set the door wide open, so that this troublesome visitant retreated with great expedition; then securing himself, by means of a double bolt, from a second intrusion, he was left to enjoy his good fortune without further disturbance.

If one may judge from the looks of the parties, they are all very well satisfied with what has passed – George Dennison and his wife are too delicate to exhibit any strong marked signs of their mutual satisfaction, but their eyes are sufficiently expressive – Mrs Tabitha Lismahago is rather fulsome in signifying her approbation of the captain's love; while his deportment is the very pink[11] of gallantry. – He sighs, and ogles, and languishes at this amiable object; he kisses her hand, mutters ejaculations of rapture, and sings tender airs; and, no doubt, laughs internally at her folly in believing him sincere. – In order to shew how little his vigour was impaired by the fatigues of the preceding day, he this morning danced a Highland sarabrand over a naked back-sword,[12] and leaped so high, that I believe he would make no contemptible figure as a vaulter at Sadler's Wells. – Mr Matthew Loyd, when asked how he relished his bargain, throws up his eyes, crying, 'For what we have received, Lord make us thankful: amen.' — His helpmate giggles, and holds her hand before her eyes, affecting to be ashamed of having been in bed with a man. – Thus all these widgeons[13] enjoy the novelty of their situation; but, perhaps their notes will be changed, when they are better acquainted with the nature of the decoy.

As Mrs Willis cannot be persuaded to stay, and Liddy is engaged by promise to accompany her daughter back to Gloucester, I fancy there will be a general migration from hence, and that most of us will spend the Christmas holidays at Bath; in which case, I shall certainly find an opportunity to beat up your quarters. – By this time, I suppose, you are sick of *alma mater*, and even ready to execute that scheme of peregrination, which was last year concerted between you and

Your affectionate

Nov. 8.   J. MELFORD

To Dr LEWIS.

DEAR DOCTOR,

My niece Liddy is now happily settled for life; and captain Lismahago has taken Tabby off my hands; so that I have nothing further to do, but to comfort my friend Baynard, and provide for my son Loyd, who is also fairly joined to Mrs Winifred Jenkins. – You are an excellent genius at hints. – Dr Arbuthnot[1] was but a type[2] of Dr Lewis in that respect. — What you observe of the vestry-clerk deserves consideration. – I make no doubt but Matthew Loyd is well enough qualified for the office; but, at present, you must find room for him in the house. — His incorruptible honesty and indefatigable care will be serviceable in superintending the œconomy of my farm; tho' I don't mean that he shall interfere with Barns, of whom I have no cause to complain. – I am just returned with Baynard, from a second trip to his house, where every thing is regulated to his satisfaction. – He could not, however, review the apartments without tears and lamentation, so that he is not yet in a condition to be left alone; therefore I will not part with him till the spring, when he intends to plunge into the avocations of husbandry, which will at once employ and amuse his attention. – Charles Dennison has promised to stay with him a fortnight, to set him fairly afloat in his improvements; and Jack Wilson will see him from time to time; besides, he has a few friends in the country, whom his new plan of life will not exclude from his society. – In less than a year, I make no doubt, but he will find himself perfectly at ease both in his mind and body, for the one had dangerously affected the other; and I shall enjoy the exquisite pleasure of seeing my friend rescued from misery and contempt.

Mrs Willis being determined to return with her daughter, in a few days, to Gloucester, our plan has undergone some alteration. – Jery has persuaded his brother-in-law to carry his wife to Bath; and I believe his parents will accompany him thither. – For my part, I have no intention to take that route. – It must be something very extraordinary that will induce me to revisit either Bath or London. — My sister and her husband, Baynard and I, will take leave of them at Gloucester, and make the best of our way to Brambleton hall, where I desire you will prepare a good chine[3] and turkey for our Christmas dinner. — You must also employ your medical skill in defending me from the attacks of the gout, that I may be in good case to receive the rest of our company, who promise to visit us in their return from the Bath. – As I have laid in a considerable stock of health, it is to be hoped you will not have much trouble with me in the way of physic, but I intend to work you on the side of exercise. – I have got an excellent fowling-piece from Mr Lismahago, who is a keen sportsman, and we shall take the heath in all weathers. – That this scheme of life may be prosecuted the more effectually, I intend to renounce all sedentary amusements, particularly that of writing long letters; a resolution, which, had I taken it sooner, might have saved you the trouble which you have lately taken in reading the tedious epistles of

Nov. 20.   MATT. BRAMBLE

To Mrs Gwyllim, at Brambleton-hall.

Good Mrs Gwyllim,

Heaven, for wise porpuses, hath ordained that I should change my name and citation in life, so that I am not to be considered any more as manager of my brother's family; but as I cannot surrender up my stewardship till I have settled with you and Williams, I desire you will get your accunts ready for inspection, as we are coming home without further delay. — My spouse, the captain, being subject to remmaticks, I beg you will take great care to have the blew chamber, up two pair of stairs, well warmed for his reception. – Let the sashes be secured, the crevices stopt, the carpets laid, and the beds well tousled. – Mrs Loyd, late Jenkins, being married to a relation of the family, cannot remain in the capacity of a sarvant; therefore, I wish you would cast about for some creditable body to be with me in her room – If she can spin, and is mistress of plain-work, so much the better – but she must not expect extravagant wages – having a family of my own, I must be more occumenical than ever. No more at present, but rests

Your loving friend,

Nov. 20.   TAB. LISMAHAGO

To Mrs MARY JONES, at Brambleton-hall.

MRS JONES,

Providinch hath bin pleased to make great halteration in the pasture of our affairs. — We were yesterday three kiple chined, by the grease of God, in the holy bands of mattermoney, and I now subscrive myself Loyd at your sarvice. – All the parish allowed that young 'squire Dallison and his bride was a comely pear for to see. – As for madam Lashmiheygo, you nose her picklearities – her head, to be sure, was fintastical; and her spouse had rapt her with a long marokin furze cloak from the land of the selvidges, thof they say it is of immense bally. – The captain himself had a huge hassock of air, with three tails, and a tumtawdry[1] coat, boddered with sulfur. – Wan said he was a monkey-bank;[2] and the ould bottler swore he was the born imich of Titidall.[3] — For my part, I says nothing, being as how the captain has done the handsome thing by me. – Mr Loyd was dressed in a lite frog, and checket with gould binding; and thof he don't enter in caparison with great folks of quality, yet he has got as good blood in his veins as arrow privat 'squire in the county; and then his pursing is far from contentible. – Your humble sarvant had on a plain peagreen tabby[4] sack, with my Runnela cap,[5] ruff toupee, and side curls. – They said, I was the very moral of lady Rickmanstone, but not so pale – that may well be, for her ladyship is my elder by seven good years and more. – Now, Mrs Mary, our satiety is to suppurate – Mr Millfart goes to Bath along with the Dallisons, and the rest of us push home to Wales, to pass our Chrishmarsh at Brampleton-hall – As our apartments is to be the yellow pepper, in the thurd story, pray carry my things thither. — Present my cumpliments to Mrs Gwyllim, and I hope she and I will live upon dissent terms of civility. – Being, by God's blessing, removed to a higher spear, you'll excuse my being familiar with the lower sarvants of the family; but, as I trust you'll behave respectful, and keep a proper distance, you may always depend upon the good will and purtection of

Yours,

Nov. 20.   W. LOYD

FINIS.

Notes

Wherever possible, information about persons and definitions of words have been drawn from the *Dictionary of National Biography* and the *Oxford English Dictionary*. Notes about clothing and colloquial speech have been supplemented by C. Willett Cunnington and Phillis Cunnington, *Handbook of English Costume in the Eighteenth Century*, revised edition (London: Faber and Faber, 1972) and Francis Grose, *A Classical Dictionary of the Vulgar Tongue*, 2nd edition (London, 1788), hereafter abbreviated as Grose.

I have also drawn upon three prior editions of *The Expedition of Humphry Clinker*: the previous Penguin edition, ed. Angus Ross (Harmondsworth: Penguin, 1967; repr. 1985); the World's Classics edition, ed. Lewis M. Knapp (Oxford: Oxford University Press, 1966; repr. 1984); and, especially, the splendid Georgia edition, ed. Thomas R. Preston (Athens, GA: University of Georgia Press, 1990), hereafter abbreviated as Ross, Knapp and Preston.

References to the Bible are to the Authorized King James Version; quotations and translations from Homer, Horace, Ovid and Virgil are taken from the Loeb Classical Library editions; and references to the works of Shakespeare, Milton and Pope are to the following:

William Shakespeare, *The Complete Works: Compact Edition*, ed. Stanley Wells, Gary Taylor, John Jowett and William Montgomery (Oxford: Clarendon Press, 1988; repr. 1991)
The Poems of John Milton, ed. John Carey and Alastair Fowler (London: Longman, 1968)
The Poems of Alexander Pope: A One-Volume Edition of the Twickenham Text with Selected Annotations, ed. John Butt (London: Routledge, 1963; repr. 1992)

Unless otherwise indicated, references to texts published during the eighteenth century are to the first editions.

Due to limitations of space, sources and analogues in other works by Smollett – such as *The Present State of All Nations* (1768–9) – are not usually indicated. No note is made either of persons whom it has not been possible to identify, or of common proverbial phrases (except where such phrases are glossed for meaning). The malapropisms – or, more precisely, Win-isms – that pepper the letters of Win Jenkins have also been annotated selectively, rather than exhaustively.

VOLUME ONE

Title page

1. *Quorsum hæc ... inquam*: From Horace, *Satires*, II.vii.21–2: 'Are you to take all day, you scape-gallows, in telling me the point of such rot? 'Tis you, I say.'

To Mr HENRY DAVIS, Bookseller, in London
(from Jonathan Dustwich, Abergavenny, 4 August)

1. *redargued*: Refuted or disproved (a Scottish legal term).
2. *mala fama*: Bad name or bad repute (Latin).
3. *in usum publicum*: For public use or benefit (Latin).
4. *in verbo sacerdotis*: On the word of a priest (Latin).
5. *quoad*: So far as; as regards (Latin).
6. *Tam ad turpitudinem ... spectans*: Bearing in mind the shame as well as the harshness of the punishment (Latin).
7. *non flocci facio*: I care not about it (Latin).
8. *vilipend*: Regard as of little value or consequence; treat contemptuously or slightingly.
9. *totis viribus*: With all my strength or might (Latin).
10. *intra templi parietes*: Within the temple walls (Latin).
11. *minatory*: Uttering or conveying a threat.
12. περι ιχθυς: Concerning fish (Greek). Galen (*c.* 130–*c.* 200) was a Greek physician and author of numerous medical works.
13. *Deo volente*: God willing (Latin).
14. *All-hallowtide*: The season of All Saints.
15. *Verbum sapienti, &c.*: A word to the wise is sufficient (from the proverbial Latin phrase, *Verbum sapienti sat est*).

To the Revd. Mr JONATHAN DUSTWICH, at—
(from Henry Davis, London, 10 August)

1. *What between . . . that kind of entertainment*: Smollett, *Travels through France and Italy* (1766); Samuel Sharp (1709–78), *Letters from Italy, describing the Customs and Manners of that Country, in the Years 1765, and 1766* (1766); Samuel Derrick (1724–69), *Letters Written from Leverpoole, Chester, Corke, the Lake of Killarney, Dublin, Tunbridge-Wells, and Bath* (1767); Philip Thicknesse (1719–92), *Observations on the Customs and Manners of the French Nation, in a Series of Letters* (1766) and *Useful Hints to those who make the Tour of France, in a Series of Letters, Written from that Kingdom* (1768); Frederick Calvert, sixth Baron Baltimore (1732–71), *A Tour to the East, in the Years 1763 and 1764* (1767); Giuseppie Baretti (1719–89), *An Account of the Manners and Customs of Italy* (1768) and *A Journey from London to Genoa, through England, Portugal, Spain, and France* (1770); and Laurence Sterne (1713–68), *A Sentimental Journey through France and Italy* (1768), in which Smollett is portrayed as the boorish and philistine Smelfungus.

2. *man of war*: A warship.

3. *the late war*: The Seven Years War (1756–63).

4. *flogged at the cart's tail*: A public punishment that involved being tied to the back of a cart and whipped from behind while being dragged along the street.

5. *C— S—*: Identified as Charles Green Say, a printer in Ludgate Street, who was fined £100 by the House of Lords in March 1764 for libelling the Earl of Hertford (Ross, p. 397).

6. *House of L—*: House of Lords.

7. *an information*: In English law, a complaint or charge against a person lodged with or presented to a court or magistrate, in order to initiate criminal proceedings without formal indictment.

8. *lend you a lift*: Give you a helping hand.

9. *Court-kalendar*: An annual handbook of royal families and their courts.

10. *toasted cheese*: A delicacy often associated with Wales, known in the eighteenth century as 'Welsh rabbit', and now known as 'Welsh rarebit'.

To Dr LEWIS
(from Matthew Bramble, Gloucester, 2 April)

1. *swallow snow-balls to cool my reins*: Adapted from Falstaff's
    words in William Shakespeare (1564–1616), *The Merry Wives
    of Windsor*, III.v.20–21.
2. *broke upon the wheel*: A punishment that involved having one's
    limbs broken upon a large wheel or similar instrument of torture.
3. *Hot Well at Bristol*: St Vincent's Well, located one and a half
    miles to the west of the city of Bristol in the parish of Clifton, on
    the Gloucestershire side of the River Avon. Attractions at the
    Hot Well included the pump-room at Hotwell House, which had
    been built in 1696, and the Assembly Rooms.
4. *demi pique*: A saddle whose peak was about half the height of
    that of the older war-saddle.

To Mrs GWYLLIM, house-keeper at Brambleton-hall
(from Tabitha Bramble, Gloucester, 2 April)

1. *neglejay*: Negligée, a loose open gown or sack fastened with pins,
    fashionable from the 1750s.
2. *French commode, Macklin head and lappets*: *French commode*:
    a tall head-dress consisting of a wire framework variously
    covered with silk or lace, fashionable in the last third of the
    seventeenth century and the first third of the eighteenth century;
    Macklin head: a head-dress made of lace from Mechlin in Bel-
    gium; *lappets*: a lappet is a loose or overlapping part of a garment,
    forming a flap or fold.
3. *bum-daffee*: Ross (p. 409) glosses as 'perhaps plum (coloured)-
    taffeta'; Preston (p. xxxvi) suggests 'laxative', from the port-
    manteau coinage created from the words 'bum' and 'Daffey's
    Elixer'. Daffy's Elixir, the 'famous purging cordial', was a
    popular proprietary medicine dating from the seventeenth
    century.
4. *Dr Hill's dockwater*: A herbal tincture prepared by Dr John Hill
    (1714–75), actor, writer, apothecary and quack doctor. Hill
    promoted dock-water as a remedy for scurvy.
5. *strong bear*: Strong beer, an ale stronger than small or table beer,
    but milder than porter (stout).
6. *fought*: Fetched.
7. *TABITHA*: A name perhaps influenced by that of the maidservant
    Tabitha ('Tabby') Runt in the popular poem *The New Bath
    Guide* (1766) by Christopher Anstey (1724–1805), or chosen in

ironic allusion to the Biblical Tabitha, who was 'full of good works and almsdeeds' (Acts 9:36).

To Mrs MARY JONES, at Brambleton-hall
(from Win Jenkins, Gloucester, 2 April)

1. *had like to have*: Was on the point of.
2. *player-man*: Actor.
3. *asterisks*: Hysterics.
4. *subscribed a repository*: Prescribed a suppository.
5. *pillyber*: A variant of 'pillow-bere', i.e. pillow-case.
6. *vails and perquisites*: Gratuities received, and entitlements claimed, in addition to a salary or wage.

To Sir WATKIN PHILLIPS, Bart. of Jesus college, Oxon
(from Jery Melford, Gloucester, 2 April)

1. *Jesus college, Oxon.*: Jesus College, Oxford; originally established to educate students from Wales.
2. *humorist*: A person subject to 'humours', or fancies.
3. *enthusiasm*: Rapturous intensity of feeling.
4. *Salute*: Kiss.

To Miss LÆTITIA WILLIS, at Gloucester
(from Lydia Melford, Clifton, 6 April)

1. *reward those . . . virtue*: Possibly a gesture towards the popular novel *Pamela; or, Virtue Rewarded* (1740) by the printer and author Samuel Richardson (1689–1761). Like *Humphry Clinker* it is written in epistolary form.
2. *Bath*: The most fashionable spa town in eighteenth-century Britain.

To Dr LEWIS
(from Matthew Bramble, Clifton, 17 April)

1. *romances*: The image of the young lady who reads romantic tales of love and gallantry was common by this point in the eighteenth century, and figures particularly in *The Female Quixote; or, The Adventures of Arabella* (1752), a novel by Charlotte Lennox (1730/31–1804), and in *Polly Honeycombe, A Dramatick Novel of One Act* (1760), a theatrical afterpiece by George Colman (1732–94). As with Lennox's Arabella, Lydia's reading probably consists of seventeenth-century French romances.
2. *jackanapes*: One who is like an ape in tricks, airs or behaviour; a pert, impertinent fellow who assumes ridiculous airs.

3.   *'sdeath*: A contracted form of 'God's death', used in oaths and asseverations.

4.   *the vagrant act*: The most recent 'vagrant act' had been passed in 1744 (17 Geo. II, c. 5). The statute divided vagrants into 'idle and disorderly persons', liable to a month's imprisonment (with hard labour) in a house of correction; 'rogues and vagabonds', liable to whipping and imprisonment of up to six months; and 'incorrigible rogues', liable to whipping and imprisonment of up to two years. As is indicated here, unlicensed actors ('strollers', or strolling players) fell under the terms of the Act.

5.   *on his high ropes*: Arrogant or disdainful; from the ropes used by acrobats in high-wire acts.

6.   *Dr Rigge*: Thomas Rigge (*d.* 1794), a physician at the Bristol Royal Infirmary.

7.   *consumption*: Pulmonary consumption or phthisis (tuberculosis of the lungs); a wasting disease.

To Miss LYDIA MELFORD
(from Wilson, Gloucester, 31 March)

1.   *tossed in a sea of doubts and fears*: Perhaps echoing James 1:6: 'For he that wavereth is like a wave of the sea driven with the wind and tossed.'

To Sir WATKIN PHILLIPS, of Jesus college, Oxon
(from Jery Melford, Hot Well, 18 April)

1.   *a mountebank's merry Andrew*: A 'merry Andrew' was a professional clown or buffoon who entertained people with comic antics in order to assist a 'mountebank', an itinerant quack-doctor and popular entertainer who sold supposed medicines and remedies.

2.   *pleonasm*: A superfluous or redundant expression.

3.   deerant quoque Littora Ponto: From Ovid, *Metamorphoses*, I, 292: '*omnia pontus erant, deerant quoque litora ponto*' ('all things were sea, and the sea lacked shores').

4.   *the Isis*: The River Isis in Oxford, upstream of the River Thames.

5.   *rustication*: Banishment to the country. Jery is possibly punning on the alternative meaning of 'temporary dismissal from a university'.

6.   *Cynic*: The Cynics were a philosophical sect founded in ancient Greece, characterized by an ostentatious contempt for ease, wealth and the enjoyments of life.

7.   *Dr L—n*: Diederich Wessel Linden, a German-born physician,

writer and frequenter of Bristol Hot Wells. A firm believer in the health-giving properties of sulphur in spa water, Linden was involved in the 'sulphur controversy', concerning the sulphuric content of the waters at various spas.

8. *Van Vloudel's translation of Horace*: By the great Dutch writer Joost van den Vondel (1587–1679).

9. *Quis multa gracilis . . . van civet & moschata gestinken*: Miscited from Vondel's translation of Horace, *Odes*, I.v.1–2: '*Quis multa gracilis te puer in rosa / Perfusus liquidis urget odoribus*' ('What slender youngster, soaked with perfume, holds you in his arms, lying on a heap of roses').

10. *toto cœlo*: Entirely (Latin).

11. *luxury*: Habitual indulgence in choice or costly items, beyond the basic necessities of life. Complaints against luxury formed an important conservative strand in eighteenth-century social thought.

12. *stercoraceous*: Consisting of, containing, or pertaining to fæces.

13. *Dr B—, in his treatise on the Four Digestions*: Dr Edward Barry (1696–1776), an Irish MP, Fellow of the Royal Society, and Professor of Physic at the University of Dublin. The cited text was actually entitled *A Treatise on the Three Different Digestions, and Discharges of the Human Body* (1759).

14. *the last Grand Duke of Tuscany, of the* Medicis *family*: Giovan Gastone (1671–1737).

15. *a close-stool*: A chamberpot, enclosed in a stool or box.

16. *assa fœtida*: Asafœtida, a concreted resinous gum with a strong odour of garlic or onions, used in medicine as an antispasmodic (Latin).

17. *tan-pits*: Vats for crushing the bark of trees, an infusion of which is used in the conversion of hides into leather.

18. *concrete*: A concretion or compound.

19. *ascites*: Dropsy of the abdomen (Latin). Dropsy is a morbid condition characterized by the accumulation of watery fluid in the serous cavities or the connective tissue of the body.

20. *facies leucophlegmatica*: A pale, swollen and flabby appearance (Latin).

21. *oedematous*: Swollen with fluid, as in a dropsy.

22. *lues venerea*: A spreading disease, especially syphilis (Latin).

23. *nodi, tophi . . . serpiginous eruption*: *nodi*: hard or gnarled tumours; *tophi*: gouty matter in the joints; *gummata*: gummy tumours, usually syphilitic in origin; *verrucæ*: warts; *cristæ Galli*: cock's combs; *serpiginous* eruption: symptom of a creeping skin disease (all Latin).

24. *communication*: Sexual intercourse.
25. *your nose . . . falling*: Possibly an allusion to the sexual wordplay concerning noses and bridges in Laurence Sterne's novel *The Life and Opinions of Tristram Shandy, Gentleman* (1759–67). Destruction of the nose, due to the use of mercury in its treatment, indicated an advanced stage of syphilis.

To Sir WATKIN PHILLIPS, of Jesus college, Oxon
(from Jery Melford, Hot Well, 20 April)

1. *a dish of chocolate*: A fashionable beverage in England since the later seventeenth century.
2. *concupissins*: Concupiscence, sexual desire.
3. *pupils*: In civil and Scottish law, pupils are minors or orphans under the care of a guardian.
4. *plain work*: Simple needlework or sewing, as distinct from fancy work or embroidery.

To Dr LEWIS
(from Matthew Bramble, Hot Well, 20 April)

1. *chop logic*: Reason through argument.
2. *calcarious*: Composed of or containing lime or limestone.
3. *a cap and bells*: The insignia of a Fool or jester.
4. *rascallion*: A low mean wretch or rascal.
5. *cheapening*: Bargaining or establishing a price for.
6. *good Lord deliver us!*: The congregation's response during part of the Litany, as directed in *The Book of Common Prayer*.
7. *pits*: Sinks in or contracts so as to form a pit or hollow.

To Miss LETTY WILLIS, at Gloucester
(from Lydia Melford, Hot Well, 21 April)

1. *Philomel*: A poetic name for a nightingale, from the ancient myth in which Philomela was transformed into one.
2. *the nymph of Bristol spring*: i.e. the water of Bristol Spring. Smollett is possibly alluding to *An Hymn to the Nymph of Bristol Spring* (1751), a poem by William Whitehead (1715–85).
3. maukish: Sickly or insipid to the taste.

To Sir WATKIN PHILLIPS, of Jesus college, Oxon
(from Jery Melford, Bath, 24 April)

1. *Alma-mater*: Fostering mother; used of a university or school by its alumni.

2. *Teucer*: Greek archer and half-brother to Ajax, with whom he fought against Troy.

3. *South Parade*: Built between 1737 and 1750, along with the North Parade, by John Wood the Elder (1704–54).

4. *turnspit*: A dog employed in turning a roasting-spit by running within a treadwheel connected to it.

5. *town-waits*: A small band of musicians maintained by a city or town at the public charge.

6. *dancing master*: A professional teacher of dancing, often a figure of ridicule during this period.

7. *Hibernian*: Irish.

8. *gra*: A stage-Irish exclamation, meaning 'my dear'.

9. *hornpipe*: A vigorous dance usually performed by a single person, associated particularly with sailors.

10. *the Abbey bells*: The Abbey bells were rung to announce the arrival of visitors to Bath.

11. *Tottenham*: Tottenham Court, then a suburban village in Middlesex.

12. *a Creole gentleman*: A gentleman born in the West Indies but of English descent.

13. *the French-horn*: A form of trumpet, the French horn was a common instrument among black musicians during this period.

14. *splenetic*: Ill-humoured, irascible or peevish. Descended from the melancholy or black bile of Galenic humoral theory, 'spleen' was one name for what was also known during this period as hypochondria, nervous disorder, the vapours and the 'English malady'.

15. *hautboys*: A wooden double-reed wind instrument of high pitch.

16. *Milsham-street*: Milsom Street, built in 1762.

To Dr Lewis
(from Matthew Bramble, Bath, 23 April)

1. *the lamentations of Matthew Bramble*: An allusion to the Lamentations of Jeremiah in the Old Testament.

2. *The Square*: Queen Square, built by John Wood the Elder in 1728–35.

3. *yard of an inn*: The Bear Inn.

4. *The Circus*: The King's Circus, planned by John Wood the Elder and completed in 1765 by his son, John (*d.* 1781).

5. *Vespasian's amphitheatre*: The Colosseum in Rome, built between AD 72 and AD 90 by the Emperor Vespasian (AD 9–79) and his son, Titus (AD 39–81).

6.   *Covent-garden*: An area in London of 30–40 acres, bounded by Long Acre, Drury Lane, the Strand and St Martin's Lane, and noted for its churches, market, fashionable houses, coffeehouses, taverns and bagnios. The arcades at Covent Garden had been built by Inigo Jones (1573–1652) in 1633–4.

7.   *frize*: Frieze, a kind of coarse woollen cloth with a nap (usually on one side only).

8.   *Gay-street*: A street which runs between Queen Square and the King's Circus.

9.   *fifteen days successively this very winter*: There were unusually heavy snowdrifts in Bath in January 1767.

10. *a Crescent*: The Royal Crescent, designed by John Wood the Younger and built between 1767 and 1775.

11. *hind*: The bailiff or steward on a farm.

12. *the mode*: The current fashion.

13. *two successive wars*: The War of the Austrian Succession (1739–48) and the Seven Years War (1756–63).

14. *country-dances*: Generic name for English dances of a rural or native origin, particularly those in which an indefinite number of couples stand face to face in two long lines.

15. *cotillons*: The name of several dances, chiefly of French origin, each consisting of a variety of steps and figures.

16. *Bedfordbury, Butcher-row, Crutched-friers, and Botolph-lane*: Impoverished areas in the 'City', i.e. the mercantile end of London.

17. *the mob*: From the Latin term *mobile vulgus* (moveable or excitable crowd). As Bramble intimates, the application of the term was not restricted to the lower orders during this period.

18. *Gengzeng*: Ginseng, a drug made from the root of a species of *Panax* and thought to possess the power of restoring virility and vitality.

19. *sophistication*: Disingenuous alteration or deceptive modification.

20. *the Pump-room*: A gathering place for drinking the waters, built in 1706, and so called because the waters were pumped to it from the spring or well.

21. *inoculation*: Inoculation against smallpox was first popularized in England by Lady Mary Wortley Montagu (1689–1762), following her return from Constantinople in 1718.

To Miss WILLIS, at Gloucester
(from Lydia Melford, Bath, 26 April)

1. *heart-housewife*: A pocket-case for needles, pins, thread and scissors.

2. The merry bells ring round: John Milton (1608–74), *L'Allegro* (1631), line 93.

3. *the Master of the Ceremonies*: Samuel Derrick (1724–69) became Master of Ceremonies at Bath two years after the death of Richard 'Beau' Nash (1674–1761). An unsuccessful actor and author, Derrick had been employed by Smollett as a contributor to the *Critical Review*, for which he was restricted to reviewing 'trash' (minor or ephemeral) publications.

4. *Bladud's-row*: Named after the legendary King Bladud – who, as a prince, was supposed to have been cured of leprosy by bathing in the Bath spring.

5. *in dishabille*: Partly undressed or dressed in a negligent or careless style.

6. *the King's Bath*: The largest and most popular of the public baths, overlooked by the Pump Room.

7. *chip hats*: Hats made from thin strips of wood.

8. *hysterics*: Fits or convulsions, imagined as a disorder of the uterus.

9. *toymen*: Sellers of trinkets, knick-knacks or small ornamental articles.

10. *Mr Gill's, the pastry-cook*: Described as '*an eminent cook at* BATH', Gill was the subject of a song in Christopher Anstey's *The New Bath Guide* (1766), and also appears in the following lines of the poem: 'If the weather, cold and chill, / Calls us all to Mr. GILL, / ROMEO hands to me the Jelly, / Or the Soup of Vermicelli' (p. 61).

11. *the Grove*: Located near the Abbey and known as the Orange Grove from 1734, when Nash had an obelisk erected there in honour of the Prince of Orange, and of the health benefits that the Prince was supposed to have received by drinking the Bath waters.

12. *Spring-garden*: Developed as a pleasure resort around 1735, the Spring Garden was located east of the River Avon, opposite the Orange Grove.

13. *the theatre*: The Orchard Street Theatre, opened in 1750. In 1768, it became a Theatre Royal, under the direction of John Palmer (1742–1818).

14. *the two public rooms*: The 'lower rooms', one erected by Thomas
     Harrison in 1708, and later known as Simpson's, and the other,
     Lindsey's, later Wiltshire's, which was built in 1728. Both rooms
     were located on Terrace Walk, between the Orange Grove and
     North Parade.

To Mrs MARY JONES, at Brambleton-hall
(from Win Jenkins, Bath, 26 April)

1.   *a frank*: The superscribed signature of a person, such as a
     Member of Parliament, entitled to send letters post-free.
2.   *as innocent as the child unborn*: A variation upon the proverbial
     phrase 'innocent as a new-born babe'.
3.   *meat for their masters*: Proverbial. Cf. William Shakespeare,
     2 *Henry IV*, II.iv.121–2: 'I am meat for your master'.
4.   *trollopea*: The trollopee or slammerkin was a loose unbelted
     garment, popular as a morning gown from 1756 to 1770.
5.   *mantymaker*: Mantua-maker, i.e. a dressmaker. A mantua was a
     loose gown worn by women, fashionable especially in the late
     seventeenth and early eighteenth centuries.
6.   *fizzogmony*: Physiognomy.
7.   *the Prades, the Squires . . . and Harry King's Row*: i.e. the Parades,
     the Squares, the Circus, the Crescent, the Octagon, the Bladud
     Buildings and Harlequin's Row. The Octagon was the Octagon
     Chapel in Milsom Street, which opened in 1767.
8.   *values not her portion a brass varthing*: A variation upon the
     proverbial phrase 'not worth a brass farthing'.
9.   *a*: Dialect for 'have'.
10. *Aberga'ny*: Abergavenny in Monmouthshire, which was then in
     England, but is now in Wales.
11. *post-chaise*: A travelling carriage, either hired from stage to stage
     or drawn by horses so hired.
12. *bumbeseens*: Bombasine, a twilled or corded dress-material,
     composed of silk and worsted.
13. *chamberlye*: Urine, especially as used for washing.
14. *pumpydoor*: Possibly a long cloak made of satin or velvet and
     named after Jeanne-Antoinette Poisson, Madame de Pompadour
     (1721–64), mistress of Louis XV.
15. *turtle-water*: A cosmetic wash containing powdered tortoiseshell.

To Mrs GWYLLIM, house-keeper at Brambleton-hall
(from Tabitha Bramble, Bath, 26 April)

1. *Non-compush*: *Non compos* [*mentis*], not of sound mind (Latin).
2. *the shirt off his back*: A proverbial expression meaning 'to give away all one's possessions'.
3. *purl water*: A liquor made by infusing wormwood or other bitter herbs in ale or beer.

To Dr LEWIS
(from Matthew Bramble, Bath, 28 April)

1. *Ch—*: Dr Rice Charleton (1722/3–88), governor and physician at the Bath General Hospital and author of three tracts on the Bath waters: *A Chymical Analysis of the Bath Waters* (1750), *A Treatise on the Bath Waters* (1754) and *An Inquiry into the Efficacy of Bath Waters in Palsies* (1770).
2. *the king's-evil*: Scrofula, which in England was supposed to be curable by the king's touch.
3. *the duke of Kingston's private Bath*: Built between 1763 and 1766 for Evelyn Pierrepont, second duke of Kingston upon Hull (1712–73).
4. *porter*: Porter is a form of beer with a dark-brown colour and bitterish taste, brewed from malt partly charred or browned by drying at a high temperature.
5. *perry*: A beverage resembling cider, made from the juice of pears.
6. *coxcombs*: Conceited fools or fops.

To Sir WATKIN PHILLIPS, of Jesus college, Oxon
(from Jery Melford, Bath, 30 April)

1. *chemists, fiddlers, and buffoons*: An allusion to the description of Zimri – a satire on George Villiers, second duke of Buckingham (1628–87) – in John Dryden (1631–1700), *Absalom and Achitophel* (1681), line 550: 'Chymist, Fidler, States-man, and Buffoon' (*The Works of John Dryden: Poems 1681–1684*, ed. H. T. Swedenborg, Jr and Vinton A. Dearing (Berkeley and Los Angeles: University of California Press, 1972), p. 21).
2. *Abigail*: A lady's maid, or waiting-woman.
3. *mulatto heiress from St Christopher's*: A mixed-race daughter of a white West Indian planter. St Christopher's, more commonly known as St Kitt's, is one of the Leeward Islands.
4. *Southwark*: A traditionally disreputable borough on the south side of the River Thames in London, known for its prisons and inns.

5. *Wapping landlady*: Wapping is a suburb in the borough of Stepney, then chiefly populated by seamen, fishermen and associated tradesmen. During the eighteenth century, the term 'Wapping landlady' came to stand for a fat woman; Preston (pp. 356–7) offers a range of illustrative examples.

6. *Shoe-lane*: Located off Fleet Street in London.

7. *the chancellor of England*: Robert Henley, first earl of Northington (*c.* 1708–72), was chancellor from 1761 to 1766, represented Bath as an MP from 1747 to 1757, and suffered from gout.

8. *a cut bob*: A brushed-back bob wig, used for informal dress.

9. *James Quin*: James Quin (1693–1766), a leading actor during the 1730s and 1740s, associated particularly with the role of Falstaff and noted for his wit and sociability – a jest-book titled *Quin's Jests; or, The Facetious Man's Pocket-companion* was published in 1766. Quin had retired to Bath in 1751. Smollett had satirized him in both *The Adventures of Roderick Random* (1748) and *The Adventures of Peregrine Pickle* (1751), but the pair had since been reconciled.

10. *Squaretoes*: A precise, formal, old-fashioned person, with strict or narrow ideas of conduct; the term derives from square-toed shoes.

11. *the Bear*: The Bear Inn in Stall Street; also a setting in Anstey's *The New Bath Guide*.

12. *sirreverence*: A euphemism for human excrement.

13. *phaeton and four*: A lightly constructed, four-wheeled open carriage, drawn by four horses.

14. *Avon-street*: A nondescript thoroughfare in the lower part of Bath town, home to lower-order families and with a high concentration of alehouses and traffic.

15. *sweet-meats*: Sweet food or confectionery, such as sugared cakes.

16. *nosegays*: Bunches of flowers or herbs.

17. *Billingsgate*: A fish-market in the city of London, noted for foul language and abuse.

18. *Puddle-dock*: An insalubrious area in Blackfriars.

19. *St James's palace*: The royal residence, located on Pall Mall just north of St James's Park.

20. *shake-bag*: A bird in a cock-fight or 'main'.

21. *quails upon the frightful porcofine*: Misquoted from Shakespeare, *Hamlet*, I.v.20: 'Like quills upon the fretful porcupine'.

22. *game*: Possessing the spirit of a game-cock.

23. *Dunghill*: Cowardly or spiritless; not 'game'.

24. *St Giles's parish*: Saint Giles-in-the-Fields, notable for its high incidence of gin shops and crime.
25. *mew*: A cage for confining animals, especially poultry, for fattening.
26. *Mrs Helen Gwynn*: Eleanor 'Nell' Gwyn (1651?–1687), actress and mistress of Charles II.
27. *John Dory*: The name of a fish, sometimes associated with Quin.
28. *O tempora! O mores!*: O the times! O the customs! (a common Latin tag).

To Dr LEWIS
(from Matthew Bramble, Bath, 5 May)

1. *wheel machine*: A large chair on wheels for invalids, also known as a 'Bath-chair'.
2. *in this high goût*: In this high flavour; with such strong relish.
3. *the General Advertiser*: A newspaper, founded in 1734 as the *London Daily Post and General Advertiser*, which became the *General Advertiser* in 1744 and the *Public Advertiser* in 1752.

To Miss LÆTITIA WILLIS, at Gloucester
(from Lydia Melford, Bath, 6 May)

1. *and wonders with a foolish face of curiosity*: Adapted from Alexander Pope (1688–1744), *An Epistle from Mr Pope to Dr Arbuthnot* (1735), line 212: 'And wonder with a foolish face of praise'.
2. *the Dog-days*: The days when either the greater dog-star, Sirius, or the lesser dog-star, Procyon, rises before the sun; noted from ancient times as the hottest and most unwholesome period of the year.

To Sir WATKIN PHILLIPS, of Jesus college, Oxon
(from Jery Melford, Bath, 6 May)

1. *Comus*: The Roman god of revelry.
2. *the Three Tuns*: A well-known inn in Stall Street.
3. *epicure*: Someone who cultivates a refined taste for the pleasures of the table.
4. *old maid*: A derogatory term for an ageing spinster, commonly used at this time.
5. *fidus Achates*: Proverbial for a faithful companion or bosom friend; from the character of Achates in Virgil's *Aeneid*.
6. *noli me tangere*: Touch me not (Latin): Christ's words to Mary Magdalene after the Resurrection (John 20:17). Also a medical

term, referring to various conditions causing persistent and spreading ulceration of the skin and underlying tissue, especially of the face.

7. *Chowder ... Newfoundland*: Chowder is a dish made of fresh fish (especially cod) or clams, stewed with slices of pork or bacon, onions, and biscuit, and eaten in such places as Newfoundland and New England.

8. *Swansey*: Swansea, a seaport town in South Wales.

9. *the puny monarch*: The Master of Ceremonies was known as the 'king of Bath', but Derrick himself lacked physical stature and suffered from comparison with his predecessor, Nash.

10. *like the red cow ... Tom Thumb*: Alluding to the tale in which Tom's mother ties him to a thistle while she milks a cow, and the cow eats up both the thistle and Tom. The tale would have been well known from contemporary chapbooks and from the use that Henry Fielding (1707–54) had made of it in his frequently staged farce *Tom Thumb: A Tragedy* (1730), revised in 1731 as *The Tragedy of Tragedies; or, the Life and Death of Tom Thumb the Great*.

11. *a penitent sinner may be forgiven*: An allusion to Luke 15:10.

12. *the offended fair*: i.e. the offended fair one; Jery mimics the language of French romance literature.

To Dr Lewis
(from Matthew Bramble, Bath, 8 May)

1. *flying-machines*: A common term for swift stage coaches.

2. *Chinese gudgeons*: Chinese variety of *Gobio fluviatilis*, a small European fresh-water fish often used for bait; figuratively, a credulous or gullible person, who will swallow anything.

3. *undertaker*: Probably a business contractor, rather than a funeral director.

4. *an Egyptian gale*: Egypt was thought to have been the source of the bubonic plague.

5. *spirit of hartshorn*: The aqueous solution of ammonia, used as smelling salts.

6. *a compound of villainous smells*: An allusion to Falstaff's words in Shakespeare's *The Merry Wives of Windsor*, III.v.84–6: 'the rankest compound of villainous smell that ever offended nostril'.

7. *hungary-water*: A distilled water made of rosemary flowers infused in refined spirit of wine.

8. *sal volatile*: Ammonium carbonate, an aromatic solution of which is used as a restorative in fainting fits.

9. *O Rus, quando te aspiciam!*: Slightly misquoted from Horace, *Satires*, II.vi.60: '*O rus, quando ego te aspiciam*!' ('O rural home, when shall I behold you?').

To Sir WATKIN PHILLIPS, of Jesus college, Oxon
(from Jery Melford, Bath, 10 May)

1. *spital*: Foul or loathsome place.
2. *the horseguards*: The cavalry brigade of the English Household troops (more specifically the third regiment, the Royal Horse Guards). Horse Guards Parade is adjacent to St James's Park.
3. *Paunceford*: Identified as Alexander Campbell (*d.* 1781). After making his fortune in India, Campbell had proved ungrateful to his former benefactors, including Smollett.
4. *Don Quixote*: The hero of the Spanish classic *The History and Adventures of the Renowned Don Quixote* (published in two parts in 1604/5 and 1614/15) by Miguel de Cervantes Saavedra (1547–1616). Smollett's two-volume translation was published in 1755. Guided by an antiquated code of chivalric conduct, and accompanied by his earthy squire, Sancho Panza, Don Quixote's behaviour represents a romantic – but also naïve and possibly dangerous – idealism.
5. *gravel*: A disease characterized by collections of urinary crystals.

To Mrs MARY JONES, at Brambleton-hall
(from Win Jenkins, Bath, 15 May)

1. *a flea in his ear*: Proverbial for an unwelcome or unexpected rebuke.
2. *siserary*: A severe rebuke or scolding.
3. *dish-clout*: Dish cloth.
4. *cowitch*: The stinging hairs of the pod of the tropical plant *Mucuna pruriens*.
5. *swinging*: Swingeing, huge or immense.
6. *mare . . . potticary*: Mayor . . . apothecary.
7. *cruperal oaf*: Corporal oath: an oath ratified by touching a sacred object, especially the Gospels.
8. *merry bones*: Marrowbones, the shin-bones or knees.
9. *gallow manky*: Calamanco, a popular woollen fabric from Flanders, glossy on the surface, and woven with a satin twill and chequered in the warp, so that the checks are seen on one side only.

To Sir WATKIN PHILLIPS, Bart of Jesus college, Oxon
(from Jery Melford, Bath, 17 May)

1. *Bristol-well ... Harrowgate*: All popular spa towns and sea resorts at various points during the eighteenth century. Brighthelmstone was the ancient name for Brighton.
2. *hectic*: Exhibiting the flushed, dry-skinned appearance symptomatic of consumption and other wasting diseases.
3. *morbi eruditorum*: Maladies of the learned (Latin).
4. *on the foundation of Queen's*: In possession of a scholarship at Queen's College, Oxford.
5. *gentleman-commoner*: A commoner was a student who paid fees, in contrast to being 'on the foundation'. Gentleman-commoners were a privileged class of undergraduates, distinguished from ordinary commoners by special academic dress, separate dining arrangements and certain academic freedoms.
6. *the advowson of a good living*: The right of presentation to a benefice, an ecclesiastical position.
7. *butt*: Target of satire; more precisely, 'A dependant, poor relation, or simpleton, on whom all kinds of practical jokes are played off, and who serves as a butt for all the shafts of wit and ridicule' (Grose).
8. *cassock*: A long, close-fitting frock or tunic worn by Anglican clergymen.
9. *break no squares*: Do no harm.

To Dr LEWIS
(from Matthew Bramble, Bath, 19 May)

1. *Golden-square*: A small square located east of Regent Street and north of Piccadilly Circus.
2. *Mr T—*: Identified as the painter John Taylor (1745?–1806), whose landscapes with classical ruins were much admired in the 1760s and 1770s.
3. *p—ts*: Parliaments.
4. *G. H—*: George Heathcote (1700–1768), sheriff, alderman, MP and, in 1742, lord mayor of London.
5. *exceptions ... a general canon*: Exceptions that prove the rule (proverbial).

To Dr Lewis
(from Tabitha Bramble, Bath, 19 May)

1. *pad*: Either a horse for riding or a kind of saddle.
2. *rogered*: From 'To roger', slang for sexual intercourse with a woman. As Grose explains: 'TO ROGER. To bull, or lie with a woman: from the name of Roger being frequently given to a bull.'

To Sir Watkin Phillips, of Jesus college, Oxon
(from Jery Melford, London, 24 May)

1. *Marlborough Downs*: A valley of chalk uplands near the town of Marlborough in Wiltshire.
2. *fairly*: Completely.
3. *the sister Furies*: The Roman version of the Greek Erinyes – Megaera, Tisiphone and Alecto – who avenged crimes against kindred blood, especially matricide.
4. *virago*: A bold, masculine woman.
5. *pinking*: Narrowing, peering or blinking.
6. *tatterdemalion*: A person in tattered clothing, beggarly fellow or ragamuffin.
7. *Humphry Clinker*: Clinker's Christian name possibly alludes to the slang phrase 'To dine with Duke Humphrey', meaning to go without dinner. 'Clinker' may allude to the coals used by Humphry in his occupation as a farrier.
8. *the poor's rate*: The 1601 *Act for the Relief of the Poore* (43 Eliz. I, c. 2) provided for the collection of money, by churchwardens or parish overseers, to furnish material for the able-bodied poor to work with; for the establishment of apprenticeships for poor children; and for the collection of 'competent Sums of Money for and towards the necessary Relief of the Lame, Impotent, Old, Blind'.
9. *guinea*: An English gold coin, equivalent in value to twenty-one shillings.
10. *Spin-Hill*: Speen hill, near the village of Speenhamland in Berkshire.
11. *Salt-hill*: A village near Slough in Buckinghamshire.
12. *all the days of his life*: An allusion to Luke 1:75.
13. *rowel*: In farriery, a rowel is a circular piece of leather or other material with a hole in the centre, inserted between the flesh and skin of a horse or other animal to cause the discharge of humours.

14. *single-stick . . . Nancy Dawson*: Single-stick was a form of fighting or fencing with one hand, using a stick with a guard or basket. A Jew's harp is a small steel instrument which is held against the teeth or lips and plucked with the finger (also known in England as a gewgaw). 'Black-ey'd Susan' was a popular song written by the poet and playwright John Gay (1685–1732). 'Arthur-o'Bradley' was the name of a popular ballad. 'Nancy Dawson' was a hornpipe – a solo dance to the accompaniment of a wind instrument – named after Nancy Dawson (1728–67), who came to public attention when she danced it during a production of Gay's *The Beggar's Opera* (1728) at Covent Garden Theatre in 1759.

15. *to dinner with what appetite you may*: An allusion to William Shakespeare (and John Fletcher), *Henry VIII*, III.ii.203–4.

16. *livery*: The clothing worn by a servant.

To Dr LEWIS
(from Matthew Bramble, London, 20 May)

1. *'London is now gone out of town'*: Quoted from James Bramston, *The Art of Politicks* (1729), p. 10: 'Such Piles of Buildings now rise up and down; / London itself seems going out of Town'.

2. *paved and lighted . . . formerly*: London's streets were much improved by the provisions of various Acts passed for that purpose during the 1760s, beginning with the Westminster Paving Act of 1762, which provided for the appointment of commissioners to pave and repair the streets.

3. *bridge at Blackfriars*: Blackfriars Bridge, designed by the Scottish architect and engineer Robert Mylne (1733–1811). Begun in 1760, the bridge was opened for horse traffic in 1768 and for carriage traffic in 1769.

4. *like a dropsical head . . . support*: A common contemporary image of London as the increasingly swollen head of the national body.

5. *the bills of mortality*: Roughly, the area in and around London; the term derived from the record of burials and baptisms kept and published by the Company of Parish Clerks.

6. *petit maitre*: Petit-maître (French): an effeminate man; a dandy, fop, or coxcomb.

7. *pettifogger*: A legal practitioner of inferior status.

8. *all tread upon the kibes of one another*: An allusion to Shakespeare's *Hamlet*, V.i.135–7: 'The age is grown so picked that the

toe of the peasant comes so near the heel of the courtier he galls his kibe.'

9. *hand-gallop*: An easy gallop in which the horse is kept well in hand to prevent excess speed.

10. *Ranelagh*: Ranelagh Gardens in Chelsea, which had opened in 1742 as a rival to Vauxhall Gardens. Evening admission was ordinarily half a crown (two shillings and sixpence), making it the most expensive, and exclusive, of London's pleasure gardens. The centrepiece attraction at Ranelagh was the magnificent Rotunda (measuring 555 feet in circumference), in which London's fashionable elite promenaded in a circular motion, listened to the orchestra, and took (non-alcoholic) refreshments. Outdoor features included the (so-called) Chinese House or Venetian Temple, while occasional entertainments included masquerade balls, firework displays and concerts.

11. *Vauxhall*: Vauxhall Gardens, formerly known as the New Spring Garden, had opened in its most recent incarnation in 1732. The most popular of London's pleasure gardens, Vauxhall ordinarily charged a shilling for admission. The many attractions at Vauxhall included a rotunda, statues, a cascade, concerts, supper-boxes, paintings and the covered walkways, which were lit up at night by more than a thousand lamps. Probably the most famous feature was a statue of George Friedric Handel (1685–1759) by the sculptor Louis François Roubiliac (1702–62).

12. *Bedlam*: Bethlehem Hospital in Moorfields, for the insane.

13. *sub dio*: Under the open sky; in the open air (Latin).

14. *pot-valiant*: Emboldened through inebriation.

To Miss LÆTITIA WILLIS, at Gloucester
(from Lydia Melford, London, 31 May)

1. *three stupendous bridges*: London Bridge, Westminster Bridge and Blackfriars Bridge.

2. *the Arabian Nights' Entertainment, and the Persian Tales*: The former possibly refers to the popular English translation, *Arabian Nights Entertainments* (1721–2), which reached its twelfth edition in 1767; the latter refers to the *Contes persans* of François Pétis de la Croix (1653–1713), which was translated into English in 1709.

3. *the famous Tenducci*: Giusto Ferdinando Tenducci (c. 1735–90), the Italian castrato, or male soprano.

4. *picturesque*: Possessing striking or effective pictorial qualities, if not necessarily the highest beauty or sublimity.

5. *the celebrated Mrs —*: Not clearly identified. Preston (p. 369) lists a number of possible candidates.
6. *scratch periwig*: A small short wig which allowed the natural hair to be combed into it; perhaps so called because it allowed easy head-scratching (Ross, p. 413).
7. *a broken head*: A head from which blood has been drawn (not necessarily a broken skull).
8. *capuchin*: A cloak and hood worn by a woman, made in imitation of the dress of Capuchin friars.
9. *Mrs Cornelys' assembly*: Theresa Imer (1723?–1797), a Venetian singer and impressario, organized fashionable assemblies at Carlisle House in Soho Square between 1760 and 1772. Admittance was by subscription only; the entertainment included concerts, balls, masquerades, dancing, refreshments and gambling.
10. *hoyden*: An ill-bred or inelegant woman.
11. *rumpt gown*: A gown with a bustle or false rump.
12. *lappet-head*: A head-dress with streamers or flaps.
13. *rout*: A fashionable gathering, large evening party or reception.

To Sir WATKIN PHILLIPS, of Jesus college, Oxon
(from Jery Melford, London, 2 June)

1. *coming*: Inclined to make or meet advances; ready, eager, complaisant, forward.
2. *panegyrick*: Discourse in praise of a person or thing.
3. *deliciæ humani generis*: Delight of the human race (Latin). From Suetonius' description of Titus (AD 41–81), Roman Emperor from AD 79–81.
4. *Augustus ... Marcus Aurelius in philosophy*: The Roman emperors cited here are Octavius Caesar Augustus (63 BC–AD 14), Titus Flavius Vespasianus (AD 9–79), Marcus Ulpius Nerva Trajanus (AD 52–117) and Marcus Aurelius Antoninus (AD 121–80). The virtues ascribed to them by Barton were commonplace.
5. *duke of C[umberland]*: William Augustus, duke of Cumberland (1721–65), known as 'the Butcher' following the slaughter of the Jacobite forces at Culloden in 1746.
6. *royal nephews*: George III's younger brothers were Edward Augustus (1739–67), William Henry (1743–1805), Henry Frederick (1745–90) and Frederick William (1750–65).
7. *the queen*: Queen Charlotte (1744–1818).
8. *the favourite yearl*: John Stuart, third earl of Bute (1713–92), controversial Scottish adviser to George III. Bute relinquished his

position as first lord of the treasury in April 1763. Smollett's ministerial, pro-Bute weekly, *The Briton*, ran from 29 May 1762–12 February 1763.

9. *shorn of his beams*: An allusion to John Milton, *Paradise Lost* (1667), I, 596.

10. *the grand pensionary*: William Pitt (1708–78), also known as Pitt the Elder. A popular war minister, formerly associated with the patriot Opposition and (in 1757) dubbed the 'Great Commoner', Pitt was granted an annual pension of £3,000 in 1761 (with a barony conferred upon his wife), and in 1766 accepted a peerage, becoming first earl of Chatham.

11. *two satellites*: Probably John Wilkes (1725–97), politician and editor of the anti-ministerial weekly the *North Briton* (5 June 1762–28 May 1763), issue number 45 of which (23 April 1763) comprised a much-noted attack by Wilkes upon the king; and Richard Grenville-Temple, second Earl Temple (1711–79), politician and brother-in-law to Pitt the Elder.

12. *lick up every knave and blockhead in his way*: An allusion to Alexander Pope, *The Dunciad, Variorum* (1729), III, 298: 'And licks up every blockhead in the way'.

13. *duke of N—*: Thomas Pelham-Holles, duke of Newcastle-upon-Tyne and first duke of Newcastle-under-Lyme (1693–1768). Newcastle was a former Secretary of State (1724–54) and Prime Minister (1754–6). Smollett's presentation of him as highly eccentric reflects the common opinion of the time.

14. *Mr A—*: Possibly John Almon (1737–1805), bookseller and political journalist.

15. *The king of Prussia*: Frederick II (1712–86), known as Frederick the Great.

16. *Dymkymraig*: A fictitious place name meaning 'no Welsh', i.e. 'I don't speak Welsh' (from the Welsh phrase, 'dim Cymraeg').

17. *Odso!*: A profane oath, or euphemistic slang, for 'God!' or 'In God's name!'.

18. *first-mover*: An allusion to Robert Walpole, first earl of Orford (1676–1745). Walpole had been Prime Minister from around 1721/22 to 1742.

19. *president of the council . . . treasury*: The office of first lord of the treasury is generally held by the Prime Minister. While Newcastle did hold this office in 1754–56 and 1757–62, he never held the office of Lord President of the Privy Council.

20. *neither profit nor pleasure*: Clinker echoes the language of contemporary sermons against profane swearing. As Thomas

Bradbury argued in *The Sin and Danger of Profane Swearing Expos'd, in Several Sermons* (1742), 'A Swearer sins without the least Temptation of Profit or Pleasure' (p. 53).

21. *own withers . . . unwrung*: An allusion to Shakespeare's *Hamlet*, III.ii.231.

22. *no distinction of persons*: An allusion to Colossians 3:25.

23. *the bon ton*: Polite or fashionable society (French).

24. *timeo Danaos et Dona ferentes*: Taken from Virgil, *Aeneid*, 2, 49: 'I fear the Greeks, even when [they are] bringing gifts'.

To Dr Lewis
(from Matthew Bramble, London, 2 June)

1. *British Museum*: The British Museum had opened in 1759. Its holdings were based upon the extensive and valuable collection bequested to the nation by Sir Hans Sloane (1660–1753).

2. *in terrorem*: In order to terrify or frighten (Latin).

3. *duty upon stamps and advertisements*: The Stamp Act of 1712 had imposed a duty on paper documents such as newspapers and advertisements.

4. *Dettingen*: The Battle of Dettingen (27 June 1743), during the War of the Austrian Succession.

5. *Lugano, a town of the Grisons*: Lugano is the largest town in the canton of Ticino, in south-eastern Switzerland. It was formerly the capital of the canton of Lugano, rather than in the Grisons, which is a large canton in eastern Switzerland.

6. *wot*: Knows.

7. *bastinado*: A beating with a stick, or cudgelling.

8. *to connive at drunkenness . . . the excise*: The 'Gin Act' of 1736 (9 Geo. II, c. 23) had placed a duty on liquor.

9. *ipse dixit*: He himself said it (Latin). Used in reference to an unsupported assertion, accepted solely on the speaker's word. The 'new Pythagoras' referred to here may be John Shebbeare (1709–88), physician, political writer and literary antagonist of Smollett.

10. *Milton . . . poetical merit*: The writers cited here are John Milton; John Dryden; Samuel Butler (1613–80), author of the satiric poem *Hudibras* (1662–3); Jonathan Swift (1667–1745), author of the prose satires *A Tale of a Tub* (1704) and *Travels into Several Remote Nations of the World* (1726), also known as *Gulliver's Travels*; William Congreve (1670–1729), author of the comic plays *Love for Love* (1695) and *The Way of the World* (1700); and Alexander Pope.

11. *a rival bard*: Possibly the poet Charles Churchill (1732–64), an ally of John Wilkes.

12. *ex cathedra*: From the chair (Latin), i.e. in the manner of someone speaking from a seat of office or professorial chair, and hence with authority.

13. *Grub-street*: The name of a real street in London, but also the symbolic location of professional authors, often regarded as venal 'hack' writers.

14. *Aristarchus*: The Greek critic and grammarian Aristarchus (*c*. 217–*c*. 147 BC). In the revised four-book version of *The Dunciad* (1743), Pope had mocked the philologist and classical scholar Richard Bentley (1662–1742) as a pedantic, modern-day 'Aristarchus'.

15. *myrmidons*: Sycophantic supporters or hangers-on.

16. *difficilis, querulus, laudator temporis acti*: From Horace, *Ars Poetica*, line 173: 'peevish, surly, given to praising the days he spent as a boy'.

17. *'change*: The Royal Exchange, which had been rebuilt in 1669, having been destroyed by the Great Fire of London. Located in Threadneedle Street, the capital's major financial district, the Exchange housed numerous business offices and shops.

18. *does nothing but smile, like Malvolio in the play*: An allusion to Maria's description of Malvolio in Shakespeare's *Twelfth Night*, III.iv.11.

To Mrs MARY JONES, at Brambleton-hall
(from Win Jenkins, London, 3 June)

1. *crumlecks*: From the Welsh word 'cromlech', meaning a prehistoric structure consisting of a large flat unhewn stone resting horizontally on three or more upright stones.

2. *fillitch*: Village.

3. *paleass of Saint Gimses*: Palace of St James's.

4. *the hillyfents, and pye bald ass*: The elephants and female zebra, owned by Queen Charlotte and on display at St James's Park.

5. *the crowns and wild beastis*: The crown jewels and the lions at the Tower of London.

6. *play the dickens*: Cause mischief or havoc.

7. *honeymils*: Animals.

8. *firchin*: Virgin.

9. *Thou shalt not . . . neighbour*: An allusion to Exodus 20:16.

10. *Sadler's-wells*: Located in Islington, Sadler's Wells boasted a spa and a theatre but was mainly associated with more plebeian

or popular-cultural entertainments, such as juggling, tumbling, rope-dancing and harlequinades.

11. *glory that shall be revealed hereafter*: An allusion to Romans 8:18.

12. *puffed up with vanity*: An allusion to Colossians 2:18.

13. *freezer*: Friseur, i.e. hairdresser (French).

14. *vanity and vexation of spirit*: An allusion to Ecclesiastes 1:14.

15. *Tabernacle*: The Tabernacle of George Whitefield (1714–70), the charismatic but controversial Methodist preacher, which was built in Moorfields in 1741. Win may possibly be referring to Whitefield's Tottenham Court Road Chapel, which was opened in 1756.

To Sir WATKIN PHILLIPS, of Jesus college, Oxon (from Jery Melford, London, 5 June)

1. *gown and cassock*: i.e. a bishop.

2. *the late duke of Ormond*: James Butler, second duke of Ormond (1665–1745), army officer, politician and conspirator in the Jacobite rebellion in 1715.

3. *wise-acre*: A foolish person with an air or affectation of wisdom.

4. *Since Grenville was turned out*: John Carteret, second Earl Granville (1690–1763), had resigned from his position as Secretary of State in November 1744, following political manoeuvrings by the duke of Newcastle and his brother Henry Pelham (1694–1754).

5. *green-horn*: A novice, i.e. inexperienced.

6. *a horsetail*: Used in Turkey as an ensign, denoting the rank of a pasha.

7. *stewed prunes*: Used as a laxative.

8. *the Five Nations . . . Kickshaws*: The Five Nations was actually composed of six nations, who together made up the Iroquois Confederation. Newcastle refers, imprecisely, to the Tuscaroras, the Mohawks, the Ottowas, the Creeks and the Chickashaws.

9. *stinkubus, and wampum*: Stinkibus means bad liquor, especially adulterated spirits. Wampum is a North American Indian currency, consisting of cylindrical shell beads.

10. *Milfordhaven*: Milford Haven is a town in Pembrokeshire, Wales.

11. *Tyburn*: Location of the hanging tree.

12. *C— T—*: Charles Townshend (1725–67), politician, who held the positions of Secretary at War (1761–2), Paymaster-General (1765) and Chancellor of the Exchequer (1766–7).

13. *the great political bully*: William Pitt, the 'great pensioner'.

14. *Hector*: The Trojan prince and warrior who leads his nation's army during the Trojan War but is finally slain by Achilles, as described in Homer's *Iliad*.

15. *preaching to the desert*: A Biblical commonplace.

16. *Spring-garden*: The old Spring Garden at Charing Cross, rather than the 'new' Spring Garden, which was now known as Vauxhall Gardens.

17. *Society for the Encouragement of the Arts*: The Society for the Encouragement of Arts, Manufactures and Commerce, which was founded in 1754 'to embolden enterprize, to enlarge Science, to refine Art, to improve our Manufactures, and extend our Commerce' (Thomas Mortimer, *A Concise Account of the Rise, Progress and Present State of the Society for the Encouragement of Arts, Manufactures, and Commerce* (1763), p. 12).

18. *Little Theatre in the Hay-market*: Built in 1720, the Little Haymarket Theatre had recently been remodelled and extended under the direction of the playwright Samuel Foote (1721–77), who in 1766 had been granted a royal patent to stage plays there during the summer season.

19. *ridotto*: A fashionable entertainment or social assembly consisting of music and dancing.

20. *hop*: A dancing-party, especially of an informal or unceremonious kind.

21. *Rotherhithe*: A seaman's district on the south bank of the Thames.

22. *Petty France*: Spitalfields, an area of London settled by Huguenot immigrants following the Revocation of the Edict of Nantes in 1685.

23. *the Fleet*: The Fleet Prison, by Fleet river; mainly a jail for debtors and bankrupts.

24. *Disputer and Ruddiman*: Johannes Despauterius (*c.* 1460–*c.* 1520), a Flemish grammarian, and Thomas Ruddiman (1674–1757), a Scottish printer, classical scholar and librarian.

VOLUME TWO

To Dr Lewis
(from Matthew Bramble, London, 8 June)

1. *fable of the monkey and the pig*: A version of this jest is reproduced in Preston, pp. 379–81.

2. *ben trovata*: Well invented or well expressed (Italian). The correct spelling is *ben trovato*.

3. *have his degree in his pocket*: Rather than taking degrees, trained apothecaries received licences to practise.

4. *in utrumque paratus*: From Virgil's *Aeneid*, II, 61: 'ready for either event' (i.e. ready for anything).

5. *the busy haunts of men*: Possibly an allusion to John Hoole (1727–1803), *Cyrus: A Tragedy* (1768). In Act I, Cyrus' father, Mithranes, states that 'for thee I've watch'd / The tedious round of twenty circling years / Each turn of fate, in this sequester'd dwelling, / Far distant from the busy haunts of men' (p. 13). Hoole may have adapted or misremembered Milton's *L'Allegro*, line 118: 'the busy hum of men'.

6. *watchmen*: Men appointed to keep watch and ward in towns from sunset to sunrise.

7. *an open aqueduct*: The 'New River' that had been built in the early seventeenth century by Sir Hugh Myddleton (*c.* 1556–1631) to supply London with drinking water from springs at Amwell and Chadwell, near Ware in Hertfordshire.

8. *balderdashed*: Adulterated with a jumbled mixture of inferior ingredients.

9. *staved*: Broken up a cask of wine (or, as here, port) into staves, or broken into it and let out the contents.

10. *right Colchester*: The English town of Colchester was famous for its oysters, which were known as 'Colchesters' or 'Colchester natives'.

11. *barrow-bunter*: Someone employed in wheeling a barrow. In London and its vicinity, a barrow was a small, two-wheeled cart pushed by the shafts – a hand-cart or 'costermonger's barrow'.

12. *draff*: The refuse or grains of malt left after brewing or distilling.

13. *drab*: A dirty and untidy woman; a slattern.

14. *cum grano salis*: With a grain of salt, i.e. sceptically (Latin).

15. *tartar*: A rough and violent or irritable and intractable person, supposedly resembling a Tartar in disposition.

16. *jucunda oblivia vitæ*: Horace, *Satires*, II.vi.62: 'sweet forgetfulness of life's cares'.

To Sir WATKIN PHILLIPS, Bart of Jesus college, Oxon (from Jery Melford, London, 10 June)

1. *S—*: Smollett himself. The author resided at Monmouth House in Old Chelsea from 1750 to 1763.

2. *Calvert's entire butt beer*: Porter ('butt beer') from Calvert's brewery.

3.   *reasons that I need not explain*: Because debtors were safe from arrest on Sundays.

4.   *flapped*: With the flaps of the hat turned down.

5.   *Wat Wyvil, the poet*: Knapp (p. 363) suggests William Woty (1732–91), a popular minor poet.

6.   *lord Bolingbroke's metaphysical works*: Works by the politician and freethinking author Henry St John, first Viscount Bolingbroke (1678–1751).

7.   *The Ballance of the English Poets*: A fictitious title. As Preston notes (p. 384), Smollett may be alluding to an essay entitled 'The Poetical Scale', which had appeared in the *Literary Magazine* for January 1758. In the essay, the English poets are rated on a scale of one to twenty for genius, judgement, learning and versification.

8.   *liberties of the King's Bench*: The King's Bench Prison mainly housed debtors and those charged with libel. As with the Fleet Prison, payment of a fee allowed prisoners to reside within the 'liberties', beyond the prison walls.

9.   *tipstaff*: An officer appointed by the marshal of the King's Bench, to take charge of prisoners on their way to court.

10. *filbert walk*: A path shaded by cultivated hazelnut trees.

11. *jemmy boots*: Stylish riding boots.

12. *Marshalsea court*: The court at Marshalsea Prison in Southwark, which held debtors and prisoners committed for crimes at sea.

13. *Ashley's*: James Ashley's Punch-House in Fleet Street.

14. *captain Pistol in the play*: Captain Pistol appears in two of Shakespeare's plays, 2 *Henry IV* and *Henry V*.

15. *larding the lean earth as he puff'd along*: An allusion to Shakespeare, 1 *Henry IV*, II.iii.17.

16. *a slip of sheep-skin*: A court order, written on sheepskin or parchment.

17. *transportation*: Deportation to a penal settlement.

18. *the Old Bailey*: Justice Hall, or the Sessions House, in Old Bailey Street next to Newgate Prison.

19. *cordwainer*: A worker in cordwain or cordovan leather; a shoemaker.

20. *Smithfield*: An area in west London, the site of a popular market and, in the summer, of St Bartholomew's Fair.

21. *a bulk*: A framework projecting from the front of a shop; a stall.

22. *St Martin's church*: The church of St Martin-in-the-Fields, located in the north-east corner of Trafalgar Square.

23. *spunging-house*: Sponging-house, a house kept by a bailiff or sheriff's officer as an initial place of confinement for debtors.

24. *act for the relief of insolvent debtors*: The most recent Act for the Relief of Insolvent Debtors had been passed in 1769 (9 Geo. III, c. 26); there were two previous Acts of this kind during the 1760s. Such Acts released all prisoners held in custody for debt on a certain date (in this instance 29 September 1768).

25. *a literary journal*: The *Critical Review*, which was founded by Smollett in 1756. Smollett edited and contributed to the journal until 1763.

26. *in petto*: Within the breast, i.e. held in reserve or undisclosed (Italian).

27. *Salmon*: Thomas Salmon (1679–1767), a historian and geographer, who had accompanied George Anson (1697–1762) on his voyage around the world.

28. *Psalmonazar*: George Psalmanazar (1679–1763), a French impostor who claimed to be a native of Formosa (now Taiwan), invented a Formosan language, and provided sensational accounts of Formosan customs, in *An Historical and Geographical Description of Formosa* (1704). Repenting of his deceit, he later settled into a life of piety and literary hack-work.

29. *Guy*: Thomas Guy (1644/5?–1724), bookseller, philanthropist, and founder of Guy's Hospital.

To Miss LÆTITIA WILLIS, at Gloucester
(from Lydia Melford, 10 June)

1. *etuis*: A small case, usually ornamental, for articles such as bodkins, needles and toothpicks (French).

To Sir WATKIN PHILLIPS, of Jesus college, Oxon
(from Jery Melford, London, 10 June)

1. *the Bull and Gate*: An inn in Holborn; also a location in Henry Fielding's *The History of Tom Jones, A Foundling* (1749) and in Smollett's *The Adventures of Sir Launcelot Greaves* (1760–61).

2. *Longacre*: A street running between Drury Lane and St Martin's Lane.

3. *light . . . the king's taxes*: A pun on *light* as 'window' and thus on the contemporary window tax.

4. *farthing candle to the sun at noon*: Adapted from Edward Young (1683–1765), *Love of Fame, The Universal Passion*, 2nd edn (1728), VII, 97–8: 'How commentators each *dark* passage shun, / And hold their farthing candle to the *sun*' (p. 167).

5. *a chosen vessel*: An allusion to Acts 9:15.

6. *Will-i'the-wisp*: Will-o'-the-wisp, something that deludes or mis-
   leads by fugitive appearances.
7. *for conscience sake*: An allusion to Matthew 5:10.
8. *Mr W——'s preaching*: Another reference to George Whitefield,
   the Methodist preacher.
9. *primum mobile*: Instigator or prime mover (Latin).

To Dr Lewis
(from Matthew Bramble, London, 12 June)

1. *innamorata*: *Inamorata*, a female lover, mistress or sweetheart
   (Italian).
2. *billet*: A short informal letter or note (French).
3. *the incomparable Hogarth*: William Hogarth (1697–1764),
   painter and engraver, noted particularly for his conversation
   pieces, satiric engravings and narrative paintings in series on
   'modern moral subjects'. The three series titled *A Harlot's Progress*, *A Rake's Progress* and *Marriage à-la-mode* achieved great
   popularity following their publication in engraved form during
   the 1730s and 1740s. Smollett is thought to have based the
   garrulous painter Pallet, in *Peregrine Pickle*, on Hogarth.
4. *justice Buzzard*: Possibly Sir John Hawkins (1719–89), justice of
   the peace in Middlesex from 1761.
5. *Clerkenwell prison*: The prison in Clerkenwell known as Bridewell – 'bridewell' being a generic name for a house of correction.

To Sir Watkin Phillips, of Jesus college, Oxon
(from Jery Melford, London, 11 June)

1. *inns of court*: The four sets of buildings in London (the Inner
   Temple, the Middle Temple, Lincoln's Inn and Gray's Inn)
   belonging to the four legal societies that oversee admittance to
   the bar, to practise law.
2. *king's evidence*: Evidence for the Crown given by the accused
   against their alleged accomplices.
3. *whore of Babylon*: An allusion to Revelations 17.
4. *mittimus*: A warrant issued by a justice of the peace, committing
   a person to custody (Latin).
5. *lime-twigs*: Twigs smeared with birdlime, for catching birds.
6. *Turenne*: Henri de la Tour d'Auvergne, vicomte de Turenne
   (1611–75), French military hero and Marshal of France.
7. *pathetic*: Emotionally affecting.
8. *Rabbit him!*: Confound him! (colloquial). Compare Francis
   Grose (1731–91), *A Provincial Glossary, with a Collection of*

Local Proverbs and Popular Superstitions (1787): '*D'rabbit it*, a vulgar exclamation or abbreviation of God rabbit it, a foolish evasion of an oath.'

9. *garnish*: A slang term for money extorted from a new prisoner, either as a jailer's fee (as here) or as drink-money for the other prisoners.

10. *Hounslow*: A heath in west London, notorious for highwaymen.

11. *Habeas Corpus*: The prerogative writ *habeas corpus ad subjiciendum*, which required a person restrained of liberty to be brought before a judge or into court, in order to determine the lawfulness of the restraint (Latin).

12. *Raphael*: Raphael Sanzio or Raffaello (1483–1520), lauded artist of the Italian Renaissance.

13. *romantic*: Used here in the sense of foolhardy or extravagant.

14. *myrmidons*: Applied here in a derogatory sense to watchmen, bailiffs and other officers of the law.

15. *to shop the evidence*: To imprison the witness.

To Dr LEWIS
(from Matthew Bramble, London, 14 June)

1. *the lord chief justice*: William Murray, first earl of Mansfield (1705–93).

To Mrs MARY JONES, at Brambleton-hall, &c
(from Win Jenkins, London, 14 June)

1. *horn-buck*: Horn-book, a mounted leaf of paper containing the alphabet, often with the addition of the ten digits, some elements of spelling and the Lord's Prayer.

2. *the gates of hell . . . again him*: An allusion to Matthew 16:18.

3. *looker of cain*: Lucre of gain.

4. *sheep in the midst of wolves and tygers*: An allusion to Matthew 10:16 and Luke 10:3.

5. *flew open at his command*: An allusion to Acts 12:10.

6. *ould Scratch*: Old Scratch, a name for the devil.

7. *fruit of generation and repentance*: An allusion to Matthew 3:8 and Luke 3:8.

8. *worldly wisdom . . . the sight of God*: An allusion to 1 Corinthians 1:21.

9. *pray without seizing*: Pray without ceasing, in allusion to 1 Thessalonians 5:17.

To Mrs Gwyllim, house-keeper at Brambleton-hall
(from Tabitha Bramble, London, 14 June)

1. *good and faithful sarvant*: An allusion to Matthew 25:21.
2. *great will be your reward in haven*: An allusion to Matthew 5:12.
3. *Martinmass*: Martinmas or the feast of St Martin (11 November), when fairs were often held and cattle were slaughtered to be salted in preparation for winter.
4. *bitchmast*: Beech-mast, the fruit of the beech tree.

To Sir Watkin Phillips, Bart of Jesus college, Oxon
(from Jery Melford, Harrogate, 23 June)

1. *his silence was pathetic*: The idea of an affecting or eloquent silence was a commonplace in sentimental novels at this time.
2. *carbine*: A type of firearm, shorter than a musket, used by cavalry and other troops.
3. *solitaire*: A loose necktie of black silk or broad ribbon, worn by men (French).
4. *paint*: Make-up; cosmetics.
5. *rappee*: A coarse type of snuff made from the darker and ranker tobacco leaves, originally obtained by rasping a piece of tobacco (French).
6. *jack-boots*: Large strong boots which reached above the knee, usually worn by cavalry soldiers.
7. *en queue*: With a plait of hair worn hanging down behind and tied with a ribbon (French).
8. *Harrigate-water*: Water from the mineral wells at Harrogate in Yorkshire, celebrated for its medicinal properties.
9. *five separate inns*: Identified by Preston (p. 392) as the Queen's Head, the Old Swan, the Sinking Ship or Royal Oak, the Crown and the Dragon.
10. *solecism*: A breach or impropriety.

To Dr Lewis
(from Matthew Bramble, Harrogate, 26 June)

1. *the New Inn*: The Dragon, established during the 1760s.
2. *Dr Shaw, in his book upon mineral water*: Peter Shaw (1694–1763), physician and author of such works as a translation of Friedrich Hoffman's *New Experiments and Observations upon Mineral Waters* (1731), *An Enquiry into the Contents, Virtues, and Uses, of the Scarborough Spaw-Waters* (1734) and *A Dissertation on the Contents, Virtues and Uses, of Cold and Hot*

Mineral Springs; particularly, those of Scarborough (1735), which was published anonymously.

3. *Pace tanti viri*: With due respect to so eminent a man (Latin).

4. *a German doctor*: Preston (p. 393) suggests Anton von Störck (1731–1803), author of two treatises on the medicinal use of hemlock, which were published in 1760 and 1761.

5. *external use of sea-water*: Recalling Smollett's own publication, *An Essay on the External Use of Water* (1752).

6. *Burdock*: From the name of a coarse weedy plant, common on waste ground, that bears prickly flower-heads called burs and large leaves like those of the dock.

7. *a mighty fox-hunter before the Lord*: Alluding to Nimrod, 'the mighty hunter before the Lord' (Genesis 10:9).

8. *dillettante*: In a neutral sense, a dilettante is a lover of the fine arts. The word is used here depreciatively, however, to refer to someone who lacks serious application, and who is thus also a 'virtuoso', or mere trifler in the arts (Italian).

9. *the count de Melville, with his lady*: Renaldo de Melvile and his wife Serafina, characters from one of Smollett's earlier novels, *The Adventures of Ferdinand Count Fathom* (1753).

10. *Macaroni*: A dandy or fop. More specifically at this time, one of a set of young men who, on returning from travel in Europe, extravagantly imitated Continental tastes and fashions.

11. *caravanserai*: A type of inn in Eastern countries where caravans put up (Persian).

12. *O che burla!*: O, what a joke! (Italian).

13. *October*: A type of strong ale traditionally brewed in October.

14. *Redstreak*: A girl with red cheeks; the term derives from a red-streaked apple that is highly esteemed for making cider.

15. *Furnival's inn*: An Inn of Chancery in Holborn, attached to Lincoln's Inn.

16. *pettifogger*: An inferior legal practitioner, who employs dubious or underhanded practices.

17. *dedimus*: A writ empowering someone who is not a judge to act in place of one (Latin).

18. *the pot of Acheron*: The pit of Hades or hell; from the river Acheron, one of the underworld rivers in classical mythology.

19. *Stygian bath*: A reference to the corrosive waters of the mythological river Styx.

To Sir WATKIN PHILLIPS, Bart of Jesus college, Oxon
(from Jery Melford, Scarborough, 1 July)

1. *the Long Room*: The Assembly Room at Harrogate.
2. *calvinistical*: Characterized by adherence to the doctrines of John Calvin (1509–64), and thus a supporter of the Calvinistic Methodism of George Whitefield, rather than the Arminianism of John Wesley (1703–91).
3. *hi joci in seria ducunt mala*: Misquoted from Horace, *Ars Poetica*, lines 451–2: '*hae nugae seria ducent in mala*' ('these trifles will bring that friend into serious trouble').
4. *jallap*: A purgative drug obtained from the tuberous roots of certain winding plants.
5. *Rippon*: Ripon, a town in North Yorkshire, situated approximately eleven miles from Harrogate.
6. *doctor Waugh*: Preston (p. 395) indicates that this refers to Dr Gilbert Waugh of Shaw (*d.* 1776).
7. *villication*: Possibly vellication, irritation of the body by means of small or sharp points.
8. *naked*: i.e. wearing only an undergarment.
9. *in foro conscientiæ*: In the forum of conscience (Latin).
10. *two public rooms*: Newstead's and Donner's, both situated on Long Room Street (James Schofield, *An Historical and Descriptive Guide to Scarborough and its environs* (York, 1787), p. 35).

To Dr LEWIS
(from Matthew Bramble, Scarborough, 4 July)

1. *York ... the Assembly-room*: The city of York is located at the confluence of the rivers Ouse and Foss. Both the Castle and the Minster date back to the medieval period; the Minster is the largest Gothic cathedral in northern Europe. The neoclassical Assembly Rooms in Blake Street were built in the early 1730s, to a design by Richard Boyle, third earl of Burlington (1694–1753).
2. *assizes*: Sessions held periodically in English counties, at which judges acting under special commissions administered civil and criminal justice.
3. *Saracen rather than Gothic*: Gothic was the style associated with the medieval period, and regarded as the opposite of classical. Sir Christopher Wren (1632–1723) had erroneously termed the style 'Saracen' or Arabic.
4. *charnel-houses*: Vaults in which the bones of the dead are piled up.

5.   *Palladio*: Andrea Palladio (1508–80), whose style formed the model at this time for neoclassical architecture, in contrast to the baroque.
6.   *fane*: Temple.
7.   *H[ewet]t*: William Hewett (1693–1766), a well-known eccentric and a member of the club of 'demoniacs' gathered around John Hall-Stevenson (1718–85).
8.   *Death in the Revelations*: An allusion to Revelation 6:8.
9.   *no religion but that of nature*: Hewett is a deist, i.e. a rationalist whose faith derives from the evidence of nature, as opposed to the revelations of the Gospels.
10.   *the cardinal Camerlengo*: The title given to the chamberlain and financial secretary to the Pope.
11.   *pope Benedict XIV*: Prospero Lorenzo Lambertini (1675–1758), whose Papacy lasted from 1740 to 1758.
12.   *Voiturin*: The driver of a hired carriage (French).
13.   *Vetturino*: Italian term for the driver of a hired carriage.
14.   *the M— of G—*: John Manners, Marquis of Granby (1721–70), commander-in-chief of the army, colonel of the Royal Horse Guards and well-known for alcoholic indulgence.
15.   *apoplexy*: A sudden attack, usually caused by an effusion of blood or serum in the brain, which arrests the powers of sense and motion.
16.   *Voltaire*: François-Marie Arouet de Voltaire (1694–1778), writer and philosopher of the French Enlightenment.
17.   *Vanini*: Mrs Mary Vannini, an English widow and landlady with whom Smollett was acquainted.
18.   *Pomponius Atticus*: Titus Pomponius Atticus (109–32 BC), who starved himself to death to escape an incurable illness.

To Sir WATKIN PHILLIPS, Bart of Jesus college, Oxon (from Jery Melford, Newcastle upon Tyne, 10 July)

1.   *prætereuntium digito monstratus*: Adapted from Horace's *Odes*, IV.iii.22: '*monstror digito praetereuntium*' ('pointed out by [the fingers of] passers-by').
2.   *ebullition of his choler*: Agitation of his bile; anger.
3.   *in the straw*: In childbed; lying-in.
4.   *lingels*: A shoemaker's waxed threads.
5.   *East Indies . . . the company's service*: The East India Company, which had been granted a monopoly of English trade with Asia by royal grant at its foundation in 1600.
6.   *Brandenburgs*: Ornamental facings to the breast of an officer's coat.

7. *a scald head*: A head diseased with ringworm or a similar afflic-
    tion of the scalp.
8. *spatterdashes*: Long gaiters or leggings made of leather or cloth,
    worn to keep the trousers or stockings from being spattered when
    riding.
9. *a resurrection of dry bones*: An allusion to Ezekiel 37.
10. *Ticonderoga*: The location of Fort Carillon, scene in July 1758
    of a battle in which approximately 14–15,000 British soldiers
    under General James Abercromby (1706–81) failed to subdue
    3–4,000 French soldiers. The 42nd Highland Regiment of Foot
    (also known as the Black Watch) suffered particularly badly
    during the battle, losing more than half of its men.

To Sir WATKIN PHILLIPS, Bart of Jesus college, Oxon
(from Jery Melford, Morpeth, 13 July)

1. *justice of the quorum*: A justice of the peace whose presence was
    necessary to constitute a bench.
2. *crusty ruttleorum*: *Custos rotulorum*, the principal justice in a
    county, who held the rolls and records of the sessions of the
    peace (Latin).
3. *Llewellyn, prince of Wales*: Llywelyn ap Gruffudd (*d*. 1282).
4. *the original covenanters*: Signatories of the National Covenant
    in February 1638, which opposed the liturgical innovations being
    imposed by Charles I on the Church of Scotland, most notably
    the introduction of a new Book of Service, popularly known as
    'Laud's Liturgy'.
5. *place in Scotland so called*: Lesmahagow, a village to the south-
    west of Lanark.
6. *Sed genus et proavos, et quæ non fecimus ipsi, vix ea nostra
    voco*: From Ovid's *Metamorphoses*, XIII, 140–41: 'For as to race
    and ancestry and the deeds that others than ourselves have done,
    I call those in no true sense our own'.
7. *jesuitical*: Having the character ascribed to the Jesuits, i.e. being
    deceitful or dissembling; practising equivocation, prevarication
    or mental reservation of truth.
8. *Miamis*: A tribe of Algonquian speakers then living in what is
    now Illinois (Ross, p. 403).
9. *sachem*: The supreme head or chief of certain Native American tribes.
10. *the Drimmendoo*: Preston (p. 401) notes that 'The *Drimmendoo*
    is an old Irish folk song entitled "Draoigheanán donn" or "Dry-
    naun dhun" (Dear Black Cow). Gaelic "Drioman-dubh" means
    a black cow with a white back.'

11. *did seriously incline her ear . . . for the dangers he had past*: An allusion to Shakespeare's *Othello*, I.iii.144–5, 148–9 and 166: 'These things to hear / Would Desdemona seriously incline . . . and with a greedy ear / Devour up my discourse . . . She loved me for the dangers I had passed.'

12. *minionette*: Mignonette, a type of fine French bobbin lace made in narrow strips.

13. *Alliance between Church and State*: Probably an allusion to William Warburton, *The Alliance between Church and State; or, The Necessity and Equity of an Established Religion and a Test-Law Demonstrated* (1736).

14. *some holy man . . . these poor heathens!*: As Preston indicates (pp. 402–3), this is 'possibly a satiric allusion to Thomas Bray (1656–1730) and the extensive missionary activities of the Society for the Propagation of the Gospel (SPG) he founded in 1700 as a companion organization to the Society for the Promotion of Christian Knowledge (SPCK)'.

15. *Salve regina*: A medieval hymn to the Virgin Mary.

16. *the creed of saint Athanasius*: An ancient Christian creed, erroneously attributed to Saint Athanasius (*c*. AD 293–373).

17. *The Ever-Green, and the works of Allan Ramsay*: *The Ever-Green, Being a Collection of Scots Poems, Wrote by the Ingenious before 1600* was first published in 1724 by the Scots poet Allan Ramsay (1684–1758). The best-known of Ramsay's original works was his pastoral drama *The Gentle Shepherd* (1725).

18. *the mind . . . her elbow-room*: An allusion to John Armstrong (1708/9–79), *A Day: An Epistle to John Wilkes, Esq.* (1761), pp. 6–7: 'When Dinner comes, amid the various Feast, / That Crowns your genial Board, where every Guest, / Or grave, or gay, is happy, and at home, / And none e'er sighed for the Mind's Elbow-room.'

19. *He's gentle and not fearful*: An allusion to Shakespeare's *The Tempest*, I.ii.471.

20. *paralogism*: A piece of false or erroneous reasoning that the reasoner is unconscious of or believes to be logical.

21. *A gentle knight . . . ydrad*: Quotations from Edmund Spenser (1552?–1599), *The Faerie Queene* (1590), I.i.1 and I.ii.9.

22. *diphthongs*: A diphthong is the union of two vowels pronounced in one syllable, or the combination of a sonantal with a consonantal vowel.

23. *recitative*: Tone or rhythm.

24.   *Cloacina*: The Roman goddess of sewers; the 'temples' referred to here are privies.

To Dr LEWIS
(from Matthew Bramble, Tweedmouth, 15 July)

1.   *that bridge*: The James VI Bridge, built in 1611–24.
2.   *noble house of Piercy, earls of Northumberland*: The medieval Alnwick Castle, home to the Percy family since 1309.
3.   *lord B—'s inglorious peace*: The Peace of Paris, which brought to an end the Seven Years War, was signed by Lord Bute on 10 February 1763. The terms of the treaty were thought by many to be disadvantageous to Britain.
4.   *which, Mr Addison says . . . an Englishman*: An allusion to the *Spectator* No. 383 (20 May 1712) by Joseph Addison (1672–1719), in which Sir Roger de Coverley is described as having 'honest Prejudices which naturally cleave to the Heart of a true *Englishman*'. See Richard Steele and Joseph Addison, *Selections from the Tatler and the Spectator*, ed. Angus Ross (London: Penguin, 1988), p. 246.
5.   *to extend it from three to seven years*: A reference to the Septennial Act of 1716 (2 Geo. I, c. 38), which increased the maximum length of a Parliament from three to seven years.
6.   *Antæus*: In Greek mythology, Antæus was a giant who possessed great strength while in contact with the earth (his mother), but who was severely weakened when lifted above it. Hercules eventually discovered his secret and killed him by holding him aloft.
7.   *paternus lar, or patria domus*: Paternal hearth or paternal home (Latin).
8.   *Wesley's meeting in Newcastle*: John Wesley was in Newcastle in early May 1766; Smollett may have heard him preaching there, as he travelled to Scotland.

To Sir WATKIN PHILLIPS, Bart at Oxon
(from Jery Melford, 18 July)

1.   *fits of the mother*: Hysteria; termed 'the mother' because thought to arise from an upward displacement of the uterus.
2.   *brocade*: A textile fabric woven with a pattern of raised figures, originally in gold or silver.
3.   *painted Jezabel*: Jezebel, wife of King Ahab of Israel; an allusion to 2 Kings 9:30.
4.   *Teague*: A nickname for an Irishman, now obsolete.

5. *Macloughlin ... Tier-Owen the Great*: Ross (p. 404) explains: 'In Ireland the MacLochlainn branch of the O'Neill (Uí Néill) family ruled in Ulster until about 1230. At that time they were displaced by the O'Neills of Tyrone, a kingdom so named (Tir Eoghainn) from Eoghain, one of the sons of Niall of the Nine Hostages. The O'Neills ruled Tyrone until they were dispossessed in 1603.'

6. *Shuffolk-street*: Suffolk Street, a fashionable street just off Pall Mall in London.

7. *came like a tief*: Alluding to the Biblical phrase, 'like a thief in the night'.

8. *the ninth part of a man*: Alluding to the proverbial expression, 'nine tailors make a man'.

9. *Tulloghobegly*: Tullaghoge, in County Tyrone in Ulster.

10. *bug*: As Grose explains, *bug* was 'a nick name given by the Irish to Englishmen; bugs having, as it is said, been introduced into Ireland by the English'.

11. *jockied*: Tricked or outwitted.

12. *Judas Iscariot ... carried the bag*: Allusions to Luke 22:47–8 and John 13:29.

13. *Mrs Humphreys*: Preston (pp. xl–xlii) identifies Mrs Humphreys as a real person.

14. *apostacy*: Abandonment of principles; by extension from the renunciation of one's religious faith or moral allegiance.

15. *could not go to Scotland but by sea*: In a letter of 1 March 1754, Smollett had written to his friend the Church of Scotland minister Alexander Carlyle (1722–1805) that in England 'Ignorance prevails to such a degree that one of our Chelsea Club asked me if the weather was good when I crossed the Sea from Scotland' (*The Letters of Tobias Smollett*, ed. Lewis M. Knapp (Oxford: Clarendon Press, 1970), p. 33).

16. *red-shanks of Ireland*: Celtic inhabitants of Ireland and of the Scottish Highlands were sometimes called 'redshanks' in allusion to the colour of their bare legs, reddened by exposure to the elements.

17. *a country inn*: Identified by Preston (p. xl) as 'most likely the Beltonford Inn'.

18. *a fortified castle ... the bottom*: The Castle, which dominates the city of Edinburgh, dates from at least the eleventh century; the palace of Holyrood House, which was founded as an Abbey in 1128 by King David I, is now the Queen's official residence in Scotland.

19. *The inn at which we put up*: Identified by Preston (p. 407) as the White Horse Inn or White Horse Stables, which was built in 1623 at the bottom of the High Street in White Horse Close.

20. *Mr Mitchelson*: Samuel Mitchelson (*d.* 1788), a lawyer and friend of Smollett.

To Dr LEWIS
(from Matthew Bramble, Edinburgh, 18 July)

1. *the Duke of Roxburgh*: John Ker, third Duke of Roxburghe (1740–1804).

2. *Lesley, at the head of a Scotch army*: David Leslie, first Lord Newark (1601–82), lieutenant-general (and effective commander) of the army at the time of the engagement with Cromwell that Smollett describes, which took place in September 1650.

3. *Philistines in Gilgal*: An allusion to 1 Samuel 13:4.

4. *a gentleman's house*: Preston (p. 408) suggests the property of Newmills, which the notorious rake, Colonel Francis Charteris (*c.* 1665–1732), had named Amisfield.

5. *Lord Elibank*: Patrick Murray, fifth lord Elibank (1703–78), a noted literary patron.

6. *Mr Cardonel*: Mansfeldt de Cardonnel of Musselburgh (1696/7–1780), a commissioner of the customs and salt duties in Scotland.

7. *Dr C—*: Alexander Carlyle (1722–1805), Church of Scotland minister, and friend and correspondent of Smollett.

8. *the Canon-gate*: The High Street in Edinburgh.

9. *the gate . . . now taken away*: The gate was removed in 1764.

10. *the Lucken-Booths*: Locked booths or shops, dating from the fifteenth century.

11. *Middle-Row in Holborn*: A block of houses then located at the end of Gray's Inn Lane in Holborn, London.

12. *a market-cross*: The ancient Mercat Cross of Edinburgh, which was removed in 1756 in the face of violent protests.

13. *lord Sommerville's garden*: At Drum House, the estate of James, thirteenth Lord Somerville (1727–96).

14. *statue of king Charles II*: This lead statue of the King, dressed as a Roman Emperor on horseback, was erected by James Smith in 1685.

15. *a steeple hard by*: The Church of St Giles, commonly known as St Giles' Cathedral or the High Kirk of Edinburgh.

16. *Lockhart*: Preston (p. xlii) identifies this gentlewoman as one of two real Mrs Lockharts.

To Mrs MARY JONES, at Brambleton-hall
(from Win Jenkins, Edinburgh, 18 July)

1. *a vixen and a griffin*: A-vexing and a-grieving.
2. *wally de shamble*: *valet de chambre* (French).
3. *Spanish owl*: Spanish wool, a type of rouge.
4. *took a French leave*: Left without permission or notice.
5. *easements*: Accommodations; with an equivocation on the alternative meaning of 'privies'.
6. *geaks*: Jakes, i.e. privies.
7. *gardy loo*: From the French phrase *gardez l'eau* ('beware of the water').

To Sir WATKIN PHILLIPS, Bart of Jesus college, Oxon
(from Jery Melford, Edinburgh, 8 August)

1. *Doric dialect*: A 'broad' or rustic dialect of English.
2. *Mr R— C—*: Robert Cullen, Lord Cullen (1742–1810), a Scottish advocate (and later judge) who was noted for his amiable mimicry.
3. *cartel*: A written agreement, more usually relating to the exchange or ransom of prisoners.
4. *The first . . . in the markets*: Preston (p. 411) identifies the reference as possibly being to William Snelgrave, *A New Account of Some Parts of Guinea, and the Slave-Trade* (1734). In the work, Snelgrave observes that 'There were likewise brought by the Soldiers some thousands of dead Peoples Heads into the Court . . . and as the proper Officers received them, they paid the Soldiers *five Shillings* for each Head'; he also records that 'one Mr. *Robert More*', a ship's surgeon, being sent to the 'King of *Dahomè*'s Camp . . . saw many strange things, especially human Flesh sold publickly in the great Market-place' (pp. 38, 53).
5. *poor Murray of Baliol-college*: Noted by Preston (p. 411) as 'Possibly an allusion to the Rev. Gideon Murray, who was at Balliol from 1729 to 1736, a generation before Jery.'
6. *antiscorbutic*: Of use against scurvy.
7. *the same hand*: The Dutch painter Jacob de Wet or James de Witt (1640–97).
8. *concert*: Held in St Cecilia's Hall, which was built in 1762.
9. *one nobleman . . . universally admired*: Thomas Alexander Erskine, sixth earl of Kellie (1731–81), director of the Edinburgh Musical Society from 1757.
10. *new theatre*: The Theatre Royal, which opened on 9 December 1769.

11. *the hunters' ball*: A ball given annually at Holyrood House by the Caledonian Hunt.

12. *the Leith races*: Horse races held each July on Leith Sands.

13. *miss R[ento]n*: Identified by Preston (p. 412) as Miss Cecilia Renton or her sister Eleanora.

14. *a toast*: A lady to whom a company is requested to drink, often as the reigning belle of the season.

15. *lady directress of the ball*: Identified as 'Mrs Murray, sister to Lord Mansfield' in Edward Topham (1751–1820), *Letters from Edinburgh; Written in the Years 1774 and 1775* (1776), p. 349.

16. *Ballymawhawple*: A comic coinage, rather than a real place-name.

17. *Seceders*: Members of the Secession, which had broken away from the Kirk – the established Church of Scotland – during the 1730s.

18. *The best in Christendom*: An abbreviated toast, explained by Grose: 'BEST. To the best in Christendom, i.e. the best **** in Christendom, a health formerly much in vogue.'

19. *Gibbs' contract*: An abbreviated form of 'Rob Gibb, and stark luif and kindness', a common toast to disinterested friendship, supposedly from a story about King James V and his fool of that name.

20. *The beggar's benison*: Explained by Grose: 'BENISON. The beggar's benison; May your ***** and purse never fail you.' There was a (so-called) 'hell-fire' club in existence from 1732 to 1836, called The Most Ancient and Puissant Order of the Beggar's Benison and Merryland, Anstruther.

21. *John Bull and his sister Moggy*: John Bull and Moggy or Margaret (sometimes shortened to Peg) were popular names for England and Scotland, as, for instance, in John Arbuthnot (1667–1735), *John Bull Still in his Senses: Being the Third Part of Law is a Bottomless-Pit* (1712).

22. *dule*: Dole; grief, sorrow or mental distress.

23. *with a toom poke at his lunzie*: With an empty bag at his side.

24. *overtaken*: Intoxicated; overpowered with drink.

25. *terra firma*: Dry or firm land (Latin).

26. *Carfax*: The crossroads in the centre of Oxford.

VOLUME THREE

To Dr Lewis
(from Matthew Bramble, Edinburgh, 8 August)

1. *the union*: The Act of Union of 1707, which united Scotland and England under one parliament, thereby creating the united kingdom of Great Britain.

2. *civil law*: Roman law, as opposed to common law (as in England).

3. *the constitution of their jury*: Scottish juries comprised fifteen men, chosen by the defendant from forty-five men; the verdict required only a majority.

4. *university of Edinburgh*: Established by a royal charter granted by James VI in 1582.

5. *the infirmary*: The Royal Infirmary, established in 1729 as a hospital for the sick poor and granted a royal charter in 1736.

6. *several hospitals*: Identified by Preston (p. 415) as 'Heriot's Hospital, founded in 1628; Watson's Hospital, founded in 1738; Trades Hospital, founded in 1704; Merchant's Hospital, founded in 1707; Trinity Hospital, an almshouse founded in the fifteenth century by Mary of Gueldres, wife of Scotland's James II; and Orpheus Hospital, founded in 1734.'

7. *the two Humes, Robertson, Smith, Wallace, Blair, Ferguson, Wilkie*: David Hume (1711–76), the famous Scottish philosopher and historian, author of *A Treatise of Human Nature* (1739–40), *Philosophical Essays concerning Human Understanding* (1748) and *The History of Great Britain* (1754–61); John Home (1722–1808), Church of Scotland minister and author of the celebrated play *Douglas: A Tragedy* (1756); William Robertson (1721–93), Church of Scotland minister, Principal of Edinburgh University (from 1762) and author of major historical works such as *The History of Scotland, during the Reigns of Queen Mary and of James VI* (1759), *The History of the Reign of the Emperor Charles V* (1769) and *The History of America* (1777); Adam Smith (1723–90), moral philosopher and political economist, professor of moral philosophy at Glasgow (from 1752) and celebrated author of *The Theory of Moral Sentiments* (1759) and *An Inquiry into the Nature and Causes of the Wealth of Nations* (1776); Robert Wallace (1697–1771), Church of Scotland minister, economist and author of *A Dissertation on the Numbers of Mankind in Antient and Modern Times* (1753); Hugh Blair (1718–1800), Church of Scotland minister, the first professor of

rhetoric and belles lettres at Edinburgh University, and author of *Lectures on Rhetoric and Belles Lettres* (1783); Adam Ferguson (1723–1816), professor of moral philosophy at the University of Edinburgh (from 1764) and author of *An Essay on the History of Civil Society* (1767); and William Wilkie (1721–72), Church of Scotland minister, professor of natural philosophy at the University of St Andrews (from 1759), author of *The Epigoniad* (1757), and nicknamed the 'Scottish Homer'.

8. *the sublime*: Rising to a great height, lofty or towering; perhaps with a hint of the broader meaning, of something great or terrible that inspires admiration and awe in the viewer.

9. *Dalkeith, Pinkie, Yester, and lord Hopton's [Hopetoun's]*: Dalkeith Palace, seat of the Duke of Buccleuch; Pinkie House, owned by the Marquis of Tweeddale; Yester House, seat of the Marquis of Tweeddale; and Hopetoun House, home to the earls of Hopetoun.

10. *Mr Phillip Miller of Chelsea*: Philip Miller (1691–1771), noted horticulturist and writer and an acquaintance of Smollett. Miller was gardener of the Botanic Gardens at Chelsea (Chelsea Physic Garden of the Society of Apothecaries of London) from 1722 to 1770, and the author of such works as *The Gardeners Dictionary*, produced in eight editions from 1732 to 1768.

11. *genius loci*: Genius of the place; the presiding deity or spirit (Latin).

12. *prudish*: Extremely prim, formal or rigid.

13. *Dr Gregory*: John Gregory (1724–73), Scottish physician, professor of philosophy (1746–49) and of medicine (from 1755) at King's College, Aberdeen, professor of medicine at Edinburgh University (from 1766), and author of works of medicine and moral conduct, most notably *A Comparative View of the State and Faculties of Man, with those of the Animal World* (1765) and *A Father's Legacy to his Daughters* (1774).

14. *Mr Smollett*: James Smollett of Bonhill (*d.* 1774), Smollett's cousin.

To Sir WATKIN PHILLIPS, Bart of Jesus college, Oxon (from Jery Melford, Argylleshire, 3 September)

1. *Ultima Thule*: The extreme limit of travel and discovery; from the name given by Polybius to a land six days' sail north of Britain, assumed to be the most northerly region in the world.

2. *Deucalidonian sea*: A coinage mixing 'Caledonian' (Scottish) and 'Deucalion', in reference to Deucalion's Flood – a great deluge said, in Greek mythology, to have occurred in Thessaly.

3.   *stately castle*: Inverary Castle, seat of the duke of Argyll.
4.   *fire everlasting, prepared for the devil and his angels*: An allusion to Matthew 25:41.
5.   *royal palace*: Linlithgow palace, birthplace of Mary, Queen of Scots.
6.   *Mr Moore*: John Moore (1729–1802), Scottish physician, writer and friend of Smollett, with whom he corresponded frequently. In 1797, Moore published an eight-volume edition of Smollett's *Works*, which included a biography of the author. Along with some well-received travel writings, Moore also published three novels: *Zeluco* (1789), *Edward* (1796) and *Mordaunt* (1800).
7.   *university*: The University of Glasgow, founded in 1451. Smollett was a student there around 1735.
8.   *regent*: In the Scottish university system, a regent was one of several instructors forming part of the teaching staff of a college, who undertook the tuition of a certain number of students from the time of their entrance to the end of the course.
9.   *inkle-manufacturer*: Maker of a type of linen tape.
10. *Mr John Wesley*: Preston (p. 418) notes that Wesley was preaching in Scotland in June 1766, when Smollett himself was there.
11. *Buchanan*: George Buchanan (1506–82), poet and historian, author of *Rerum Scoticarum Historia* (1582), a history of Scotland.
12. *arx inexpugnabilis*: Impregnable fortress (Latin).
13. *Change-house*: Scottish term for a small inn or alehouse, which may originally have referred to a wayside inn at which horses could be changed.
14. *a chopine of two-penny*: A chopin is a Scottish liquid measure, equal to a Scottish half-pint; two-penny was ale originally sold in Scotland at twopence per Scotch pint (equivalent to three imperial pints).
15. *a gill*: A measure for liquids, containing one fourth of a standard pint, although sometimes equivalent to a half-pint, as perhaps here.
16. *whisky*: Whisky was primarily a Highland drink until the middle of the eighteenth century.
17. *geneva*: A Dutch spirit, distilled from grain and flavoured with the juice of juniper berries. The shortened form of the word, gin, refers mainly to a British imitation of geneva, which is usually flavoured with a substitute for juniper.
18. *confluent small-pox*: The eruption in smallpox, when the vesicles run together.

19. *the duke of Argyle*: The current duke was John Campbell, fourth duke of Argyll (1693–1770).

20. *disarmed . . . their ancient garb*: By a parliamentary Act of 1746 (19 Geo. II, c. 39), titled 'An Act for the more effectual disarming the Highlands in *Scotland* . . . and for the more effectually securing the Peace of the said Highlands . . . and for restraining the Use of the Highland Dress . . .' As Jery goes on to note, along with kilts and other kinds of Highland dress, the Act specifically debarred the wearing of Tartan coats.

21. *russet*: A coarse homespun woollen cloth of a reddish-brown, grey or neutral colour, formerly used for the dress of peasants and country-folk.

22. *The poems of Ossian*: The poems of Ossian were published by James Macpherson (1736–96) as his own translations of poems in Gaelic by the ancient Scots bard, Ossian. The main Ossianic publications were *Fragments of Ancient Poetry, Collected in the Highlands of Scotland, and Translated from the Galic or Erse Language* (1760), *Fingal, An Ancient Epic Poem, in Six Books* (1762 [1761]), *Temora, An Ancient Epic Poem, in Eight Books* (1763), and a two-volume edition of *The Works of Ossian, the Son of Fingal*, published in 1765. While the Ossian poems drew upon Gaelic ballads, a controversy over their authenticity soon developed, especially in England. They were, though, extremely influential in Europe, particularly in Germany.

23. *the laird of Macfarlane*: Walter Macfarlan of Arrochar (*d.* 1767), antiquary and chief of the clan of Macfarlan.

24. *Sassenagh*: Sassenachs.

25. *patronimics*: Patronymics, family names derived from those of fathers or male ancestors.

26. *penetralia*: Innermost parts or recesses.

27. *coronach*: Company of mourners.

28. *Gaelly's*: Gillies, attendants on Highland chiefs.

29. *kilderkin*: A cask for liquids. A kilderkin for beer holds eighteen gallons, while a kilderkin for ale holds sixteen gallons.

30. *bickers*: Bowls or dishes for drinking.

31. *Boreas*: The Greek god of the north-wind, and bringer of winter.

To Dr LEWIS
(from Matthew Bramble, Cameron, 28 August)

1. *iron-work*: Identified by Preston (p. 421) as probably the Carron Works near Falkirk, established in 1759 by John Roebuck, Samuel Garbett and William Cadell.

2. *colliquative sweats*: A disease characterized by profuse discharges of perspiration which cause the body to waste away, as in consumption.

3. *rack rent*: A very high, excessive or extortionate rent.

4. *cathedral*: The Gothic-style Cathedral at Glasgow, also known as the High Kirk of Glasgow and St Mungo's Cathedral, was consecrated in 1197 but not completed until the fifteenth century.

5. *Mr Cochran*: Andrew Cochrane (1692/3–1777) was provost of Glasgow six times during the period 1744–62. In 1749 he secured £10,000 from Parliament as compensation to Glasgow for its losses during the Jacobite rising of 1745/6.

6. *Mr P—*: Either Henry Pelham or William Pitt.

7. *Dr John Gordon*: One of the surgeons to whom Smollett was apprenticed in 1736 (the other being William Stirling).

8. *Mr G—ssf—d*: John Glassford (1715–83), one of the richest of Glasgow's tobacco merchants.

9. *the reign of Antonine*: Antoninus Pius, Titus Aurelius Fulvius Boionius Arrius Antoninus (AD 86–161), Roman Emperor, AD 138–61.

10. *canal*: The Forth–Clyde Canal, begun in 1768 and opened for navigation in 1790.

11. *cambrick*: A kind of fine white linen, originally made at Cambrai in Flanders.

12. *flowered lawn*: A fine linen, embellished with a floral design.

13. *The Black Book of Paisley*: The 'Black Book of Paisley', an early history of Scotland, forms part of the *Scotichronicon*, which was actually written by John Fordoun (d. 1363) and Walter Bower (1385–1449), rather than by the monks of Cluny.

14. *the earl of Dundonald*: The current earl was Thomas Cochrane, eighth earl of Dundonald (1691–1778).

15. *isthmus*: A narrow portion of land, enclosed on each side by water, and connecting two larger bodies of land.

16. *ODE TO LEVEN-WATER*: Smollett's 'Ode' was first printed at this point in *Humphry Clinker*, but later published separately.

To Dr LEWIS
(from Matthew Bramble, Cameron, 6 September)

1. *A captain . . . Mr Anson*: Captain Robert Mann (*d.* 1762), Smollett's neighbour in Chelsea, and George, Baron Anson (1697–1762), first lord of the admiralty (from 1751), admiral of the fleet (1761) and author of *A Voyage Round the World* (1748), which contains a description of the Island of Juan Fernandez (in book 2, chapter 1).

2. *a person . . . his own planting*: Donald Govan, a former owner of Cameron House.

3. *alga marina*: Seaweed (Latin).

4. *the Earl of Breadalbine*: The current earl was John Campbell, third earl of Breadalbane and Holland (1696–1782).

5. *They attacked . . . service*: The Jacobite victories over the English at Prestonpans (September 1745) and Falkirk (January 1746).

6. *Divide et impera*: Divide and rule (Latin).

7. *feudal system . . . patriarchal*: As Preston notes (p. 424), the feudal system was a set of legal relationships, whereas the patriarchal system was based on personal loyalty.

8. *Mr Cameron of Lochiel*: Charles Cameron (*d.* 1776), son of the Jacobite army officer Donald Cameron of Lochiel (*c.* 1700–1748).

9. *the remains of a castle . . . formerly resided*: Finlaggan Castle, residence of John of Islay or John MacDonald (*d. c.* 1387), chief of Clan MacDonald and self-styled 'Lord of the Isles'.

10. *Mackcrain*: Gillouir Mack Crain or Mackirain.

11. *John duke of Argyle*: John Campbell, second duke of Argyll and duke of Greenwich (1680–1743).

12. *St Columba chose for his habitation*: Saint Columba of Ireland (*c.* AD 521–97) is supposed to have arrived at Iona in AD 563.

To Miss LÆTITIA WILLIS, at Gloucester
(from Lydia Melford, Glasgow, 7 September)

1. *Aimwell*: One of the beaux in *The Beaux' Stratagem* (1707), a comic play by George Farquhar (1676/7–1707).

To Mrs MARY JONES, at Brambleton-hall
(from Win Jenkins, Glasgow, 7 September)

1. *the land of the living*: A common Biblical phrase.

2. *musician*: Magician.

3. *waves . . . hyland*: Win invokes an ancient folkloric belief by

which Loch Lomond possessed waves without wind, fish without fins, and a floating island.

4. *Kairmann*: Preston (p. 426) suggests Ptarmigan, the western shoulder of Ben Lomond.
5. *a taster*: A tester, i.e. sixpence.
6. *birth-day soot*: Birthday suit, i.e. naked.
7. *selvidges*: Savages.
8. *sounded*: Swooned.

To Sir WATKIN PHILLIPS, Bart at Oxon
(from Jery Melford, Carlisle, 12 September)

1. *land of cakes, where bannocks grow upon straw*: The name 'Land of Cakes' (i.e. of oaten bread) was applied in jest to Scotland, or to the Scottish Lowlands specifically.
2. *Lord Clive*: Robert Clive, first Baron Clive of Plassey (1725–74), army officer in the East India Company and administrator in India.
3. *Drumlanrig ... the duke of Queensberry*: Drumlanrig Castle, owned by Charles Douglas, third duke of Queensberry and second duke of Dover (1698–1778), courtier and politician.
4. *Syrtes*: The name of two large quicksands (*Syrtis major* and *minor*) off the northern coast of Africa.
5. *in propria persona*: In proper person, i.e. himself (Latin).
6. *a subaltern's half-pay*: The half-salary paid to a subaltern – a junior army officer, below the rank of captain – when not in service or when retired.

To Dr LEWIS
(from Matthew Bramble, Manchester, 15 September)

1. *cale or cole*: Cabbage.
2. *big*: Bigg, four-rowed barley.
3. *sowens or flummery of oat-meal*: Sowens consists of starchy matter extracted from the bran or husks of oats by steeping in water, allowing to ferment slightly, and boiling. Flummery is a synonym for sowens.
4. *now in possession of his great fortune*: Since 1769, when the House of Lords voted in favour of the claim of Archibald Douglas (1748–1827) to inherit the estate of his uncle, the late duke of Douglas (1694–1761), against the challenge of the Hamilton family – thereby ending one of the most famous legal disputes of the eighteenth century.
5. *The dutchess*: Catherine Hyde, duchess of Queensberry and

Dover (1701–77), second daughter of Henry Hyde, the fourth earl of Clarendon (1672–1754), and a noted literary patroness.

6. *but little honoured in his own country*: An allusion to Matthew 13:57 and John 4:44.

7. *you have made ... den of thieves*: Alluding to Matthew 21:13, Mark 11:17 and Luke 19:46.

8. *manes*: Spirits (of dead ancestors).

9. *olla*: A Spanish stew of meat and vegetables.

To Mrs GWYLLIM, house-keeper at Brambleton-hall
(from Tabitha Bramble, 18 September)

1. *Devil's Harse a pike, and Hoyden's Hole*: The Devil's Arse-a-Peak (a large cavern) and Eldon Hole (a deep limestone pothole), both located in the Peak District of Derbyshire.

2. *baiting an ass*: Bating an ace, a proverbial expression meaning to abate some minor thing, or to make the slightest abatement.

3. *bring forth fruits of repentance*: An allusion to Matthew 3:8 and Luke 3:8.

To Dr LEWIS
(from Matthew Bramble, 20 September)

1. *Fabricius, Cincinnatus, and Regulus*: Gaius Fabricius Luscinus (*d.* after 275 BC), consul of Rome, known for his integrity and incorruptibility; Lucius Quinctius Cincinnatus (*c.* 519–438 BC), farmer and dictator of Rome, regarded as a model of virtuous simplicity; and Marcus Atilius Regulus (*d. c.* 250 BC), a general and consul.

2. *Darien company*: A company founded in 1695 as the Company of Scotland Trading to Africa and the Indies, which in 1698 made an (ultimately unsuccessful) attempt to establish a trading colony in the Isthmus of Darien (Panama).

3. *premunire*: A difficulty or predicament.

4. *mucilaginous*: Of a soft, moist and viscous quality.

To Sir WATKIN PHILLIPS, Bart of Jesus college, Oxon
(from Jery Melford, 28 September)

1. *throw the stocking*: An old custom whereby, on her wedding night, the bride's stocking was thrown among the wedding guests. The girl hit by the stocking was supposed to be the next person to be married.

2. *knight of La Mancha ... Panza* : Don Quixote and his squire, Sancho Panza.

3.   *gens foutre*: *Jean-foutre*, a vulgar French term for a simpleton or imbecile.

To Dr Lewis
(from Matthew Bramble, 30 September)

1.   *punctilios*: Petty formalities in behaviour.
2.   *ruling passion*: Dominating enthusiasm or behavioural predisposition; an idea most famously articulated in the poetry of Alexander Pope, for instance in his *Of the Use of Riches, An Epistle to the Right Honourable Allen Lord Bathurst* (1733), lines 155–6: 'The ruling Passion, be it what it will, / The ruling Passion conquers Reason still'.
3.   *the habit of a hussar*: A military uniform of the light cavalry, characterized by brilliant colours and elaborate ornamentation.
4.   *scorocconi*: Sharpers or swindlers (Italian).
5.   *ciceroni*: Guides to the antiquities or curiosities of a place (Italian).
6.   *dutchess of B[edford]'s conversazione*: Possibly referring to Gertrude Leveson-Gower (1718/19–94), second wife of John Russell, the fourth duke of Bedford (1710–71). *Conversazione* is Italian for an evening assembly held for conversation, social recreation and amusement.
7.   *biglietti of invitation*: Italian for tickets or letters of invitation.
8.   *fable of the frog and the ox*: *Aesop's Fables*, II, 20.
9.   *kickshaws*: Contemptuous term for fancy but insubstantial dishes, from the French *quelque chose*.
10. *rotis*: Main courses consisting of roasted meat (French).
11. *fumet*: The smell of game when high.

To Sir Watkin Phillips, Bart at Oxon
(from Jery Melford, 3 October)

1.   *arietta*: A short air.
2.   *cara*: Beloved (Italian).
3.   *Pargolesi . . . Corelli*: The Italian composers Giovanni Battista Pergolesi (1710–36) and Arcangelo Corelli (1653–1713).
4.   *Burn*: Richard Burn (1709–85), legal writer, Church of England clergyman, and author of *Ecclesiastical Law* (1763) and the popular justices' manual, *The Justice of the Peace, and Parish Officer* (1755).
5.   *plague water*: An infusion of various herbs and roots in alcohol, taken as a supposed remedy against plague.
6.   *coup de maitre*: Master-stroke (French).

7. *camisciata, scagliata, beffata*: Roughly: a low-down or dirty trick; a demeaning prank; and a jesting prank. Preston (p. 432) provides a more detailed explanation of these non-standard Italian terms.

8. *O, che roba!*: What a nonsensical business!; What nonsense! (Italian).

9. *caricatura*: Caricature (Italian).

10. *a Rosa, a Rembrandt, a Schalken*: The Italian painter Salvatore Rosa (1615–73), and the Dutch painters Rembrandt Harmenszoon van Rijn (1606–69) and Godfried Schalcken (1643–1706).

11. *Zooks*: An exclamation or minced oath, expressing vexation, surprise, or other emotion.

12. *catastrophe*: The change or revolution which produces the conclusion or final event of a dramatic piece.

13. *saturnine*: Sluggish, cold and gloomy in temperament.

14. *mull*: Mill, a snuffbox in which tobacco could easily be ground to powder.

15. *done my business*: Done for me or ruined me, possibly with a pun on 'caused me to ease myself'.

16. *a glyster*: An enema.

17. *Christ, have mercy upon us!*: An allusion to the Order for the Visitation of the Sick, in *The Book of Common Prayer*.

18. *cut off . . . a flower of the field*: An allusion to the Order for the Burial of the Dead, in *The Book of Common Prayer*.

19. *antimonial wine*: Sherry containing tartar emetic.

20. *oxymel of squills*: A medicinal drink or syrup made with honey and with vinegar from the bulbs of the squill, or sea-onion.

21. *egesta*: Excreta.

22. *payed me Scot and lot*: Fully settled with me; paid out thoroughly.

To Mrs MARY JONES, at Brambleton-hall
(from Win Jenkins, 4 October)

1. *Mathewsullin*: Methuselah (who, according to Genesis 5:27, lived for 969 years).

2. *Dunquickset*: Win presumably means Don Quixote.

3. *steeling of kettle*: Stealing of cattle.

4. *impfiddle*: Infidel.

5. *a nubjack*: An object.

6. *I vow she would . . . for an owl*: A variant of lines from a popular song titled 'The Gossips' or 'The Gossips Tale, under the Rose', which appeared in various lyric miscellanies and jest-books

during the eighteenth century, such as *The Lark* (1740) and *Ned Ward's Jests, or Repository of Wit and Humour* (1752). The original lines read 'In troth he would fain have a Bird, / That would give a Groat for an Owl'.

7. *the devil and all his works*: An allusion to 1 John 3:8.
8. *cuddling*: Coddling.
9. *viol of assings*: Vial of essence.

To Sir WATKIN PHILLIPS, Bart of Jesus college, Oxon
(from Jery Melford, [6 October])

1. *horse-fleam*: A lancet for bleeding horses.
2. *like Father Thames . . . urn*: A common poetic image, as in Pope's *Windsor-Forest* (1713), lines 329–48.
3. *Blessed be his holy name*: An allusion to Job 1:21 and Psalm 103:1.
4. *through fire as well as water*: An allusion to Psalm 66:12.
5. *cornelian*: A variety of chalcedony, a semi-transparent quartz, used for seals.
6. *the very moral of*: Colloquial phrase meaning the likeness or counterpart of.
7. *a poor object . . . in iniquity*: An allusion to Psalm 51:5.
8. *Dolly's*: Dolly's Chop House in Queen's Head Passage, Paternoster Row in London.
9. *hot and hot*: Said of food dishes, especially of meat, served as fast as they are cooked.

To Dr LEWIS
(from Matthew Bramble, 8 October)

1. *coadjutrix*: Female helper (Latin).
2. *a second brother*: Under the terms of primogeniture, the rights of succession and inheritance fell to the first-born son. The younger sons of privileged families often followed a career in one of the professions (the Church, medicine or law).
3. *health of body, peace of mind*: Possibly alluding to Pope's 'Ode on Solitude' (1717), line 11: 'In health of body, peace of mind'.

To Dr LEWIS
(from Matthew Bramble, 11 October)

1. *tower of desolation*: As Preston notes (p. 435), this may be an allusion to Ezekiel 29:10, an ironic allusion to 2 Samuel 22:51 ('He is the tower of salvation for his king'), or an allusion to

Milton's *Paradise Lost*, I, 181 ('The seat of desolation, void of light').

2. *usquebaugh*: Either whisky or an Irish drink made from honey, wine and herbs.

3. *pepper-pots, pillaws, corys, chabobs, and stufatas*: Pepperpots: Caribbean soups or stews consisting of pieces of meat cooked slowly with red peppers, cassareep, sugar and other seasoning; pillaws: dishes partly of Middle Eastern and partly of South Asian origin, generally consisting of rice cooked in stock with spices, meat, and other ingredients; corys: curries; chabobs: kebabs, dishes consisting of pieces of meat (usually lamb) grilled on skewers; stufatas: Italian stews.

4. *chuck-farthing*: A game in which coins are pitched at a mark, then tossed or 'chucked' at a hole by the player who came nearest the mark.

5. *Lyle, Tull, Hart, Duhamel*: Edward Lisle (*d.* 1722), author of *Observations in Husbandry* (1757); Jethro Tull (1674–1741), author of *The New Horse-Houghing Husbandry; or, An Essay on the Principles of Tillage and Vegetation* (1731); Walter Harte (1708/9–74), author of *Essays on Husbandry* (1764); and Henri Louis Duhamel du Monceau (1700–1782), author of *The Elements of Agriculture* (translated and revised by Philip Miller, 1764).

6. *furze*: The popular name of *Ulex europæus*, a spiny evergreen shrub with yellow flowers.

7. *As the law requires ... resident in the parish*: According to the requirements of Lord Hardwicke's Marriage Act of 1753 (26 Geo. II, c. 33), 'An Act for the Better Preventing of Clandestine Marriages'.

To Sir Watkin Phillips, Bart at Oxon
(from Jery Melford, 14 October)

1. *commerce, loo, and quadrille*: All card games. Commerce is a game in which exchange or barter is the chief feature; loo is a game in which a player who fails to take a trick or breaks any of the laws of the game is 'looed', i.e. required to pay a certain sum, or 'loo', to the kitty; and quadrille is a game played by four people with forty cards, with the eights, nines and tens being discarded.

2. *Scrub ... Captain Gibbet*: Characters in Farquhar's *The Beaux' Stratagem*; Scrub is Squire Sullen's servant, while Gibbet is a highwayman.

3. *Harlequin Skeleton*: The popular pantomime *The Royal Chace; or, Merlin's Cave* (1736), sometimes known as 'Harlequin Skeleton', by Edward Phillips (*b.* 1708/9).

4. *dulcified*: Sweetened.

5. *jointure*: The holding of property to the joint use of a husband and wife, as a provision for the wife in the event of her being widowed.

6. *a month's mind*: An inclination, fancy or liking.

To Mrs MARY JONES, at Brambleton-hall
(from Win Jenkins, 14 October)

1. *matthew-murphy'd*: Metamorphosed.

2. *was out at elbows*: Had his coat worn out at the elbows, or (more generally) was in a bad condition.

3. *shilly shally*: Irresolute or undecided.

4. *on the wrong side of the blanket*: Illegitimately, i.e. out of wedlock.

5. *tackle*: Obsolete slang term for a mistress.

6. *chaps*: Chapmen, i.e. customers.

To Dr LEWIS
(from Matthew Bramble, 26 October)

1. *draught animals*: Animals used for pulling a cart or plough.

2. *unclog the wheels of life*: Possibly alluding to John Armstrong's poem *The Art of Preserving Health* (1744), II, 259–61: 'Besides, a meagre day subdues / The cruder clods by sloth or luxury / Collected; and unloads the wheels of life' (p. 40).

3. *quondam*: Formerly (Latin).

4. *Lady-day*: A day kept in celebration of some event in the life of the Virgin Mary. The day meant here is 25 March, the Feast of the Annunciation.

5. *upholder*: A dealer in small wares or second-hand articles.

6. *Naiads*: Mythical freshwater nymphs.

7. *tergiversation*: The action of 'turning one's back on', i.e. forsaking something in which one was previously engaged, interested or concerned; to a lesser extent, shuffling, equivocation or prevarication.

8. *out of the hands of the Philistines*: A common biblical phrase, for instance in Judges 13:5.

9. *peltry*: Furs and skins prepared for sale.

To Sir WATKIN PHILLIPS, Bart at Oxon
(from Jery Melford, 8 November)

1. *sentimental*: In a favourable sense, *sentimental* would mean characterized by or exhibiting refined and elevated thought, feeling or moral reflection; less favourably, it suggests someone who is apt to be swayed by sentiment, or addicted to indulgence in superficial emotion. In this instance, Jery perhaps adopts the first (favourable) meaning, but with an unfavourable evaluation of his sister's sentimental reflectiveness. The word itself had been fraught with ambiguity since its recent appearance in the English language; the first recorded use of 'sentimental' occurs in 1749, in a letter from Dorothy, Lady Bradshaigh (1705–85) to Samuel Richardson that is concerned to ascertain the meaning of this seemingly voguish term (*The Correspondence of Samuel Richardson*, ed. Anna Letitia Barbauld, 6 vols (1804), IV, pp. 282–3). It was subsequently popularized by the publication of Sterne's *A Sentimental Journey* (1768).

2. *Death in pursuit of Consumption*: Possibly an allusion to the consumptive narrator's dialogue with Death in volume 7, chapter 1 of Laurence Sterne's *The Life and Opinions of Tristram Shandy, Gentleman* (1765), or else to the painting by Thomas Patch (1725–82) of 'Laurence Sterne and Death', two engraved versions of which were issued during the late 1760s.

3. *opima spolia*: The spoils taken from an army's general when slain by the general of the opposing army (Latin).

4. *tye-periwig*: The tye-wig, an undress wig worn by graduates, in which the hair was drawn back and the curls bunched together to form a queue – a lock of hair hanging down behind – which was tied with a black ribbon at the nape of the neck.

5. *in buckle*: The state of the hair when crisped and curled, from being kept a long time in the same state.

6. *the pas*: The precedence, or right of going first (French).

7. *French coat . . . his thigh*: Short-skirted coats were still fashionable in France, but had been out of fashion in England since the 1750s (Preston, p. 438).

8. *Hymen*: The god of marriage in Greek and Roman mythology.

9. *Saturn and Cybele*: Saturn, a Roman god, was associated with melancholy; Cybele, identified by the Romans with Ops, was Saturn's wife and the goddess of plenty.

10. *benediction posset*: Drink of blessing.

11. *the very pink*: The highest state or most perfect condition of.

12. *back-sword*: A sword with only one cutting edge.
13. *widgeons*: Fools, simpletons or ninnies; in allusion to the supposed stupidity of wild ducks.

To Dr Lewis
(from Matthew Bramble, 20 November)

1. *Dr Arbuthnot*: John Arbuthnot (1667–1735), physician, satirist and member of the Scriblerus club of wits. While he did not publish extensively under his own name, Arbuthnot provided many ideas for others, most notably his fellow Scriblerians, who included John Gay, Alexander Pope and Jonathan Swift.
2. *type*: A foreshadowing or prefiguring – as in the theological sense in which a person, object or event in Old Testament history prefigures some person or thing revealed in the New Testament.
3. *chine*: A joint of meat, consisting of the whole or part of the backbone and the adjoining flesh.

To Mrs Mary Jones, at Brambleton-hall
(from W. Loyd, 20 November)

1. *tumtawdry*: Preston (p. xxxvi) suggests 'rough wool cloth'.
2. *monkey-bank*: Mountebank.
3. *Titidall*: Titivil, the name of a devil or demon in the mystery plays.
4. *tabby*: Waved or watered silk.
5. *Runnela cap*: The Ranelagh cap or 'mob', an informal head-dress fashionable in the 1760s, made from a piece of gauze or other fine material folded diagonally and tied under the chin or behind.

PENGUIN CLASSICS

MOLL FLANDERS
DANIEL DEFOE

'I grew as impudent a Thief, and as dexterous as ever *Moll Cut-Purse* was'

Born and abandoned in Newgate Prison, Moll Flanders is forced to make her own way in life. She duly embarks on a career that includes husband-hunting, incest, bigamy, prostitution and pick-pocketing, until her crimes eventually catch up with her. One of the earliest and most vivid female narrators in the history of the English novel, Moll recounts her adventures with irresistible wit and candour – and enough guile that the reader is left uncertain whether she is ultimately a redeemed sinner or a successful opportunist.

Based on the first edition of 1722, this volume includes a chronology, notes on currency, and maps of London and Virginia in the late seventeenth century.

Edited with an introduction and notes by David Blewett.

PENGUIN CLASSICS

ROBINSON CRUSOE
DANIEL DEFOE

> 'A raging wave, mountain-like, came rowling a-stern of us
> … we were all swallowed up in a moment'

The sole survivor of a shipwreck, Robinson Crusoe is washed up on a desert island.
In his journal he chronicles his daily battle to stay alive, as he conquers isolation,
fashions shelter and clothes, first encounters another human being, and fights off
cannibals and mutineers. With *Robinson Crusoe*, Defoe wrote what is regarded as
the first English novel, and created one of the most popular and enduring myths
in literature. Written in an age of exploration and enterprise, it has been variously
interpreted as an embodiment of British imperialist values, as a portrayal of
'natural man', or as a moral fable. But above all it is a brilliant narrative, depicting
Crusoe's transformation from terrified survivor to self-sufficient master of his
island.

This edition contains a full chronology of Defoe's life and times, explanatory
notes, glossary and a critical introduction discussing *Robinson Crusoe* as a
pioneering work of modern psychological realism.

'Robinson Crusoe has a universal appeal, a story that goes right to the core of
existence' Simon Armitage

Edited with an introduction and notes by John Richetti

PENGUIN CLASSICS

DON QUIXOTE
MIGUEL DE CERVANTES

> 'Didn't I tell you they were only windmills?
> And only someone with windmills on the brain could have failed to see that!'

Don Quixote has become so entranced by reading romances of chivalry that he determines to become a knight errant and pursue bold adventures, accompanied by his squire, the cunning Sancho Panza. As they roam the world together, the ageing Quixote's fancy leads them wildly astray. At the same time the relationship between the two men grows in fascinating subtlety. Often considered to be the first modern novel, *Don Quixote* is a wonderful burlesque of the popular literature its disordered protagonist is obsessed with.

John Rutherford's landmark translation does full justice to the energy and wit of Cervantes's prose. His introduction discusses the traditional works parodied in *Don Quixote*, as well as issues surrounding literary translation.

'John Rutherford ... makes *Don Quixote* funny and readable ... His Quixote can be pompous, imposingly learned, secretly fearful, mad and touching'
Colin Burrow, *The Times Literary Supplement*

Voted greatest book of all time by the Nobel Institute

Translated with an introduction and notes by John Rutherford

PENGUIN CLASSICS

GULLIVER'S TRAVELS
JONATHAN SWIFT

> 'I felt something alive moving on my left Leg …
> when bending my Eyes downwards as much as I could,
> I perceived it to be a human Creature not six Inches high'

Shipwrecked and cast adrift, Lemuel Gulliver wakes to find himself on Lilliput, an island inhabited by little people, whose height makes their quarrels over fashion and fame seem ridiculous. His subsequent encounters – with the crude giants of Brobdingnag, the philosophical Houyhnhnms and brutish Yahoos – give Gulliver new, bitter insights into human behaviour. Swift's savage satire views mankind in a distorted hall of mirrors as a diminished, magnified and finally bestial species, presenting us with an uncompromising reflection of ourselves.

This text, based on the first edition of 1726, reproduces all its original illustrations and includes an introduction by Robert Demaria, Jr., which discusses the ways *Gulliver's Travels* has been interpreted since its first publication.

'A masterwork of irony … that contains both a dark and bitter meaning and a joyous, extraordinary creativity of imagination. That is why it has lived for so long'
Malcolm Bradbury

Edited with an introduction by Robert DeMaria, Jr

PENGUIN CLASSICS

THE HISTORY OF TOM JONES
HENRY FIELDING

'He was indeed a thoughtless, giddy youth, with little sobriety in his manners, and less in his countenance'

A foundling of mysterious parentage brought up by Mr Allworthy on his country estate, Tom Jones is deeply in love with the seemingly unattainable Sophia Western, the beautiful daughter of the neighbouring squire – though he sometimes succumbs to the charms of the local girls. But when his amorous escapades earn the disapproval of his benefactor, Tom is banished to make his own fortune. Sophia, meanwhile, is determined to avoid an arranged marriage to Allworthy's scheming nephew and escapes from her rambunctious father to follow Tom to London. A vivid Hogarthian panorama of eighteenth-century life, spiced with danger and intrigue, bawdy exuberance and good-natured authorial interjections, *Tom Jones* (1749) is one of the greatest and most ambitious comic novels in English literature.

In his introduction to this new Penguin Classics edition, Thomas Keymer discusses narrative techniques and themes, the context of eighteenth-century fiction and satire, and the historical and political background of the Jacobite Rebellion. This volume also includes a chronology, further reading, notes, a glossary and an appendix on Fielding's revisions.

Edited by Thomas Keymer and Alice Wakely

With an introduction by Thomas Keymer

PENGUIN CLASSICS

THE LIFE AND OPINIONS OF TRISTRAM SHANDY, GENTLEMAN
LAURENCE STERNE

'L—d! said my mother, what is all this story about? –
A COCK and a BULL, said Yorick – and one of the best of its kind I ever heard'

Laurence Sterne's great masterpiece of bawdy humour and rich satire defies any attempt to categorize it. Part novel, part digression, its gloriously disordered narrative interweaves the birth and life of the unfortunate 'hero' Tristram Shandy, the eccentric philosophy of his father Walter, the amours and military obsessions of Uncle Toby, and a host of other characters, including Dr Slop, Corporal Trim and the parson Yorick. A joyful celebration of the endless possibilities of the art of fiction, *Tristram Shandy* is also a wry demonstration of its limitations.

The text and notes of this volume are based on the acclaimed Florida Edition, with a critical introduction by Melvyn New and Christopher Ricks's introductory essay from the first Penguin Classics edition of the novel.

'The excellent Florida *Tristram Shandy* ... will be the definitive edition'
Studies in English Literature

'The book that I would never tire of ... Sterne was about 250 years ahead of his time' Roy Porter

THE FLORIDA EDITION
Edited by Melvyn New and Joan New

PENGUIN CLASSICS

PRIDE AND PREJUDICE
JANE AUSTEN

'Vanity, not love, has been my folly'

When Elizabeth Bennet first meets eligible bachelor Fitzwilliam Darcy, she thinks him arrogant and conceited; he is indifferent to her good looks and lively mind. When she later discovers that Darcy has involved himself in the troubled relationship between his friend Bingley and her beloved sister Jane, she is determined to dislike him more than ever. In the sparkling comedy of manners that follows, Jane Austen shows the folly of judging by first impressions and superbly evokes the friendships, gossip and snobberies of provincial eighteenth-century middle-class life.

This edition also includes a new chronology, additional suggestions for further reading, and the original Penguin Classics introduction by Tony Tanner.

'*Pride and Prejudice* has always been the most popular of Jane Austen's books … with its good humoured comedy, its sunny heroine, its dream denouement'
Claire Tomalin

'These modern editions are to be strongly recommended for their scrupulous texts, informative notes and helpful introductions'
Brian Southam, The Jane Austen Society

Edited by Vivien Jones with an introduction by Tony Tanner

PENGUIN CLASSICS

THE COUNT OF MONTE CRISTO
ALEXANDRE DUMAS

'On what slender threads do life and fortune hang'

Thrown in prison for a crime he has not committed, Edmond Dantes is confined to the grim fortress of If. There he learns of a great hoard of treasure hidden on the Isle of Monte Cristo and he becomes determined not only to escape, but also to unearth the treasure and use it to plot the destruction of the three men responsible for his incarceration. Dumas's epic tale of suffering and retribution, inspired by a real-life case of wrongful imprisonment, was a huge popular success when it was first serialized in the 1840s.

Robin Buss's lively English translation is complete and unabridged, and remains faithful to the style of Dumas's original. This edition includes an introduction, explanatory notes and suggestions for further reading.

'Robin Buss broke new ground with a fresh version of *Monte Cristo* for Penguin'
The Oxford Guide to Literature in English Translation

Translated with an introduction by Robin Buss

THE STORY OF PENGUIN CLASSICS

Before 1946 ... 'Classics' are mainly the domain of academics and students; readable editions for everyone else are almost unheard of. This all changes when a little-known classicist, E. V. Rieu, presents Penguin founder Allen Lane with the translation of Homer's *Odyssey* that he has been working on in his spare time.

1946 Penguin Classics debuts with *The Odyssey*, which promptly sells three million copies. Suddenly, classics are no longer for the privileged few.

1950s Rieu, now series editor, turns to professional writers for the best modern, readable translations, including Dorothy L. Sayers's *Inferno* and Robert Graves's unexpurgated *Twelve Caesars*.

1960s The Classics are given the distinctive black covers that have remained a constant throughout the life of the series. Rieu retires in 1964, hailing the Penguin Classics list as 'the greatest educative force of the twentieth century.'

1970s A new generation of translators swells the Penguin Classics ranks, introducing readers of English to classics of world literature from more than twenty languages. The list grows to encompass more history, philosophy, science, religion and politics.

1980s The Penguin American Library launches with titles such as *Uncle Tom's Cabin*, and joins forces with Penguin Classics to provide the most comprehensive library of world literature available from any paperback publisher.

1990s The launch of Penguin Audiobooks brings the classics to a listening audience for the first time, and in 1999 the worldwide launch of the Penguin Classics website extends their reach to the global online community.

The 21st Century Penguin Classics are completely redesigned for the first time in nearly twenty years. This world-famous series now consists of more than 1300 titles, making the widest range of the best books ever written available to millions – and constantly redefining what makes a 'classic'.

The Odyssey continues ...

The best books ever written

PENGUIN CLASSICS

SINCE 1946

Find out more at www.penguinclassics.com